I0760504

Whispers of Ghosts

Sundering the Gods
Book 3

by

L. James Rice

TWELFTH
STAR

Whispers of Ghosts is a work of fiction. Names, characters, places, and incidents are the product of the author's imagination or are used fictitiously. Any resemblance to actual events, locales, or persons, living, dead, undead, possessed, or anywhere in between is purely coincidental.

Published by Twelfth Star Publishing, Council Bluffs, IA, USA

Cartography by Jenna Jing Rice

ISBN: 978-1-951068-06-6 paperback
ISBN: 978-1-951068-05-9 e-book
ISBN: 978-1-951068-07-3 hardback

Join the Sundering the Gods newsletter `for updates,
promotions, and exclusive short works at:
sunderingthegods.com

Dedicated to my beautiful wife and
two lovely daughters for continuing
to tolerate my writer's life.

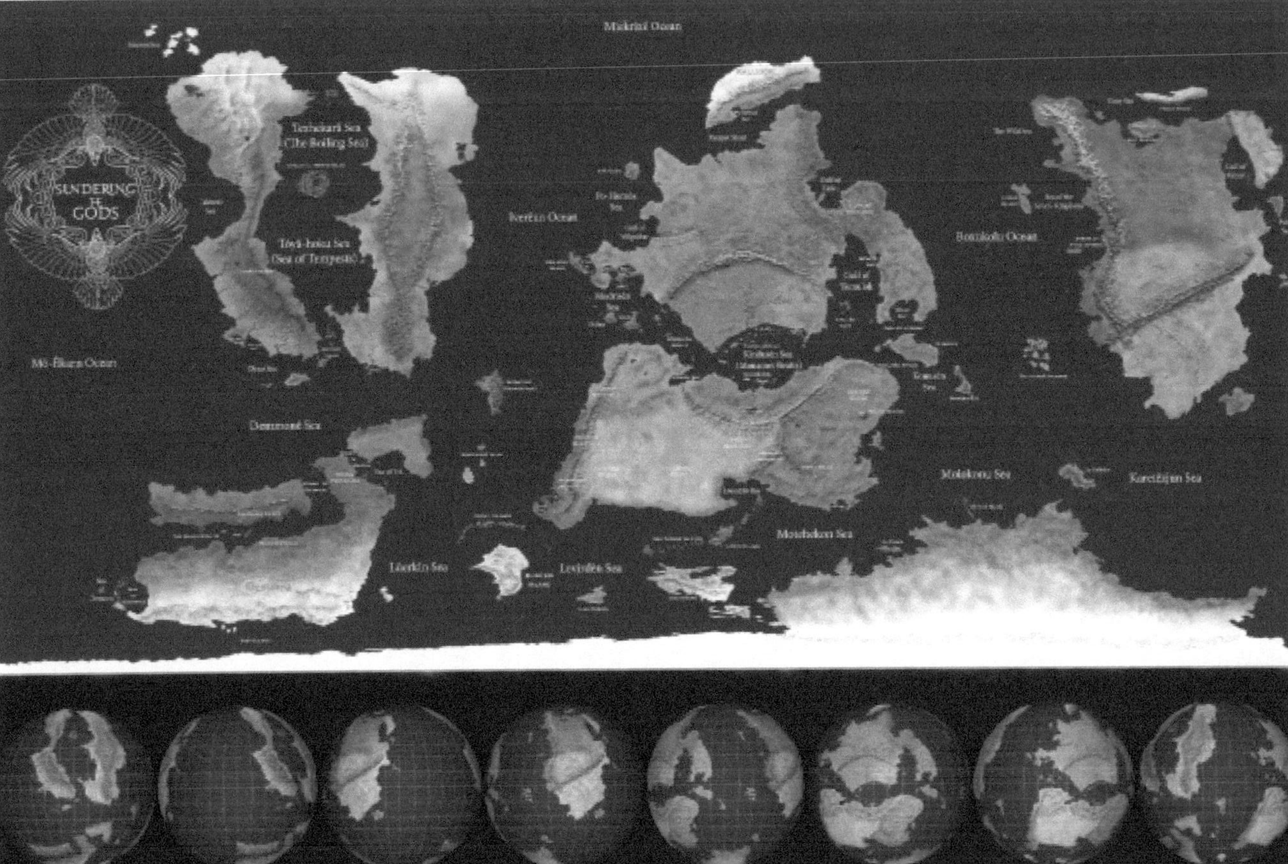
SUNDERING
GODS
(The Boiling Sea)
(Sea of Tempests)

TERRITORY OF THE CLAN CHOERKIN

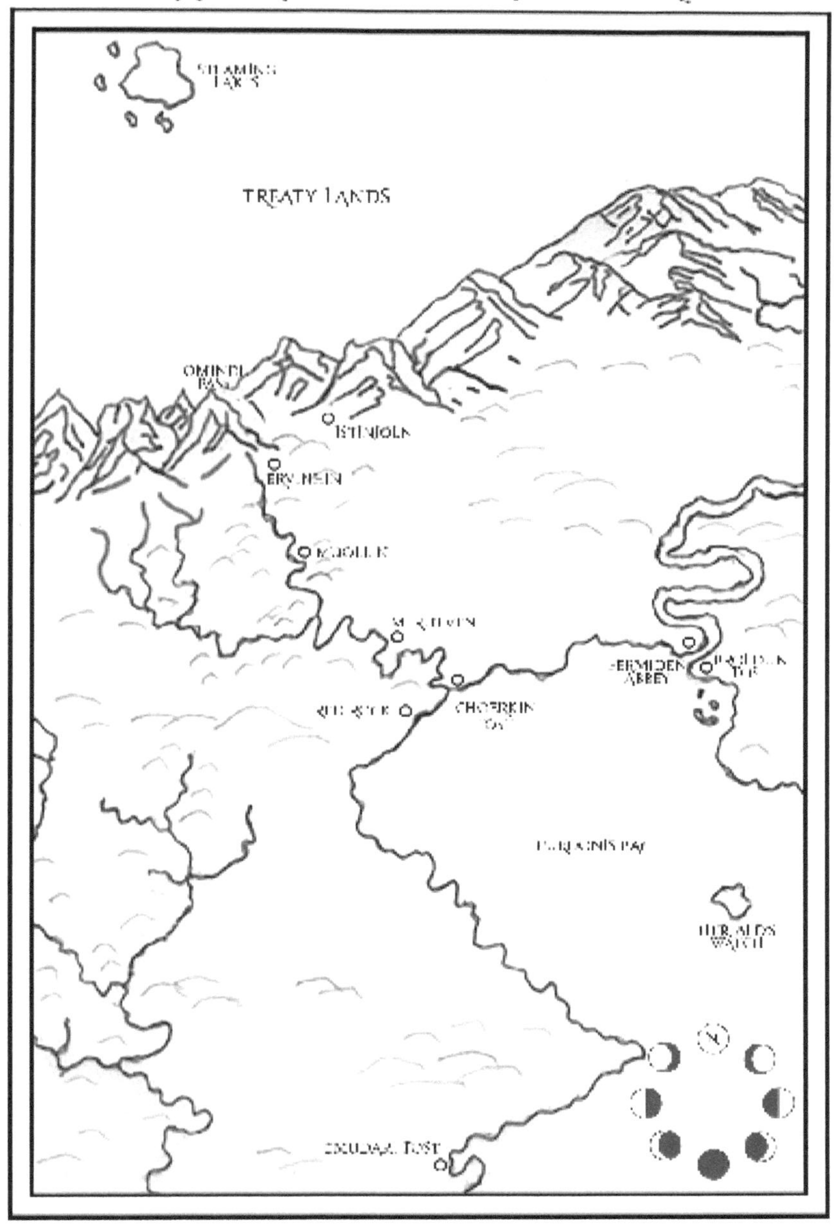

Ôfelun
Helebôm
Ilu-Strono Plains
Mulshahar
Ômkinter
Kamar
Ôsho
KÔNU BAY
STRAIT OF KÔNU
Înlark
Barkûsh
Œrinklin
Danlok
Medrisên Sea
Pôn
Todyûl
Bêmerû
Zágarn
Yungilêtunu
Rôqwu
Arkudân River
Tebûul River
Môndeu River
Mèsrân River
Tebôhûu
Chitorâ
Kelêf
Môtûu
Choru
Llopu
MEDRISÊN STRAIT
Toltûk

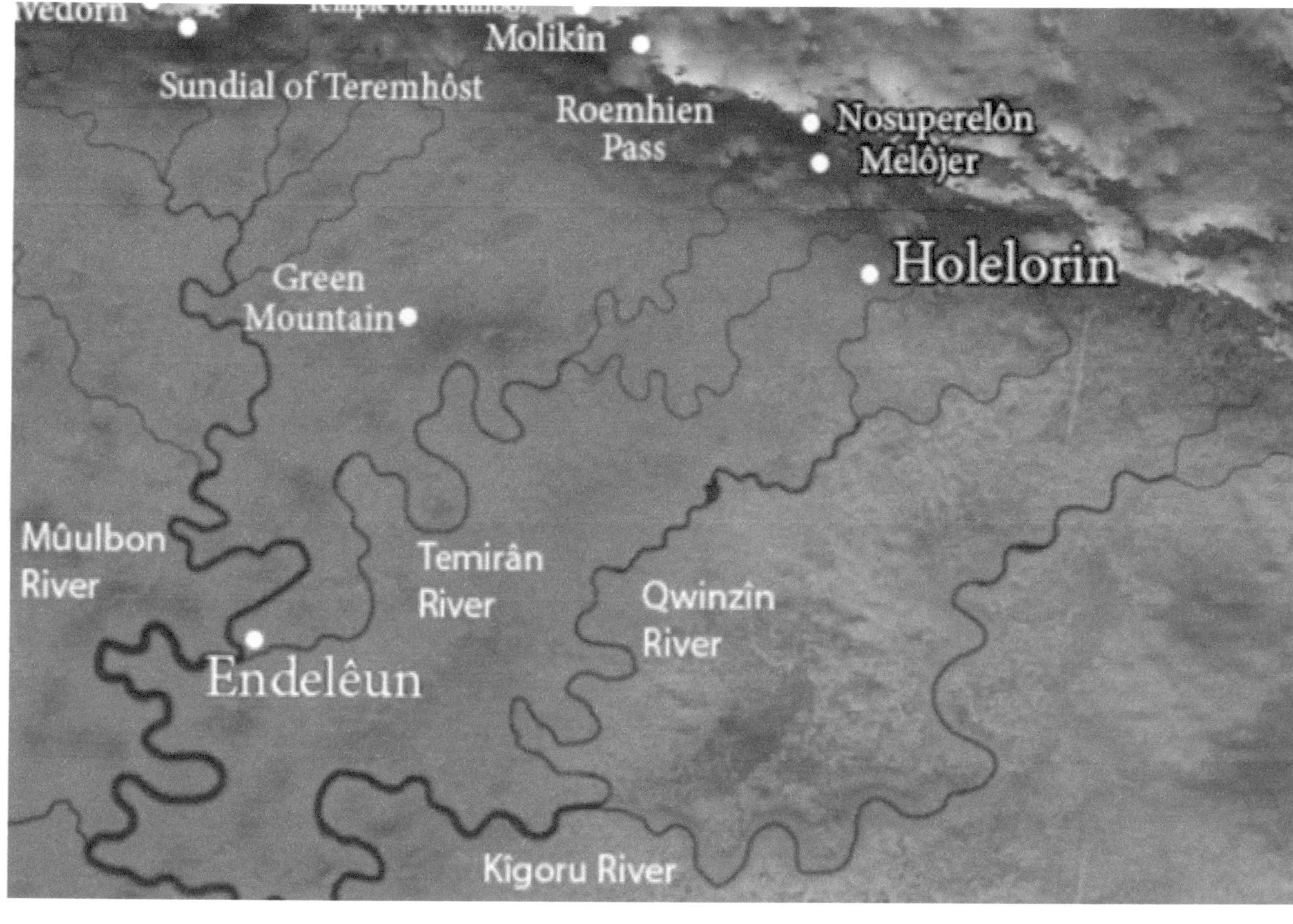
Molikîn
Sundial of Teremhôst
Roemhien Pass
Nosuperelôn
Mélôjer
Holelorin
Green Mountain
Mûulbon River
Temirân River
Qwinzîn River
Endelêun
Kîgoru River

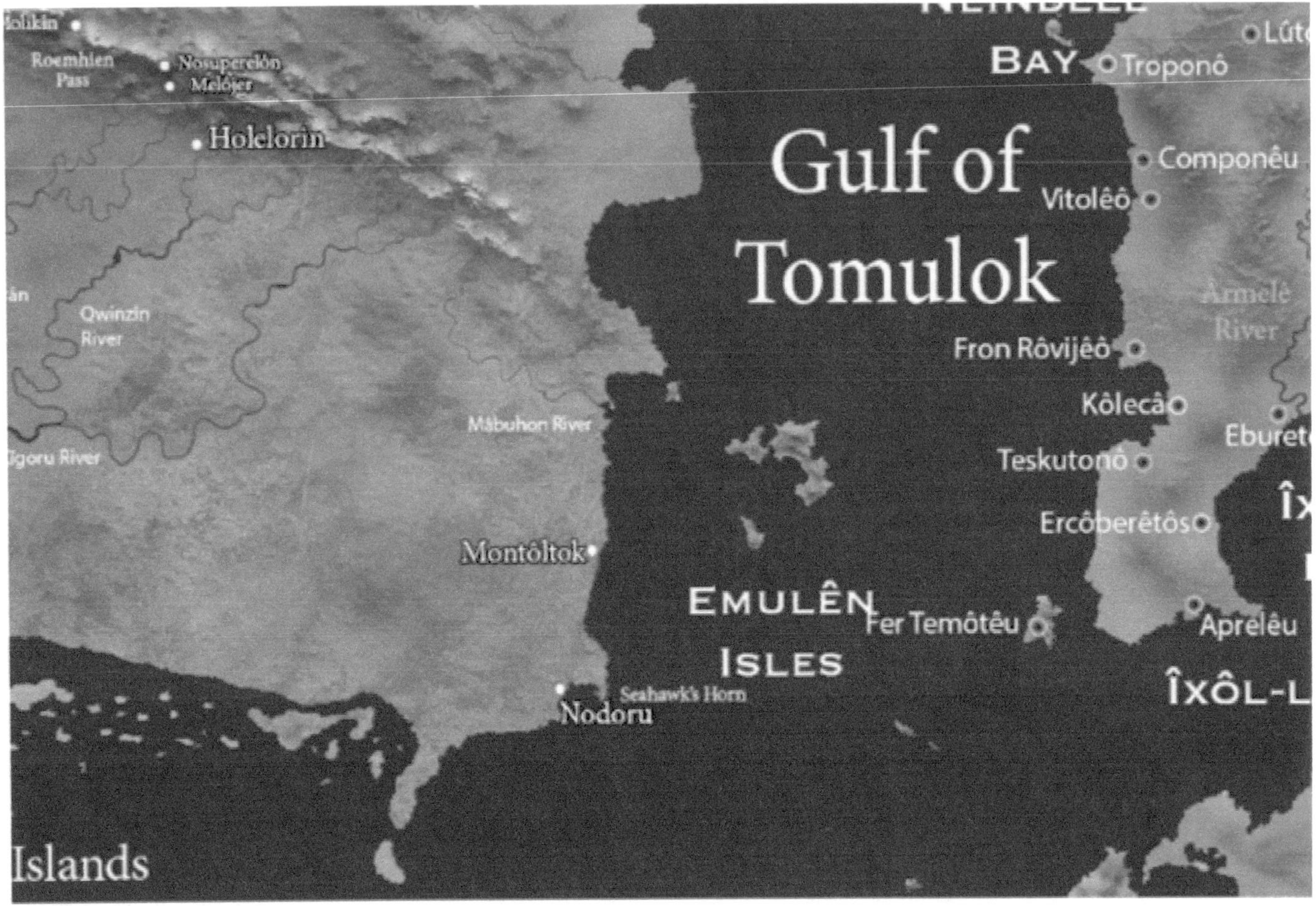

Roemhien Pass
Nosuperelôn
Melójer
Holelorin
Qwinzin River
Mâbuhon River
Montôltok
Nodoru
Seahawk's Horn
Islands
BAY
Troponó
Gulf of Tomulok
Componêu
Vitolêô
Fron Rôvijêô
Kôlecâ
Teskutonô
Ercôberêtôs
Armelê River
EMULÊN ISLES
Fer Temótêu
Aprelêu

The Sundering the Gods Saga

Eve of Snows

Trail of Pyres

Whispers of Ghosts

For additional maps and information head on over to:

www.LJamesRice.com
and
www.STGWiki.com

One

Rain Forest Hunters

There's a seeping in your brain,
a trickle drip drop drip,
memories past fading into future memories
to forget again.
There's a sleeping in your brain,
a tickle flutter flick flutter,
memories imagined sewn into true memories
to forget never.
Why do your dreams, so often of her,
feel so much more real than standing by her side?

—*Tomes of the Touched*

505th Year of Remembered Time

"A peculiar scent on the winds." Edlmir scrunched his nose, and if he'd raised his lip, he would've looked like a stud smelling for a mare in season.

Imagining the bastard as a horse brought a grin to Rinold's face, but he'd noticed the odor a wick before. It wasn't the first time that the breeze carried a hint of basil and urine; some sort of flower he guessed. If it wasn't a flower, he wasn't sure he wanted to know what the hells it was.

But the forest was full of smells, and most he tracked to wet and decay. Every piece of low ground collected water from the damned-near daily rains, pools of stench covered in green muck, and how often a rack of skin-scattered ribs sat by these bogs proved you didn't want to drink the water even if it was potable. No one in their party had seen anything living in these still pools, but they avoided them at every step as if they might lead to one of the Twelve Hells.

Rinold rubbed the scent from his nose, glancing high into the trees. The canopy here was thick with leaves big as a man... Hells, he swore some of them could blanket a horse. A few might make sails on a small boat. Hundreds of flowers big enough to swallow his face dangled in clusters from the thigh-thick branches, their petals painted with every hue of the rainbow. The trunks of the trees here wore a scaled armor-bark, the plates bigger than his hands and offering grips to climb high with ease.

They were three weeks in the woods and deeper south than they'd traveled before. Most times they entered the forest to find meat and fruit, but those forays proved easy; food in these wilds was abundant, and this fact drew more and more Silone over the Rôemhîen Pass. No, this time Edlmir talked him into exploring south. Puxele had given him the demon's eye at the notion of his leaving, but after a couple of days, it was all he could do to keep her from joining them.

The big promise? He'd be back before their child was born. Only three months along, it was a vow easy to keep so long as he stayed alive. The other promise was to name a river after her. He figured this promise could be tricky as some muddy stream wouldn't suffice.

Uncertain of what to make of the smell, he focused his ears. If getting used to all the reeks of the forest confused his senses, after a lifetime in cold mountains, the constant buzz and call of life put the shivers to his skin. Bugs, birds, bog-deer, frogs, lizards, lemurs, squirrels, and monkeys swinging from trees or hanging from their tails, every damned one and a hundred more critters filled the universe with a constant clamor that grated his nerves. What worried him more were the things you wouldn't hear until their fangs tasted your flesh: prowling cats or snakes they'd seen and avoided, but there were rumors of fouler beasts. Hells, more than rumor, one pile of shit they found was bigger than a Choerkin.

He grinned. *I'll have to use that on Ratsmasher next time I see him.*

They followed a river the party named the Swimming Monkey after coming across a family of the hairy critters taking a bath, and it traveled with steady southwestern crooks. It started as little more than a stream, though every rain drove it wider and swifter, but by now more than a dozen similar streams had joined into a twenty-stride flow deep enough they'd need to swim to cross.

A hillock covered with trees and grass rose before them, and the river cut a sharp channel with rocky cliffs maybe three poles high on their side. Skirting the bank low looked a tricky proposition with steep, water-worn rock for footing.

Edlmir clucked as he stared. "We could swim across."

"If I can't see bottom, I ain't sticking my toes in it, let alone swim."

Kurin slipped to their side. "You smelled that?"

Rinold turned to the Kingdomer, a Wayfinder who Puxele had insisted join them. She was a stout woman of a similar height to his own, and no doubt she outweighed him. If not straight out, the magnetic stones she carried in her pack tipped her over the edge. "Aye, smelled it. Not for the first time."

"Not a smell I've met before yesterday, and I thought it belonged to a flowering bush. Today, a tree smelled that way."

"In this wet hell, I'm betting some sort of mold or fungus." The woman snorted, and Rinold trusted her instincts: She didn't think him right. "What the hells do you think it is, then?"

"Just like it smells, we're in something's territory."

"Piss marks?" Not once had he smelled the mark of an animal without kneeling to catch a trail. "That there's some pungent pee if yer right."

"Or a lot of it. I'd be curious to see what made the marks."

Edlmir huffed a curt chuckle. "Not me, no ma'am. Critters who mark tend to be critters who ain't so worried about being eaten."

"Likely as not, it's one of the big cats." Rinold's eye twitched and he pursed his lips. There was a reason half the men carried spears and pikes and the other half longbows; sword and ax range meant you were headed for dead against the monsters stories spoke of. "But I'm thinking my man here has a point. Let's keep moving."

They scratched and hauled themselves up the steep hill and gave the world a good look while catching their breath and resting their muscles. The river moseyed on south-southwest, and amid the deep greens and browns of the forest, a stone outcropping rose above the canopy in the distance; it stood overgrown by patches of vines and small trees.

Kurin stared at the distant hill as Rinold had seen her do to a multitude of landmarks over the past several months. He didn't understand what she was doing, to the detail, but once the woman had an eyeball on a location and made its mental map, she was sure as Puxele's arrow to find her target. She pulled a folded parchment from her pack, scribbled marks and a quick note.

Rinold turned his eyes back to the jutting hill and the creeping green up its rocky sides. He squinted, eye giving a twitch as he surveilled a squared corner of rock. "That ain't no mountain, it's a structure of some sorts. Look at how that yonder crag squares so neat."

"*Hefmulu telû*. I believe your eyes true."

The smile on her face caught his attention as much as the rock. "What the hells is it?"

"I don't know. Kingdomer explorers have called them *Yudulê Omu*, green mountains, because the forest has overgrown them. Pyramids... Maybe temples, shrines, signal towers, and some claim they have secret entrances. People who built them are dead and gone. Most have more ruins around."

Rinold stood accustomed to ancient places buried in snow... or sitting in a steaming bowl with some babbling pile of bones ready to spew riddles. What were the odds of there being a second Touched? "What do people find around these places?"

"Often nothing, nothing no one admits to anyhow. Rumors abound, as you'd imagine."

"Treasure." He laughed. "I ain't never heard of ruins that someone didn't claim held a treasure. Sometimes they aren't a lie." Puxele's ring came to mind, though it'd been a gift.

"Perhaps our peoples aren't so different."

Edlmir grinned. "After I heard treasure, I stopped listening. What're we waiting for?"

Rinold sucked his teeth. "That's a stretch from the banks of the river, I figure. But it ain't like we can get *too* lost with the Dragonspans covering the north, even if, gods forbid, we lost our Wayfinder."

Kurin grinned. "If I'm lost, you're all dead."

Every Wayfinder he'd met lacked humility, but at least Kurin tempered her cocky with a hint of smile.

They descended steady but slow, clinging to vines and slippery rocks until reaching bottom. The ground squished beneath their feet, sucking at their boots until they reached an animal trail; fresh Srôbu boar tracks marked the turf, biggest godsdamned pigs Rinold'd ever seen. An adult sow Puxele dropped over a year before weighed three hundred bricks and fed several families through a tough stretch. Every soul here would be scrambling for a tree if a sounder of the beasts carried a charge their way.

Kurin took the lead with a nod, and Rinold slipped in a few steps behind her. It was in his nature to be out front when exploring or hunting, but the Kingdomer's skills made his considerable directional wits fall behind without complaint.

He glanced into the trees, to Kurin's back… back to a tree limb. He stopped in his tracks, warriors behind stumbling to a stop. The eyes of a gigantic eagle stared at him from beneath two tufts of feathers rising from its head, like some demon with blunted horns. White chested, dark gray wings and head, and a black band around its neck, the creature's hooked talons were as long as his fingers, and it was at least four feet tall; but it was the calm, intelligent gaze that transfixed him.

"What the hells you call that thing, and does it eat people?"

Kurin strode back to him for a better view. "Ah! Griffon Eagle is the easiest translation. Legends say they served the Griffon Lords during the Age of God Wars. No one's ever seen one take more than a child. So, if you consider children people…" She shrugged.

Rinold stared; it stared. "Beautiful and disturbing. Let's keep a movin', shall we?"

Kurin led them into a dense thicket following the trail, and most of the men bent beneath the low ceiling to avoid thorns. Sometimes, short was useful. "Who were these Griffon Lords?"

"No one knows. The Cliffs of Knowledge mention them but give scant details. Some people believe they were men who rode on the backs of griffons, others believe they were *actual* griffons. Some hold that these lords spoke human tongues."

Rinold pondered before taking a drink from his canteen. "That eagle looked like it had smarts, wouldn't have shocked me a bit if it spoke." Not after the Colok reeducated his expectations.

Kurin chortled as she swept branches from her face. "No one I know has ever heard of a griffon speaking to men, but plenty of Kingdomers have died trying to tame one, to become a Griffon Lord. Stealing eggs… most die right there." She laughed.

Lion-eagles bigger than a horse… Griffons. Half of Rinold's brain craved seeing one, the other half dreaded seeing one too close. "I heard you Kingdomers hunt griffons."

"Mmm, only when needs be, to save our herds, or a wounded griffon feeds on a villager. And then, more often we convince them to leave the region instead of kill them. Their feathers are a more formidable armor than you might imagine, killing one tends to cost Kingdomer lives."

"But you esteem their feathers."

"We esteem their lives! They are a holy animal. It is said that a soul who stares into the eyes of the griffon and lives has been judged pure by the Foundationals. The gods judge many souls impure every year."

Rinold's eye twitched as he squinted. "You mean people go to look one in the eye?"

"*Sotodu Emûel.* The Pilgrimage of the Eyrie."

"No offense, but that's plum crazy."

Kurin laughed. "I'm not so ignorant as to consider myself pure, nor so bold to consider myself so lucky. I've seen them in the skies from way below; this is close enough. Tssht!"

She raised her hand and crouched; Rinold dipped a knee beside her. "What?"

She shook her head, eyes plying the woods from ground to canopy.

A griffon eagle lit in a nearby tree, the branch bending and swaying with its weight. Its eyes, he swore the damned thing stared at him alone.

Kurin stood, her breaths easier, but her eyes still scanned the trees. "We seem to have a friend. I've never seen one follow a party."

"Griffon Lords keeping an eye on us?" He tried to grin.

"More likely it hopes we stir up some game… Or, it's telling us to shut up and pay attention to the surrounding forest."

They spoke less and stopped more often to take in their surroundings afterward, and damned if the bird didn't follow them. Rinold considered they might be near its nest, but after a couple horizons, his theory no longer made sense. By afternoon, he'd named the eagle Hirk. He hadn't thought of Hirk in years, a dog that had adopted the Wolverine and followed his wardens around for a long stretch. The goofy thing wouldn't come so close as to take food from a hand, but the hells if it would leave even if you threw rocks at it. One day, after two years, Hirk disappeared and every man who'd made fun of the animal murmured prayers for the beast.

The sun cast long evening shadows by the time their winding trail brought them to the base of the Green Mountain. Overgrown by vines and bushes growing from its ancient cracks, the pyramid's base was maybe two hundred and fifty strides across, and it rose at least a hundred strides, standing well above the mighty trees. Massive stones twice his height stood pieced together in steps toward the summit, and from their vantage, it wasn't an easy climb. A stone-covered road, overgrown by grass, weeds, and lichen, spanned the side of the structure and split into the forest in paths marked by a lack of huge trees. No doubt a careful search would yield the remains of other buildings.

They struck camp at the pyramid's feet and scratched together a meal of dried fish, while Hirk watched from the bare-branched heights of a dead tree, tearing meat with its massive beak; the bird's meal was fresher than theirs and furry. Rinold suspected it some type of monkey.

Kurin eased in beside him. "Our friend joined in our meal."

Edlmir plopped to the ground. "That godsdamned bird gives me the jitters. Anythin' eats a monkey might as like eat a man."

"Some Kingdomers eat monkey."

Edlmir chortled. "Remind me to keep an eye on you."

Rinold puffed. "I figure we're better off with its belly full."

"True enough." Kurin turned her nose to a breeze drifting in from the east. "Smell that?"

He didn't until she asked, then the odor became unmistakable: basil and urine, but it was faint. "Aye. Hey, Hirk? How about you let us know what the hells pisses that smell?"

The eagle's gaze locked with his, and he imagined if it were a griffon it'd be judging him and on its way to killing him. Instead, Hirk dipped its head for a rip of monkey.

"Our friend is a quiet sort."

Rinold grinned. "Aye." He leaned against the pyramid's cool stone; it felt good to have something solid at his back. "We'll stay here the night, up a couple tiers to get us off the ground. Come mornin', we'll see if our friend shows us where the treasure hides."

Edlmir grinned. "If the bird does that, I'll forgive his demon's gaze."

Rinold awoke with an uncomfortable twist in his gut but no memory of a dream to explain his unease. In the east, the sun brought a faint glow over the canopy of monstrous leaves and the swooping swarms of flittering birds ducking and diving into their shadows.

He eased into a crouch, planting his hands to the stone of the fourth tier of the pyramid where they'd slept. His eyes flicked to the four sentries to make sure all was well. Two sat high above, and the two below stood with spears in hand, one stretching his arms. Quiet. Normal.

It did nothing to unbind the knots.

Edlmir stirred a couple feet away, and Kurin stepped to his side, bright-eyed as ever. "Ready to explore this Green Mountain?"

The morning glow spread in the east, scattered clouds drifting into oranges and yellows; the deep green leaves of the forest glistened with dew, still on a windless morning. "No. Something's watching us."

Edlmir huffed. "So much for taking a piss… Sure it ain't your feathered pal?"

"Hirk wasn't no shy bird."

Kurin said, "I haven't seen nothing, and I've been awake a candle."

"I know it by the twitch of my eye, but I don't see a damned thing. Wake everyone but keep 'em quiet. Anyone needs to piss or shit, they stay on the pyramid. And watch them godsdamned woods."

Edlmir slipped away, shaking men from their sleep.

Kurin squinted at Rinold. "You're certain? I don't miss much."

"If I were certain I'd put an arrow in it."

"Only one?"

The notion of more than one set of eyes hadn't crossed his mind. "I think so." His eyes swung back to a stretch of woods straight beneath the rising sun and he cupped his ears. Vines, bushes, massive tree trunks, a thousand places for critters to hide, but not a sound carried from the area. He pointed. "You hear that? We've got noise from all around… birds up high, bugs godsdamned everywhere, but not there."

The Wayfinder squinted. "You're right… See that line of vines and bushes farther out? Could be the remains of a wall."

It took a flicker to discern what she looked at. "Could be."

"Want me to take a look?"

The woman could disappear in the forest with her outfit of rags and sticks, but animals weren't men and used senses other than sight to hunt. "Not so sure it'd be wise."

"So, what *do* we do?"

Rinold glanced at the warriors and raised his voice. "Everyone at the ready. Keep your eye out for any movement." He slipped his bow from its harness and nocked an arrow, taking aim… hells, he didn't have a target. He picked a spot between two trees and loosed. The arrow sailed into the gap and disappeared into the underbrush, whipping a few branches, but nothing else gave a twitch.

"Where the hells are you?" He took aim at a tree and loosed a second arrow. It struck and protruded from the trunk, but he'd figured on hearing a little something even from this distance. The longer he stared… "Something ain't right." The arrow rose higher from the ground, then lowered. Difficult to see from this range, and it made no sense. Unless… "Breathing. The arrow hit *something breathing.*"

Edlmir took a knee beside him. "I see it. Trees here breathe?"

Rinold turned to Kurin.

"They say there're man eating plants deeper south in the Summer Jungles, but never have I heard of a tree with lungs."

Hoemulus, a hunter from Emudar who knelt thirty paces down the pyramid, said, "It didn't hit the godsdamned tree."

"What the hells're you talking about?" Plain as the scar on his face, the arrow stuck in the tree's trunk.

"It just ain't, come take a look."

Rinold jumped to his feet and trotted to the man's position with Kurin and Edlmir on his heels; he kneeled, eyes pinned on the arrow. The fletching rose and fell as before, but the angle of view… the tree shifted, or rather, the tree wasn't where it seemed to be. "It's like the godsdamned thing is stuck in a wall of clear water and we see the tree through it."

Edlmir huffed. "Some kind of Water *te-xe?* Like that frozen one you met in the Treaty Lands?"

Kurin answered for him. "*Te-xe* are tiny, even the most powerful are maybe the size of a hare."

Revelation struck, and Rinold stood with his eyes trained on the arrow. "We aren't seeing through the creature…" He looked to Kurin. "That lizard you showed me, one that changed colors? They matched whatever they stood beside."

"Chameleon?" Her eyes darted back and forth in thought. "If you're right, whatever this creature is… the way it blends is beyond anything one of those lizards can do. The way the real tree blends with the false trunk… how would anything do that?"

Rinold could read the woman's mind because he too wondered if it wasn't some trick they might be able to mimic. "The how don't matter much… It's the why. Does it hide to stay safe, or is the camouflage a predator's trick?"

Edlmir said, "The beast slunk to the edge of camp in the middle of the night and took a nap? No, I'd wager it rested in wait for us to awake."

"Which means it's got the smarts to recognize guards at the watch… or it can't climb."

Kurin said, "Now I know what I'm staring at, I think I spot ripples, distortions… if I'm right, the damned thing is huge. Thirty paces, maybe more. Stealth hunters tend to be slow overall, but quick in a tight space, like the head of a snapping turtle. Might be we could just walk over the pyramid and stroll away."

"Gather the gear, but we're here, so we might as well see what can be seen before headin' on. Constant watch on whatever the hells that thing is."

Rinold put a dozen sets of eyes on the creature as the rest poked around the giant blocks of stone. While Edlmir oversaw the guards, others lifted and pulled each other up the tiers of stone. Rinold and Kurin took a stroll east. Neither of them was tall enough to enjoy the idea of climbing the escarpments.

Rinold's eyes flicked back and forth from the woods and the seams between stones. "You think there're passages in this place?"

"I do, but from what I've heard, the entries are in the surrounding area. But rumor speaks to hidden contraptions and levers as well."

They rounded the northeast corner, and the eastern side looked like a mirror to the north, but when they reached the southern side, Rinold grabbed his ribs and laughed; built-in stairs led from the forest floor to the peak of this man-made mountain. Rinold hit the steps at a jog. "Won't they piss when they reach the top and we're there?"

They didn't piss, but a couple of them did moan. He didn't pay attention to a wit of their grumbling banter; the overlook of the forest was beautiful, a sea of green with colorful birds and butterflies rising and falling into its still waves. They stood on an island without another sight of land; to the north, even the Dragonspan Mountains had sunk from view. He turned southwest, guessing where the river might flow, and his mouth opened to ask how far these forests stretched, but he didn't utter a single word.

"It's moving!"

He spun. "Which way?" But when he looked, he didn't need an answer. A wrinkling distortion shifted southeast at the edge of the forest, crushing shrubs and grasses under its invisible weight. Forty paces long if a hair. "Heavens have mercy. Run west! There're stairs on the south!"

Kurin grabbed his shoulder. "It's turning into the trees."

His eyes followed the beast into the woods, its path winding between trees before turning onto an ancient, bramble-covered road and came their way. He whipped his bow from his back and nocked an arrow. "Nock 'em! This thing ain't lettin' us leave!" Its trail wasn't silent now, as small trees cracked and ground beneath its weight. "At the head! Loose!"

He held his string tight as bows thrummed around him. The arrows struck twenty paces in front of the base of the pyramid; they skipped and tumbled from the target.

Kurin muttered beside him, "*Sheketu.*"

Moments later the world quivered under their feet as the creature rammed the lowest tier, and for a split flicker, a great slitted eye appeared, rising straight and falling. *Serpent.* Rinold twitched his fingers and the arrow flew true, but the eye disappeared and his arrow ricocheted into the grass. He squinted, trying to track the distortion; the thing fell back from the third tier but slithered east along the second.

His breaths rushed, eyes flicking back and forth. *That thing reaches the stairs…* "West! Down now! Hit the trees and scatter, get across that damned river and we'll meet up on the other side!" He tugged Kurin into motion and jumped down, staggered several steps, and leaped again. His knees weren't as young as they used to be and they ached by the third landing, but it was better than whatever that godsdamned snake had in mind for him.

He slumped to a knee on reaching the turf, catching his breath as others raced past and into the forest.

"Move!" Kurin kicked him in the ass, and he lumbered back to his feet; it took a dozen strides for his legs to stiffen from the limp leather the descent had turned them into, but once in stride confidence returned, and he glanced back.

It wasn't hiding no more. Smaller trees bent and brambles cracked before the monstrous serpent, its head covered in plates of lustrous-green scale that rose as horns above its eyes. "Split up!" Men running nearby veered, but Rinold kept a straight line, hoping it'd follow him. So far, success. He glanced to Kurin. "Get out of here!"

But she held firm by his side, and he didn't have the breath to argue.

They tumbled as the world fell away, and his bow fell from his hand as he bounced and skidded on his belly and chest down a slime-covered hill, his nose stopping so close to a stream's edge he could see his muddied reflection. *Streams lead to rivers.* He bound to his feet and glanced back. Kurin rose slow, covered in green ick, and trotted his way. He snagged his bow from the turf as brush crashed from above, and they ran.

The creek was no wider than a pole, and as soon as they reached a rushing narrow they leaped to the westward side. He held no hope the gurgling brook would stop this thing but slowing it a flicker would be nice. He caught his stride and a second wind; he could damned near run all day like this. Hells, this was drinking sweet wine compared to running out of the Crack of Burdenis. Then, he realized the serpent's armored head was damned near straight across from them, racing them southwest.

"Hells!"

Kurin nodded but didn't waste her breath on a word. He glanced at the beast, the creek, and the path ahead.

"Water and its channel are wide as this beast… it'll struggle to cross moving parallel or it would've already."

"Wonderful."

There was no missing the sarcasm, but he lacked the breath to laugh as they ducked branches and leaped over a streamlet that fed the creek. His boots sucked the mud on the opposite bank, and he stumbled, fingers sticking into grass-twined muck, and he prayed he didn't leave his boots behind as he lunged forward.

He kept his boots and straightened to catch his stride. "The river!" A murky green flow appeared ahead.

"Who's to say... this damn thing... don't swim... fast as it slithers?"

It wasn't the first time Rinold took to disliking logic. The current of the river ahead would take them right past their scaled friend's mouth, but the creek they ran beside widened ahead, and its cut in the forest floor deepened. *Let's see what this bastard can do.* "Follow me."

He cut northeast, winding his way around the base of a felled tree larger than a ship could handle for a mast, looking for a tree near the river's bank, a tree whose heights might help starve this critter. Four poles high and bigger around than a Colok's chest, it was larger than he'd seen this thing knock over, and it bore branches low enough to grip; a nut tree of some sort. He glanced back; the serpent squared itself to the stream bed and was barreling toward them to make its crossing. Thank the heavens this damned thing didn't turn its corners like a regular snake. "Climb!"

Rinold leaped for the lowest branch, caught, and swung his legs up and over, showing why he'd earned his nickname long before the Wolverine came around. Kurin stuttered her leap and slipped, fingers unable to even tickle the branch's bark.

He wrapped his legs and reached his arm to her hand, pulling her up as her feet scrambled against the bark for a toe hold, and together they sat breathing heavy.

The serpent rose through the air and hit the near side of the stream bank; dirt and debris scattered into the air with impact, and its horns wobbled above its brow.

"Mercies be. Climb!"

Branches clung to his clothes and ripped at his skin as they shimmied higher, not bothering to look down to see what he knew was coming. They were twenty feet high and rising when the tree shook as if struck by a runaway boulder in a landslide. Branches waved and his foot slipped, leaving him dangling as nuts clattered from above to dance on his head and shoulders. He closed his eyes and bellowed, bleeding hands slipping as tired arms hauled him high enough to catch a heel over a nearby branch.

Kurin snagged the nape of his shirt, and with her as a steadying guide he managed to a seat. He hugged the tree and laughed. "Take that, you godsdamned snake!"

Kurin giggled, but after she caught her breath, she said, "My people have a saying... never taunt the Traitor."

Rinold snorted. "This thing ain't a climber... it didn't even like the pyramid. In a couple candles, this bastard'll give up like a bear circling a bee's nest it can't reach."

Circle it did, surrounding the tree's trunk, the edge of its body slipping into the river's current. Rinold marveled at the creature's tenacity. "Stubborn prick." And stiff as a board compared to most snakes, no way it could wind itself around a tree this size. But after making its loop, it stared up at them, slitted black eyes unblinking, tongue tasting the air. Its head tilted to give them a better look.

"Can't even raise yer head like a snake, can you? Ha!" He plucked a nut from the tree and winged it, beaning the serpent between two nostrils each the size of his forearm. "Next one goes right up your nose! You bring any whiskey, we got time ta kill."

Kurin snorted, then pointed as her eyes widened. "Fifth Earl, what's it doing?"

Scales shifted at the side of the thing, and its head rose a couple feet from the ground as it slithered toward the trunk. The giant nose kicked up as it eased into the base of the tree, and scales farther down the body shifted, lifting? Branches shattered and fell from the creeping head's path. The good news was it moved slow as molasses.

"Son of a godsdamned whoreson." It wasn't often he borrowed the Wolverine's curses, but the moment was worthy. He rose to stand on his branch and shimmied around the tree. "Back to my first notion. It's time for a bath." He reached the tree's riverside and shuffled out on a branch, his hands guided by twigs and leaves to help steady his balance.

"Are you crazy?"

He glanced back; her tone was incredulous, but it didn't slow down her following him. "Wait there until the branch steadies... if the thing follows me, stay here. It keeps coming for you... well, you better get crazy."

She nodded. "Good luck."

The golden-green snout cracked branches beneath them, and he took three breaths to steady his nerves. "I don't know what damned god to pray to for this one. If I make it so far as the river, at least no one will realize I pissed my britches." He turned and winked, then let go of his handholds. Two strides then three before the heavy branch bucked beneath his weight, and he sprang. Twigs and leaves slapped his face and he bellowed; he was going to land right on the damned thing. He threw his legs forward and ricocheted off the serpent's back, somersaulted sideways into the river before thinking to hold his breath.

He sputtered, gasped, and flailed, transitioning from murky blindness to blinding sun, and let fly a stream of water that left an oily coat on his tongue. Soon as he knew he wasn't drowning, he struck his arms forward and swam with the current. Ten strokes then twenty before he looked back; the good news and bad were the same; the serpent lowered from the tree and was coming after him.

He settled into a swimming rhythm and his brain was brash enough to think this was better than running, considering his knees and all the jarring jumps before.

The currents in the middle of the river changed his mind, moving fast with an occasional twist and curl that threatened to turn him around or dunk him for good; he appreciated land again. He glanced back in time to see the serpent's head surrounded by a halo of watery splash as it collided with the river.

Damn Kurin for being right about the thing swimming.

No time to piss and moan. He stroked faster, angling the best he could upriver in the hopes of not getting carried past an outcropping ahead, and as he grew closer, he realized there were cliffs beyond. *Shits!* Those cliffs were death; no way he'd climb his way from the waters before being eaten. He kicked his tired legs and drove himself on, spitting vile water that sloshed his mouth after damned near every breath.

His shoulders ached and he didn't dare look back; all his focus was on slime-covered rocks ahead.

Stroke. Breathe. Stroke.

His hand struck algae and stone, and he lowered his legs, knees clunking the river bottom. He scrambled toward the outcropping; he was going to make it. He hollered and laughed. "Hells yes!" And in flickers he stood atop a dry boulder, a half-drowned squirrel but very alive.

He turned and whooped, watching the currents carry the serpent past him and into the steep-walled cliffs beyond. He flicked his nose at the beast and pointed. "Goodbye, snakey! Best of luck next time!"

The crack of a twig from behind ended his laughter. *No way that's Kurin so soon.* "Hirk? That you?" He turned, his eye spasming in twitches. A dozen men and women stalked his way, their armor fashioned from strips of wood to cover their chests, but other than that, they were damned near naked. They were normal enough with ruddy skin and black hair, but the eyes of every one were a hue of topaz lit as if they held fire in their skull. Every damned one of them pointed an arrow at him with bows as long as Rinold was tall.

Kurin was right again: Never taunt the Traitor. His shoulders relaxed, and his head slumped. He raised his hands and smiled with a mutter beneath his breath. "Gotta be shittin' me."

Two

Born of Stone

Assassins silk stretched taut,
sought and fought into a rout,
the lout, a bout about the vows and soot,
your foot, my foot, five foot who?
My hand, your hand, six foot underland,
Wrist to wrist, silk tied taut,
sealing love, bringing love,
eliciting joy or fiery Damnation,
the pathetic and prophetic,
to Heaven can a man rise when a man never dies?

—*Tomes of the Touched*

Sîkômu Rekrôm, East-Wall Quarry, stood less than half a horizon from what the Kingdomers named Rôemhîik, the wall and fortress so many Silone had taken to calling Castle Choerkin. For his part, Ivin stuck to the Kingdomer name as close as he could pronounce the nuances of the foreign tongue. In his years on Herald's Watch, Ivin never had the opportunity to witness the construction of anything more than a brick warehouse. Hells, he never once bothered to consider how people chiseled gigantic blocks from mountains, let alone how they transported them, let alone how they lifted them into place, let alone how they interconnected them for strength and stability. It was no wonder folks imagined giants hard at work.

Ivin stood beside Morik of Shuntiskâ overlooking the quarry where several hundred Kingdomers and Silone worked together. They hammered and chiseled grooves into amber-hued travertine, all to sizes specific to Lordbuilder Hîekôn's specifications. Once grooved into a rectangle, square, or other shape, hammers and chisels and crowbars went to work to separate the block from its base, and it was slid out onto logs. They left two protrusions on each long edge, used later to lift the blocks into place along the wall by a crane fifty-feet tall. Once separated from the mountain, the undeniable genius of the Kingdomers came into play; they fitted the ends of the blocks into wooden forms, and when they finished, the blocks of stone, which could crush a man into jelly, became axles between oaken wheels to be pulled by oxen to the wall. The largest he'd seen was twenty-seven feet long, thick as his forearm, and deep as he was tall.

"How's that future wife of yours getting along?"

Ivin's eyes dropped to his toes, and he snorted before raising his gaze to look the Kingdomer in the face. "She'd be better with word from Solineus."

"Once past Barkûsh, there aren't no pigeons. But that isn't what I was talking about."

"Which is why I answered the way I did." They shared a laugh. "Ah, hells. She spends more time with the pigeons than me, and I spend more time staring at rocks."

"Stones are the bones of the world! But they aren't pretty as that little gal."

Ivin sighed. "A day less than a month until a wedding neither of us is keen on, but Tedeu will stomach no further delays."

"Here's a story I never told a soul; repeat it to the wrong ears and I'll box yours. Solineus climbed the Twelfth Foundation—"

"I've heard that tale." He grinned and twined his hands behind his back.

"You Silone are an impatient sort. I climbed that same mountain, though I stopped well short of the summit. I was in love! I had to get back to my love or my heart was bound to shittin' burst. When I got back to Shuntiskâ I found she'd been promised to a man of Molikîn. I thundered, I wept, I cursed the gods and my mother for arranging the girl's marriage. Turned out the Ironwing had different plans for me, and I was wed to a young lady from the Vale of Herindet, a place I'd never even heard of. Istilu and I, we *hated* each other. She didn't want to move to Shuntiskâ, I didn't want to so much as see her face. Twenty years on, the only thing that separates her and me are you godsdamned Silone." He grinned and slapped Ivin on the back.

Ivin chuckled. "How many years did that take?" The man paused, the twitch to his lip and his gaze to the ground suggesting he thought to lie. "No lies now."

"Five *agonizing* years. Two before we tolerated one another. I think you're ahead of us in this regard."

"So maybe I only have three years of misery to look forward to?"

"You're a brighter bastard than I ever was, I reckon. And she's sweeter than my lady in those days. We both bore tempers and broke many fine antiques between the two of us. You two don't seem the sort. Well, you don't anyhow."

"I should be grateful I got the gentler sister, I suppose."

A guffaw. "Come! We should get back to the wall, make sure pigeon-girl hasn't flown the coop to escape you."

They hopped down the mountain's chiseled tiers before edging to a smooth trail leading to the grass-covered Rôemhîen and its footpaths. For a long time, the trails here traveled three directions, east, west, and north, from the wall to the eastern and western quarries, but a trail traveling south was now beaten clear. Silone headed for the dense forests to the south for meat, furs, wood, and other supplies, so much travel that the villages of Forest's Gate and Foggy Vale already sprouted at the southern end of the Roemhien.

So it was that when they turned their heads to the sound of riders from the south, it wasn't a surprise: Kurin of Kîlît and a handful of Silone men. The group spurred their horses from a walk the flicker they spotted Ivin and Morik. The woman slipped from her saddle and into a graceful kneel. "My apologies for all that has happened and for all that will come. Mountain Lord, we found trouble in the south."

"Rise, Kurin. What kind of trouble?"

Ivin's thoughts spun to the Ôgrihîn or some other monster. "Where's Rinold?"

The woman didn't even glance at him. "Men."

Morik huffed. "The Histê don't travel so far east."

"Not Histê, best as I can tell. I've never seen these people before."

Ivin kept his calm. "Rinold? The other men with you?"

"These people attacked as we fled a snake so damned big it might swallow a griffon. We ran. It was a blur. It followed Rinold and me, and he led it into a river with me up a tree. The beast didn't get him, but a hunting party did. They were half-naked and armed with bows. I rounded up most of the Silone and tracked them to a camp... Every soul who wasn't with me was tethered to poles or caged. We lacked the numbers for a fight, and the next morning they attacked again, took three more of us in nets, and later in the day, two more. They tracked us, led us into a trap. All of us you see here, we got lucky to make it through. Soon as we got past them, we moved north straight until we got here."

"Tethered? Caged?" Morik grunted. "Sure sounds like Histê, cursed slavers."

Kurin shook her head. "The language was wrong… they painted their bodies instead of tattoos. Smaller builds in general, more Rinold's size than the Histê."

Morik snorted, spat, and ground it into the stone with his toe. "I don't know what the hells to make of it."

Ivin's brain spun with the turning of days. "How much time are we talking about? A month since they were taken?"

Kurin's head drooped. "Just over a month, thirty-two days. By my reckoning, they were taken just under a hundred horizons from Foggy Vale. As the griffon flies. It'll take twenty days to get people down there, more apt to add a week in that terrain than move faster."

Morik grunted. "A sixty-day lead and that if we move fast. If we knew who these people were—"

Ivin said, "I don't give two shits who they are or why they took our people. I'll spread the word through the clans, we'll have men ready to ride for the forest by tomorrow morning. Will you lead them?"

Kurin glanced to Morik. "I will. We found a Green Mountain, a ruin, that's where the beast first attacked. We'll begin the search there."

"These ruins, are they defensible? And how many enemies can we expect?"

"Most walls are down or covered by forest, but with work… maybe. Difficult to pin a number on these bastards, way they glided through the woods. I'd guess half a hundred, give or take a handful. If they're slavers, there'll be a bigger camp."

Morik said, "I can spare twenty guards from the quarries, and the Ironwing will want word on this… we've loggers in them woods often enough."

"I appreciate the help, but this fight isn't yours."

"No, Choerkin, we don't know whose fight this is. And tell me you wouldn't do the same?"

The story of Solineus' trek up the mountain and subsequent journeys were familiar, but he forgot or underestimated how these two men bonded. It was more than a favor owed. Ivin chuckled and shook his head. "A brother of a brother is a brother."

"You say it as if it's funny."

Ivin shook his head. "After all I've seen, I find it amazing someone means it. I welcome you and your people to travel by my side."

Morik coughed. "I reckon I don't know your customs so well, but I expect the groom should attend his own wedding?"

Ivin's head rolled back and he stared at the sky, wondering if he might put off the ceremony for a while… a few years, maybe. "No, I wouldn't expect the Lady Ravinrin to go easy on that plan."

"Nor the Ironwing… nor my wife… Sufficient to say I won't be seeing the forest's depths. But my people will assist yours."

Ivin turned toward the wall and walked. "I'd send an army if I could, as it is, I doubt the clans will spare a hundred men."

Kinesee's fifteenth birthday had been a celebration she would never have imagined for three reasons. First, there'd been at least three hundred party-goers. Second, Tedeu allowed her to drink wine for the first time, and she *hated* it; the stuff was a sinister plot against her palate and expectations, but after three glasses she ignored her tongue, thankful for the drink helping to numb the third: The party doubled as a celebration of her pending nuptials.

Marriage!

She wanted to hurl curses, but she saved her sharpened tongue for those times when she was alone. Maro and the other guards relaxed month by month as there hadn't been so much as a whisper of assassins, but time alone was still rare and precious, even here on the wall spanning the Roemhien Pass. She and Ivin had delayed the woman's plots and plans for a month, but they'd run out of excuses. Tedeu would see them married before the new year, even if she had to take a stick to both their heads to do it. The breezes this afternoon passed from warm to chill, depending on the moment, making it a pleasant day to wrap herself in a fox-skin robe as she walked with Maro shadowing her.

She was a princess with a castle now, even if it wasn't like what she'd imagined a couple of years ago, but compared to the harrowing alternatives she shouldn't be complaining. The Western Tower, the Pigeon's Nest she called it, was complete. It was more a castle unto itself than a tower, or perhaps a keep (the proper names of such things eluded her), which housed a stable, garrison, the pigeon-master Kekoru, and herself. Kinesee would live at the central tower once married, but for the time being the Pigeon's Nest was her home. And she loved it, most days at least.

The wall proper might as well be finished, thirty feet of solid stone thick and a pole higher, and the approach from the north was a steep rise an army would hate to march. Despite being a horizon wide, it would take few men to defend its perch; the Kingdomers assured her that so long as the wall had ample men in defense, no army would defeat their master construction. She didn't doubt them, and she understood that a siege would be fruitless; with a forest full of food at their backs and fresh wells and springs for water, an army could hold here until growing old with age. But there were still two main towers to finish and talk of a walled city had already begun.

She didn't know what her father had done to earn such respect from the Kingdomers, but they were feverish in their insistence to help. Oh, Solineus' letter had spoken of a "coin" on a mountain, but she'd never grasped why such thing was so valuable.

The Central Tower grew before her as she approached, and so too did the number of guards she passed, which meant Maro and his men drew closer to her side. She slowed to drop in by the big man's side. "We should bring horses atop the wall, it'd be a fun gallop."

The man's mustache drooped. "Can't say I've ever entertained that notion any more than the idea of being bucked over a cliff."

"You're such a gloomy fellow, the wall is wide enough for two wagons. A well-mannered horse would be no trouble at all."

"You know why no assassin's come for you since that night? Because they figured out you'll do something stupid to kill yourself without their help."

She laughed. "You might be right." Kinesee turned and leaned against the parapets facing south. A pair of oxen pulled a slab of stone down the hill, two men riding beside the wheels, leaning on hand-brakes to make certain the chiseled piece of mountain didn't get away. Even with these smaller stones, the system never failed to impress.

Her eyes rose as riders poured over the rise to the south and galloped around the oxen. They rode with a speed that spoke of a purpose, and it didn't take more than a few flickers to realize one of them was her betrothed and another was Morik.

"I didn't know the Kingdomer was here for a visit."

"I've little doubt the man has more to do than visit you and your pigeons every time he leaves Shuntiskâ."

"Did somebody punch you awake before sunup? You're a grump today."

"I'm warm as the sun, m'lady."

Kinesee glanced at the cloud-covered glow in the sky. "Mmhmm. I see."

The horses approached fast and she leaned and stretched, waving to Ivin. In her mind she wasn't some girl in a day dress; she was a princess draped in a silver-laced gown like she'd worn on her birthday, the one that made Ivin's eyes go wide like enraptured men were meant to. But this time he wasn't even looking. She stretched to her tiptoes and waved with her broadest smile, and the thick-headed man rode straight into the gates without so much as a glance up.

She raced to the northern parapets in time to see the horses streak through and down the rise. "Ivin!" She waved and jumped, then stomped her foot and scowled the flicker she realized her prince was a thick-headed warlord and she was just a girl in a plain dress. "Men are so blind."

"Don't blame the boy, if he'd seen you—"

"A man should *know* his lady is waving."

Maro laughed but cut the guffaw short as she turned her stare on him. Her other guards looked everywhere but at her. "Now who was punched awake this morn? I'd be more curious about what had them riding so fast."

Kinesee snorted. "That's because you're a lunkheaded man as well. Maybe even lunkier than that Choerkin." She turned to the gate towers and stared; her walking mood had turned sour, but there was no way to avoid a walk one way or another, seeing as she was in even less of a stand-around mood. She spun west. "We should check on the pigeons, see if Solineus has sent word."

Maro puffed his mustache with a breath. "We spoke to the pigeon-master not much over a candle past."

"And we'll talk to her again!" She tromped along the wall as if she were some legendary dragon trying to tear down a mountain. A hundred stomps later, she admitted she was behaving like a peevish brat, but only to herself. She lightened her steps, to save her ankles from the pounding, and took deep breaths before releasing her lips from a pouting frown.

After a half candle to walk off her irritation they reached the Pigeon's Nest. Guards nodded and opened the single oak door, and she strode into the shadows of the tower's hull. She headed straight rather than left and down.

"You've decided to not visit the pigeon-master?"

Kinesee sighed. "Kekoru can wait a few wicks. I'm going to rest my feet a little." Her boots were new and comfortable, but they'd rubbed a couple spots sore in the early part of her walk.

She ascended a flight of stairs with her train of guards marching behind, and she threw the door open, but it should've been locked.

"Hello, Kinesee."

The woman's voice startled her toes off the floor, and her heart thudded as Maro's sword whispered from its sheath. She turned to stare at inhuman eyes. "Lelishen! Gosh be darned; don't do that." Maro's sword remained leveled at the woman until Kinesee pushed his hand down.

Lelishen sat in Kinesee's favorite chair by a stained-glass window depicting vines of red roses. "I am sorry for my entrance."

Kinesee moved to a stool beside her bed as Maro sheathed his blade and motioned the other guards to remain outside the door.

"Do tell, what brings you to my palace?"

Lelishen straightened in her seat, her face calm as if still in deep thought. "Have you had word from Solineus?"

"It's been many months, but the Ironwing let us know he'd passed through Barkûsh. Where he went from there and why nobody knows."

Lelishen sighed and couldn't conceal her worry. "May we speak alone?"

Kinesee nodded. "Maro, please leave us be, and close the door."

The big man glared and puffed his mustache. "Yes, m'lady."

Lelishen waited until the door closed behind him. "Your pearl, can you call him?"

Maybe it shouldn't have shocked her that the Trelelunin knew, but somehow it did. "My... I can tell that he is alive."

"He mentioned hearing your voice."

She blushed, a tad annoyed at what she knew. "Yes, but only when he was close... and when my need was desperate. Alu heard him once."

The woman stood and glided to tower over her, but Kinesee didn't feel threatened. She felt sadness and concern. "Rub the pearl for me, tell him I need him."

Kinesee pulled the pearl from beneath the hem of her dress as she stared into the woman's large, beautiful eyes with their flecks of silver. It'd been over a year since Lelishen had been here last, and looking back, she figured she should've seen the worry in the woman's gaze when she asked after Solineus. She rubbed the pearl between her hands, soothed by its familiar warmth, and she felt a connection to the man's soul grow. She closed her eyes. *Lelishen is here, she needs you.*

Lelishen's stare didn't waver. "Anything?"

Kinesee shook her head. "No. I mean, I *feel* him, so I guess he feels me, but... I have no idea."

"Rub the pearl again."

The pearl grew warm and Lelishen clutched her hands, long fingers enveloping her grip on the pearl. Her touch was warm, so hot she wondered if the woman maybe had a fever. Then she heard Lelishen's voice in her head: *I need you. Come to me.*

Lelishen's eyes blinked open and the two stared at each other, the pearl's warmth fading. There was no response from Solineus.

"I didn't hear him, but I heard you."

"I heard nothing as well." The woman's chin sank to her chest, and if a tear had fallen, Kinesee wouldn't have been surprised.

"What's wrong? Maybe I can help."

Lelishen released her hands. "No, but you can rub the pearl every day, try to let him know. If you speak to him, tell him to find me between the snow and the sun."

"Between... What do you mean?"

"He'll figure it out." She turned to leave.

Kinesee stomped her foot. "Tell me what's going on."

Lelishen stopped, her arms dropping to her sides. "Can you keep a secret? One a life depends on."

"Of course."

Lelishen stepped close, and the whisper in her ear brought a chill to her spine. "Solineus and I have... an impossible son. If the wrong ears hear this, he will die. Not a soul except you and Solineus may know this."

Kinesee's head rocked back, the chill gone. "I have a little brother?" Lelishen's smile fought through a fear fraught face. "What's his name?"

"Veldehar. It means untold blessing in the tongue of the Helelindin." She turned, opened the door, and disappeared down the hall.

Maro's head stuck through the gap in a flicker. "What did the woodkin want?"

Kinesee stifled her grin. "Leaving a message for Solineus, is all."

"If you say so, m'lady."

"Nothing for you to worry about. Womanly things. I need to sit and think. Leave me be a for a while."

The door closed, shutting off a grumble from the man, and Kinesee flopped in her chair. *I never considered having a little brother, even if he isn't blood.* With all the death and misery she'd faced over a lifetime, let alone these past couple of years, the notion left an unexpected warmth in her breast. Except, *who would want to kill a baby?*

THREE

Western Reach

The Five-Handed Finger, the Mute and Madcap Singer,
to linger into anger unending,
fending inanity and rending insanity, the words come fast at a dash
rash lash slash mash bash.
And blend. Until the end.
A million eyes.
Molasses lipped in a single gem.

—*Tomes of the Touched*

"A Warlord Choerkin... And the runt of the litter, no less."

Solineus swished warm ale around his tongue and swallowed as he stared at his aging mirror. He and his father had talked for three candles, consumed four mugs apiece, and his wits still hadn't swallowed the enormity. "He's twenty by now, I reckon, and plenty tall. But enough of my tales, how the hells did you end up here in Mulshahar?"

Adinvan frowned into his mug before raising his eyes. "Ours isn't much of a tale compared to yours. I'd just docked back at Emudar Fost on the Eve of Snows, having sailed up from Ôfelun, when I learned someone killed Lord Lidin Emudar and his family in their sleep that night. The Fost was godsdamned chaos. I sent your sister, Ederu..." Adinvan stopped to stare. "You've a sister, she's on the Isle of Pôn last I knew."

"Maybe when I see her, I'll remember. The name is familiar, at least." It was a cozy lie to ease their souls; not a lick of his memory recalled a sister or the name.

"Germund Ilô, that sack of wind, was strutting around like a king as the Fost crumbled."

Hadin snorted, foam from his ale spattering the table as he wiped his mouth. "That preenin' prick thought his shit were an order to be followed."

Adinvan grinned. "Wasn't more'n a few candles before a rider came in from Istinjoln warning of demons, the Shadows of Man you called them, and Taken."

Riders from Istinjoln took days to reach Emudar Fost; the incongruity brought a squirm to his seat. He recalled how Ulrikt gave Meliu the *Codex of Sol* with the note to flee Kaludor. It was as if the lord priest had the heads of the clans killed and warned the clans of his own failure to summon the gods before it happened. A thousand horizons or more away, and he could still smell Istinjoln's stink. "And on that word, you sailed?"

"Wish it were true, but no... no one knew what to trust. We spread the word anyhow, had folks prepared the best we could... and a couple days later word trickled in: sightings. When Morgîth Shorkin rode in from Delkin Tower we raised the alarm and ships set sail. Still, it took days to get so many folks to sea, and I saw firsthand what came for us before fleeing."

"Word I heard was the Tek Brotna were attacking Emudar ships."

Adinvan shrugged. "Didn't see it m'self, but I reckon it's likely as not. We had damned poor timing all around. A day out, one hells of a storm blew in off the Iverêun Ocean, and we bobbed bare poles for a day and a half; winds died down we saw Thon sails moving into the Parapets. They ignored us, but we didn't push our luck and bore south."

"All the way to Mulshahar?"

He chuckled. "We gathered on the west coast of Resharm Island first. Late arrivers brought word of the clans gathering in Hidreng, but there was word of Brotna and Thon as well. South was our best option, Ôfelun City was the goal. We lost a lot of boats on the way; others gave up the journey and stopped off in Tek cities. Can't blame 'em much. The holies kept our fresh-water supply stable, but food ran short after a time."

"How many made it with you?"

"We're scattered, no count. The Lord of Ôfelun called us the lost herd and counted us at six hundred sea-worthy vessels plus smaller ships. Folks packed the decks."

Six hundred ships were more than the rest of the clans combined. "A guess?"

"I'd say sixty thousand, if'n you include those who stopped off in Tek cities. Twenty thousand maybe made it to the peninsula right off, but more and more have trickled in from the Tek cities."

"That's as many or more than who made it to the Dragonspans, by my reckoning. Where's everyone living?"

"Folks who're able have been hiring out their ships, fishing, docking or dropping anchor anywhere they're welcome. But, there're a few islands south of here... so hot you wanna run around naked all day and burn to a cinder, and the native folks welcome us. Or others haven't anyone living on them at all. We've been settling them slow and steady."

"A new home."

"Aye. From what you say, sailing back to Kaludor isn't much of an option."

"It isn't. Not yet."

Adinvan stretched and quaffed his ale. "I hate to say it, my boy, but I don't reckon many folks once settled would move back north even if they could. A long godsdamned journey just to face ice and winds. Twelve Hells, I didn't spend so much time trading in the south for the gold alone!" He laughed. "Not a soul loses fingers nor toes to frostbite hereabouts."

Solineus chuckled, rubbed his face. "The rest of the clans could use our numbers."

"There's nothing for that, son, unless you plan on cuttin' a canal all the way to... wherever the hells they are."

Solineus snorted. "We've got Silone scattered across Northern Vandunez. Secure them islands, and we might be able to get some Kingdomer birds for communication."

"Birds? They got talking birds?"

Hadin leaned in. "We got eyes, more'n one set to watching us."

Adinvan leaned in his seat, hand loosening his sword in its scabbard as he laughed at nothing. "What the hells for, you think? We aren't flashing gold. You flirtin' with some woman who one of these gents claims?"

Solineus squinted. "I haven't been here so long, but I might've exchanged enough coin to gain some attention." He doubted the lady at the exchange, or her husband, said a word, but maybe a hundred people wandered through the lobby while he sat there. He glanced at the folks sitting and drinking; he reckoned most were merchants and not a one wore armor. "City official maybe, checking on a large exchange?"

Hadin's eyes flicked back and forth. "Ain't no way you carried so much... How the hells much did you bring?"

"Two hundred and fifty thousands, or thereabouts."

The man's eyes bulged. "Sâguts?"

"Smedên."

Adinvan spat beer across the table as Hadin stared at the ceiling and tapped his finger to thumbs in calculation. His voice came as a raspy whisper. "That's over five million sâguts. You shittin' me?"

"I don't even know what a smedên *is* to *be* shittin' you."

The three men stared in silence as Adinvan wiped the table with his forearm. The old man huffed after a spell, rocked back in his chair. "I always knew you had a way with the ladies... known you attracted coins like that I would've brought you south long ago."

Solineus scoffed. "Sure we got eyes? This don't seem the sort of place for a brawl."

"In Mulshahar, death is more apt to wear silk than burlap." Adinvan smiled and waved a serving lass to their table. "A cask of your finest ale to go... he's buying. A *sâgut* should cover it with gratuity."

Solineus dropped a small coin on the table, impure silver, which he believed to be a sâgut. "So, you're sayin' I won't want for ale in my lifetime."

"I reckon that's what I'm a sayin'. Hadin, stick your nose outside and see if you smell any outlaws who might want my boy dead."

The sailor returned the same flicker their ale arrived. Adinvan tucked the little cask under his arm. "Well?"

Hadin smacked his lips and licked. "I'll be lettin' you see for yerself."

Solineus reached over his left shoulder to unbind the sister's cover; they concealed the Ikoruv but could slip the grip if a real fight came. Adinvan glanced. A triple take at the hilts.

"You shittin' me?"

Solineus grinned. "You don't know the half of it." He walked to the doors, his foot shoving them open to stride beneath the eve. People lined the broad boardwalks, and horses and carts plied the streets, but nothing felt out of place.

Adinvan brushed his left shoulder as he strode past, heading east. "You haven't been in Mulshahar long enough. Three men ahorse yonder? They aren't watching you; they're throwing shade for the one who is. I've only seen one twice. A Vikarê. Come on, but don't stare."

His father ducked into the street, stepping around horse dung, and Solineus followed. His eyes flicked to the horsemen, natural enough seeing as they strode that way. It took a second glance to catch black eyes beneath an umber hood staring at him; it was difficult not to stare back. He broke the gaze to look to clouds rolling in from the east, but he couldn't restrain his curiosity as they drew closer. Beady eyes set in a narrow face, tan skin patterned with diamonds; the person wore a mask, or wasn't human.

The being stood maybe five feet tall, hunched with massive shoulders beneath a cloak fashioned with a fine weave. After Adinvan sidestepped through the street's traffic and stepped onto the boardwalk, Solineus was close enough to discern the flat face was more forehead, and what he'd assumed the chin was instead its snout.

Adinvan spoke with a raised voice. "We'll make for the *Evening Sky*, got her docked yonder at the end of the fourth bay. We're in no hurry to set sail, so you've plenty of time to get to know this beautiful city."

Solineus dragged his eyes back to his father's shoulders. "Sounds good."

Several strides later: "You stared, didn't you?"

"Who was that?" It'd taken a while to get used to the Luxuns, but like the Edan, they'd had a human-like familiarity.

"All these people you see in the streets are just that, people who live and trade here. The rulers of Mulshahar... indeed, the whole of the peninsula, are the Vikarê."

"The face..."

"Aye, they walk with their faces tucked to blend more with the surrounding folks. I've never seen what's beneath the robes, but by the size of 'em, I'd say they weigh damned near two hundred bricks."

Hadin said, "Folks say their backs bear armor like an armadillo, their hide thicker than a bull's."

"Two hundred bricks. Armadillo." He'd heard of armadillos enough to know of what he spoke but had never seen one. "So, the men in the tavern were its associates?"

He turned south toward the docks. "I'd wager not, but I reckon their eyes're on you for the same reason: gold." Adinvan stopped so fast Solineus ran into him.

A stocky man wrapped in yellow and brown silks had stepped in front of him. He blurted gibberish, but his father must've understood him.

"This bastard says there're crossbows on us from the windows. He wants us to go with him to that building there."

Solineus eyeballed windows all around but saw nothing in particular. "What're the odds men knew our route?"

"Plum poor, I'd reckon."

Solineus stepped close and nudged Adinvan to the side. He glanced at a three-story building built from fired clay, its orange hues showing through a coat of paint flaking away. He pointed. "That building right there?"

"*Yostuvu. Seru-tê menid sômu ûballamâor.*"

"He says yes and wants our weapons."

Solineus raised his hands in peace and lifted his shield from his back with a smile; cracked the man upside the head with its face, and the shield sang a melodious tune as the man crumpled to the street bleeding.

Adinvan clucked. "Reckon he didn't see that comin'."

Solineus strode toward the building, Hadin on his back. "What the hells're you doing?"

"Finding out why he wanted us in that building."

"You crazy? Your boy is crazy."

Adinvan shrugged. "We don't wanna stand around in the street over a bleeding man anyhow. So, boy, you know who these people are? Have a plan?"

Solineus hopped up a single step in front of the door. The building's face ran thirty paces in either direction and without a window at eye level, he figured the openings in the wall above supplied light from a high ceiling. "Nope. Hadin, you might want to hang back." He had to remember that these two weren't fresh off the trail and still wearing their armor. "Maybe both of you should."

Hadin snorted, and Adinvan said, "Hells no. You step through, I'm with you. But I hope to the Forges you know what you're doin'."

"Crazy has worked out for me so far."

They entered to silence and stared. The sun lit the room in dusty beams of light from the windows high above, showing off a tall room held aloft by pillars and stacked with crates lined in rows. There were plenty of places to hide and a half dozen routes to traverse amid the stores, and no doubt more stood outside his view. He nodded straight ahead and strode forward until reaching a broad open space in the center of the building. Wood creaked, and he drew the Sister before taking three more steps.

Six men stepped in front of them, and he guessed more had arrived from behind from the sound of hushed steps. Silks wrapped the men from head to toe, colors ranging from muted earth tones to vibrant flowers, and to a man, they bore some weapon or another. Most carried smallswords suited to the streets, but two of them carried short-hafted, leaf-head spears. "Hadin, how many behind us?"

"Three."

A man with his face wrapped in brown silk stepped forward and spoke, Adinvan translated. "He says to hand over all our valuables, starting with that fancy sword of yours. Speaking of which, you skipped those in your story."

"That's a whole 'nother tale. Tell him he doesn't want this sword." Solineus flipped the sword's grip and caught the blade with a gentle touch; he smiled and held it out.

The brigand's eyes glanced back and forth as he spoke. Adinvan said, "He's quite convinced he wants it and tells us not to move."

"I'm not sure what's about to happen but be ready for a fight."

"I'm ready for a fight the moment my eyes open in the mornin'."

Ginger fingers reached for the hilt and snagged the sister, the man jumping back as if he saw a snake curling to strike. His eyes widened, and the surrounding skin went ashen. His smallsword hit the floor with a clatter as he took the sister in two hands, dropped to his knees, and slammed the blade through his chest until guard hit bone.

The brother sang between Solineus' ears when drawn, and he charged the nearest man; steel flashed to his left, and he raised his arm, the point of a spear striking off the Kingdomer shield with a chime. The brother shaved steel as it redirected the thrust of another's sword, striking and cleaving the guard and half the man's hand. His scream ended when Latcu split him from groin to shoulder on the return stroke.

A whisper in his mind and he spun, the shield smashing a sword before the brother pierced the man's silks to find his heart. He spun on two more men; one thrust his arm and took a half-hearted throw at him with a spear before turning to run. The spear sailed over Solineus's head to stick in a crate. The other man half-stepped toward him before spinning to bolt.

The clatter of a sword behind him and he turned to see his father standing over a dead man, and Hadin with two daggers plunged up and under a man's ribs; he withdrew the blades and plunged them twice more before the brigand fell.

Solineus turned a circle, eyes focused for any movement, his ears open for any sound. *Steps coming.* He raised his shield and crouched. "We've got company."

Four men with halberds, mail, and red robes charged into the room. "*Sumâlu* Mulshahar!"

Adinvan stood straight and wiped his blade before slipping it in his sheath. "He's telling these dead men to surrender to Mulshahar, I believe." Adinvan raised his hands wide and spoke to the man back and forth. "He says he'd gotten word of thieves attacking foreigners in this warehouse, and he is happy to see we are alive." Adinvan strolled close. "How many sâguts you got on you? Give these men some coins and thank them for their concern. Don't ask, just do it."

Solineus sheathed the brother and smiled at the lead guard as he opened his pouch and palmed a dozen coins. He held out the prize to the officer and dropped them into his eager hand. "Tell this man how much I appreciate his service, and of course, to keep his eye on our backs."

"*Syet Syet!* Honor. *Humum tûê.*"

"He says yes, it will be his honor, and to not worry about this mess."

Solineus bowed then meandered to pull the sister from the brigand's chest. He sheathed the blade and hung his shield on his back. "We are free to go?"

Adinvan laughed and slapped his back while guiding him toward the exit. "Very free. Even after he splits those coins with the surviving thieves, it'll be more than he earns in a month."

"I overpaid then..." Solineus cocked his head. "What the hells are you talking about, share with the thieves?"

"Someone meant those guards to save us from brigands... to make a point to a wealthy foreigner that he needs to pay for protection."

Hadin said, "I think yer old man's got the right of it. Didn't work out so well for the deaduns."

Solineus sighed. "So, we just killed a theater troupe? Tell me that won't happen again."

Adinvan laughed again as they stepped onto the boardwalk. "Tomorrow, we'll make our way to the captain of the guard and city officials to make a generous donation to their coffers. Then you won't have to worry about another incident."

"Wealth has a price. A peculiar way to do business."

"Welcome to Mulshahar, my boy, welcome to Mulshahar!"

Four

North South North

The Mêômbar of the Tostolu hung stretched into the Diving Bird, head-first before the Temple of Sângmûer, ankles bound above his head and wrists stretched to his side. Every day for twenty-two days did King Priest Îmund the Second offer the man a journey to the Stars, but on the twenty-third day, Îmund kept his promise to free the man: The Black Sword of Muzdar severed the man's ankles without blood so he might walk free again, and severed the ties at his wrists so that he might still play the harp. From this act of kindness, we still have the song Holy Stars on High, the Mêômbar's ode to the honesty and generosity of Îmund.

-Codex of Sol

The *Codex of Sol* thwarted Meliu at damned near every turn of the page, giving her hints and glimpses, but whatever knowledge she gleaned cast more shade than daylight. Half the damned book contained histories instead of prophecies, giving her names and events, information that, without context, was pert-near worthless. And it bored her to tears. Wars, murders, executions, and assassinations blurred from the distinct colors of a rainbow into dull mud.

The cryptic words of the text reflected how she felt about the years since the Eve of Snows: She was missing something. Hundreds of keys to ciphers littered the text; *no one* went to this depth of toil to hide nothing.

Her brain flitted around the keys to secrets, and maybe even fiddled with them in the lock, but she never quite got the tumblers to roll. Two years of fatigued wits and stifled yawns to learn how many warriors died at the battle of something or another and how some city or territory (that no longer existed, as far as she knew) conquered another.

If Ulrikt ever showed a face she knew was his, she might give the damned book back to him for good. But she wasn't even that lucky. Or maybe it was lucky... hard to decide which his absence was.

She rubbed her eyes and retrained them on the latest bit of translation:

On this, the 5th of Kelevrâ, in the year 387 by the reckoning of Sôl, the Forty-Fifth Warlord Broldun beheaded the thirty-ninth Warlord Emudar, claiming his helm and reign, becoming the Fortieth Warlord Emudar under the watchful eyes of King Priest Mestofin the Third.

By this time, there had only been twenty-four Warlord Choerkins, speaking to stability at the top of the ladder. It was chilling and funny to realize that despite all the clan hatreds which brewed over the past five hundred years, the Age of God Wars was more brutal by far. And from what she figured, there was an irony to the hierarchy: Choerkin, Emudar, Broldun, and Ravinrin back then mirrored life on Kaludor for power and influence before they fled. In the Age of God Wars, the Warlords were interchangeable in power and prestige, and they didn't follow bloodlines, but every one strove to be Choerkin.

Irony required coincidence; what if it wasn't coincidence?

She rubbed her eyes, and they reopened to the pleasant surprise of a bottle of wine sitting in front of her.

Sedut peered at her ink scratches. "Killing each other again?"

Meliu giggled. "Nothing like a grand victory to warrant an execution." In a few instances, lords rose or fell without blood, but most often, someone's head rolled. Hells, these people didn't even play games without someone's soul departing in gruesome fashion. She poured a glass of wine and swished the cherry tones around her teeth.

"We've word from the Choerkin wall."

Meliu's head rolled back as she swallowed, as if reading the name Choerkin every day wasn't enough. "Let me guess... we're invited to the wedding?" The woman's grin was difficult to read, insulted or insulting? "I know, get the fool man out of my head."

"After two years of pining... Two years minus several ill-advised rendezvous, it's good to know I don't have to say it. No, a group of hunters was attacked deep in the southern forest. The Rat... I should say, Rinold, and others are missing."

"Rinold's one of the best hunters we've got. What the hells kind of creature got him?"

Sedut wandered to Meliu's haphazard pile of books and scrolls, grabbed a map. "The two-legged kind, and I don't mean some bird. A Wayfinder and several Silone made it back... Rinold and the others were captured by men."

"Men? The Histê don't come so far north."

"So the Kingdomers say."

The way the woman sauntered her way with a smirk, there was more. "Yes?"

"They're gathering folks to go find them." She unrolled the scroll over the Codex. It wasn't what Meliu expected: It was the ancient map upon which Lelishen had located Meliu's mysterious goal and which taunted her with a name and unknown locale.

"What the hells has this got to do with Tomarok?" The map was a simple one, with major rivers and scattered mountains on its northernmost edge, but near its center rested the holy mountain.

Then Sedut unrolled a parchment a quarter the size of the map. "The Ravinrin messenger carried this, a copy of the Wayfinder's scribbles."

Meliu looked, but she couldn't read the Kingdomer words any more than she could crack the more difficult codes in the *Codex of Sol.* "What am I looking at?"

"You've stared at that tome too long; you're looking at the words. Imagine the scales more similar." She pointed at the edge of mountains on both maps, a river and several tributaries, a couple of circles, and a triangle. "These circles are minor ruins, the triangle a pyramid."

She squinted, visualizing the maps overlapped. The circles and triangle were exact if her reckoning was right. "You're thinking these circles are Mekelên, Jûmjôlu, and Setemêz?"

"If we've learned a thing about Wayfinders, it's their precision. And the symbols the Wayfinders use are centuries-old tradition. The Tomarok map bears similarities to suggest a Wayfinder made it." She pointed to a triangle far to the southwest on the ancient map.

Meliu sucked her teeth, released a whistling breath. "Tempting to see what I want to see... but the rivers are off."

"A river's flow changes over time, and don't forget, the world changed. Entire lands disappeared with the Forgetting."

Meliu still wanted to believe the world's dismemberment a myth, but how? "So the rivers changed. Let's assume this triangle is Setemêz, it still puts Tomarok several hundred horizons to the southwest."

Sedut grinned. "The Wayfinder thinks these people were slavers, if they aren't Histê, they're probably selling their catch *to* the Histê. That means southwest."

"You're suggesting I go on the search?"

"You've had your nose in that book too long, the air would do you good."

"Air and rain and bugs and snakes... I think you should go."

Sedut laughed. "Our lord priest would have my hide. I can't leave the north without Ulrikt's direct order."

The best Meliu knew Ulrikt remained busy fomenting war between a half dozen Tek Nations to ensure none set their spears on the Silone people. Before reading of the wars in the Codex, she'd wondered if any man had more blood on his hands than Ulrikt, but these pages made her error clear. "Ulrikt did tell me to find Tomarok."

"He did." She drained her glass and poured another. "It wouldn't be without risk."

"And I'd be forced to speak with the Warlord before going."

Sedut grimaced. "Strike my every word. You're better off here."

Meliu unleashed an indignant snarl. "What? I... You don't think I can keep my hands off him?"

"I don't think it's your hands the goddess Januel worries about, with a man so close to marriage. If you do this, no more 'last times'."

"Our last time was our last, last time."

"So I heard the last time before last. Sometimes I wonder if I shouldn't bed the boy to see what's got you so enthralled."

"Shush."

And they laughed into their cups.

"Have you had any word from our esteemed Lord Priest?"

"Last I knew, he was at the siege of Qwôhar making sure there would be no peace in the north."

"Do I want to know how?"

"I doubt either of us does. I might disapprove of his methods, but he's effective."

Meliu flicked a barbed comment about how effective the Eve of Snows had been from her tongue, smiling instead. No kind words came to mind despite her hopeful expression. "When will the expedition head south?"

"The Warlord has called a Circle Meet in three days, giving other lords time to arrive."

Meliu grinned and stared at Tomarok's mark. "Been a while since I've been to the Bickering Tent. I'm surprised Ivin is moving so slow."

"Not by choice, as I hear it."

"If Solineus were here, men would've left before word reached us." She grinned at the thought of the handsome man with a reputation for running into fire. Ivin might be off-limits, but... Silly thoughts. "How do I explain wanting to go without revealing Ulrikt and Tomarok?"

"That's for you to figure out. It would be improper to send a high priestess alone. We'll gather enough monks and priests for a proper escort."

"I'm ready to go!" Deelee the Pious' voice came from the tent's flap. She was older, with longer, untangled hair, but no less loud than ever.

Sedut's gaze was cold. "You've a postulant's work to keep you busy for the next ten years or so."

Meliu appreciated the girl's spunk. "Where I'm headed won't be a place for children."

"Looks to me everyone's heading south anyhow."

Meliu glanced at Sedut, and the woman shrugged. "What the hells do you mean, girl?"

"I mean... take a look!"

Meliu strolled from the tent with Sedut on her heels. She'd struck her camp high on a rocky crag in the foothills several candles' walk from Choerkin Castle, sheltered from winds from three directions and with a view in every direction but southwest. It was a beautiful spot in the morning, overlooking green valleys with an orange sun over the forest to the northeast, and folks called the place Northern Flower. What she watched wasn't obvious at first; the town of wooden homes and animal-hide tents had blossomed below, and people were always traveling to and fro. It wasn't until she'd eyeballed the scene that she realized the patterns were off. There wasn't enough fro; it was damned near all to, and that pointed south.

"What the wicked winds is going on?"

Sedut glared at Deelee. "What do you know, child?"

"Nothing! I heard Fomus shouting to pack their gear and go."

Meliu cringed. Fomus had the largest general store in the valley, buying pelts from every hunter and trapper who came through, and his building was beautiful hardwood. He wasn't going nowhere without cause. "Deelee, start packing my gear."

The girl stared, and Sedut cuffed her head. Hard. "That's an order to a postulant from a high priestess." She scrambled into the tent holding her ear.

"You didn't need to strike her."

Sedut pursed her lips. "She needs to respect you."

Meliu took three steps down the side of the steep hill. "She doesn't need to fear you."

"Maybe she doesn't need to, but she should."

Meliu ducked her head to watch her footing on the rocky descent. "As you say, high priestess." The past two years had made it easy to forget that they weren't two friends jabbering over boys and history and prayers; Sedut might be Lord Priest right now if she hadn't lobbied to deny an election by the Council of High Priests. Most folks still believed Ulrikt and the rest of the lord priests dead. It was the first time without someone bearing the title since the second year of Remembered Time, and somehow this stubborn woman had prevented nominations and votes without revealing the truth of Ulrikt. She was as faithful to the lord priest as she was the gods in their heavens, and she was capable of monumental butchery without a bat of her eye; combined, these should be enough to keep Meliu biting her tongue, but sometimes her teeth lost their grip.

On reaching the base of the hill, they strode toward a wagon laden with goods and surrounded by people. Sedut called, "Good people! What drives you south?"

A man peeled from the group, trotting their way until he stood within strides and bowed. "High Priestess Sedut, you should head for the Gediswon... Clansmen awoke us before dawn, warned us of Tek on the northern shore."

"Crossing?"

"No, priestess. Not as I heard, no how."

"Thank you, sir. I wish you well." The man bowed again before trotting to rejoin his people.

Meliu licked her lips, huffed. "We knew this day would come."

"Question is whether this is the day they cross the ford, or are they just playing games?"

Meliu shrugged and glanced at a nearby stable held by Clan Ravinrin; men were throwing saddles on horses and fitting bits. "There's one way to find out for certain."

Meliu and Sedut rode with Yustof Cormîn, a Ravinrin cousin, and fifty warriors within a candle of Deelee stepping inside the tent; all she needed was the *Codex of Sol* and the Tomarok map in hand with all her notes to be ready. The party made good time, and instead of eating dust the whole way, the priestesses rode to the western side and rear. It was more polite than arguing about whether valuable lives such as theirs should ride at the fore.

They were maybe five candles into the ride when they spotted Gediswon Keep atop Crossing Hill, the small fortress built in haste to house a garrison and provide a distant view of Tek territory. It was plain and square with thirty-foot round towers at the corners and a central keep with a high spire for observers to stare north. By the time they arrived, the small castle was swarming with bows and swords, all Silone, which brought a smile. And when Meliu gazed across the river there was grass, not the chest-pounding army she'd expected. "So, just where are these Teks?"

Sedut reined her horse to a stop, took several breaths, then closed her eyes. "If I start to fall from the saddle, stop me."

Meliu giggled and put a hand to the woman's shoulder as Sedut prayed. Flickers later her eyes opened, and a scowl wrinkled her face. "What'd you see?"

"Armored horse, a few hundred, and footmen enough to make a thousand total."

"Not enough to invade. What're they doing?"

"Nothing far as I can tell. It's either a vanguard for a larger force... or who the hells knows. We need to find Xenê Broldun, see what he knows."

Xenê was strutting the castle's courtyard when they found him, a Broldun through and through, even if his clan-blood was wrong-eyed thin; dark-haired, loud, blunt, and drunk. He was shorter and thinner than most of his kin, which maybe made his attitude even worse. The runts in the litter always barked the loudest.

"Huh? How the shittin' hells should I know what those goat pokers want? Why don't you ladies go ahead and pray yerself up an answer. Mmm?" No doubt the bottle in his hand contributed to more than his foul breath.

Meliu held her hand up, cutting Sedut off before sliding from her saddle, landing right at his feet so close he stumbled back. "You're an ugly, fish-sucking bastard, and you hold your liquor like a child. Who the holy hells is *really* in charge here?"

"I don't answer to the Choerkin's whore, you little—"

This time her hand cut him off, the butt of her palm a finger from his chin. "Unless you wanna piss yourself in front of all yer men, I suggest you cut your tongue off. Who knows what the hells is going on with them Teks?" Men glanced back and forth, and one stared at his own toes; she made straight for him. "You look smarter than a donkey's asshole, who the hell's in charge here when he's passed out?"

The man's voice was a croak. "Nils Mulvarn, high priestess."

"Where is this Nils?"

"At the river, m'lady... m'priestess."

Meliu clapped his shoulder. "Good man." She put foot to stirrup and swung into the saddle.

Sedut glared at the Broldun but smiled soon as they'd turned for the gatehouse. "That was worth the journey."

"I've moments my father would be proud of."

"This Mulvarn better be worth a spit, or the river won't hold a day against the Tek."

"It would take Anzelok himself to hold this river if they come in force." It'd be delusional to believe otherwise. Castle Choerkin would be another matter, the Kingdomer wall wasn't finished, but its height and location made it damned near unassailable by her eye, and a typical siege impossible.

"Two years of slaughtering each other, they may not be as capable as you think. These are lesser nations, not Thon or some other *true* power."

"I hope you're right, and I hope not to find out."

The river was wide with rain, an extra thirty strides compared to the day Eredin Choerkin died, and they struggled across the currents then, which might help explain the Tek reticence to ride closer; without rebuilding the northern bridge, crossing now would invite slaughter. Maybe two hundred archers lined the banks of the Gediswon with wall shields driven into the ground. The Kingdomers helped them construct an "archer's wall" spanning the width of the ford, ten feet high with a walkway halfway up to give bowmen cover, but the river was so wide a person needed to wade ten strides to reach its stair. Thirty or so archers manned its low parapets despite the flood, and Meliu wagered that the one with a dun horse's tail dangling from his helm was the Mulvarn.

They rode to the river's edge, both horses shying at the flow passing their hooves. "Nils Mulvarn?"

The horsetail turned to reveal a face with a mustache damned near as long. "Aye! Who might you be?"

"This is the esteemed High Priestess Sedut, and I am Meliu."

"Those names I know." He stood stone still a flicker, then stepped from the walkway and splashed into the river, sauntering their way with a dangerous man's swagger. Maybe forty, his face was long and bore a scar on either cheek, and when he spoke, his words carried a light whistle through the gap in his front teeth. "It takes a Tek army to attract pretty holies to our shore." The funny thing was he eyed Sedut instead of her.

Meliu cleared her throat. "Any word from the Teks?"

He stepped from the river and shook his oiled boots to shed the water. "Aye, men came bearing a yellow banner and demanding words with clan-blood."

Sedut asked, "What's your last name?"

And he laughed. "They ain't never heard of no Mulvarn, no. They wanted a Choerkin, Ravinrin, or Broldun."

Meliu said, "You got one of those, too."

He scoffed. "At yonder castle? Hells, ladies, that ain't no Broldun, that's a whiskey pissin' dog with a high and mighty name. He weren't gonna lug his ass all the way down here to chat. We sent word onward south this morn... In fact, I think a real Broldun is here now."

He pointed over their shoulders, and Meliu turned. A giant of a man sat atop a Tek warhorse, so big he made the sixteen-hand horse look ordinary. "I'll be damned, Polus." She dismounted, tossing her reins to the Mulvarn, and waited for the Broldun and his entourage of a hundred cavalry to wind their way to the shore.

On arriving, Polus slid from his horse and strode her way with arms wide, his smile bright in the mass of his red beard. "High Priestess Meliu! It's been too long." He crushed her in a hug so tight it prevented a reply, and on releasing her, he turned to Sedut with monotone words. "And you. Mmm. Good to see you alive."

Meliu slugged his mail covered chest. "You be nice. How's your wife and youngin'?"

"The little one grows like a sunflower. Don't need no new wife yet, if yer askin'."

Meliu shook her head with a grin. "I expected you'd be headed south to the Circle Meet."

"My sister rode that way, the woman was barely out of camp when I got word of our visitors." He turned to Nils. "No need to dawdle, light a smoker and let's get this meeting over with."

Nils handed Meliu her reins and strode toward a cluster of archers. "Get us a fire and make it smoke!"

Meliu eyeballed the Broldun. "You've a clue what they want?"

He laughed. "Our blood? Hells, we ain't heard much more than a peep for two godsdamned years... traded furs here and there with trappers and the sort, but nothing official. What do Sedut's long eyes have to say?"

"I'd say near a thousand men, three hundred horse."

"Mmm. Too many men for a dinner invite, too few for a war."

Meliu giggled. "I appreciate your trimming the options."

"Wisdom is what I do... Or is that break things? Neither, I drink." He stalked to his horse and its saddlebags, pulled out a bottle of something certain to create profanity strewn sentences and hangovers. He bit the cork and gave it a pull then handed the bottle to Meliu.

"I won't go blind?"

"Not right away."

She took a swig and cocked her head to swallow; she couldn't identify the fruity edge to the whiskey, and the burn going down stole her breath. "Yum."

She handed it to Sedut quick to avoid dropping the bottle as she coughed.

"We used some fruit from the Southron Forest to add a wee lick of flavor and to take the edge off."

"No shits. That's edge off?"

"Might be it needs more time in the barrel."

Sedut took a sip and shrugged. "Not so bad." But by the way the woman blinked, Meliu would swear she was holding back tears.

Polus snatched the bottle back and filled his mouth before handing it off to his men. "Ahhh! That'll take the godsdamned edge off o' any man's blade."

"It'll clean a wound, of that I'm sure."

"Now, what's all this about Rinold captured? Ivin won't take kindly to taking his friends."

"No, he won't, but you might know more than we do."

"In that case, we ignore our troubles to the south and await the troubles from the north."

And so they waited, and Meliu learned the truth of the Broldun's wife; Irose was ecstatic with her now toddler and was taking in orphans from all through the clans, which Polus didn't mind so much seeing as the youngins didn't drink his booze. The Broldun territory had swollen to more than fifteen thousand souls, and set up as they were, they had dealings with the Kingdomers on a regular basis, with traders traveling as far as Ôshô. There were also two Tek nations to the west who weren't at war with no one, so traders willing to risk the travel opened new and profitable markets. It also opened up an exchange of languages, and the Broldun claimed several merchants spoke enough Tek dialects to speak to any of the bastards who might come this far south.

They spoke for a candle before a horn blew, and wicks later dust rose on the northern horizon. A score of horsemen cantered their way, men and animals alike covered in draping mail and faces covered by plates of steel. Three men rode ahead of the main group to stop at the river's edge.

The man in the middle dropped his reins and stood in the saddle with the grace of a woodkin, and the horsemen to either side pressed their animals close to keep his mount steady.

He raised his arms and spoke in broken Silone, his voice carrying the distance with ease: "I am Ôlisbenar the Razer! Scepter of the King of the Malstefnê! Spear of the Fourth River! Partisan of the Night Sky! Crown of the mighty city of Qwôhar! And I bring joyous words! The city of Qwôhar is saved by my hand. The Malôbund are defeated." He leaned and yanked a bundle from the side of his saddle, but when the cloths fell away, it revealed a head, bloodied and misshapen. "The spy of your Choerkin Warlord is dead. Never again will he change his face to sew hatred amid my people!"

Change his face... Meliu prayed for vision as the man raised his grisly prize above his head. Her heart pounded in her chest, but the flesh of the head's face sloughed and was covered in dried blood.

Ôlisbenar dropped the head on the rocky shore and spit. "Tell your Choerkin Warlord I will hold his head soon, and I will pass his bleached skull to my son, to his son, until my lineage runs without blood." He dropped in his saddle, and his men hooted and hollered and screamed until their backs disappeared over the horizon.

Polus bit the cork on a second bottle and took a long pull. "Since when did the Choerkin have a spy up north?"

Meliu shivered. "I don't know, but we need that head."

Polus nodded. "You men, go fetch that there... face."

Meliu froze and turned on the Broldun, for a flicker wondering if this was the *real* Polus. She stared and figured it more likely that neither the head nor this man was Ulrikt.

Sedut said, "The Church did have a man at Qwôhar, his goal was to pour oil on the fire."

Polus sucked his teeth and took a big swallow of his fruity fire. Meliu grimaced. *Could anyone but a Broldun drink that with a straight face?* "No doubt we've lost that advantage."

Polus grunted. "Cocky ass atop his horse didn't let me get a word in."

It occurred to Meliu then: "He wouldn't have heard you... it's too far. His voice was given power by prayer."

Sedut snarled and snatched Polus' bottle. "The Elements for certain... I'm not sure what it means, but I don't like it."

They stood in silence, passing the bottle, and even Meliu's tongue grew used to the infernal concoction before Nils returned the head.

"You ladies know this man?"

Meliu covered her mouth and nose before leaning in with a squint. Her impression from a distance proved correct: Alive, the man might've borne a thousand different faces that would've been familiar, but battered and broken, with his eyes and nose missing, there was no way to give him a name. She glanced at Sedut before straightening her back. "I can't tell you who he is... was."

Sedut exhaled through pursed lips. "Until we know otherwise, we assume it's our man."

Polus snorted. "Bury him, then. Say some prayers for his soul. Mmm. Don't matter two shits who the man was; if there's no peace to the north, we got bigger troubles."

Meliu pulled her eyes from the dead face to stare at the rocks between her feet.

Sedut said, "We need word sent to the clans, the Kingdomers, and the Helelindin... We need to know where we stand with everyone."

"Mmm, it'll be done. If these shit suckers are comin', we need everyone beyond Castle Choerkin. Question is, will it hold?"

Meliu grimaced, this news would burn the spirits of every Silone still this side of the Dragonspans. "It'll hold. It must."

Polus nodded and turned to his men, shouting orders, as Meliu grabbed Sedut's arm and drug her to the side.

"Do you think it's him?" She couldn't bring herself to say Ulrikt's name.

"I pray not, but..."

Meliu clutched her head, sorry for the alcohol fuzzing her thoughts. Or was it the fire the Malôbund had set blurring her senses?

No matter.

"There's a way... Ulrikt's abilities, how would he be caught, let alone be killed?"

Sedut's eyes went cold. "When was the last time you heard a man's voice carry so far, so strong?"

"What the hells are you..." *Ivin, reading the scroll of the Mercies.* Her heart thudded in her chest and paused too long before beating again. "What the hells are you saying?"

"I'm saying we don't know what doom the Forges have sent us in the form of this Ôlisbenar the Razer. Until we know, assume the worst."

Lord Priest Ulrikt is dead. She could assume the worst, but she couldn't bring herself to believe it.

FIVE

Slaver's Tongue

The fading flowers in the dying hours
hide the Brave Man Who Cowers.
Bring no love for the flirty,
bring no soap for the dirty,
wallow and wallow in the misery and mud,
you the eaten, you the cud.

—*Tomes of the Touched*

Not so long ago in Rinold's life, if he'd been stripped of everything but his trousers and boots and forced to sleep in a rickety wooden cage hanging from a tree, he'd assume himself dead within candles, or at the least his fingers and toes would be black or fallen off. The notion of sweating at night wouldn't have occurred to him.

He awoke each morning thankful for the water the yellow-eyes brought him, even if it was cloudy and warmer than the rain that fell damned near every day. What he didn't appreciate was the descent from the canopy. The bastards lobbed arrows with strings attached over branches higher than he'd want to climb, then pulled the cages to dizzying heights every night. Heading up didn't bug him so much as down the next morning. The yellow-eyes took joy in the herky-jerky stops and starts while laughing at him as he clung to the bars of his cage.

But the cage was only the beginning of his misery. His beard itched from sweat and bugs wriggling toward his face to make lunch of him, or to lay eggs, or just hide from the rain; he never bothered to ask their motives before crushing their guts between his fingers. If anything made him miss the cold of Kaludor, it was the godsdamned bugs.

While he wasn't forced to share a cage, Rinold wasn't alone. Edlmir and seven other Silone were hoisted into the trees every night, where they were free to talk so long as they kept the words under their breath. When a man spoke too loud the yellow-eyes took pleasure in sticking slivers of stick into their skin with a puff of breath and a blowgun. Sometimes they shot small rocks instead, but either way, it kept conversation to a whisper.

They'd traveled by canoe for ten days before reaching the first village, or perhaps it was a hunter's camp. A dozen lean-tos fashioned from hardwood poles and giant leaves lashed into roofs stood beside massive trees, and a couple huts looked like they were permanent, but their captors slept in simple tents. The tents varied in shades of greens and browns, and Rinold suspected them cut from some giant snake. Whatever they were made from, they repelled rain a hells of a lot better than his hands held over his face.

They spent three days in the village dangling low enough in their cages to receive food and water without being lowered. He appreciated the altitude, but the lack of stretching his muscles and not being able to relieve himself without feeling a spectacle for the yellow-eyes were irksome.

He'd tried his damnedest to catch a word or phrase and piece together a meaning, but they spoke so fast he couldn't tell one word from another as the garbles strung together. Maybe if he was Meliu or some other educated holy he'd learn himself something of their language, but the Squirrel was a boy of the wilds who'd grown into a man of the wilds and book learning had never come easy no how. Listening to the bastards was pointless, but he tried anyhow to ease the boredom.

It was the fourteenth day of captivity that the barge arrived, full of yellow-eyes draped in dyed clothes and with gold and silver dangling from their ears and wrapped around their necks and wrists. Rinold puzzled on them a flicker before realizing they were all men. Silone women wore jewelry, but few men, and neither wore so much in garish displays of wealth. It was damned near as peculiar as the only pieces of armor he'd seen being made of wood and wire.

Within a candle of the barge's arrival, a man with his head shaved of every sprout of hair including eyebrows wandered over to cast his gaze at the Silone in their cages. If the weight in gold a man wore was the measure of his worth, he was an important bastard. The necklace he wore must've weighed a brick, with its heavy links and medallion shaped as the face of an ugly, screaming woman bouncing against his chest. The lobes of his ears stretched three fingers from the weight of his earrings. If the size of a man's belly spoke of importance, this too set the man apart. Every yellow-eye he'd seen before this hefty fellow ranged from lean to scrawny.

Two of the warriors who captured them, a man and woman, trotted to his side, pointing at the Silone and rattling off words faster than a flute's notes.

Rinold muttered, "The Bossman."

Edlmir dangled nearby. "What the hells you think they're doing?"

"Judging by the belly and gold on the Bossman there, I'm guessing they're haggling a price for our skins or talking recipes before eating us."

Edlmir chuckled and tiny rocks pelted him while others clacked off the bars of his cage. "Godsdamned bastards. Slavers or cannibals, I love this forest so much I'd like to burn it down."

"Too damned much rain for a big enough fire. But, if you ever wondered what yer life is being worth, you might just find out."

The Bossman pointed and a hunter lowered Edlmir's cage to the ground. Three spears faced the Silone as Bossman approached. Edlmir was taller than any of them by a head or more and broader of shoulder, and Bossman seemed pleased as he motioned to every cage and they were lowered.

Rinold was the last inspected, and Bossman didn't appear impressed. Still, he stared at him longer than most, then smiled when Rinold refused to blink. A rattle of words and this time both the man and woman answered, gesticulating with hands and arms, all their motions exaggerated from steps and spins to smiles and frowns; the haggle was in full motion.

"Slavers, or we're a damned expensive supper."

Edlmir resisted the humor this time, and within a wick or two Bossman stood staring at them with his hands crossed to rest on his belly, and a broad smile showed teeth carved and filled to form tiny characters Rinold couldn't make out; runes or letters he presumed.

Their rope bonds were exchanged for iron manacles and chains, but it was a trade Rinold could live with if it meant no more rides in wobbly dugout canoes and being hoisted into the trees. Rinold watched as the Silone were led onto the barge and stuck into a single cage, but Bossman made certain Rinold was the last to jump aboard, and soon as his foot struck the deck the man spun him, barked something, then punched him in the gut.

But Bossman didn't look at Rinold as he struck, he stared at the Silone in their cages, and as Rinold straightened Bossman grabbed his manacles and led him to the rail, pushed him to sit on a coil of rope. A sturdy chair arrived a flicker after and the big man settled into his seat to stare at him.

"Sokûtu."

It was the first time Rinold had heard one of them speak slow enough to understand. "Sokûtu?"

The man grunted, pointed to his chest. "Sokûtu."

He mimicked the man. "Rinold."

Bossman pointed at himself then his sailors, oarsmen, and warriors. "Wiirê. Rinold... Helmveline?"

Rinold's head rocked back and he scratched his head before crossing his hands in front of him. He spoke in Silone first, then repeated the words in the Kingdomer tongue. "No. I am from the far, far north. Not Helmveline. Not Kingdomer."

"*Sêem* Helmveline. Barkûsh? Ôshô?"

Rinold groaned. The bastard didn't know Kingdomer, he just knew the names of kingdoms. He waved his hands back and forth. "*Sêem*. No Barkûsh. No Ôshô. Silone."

"Silone."

Rinold nodded, pointed at the crew. "Wiirê, no Histê? Sêem Histê?"

"Sêem Histê." His arm made a sweeping gesture to the west and southwest. "Histê."

Who the Twelve Hells are you people if not part of the Histê? The Kingdomers never mentioned another people living south of the mountains, nothing human no how. He pointed to his chest. "Rinold."

The man snapped his fingers and babbled something to a young man, naked but for a loincloth, with his body painted in blue and red streaks. Bossman smiled and Rinold could see the peculiar symbols carved in the man's teeth; hard to say what they represented, but they were filled with an ivory white material to stand out against his yellowed teeth.

A wick of staring at the man later, the boy returned; in his hands, he carried Rinold's mail cuirass, leather jerkin, and arming sword. Bossman rattled the mail with a fist and pointed at him. "*Telmet?*"

Rinold shrugged and shook his head.

"*Telmetet?*"

It took a flicker to click; it was close to the Kingdomer word for warrior. If he was right, did he even want to let the man know the truth? His eye twitched. "What the hells can it hurt? *Telmetîn?*"

The big man laughed and slapped his knee. "*Kî! Kî. Telmetîn.*" He made a slashing gesture with his hand, as a man who knew what a sword was, but not how to use one.

Rinold mimed drawing a bow. "Hunter. *Iniseld.*" He pointed at Edlmir. "*Telmetîn*. Warrior."

Bossman nodded with a scrunch of his lips that suggested he'd made some sense of Rinold's words even as Edlmir asked, "You tryin' to get my ass baked over there?"

"I have no idea what the hells I'm doing."

Bossman watched their banter with a grin, then snapped his fingers and babbled at the boy again. A wick later, two men dragged a crate across the deck before they unlocked the cage and motioned for Edlmir to step forward.

"What the Forges have you gotten me into, Squirrel?"

"What's in the box?"

"Our armor and weapons."

Bossman took Rinold's armor and held it against his chest, rattled it with a slap.

Rinold said, "I think he wants you to take your gear from the bunch."

The man planted his foot. "So he can shittin' kill me?"

"If he's gonna shittin' kill you, you might as well do it with fight."

Bossman stood and yelled, a man with a body length shield and short spear turned. Like most of these people, his skin was bare, but he wore lamellar cut from some sort of bark covering his chest and abdomen and thick leather wraps on his forearms and shins. Rinold's gut twisted as Edlmir slipped into a jerkin and mail, buckled his swordbelt, and couched a shield.

"*Ereti*!" Bossman mimicked jabbing with a spear and slashing with a sword.

Edlmir glanced to Rinold. "What the shits? Is he serious?"

The spear punching Edlmir in the gut suggested just that. Edlmir stepped back from the unexpected attack with a smirk and knocked the spear away before stepping forward. The arming sword's steel severed the shield's rawhide edge and split the wood damned near to the middle. He struck next with the edge of his shield, breaking the man's nose, before the sword cleaved into the shield, and blood sprayed where the man's hand had been.

The bastard howled in agony before Edlmir lunged, driving the blade's tip straight through the warrior's bark armor and out his back. The scream turned to a rushing breath as he drooped and slid from the blade, collapsing, his breaths struggling for the next half a wick before ending.

Edlmir turned; as far as Rinold could tell, the spear hadn't damaged a single link in the riveted mail.

Bossman whooped and clapped and rattled off sounds too fast for Rinold to even recognize as words.

Edlmir said, "Say the word and I'll kill as many as I can."

A warrior pointed at Edlmir's sword then the ground, but kept his distance.

It wasn't the worst notion; with steel armor and a steel sword, he might well cut his way straight through the bastards. But there were at least a dozen bows in the hands of skilled hunters. "If you wore a helmet, I might say yes." By now, Bossman gave Edlmir a hard stare. "Go ahead and put the weapon down, we'll get out of this another time."

Edlmir wiped the blade clean, sheathed the sword, then removed the belt and stuck them back in the crate.

Bossman stepped between Edlmir and the weapon with a smile damned near as big as his belly. Vibrant yellow eyes. Rinold had seen that glow in men's eyes before; it was the glow of a man eyeing gold.

He pointed at the dead man. *"Mîuk. Mîuk!"* And he laughed, thumping Edlmir's shoulder and appraising his size and power while staring up at him. "*Telmetîn.*" Bossman tapped his shield and armor and Edlmir dropped them back in the crate.

"I'm thinkin' we woulda been better off taking our chances on my killin' 'em all."

Rinold's eye twitched and he smiled, though not with the confidence he wished for, but his words dripped with bravado. "Might be we just proved more valuable than being their dinner."

Edlmir chuckled as a guard shoved him back into the cage and locked the door. "If nothin' else I got to kill one of the sons of bitches."

Two men strode forward, picked up the dead man by the ankles and shoulders, hauling him to the edge of the barge and casting him overboard. One thing for certain, Bossman didn't care much for the lives of his people, nor did he care much for their bodies. Rinold knew from Kingdomer tales that the Histê kept slaves, so it only made sense they were being kept alive for a downriver profit.

His eyes followed the body floating away from the barge. *Slaves don't fight battles.* Not in the stories he'd been told anyhow. In the Slave Fields the gods forced folks to till the land, plant the seeds, bucket the water, eat the bugs from the leaves, and to harvest the crop to only burn the fruits of their labor and begin again. Neither did stories of the Tek speak of warrior slaves, but here down south, it was another world.

The ripples of the river thrashed white and massive jaws surged from the murky waters to take the dead man; the body flailed in the beast's toothy grip then submerged, and the wake of its consumption disappeared in flickers. Rinold snorted and spit into the river. Another world, indeed.

Six

Charted Waters

Forever old, forever young,
forever beginning, forever done,
your song,
forever forgotten, forever sung,
never ending or never begun.

—*Tomes of the Touched*

A night aboard a ship where every soul spoke Silone was welcome to Solineus' ears and tongue, but the celebration left an alcohol echo in his head that made him cringe when the sun struck his eyelids. He crawled to his feet, found a barrel of water, and splashed his face. In the morning sun, he spotted silver coins at the bottom, resting unspent to keep the water pure and drinkable.

Adinvan strode to his side, sniffed the air. "I'm thinking you need more'n a splash of water before greeting the keepers of Mulshahar."

"You smell like a skunk who dragged himself from a pigsty yourself. I doubt the keepers nor mother would approve."

"I'm safe; she's days away, probably swimming naked with the natives in some pool or another. No doubt she smells better than we do."

"Mother... Naked?" Lack of memory didn't keep him from a cringe.

"There're enough bare breasts on the islands to make a man bored of seeing them... almost." He flashed a grin and a wink. "Your mother is still a fine-looking woman, so my eyes don't wander so far I get slapped."

Solineus grimaced and reached for a change of subject. "You spoke of a bath?"

Hot water and soap felt a luxury when first he slumped into its steaming ripples, but within wicks he stood, toweled off, slipped into his jerkin and armor, and waited for his father. It was another half candle before the old man moseyed from his private tub with his silver hair wet and combed back, his face shaved and pampered with oils.

"How the hells long you been out here?"

"Too damned long; you soak like a woman."

"I reckon you've had some long soaks in your day, though unalone. These past coupla years might've ruint you, you need to learn to slow down and enjoy again."

Solineus tossed his father a pair of trousers and waited for him to dress before speaking. "In all our chatter yesterday, there are still questions I need to ask."

"Like your mother's name?"

Solineus huffed and looked to the floor. "No, like why was I on the Resten?"

Adinvan squinted, cocked his head, then strode for the exit. "You aren't interested in your mother and sisters? No one?"

Solineus followed close on his heels, his thoughts bouncing in his skull without reaching his tongue until they stepped outside. "I know I should... After two years of knowing nothing, it's like a different person's past."

Adinvan slipped into the boardwalk's traffic. "Well, you aren't no one else, you're my son, the next Lord Mikjehemlut and but a few steps from becoming the Lord of the Emudar. You might want to start thinking on such things."

"I know you're right." Shame heated the beat of his heart. "And I will, but I need to piece other things together as well."

"The Resten, eh? Why you were on it? The captain's daughter, for one. Lord Lidin Emudar for another. I was far to sea, but I know Lidin was worried before I set sail. Lord Priest Serxuk blew smoke when we captured Thonian smugglers slipping toward that citadel of theirs a couple months before the Eve of Snows."

"Whiskey?"

"Two kegs were marked whiskey, but tapping one did more'n blind a man: he died. If not for the dead man's thirst it would've been sent through."

"What was it?"

"Wyvern's Flash. I was there with the Lord Emudar or I wouldn't have believed it m'self, I reckon. A thimble from one and a thimble from the other, when we poured them together a flaming hell broke loose. Blackened the stone floor and burned for five wicks or more with pure white flames."

"Any idea what the Church planned with the stuff?"

"Your guess is better'n mine considering what you've seen, but the Lord Emudar damned near sent you straight away to Choerkin Fost with word. He and Lord Lovar Choerkin were passing notes for months leading to this, but a couple riders disappeared."

"But he didn't send me."

"To my shame, perhaps, I talked him out of it. Told him to wait until he knew more."

"Why'd he send me then?"

"Hell's if I know for sure, but I'd wager he waited until he knew *more.*"

Solineus stopped cold in his tracks outside the currency exchange. "You're saying I might've carried information that could've prevented all this?"

Adinvan sighed and shook his head. "Don't be flogging yourself, boy. From what you know, is there anything you could've said to stop the horror?"

He admitted to himself it seemed impossible, but not knowing for certain would be a hornet in his boot for a while. "Backwards is no way to live. Come on."

He pushed the door open and stepped into the luxury of the exchange; the street's noise disappeared behind him as the thick doors closed. Three women with sincere smiles didn't leave him standing in the lobby today; they fawned over him and led him straight to the desk of the woman he'd dealt with before.

The lady curtsied in a plush, green-velvet dress and she'd bothered to paint her face this morning, highlighting her eyelids sky-blue and her lips red. She spoke in Kingdomer. "Solineus Mikjehemlut. So good to see you. You are here for the exchange?"

"I am. This is my father, Adinvan, now Lord of the Emudar."

"Indeed! Oh my. We are blessed today! I am Sêeloru Ledun, at your service." She bowed.

Adinvan grinned and stuck his thumbs in his belt. "My boy is far wealthier than I am."

Her smile slipped lower and her eyes retrained on Solineus in a heartbeat. "You come for the exchange?"

"I do."

"This is well. I should also inform you that we operate as a bank to hold such sums safe. We also offer various investments. Yesterday was such a blur! I neglected so much... did I even say my name?" Sêeloru's laugh was nervous, as if she risked reprimand for having failed the exchange. "I don't often... never have handled an account such as this. Not sure if anyone has."

"Well, the account is yours. You can tell your superiors that I deal with you alone."

"I... Most gracious."

Adinvan slid into a seat, fingers tracing the leather-covered arm; he spoke in Silone. "Some fine leather here. How much for this chair?"

Solineus eased into a seat, attempting to realign the conversation. "My father jests."

"No I don't, I'd like this on my ship. How much?"

The smile on the woman's lips fought off a scrunched purse as she tried to ignore Adinvan. "I... I am certain something could be arranged."

"Five smedên sounds fair."

Solineus glared. "If I buy you the damned chair can we move on?"

The old man threw his arms in the air. "If you bathed longer you mightn't be so testy."

He ignored his father. "I will buy this chair to shut my father's mouth, and I will need smedên to take care of a little issue with the city guard."

Her smile turned to sincere concern. "Oh dear, you ran into thieves."

"More they ran into me, but I'd prefer not to leave bodies behind a second time. How much will I need to buy my protection?"

She coughed. "Well, indeed... special attention from the guards, a few hundred smedên should handle this detail. You should carry plenty from yesterday's exchange."

"I'm also in the market for a map."

Her tell-tale face shifted to a curious grin. "What sort of map?"

"The coast here and south; islands, inlets to the mainland."

"These are easy, and I'd suggest your father might even possess such charts. A smart woman such as myself might suspect you want something more specific, more rare."

"Maps I've seen show Chitorâ Island and others to the southeast, as well as the coast of Southern Vandunez, but in between the charts turn blank."

"The Kindusên Sea, yes. Charts of those dangerous waters are privy to powerful captains and lords, and they don't like to share."

"My fool of a boy wants a map of the Monsoon Strait; do you know of a seller or not?"

Solineus eyed his father; he'd uttered Monsoon Strait with gravel for emphasis. "My father is proud that his son can handle any waters. Do you know of a seller or not?"

"With the smedên in your account you might buy a thousand charts and overpay for each. What you want is accuracy."

"I saw Luxun vessels—"

"You couldn't find better sailors, but the Luxuns rarely sail the Strait. From here they sail to their home of the Crown Islands or north for further trade. The Exchange employs a variety of vessels, some do business with the Gorotan and Boboru across the sea. I won't swear to a copy, but I'd wager Captain Edmordô would give you a look. Red-Diamond dock, a ship called the *Fefemor.* Tell him Sêeloru sent you."

Solineus nodded, reached into his pack, and withdrew the rub of the timôu coins he'd turned in. "I would like to keep the bulk of my fortune here, secure, and withdraw two thousand smedên."

She took the paper and unfolded it. "This count of remaining smedên, it would be a shame not to invest."

"If the map proves fruitful I'll be wanting ships, two to three."

"Trade cogs?"

"No, seaworthy but able to navigate rivers."

She straightened and rested her hands in her lap. "Less easy; you might need to consult the Lulcaster Shipyards, they've shipwrights of renown who work with such designs."

"See well to my wishes and I will see to you managing my investments in my absence."

The woman blanched, lips pursed, but as her muscles relaxed, she smiled again. "Hardly my area of expertise..."

"I trust you to not rob me."

"Then you should entrust me to find another more skilled in these matters. The Exchange has rules, and Mulshahar's laws governing such transactions and theft would make your swords a mercy."

"The finest banker you know, but... they must converse in the Kingdomer tongue and ways, and be willing to learn Silone."

"I'll be certain to arrange these things."

And so it was, but what Solineus hadn't figured on was spending the next four candles arranging security measures and the inheritance protocol, signing so many sheets of vellum he figured his signature improved by the time he finished signing documents, but on the bright side his father caught his first nap in his new over-priced chair. They strode from the Mulshahar Exchange with the hefty sum of two thousand smedên in his pouch and a scroll worth ten thousand more—if endorsed by yet another signature and password—on the chance he needed payment on ships to secure purchase. His well-documented stash of gold was also a little lighter to secure a manager and their lessons to learn Silone.

The sun had already passed noon when they found fresh air again, and Adinvan stretched his arms after waking from his nap. "So, what the hells are you up to, boy?"

"I need a map. I need a ship. I need a guide. I've crossed dozens of rivers big and small, it's about godsdamned time I went up one." He crossed the street and headed for the wharfs; the Red-Diamond Dock wasn't far from where the *Evening Sky* was tied off.

"A river, why?"

Solineus paused so as to not get run over by a wagon, then headed straight downhill toward the harbor. "Way I reckon it, whether the clans outgrow their new home in peace or are faced with war, they'll need to move south over the Roemhien Pass."

"That's gibberish to me, boy."

"The Roemhien leads over The Foundations... the Dragonspan Mountains. Mountains are where the rains fall, and rains make rivers; all I need to do is find the right river to reach them."

His father spit, almost hitting a small dog scurrying past. "Sorry, pooch. You know how godsdamned far that is?"

"I've already put enough horizons beneath these feet to make it to the Monsoon Strait, so yeah, I've got an idea. This time I want a boat, sails, and oars doing most of the work."

"I follow your thinking just fine; I won't even bother to argue, but we've got longboats and men."

"Just the way you say Monsoon Strait speaks to dangerous waters. I'll hire a crew who knows the currents, the reefs, the storms, the locals."

Adinvan strode wordless by his side for a stretch, but the silence didn't last. "You'd trust some foreign crew?"

Solineus laughed. "Hells no, but we need to decide which is more dangerous, wind, water, and weather, or foreign sailors."

"Pirates. Don't forget Boboru pirates." Adinvan snorted but remained silent until they found the *Fefemor,* and at that point he had to speak in order to bribe their way to Captain Edmordô; a single smedên had every finger on deck pointing to the same door. They entered with an escort of two sailors to find a man with a waxed mustache stretching to dangle from hooped earrings in both ears, a fashion Solineus hadn't seen before.

The man's dark eyes relaxed with Sêeloru's name and brightened with the glint of gold. "Charts of the Monsoon Strait? I possess the finest, some of the most detailed, all by my own hand."

Adinvan translated. "We would like to take a look at them."

The captain stared with a smirk. "A look. Why?"

"I seek a river which will lead me north to the Dragonspan Mountains, those the Kingdomers call the Foundations."

He plopped into his seat, shaking his head and raising his arms as if auditioning for a theater troupe. "Again, why?"

"In my journeys I befriended the Kingdom of Helmveline, and my family remains in their mountains. I must get back to them."

A cocked head and a sigh as the man's fingers drummed his desk. "I do love my family, but if I loved my family so much, I would go back the way I came."

"A hundred smedên just to study your map."

Edmordô opened his desk, eyes never leaving them, and withdrew a long roll of parchment. He stared and studied them as he tapped its end on the desk. "I don't sail up rivers; all I have are the locations of their mouths."

"The river will be wide."

He unfurled the map, revealing a broad stretch of water sitting between continents and dotted with islands along the coasts. "Three mouths feed the Monsoon Strait, wide as you say. The Tebûul is too far west, I'd suggest, while the furthest east... If that is the mouth you need, you've trouble. The Mûulbon Delta here is a monster undoubtedly fed by thousands of streams and smaller rivers to the north. There are ruins at this mouth, some fortress or city reclaimed by the forests. No men I ever seen."

Solineus followed the coast beyond the delta until it reached the Gulf of Tomulok and he pointed. "Could we sail north into the gulf? The land we'd need cross to reach Helmveline would shrink considerably."

Edmordô laughed. "The gulf is at war. Unless you can fly the colors of both the Gorotan and the Boboru, you will not risk these waters. Perhaps a ship of the Free Cities. No. I doubt you will survive your trip by river, by the gulf?" He shook his head.

Solineus glanced to Adinvan. "We should be able to hug the coast, hard as the Twelve Hells to miss that river."

"You haven't heard the tales of the strait I've been blessed with. All these islands, reefs, storms from all the hells... I guarantee you this man knows every twisting current and safe harbor to throw an anchor, and they aren't marked on any map, they're in this bastard's head or he's got himself a chart-master to keep his secrets."

"If what you're saying is true, we need him to finish his charts."

Adinvan tapped the islands near the coast as if chasing a tiny and speedy bug. "Every shittin' stretch through here is a trap. No, we need him to guide you. No two pisses about it, you want someone who knows the waters, not just his chart. If not him, another captain."

"Tell him two thousand smedên for a copy of the map *if* he marks out his secrets."

"I just told you—"

Solineus shrugged. "Just tell him."

Adinvan sighed. "Two thousand smedên for a copy, but only if you mark out the secrets you keep."

Edmordô's brows rose and twisted, an expression blending shock and bemusement, and his chortle turned to an awkward cackle before he cut it short. Solineus didn't let him off the hook.

"Five thousand." The man's face went blank. Solineus pushed harder. "Ten thousand."

The blank stare turned to pursed lips and his hands planted on the desk as he leaned. "What game are you men playing?"

"Ten thousand smedên, yes or no."

"No! What game are you playing?"

"No game."

"And no man pays a king's ransom for a chart. A smart man knows a game when he sees it."

"A smart man worthy of our coin should recognize the game."

Solineus grabbed Adinvan by the shoulder as he finished the words and walked toward the door.

"Wait. Wait."

Solineus turned and his father translated: "What dice am I rolling?"

Edmordô arched his back and scratched his cheek, puzzling together an answer Solineus didn't even know. "Golden dice forged by the smiths of Helmveline. You want to open trade between Helmveline and Mulshahar by river. I am right."

Solineus smiled; it was a good idea the man hatched, but he could make it better. "I have connections with Helmveline and the Helelindin, as well as the Trelelunin. Now you see the truth; ten thousand for the chart. Yes or no?"

The captain's mouth dangled open. He waggled his finger the moment his mouth closed. "No, oh no. I want a cut, a partnership."

Solineus chuckled with a shake of his head. "Your map is worthy the ten thousand, maybe, no mere chart is worth the fortune I stand to bring down that river."

Edmordô stood straight and pounded his chest. "Captain Edmordô will lead you to the delta, it is the only way you make it without learning to breathe seawater." His gaze was fierce and determined.

Solineus exhaled and paced. "How do I know you are trustworthy?"

"I am Edmordô. Sêeloru of the Mulshahar Exchange sent you, and they will speak to my honor. How can I trust you?"

He glanced back and forth with his father. "A contract overseen by the exchange."

The Captain nodded. "Agreed. Fifty percent of profits."

Solineus and Adinvan both scoffed. "Ten percent will make you the wealthiest captain in these waters."

"Less than forty percent leaves you drowning in a storm."

"Twenty-five and you get the ten thousand smedêns."

"Thirty-five plus the smedêns."

"Thirty percent and no smedêns."

"Thirty percent and a thousand smedêns for my crew, now, in case we never return from this caper."

Solineus counted out ten hundred-marks from his pouch and slid them across the map. "Done. I will meet you at the exchange tomorrow at dawn to seal the details."

Edmordô smiled. "Done. And here is the first time I will save your life: We don't sail for two months or thereabout, storm season in the strait isn't a thing you wish to see. But if we aren't out of here round-about then, we might be heading back in storm season, as I imagine your trip north will take a while."

"And that isn't a thing we want to see." Solineus stared into the man's black eyes and saw no deception. "Fine. Well enough. We've ships to buy, anyhow."

Edmordô laughed as they strode for the door. "Ships to buy? Trade with the Helmveline? By the gods man, who are you?"

Father and son strode the gangplank to the docks and moseyed toward the streets that would take them to the shipbuilder, silent until out of earshot.

"Holy hells, boy!" Adinvan laughed. "I sure as shits failed in never taking you on our trade runs. Are you shittin' me?"

Solineus exhaled with a smile so wide it hurt. "The rush of battle without the blood."

Adinvan smirked. "Not quite."

"No, not quite." Nothing compared to battle; standing alive in the middle of death and dying, a beating drum in the middle of hundreds of silent and fading hearts, a thrill in the middle of despair and darkening visions; being the surviving predator to walk from a battle of thousands of monstrous beasts was a sensation unto its own, different from even single combat.

But a bargain well-struck *was* worthy of mention if not song.

"You've set the mark high for negotiating ships, boy! I expect to pay no more'n what I got in my boot." Solineus rocked in his stride at the congratulatory blow to his back.

"Somehow I don't think we'll leave so heavy in the pouch this next time."

The Lancaster Builders rested just inland of the shore beneath the cliffs west of Mulshahar and would put a host of beavers to shame. Adzes, axes, hammers, saws, draw knives, chisels, and planes of all sizes hewed and shaped massive logs hauled in by ship, fashioning the roughest plank of the hull down to the finest details of the eyes of the statue destined for a prow. Solineus would wager the yard employed five hundred people in one capacity or another.

Their guide was Horik Lancaster, a barrel-chested man whose hair had slipped from his head to cover his face, his bald pate revealing a variety of bumps and scars from a time he served on ships instead of building them. He was Tek Malstefnê by birth, which brought a twinge to Solineus' gut, but as it turned out the man wasn't aware of recent events to the east, and better, he spoke Kingdomer well enough he didn't need his father to translate the local tongue.

Horik's great-grandfather had founded these yards two hundred years earlier and today he was proud to point out his family's legacy. "If it's wood we work it here, fresh from logs brought in from the Utumwu Forests, oaks and pines mostly, and keep them soaked in our lake yonder to keep them flexible. We strip the bark and that's hauled over to Tanner Row in trade for leather straps and a variety of goods. I haven't paid for a boot since arriving in Mulshahar!" He pointed to men pounding wedges into logs with heavy hammers to split them. "Our craftsmen have experienced eyes, selecting timber with natural shapes to suit our needs, and we radial split the wood for even more strength; you won't buy a sturdier ship on the water than a Lancaster vessel."

"Not even Luxun?"

"Give me Luxun wood and I'd show them a thing or two." The man grinned. "Either way, good luck buying one. Plus, I've never seen a Luxun ship meant to ride up and down rivers. We do everything here except spin the ropes and weave the sails. Every plank, every oar, every nail for the clinker build is crafted here."

Adinvan said, "I'd seen these yards from afar, impressive to see it close."

Solineus agreed even if he didn't know the first cut of wood about building a boat. "Three longships, fifty to sixty feet from nose to tail, how long and how much?"

Horik pulled his beard. "A thousand smedên each, maybe a year to see the third into the water. We've a long list of commissions, though most are for deepwater vessels."

"Three longships, two months; five thousand now, five thousand when they hit the surf."

Horik sucked his teeth then cleared his throat, muttered to himself as much as to them. "I could take the timber from the Hedinrôp ship that just arrived. It would cause delays and I'd need to hire more hands... More hands, skilled hands. Where, how? Three months maybe."

"I've a writ for ten thousand smedên from the exchange, right here, right now, on your word of delivery. Three thousand more on completion and a hundred smedên on top for every day under two months."

"If I bring 'em in a month? I'm not saying it can be done—"

"I'll pay."

The man whistled and Solineus knew the deal was struck. "A foreigner casting smedên like the pedals of daisies will draw eyes."

"I'll be speaking to the officials of Mulshahar soon as I leave here."

He smiled. "This would be wise; wheels left ungreased in Mulshahar are prone to falling off the axle and hitting you in the head. Trouble is, most foreigners think there's only one wheel, but how many wagons you seen with only one wheel, eh?"

When Solineus translated, Adinvan snorted. "Shits, man. How many wheels has this city got?"

Horik tapped his lips. "Feed the driver so he don't forget to keep the wheels sound, if you catch my meaning."

Solineus said, "And who is this driver?"

"Depends on how much gold you have. Guardian Zerik Mô'od will serve for all but the wealthiest of men. There are maybe a dozen merchants in all of Mulshahar who need higher protections; protection from the true masters of Mulshahar."

They spent the next candle staring at scribes scribbling contracts; excitement turned to boredom, boredom turned to impatience, and impatience turned to hunger, as he perused and signed a dozen contracts scrawled on parchment, including the writ from the exchange. Then the terrible weight of gold spent fell on his shoulders, a peculiar sadness despite knowing he'd done what needed done.

They strode from the shipyard, Solineus breaking the heavy silence. "That was a hells of a lot of treasure."

Adinvan laughed and he stood straight as if relieved to hear the words. "By the gods, I'm glad you said it. You overpaid by a horizon, boy!"

"I reckon it got us ships in a hurry."

"If you trust the Tek bastard. He's Malstefnê... not a friend of yours as I recall."

"This one isn't my enemy until he proves otherwise. And he's under contract now."

"Aye. But there's a thing to remember about contracts... dead men can't dispute them."

Solineus snorted, but not at his father's words; his nose caught the scent of spiced meat over a fire, and in a wick they both held skewers of pork and a variety of fruits Solineus didn't have a name for. But the hells if every green, orange, red, and yellow one wasn't delicious.

By the time they reached the Prâterêut of the Central District, a three-story building surrounded by walls capped with barbed spikes from both directions, grease covered their lips; by the time they'd bribed their way to Guardian Zerik Mô'od their skewers were empty, and their stomachs satisfied. Zerik didn't meet expectations, whatever the hells they might've been. He was a gaunt, spindly man who wobbled as he walked, like a snake forced to stand rather than slither. Two canes stood stashed in the corner, hidden from casual eyes but within reach.

He spoke fine Kingdomer with a western twang that drew out the vowels. "Solineus Mikjehemlut of the Clan Emudar, what might I do for you this day?" He stumbled into his seat more than he sat; curious, that the man didn't take a seat before they arrived to hide his infirmity.

"I am but a newcomer to your glorious city, though my father has traded here on occasion. I arrived bearing no small wealth, and it has come to my attention that a wealthy soul might pay for eyes to guard their travel and business."

His brow crinkled. "The guard is not a mercenary force."

"Not my meaning, sir. I merely mean that the guards in the streets might be made aware of me and my kin, and if they should see some suspicious eyes at our feet?"

"That they would interdict? This is a possible thing. The taxes are low and the pay barely enough to give weight to a guard's pouch. Given your name and description, and a rattle for their numerous pouches, you should walk free and safe at any candle. No guarantees, of course! Cities and their people are wild things, but at the least help would be near. Very near."

Solineus bowed. "This is as I'd desire; blood is never my intent."

"But those swords speak not only of wealth but of a man capable of keeping that wealth. Pray, what brings you to our noble city?"

The squint in the man's eye suggested the answer might be as important as Solineus' gold. The haggle with Captain Edmordô might pay off again. "Trade with Hemvelîn; I served the Ironwing not so long ago and if I can find a river route to the Foundations, I believe it possible to carry fortunes on those waters."

"You don't say." The man sat silent, studying him with suspicious eyes. "Bold. Perhaps folly."

"I've partnered with a guide for the Monsoon Strait and secured purchase of several sea- and river-worthy vessels already."

"What goods from Helmveline? What would they desire from Mulshahar?"

Solineus smiled and leaned with palm to the man's desk. "I only share those secrets because you could learn them yourself. The remainder of my plan is my own."

Zetik's fingers drummed his desk. "Two thousand smedên will make the Guard of Mulshahar smile upon you. If you succeed... On your return you may need to speak with the Smiling Men for your continued protection."

He glanced to Adinvan and translated, but all he got was a shrug. "I've not heard of these Smiling Men."

"Higher Men. Higher than you, higher than me, higher than every man in the streets; so high, they are always smiling, for nothing worries them. And so we name them such."

"They rule Mulshahar?"

"Rule? As a king, magistrate, or priest? No, they do not rule. But if you trade with Helmveline as you say, you will make the Smiling Men of Ôfelun and other cities jealous, and if their smiles turn toward the dirt, you will need the blessings of Mulshahar to survive."

Solineus crossed his arms. "Mulshahar can't guard its own streets? It's merchants?"

Zerik raised his pasty white arms with bulging blue veins. "Ever we try!" He leaned on his desk and whispered. "But when Smiling Men frown there will be blood."

Solineus grunted with a grin and waved it off. "The city is what it is. But there's another task you might be uniquely capable of handling for me, no small thing, and I'd pay well. I need a message sent to Barkûsh so that it might pass on to Molikîn."

The captain's brow arched. "There are a hundred men who could handle such a thing."

"If I hire it done, out yonder and in public, the messenger may not survive. With your name on it, with your connections..."

"Uniquely suited I am not, but I know people who are. I can see it done."

Solineus eased his hands to his hips, nodding, then opened the mail-lined pouch at his belt; he counted out forty hundred-marks in smedên and slid them across the desk. "The utmost secrecy. A thousand for the message. Two thousand for your guards, and another for you, so that the details of this conversation stay in this room."

Zerik pushed ten coins to the middle of the desk. "I regret that I cannot make this promise. If a Smiling Man asks, I can't lie."

"Lies make them frown."

The captain tapped his nose with a wink and nod.

"Keep these as a bonus for your guardsmen, then."

"This I will do." Zerik stood on frail, wobbling legs and gave them both an unsteady bow.

Solineus leaned low. "I will reach out to you, seeking the Smiling Men, on my return."

"Oh! My dear boy... No need, no need. They will come to you."

Solineus stood straight and smiled before turning to walk through the door. This time Adinvan didn't wait until they were out of earshot. "You throw coins around like their pebbles into a stream."

"You'd rather we watch our backs every step we take?"

Adinvan grumbled and stomped. "I'm gonna have to think on that one. Hells, I've sailed months to earn so much coin."

"The world doesn't spin on gold alone."

"The hells... I think that knock to your head was worse than I reckoned. Gold spins all the wheels."

"Gold can't buy you blood when you're bleedin'. And gold can't buy you blood-kin."

Adinvan strode silent by his side until they reached the street. "So, blood and gold spin the world."

He cast his father a smile. "I reckon so. And we've got a month or two before the longships hit the surf. Two months to keep our blood where it belongs, then we sail to see *blood.*"

Adinvan whooped and thumped him on the back. "Your mother! Aye, not a woman alive who'd love to see her son more than that one. What the hells do we do for so long?"

"We learn this city and its ways as wealthy men." His father's squirreled lips weren't impressed. "And we find out which brewery is best." That brought a smile.

Seven

Council of Highs

Low and High,
Crawl and Fly,
the Tri-Forked Tongue hisses the double speak,
preys on the weak and feeds them the dung,
prays without gods and greases the rung.

—*Tomes of the Touched*

The Council of Lord Priests: The histories of the Pantheon of Sol spoke of the seven gathering every two years, but the tradition had transitioned into idyllic fancy by Lord Priest Ulrikt's time; to the best of anyone's knowledge, the lord priests gathering for the Eve of Snows at Istinjoln was the first time they'd all been together in living memory, and it might well be the last time seven lord priests would ever lead the Church.

There are no lord priests attending the meeting of elders today... or at least, none I know of. Meliu scanned the faces in the room knowing Ulrikt might be any one of them and the only way she'd know was if he revealed himself through some wink or sly gesture. Or, his head might be buried a horizon from the Gediswon River. The table in the middle of the cavern sat seven, but every butt in a seat belonged to a high priest selected to represent the adherents from the clans of Kaludor with no one daring to claim the moniker "lord".

High Priestess Sedut represented Istinjoln, an obvious choice; even if you didn't like or respect her, there wasn't a robed soul here who didn't fear her, and she directed most of these meetings. Far as Meliu knew, Sedut was the only one here who knew of Ulrikt and his Face.

High Priest Bekid represented Fermiden Abbey from Broldun territory. He stood as the eldest of all surviving high priests, and as far as Meliu could tell, this trait alone earned his seat at the table, for no one respected the weasel-eyed man. His body-racking cough and slow wits suggested he was a temporary figurehead.

High Priestess Jelodu represented the Citadel of Rôkân from Emudar territory, and she was the opposite of the other two. Tall and blonde and learned as any, her face and tone were soothing to the soul; gentility flowed from her presence, and so if the council sent anyone to the people to speak for them, it was her. Some claimed a volcano lay beneath this trained facade, but Meliu had never seen it.

High Priestess Lizel represented Zarstok Monastery from the Ravinrin territories. She was plain and humble, a woman in her fifties who didn't speak often, but when she did, the others listened. Perhaps it was deference to her years of service as Canon Scribe, or the fact she was the deciding vote on so many issues, but no one ignored her.

And with those four, normality ended. From there the council transitioned from southern to northern clans, and in Meliu's guarded opinion, all these northerners could sing a tune for the Dancing Bastards.

High Priest Runker was a whoreson and hailed from Hîgun Abbey in Mulharth's mountains. What teeth remained in his mouth were black, probably from the fire he breathed at every perceived insult. Over six feet tall and broad as an ox, he looked more a clan warrior than priest, and when he walked, he did his best to pound the dirt like a giant from some scaredy-white tale.

High Priest Merduun was a vile, back-biting bastard with a thick northern accent to make his every pronouncement denser than need be. He looked ordinary enough except his lips were so fat you'd swear someone punched him a candle before; Meliu would've been happy to fatten his lips every time she met him, and maybe push a couple teeth down his throat. Meliu had always heard that the Restutin Monastery in Bulubar was a rat's nest in need of a strong lord priest's hand; this rumor hadn't been a lie.

But the high priest who sang loudest for the Dancing Bastards was Olum of Benet. Meliu refused to think his name with the title attached after they first met; he'd stared, damned near drooling, over Deelee. Even Lord Priest Dunkol restrained his tastes to double-digit years. Black hair, black eyes, and a black soul, it made perfect sense his breath reeked of rot. If Sedut offered the bastard a hundred bricks of gold he'd scream and shout how unfair and hateful the soft southern bitch was.

Meliu didn't get a count of the other high priests attending; one hundred and twelve had survived the flight to the Dragonspan Mountains, and the Church had ordained seven more since crossing the Gediswon—including Meliu—but she figured three dozen at most kneeled in the shadows of the cave.

The conversation so far had bored Meliu to yawns and blinking eyes to fight the desire for a nap, but Sedut hadn't allowed her to skip a single council meeting and made certain she didn't *forget* to show up this evening.

Sedut banged the floor with the leaf-headed Spear of Istinjoln, its red-gold head polished to a sheen. Meliu didn't know if it foretold something important or if the woman was just trying to keep her awake.

"We've a matter before the Council of High Priests of some importance, one I have stalled for too long. Two matters, truth be told. They are related, and both concern the Canon of Justef."

Meliu's fatigue disappeared; her back straightened and she turned to gaze on the council as mutters echoed through the room. Contention over healing witches had been growing in the ranks of the adherents since settling the valley.

Sedut banged the spear and cast a subtle glare over the attending priests in the shadows. "We well know that the Warlord Choerkin has trod upon the laws of the Church regarding those deemed Defiled by the Vanquished Gods."

Merduun cursed the loudest. "Rumor has it the priestess Eliles who brought Fire to the Watch was a child of the Vanquished."

Sedut laughed. "If you believe Lord Priest Ulrikt so blind as to allow one so touched to reach the priesthood, we can finish that conversation with your blood here and now."

Meliu pinched her lips to hold back the smile; no one would mutter that rumor aloud within earshot of any adherent of Istinjoln again.

Olum puffed his chest. "The Choerkin overstepped his authority and he will suffer in the Twelve Hells. The Canon is iron."

Sedut said, "The Choerkin seized an authority never considered before, it was bold to outlaw their capture and execution, and indeed, to accept their help; authority is only an overstep when it fails."

"Then we shove hard! Push him across the line he should never have crossed and cleanse the people of this infestation."

"Infestation is it?" Sedut sighed and stared at the ceiling before lowering her eyes and addressing the table of priests. "I've an unofficial count of healers among the clans, over two hundred. *Two hundred!* They were in hiding until desperate times forced them forward. These people who we deemed heretics, witches, or worse, have been keeping our people alive while our prayers are spread too thin."

Runker stood with an ugly snarl on his face. "What the Twelve Hells're you suggestin'? The Canon of Justef has served the Church for five hundred—"

"But it did not serve before then; it did not serve in the time the gods shepherded their people. What if Justef was wrong?"

Meliu's heart thudded hard. *Holy shittin' hells!* Sedut was lighting a fire, one Meliu figured hard to contain.

The cavern exploded with a din of protests, but it was Runker's voice which cut through the outrage. "Heresy! You should burn!"

The chamber flashed with brilliant white Light and Sedut's gem glowed in her hand; the suggested threat ceased the loudest cries and brought the remainder to a murmur. "It is not heresy to question the judgment of mortals."

Runker cast his eyes about the table of silent priests but was uncowed. "You think yer threats'll clamp my mouth?"

"Yes, I do. One more word before I have my say, and I will paint the floor in your blood."

Runker's mouth opened, but he sat.

What the hells is Sedut doing? Enchanted stone or no, the woman was playing a dangerous game. For what prize did she play?

"More than two hundred healers. Some mix salves and potions, others heal with a thought, some with a touch which heals the patient but brings the wound to the healer. Many serve as midwives bringing our much-needed heirs into the world. Their powers aren't so potent as prayer, but they are enough to stave off infection, heal wounds, and at times fight disease. More than two hundred; could they all be Defiled? Would Sol allow such a thing? Should we hunt them down and burn them, and turn the people forever against us?" Grumbles arose and she spoke over them. "Do *not* be fools! When we lead prayers for the people, how many arrive who haven't taken the adherent's vows?"

Sedut's gaze traveled the room, and Meliu stood. "High Priestess Nedei held prayers just yesterday that brought fourteen clan souls into the world."

Lizel stood, leaning on the table. "What is right is right. The Canon of Justef is law, even if we are unable to enforce it. Even if it is imprudent to enforce."

"And again, I ask: What if Justef was wrong? Or at the least, misguided?"

"Your Lord Priest Ulrikt sought the Defiled as no other before him, raising the reward to such heights that parents turned over their own children, and Lord Priestess Sadevu before him began this practice. Do you claim they too were wrong?"

Sedut smiled, but the glow of the gem cast her face as a haunting vision. "I make no judgment for following canon, but I do question the canon itself."

High Priestess Jelodu was next to rise. "On what grounds would we overturn canon?"

"On the grounds of the numerous lives these people have saved."

"It is a sentimental answer, but reason, not emotion, is required to entertain such a drastic change in canon."

"Sol would not allow so many children to be Defiled, and if Defiled, why do they perform so much good?"

"The Vanquished seek a return to our world; performing virtuous deeds is the surest way to earn trust."

Lizel added, "And even ignoring Jelodu's concern... Historically, such decisions would need more than a simple majority vote from the seven Lord Priests."

Sedut nodded. "I am not here to break the laws of the Pantheon. Lizel, correct me if I am wrong. A proposed canonic change requires three votes for consideration, at which time all parties may research the question at hand for two years, the traditional time between meetings of the Lord Priests. A call of Five-Voices-Aye then alters canon, and a vote of Four-Voices-Aye continues the debate another two years."

Lizel stared with a squint. "All you have said is correct, but there is one thing lacking, a cause to overturn current canon. There must be evidence and I do not see how such thing is possible."

Rusker bellowed, "It ain't! She blasphemes the gods with her words."

Sedut didn't waver, and even as Meliu mused upon what parts of Rusker would paint which wall, Sedut's gaze fell on her.

"I propose rewriting the Canon of Justef based upon the *Codex of Sol.*"

The cavern exploded in murmurs and shouts, and again Rusker's voice spoke loudest. "Outrageous! The *Codex of Sol* burned centuries ago. This is a mockery of Justef's words."

Sedut nodded Meliu's way. *The codex speaks nothing of the Vanquished.* But she stood and walked to the table as the crowd hushed. She pulled the tome from her pack and eased it onto the table; the chamber went silent and none of the seven remained seated. "The *Codex of Sol* survived. I rescued it from the Crack of Burdenis and Lord Priest Ulrikt entrusted me as its guardian before the Eve of Snows."

Lizel muttered, "I'd heard whispers, never had I thought..."

"The Lord Priests met in Istinjoln because of prophecies found in these pages, but their translations were lost."

Sedut banged the Spear of Istinjoln, its red-gold head glinting in the light. "The prophecies are irrelevant; the histories bring us here this day. High Priestess Meliu has been working on fresh translations, and while the prophecies are slow to read, she has progressed in lore dating to the God Wars."

More whispers, but Meliu silenced them by clearing her throat. "This is so, though there is no mention of the Vanquished."

Olum said, "Forges woman! What is your point?"

Sedut grinned at the man, teeth aglow in the Light of the gem. "Meliu, read the passage on the Battle of Ulimbibor, skipping the tallies of dead and heroics."

Meliu scratched her ear in a moment of thought, the woman's purpose a mystery to her, then flipped the tomes' pages until finding her destination. She cleared her throat. "Ten thousand voices rose in prayer, and behold! Anzilok stood before them in the glory—"

"Next paragraph."

"Anzilok pointed to Lord Priestess Ilumbôwarê: 'Bring me your child' and the young girl was carried on the shoulders of the Warlord Choerkin to stand before Anzilok, God of War, and Shetuharu, Lady of Maimers. Anzilok spoke again: 'Strip this girl of her clothes on this her sixth birthday.' Naked but without fear the girl kneeled, and the Lady of Maimers struck the Whip of Scars to her shoulder. There was blood; there was no scream; there was no cry. The child gazed into the eyes of Anzilok, and as everyone watched, her wound healed"—Meliu swallowed as she recalled what came next—"leaving not a scar.

"And Anzilok raised his hands wide to praise his father in the Conqueror Heaven above: 'Behold this child! Behold the chosen of the Father, Sol, and the Mother, Elinwe. She strode before me as a child, she leaves as a Priestess of Erginle—"

Sedut said, "This is enough."

Meliu closed the Codex. The first time she'd read this passage she'd paid little attention to the details; what struck her now was the pronunciation of a six-year-old as a priestess; what struck her now was that the only similar event she knew of was Eliles at the Night of

Bones in Istinjoln, and she felt once again that she didn't understand a godsdamned thing about the past couple of years.

Rusker flailed his arms. "This proves what? You're wasting all our time."

Sedut gestured to the priests at the table. "In the time of the God Wars the Lord Priests under their King Priest were known as the *Mordelotê*, the Council of the Highs, and today we sit in their places at the head of the Church. Bear with me, my peers." She turned to the cavern entrance. "Bring me the girl."

Liermu, Mistress of Trials, strode into the cave with a frightened girl clinging to her side. It shocked Meliu to see Liermu after so long, but it wasn't this wicked woman who held her gaze. A chill pricked Meliu's flesh as she recognized the child. Cleaned up now, she was blonde and pretty, thin to the point of looking underfed. She was the child she and Sedut had witnessed healing a wagon-driver's shattered leg a couple months back.

Sedut faced the table. "Does anyone doubt that the Lady of Maimers and her Whip of Scars is of the same power as the Maimer's Lash? For more than four hundred years the Maimer has tested postulants on their journey to the priesthood; for those four centuries every lash has healed to a scar, unable to mend through salve or prayer."

She nodded to the girl and the child slipped from her robes, kneeling, her head bowed, her hands shaking. Liermu took two steps and turned, the whip flashing and striking the girl's shoulder. No scream, no cry, only the crack of leather on tender flesh. The child leaned and Meliu imagined she fought tears.

Blood congealed and skin mended before their eyes; Meliu's shoulders ached in sympathy for this girl, until Liermu wiped a wet cloth across her shoulder, cleaning the black blood, revealing a girl without a scar.

Hushed silence as the girl's face rose, calm as if nothing had happened.

Sedut strutted to the girl, kneeled to assist her back into her robes, then stood hand in hand with the child, her cheeks burning red with her broad smile, but her eyes were granite. "We are the Mordelotê now and it is we who must decide! Is this girl defiled? Or is she the chosen of Sol the father and Elinwe the mother?"

Meliu's legs quivered. *This child is a little Eliles, only not Fire.* She stumbled backward a step and fought breaths that clutched at her heart.

Sedut said, "We vote here and now as the Mordelotê. Four-Hands-Aye moves the proposal to strike Justef from the Canons of Sol forward two years hence for a final vote."

Five hands rose, and it was no surprise that the one northerner to vote "aye" was Olum, with his taste for naked young girls. But that slimy bastard didn't matter. What mattered was Meliu's world had once again changed before her eyes, this time in an instant for which her translations were a root cause, but it was an embarrassing shame she'd missed what the *Codex of Sol* had been trying to tell her.

She pledged then to pay more attention to the histories.

Eight

Bones Forgotten

Fermentation in time, a fine line of wine,
a bubbling stream of stain leaking and seeping
to cross your heart.
Worry not for its meaning.
Drink the fruits of the yeast and untame your beast.

—*Tomes of the Touched*

Eliles popped a purple grape into her mouth and bit; an explosion of acidic sweet brought a smile to her face. "Oh gods, so good." She snagged a bunch and sheltered them from Artus. "We're not using them *all* on wine."

Artus snorted, plucked a grape and bit... a slow, grinding chew with wide eyes. "Gods. Better than the sweets my ma fed me as a boy. Or it's been too long since I tasted such a treat."

It was the third harvest since she'd remedied the Elemental issue with growing plants, and it was by far the tastiest fruit found on the island. So far, the trees still proved resistant to producing quality apples and pears, but everything else grew well. Sometimes too well. The gardens were more than a handful of part-time help could tend to Wilu's satisfaction. The woman possessed a fervor for gardening that brought her out day by day without fail, but for the past six months her grousing over a lack of help grew. The labor took its toll on the woman, and it wasn't simply the work; she was the only one whose hair grew enough to cut since the tower of flame, which meant she was aging while tending the garden.

Artus trimmed his beard a few months back after so much time watching the grapes, but after that, even he avoided the gardens as much as he could. The notion of immortality had caught on and folks weren't keen on letting go. And the priests from the stars? They didn't show their faces to work anywhere, they hid away or strolled the island as if they lorded over every speck, and they only seemed to speak to anyone when claiming food or drink.

At some point there would need to be a reckoning between the two camps.

Eliles sighed. It wasn't fair that one sugary fruit would trigger so many stresses. "Everyone who drinks wine should assist your picking."

"I'm sure they should..."

The man's voice trailed away, and Eliles followed his eyes: Jinbin, with a smug smirk on his face. "What? You brewed the greatest ale ever... again?"

"Indeed I did, but this boyish grin isn't because of that." He pointed to his face and his smile grew. "You recall how you and Artus promised me half the grape crop if I found the buried shrine?"

Once Eliles had straightened out the gardens, every now and again they searched for the shrine that Kotin buried after Peneluple's death, but they'd never found a thing.

Artus planted his feet as if ready for a fight. "You didn't."

"I might have."

The burgeoning vintner relaxed. "Might, you say. And where *might* this shrine be?"

"The shrine is under the Watch, that's what you always said, but we explored that godsdamned place a hundred times. There's a cave that leads *under* the Watch, and I found it."

"Ain't never heard of no cave on the Watch, outside of the root cellars."

"Sure you did! It leads to an old shrine."

"Cocksure, ain't ya, boy?"

"Willing to wager the other half of your grapes?"

Eliles smiled back and forth before the Choerkin gave his gruff answer. "No. Where the Twelve Hells do you claim this cave is at?"

Jinbin turned with a jaunty bounce to his step. "The eastern shore, follow me."

Artus cursed under his breath but followed, and Eliles was close behind. "What were you doing on the eastern shore?"

"I was stretching my legs with Deleu. We circle the island once or twice a week."

The girl had a crush on the monk, or enjoyed his ale, Eliles wasn't certain which. "Will a false claim cost you ale?"

Artus perked. "Oh, I like the sound of that."

Jinbin chuckled. "There won't be any adding new rules after the fact."

He led them through the main gates and near the docks before swinging north onto a rocky trail which wound their steps to the shore. Jagged rocks stuck from the surf, catching waves and crashing them into white showers and rainbows. If rumors were true, more than a few boats found their resting place here. The stroll which started flat took a rise and soon after their trail turned to ankle-bending rocks.

"I never want to hear you crying and moaning if you break a leg out here."

Jinbin shot her a smirk. "That's why I always walk it sober."

They picked their way with caution for a half candle farther before their trail cleared of scree, but on their left hand was a four-pole fall from a cliff, the bottom of which was jagged crags to break a body. She was happy to see that except for a couple of tight spots, their route was plenty wide.

"I've walked around this island maybe a hundred times, but it wasn't until the other day I noticed it." Jinbin stopped and pointed. "There's a stretch there and there, looks like feet beat those paths, but they don't connect, right?"

Artus snorted. "Aye, folks who made repairs to the Watch's mortar and cleared brush, they used that trail. I walked it once or twice. Ain't no cave."

"Don't be weighing your grapes just yet." Jinbin picked his way between boulders, zigging up what passed for a trail. "This morning Deleu didn't walk with me, so I decided to see what's what, and on my way down I split from the way I went up, and I damned near broke my ankle in it. It's over yonder."

"A man don't break his ankle on a cave."

"He might when it's been filled in."

They struck a hard angle across a steep stretch until he put a hand to a cliff almost twice his height and pulled himself up, then assisted Eliles. Artus didn't accept his help and cursed plenty on the short climb. They stood atop a flat shelf near a heap of rubble, and Jinbin pointed to a black hole. "I think this area was filled in, but the rock shifted, and when my foot went down, I heard stones tumbling for a ways."

Eliles grinned. "This is all good fun, let's see what a little Fire has to say." She raised her hand and a little friend appeared on the tip of her finger.

"Oh no! I found this cave; you aren't seeing what's down there before me."

Eliles glared. "A peek, just to see if its worth the work... because I'm not moving all those rocks."

Jinbin nodded and the Fire darted into the hole that was big enough to take a man to his thigh. She closed her eyes, willing to see through the Fire. "It's big for sure, tall enough not to stoop and it leads into the island."

Jinbin's smile was downright obnoxious. "*Exactly* the kind of place the Church loved to put shrines."

Artus snorted. "We'll see about that." He went to his knees and lifted rocks, tossing them to the side. He glared at Jinbin. "We're doing this, right?"

"Oh! We're doing this all right." Jinbin kneeled and grabbed a rock.

"You boys are doing this; I'll be sitting over here watching you fools."

Artus smiled. "I wouldn't have it another way."

"I'll move more rocks than this old man."

Eliles rolled her eyes. "Don't either of you go hurting yourselves." It was a silly statement, considering how easy it'd be to heal either of them.

Jinbin heaved rocks with determination, but youth wasn't enough to defeat the Choerkin. By the time they picked a hole big enough to slip through the rubble, Jinbin collapsed to his back to stare at the sky, puffed and groaned. "I knew the challenge would make you work all the harder."

Artus laughed from the bottom of the dig. "You think the challenge from your puny arms made me work harder?"

"Arms hells, it's the shoulders and back. Godsdamn, I'll need healing to be able to move tomorrow."

Artus peered up from the shaft. "Too damn sore to climb down?"

Eliles dangled her legs on the rubble, most of the remaining stones the size of a head, and eased her way down. From above she heard Jinbin's groan, and when she looked up the man's face appeared; he must be on his hands and knees. "Damned happy I took the monk's robes instead of going back to the mines with my father."

She turned and took a couple steps into the dark tunnel to make room for Jinbin. Fire blazed above her head, lighting the area; she didn't even recall inviting her little friend. The cavern was natural as far as she could tell and of the same plain gray rock as the rest of the island and its common buildings. The walls and floor were worn smooth or at the least rounded by water while the ceiling remained jagged. "I'd say a lot of water used to flow through this passage, might be another entrance up higher."

Artus said, "Could be Kotin buried 'em both."

Jinbin brushed the legs of his trousers and looked around. "*Or*, the Church sealed the upper entry when building the shrine."

Eliles grinned. "Good, we can at least agree there was water."

Artus snorted and puffed his mustache. "Can we agree to walk?"

She strode forward and sent the flickering ball of fire ahead several strides. The tunnel snaked left and right just enough not be able to see ahead and with a mild grade lifting toward the city above, but it ran straighter than she expected. She pushed her vision into the

Fire, awkward to walk seeing the world through two sets of eyes, but she managed. Nothing out of the ordinary came to either vision until the Fire rounded a corner and her contact with her friend vanished into black.

She stopped and the men both bumped into her.

Artus grumbled. "What the hells you stopping for?"

"I can't see with the Fire's eyes, but I know it's still ahead of us."

Jinbin planted his hands to his hips. "You cheating wench!"

"Hey! Cheating to try and keep us alive."

"Says you."

Artus nodded. "I agree, cheatin'." But he pulled his sword and scrunched to her side, leaving Jinbin in back.

The monk snorted. "Now you're both cheating."

Their next twenty steps were slow and when they rounded the corner, she shielded her eyes from a golden glow. "Fire, less light."

Her eyes adjusted as the Fire dimmed. The cavern was more or less round, fifteen strides from the center to any wall, and was more a piece of art than an act of nature. Rows of yellow garnets were set in the walls, but they weren't ordinary stones; they absorbed the light of the Fire and glowed with an intensity that hurt if she stared at one. In the middle of the chamber stood a stone dais chiseled in a shape similar to a sand-glass timer. Her eyes were drawn to its top, expecting something, but it was empty. Instead, it was what knelt before it that stole her breath: A robed figure.

Artus stepped in front of her, sword leveled. "You there! Show your face."

But the person didn't move. She edged around the figure, blinking to see clearer, and ducked for a glimpse with the expectation of finding a priest from Skywatch. A skeletal face, and after her eyes adjusted further to the glow, she realized the robes were ancient and tattered, not so far from turning to dust.

Jinbin shaded his squinting eyes. "Who is it?"

"No idea. Dead."

"Another murder?"

"No. This one walked the stars long ago."

Artus sheathed his sword and stepped to her side. "What the Twelve Hells you yappin' about? Oh! Shits, guess we ain't worrying none about this one's killer."

Jinbin joined them to stare, his eyes flicking to Eliles. "You think?"

"Check the back of his skull."

The man snorted and folded his arms. "I found the place."

Eliles took a ginger step and lifted the cowl with two fingers, meaning to shift it to the shoulders, but the seams disintegrated, and it fell in a puff of dust. She leaned close and spotted two holes at the base of the skull about as wide as if she spread and hooked her index and middle finger. "This is... unbelievable."

Artus said, "Forges be damned, what're you talking about?"

"In the Age of God Wars, when many of the shrines were built, a priest offered themselves as sacrifice and in return their soul was guaranteed a safe journey to the Seven Heavens. The lord priest struck the devout with a snake-bite dagger to the back of the skull and their body was posed in kneeling prayer."

"I ain't no devout man, but I've seen me dozens of shrines with no such thing."

"Lord Priest Elemeru ordered the sacrificed taken from the shrines in the fifth decade of Remembered Time."

"Why? And how the hells is he still kneeling like that?"

"The dead disturbed pilgrims visiting the shrines. And it was a new age." She kneeled and looked close at the skeleton's exposed fingers. "They used prayers to fuse the bones together, turned this man into a statue."

Jinbin shuddered and kissed two fingers before placing them to his forehead. "Before or after spiking his brain with the dagger?"

Eliles stood, kissing her fingers as well. "I'm praying for after." She stood and turned a circle. "A shrine to whom?"

Artus said, "Bontore is who they always spoke of."

"The dais is bare; something should carry his symbol. It's not as if the God of Knowledge didn't have enough of them."

Jinbin said, "God of Knowledge and Patron of the Oracles of Bones... They say Lord Kotin bore a mighty grudge for this particular god."

Artus walked the wall looking up and down. "Oh aye, he did at that. I'd say the man mighta taken and destroyed any symbols."

Eliles sighed. "Then why not destroy the dais itself? And the skeleton? We're missing some..." A scant streak of silver glinted, inlaid in the wall, its left end pointed? *Fire, dim.* As the ball of Fire and the resulting golden glow of the gems faded, the silver stood out. Thin and only a hand's length under the glow, it was clear to see now: Three feet long and with the leaf-shaped head of a spear on its left end angling down. She glanced right to see another straight streak of silver with its right end angled down.

Jinbin edged to her side. "The Spear of Bontore, but its all wrong."

Artus said, "Aye, his constellation is the Bent Spear not the broken spear, even a heretic bastard like me knows this much."

Eliles gasped and her heart beat fast. Her smile was broad but nervous as she turned to them. "Dareun told me a hundred stories of Bontore as a child. Do either of you know why his spear is bent?"

Artus shrugged. "He pissed off his woman?"

Jinbin guffawed, tears in his eyes as he stifled further laughter beneath Eliles' glare.

"Men. No. After the Great Forgetting, when the gods could no longer reach the world, they noticed that his constellation in the sky was broken, once straight, but now as if snapped in twain. But when the priests learned to communicate with him through the Oracle of Bones, the spear was no longer broken, the stars had moved, making it the Bent Spear."

Jinbin groaned. "The stars moved, you say?"

"Yes, because Bontore could once again speak to us, but his words would never again be straight." She ducked her head, it sounded like a silly tale for children. "That was the story."

Artus traced the head of the spear, tapped its tip as if to see if it was sharp. "Ain't no way I dismiss nothin' these days, girl. So, what do you think this story might say about this here shrine?"

"It would be a shrine of the... of the in between times. Not from the Age of Gods Wars, and not... Well, I don't know when this was built. Our historical knowledge is bent and broken, much like the spear, and there are inconsistencies..." A rush of excitement brought a tingle to her fingers, but she kept the revelation private: *The constellation in Skywatch might answer some questions.*

"Either way or some other, we know godsdamned well why Kotin covered this hole. Might be we shoulda left it that way."

Jinbin turned to the skeleton. "It would be unbelievable that the Church didn't know of this shrine, so why leave this skeleton while removing all the others?"

Eliles leaned to take in every finger of the dais' surface; the stone was white marble, she figured, and streaked with grays and yellows, but it showed not a single sign of writing. "It wasn't an accident. I've no idea if the reason is important now or not, but there was one."

"Think them cloistered holies might know why the hells he's here?"

Eliles glanced to Artus. "Possible, but this shrine was as much a secret as the Crack of Burdenis... more so, at least in Instinjoln we had rumors of the Crack. Most of the priests here are young, I doubt they know much." *The old priestess in the street is another matter,* but Eliles hadn't seen that old woman—outside of wishful thoughts—since she disappeared two years ago.

Artus huffed. "You calling me old or wisened?"

Eliles grinned. "Neither." She eyeballed the both of them. "Let's keep this shrine a secret for a time."

Jinbin raised an eyebrow. "Folks don't like secrets. Everyone promised."

Eliles grimaced, then shrugged with a smile. "We only promised the denizens of the Salty Frog. You two let our people know but leave no doubts they aren't to speak of it with anyone. I don't want Skywatch to know until I want them to know."

Artus grunted in agreement. "You got a plan, then?"

"No, but Skywatch and this hidden shrine to Bontore are both on this tiny island... they're connected. Or at least they were." And she wanted a chance to shake the truth from the stars before they had a chance to shine down lies.

Nine

Tethered Silks

Love rests in the heart of the Mother;
Joy rests in the heart of the Father;
Pain rests in the heart of the Sister;
Sorrow rests in the heart of the Brother.
Which inbred kin are you?

—*Tomes of the Touched*

The day before the wedding, Roplin and Inisfer shuttered Ivin away in a room, alone except for a mottled-brown sparrow that visited to share in his loaf of bread and jug of water. From midday to midday, he was to sit and reflect, purifying his body and soul in preparation for his vows. As a boy, he'd considered the notion philosophical if not romantic; reality turned out boring as he tried to make sense of the growls his stomach made, as if his gut was trying to tell him something of import.

Turned out his belly knew nothing about nothing except being hungry.

His thoughts skipped from one worry to another; marrying a girl he cared for but didn't love to the woman he did love but couldn't marry, to a woman, lost to him, that he loved but barely knew—*how silly is that?*—to the one woman he could never not love, his mother...

and yet, most of his waking candles he spent staring out the south-facing window and pondering what Daksin Ravinrin and his party of hunters faced in their journey.

They'd ridden out a week and a half earlier; fifteen days of travel into dangerous and unknown forests to find a man *Ivin* should be searching for. Rinold was a Warden and a brother who was only months from fatherhood.

What the hells am I going on about? He stared at the down-stuffed mattress on the bed and the oak tables and chairs in the room before taking a seat, remembering a far more uncomfortable tower. He spoke to the plush chair. "I once killed a distant relative of yours far to the north, hoping to use him for an escape." He blinked and rubbed his eyes. "There I go, talking to furniture again."

Thank the gods someone knocked on the door. His sister-in-law Inisfer stood with a beaming smile on her face and clothes draped over her outstretched hands. She curtsied. "Kinesee will swoon when she sees you."

"I'll be content if neither of us runs. Place them on the bed, please."

She straightened her face and spoke in a gruff voice. "At your request, Warlord Choerkin."

He cracked a grin and chuckled despite himself. "I like you, don't push it." His brother had married the right woman. A part of him was happy for Roplin; a part of him cursed the couple for their luck.

She placed his clothes on the bed and straightened them before turning for the door with a smile. "Don't be late for your own wedding."

"Dear sister, the only thing a warlord can be late for... is a war."

"Late for your wedding will start one."

He tipped an imaginary hat as she closed the door and changed his clothes. The trousers and shirt were spun from fine black silk, and the shirt shimmered with silver griffons. He tied a golden sash around his waist, a gift from High Priestess Sedut, and, to finish the ensemble, he slipped into calfhide boots from Lady Tedeu's favorite shoemaker. He dabbed a pungent, musky perfume on his neck and wrists, snorted at the odor, and shook his head like a dog who'd sniffed a stink bug. Everyone assured him it was a favorite of Kinesee's, but he wondered if anyone had bothered to ask. Likely as not, Roplin was setting him up for some joke.

He opened the door, stepped into the hall, and was no longer alone. Armed and armored men stood stiff every few steps along the hall; Ivin hated to imagine what security would be like if someone *had* made an attempt on Kinesee's life in the past two years. Lady Tedeu wasn't going to allow either of them to die today... or perhaps they were here to keep him from skedaddling.

Ivin chuckled to himself as he meandered down the hall to meet Roplin. His brother eyeballed his shiny vest. "You look dashing."

"Any word from the south yet?"

His brother clutched Ivin's head in both hands, stared into his eyes. "Forget the south for a day. You are the groom about to wed a beautiful young woman. So, shut your yap and follow me."

The passage wound in squared turns until exiting the tower. A field of green spread before them on the southern side of the wall, tall poles bore green and yellow silk banners flapping in the wind as they stretched pole to pole; four concentric circles shrinking until reaching the middle.

He cleared his throat and stared as he slipped from his boots so his feet could feel the world. They'd told him two hundred people would attend, but it looked more like a thousand; he grew warm with a racing heart and sweating palms. His knees locked, refusing to move. A fake smile as he muttered, "What the hells am I doing?"

"You better be walking."

His feet trudged into a dreamer's stroll, where his legs didn't quite connect to his body, and everything around took on a blurry, uncertain character. The crowd of smiling faces parted before him, a canyon of people leading to Kinesee. She stood tall, her blonde hair braided with white silk and penetrated by golden pins with heads of ruby—gifts from the Ironwing of Helmveline—and begowned in white silk sewn with strands of gold in the shape of flowers—a gift from the Shining-Queen of the Helelindin—but it was her face that brought goosebumps. Her face was painted as a noble lady today, not a child, highlighting her eyes and lips, emphasizing both her beauty and trepidation.

This vision of his bride returned the world to reality, the fuzzy dreamscape reshaping its focus on a single face and the trembling corner of a nervous smile, and Ivin's own smile, moments before terrified and fake, became real. He knew it real because, of a sudden, he wanted to ease her fears more than indulge his own.

Twenty barefoot strides cushioned by dense grass, blades slipping to tickle between his toes, a sensation reminding him he was in a different world from the one he'd left; on Kaludor, naked feet were for firesides, beds, and baths, as even when there wasn't frost or snow, the rocky terrain bit the soles. A different world, a different Ivin, and a different Kinesee; would all three be different again after accepting the vows?

He stepped to stand in front of her and took her hands in his. He whispered, "Are you ready for this?"

"Are you?"

"No."

"Me neither. But Pa always told me I did a lot of things before I was ready."

Two priests robed in black and carrying a ribbon of red silk strode from the center of the circle, stepping to either side of the couple until draping the silk over Kinesee's shoulders first, then his. They intoned: "The bond of man and woman before Sol and his seat in the Conqueror Heaven is of soul and blood, of spirit and heart."

The duo circled them with the silk then led them to the center of the gathering where they kneeled on pillows, facing one another, slippery fingers still entwined.

The priest pulled a red silken sash from his robe and draped it over Ivin's wrists, and at the same time, the priestess pulled a white silken sash from her robe and draped it over Kinesee's wrists. Ivin's mouth went dry.

The delicate touch of silk fluttering to land on her outstretched hands set Kinesee's heart into a racing panic from which she couldn't flee. Her teeth clenched; she feared that her eyes bugged but prayed they didn't. *What the jibber-jabber am I doing here?* She'd rubbed the pearl a thousand times in the last two days, comforted by its light and warmth, but knowing Solineus was too far away to save her. And save her from what? Marrying a handsome warlord who was nothing but kind to her?

Yes, to save her from exactly that.

Quit yer bleating, little sheep; Pa and Father would both approve.

She sucked a breath, and this time her eyes *did* bug; she choked and coughed and took a wheezing breath before recovering. Thank the gods, and all that was holy, she didn't do that while he spoke. She smiled at him the best she could, tears seeping from the corners of her eyes.

He leaned a hair closer to whisper, "You're all right?"

She could only nod and smile.

He straightened and took his hands from hers, tying one end of the red sash to his left wrist, then reaching to lay the other end across her right wrist. "I bind my blood with love and offer my heart."

She took the red silk and tied it; cleared her throat, twice, before attempting to speak. "I accept your heart into mine and bind it to my blood, so they may flow as one in this mortal realm." Not choking again was a blessing from some god or another! W*hich god would that be? Shut up and tie the white silk.* But she already stared at the red knot long enough that others stared at her. She fumbled with the white sash before getting it tied but managed to lay it across his hand without making a further fool of herself. "I bind my spirit with love and offer my soul."

She stared at him, and he licked his lips. *Even warlords have nerves.* The thought was soothing.

"I accept your soul into mine and bind it with my spirit, so they may rise and be as one in the Seven Heavens."

She smiled, and he smiled back, and she figured his heart might be racing as fast as hers as High Priestess Jelodu stepped from the crowd. Kinesee had demanded one thing before this ceremony: Neither Sedut nor Meliu could bless the vows. Jelodu was the perfect choice, a woman with a voice as soft as her eyes, plus she'd never kidnapped Kinesee nor slept with her betrothed.

Jelodu raised her arms toward the sun above. "Before the Fire of Sol, Ivin Choerkin and Kinesee Mikjehemlut have spoken their vows, and I feel the heat of Januel's love in approval for this twining of bodies, of lives, of souls, and of futures. In the eyes of Januel, Sol, and all the pantheon, you are now husband and wife."

They stood together as the surrounding crowd erupted into cheers. Within flickers music played, a lap harp, a flute, and drum accompanied by a choir of holies singing a frolicking tune. All those gathered around them, except the rings of guards, danced in a chaotic swarm until forming lines to come and touch each of them on the shoulders, giving their own silent blessings before they'd feast and drink themselves into a stupor.

Ivin cocked his head as Maro was the first to lay a hand on his shoulder, and the way Ivin's face twisted, she knew he fought a laugh at whatever the man had whispered. "What did he say?"

"That he was godsdamned happy there was one less man he had to protect you from."

She glanced at Maro, who only managed to get ten strides from her, and caught his wink. "I suppose it makes his job a little easier." They stood in silence for a time, dozens of folks touching their shoulders and moving along until their lack of words grew awkward. "I can't believe I choked on my own breath."

Ivin grinned. "I can't believe I got the words out; my tongue was stuck to the roof of my mouth. But we made it. We're married."

She glanced at the silks tethering their wrists. "Married, which means we're tied together for the next six candles or longer. Walking together, feeding one another..."

He leaned to her ear. "I just pray I don't need to pee."

Her eyes flew wide. "Oh gods! Oh dear." And she laughed, even as she prayed both their bladders stayed strong.

"And—"he coughed"—by tradition, the silks shouldn't be removed until after..."

Her laughter turned to a choking giggle as she patted her bodice. "I have a knife to cut those if need be."

"The silks or my—"

Kinesee laughed again. "The silks. You'll need the others. Eventually."

He gazed at her, and she fell into staring at his eyes until he spoke. "I like you."

She blushed. "And I like you." It was awkward to hear and awkward to say, on both ends of the conversation judging by the quiet that followed.

It felt like a candle before the lines of blessing came to a merciful end, and joyous music turned to a soft serenade.

"It's tradition that we dance now."

Kinesee raised her hands into his, and they pressed close, and she managed not to step on his toes as they bobbed, weaved, and stepped to the beat of the drum. "I've been practicing with Alu for three weeks."

He smiled as he leaned over her, so close she felt his breath. "It's also tradition that we kiss."

Her heart fluttered in a buzz of terror and excitement. "That I haven't practiced—" His lips met her words, and she mumbled before going silent.

The kiss didn't melt her soul like it would've in her stories of princesses and queens, but neither was it as horrible as nightmares had foretold. She relaxed her fingers in his grip and returned the kiss, and there was a tug at the hem of her dress. But she wasn't going to let some child interrupt her wedding kiss now that her lips had found the right shape.

Another tug.

"Kinesee." Ivin spoke through the kiss, and she could feel his lips smiling. "There's a black goat trying to eat your dress."

She rolled her eyes. No doubt Tengkur would be the talk of the party. "Sometimes, you just have to learn to ignore her." She clenched his hands, closed her eyes, and took his breath into her mouth.

TEN

Tangled Triangle

I was born a Child of Hope in a time of greatness.
We climbed atop the shoulders of our ancestors,
the stars tantalizing to touch.
Atop them shoulders we stacked our bodies
dead one by one to scramble and climb.
I reached the apex the sole survivor and fell,
the plummeting fall;
in my death I lived forever.

—*Tomes of the Touched*

Ivin and Kinesee untied their wrists after climbing into bed together, the extent to which they both agreed to the mandates of tradition. He lay awake most of the night staring at the ceiling, wondering on the fate of the Squirrel, wondering whether Daksin Ravinrin's party had found a trail or were themselves prisoners or were perhaps dead by now. From stories told of the south, two hundred armed men might be safer from the natives than they were the critters swinging and flying through, or wandering beneath, the dark canopy of the forest.

His eyes drooped, and perhaps he dreamed of lying awake, for when the knock at their bedroom door came it was accompanied by the first creeping rays of the morning sun. He glanced at Kinesee's curled lump beneath the blanket and eased his feet to the chill stone of the floor, cursing as he strode to the door with once warm toes.

A glance through the peephole revealed Maro; his eyes were bloodshot and his hair unkempt, no doubt a reflection of his having tipped a dozen mugs the night before. Ivin cracked the door.

"What is it?"

"A rider from the south wants to meet with you soon as you're rousted."

"What news?"

Maro shook his head. "I don't know the details, but nothing happy I guarantee."

Ivin sighed. "I'll be in the side-chambers, bring the rider to me soon as you can."

Ivin closed the door as Maro disappeared down the hall, then snuck to the maple wardrobe for a change of clothes and a pair of boots. He was proud of his stealth right until the wardrobe creaked the final finger before clicking shut.

He spun to stare at the bed; no movement, but after two steps toward the door to the side-chamber the voice came.

"That was Maro?"

"Aye, it was. Nothing to worry about, just a messenger."

She sat up, still in her wedding dress. "*Just* a messenger? You think me a foolish girl?"

He smiled at her. "How long have you been awake?"

"All night... Or may as well have been." She swung her legs over the edge of the bed, stood, and straightened her dress before making her way to a mirror. "I wish to hear what word this messenger delivers."

Ivin grimaced. "I'm sure it's no worry of yours. Rest."

She turned on him, fists to her hips, and he was happy he hadn't gotten around to giving her his wedding gift. "I am the bride of the Warlord Choerkin, what the hells business of yours shouldn't worry me? And yes! I am married now; I can say *hells.*"

"You really didn't sleep, did you?"

"You snore."

"I..." He'd learned many lessons from Meliu and fighting the Tek, one was picking your battles. A second was that if you were going to lose, at least slow your opponent's pursuit. "Your point is taken, but don't you think you should get out of your wedding dress first?"

Her stare softened. "Hmmm, I suppose we don't want rumors of our not earning the silks cut to spread. All my clothes are at the other tower!"

"Well, then. Soon as you've changed, join me." He stepped into the side-chamber with a cocky grin and closed the door behind him.

The room was maybe ten by fifteen strides and the walls stood lined with shelves for books, but only a dozen tomes stood at the ready for reading, barren as many ruins, except the oak was fresh-polished and golden hued. It reminded him of the tale of King Olimen the Hard-Headed—a favorite tale of his mother's—who would speak of the poor king who built a fabulous palace only to find that he'd spent his every song and could no longer afford a throne, or indeed, any furniture at all, and how he sat alone on the floor of his empty library every night. Ruining this impression were the eight chairs, a table with a brass lantern, a mahogany serving cart—stocked with Broldun whiskey—and a silver-gilt mirror taller than he was.

He meandered to the fireplace and opened the flume, struck flint to steel until the kindling smoked, then tossed two small logs into the growing blaze. The fire was more for light than heat, perhaps an equal part of something to keep busy while waiting. But he no more than took a seat with his feet by the blaze when he heard a door open. He turned, expecting Maro and the rider.

Kinesee said, "Good, they aren't here yet."

Ivin squinted, suspecting his bride a magician, as she stood in a mauve velvet dress hemmed in forest green, but as impressive was how her hair lay so neat. She'd even managed a dab of powder to her face and red for her lips. He'd be peeved by her defeating him, but... "You look lovely."

The compliment appeared to startle her, but she recovered with a grin before making her way to the mirror, dabbing a pinky at a speck marring the corner of her lip. "I'm atrocious."

"Far from it." His chin lolled to his chest. "You stripped your poor serving girl of her dress, didn't you?"

"The Lady Tedeu taught me to always have ladies around who are about your size... Now I know one reason—"

A knock resounded and she rushed to take a seat beside the fire as he stood to open the door.

Maro stepped inside and came up a step short, as if an unexpected splash of water had struck his face, and a smaller man covered in dirt damned near ran into his back at the abrupt halt. "Kinesee... You look beautiful this morn, glowing one might say."

She blushed. "It's the fire I'm sure."

Ivin gestured to chairs. "Please, sit. I've been anxious for news from the forest."

Once out from behind Maro, Ivin recognized the other man as Mekrin but didn't recall his family name. He was a mountaineer, a hunter and trapper, of Choerkin stock who'd made a name for himself stalking wild hogs. He sat in a chair as far from everybody as he could find. "Pardon, m'lady, my dirt and grime."

Kinesee shrugged. "I hadn't noticed, sir."

Ivin stifled a chuckle; the Ravinrin training was making her more a lady than Ivin was a lord. "Tell us of the south, any word of Rinold and his people?"

"Nah, nah. We stumbled and fell into a pile of shit... excuse my tongue, m'lady."

Ivin felt an urge to strangle the man. "Be free with your words and apologize later."

"Aye! Yes, Warlord Choerkin. Lord Ravinrin led us to the Foggy Vale as you suggested, we traveled on foot from there, keeping a dozen horses at the ready for any messages needing sent north. We made good time according to the wayfinder, eighteen-day trek to reach Green Mountain from Forest's Gate. We lost two men to some godsdamned fever after swarms of black and yellow bugs bit them while they took a squat... but other'n that nothin' much stood in our way. Once at Green Mountain, Daksin sent out patrols as we cleared woods and weeds around the pyramid. Turns out there's a godsdamned ruined city all around the mountain."

"Usable?"

"Mayhaps, down the line, plenty of stone we might shuffle around with the right tools and time. We claimed the top four tiers of the pyramid, built us a gate and wall of sharpened stakes right off. We sent a rider north, but seems he never made it back to the Bluff. Seven days in, a patrol didn't return; that was the first real trouble we knew. Ten men gone. Took another five days before the Wayfinder led us to the poor bastards. I was there. Must've been fifty of these damned-near-nekid bastards in a camp, our boys hanging in cages from the trees."

Ivin groaned. "I'm guessing Daksin couldn't sit idle for that."

"Hells! No one could. Fifty half-nekid against our armored men? Forges, there wasn't a one of us who wasn't strappin' their ax to their belt. Folks rolled dice to see who'd have to stay behind at the Green Mountain! I was itching-mad being the rider trailing the rear in case things scattered on us. It wasn't even a fight." His head slumped.

"Killed to a man?"

Mekrin sucked his teeth. "Nah, don't think so anyways. I mean it weren't a fight at all. I was on a yonder hill thinkin' I should charge to get me some glory when the first men fell. Stumbled and just slumped to the ground, dead or knocked cold I couldn't tell. A hundred and ten men fell without a drop of blood; I stared long enough to see the yellow-eyed shits drag off a few of our people. Then I rode like the hammers of the Forge were chasing me."

Maro interrupted. "And Daksin Ravinrin?"

Mekrin shook his head. "One of the first to fall alongside the Wayfinder."

"And who do we have at the Green Mountain?"

"Seredon Tutlif commands more 'n sixty men there, including Helmveliners. I swapped horses, and this time three of us made for the Bluff; we all got through. After a nap I figured it best to bring the message personal like."

Ivin stood and paced. "How many Kingdomers did they take?"

Mekrin's head weaved in thought. "I'd put the number at thirty or close enough."

"We'll talk some more, but first you get some rest; you'll need to tell this tale again. Maro, gather the clan-blood who were here for the wedding. Set a meeting for noon in the Sun Chamber."

Maro stood and puffed his mustache. "It'll be done. Hearing of her son's loss will displease the Lady Ravinrin but at least there is hope. How much should I tell them?"

"As much as you need to." He turned to Kinesee with a smile. His bride had sat quiet and poised through the entire story, in retrospect a surprise. "Your thoughts?"

Her brows shot up as if surprised he asked her opinion, but it took no more than a flicker for an answer. "We need to send word to the Ironwing of Helmveline and to Shuntiskâ."

"Aye, indeed. You know the pigeon-master well, would you do the honor of writing the messages and seeing to their delivery?"

"Of course."

Ivin noted the snarl shaping Maro's mustache. "No need to hurry until Maro has returned for escort."

The man snorted with a grin. "I'll get on the clan-blood." He strode for the door and disappeared with a bellow: "Vernik! You're on the lady's guard until I get back."

Kinesee had already pulled quill, ink, and parchment from the table's drawer by the time Ivin turned back to Mekrin. "Tell me everything you recall of the terrain around Green Mountain... ruins, hills, rivers, streams...and for that matter, the route there."

Kinesee had wanted to ride from tower to tower along the wall since—well, since seeing the wall—so she wasn't going to waste her excuse to ride fast. She commandeered a dress cut for riding from her handmaiden and leaned into the horse's mane as she heeled the beast into a straight-tailed run.

"Holy Heavens, girl! Slow it down!"

Maro's voice faded behind her; she hadn't spent a couple hundred candles training on horseback to ride slow.

"You're a crazy child!"

A glance back at Maro proved him at least as crazy, considering the smile on his face. So she leaned deep into the mane, breathing the musk of the horse's sweat, enjoying every breath, every bug that ricocheted from her forehead, and every stare from guards when they thundered past. In a matter of wicks, the clatter of hooves had carried them to the western tower; she tugged the reins and relaxed, sitting up into a cantor that eased to a trot and walk. When they passed beneath Ironwing Arch they entered the round, as folks called it, where the wall broadened into a circle that resembled a castle's bailey, except it stood perched four rods above the ground. Stablehands trotted to take their puffing horses.

With a racing heart and a laugh she dismounted to find Maro looming over her. "I suspect we'll be riding back the same way?"

She smiled. "We'll want fresh horses for speed."

"Gods girl, there's no hurry riding back."

She turned and strode into the tower, heading for the stairs up. "A wise person once said you should live in a hurry."

"What confounded idiot ever said that?"

She shrugged; far as she knew no one had said it, but someone must have, even if they weren't wise. "I don't know. Someone who lived too slow, I'd wager."

They stepped from the guts of the tower to stand in Pigeon Hall. It stood a level below the top of the top of the tower and instead of being enclosed except for arrow-slits, it felt more like standing on a stone balcony with a rail and roof. Shutters could block the wind from any direction but there was always one or two open in case a bird arrived.

Kekoru loved her pigeons more than people, or that's what folks whispered, and she was a squat Kingdomer who had to look up at Kinesee. Not that this was so unusual anymore, as she'd grown like spring wheat the past couple of years. She was still getting used to adults looking up *at* her, let alone adults looking up *to* her, let alone understanding the expectation to behave as one.

Between her studies and spending time with the pigeons, Kinesee's Kingdomer was better than most other Silone. "How are my favorite birds today?"

The woman smiled. "They've flown under the Griffon's wings." A saying which meant they all returned safe from hawks. "But your favorite pigeon today is Broken Toe."

She was a pigeon whose one toe had been broken when a fledgling, and it had grown crooked. "Broken Toe? Why's that?"

Kekoru slipped a sealed letter from behind her back and held it up. "One guess who it's from."

She didn't need to guess. A hand swifter than the pigeon master's swiped it from her grip and Kinesee broke the wax-covered thread tying the note. She couldn't stay silent after the first line. "My father is in Mulshahar."

Maro said, "This is fine news." Then he grunted and cocked his head. "Where the Twelve Hells is Mulshahar?"

Kinesee shrugged and they both stared at Kekoru. "Beyond the Foundations, a trade city of renown beside Kônu Bay. You want more than that, you need to find another."

Her breath left her as she read. "Gods!"

"What?" Maro eyeballed her and she held up her hand to stall him.

"He's found the Emudar... they're scattered, but thousands are on islands south of Mulshahar."

Maro stared as if she might be crazy. "Graces of the Seven Heavens, that is good news. Is he on his way back?"

She dropped the note on the table and sat. "No."

"No?"

"Yes, but... He and his father are sailing to visit his mother, then he's going to try and sail upriver to reach us, from waters he calls the Monsoon Strait." She turned her eyes to the pigeon-master.

"Don't look to me this time, I've barely heard of Mulshahar."

Kinesee huffed, then squinted at Kekoru. "Does Helmveline trade with Mulshahar?"

Kekoru tossed bread to a cage of pigeons. "Some, but the roads are either filled with Teks and their wars... bandits, or goods need wind through the Foundations, no small feat as your father will attest."

"Solineus looks to find a trade route between Helmveline and Mulshahar..." The woman's eyes bulged for a split-flicker. "Would this interest the Ironwing?"

A snort-chuckle came from the woman. "Men have tried afore to no good end. I forget the man's name, but one explorer made it down some river or another, maybe all the way to this Monsoon Strait, but keeping a route open was plum impossible. The manpower..."

"As impossible as claiming the coin from the Twelfth Foundation?"

The woman's lips pursed. "As impossible as. But a single man can no more hold a thousand horizons clear than he could hold back a river."

He won't be alone. "If he's to come up from the south, he'll need to get by those who took Rinold and our people."

Maro said, "From what I know of the man the yellow-eyes would be happier letting him pass."

Kinesee giggled. "Still... He's trying to unite the seven clans. Kekoru, I need to add a request to my note."

The woman's brow wrinkled. "You've the look of a girl with purpose."

"I'm a girl in need of maps... old, unreliable maps."

"Another hundred or two hundred men sitting on the Green Mountain? I ask, how will this help us?" Ivin stood in front of the gathered clan-blood, already several candles into the bickering. He glanced to Kinesee, who had strolled into the fray with Maro on her heels over a half-candle earlier. She sat three strides from the speaker's circle with a curve to her grin that he would call smug, but as yet she hadn't said a word.

Danwik Mulharth stepped into the circle with him, his stubbed right hand pointing at him. He spent most of his days in Forest's Gate but had returned to visit kin. "How would ten thousand help? This is why we needs stay here. Peace with the Tek is dead, it's a matter of time before they strike. We can't afford to be sendin' our kin south on a fool's bidding."

"Aye, peace is dead, yet only their arrows have crossed the Gediswon. Our people are behind the wall now, many thousands more than needed to man these walls and repel an army. If this wall falls, it won't be because of any number of men we send south."

"Oh, aye... says you, mighty Warlord. How many would you send to their doom, where the enemy puts warriors to sleep without a battle?"

Ivin paced the circumference of the circle around the man. "A thousand, fifteen hundred, maybe." The door to the room opened and Ivin blinked twice at who he saw: Sedut and Meliu. No doubt Kinesee noticed her as well; the smug disappeared from his bride's face. "Perhaps the holy have something to say?"

Meliu lurked by the door, not even looking at him, while Sedut treaded to the circle with soft steps. "I thank you, lords of the seven clans, for this opportunity. The Council of High Priests has been in conversation since first word of the captures. Slavery is of the highest sins in the eyes of Sol, and to know our people should suffer such depravity draws our ire more than even murder. Like you, we assumed these people primitive, weak, but they have proven this to not be true. The council has determined to send nineteen high priests with whatever contingent the lords deem to send south."

Murmurs passed through the room, and the Mulharth spoke next. "Will you bear the artifact in this fight?"

"I head the council and will remain here where I am needed most... at the wall facing the Tek. High Priestess Meliu will lead the nineteen."

Ivin muttered to himself, "Shits." His plan to lead the force south just hit a snag; Kinesee would erupt if he and Meliu traveled together. Hells, she wouldn't be the only one. The wrath of Lady Tedeu and Alu and untold others would shower upon him. Soon as his mind reconciled this, suspicion took over: why the hells would the holies send so many ranking priests south?

The Broldun strode to the circle and shoved the Mulharth from his way. "This all sounds grand and mighty, but who the hells would lead such a thing?"

Ivin stood straight. "I will lead the force to Green Mountain and beyond."

The room erupted in shouts that didn't settle until the Broldun raised his arms. "Silence! The circle is speaking. Still, these lords are right, the war is to the north, and *you* are the Warlord Choerkin."

"It's been weeks without a single Tek crossing—"

"No matter, and you know it. The wall is your command until we have peace. If... *If* we send men south, you won't be one."

Sedut said, "It is my opinion that we must face this new threat, but, indeed, I would see the Warlord here by my side to defend our people."

And for me to be clear of Meliu. But Sedut's words were the words of the Church now; with her say the odds of an expedition moving south improved.

He turned his gaze on the Broldun. "So be it. A force of fifteen hundred led by Polus Broldun." Ivin smirked, hoping the man regretted his stance, but Polus smiled and puffed his chest.

"You trust a Broldun with this? Mmm, I am honored, if the clans should agree."

Shouts of "aye" and "nay" arose from the gathered, enough of both to keep the question from being settled. Frustration burned in his gut, but the return of the smug grin to Kinesee's face proved the advantage to his staying between the canyon walls of the Roemhien.

Polus said, "This is a choice for the heads of the clans, and all seven are here. Do we have a count? All in favor?"

Silence. Not a single damned one of them agreed, not even Roplin. Ivin stared at his brother, but all he got in return was a shake of the head.

"Damn it! We can't leave them to the fates of foreign gods and slavers."

Kinesee sauntered into the speaker's circle and raised her hands for silence. Her grin was no longer smug, it resembled a cat with the mouse's tail still sticking from its lips. "While you lords consider my husband's words, I have news."

Polus said, "The lords should decide one matter before broaching another."

His bride stood her ground, and Ivin stepped to her side, proud as she answered. "The matter may sway a few minds."

Polus flicked his wrist. "Mmm, speak further."

"I bring word from my father, Solineus Mikjehemlut, born by pigeon. In the city of Mulshahar, he has found Clan Emudar—" A chorus of voices and shouts erupted. She waved her hands. "Please! Please. Quiet."

Kinesee closed her eyes and counted the length of her breaths to maintain her calm as the room eased to a hush. She needed to get things right, present what she knew in a way to move opinions. "Adinvan Mikjehemlut is lord of the clan now and some sixty thousand Emudar are scattered along the coast, but they are gathering on islands south of this Mulshahar."

Lady Tedeu stood, not bothering to walk to the crowded circle. "This is wonderful to hear, but they are thousands of horizons from us. It has no bearing on the question at hand."

She smiled at the woman and thanked the gods it had been her to make the point; it was like talking to her gramma. "This *would* be so, but for the fact he plans his return by river. Longships for as far as the waters allow."

Tedeu cut murmurs short with a raised hand. "Speak plainly, girl."

"Mulshahar is a trade city to rival any in the Tek nations and Solineus plans to open a trade route to Helmveline. I sent a pigeon to the Ironwing requesting to view any old maps he has and mentioned my father's goal. The Ironwing has invited me to Molikîn to study these maps and discuss his venture."

"And how does this alter our plans?"

A sharp exhalation before Kinesee seized her gambit. "We know well that Helmveline is hesitant to wage a war here in the north, and like you lords, I doubt they wish to risk more lives in the south. What my father is doing *could* open Helmveline's trade with Mulshahar, trade harried by taxation and blood, if the pigeon-master speaks true. A trade route would be worth a fortune to the Ironwing. I wager it's worth enough to risk lives to meet my father part way while trying to save the Helmveliners lost thus far."

Locust Mulharth piped up. "On whose word, yours and some woman who plays with birds?"

Kinesee turned her glare on the Mulharth. "Kekoru is a master of messages and entrusted with knowledge beyond most Kingdomers. Her intrigue was palpable, and the invite from the Ironwing himself? This is no small thing. Morik of Shuntiskâ is still here from the wedding, ask him."

Tedeu said, "Perhaps I will. Have you a proposal to consider?"

"I do, Lady Tedeu. Morik will escort me to Molikîn to study the maps. They are old and outdated, by the word of the Ironwing, but still they might suggest a passage my father could be following. I will convince the Ironwing that it would be in his interest to match whatever number of warriors we send south."

"So simple is it?"

Kinesee smiled, recalling a piece of one of the woman's lectures. "It is. You once told me that there are two ways to tempt a stubborn man, by crotch or by pouch. This is a straight route to the latter."

Chuckles spread through the room and the Lady Tedeu blushed. "That was in the strictest confidence, my dear."

"When I gain his commitment, Polus Broldun leads the way south."

Sedut stepped into the circle with a cough. "If you're getting a look at the maps of Helmveline, I recommend taking Meliu with you."

Kinesee's gut twisted but she managed a smile... she hoped. "Pray, what for?" She wanted to bite her tongue. *That came out nastier than I meant.*

"It happens that she too holds an ancient map; it might prove useful in your negotiation."

Kinesee wanted to scream through her clenched and smiling teeth. "Fine. She may travel with me." *At least I'll know where she's at.* "The lords need pick a number of warriors and I will get the Ironwing to agree to match the count. One or two hundred *will not* prove we are serious. Gather them for the ready and I will send word by pigeon when it's settled. Polus Broldun will lead them with High Priestess Meliu, while my husband remains here at the wall."

Ivin raised his voice. "Any naysayers?" Kinesee smiled at the silent mouths in the hall as Ivin continued. "Settled, Polus Broldun will lead an expedition of fifteen hundred to Green Mountain, contingent on word from the Lady Choerkin and the Ironwing of Helmveline. This time we will not be so brash. We secure the Green Mountain, fortify this position, and only then strike south to find our new enemy and bring our people home." Ivin turned to

Polus. "But no mistake, friend, you find the whoresons? You bleed them into the dirt." Ivin grabbed Polus' shoulders and gave him a shake. "Understood?"

The Broldun clamped his shoulders. "Aye, brother, it's what I do best." Then the big man slapped Ivin in the head and Kinesee overheard his whisper. "I saved your life, Kinesee would've killed you before you set foot to stirrup."

Kinesee had never been so proud and angry at the same time. She turned her back on her new husband and the big-bastard Broldun, her eyes alighting on Meliu hiding in the shadows. *Precisely which hell have I fallen into?*

ELEVEN

Archiver's Work

Sondonumâ, Third King of the Jûntu Dynasty, dismissed the wisdom of his forebears in the quest to befriend the White Eyes, and instead sought their capture. Rondinumîn, Seventh King of the Jûntu Dynasty, grasped the hopelessness of the ploy but he believed a return to peace impossible, so instead sought their extermination. And so the Jûntu Dynasty ended in a Fire only the White Eyes could see coming.

—*Oxeum Codex*

Crafting a precise copy of the Oxeum Codex was not a simple endeavor. Glimdrem's first thought involved ink, a quill, and a lot of blank pages to fill, but this notion declared itself foolish the moment he struck ink to paper. The precision he needed went beyond symbols. Ciphers could be hidden in the text with a tiny mark throwing all his work to the wind. He needed Archival Parchment. This valuable material started sheep hide, before being treated and stretched so thin you could see the print of your finger when pressed to its surface, but the final bath in its manufacture made it special. Artisans stretched the hide taut and soaked it in *inbelêud,* an Elementally charged liquid. Once dried and finished an archiver could press it tight to the page of a book and a flash of Elemental Light used to burn a perfect copy onto the Archival Parchment.

There were two problems: First, the Edan controlled the limited supply of parchment, and second, Glimdrem did not have a legitimate cause to make a request. There were also two positives: First, he could purchase the base parchment of the quality he needed, and second, Glimdrem could learn to make *inbelêud* himself.

One year, two months, and seventeen days after perfecting his version of Archival Parchment he copied the two hundred and fifty-fourth page, the final page, but it still took him another month to sneak back to Uvin's chambers and return the codex to the Blind Monkey's base without attracting attention.

Twenty days later he lay sprawled in bed wide awake, staring at the ceiling, enjoying Ilsferu's warm breaths on his chest as she slept nestled to his shoulder, his mind slipping over and over to a single question: Is today the day? The words of the Codex defied his every glance, so far he didn't even have a name for the language it was written in. If Lelishen returned to the Mother Wood, she might know, but could he trust her? It did not matter, since she had disappeared with the humans far to the south. The only word from her the Edan shared was that she worked with the Helelindin to secure a new home for the odorous Silone. *Pathetic humans.*

Ilsferu moaned and rolled to an elbow, her golden eyes fluttering open to the first rays of the sun's light peeping through the window. "You're awake early."

Lelishen was less important than ever, a forgettable figment of lust to bury in his past. "I had a dream. In my dream I found the Oxeum Codex."

"I worry for your obsession."

He chuckled and ran fingers through her hair. "My obsession is you. The Codex is—"

"I am your love, the Codex is your obsession, and I am satisfied with this."

"But I know where it is."

"The last time you looked, I almost died."

Glimdrem knew her memories of that day were shaken and scattered. "Do you remember the monkey statue?" Most days he asked she recalled little to nothing of its story, let alone examining it.

"That hideous little thing? What about it?"

He kissed her forehead then sat up. "It holds the codex, I'm certain of it. And I know how it opens."

She groaned and pulled silk sheets to cover her breasts. "And you are off to see the Lord Chancellor to get permission to try."

He stood and leaned over her with a smile. "And then you will be life-bound to one of the most famous Trelelunin in the history of the Eleris."

"I know better than to argue. Just this time, promise not to almost kill me?"

"On my life." He kissed her lips and grabbed a robe to throw over his shoulders before setting out to claim what he figured was the next step to his destiny.

He found the Lord Chancellor of Knowledge sitting with her sister, Limereu, on the banks of the Reshfuon River and he didn't know if he was interrupting a personal or professional moment, but he had made his decision this morning: He must treat this as an urgent revelation.

Fesele reclined in a life-sculpted tree, its leaves draping to cover her eyes from the sun. "Inslok returned from a foray of Kaludor with nothing new to report. You may as well know this as well, Glimdrem."

He grinned. No matter how silent his steps, he should have known the Chancellor would know of his arrival. "Then I am happy that I might have some thoughts of importance."

Both women turned to face him. Limereu's blank expression lacked the emotions he'd seen upon her return to the Eleris; she was becoming more Edan the longer she was in the Mother Wood. "What news have you?"

"Not news. A thought." He strode close and leaned on a tree. "Two nights ago I dreamed of the Vale of Resting Winds, a vision of that night, except I watched myself and the Twenty-Five from the trail leading down. As my eyes adjusted to the explosion and I watched myself lean over the twenty-fifth, I realized that Uvin stood by my side. He spoke to me again of the Blind Monkey, but instead of calling it a temple, he said a statue."

Limereu's head cocked, the squint to her eye proving that the Mother Wood had not stolen all of her emotions yet. "You reference the statue in his home?"

"I do. He also mentioned the Latcu and Ikoruv experiment which led to his understanding how a smith would forge the two materials together. Not demonstrate but led to. As if it might be a key."

Fesele leaned to grab something, and when she turned she held the combined needle of Latcu and ball of Ikoruv in her hand. "You believe this is a key?"

Glimdrem's heart dropped, his soul a flicker from panic, but he forced his eyes straight. When returning the Codex, the needle had still sat in Uvin's desk. "I do." *How much does she know? Was I followed?*

She held the monkey's key aloft, the sun's light creating a rainbow as it passed through the Latcu. "It is spectacular. What is your theory on how it works?"

He cleared his throat to give his breaths more time to calm. "The Latcu and Ikoruv must create some sort of force, a polarity like a magnet. It could operate, then, as so many magnetic locks."

Fesele glanced to Limereu. "No one has ever detected a force. You've seen the statue in person, your thoughts?"

Two blinks later: "The shape of the base suggests that it could house a tome. There is no harm in trying, and if true, it might assist in understanding the Elemental dynamic forcing the materials apart."

Glimdrem cleared his throat. "If my theory proves correct, I request observer status during the Oxeum Codex's translation."

Fesele gave him owl eyes with a slow blink. "No. Such a thing would be outside protocol and your expertise."

"It is without fault of my own that I am embroiled in this mystery. I have spoken with the Touched and seen Celestial Gates twice, if my advice reveals the Oxeum Codex, I feel I will have earned access."

The Lord Chancellor of Knowledge stared without a word, meaning she at least considered his position. "You may be present as we test your idea, but I deny full access to the translation."

Glimdrem anticipated the answer and chuckled. He wanted to proclaim that the Chancellor had misunderstood, but he knew not to poke an Edan ego. "Witnessing its opening would satisfy me, and its first words. Of course, I would include any section dealing with Celestial Gates." What he really wanted to know was what language the Codex was written in.

For a flicker he thought they would deny his request, but Fesele's jaw cocked a nudge sideways before nodding. "This is reasonable, if you volunteer to witness any attempt to close the gates."

To volunteer in the Eleris was the illusion of self-determination, but in this instance, it was a courtesy that purchased what he desired most. "I would have it no other way. I want nothing more than to witness the defeat of the gates and the minions seeking entry to our world."

Fesele glanced to her sister: "Fetch the monkey, if you would be so kind."

Limereu eased from her seat and glided through a door in the tree's wall as Glimdrem choked on spit his throat refused to swallow; he coughed, pounded a fist to his chest, and coughed a second time with a grinding hum and rasp.

The voice came: *You were careful.*

"I was."

Fesele's eyes turned on him, unblinking and wide, glittering, in his mind's eye the metallic flecks turning to blood, a hallucination he smiled away. "I wasn't expecting the statue to be here."

"I had them retrieved just over a week ago. Lucky for us, as it saves time investigating your dubious theory."

Mere days after he'd replaced the Codex. Either he had the luck of the Golden Dice or the Lord Chancellor played him, waiting for him to confess, to trip himself up, or to run like the deer his thundering heart begged him to mimic, but he stood silent and smiling, hoping to exude a confidence unbetrayed by his twining gut. The Edan's stare betrayed nothing more than you might expect from a stone or tree, so he strolled near a dangling branch Life-sculpted into a reclining seat, a seat which would force her to turn to see him. "May I?"

"Of course."

Her eyes broke from him as he sat, and having escaped the uncomfortable gaze, he relaxed. "Have you found any new information on Celestial Gates?"

Her head tilted back to stare into the leaves rustling above their heads. "References abound throughout the God Wars, but what you've reported is unique in its details."

"A pity."

"Even the Shadows of Man, Marukane, and this queen defy our knowledge to date, but we've twenty thousand three hundred and sixteen tomes untranslated in the Halls of Knowledge. Time will reveal what we need to know."

His brain numbed at the number and he blinked just conceptualizing the library. "Twenty thousand..."

"Not including dead languages."

Limereu's voice echoed from the door as she entered. "We know so much and so little." She cradled the monkey statue in both hands, its empty eyes staring straight at him as she turned, and between blinks he swore the thing grinned at him.

He resisted the urge to stand, to snag the key, to run to his treasure and claim the fame he deserved, the fame which could reveal his lies and end with his banishment from the Mother Wood. He stared and smiled instead.

Limereu placed the Blind Monkey on the table near a decanter of wine, and Fesele held forth the mystic key of Latcu and Ikoruv, her voice smooth and without a hint of malice nor suspicion. But then, he doubted her tone would change if pronouncing his death sentence. "Would you care to test your idea?"

Glimdrem's heart lurched and he pinched his lips before the Edan could see them twitch a second time. "Me? Well, I... Pride is a pitiable trait, but yes, I would."

He stood and grasped the key, its Ikoruv warm from the Edan's grip, rolling its weight and peculiar balance in his hand. He towered over the monkey first, then kneeled to gaze into empty eyes.

"Your dream didn't tell you how the key worked?"

The tone was dry and flat, without a hint of the sarcasm one would expect if dealing with a human or even a Trelelunin, but a smirk forced its way onto Glimdrem's lips, knowing that somewhere within the woman's soul there rested a bitter humor. "No, it didn't. Still... I always assumed Uvin spoke of the monkey as being blind for the missing gems." The rustle of leaves died as the breeze disappeared, leaving them in utter silence as he glanced from key to monkey. "I wager it's a perfect fit." He flipped the key until he held the Latcu and stuck the ball of Ikoruv into the right eye. Nothing, and he could feel Fesele's laughter even if the woman hadn't laughed in over five hundred years. He heard her intake of breath, no doubt to empower cutting words, before he twisted the key a nudge. Ikoruv slipped into a perfect fit and a click resounded.

The Lord Chancellor loomed by his side before he realized she had stood. He backed from the table, the needle of Latcu pointing straight at him from the monkey's eye.

Limereu said, "Careful, sister."

Fesele looked at him. "Do you think Uvin would have left a trap armed?"

"No, I do not, but I suspect you knew him longer and better than I did."

The Lord Chancellor slid a fingernail into a tiny crack and pulled. "It amazes me that the seam is invisible when it's sealed." She lifted the Oxeum Codex from the statue's drawer with the calm of someone putting their hands to a thing no more special than a clod or broken branch rather than a legendary tome the Edan wondered upon for at least five hundred years.

Glimdrem smiled, his heart racing despite having spent the last two years with it hidden away. Its secrets were still secrets, but they were out in the open now and ready to decipher. He did his best to mimic an Edan's disinterest. "A peculiar leather."

Fesele nodded and she flipped the book to glance at all sides. "A thick leather, crocodile I imagine." Her head cocked and she squinted. "This is but one book in a collection."

The skin of Glimdrem's face chilled as his smile sank. "What?"

"Oxeum seven thirty-three to seven thirty-five, so reads the spine."

"You know the language?"

"We call the language Oxeridinun, I familiarized myself with the writings in anticipation of the Codex's discovery." She lay the book on the table, opening the first pages with a gentle touch, pointing to curves, hooks, bars, and dots which were scribbles to Glimdrem. "Three historians inked this tome, their names are here, but I won't embarrass their memories by trying to pronounce them. Indeed, the tome begins in seven thirty-three upon the Toltorûoc calendar."

The Tolturûoc was a dead calendar much like so many languages, but he puzzled together what he recalled from his studies before heading for Sutan. "Between three and four hundred years before the First Forgetting, near the end of the God Wars. How many translators are learned in Oxeridinun?"

"I will lead a forum of three in the first translation. The language is, at its core, uncomplicated, but as with all histories there are biases and conflicts with known and suspected realities, pieces to be puzzled together."

Glimdrem dipped his chin with a solemn nod. "I only care for the Celestial Gates and how to close them."

The Oxeum Codex slapped shut with Fesele's long fingers clamping its covers. "This is well. I will inform you the moment we come upon such information and invite you to sit in on associated sessions."

He bowed with his eyes pinned on Fesele rather than the book. "I look forward to the day you summon me."

Inslok's voice startled him. "Consider yourself summoned. I just departed the Hall of the Volvrolan, he has a mission for us."

"Us?"

"The Silone have sailed for Kaludor and the Volvrolan wishes us to intercede on the behalf of the Silone in Istinjoln."

"Intercede how? We know nothing."

"In whatever way we can. We leave in two days for Choerkin Fost. If Limereu wishes to join us, the Volvrolan accepts her desire."

Glimdrem turned to stare. Either the Edan left the Mother Wood more often than he knew, or something monumental drove them to risk the outer world. It was one thing for the two to travel a couple hundred horizons on Northern Vandunez, another to visit a dangerous island.

Limereu's head tilted. "I risk very few memories if I go. But why me?"

"Three hundred and fifty years ago you banished the Lôdôkohoxi-kê from the mortal realms, sealing it for eternity."

"You say I did, but this is the first I have heard such a thing. I recall nothing."

"Facing similar events can induce memories of the past. The Volvrolan hopes, if you choose to take this journey, that it will inspire recollections of your history."

Glimdrem shifted his feet; the tactic made perfect sense despite its risky nature. The Lôdôkohoxi-kê threatened to rend the Eleris during the Age of Warlords, but the great demon summoned by the Tek nations was banished from the world, a ritual involving infused and enchanted gems crushed into a powder. If her memories of this event returned, she might provide clues on how to control the demons on Kaludor, perhaps even hint at how to close the Celestial Gate. The question was whether the woman was willing to depart the safety of the Mother Wood. She didn't allow the question to linger.

"I will travel with you."

The Chancellor turned to her sister. "You are certain?"

"I am. It is a risk, but one with many potential benefits, personal as well as for the greater good."

Inslok bowed with a gracious sweep of his arm. "It is settled."

Glimdrem stood enthralled. The humans mattered naught. Returning to Istinjoln interested him in itself, returning with these two Edan brought goosebumps. "If you will excuse me, I will prepare for our departure."

Inslok nodded and Glimdrem turned to leave, but the Chancellor's voice stopped him. "One more item. There is a fine residue from archival parchment on the pages of the Oxeum Codex. Do you know if Uvin copied the codex?"

Glimdrem swallowed and turned, his eyebrows bunched. "He said nothing to me."

The sisters nodded, and when their eyes turned from him, he spun on his toe to escape the chambers with steps he assured himself were unhurried. *Is that why they send me to Kaludor? Do they know? Do they suspect? Are they playing with me?*

The laughter of the voice ricocheted from ear to ear before speaking. *We are the poisonous frog the cat regrets pawing.*

TWELVE

Living Bones

The lens of glass traveling fast,
to see, to find,
reality through a distortion
more filtered than your own eyes.

—Tomes of the Touched

"Elinwe, show me the way to the Great Forgetting." Eliles figured herself clever until the stars didn't move. It had taken a week to walk into the stars and find herself alone, the irritating priests acting as if she were a house guest out to steal the family jewels, and she didn't want to waste the opportunity. She planted her feet for balance. "Elinwe, show me five hundred and six years ago."

The stars blurred, and her head swam; she clenched her eyes shut until her wits stopped spinning, and when she opened them, she sought out the Spear of Bontore.

Broken.

The five stars of its shaft didn't hold their familiar arch; the first three stars were straight, and the next two were also straight but shifted at an angle approaching square. "Heavens, it's true. Elinwe, show me five hundred and five years ago."

The blur of stars was minor, and as she stared, the Spear of Bontore came back into focus, a perfect arch in the sky.

She exhaled and put her hands to her hips. "The Great Forgetting bent the Spear? Elinwe, show me the Seventeenth of Velôbrâ, five hundred and five years ago." The sky twitched because it was just an extra day back in time, and the spear remained crooked. She shifted the sky with prayers to Elinwe until the Spear snapped. She whispered to herself, "The eleventh of Velôbrâ, the day before the Great Forgetting."

"Clever Dame."

"Holy hells!" Her toes left the latcu floor and she spun, landing with tinkling chimes to face the Touched. His eyes twinkled with mischief and the light of the stars.

He touched his face, dimpling his cheeks with his fingers. "I once enjoyed eating the meat from bones; now I enjoy *being* the meat on bones. Ha ha!"

"You should warn a person."

Silent steps brought him close to loom over her with a playful smile. "What fun would you allow me? But here you are a swallow swallowed and flying through time, beating wings and beating heart to find what scholars also found in the time of the stars, even without this mystic view."

"I never knew what day it happened."

"What minds find, they often don't care to share, and in this instance, the instant taught so little, spittle in the spittoon of important things to ponder into insignificance."

"Well, it feels important to me. Wait a flicker, how are you here? Last time—"

"This time, I came looking for the Dame of Fire, in her pyre, surrounded by liars."

"Looking for me? Liars?"

He waggled his fingers. "Truth be told, in fold to hold not so bold, I was bored! No, that wasn't it, not this time, fine, fine, in this time. Ah. Maybe. Did I mention before that I made a mistake? Or perhaps I created, crafted, drafted, a ratted and fattened mistake? A blunder asunder, a—"

"No, you didn't."

"I came for that then." He stared at her and nodded. Stared some more.

"What mistake?"

"I didn't tell you? I thought for certain I did. Just now."

"I fear not."

He flailed his arms in a fit. "That is an outrage! How dare I not tell you? Have you spoken to the smudged man, Solineus, since your tower, this flaming flower?"

She didn't know if glaring at the Touched would do any good, but decided it was worth a try. "Just how the hells would I talk to him?" She met his stare with her glare, focusing on his brown eye. "No, I have not."

"You will."

"I will?"

"Indeed."

"And?" She glared into his blue eye this time.

"I told you."

"No, you didn't."

"I will tell you again then. I made a mistake, I told the smudgeon, the curmudgeon, who sat, sits, or will sit in a dungeon, that Almost would *never* travel to the gate. No, no, only me to see. I am wrong."

"You were wrong?"

"I *was* right, but *now* I am wrong."

"So, you want me to tell him that you were… are wrong?"

He waved his hands with a chuckle. "No, wrong is of no importance; it is the mystery of *how*, and that other puny and looney word, *why*, that he needs to know."

"How?"

"And maybe who. Yes, who who who the Blind Owl sings for the Craven Raven, a Mad Maven, a Bloody Maiden, the Fire-Licker and the Fire-Breather, the Hate-Seether."

"If you thought you found me, you lost me again."

"Now she speaks like me!" He laughed, doubling over as his humor echoed through the universe. "Oh! Oh. I *miss* our conversations, even if we have them daily."

"Our chats aren't boring."

"Not, not, tie the knot and swing and rock, to rot and break in poisonous embrace, to fall for the Dame a second time. Marry me."

It was her turn to laugh. "We would make a couple, wouldn't we?"

"A couple of what is the question, the lesion bleeding the legion of answers unfound and unsought. But no, tell the smudge that Almost would not have gone to the gate's Eye again, if I had not said he would not. Irony yes? Irony no? To what crop did my seed sow?"

"Solineus is the smudge? If I see him, somehow, I'll tell him. Will the stars take me to him?"

"Yes, he is, and no, they will not. Someone overheard our conversations one and two at the same time and different times, and whoever, whatever listened, made sure Almost would return to the eye of the queen to be seen or stolen, gleaned or broken. Who or why I would not say even if I knew these answers."

"The eye from the gate, not in my Fire."

"Different eyes indeed."

"Well! I'll pass your words on, even if I don't understand."

"Good!" He patted her on the back like she was a fragile or aged pet prone to falling over. "Now, clever girl, you weren't really so clever."

Eliles stepped back and planted a foot. "I was pretty clever, thank you."

"Pretty and clever, two different things you often pull together, but... eh!" His smile through pyramided fingers teased her. "You only discovered what others already knew, even if you yourself didn't know, now show me what nobody else knows but so many scholars dream of surmising, surprising even the haunt of Meris in her decades of not being so clever amid the stars, from string to chuck, the answer isn't found with luck."

Eliles squinted at him, ready for his game, whatever it might be. "I could find the candle, the wick, that the Great Forgetting took place."

He clapped his hands with a smile so big she knew she was wrong about something. "Yes, you could."

"The flicker?"

"Clever girl, lucky girl, or patient girl? Stretch a flicker from one end of the universe to the other"—he pointed from one horizon to the other—"and chop slice chop? How many slice chop slice?"

"You're saying the Forgetting was an instant amid infinite instants."

"Clever Dame, for sure, but clever to endeavor enough?"

"You think I should find something else?" Her temper stood on the precipice of a flare when the obvious struck her and she wanted to slap herself. A day no living scholar knew. "The First Forgetting, when the Spear of Bontore was whole."

He leaned over her, his breath wafting pleasant basil into her nostrils. "Clever Dame."

She sat and crossed her legs to keep from falling over. "Elinwe, show me one thousand years ago." The blur muddied her brain and thoughts, but she recovered to find the Spear of Bontore still broken. She took several deep breaths to still her gut. "Elinwe, show me two thousand years ago." But nothing happened.

"The sky cannot reveal what it did not watch."

"So Skywatch didn't exist yet? Elinwe, show me one thousand and five hundred years ago." As her eyes focused, her breath left her; the spear wasn't just straight and in one piece, the star at the tip of its leaf-head point glowed brighter than any in the sky, and the haft was a star longer.

"I remember these skies well. Continue."

Eliles prayed back and forth through time by centuries, then decades, then years, then days: One thousand, one hundred and twelve years ago, on the twenty-first of Beldrên, the Spear of Bontore broke. She smiled at the Touched, but his eyes were lost to the stars, his face so solemn that a tear wouldn't have surprised her. "Is something wrong?"

His stare didn't leave the constellations as he spun a slow circle, taking in the sky, and for the first time his feet produced a song, soft and gentle, as reflective as the man appeared. "No. It is... This is the last day I lived, to die, to live forever dead, in a manner of speaking."

"The First Forgetting?"

"The day I remembered more than I ever knew before."

"You didn't forget?"

"I was unfortunate to know so much more than when I started, awaking, taking, seeing and being, discord, the under-Lord, the storm in being born."

She jumped to her feet, tired of straining her neck more than necessary. "How did you not forget?"

"Oh, my lovely Dame, I went insane, didn't you notice?"

Her giggle shifted to a laugh before it sounded fake even to her. "You are perplexing, but insane? I don't know."

"That is kind of you." He sighed, staring at the sky. "I wish I could tell you what happened beneath these stars, but despite the blur of time that hides us from eyes, there is no hiding from lies."

"Nor rhymes. Why are we here?"

"We haven't gone anywhere."

"Haven't we? I'm not so sure."

"An argument moot as a conversation with a mute. No, it was to see these stars again and remember. And to challenge you, perhaps."

Eliles rolled her eyes. "Challenge? You guided my way."

"To a time you would find, but this way, you earned my favor."

"Do your games ever end?"

"My games never begin nor end, they run one into the other like the waters of oceans into seas into currents predictable yet unknowable. You know why I came here, why did you? What of the Spear bent, broken, and straight skewered your curiosity?"

"I know something you don't?"

"You know your heart, how could I?"

She nodded and wandered a ringing circle around the Touched. "This is the challenge, to challenge you, isn't it? Fine. I found a shrine to Bontore."

His shoulders slumped. "Tut tut, you've nothing better than that?"

She blushed. "Let me guess. You once prayed at the shrine with some King Priest or another. Or you met there with Bontore himself?"

"Bontore is not one you forget once met, but I only know the Shrine of the Undersky by reputation."

She took advantage of a breath to speak. "It has a name?"

"They *all* have names even if they are forgotten and unearned with certain rings to the ear, in particular pitches and particular keys to play a sound to a particular song without a gong... Why don't more songs include gongs? What of this hole in the ground gives you trouble?"

"The Snakebite Skeleton... priests removed them from every shrine on Kaludor but this one. Or so they claim."

His face went blank. She'd challenged him, or if not, she at least forced him to question how much he would reveal. "Elimwoth is the name of the bones fused, a name little used, of the abused and dead. Some said he had such a lazy eye that he could stare at two things twice! What good to you is this answer?"

"None, as you know well. Why would they *not* remove this individual?"

He stared at her, his playful smile still gone, his eyelids blinking fast. "I know not your heart, so how could I guess the hearts of those who did such a thing? A thing done which shouldn't have been."

"Shouldn't have left him, or shouldn't have removed the others?"

"Sol taught and fought and sought, to go to war is to kill your enemies all, unless you have reason or cause to let your foe not fall."

"You're saying there is a purpose..." The sensation of a presence overwhelmed her mind, and she crouched as if ducking a blow before she noticed the Touched staring to the stars; her eyes followed.

The Fire of her wall burned through, hiding the sky with its bright glow, but above, a great eye blinked.

The Touched spoke, but no longer to Eliles. "Of course. The Slaker of Dreams will come to drench the wench and heave the winch, but my tongue has flapped too long. A song I will sing of the damnedest thing, and in this heart, I will linger."

In an instant, the stars and night sky returned, her Fiery tower and the mysterious eye gone. "What is that thing?"

"*She* has warned me, oh Dame, to cut my tongue and run. Fear not the eye, dare the lie and inhale the sigh. Goodbye." But he stopped, raising a finger to silence her. "The lion of white's whiskers sense and search for you. Speak not the name he earned." In an instant, it felt as if she'd been standing alone the entire time.

"And what's that supposed to mean? How can I speak a name I don't know?" Eliles sighed and stood alone in the empty silence of a sky twelve hundred years in the past; the only mystery solved was one she hadn't sought the answer to. She tapped her foot for a rhythm of chimes and hummed a tune to regain a hint of control and calm, then sat to breathe, eyes closed. "Elinwe, show me today."

The Spear of Bontore was bent in the sky above but bent less crooked than her understanding of what just happened. *She warned him. Warned him of what? Me? Or revealing too much? A lion of white?*

"There you are."

Startled, Eliles spun on her rear to face Jinbin. "I am. And you. Why?"

"The wing in the Fire, it's returned. Saw it myself."

The wing remained hidden for two years, like the eye, like the Touched, like the old priestess in the street. "When we found—" She cut off her own words; how many ears could hear her?

"You don't seem surprised."

She stood and smiled. "I've been surprised too many times today to make much of it. Come, let's see if this wing appears again." *And then, we find out why it... they... are here.*

Thirteen

Blow Holes

Flickering flames on dancing waters,
breakers and takers, singers and sayers,
the Mended Skull aboard the broken hull.
What thought have you?
What word?
Blending and bleeding into the absurd,
a curd, a way, and a four-legged spider
plucked by a child's game.
Eight eyes and a web of lies,
all you need to survive.

—*Tomes of the Touched*

Water spouted in the air to their south with a roaring blow, and drake-whale humps rose and dove into the waters of the Parapet Straits. Pikarn leaned on the rail, staring at these visitors and wondering if such giant creatures had any predator except men and monstrous beasts he'd once assumed legend. *I suppose a dragon might eat one easy 'nough.* It seemed peaceful out in those waters, but a turn north remedied his easy calm.

The *Soaring Gull* and four new longships sat anchored near the mouth of the Kiubor River, and scattered along the shore to stare back at him, whenever he bothered to look, were the Shadows of Man.

Silent as ever, unflappable as ever, fearless as ever, until the rains came and they disappeared for a time. And again today, all day, no Taken.

They'd sailed near enough to the coast to spot Shadows for five days, but not a single Taken had made an appearance, which was peculiar enough, but bobbing on the waves just outside Broldun Fost, the lack of Taken ate his nerves. Not a soul on board could explain why, but he seemed to be the only one concerned. The reason could be a boon or a bane or nothing at all, but at this juncture, he didn't like mysteries.

Broldun Fost was nothing more than cold, lifeless stone, no fires, no sounds, no action. The last time he'd set foot here, the docks swarmed with sailors, and fires burned all night, or at least until everyone got too drunk to keep them lit. *Even if we slaughter every last godsdamned one, there ain't no way to bring back the past.* The gloom brought on a malaise every time they had passed an empty village, but for the mighty Broldun Fost to be so dead? He glanced at cloudy skies with a snort and pulled his cloak around his shoulders. It was sure as hells damp enough to rain, but the clouds thus far refused to do them the favor despite drenching them for three days straight before their arrival. If he needed a forecast for the continued drought, all he needed to do was watch the Shadows watching them.

"Well, Gull Droppings, d'ya think it's gonna rain today?"

Captain Swolis turned to the sound of his nickname. "Ain't you in a sour way this mornin'."

"Aye, I am at that. What days these have become when a cold rain would make me smile."

"Hells of a time for a drought." Rikis strode from behind him. The eldest Choerkin was more than healed, he strutted muscles even Kotin didn't rival in his heyday. The boy spent every day of the past two years swinging axes and adzes, dragging and carrying lumber for daily labor, and hauling heavy packs up and down ladders for what he called fun. If the Choerkin's enemies were mortal, they'd fear him.

Pikarn envied the boy and his youth, but he was proud of his own count of swinging the ax, even if his old body didn't show the fruits like a young man. "We've got food for a month or two."

Swolis raised his nose to the wind. "You won't be waiting so long."

Pikarn glanced to shore; Shadows whisked toward the gates of Broldun Fost. The city was once home to fifteen thousand or more Silone, but he figured a mind-bending number of Shadows could squeeze into hidden places. "They're taking cover."

The Captain said, "There's that, and..." He pointed west. A wall of dark streaked from the sky as if the clouds fell in a tidal wave.

"Unholy shits, when I prayed fer rain, I should've specified a pleasant shower."

They laughed then, but the squall blew in with a ferocity that tested the seaworthiness of the new ships; while the blow slowed their plan, it didn't stop them. Pikarn and Rikis stood braced against the rails of the *Singing Dolphin,* a longship helmed by Captain Bour, as the power of men's shoulders sitting on two decks of oars powered her north. They pushed through the broad mouth of the Kiubor with the rains so heavy they couldn't see the Fost's buildings, let alone a Shadow.

Pikarn stumbled and weaved to Captain Bour, a man who claimed some drips of Broldun heritage, but more to the point, one of a few men at New Fost who'd navigated the Kiubor's currents. The man's calm as he swayed with the roll of the deck, staring north with arms crossed, built a confidence in the man Pikarn didn't have before.

Pikarn yelled over the wind's howl. "How far you thinkin' we make it in this here wickedness?"

Bour eyeballed him. "Mmm! I'm supposin' we damned well better make it to the Sogenden Bend. The river turns easterly there, and we can raise a little sail, get plenty of horizons between us and Shadows in Broldun Fost and Fermiden before this storm blows over. From there, the river twists northwest for a spell. If we keep some wind, we'll make ground."

Pikarn snorted with a nod and wobbled a dozen steps to a lean-to covered in canvas and packed with men. They made space for his ass without comment, in part because he was the Wolverine, and in part, because of the strips of jerky he handed around. He ripped a strip for himself and chewed as he waited.

It was hard as hells to see a thing, but he felt the boat turn, and in a wick, men raised a sail maybe a quarter its full height on the mast. The winds didn't disappoint, filling the canvass with a snap. The captain's yell came garbled to his ear, but sailors must've understood as men leaned on the starboard rudder, the starboard rowers pulled their oars from the water, and on the port side, oars dipped to help steer. The ship drifted sideways. Pikarn grunted and kept his seat, figuring either Bour knew what the hells he was doing, or sitting would be useful when they crashed into the bank. His iron gut rusted as they rocked on the waves, and he grumbled with the twists and turns, but the hells if he'd admit his unease to any of these sods.

The *Singing Dolphin* rammed nothing more than a few drifting logs, and Bour hollered out half the day, with rowers from both sides assisting the helmsman in keeping them more or less centered in the Kiubor as it twisted and turned. Pikarn didn't stand until the rain ceased, and the oarsmen relaxed, and by then, the sun drifted west in the sky.

Bour stood tall and damned near unmoved, his woolwaxed coat still dripping. "I once sailed down Nôduk River to raid some Tek village, I'd forgotten the whistle through my soul navigating a river in a storm with speed." His smile made Pikarn wonder if the bastard's mind wasn't a nicked sword: Still sharp and deadly, but damaged.

"You got us here, by the gods, wherever here is. Any guesses where that be?"

The man's face went blank as he pondered, then a corner of his mouth scrunched. "We're on a northeasterly stretch now, so bettin' we made some horizons. Long stretch of river ahead of us, though. But just as important..." He stretched an arm and pointed to the banks of the river.

"Not a Shadow in sight." Pikarn chuckled and slapped the man's back. "For Broldun blood, yer tolerable."

Bour guffawed. "Better'n tolerable, I'd wager we reach Ulmun Island by nightfall. It's a barren chunk of rock sticking out of the water, but we should be able to row up to its southern shore and stretch out for the night."

Turned out, the captain underestimated himself. The orange protrusion of Ulmun appeared on the horizon well-before sunset, but the man was wrong about its being barren. A horn blew as they approached, and Pikarn didn't know what he saw at first, or his eyes chose not to believe it; a palisade wall ringed the island, and men and women jumped up and down on its heights yelling at them, the horn sounding over and over. Every man aboard the *Singing Dolphin* stood to stare, and Pikarn guessed every one felt a shift in the beat of their hearts akin to his own; his blood raced but his muscles relaxed, loosening a tension he'd come to accept as normal with a single breath; he didn't smile, he couldn't with his jaw drooped.

Then his feet left the ground in Rikis' bearhug. "Son of a bitch! People."

Pikarn puffed his chest to keep from being crushed then squirmed from the exuberant grip. "People, aye." For some reason, he'd never entertained the thought of survivors outside of wishful thoughts. He turned to the captain with a grin. "Probably godsdamned Broldun, but I guess I'm happy enough to see 'em."

Terunt Gijiv poked at the fire with a steel rod after supping on smoked fish. "Them cursed don't bother with us in the spring and summer, but soon as winter comes and ice flows, the Taken will do their damnedest to reach us. After that first season, we got the wall up, bringing in wood every rainy day we could. Hasn't been much trouble since. We travel to shore for supplies when it rains, but mostly we live on fish, we got plenty of them. We grow a couple tubers, and blister-berries grew wild when we got here. Boiled into a sauce, they taste right fine."

Pikarn sucked the remnants of meat off a catfish rib. "How the hells did you end up here?"

"We first fled to islands farther upstream and figured to float on down to Broldun Fost before... Dunno, we didn't have much've a plan except stayin' alive, you know? Others were here when me and my family arrived. We'd see Shadows on the banks... hells, far as we knew everyone else was dead or Taken. Some of us headed for the Fost or the Abbey, but for us, the choice to stay put was easy."

Ships might've found them floating in their tiny boats outside the Fost or carried them farther into Purdonis Bay, but Pikarn wasn't about to haunt them with that chance. "Aye, you chose right, I'd wager. You missed death and war and disease... You chose right."

Forty men, women, and children nodded at his words and murmured their agreement: forty more souls than Pikarn had hoped to find.

Oleana, Terunt's wife, was the next to speak. "What brings you back? What hope is there against this enemy?"

Pikarn squirmed. "Hope lingers, but aye, its no more'n a spark in wet kindling. We plan on moving up yonder to Berul Island and make a home of it."

"A home? For what?"

"To take Istinjoln Monastery."

Terunt said, "Istinjôln. How? Why?"

"The why is easier than the how."

Rikis laughed, then sighed. "The Shadows of Man, these demons, they enter our world through Istinjoln. Through a Celestial Gate."

A scatter of murmurs erupted around them, but Terunt kept his calm. "You speak to us of legends and children's stories, but... You've a way to close this gate?"

Pikarn said, "No! Not yet. But we spoke with the Edan, and they look for answers. Meantime, we needs to chat with the Colok and see if they're willing to aid us."

Oleana stared at them as if their wits were draining out their eyes. "Colok?"

"Long story, but yes, Colok." Back at New Fost, the tale of Ivin and the Colok was folklore heading for legend; he needed to remember how isolated these folks had been. "An unlikely ally, aye, but some can speak Silone."

This drew mystified stares from all gathered, but a young girl squirmed her way through folks to peer at him. "Are you taking us from here? To a better home?"

Mumbles and grumbles ensued; leave it to a child to speak everyone's mind. Pikarn smiled, but it must not've been as kind as he intended, as the girl hid behind a woman's leg. "Aye, little miss, we will. But only on our way back downriver. That is if folks want to leave. Sailing to New Fost ain't without risks, with bergs and Tek warships."

Terunt huffed. "I'd just as soon stay put, so long as there's hope. I never was one for open water."

But his wife, Oleana, pursed her lips, and Pikarn could feel a family squabble coming on. "No need to hurry or worry on it, folks. Now, has anyone heard word of Berul Island? If there are people there?"

Oleana nodded to three women hanging to the side with a dozen children clustered around them like a clutch of chicks. "Keemu and them sailed down from up that way."

A thin woman, who showed the sag of a person who'd once been plump, nodded. "Mmm, we left Berul and them islands over a year ago. Last we seen there were maybe two hundred people there and not enough boats to carry 'em all."

"Two hundred?" Pikarn tugged his beard. "But you left?"

"When the freeze came... The river there is shallow and not so wide as you'd like, mmm. When it iced, Taken sometimes made the jump. We loaded the women and children onto what boats we had, and men drew straws. Most of us done died makin' it this far."

Rikis said, "So maybe we got more survivors, some help when we get there."

"The north was worse than here down south. But, could be."

Pikarn said, "We can all do with some more hopeful thinkin'. Who commanded the island?"

"Oldenu Broldun."

Rikis said, "Never heard of the man."

Pikarn laughed and slapped a knee. "That's damned obvious, Oldenu is one of the meanest women you'll ever be sorry to meet. She could cook a goat with her hard stare, and she's put the eyes out of more'n a few men who told her so."

Keemu said, "Mmm, sounds like the same woman."

Rikis shot him a grin. "You aren't blind."

"'Cause I've the wits not to say stupid things to her face, even when I was young and foolhardy. If anybody's still alive and fightin' on Berul, she'd be the one." The last time he'd seen Oldenu, she stood in an inn's window holding a sheepskin over her naked breasts, and she blew him a kiss as Huverd Broldun chased him down a muddy street with a mace swinging for Pikarn's head. Pikarn stripped a piece of jerky with his teeth and smirked. "Our journey just got a li'l more interesting."

FOURTEEN

Slaver's Pit

Step to stop and stop to step,
every finger creeped and crawled chancing to live,
Chancing to die, dancing the fib and fancying the lie.
A flicker to breathe, a flicker to leave,
A flicker to play, a flicker to pray.
Every chancing step in a flicker may cross
the fine line between vinegar and wine.

—*Tomes of the Touched*

Bossman's barge floated at an unhurried pace; instead of men manning oars, they used poles to guide them downstream with no concern for time. They stopped days at a time to bicker and haggle with small villages, or for traders to leave them as they traveled into the woods, but the yellow-eyes never allowed the Silone off the barge. The only worry was when some critter in the deep took hold of the pole and tried to use it as a fishing rod in reverse. Rinold had seen six poles disappear into the water, but so far, no steersmen. The yellow-eyes foraged the forest every morning and evening and fished for hours at a time while half asleep, but lounging seemed their natural state.

Fish, raw roots from a flower that grew in mucky-green eddies, and a cup of murky water were the staples Rinold and the Silone survived on, bland, but it managed to fill their guts and keep them alive. The yellow-eyes covered everything they ate with a yellow powder that didn't look so different than salt that'd spent a candle between mortar and pestle, and no doubt they enjoyed their meals more than Rinold did. Most days, the water had more flavor than the food, and after twenty-seven days of scraping muck from his teeth, he was ready to try the amber powder without a clue of its taste.

The only good thing, outside of being alive, was that Bossman was teaching him bits and pieces of their foul language. Today marked his twenty-fourth lesson, and by the time his guard escorted him to the front of the boat where the cages stood, he was frustrated as the Twelve Hells. The yellow-eye shackled his wrist to a post and poked him in the forehead with a finger as he laughed with a prattle of words.

Edlmir leaned on the bars of his cage. "I might be wrong an' all, but I think that there bastard was calling you a genius."

"Close as I can figure, he said I'd be smarter if he put on arrow through my head." Rinold laughed as he shook his head. "I'm piss-sucking poor at their words, but if the bastards order me killed, at least I'll have the gist."

"That there's worth a song or two."

"Worst thing is, even if I survive this, Puxele is gonna gut me fer sure."

"You might consider settlin' down with a yellow-eye bride; you might be livin' longer."

Rinold was a flicker from agreeing when he spotted smoke on the horizon. He stood for a better view, but his chains clanked and held him down. "Might be we're comin' up on some camp."

"Some thick smoke for sure."

Edlmir was right and wrong. As the boat followed a twist in the river, the smoke split into two pillars, then a third and fourth rose above the trees. "A godsdamned village."

A guard prodded him in the ribs with the butt of a spear and spoke slow enough he understood. "Foreigners shut mouths."

Rinold cocked his head with a smile, batted his eyes at the man, and the guard huffed and strode away.

Edlmir whispered, "You did that shit to me. I'd knock you into the river."

"Have ta get out of yer pen first, cage-dweller."

They shared a quiet chuckle and sat back to see where the current took them. The river here was broad and slow, carrying them nowhere fast, so it was at least half a candle of watching smoke before they caught a brand-new sight: children.

A half-dozen youngsters splashed in a pool of mud beside the river, with spear-bearing women watching over them. Like all these people, they ran around damned-near naked, with wooden and metal jewelry covering almost as much skin as their clothes spun from tree fiber, but what kept his attention were the youthful eyes. They weren't yellow. They looked as ordinary as any child on Kaludor.

The river eased them past the outskirts of the village, and a clearing with a dozen huts came into view, plank walls with bark roofs, and every one stood on stilts ten feet off the ground. Men, women, and children ignored them, never making eye contact, and soon they passed back into the forest.

Edlmir said, "I guess that's it then, our first village."

But when their boat rounded the next bend, Rinold got to rub the man's nose in his error. "That were just the poor folks' homes."

A stone wall lined both sides of the river, a flood barrier of some sort he figured—until he remembered the lizards swimming in these waters—and behind it stood a thousand strides of cleared forest with dark brown buildings rising as high as three stories. These were sturdier than anything he'd seen thus far, built from fire-baked clay with a cream-white mortar that stood out against the mud-brown bricks.

It wasn't long before men snatched up poles and started shoving them toward shore, and within wicks, Bossman stood onshore bickering with a woman whose gut would give his a challenge if they started shoving.

The cages were unlocked, and the Silone bound in heavy shackles hammered from bronze that carried a green patina before they shoved to shore. Rinold figured if given a good rock, he might be able to bust his way free, but against his flesh and bones, they might as well've been the finest steel. Yellow-eyes threatened them into silence and prodded them with spear butts until they formed a neat line of properly humble foreign *chiûku,* their word for maggots, if Rinold had learned his lesson right.

Bossman strode in front of them with a strut that would've made a bantam rooster proud, and people stopped what they were doing to stare. Foreigners with skin pale as a maggot's and children's eyes, it was about time the common folk got an eyeful instead of hiding their faces.

Rinold stared into the eyes of a child as he passed, and a strange pang struck his gut. *I might orphan this child one day, and if I don't, the clans will to free me.* It felt wrong and necessary at once. Bossman had ignored his threats of thousands marching from the north in steel armor, or he didn't understand Rinold's babbling.

They passed through the riverside clearing and entered forest, but after a hundred strides, he realized they walked on a paved road covered in leaves and moss. A hundred strides more and they arrived at stone ruins in the process of being reclaimed from the forest, with folks stripping vines and chopping trees. No more wood, no more mud bricks, these buildings and walls were heavy stones worthy of castle walls.

Bossman turned onto a wide road that ran straight west, a bustling street filled with merchants in stalls selling animals alive and dead, furs, fruits, nuts, stones uncut or polished, copper trinkets, and gold jewelry to a crowd of shoppers. The din of barkers and haggling brought a pound and rattle to his skull.

Then he locked eyes with a man. Brown eyes, not yellow. He stood taller than the Yellow-Eyes and carried himself with airs. A tattoo of diamonds and circles ringed his neck, and heavy gold rings pulled his earlobes, damned near stretching them to his shoulders.

Histê. He couldn't know for certain, but they'd already been captured by the Yellow-Eyes, a people no one had heard of, it seemed logical that a new people would be one they *had* heard of. And if he was right, it meant one thing: Slavers.

It was their third day in the hole with four bars of light shining on the floor during the day to prove the world above hadn't gone dark. They ate meat for their meals now, well done and still on the bones—one deer-like critter still had a face, but the yellow-eyes had taken the horns to not give the Silone a weapon—but it was still bland. Edlmir figured he could bash a head with the critter's femur, but in the end, they cast it to the side and hoped their escape didn't come down to such desperation. Rinold wanted to believe it was general kindness that brought them better food, but the men shared more than a few laughs over being fattened for the auction. Rinold figured the latter funnier because it was more apt to be true than not. A strong warrior would always fetch more than a starving scrub.

A vine-covered door creaked open where they hadn't even know there was a door, and torchlight lit an alcove where several men spent their nights sleeping. Spears were the first things Rinold saw in the light and yellow-eyes with shackles and chains for their wrists followed close behind. A few brave words passed Silone lips, but the shackles went on, and they were thirty strides down a hall before turning left. The ground vibrated with a noise that grew louder the farther they traveled, and when they veered right, bright sunlight lit an exit and the sound turned to a dull roar, the source for which he feared he knew.

When they stepped into the light of day, covering their eyes and cursing the sun, the noise turned to the bellow of a thousand voices, and from the looks of it, every one of them jumped up and down to shake the soil. Once his eyes adjusted, there was no doubt where they stood.

Rumors of fighting pits in the south had made it to Kaludor decades before, but Rinold never expected to see one, let alone to stand on its blood-stained turf as an offering. In Thon, warriors would fight in the pits for treasure or the honor of feeding a virgin's heart to Fîkêzê; in the Gorotan, it was criminals who fought for the pleasure of the crowd and their freedom; and in the Free Cities those who fought were slaves—a peculiar irony considering the region's name—or fame seekers. Rinold had no idea what he was about to fight and perhaps die for.

He scanned the crowd as spears pointed at his chest, and a skinny old man unlocked his shackles. As hard metal fell away and he rubbed his wrists, he turned. Yellow-eyes hooted and hollered, leaping up and down in unison, but one section of the crowd sat quiet, aloof, and leaning to speak to each other rather than paying attention to the Silone. These were the bastards they'd be performing for.

A gate opened at the end of the pit, and a yellow-eye led a long-necked, big-eared critter with a hump in its back, pulling a cart into the arena, and behind it walked Bossman, waving to the crowd with a golden scepter in his hand. Next came a man wearing the wooden lamellar armor so many of these people wore.

There wasn't no way he'd be lucky enough to fight Bossman.

Edlmir stepped to Rinold's side. "What the Forges you think is happnin' here?"

Rinold's eye twitched. "I don't suspect we're gonna fight a pack animal, so I'm confused as the hells, but we'll know soon nuf."

Bossman ordered the cart stopped within several strides of Rinold, and he could see their arms and armor inside. "Fluff-Tail, come."

Rinold grunted, regretting trying to explain to the bastard what a squirrel was in Silone. "Three godsdamned words he remembers."

Bossman gestured and spoke in the yellow-eye tongue, but Rinold only understood fragments. "Bow, arrow that man." And he pointed at the armored yellow-eye.

"The hells, you say?" But Bossman understood not a word. "Bow? Kill him? His armor won't stop this arrow."

"In his heart, reward clean kill. Yes?"

The man's jovial smile brought a twist to his gut as he grabbed his bow from the cart and knocked an arrow. He glanced at Edlmir, and the warrior just shrugged, then he gazed at his intended target. The man stood bold with his chest puffed and a defiant stare. "This poor son of a bitch don't know what steel is." Then in the tongue of the yellow-eye, "Sure of this?"

The scepter tapped Rinold's shoulder. "Knock your head."

The arrow he grabbed bore a long, thin head meant to penetrate armor, not a broad-head, and when he loosed the arrow, it was only a flicker before its tip threw dust in the air as it struck the arena floor behind the man. The crowd was silent, and Rinold imagined they believed he'd missed, but he knew better. The warrior's proud stare went blank, and he crumpled to his knees before collapsing to bleed out. Taking a deer with such precision would've been a moment of pride, but he ducked his chin to his chest as the crowd roared in a frenzy that coalesced into a chant.

Bossman took the bow and raised it above his head. "Breaker of armor!"

"It's the arrow, you idiot." Rinold smiled, knowing the man didn't understand a word, but as his eyes wandered to the section of stadium where the Histê sat, he noticed a yellow-eye with a silver collar around his neck sitting on the ground beside a wealthy woman covered in gold and jewels. His face and body bore white scars, and he squinted at Rinold as a man accustomed to killing. Here was a warrior, not a plump man used to soft chairs and full plates. Here was a man who understood what he'd witnessed, even if Bossman hadn't a clue.

Sokûtu tapped his shoulder with the scepter and pointed to the crate. "Men. Dress, swords and axes."

He didn't like the turn in direction, but he figured they'd be dead fools if they didn't do as commanded. Rinold turned to the men. "Armor on, men. I think he wants us with hand weapons."

Rinold let other men pick through the armor and weapons first, but Edlmir held up a mail cuirass. "This'n looks wee enough to fit a squirrel."

"You're a funny lug, ain't ya?" But he took the armor without an argument, and within a few wicks, the Silone stood ready for a fight. Rinold adjusted the helm on his head and shrugged several times to settle the mail's links on his shoulders. It wasn't a perfect fit, and it was heavier than he was used to, but it was better than a shirt and trousers. Then it clicked in his head; Bossman had more Silone armor than he had Silone, meaning it came from other men captured or dead. But he didn't have time to think.

Four men labored to open a rusty iron gate at the eastern end of the arena; it ground open, its lengthy bulk carried by squealing wheels in desperate need of oil. Eighteen men in wooden armor strutted through the opening with blue and black plumes rising from bronze helms. They carried spears, and at their waists, rode either a broad-bladed gladius or ax.

"Two to our one. Bossman is a confident bastard."

Edlmir snorted. "He underestimates us."

Rinold couched his shield, limbered his fingers with a twirl of his sword's hilt, and hopped twice before puffing a nervous breath. "Let's hope you're right."

Sokûtu prodded him in the back with his scepter, and he stepped forward with his men in a line, their shields side by side and swords ready to strike over their tops. The yellow eyes chanted and howled at the sky, and then they rushed in a chaotic fury of hoots and shrieks. In a flicker, Rinold knew it would be a slaughter.

The dumb bastard sprinting straight at him leaped in the air with a trilling scream, and his spear struck Rinold's shield with impressive power on his descent, but with a nudge, Rinold redirected its tip. The Wolverine hadn't given him too many formal lessons in the ways of war, but one lesson he remembered well was "only a fool leaves his feet". Rinold's sword split armor and sternum with the momentum of the man alone, and he spun, directing the man into the dirt before he brought his sword up in a backhand swing as he ducked under a second spear.

His sword caught the man in the armpit just as his wooden shield hammered Rinold in the shoulder. He took a knee in the spray of blood. The yellow-eye surged past, and Rinold spun to stand, bringing his sword down on the shoulder to remove his arm clean with the second strike.

His heart pounded, and the combat around him was a blur, but the third yellow-eye's face was fine in its detail—the carved teeth, the pitch pupils in sun-like eyes, the scar across his nose and eye. Rinold screamed and charged straight into him, smashing his enemy's spear high with his shield, his sword splitting the other's shield. They rushed past one another; he turned as the spear soared past his head, and the Wiirê pulled his ax. Rinold led with his shield straight into the other's shield, and as the Wiirê leaped high to bring his ax down, Rinold ducked to his knee and brought his sword straight up into the man's groin and gut.

The man split open with a stench as he fell, and Rinold wrenched his sword free as he stood, eyes wide and expecting another attack. He stood panting, his hands quivering with the urge to fight.

Dead yellow-eyes lay scattered around them, many dead, others moaning and rolling in bloody mud. But far as Rinold could tell, not one of his men rested in the dirt. In fact, it'd be hard to tell they were in a fight if not for the enemy blood spattering their armor and faces.

Edlmir stood nearby, and Rinold hollered, "See that? I killed three of the bastards!" He'd been in many fights in his day, but most were nothing like this.

Edlmir glanced at a one-armed man rolling in the dirt and stuck his sword through his throat. "Technically, you only killed two right like."

"I'm claiming that one."

A shout came from behind them, "Slow down and die, you bastard!"

Silone laughed, the crowd cheered, and when Rinold turned, he saw Rûflun and two other men chasing the only surviving Wiirê. Rinold dropped his sword and shield as he walked to the wagon. He grabbed a bow, nocked an arrow, and waited for the sprinter to reach a straightaway. The bow sang, and in a flicker, the runner dropped in a tumble of dust; Rûflun swept the wounded's head from his shoulders.

Rinold turned to Edlmir with a scowl. "I'm a countin' that one too."

"I'll give ya three total."

"Fair enough." He turned to Bossman and dropped his bow to the ground.

The crowd roared, and even a handful of Histê stood and whistled as Bossman strutted an arc back and forth with his scepter waving high and low. When the crowd quieted, Bossman's voice boomed out a string of words that came so fast Rinold could only catch the meaning of a few. "Warriors—Armor—Unbeatable—"and for a flicker, he held hope that maybe the man was smarter than Rinold had given him credit, that he was warning these people of a powerful enemy from the north, but hope died"—Men—Armor—One price!"

Edlmir wandered to his side and spat on a yellow-eye bleeding and moaning at their feet. "We're being sold is what I'm thinkin'."

"Question is for what? We're a godsdamned small army."

"Fighting pits, I'd wager."

"Or somebody might want us for our steel. Hard as hells to say."

Bossman yelled, "*Guber!*"

A cacophony of shouts erupted amid waving arms, but only in the Histê section of the theater. The Histê noblewoman and her yellow-eye slave conversed but sat calm, as did several of the other wealthier looking men. One, in particular, caught his eye, a muscular man amid the soft and bulging who strode down the steps to stand at the arena's rail. Intense eyes and three javelin points protruding from above his right shoulder set him apart from every other.

The noise and gyrations of the crowd slowed until only a couple of men raised their hands, and in a moment of contemplative silence, the woman raised her hand and spoke with dignified airs, even if Rinold hadn't a clue what she said.

Dead silence followed until the muscled man stood straight and raised his hand.

The two chirped back and forth like two strutting cardinals arguing over territory, but Rinold's eyes wandered to the slave chained to the woman. Rinold locked the slave's eyes with his own, and when the bidding stopped with the man making the last bid, Rinold mouthed two Wiirê words he'd learned so well, "You understand."

The slave's brow crinkled, he whispered something to his mistress, and after a flicker of thought, the woman raised her arm, and the chirping surged into a new frenzy. All the while, Rinold and the slave stared at each other. The shared gaze grew uncomfortable, but instead of shifting his eyes, Rinold grinned. The slave smirked.

But when the woman won the bidding, the slave didn't break their stare until giving a single nod with his toothy smile.

Rinold sighed and smiled back, but his mail rattled when Edlmir cuffed his shoulder. "What hells was that, Squirrel? You leavin' Puxele for that there yellow-eye boy?"

Rinold snorted. In truth, he didn't know what the slave understood; it might be nothing. "I don't know, but we might've just made our first friend... or, he'll get us all killed."

Fifteen

Out of the Valley

And Senderêun slithered to his master's table, rising without arms to sit without legs. His jaws opened wide to feed, but when he swallowed, he found his gut gone. He dreamed this dream a hundred times and feared it a prophetic riddle. He poisoned his master and assumed his crown, all to make sure a dream would never come true.

—*Ôxêum Codex*

A pigeon's flight from Castle Choerkin to Molikîn was shorter than the flight to Shuntiskâ, by half a day depending on the bird's mood, but by horseback, it required a four-day ride no matter the destination, with the road winding north before wheeling around mountains for a safer journey. Maro rode as Kinesee's constant shadow along with a dozen Ravinrin and a dozen Choerkin warriors, and while Morik's contingent had tripled this number when they set out, only half a dozen Helmveliners remained with them after most forked toward Shuntiskâ on the second day out.

They were three days on the winding road to Molikîn, on a section Morik named the Nînik Pass, a broad, U-sloped valley whose walls turned to bare stone after turning steep. A cool midmorning breeze puffed Kinesee's hair, and polite conversation droned all around, horses beating the base rhythm; for her part, Kinesee avoided the chatter while keeping Meliu to her backside. The high priestess' mouth had stayed blissfully shut, but still, the silence between them was a rock in Kinesee's gut. *This is silly.* Silly, yes, and sillier that she thought the same thing at least twenty times a day. She sighed and tugged her reins to slow the horse's walk until she fell in beside Meliu's roan gelding.

"I still wear the trinket you gave me."

"Alongside the pearl, I am honored."

The silence returned with a vengeful pinch to her gut, stealing any words she might otherwise have managed. She stared at billowing clouds rushing over mountain peaks.

Meliu cleared her throat. "The thing between Ivin and I, it *is* over. I want you to know that."

"You love him, don't you?" The words blurted out, and Kinesee regretted them, but the priestess took them in stride.

"I did. I do, I suppose. But love between a man and woman never need find its way to a bed."

"It already has." She regretted her words again. "But I appreciate the sentiment."

Meliu sighed. "I understand we may not be friends like once we were, but know that I bear you no ill wishes. You married a fine man, and he married a fine lady. Happiness should be yours."

"It should be. But I don't know if it ever can be."

"Time changes most things. Not so long ago, our people were harried by Shadows of Man and Taken, then by Tek nations able to snuff us into history; disease, starvation, and determination brought us to a new place. People feast and wed and bear children. There is hope where there was none. If the Silone are capable of such feats, you and Ivin are more than able to forget little old me."

"Fine words, but there is war coming from the north, and gods know what to our south."

"We handle what we can as it comes."

A Kingdomer shout echoed. "Lôkêtu!"

Kinesee's grasp of the Kingdomer tongue was better than her Edan, but it still wasn't perfect. *Rider? Riders. Enemy riders?*

She glanced up to see dust in the distance, and Meliu stood in her saddle, muttering. “Dancing Bastards, what the hells now?” The priestess’ eyes pinned wide. “Tek!”

“They repaired the bridge?”

“No godsdamned idea.”

Maro reined in by Kinesee’s side as warriors couched their shields and drew weapons. “Protect the Lady Choerkin!”

Morik’s voice pierced the din. “You’re certain it’s Tek? Shouldn’t be any in these mountains.”

“Sure the hells look like Tek.”

“I should’ve kept my men with us. Got a count?”

“No. More than we want to fight.”

Kinesee’s breaths tightened in her chest. With no armor and nothing but a petite dagger between her breasts, the notion this might be the day she died spiked every lick of wits she possessed. Her skin chilled. “We need to get out of here.”

Meliu said, “Won’t a single Tek make it to us on horseback.”

Maro’s hand took Kinesee’s shoulder, his voice soft and soothing. “Breathe, m’lady.”

Kinesee tried, but the next shout sent her head into a spin.

“Riders rearward!”

Meliu’s head spun east, and she jerked her reins harder than she intended; her horse pulled back and nickered, and she patted his neck. Her prayer for vision remained strong. A line of riders five wide with sabers and shields rounded a corner. Behind them in a trail of dust, she wagered there were twenty more. This was no coincidence.

“Dancing shits.” Her heart fluttered, and she grabbed Kinesee’s arm. The girl was the white of the purest tin-glazed ceramic, her hand clutching her pearl beneath her blouse, and she knew the girls’ thoughts, Meliu’d had them before. “This isn’t the day you die.”

The girl managed a nod, the bride of a warlord but still a child.

Maro shouted, “Ravinrin to the fore! Choerkin the rear!”

Meliu blurted, “No. Everyone to the fore.”

Maro eyeballed her over his nose. “We don’t have time to bicker—”

He was right. "Everyone to the fore, godsdamn it! I've got the rear." And she winked, hoping to pass on confidence she didn't have herself.

"You heard the high priestess! Every man to the fore!"

Meliu wheeled her horse and put spurs to the gelding's ribs, and the animal skip-bucked a half-dozen strides before settling. She prayed for Light, absorbing the prayer's tranquil warmth; the knot in her gut unwound, her heart slowed, and when she leaned, putting her hand to her horse's neck, the animal too calmed under Erginle's grace. *Kibole, feed me your will straight from the Forges, hammer my senses into steel and melt the will of my enemies.*

Her horse pranced from the group of Silone, Dark straightening her spine even as she no longer felt she sat in her saddle; she was risen above, gliding on the favors of the Seven Heavens. *Dark... no, Light.* The world distorted in front of her, a window of wavering mirage as she willed Light to mirror nothingness in her path. She heeled her horse, and he moved into a full run. The Light's effect wouldn't be perfect, it couldn't be at this speed, but she wagered her life on the enemy not looking for her.

Light was the bellow pumping the fire of her confidence, but the ferocity of the Dark boiling in the aura of her soul held the promise of hardened steel in hand. The gelding's breaths pumped in rhythm with his hooves, and the distance between charging enemies closed.

There are two ways to blind a man with Light, she recalled her master telling her: *to bend or reflect Light so you aren't seen, or to direct the force of prayer into their eyes,* but Dark gave Meliu two more options, impenetrable shadow and fear. Fear was perhaps the greatest blinder of them all, capable of not only keeping a man from seeing what was in front of him but making him see things that weren't even there. Today, she would use all four.

She pressed her cheek into the coarse hairs of the mane, balanced and one with the horse, Light giving courage to the both of them. She squinted and stared hard at the lead riders, their faces calm even as they thundered her way. Two hundred strides from colliding straight into him, one man's mustached face cocked to the side; he was seeing something that confounded his eyes, a wavering blur coming fast, she imagined, but even if he saw straight through her mirror it was too late.

A hundred strides, fifty, twenty... *Erginle, blaze my way.*

Light erupted with a force she'd never imagined, so bright she turned her head and her gelding thrashed until she reined hard and held him straight.

Tek horses neighed, riders lost control. Two horses crumpled to their knees, three hundred bricks of muscle flailing with steel-shod hooves, one rider thrown, another crushed. Others careened, running into each other, shoving and tumbling, opening her way straight into the heart of their charge. Her horse leaped a man dragging his broken legs, a hoof splitting his head; he might be the lucky one. She reined hard, and her horse's rear slouched into a sliding stop, and when he stood straight again, she unleashed Dark in a wheel with her as its hub, the only place the sun shone in her little world.

The terror around was shrill in her ears, but it was the deep sense of *knowing* their horror that brought a smug grin to her face.

A biting, kicking, bucking horse burst from the oblivion of Dark and careened into her horse's flank; riderless it spun, reared, and a hoof clipped fingers above her ear. Screams turned to a deafening ring in her skull, and she felt the world rising to meet her fall. Her horse spun from beneath her, kicking the other animal. She landed shoulder first and her body buckled as it struck the turf, pain lancing through her side. The sun ignited her world as Dark disappeared from her grasp. Horses and men scrambled, some still attacking their demons. Not a warrior sat their seat, and most of the animals were scattered and nowhere in reach of their rider, except for one who bounced beneath his bucking mount with a foot stuck in the stirrup.

She reached for her horse's reins and missed, stumbling to a knee. The gelding puffed and reared, and she saw the Tek coming for her. *Kibole.* A whip of Dark ensnared the man's face and neck, so much less than she'd hoped, but enough to force a scream and stop him in stride.

She glanced to the ground; an ax lay stuck in the dirt, its spiked end bloody and sticking up. She grabbed the haft and charged; the curved edge struck his face as Dark faded. Blood erupted from between the cheek plates of his helm, and he collapsed. She wobbled as she turned a circle. No Tek came for her, but a dozen men appeared healthier than she'd like. Her legs straightened to stand tall, and she puffed her chest with several breaths.

"Kibole, save me." She focused her will, and Light and Dark came, but she struggled to find a sense of cohesion within the energy as it fluttered her soul in wisps rather than a flood. She stumbled and strode, raising the ax and dropping its spike through the helm of a man writhing on the ground. The weapon penetrated with unnerving ease, but she yanked three times to get it free of the helmet's steel.

A man screamed, and she turned to face him; his arms flailed with a saber and shield in either hand, his eyes wide and looking at nothing. She couldn't tell if he was trying to kill her or a figment of his fears, or perhaps he saw her *as* his demon. Maybe she was.

She raised a hand, and Dark swallowed the man's face. Anticipated screams never came as he collapsed in a twitching heap. But there wasn't a joy in the power over life and death this time, just a need to blacken her enemy's thoughts, saving herself and her people. She approached another man, and Dark dropped him wailing to his knees. The ax's spike popped his throat. A second fell on his sword to escape her as she drew close, the third dropped to his belly and covered his head, blubbering before she severed his spine at the base of his neck, and the next charged four strides before Dark sent him careening into the dirt to flail and die like a sick bug. Weak and powerful at the same time, she killed the lot of them, and each reached their destination on a unique path, until the last man.

She saw him as he stumbled over a dead man's foot, his arms outstretched, waving at the air. "Rôt! Kîg!" He rattled off names with every ginger step, and Meliu sighed as she drew near him. She stepped in his path, and he came forward, clueless she was there.

Light had blinded him.

"I am here," she said in Tek.

He stopped in his tracks, face twisted. "A woman?"

"Your doom." She raised the ax as the man stood with a blank stare, unaware of the steel a flicker's fall from his face. But her side ached, and her arm froze. Not for the first time, she was frightened of what she'd become, and she lowered the weapon. "Your eyesight may return, it may not. But there will be a thousand sunny days ahead, whether you see them or not."

She strode several strides searching for her horse but wasn't sure what trail of dust might be his.

To the southwest, fighting raged, but it'd be over by the time she walked there. She released her prayers, and the ax fell from numbed fingers. Her hands went to her knees to stay upright, head spinning. She breathed deep, and her left hand reached for a pain in her side. Her finger slipped into a deep wound, and she felt the chill wash of her face turning pasty white. A whispered prayer for Life kept her conscious, but the energy was too weak to heal. She glanced to the ax on the ground, wondering if the first blood it spilled had been her own.

She rubbed her cheeks and grimaced as blood smeared from eye to chin, but when she looked up, all thoughts for herself faded. A horse with a blonde and begowned rider bolted from the battle, making straight for the valley's northern rise. Alone. *Where the hells is Maro?*

Meliu's feet broke into a limping, stumbling trot before she questioned whether she had the strength to make the run. *Erginle, give me strength, strength to save Ivin's bride.* A wisp of energy and the wound in her side tickle-tingled, a sign of meager healing, but more than she'd expected.

Then came the rush.

A flood of energy drove her into a sprint, spirit guided and unquenchable. Neither muscles nor lungs burned, and her eyes were keen, unclouded by exhaustion and pain and Dark. *I'll kill every damned one and die myself to save you.* The thought was hers, but the sentiment triggered a vision of a woman defending her child from wolves, a bedside tale her mother had told her on sober nights. The energy in her bones was the urgency of a mother protecting her child.

She had prayed to Erginle, but the Goddess of Love and War had answered: *Januel.*

The collision of armored horses and men was thunder, fleshy drums, and cymbals punctuated by hollers and screams. Kinesee was more familiar with battle than she'd ever imagined as a child building castles, but sitting horseback on the receiving end of such a charge terrified her more than anything since the attack on the beach when she was the assassins' target.

Shouts and ringing steel. Blurred vision as her horse spun in circle after circle with her clutching at the reins. Her heart thudded in her chest, and she forced herself to remember to breathe before turning blue. Then the horse reared, and she clung to her neck and mane, slipping in the saddle until Morik grabbed the animal's bridle. Frazzled, she didn't bother to wonder why the man was afoot.

"Ride up that hill, child! Ride hard! Half a candle from an outpost! Ride!"

Kinesee's eyes searched for Maro, but in the press of battle, she didn't find him.

Morik turned her horse and let go of the bridle, slapping the mare in the flank. Kinesee's training returned in an instant as the powerful animal thundered and puffed beneath her. She raised her seat a finger above the saddle, settled her feet in the stirrups, relaxed her knees, and leaned low, clutching rein and mane. *North.*

The slope rose in a gradual climb at first, but danger loomed as grass gave way to rocks on a steep ascent. She tugged the reins left then shifted back right to gain a better angle. From the corner of her eye, she caught sight of riders, and a glance brought fear. Three Tek had broken free to chase her.

Me? Why me?

No time to think nor worry as the horse scrambled up the sidehill, surging and lunging up the steep slope, slipping on rocks with a snort and whinny before charging on. The climb eased into a natural trail, and her mount bolted even as foreign shouts and screams came from behind. She didn't dare glance, but she did. A horse tumbled and rolled with its rider, but the other two still pushed hard. But for the moment, she gained ground.

Treacherous footing slipped beneath her horse's hooves, and looking ahead, something was wrong, but her mind wasn't piecing the puzzle. Kinesee reined hard to a stop, spotting the drop-off at the last flicker. The trail washed out in front of her, a gulley dropping sheer to a hidden end. No way in all the heavens would she risk her horse making the jump. She pulled the mare's neck to zig up the slope in the other direction, but in flickers, the animal's hooves slid downhill, and like a fool, she yanked the reins. The horse bellowed and rose, threatening to flip.

She slipped her feet from the stirrups and let go of the reins, sliding from the saddle to the ground. *Nothing to do but climb.* She still had a lead as she scrambled up the scree-covered slope but glances back showed the Tek gaining fast.

Her boots were fashioned for comfort and riding, not climbing, and at every tiny cliff, she scrambled on all fours, scraping hands and elbows. More horses came from below. Maro maybe? It didn't matter; they were too far behind. Her chest pumped until she felt she could climb no more, so she slowed, looking for a place to hide. Anything offering hope. She reached a stretch of flat stone, picked up a rock and heaved it at the men below, but it clattered past them. Three breaths and she ran, but she reached another washout with a cliff to her side. It was backtrack, or... across the washout stood a ledge beside a towering slab of granite. *Fifteen feet then ten down?* Even if she made the jump, it'd hurt like the Forges.

She retraced her steps and found a scree-covered trail arching higher, but she could hear the grunts of her pursuit straight below. They were close. She determined then that she would reach the ledge alive by the grace of the gods or make a quick trip down the mountainside to visit the gods. Her feet struck the ground, and she ran like the day the rapers chased her, light on her toes, and when the ledge came into view, she imagined Solineus on the other side with his arms outstretched to pull her in for a hug.

She leaped. Plummeted. Then her feet struck stone and her body crumpled, bloodying her knees on the ledge and rocking her shoulders as she broke the fall. She dove forward to clutch at the trunk of a small juniper, but she didn't need the little tree. She rolled to her back gasping for air, safe. Until she saw the Tek standing on the trail she'd jumped from. She leaped to her feet and pulled the knife from her bodice, glanced around. The only way off the ledge was down, and instead of jumping, the men slung bows from their shoulders.

"Cheaters." She squeezed tight into a crease between the slab of granite and the washout until she couldn't see her enemy. She prayed they too couldn't see here. An arrow skittered off stone and ricocheted by her knees before rattling down the washout.

The head of an arrow scratched her thigh, and she pressed tighter and tighter as arrow after arrow clattered past—silence, then the sound of swords.

She took a breath and braved to look from her hiding place. Three Tek fighting with their backs turned, and when she saw Maro's face, she smiled. Beside the Ravinrin stood Junt, and behind them at least one more man she couldn't see well enough to name. But her joy fled with a scream when the saber thrust through Maro's gut. *Your armor! Where's your armor?* The big man's eyes went wide, and he smashed his helmeted forehead into his enemy's face before kicking him backward. The Tek stumbled and fell, careening to bounce down the steep slope with a howl that ended in a yelp.

Junt reached over Maro's shoulder and forced himself between his commander and the Teks. A saber slashed Junt's mail, a blow that would've opened Maro's chest, but as Junt brought his ax to bear, the second Tek struck the side of his head with a shield. The warrior's knees buckled, and a single misstep sent him over the edge.

"No!" Kinesee stood panting, her throat in agony as she screamed to the gods. The third Ravinrin, who she recognized as Kulor, held his shield high to save his own life as Maro collapsed to his knees, blood leaking from his mouth to darken his beard. The Tek towered over him, raising his saber.

The faces of the Tek warriors disappeared in darkness, and for a flicker, her mind flashed to the Shadows of Man. The men screamed, dropping their weapons, but instead of taking their bodies, these shadows drove them mad. The Tek flailed at the air, then bolted straight into each other, clinging, scratching, clawing, punching, even as they went over the edge of the washout.

Kulor dropped to Maro's side to keep the man upright, and a flicker later Meliu skidded to a stop, eyes wide.

"Meliu! I'm here!"

The priestess smiled. "Thank the gods." But then she sat. And Kinesee noticed the blood staining her side all the way to her ankle.

"Don't you dare die!"

"I won't if you won't."

Maro said, "No more dying today, godsdamnit."

Kinesee kneeled and ducked her head, smiling, but she knew these were vows uncertain of being kept. "No more."

It was a quarter candle before Morik and more men arrived, and despite Meliu and Kulor doing their best to staunch the flow of blood, Maro grew weaker. The Kingdomers threw Kinesee a rope, and she tied it around her waist and jumped, swinging into the far wall with a bone-jarring collision as she spun out of control, but the pain mattered little. She clutched the rope as they pulled her towards the precipice, and she scrambled over the edge as soon as she could reach. On hands and knees she reached Maro, the man sitting with his back to the wall.

He smiled at her. "Why so glum?"

Kinesee laughed through sobs, and her eyes flashed to Meliu. "Save him."

Tears wetted the woman's cheeks, and her lips quivered in a prayer Kinesee couldn't understand. She shook her head. "I'm barely keeping myself alive."

Kinesee wrapped her arms around the man. "You keep strong."

Morik said, "Men are on their way with herbs. If my runner makes the outpost... If there's a healer." He bowed his head. "This is my shame; you were under my protection."

"Don't no one blame another. I shouldn't have shed my armor." Maro tried to laugh, but it turned to a grunt. He put a hand to Kinesee's shoulder. "It's fine, girl. I'll be fine."

"Liar."

Meliu crawled to his side and put a hand to his shoulder, but the warrior scoffed. "Don't you dare die trying to save me, high priestess. I've had thirty more years in this world than maybe I deserved."

"We'll wait for the herbs, then." And Meliu sat back, eyes closing, her hands clutching her side.

Kinesee ran short of tears by the time the unctuous healing pastes arrived, and the man howled as fingers pushed the concoction into the hole in his body. There was no way to know if it would save his life, but she was certain it eased his pain.

Maro passed to the Road of Living Stars with the sun high in the sky before the runner returned with a healer. Kinesee clung to the man and wept her goodbye onto his shoulder, blaming no one but herself.

Sixteen

Breaking the Old Ways

The slender sunshine of narrow days
found short between canyon walls tall,
heatless cold with clouds descending,
finding and blinding the White-Eye seekers,
the drinkers and the slaked, never thirsty,
never lost, never found,
these finders of trails before they're traveled,
these finders of trails centuries old.
You will only find the finders when they find you.

—*Tomes of the Touched*

They intended to stay on Ulmun Island for two days to rest the crew, but when a perfect wind arrived the next morning, they bustled their gear together and jumped aboard the *Singing Dolphin.* Captain Bour was giddy as a child to be back on the water with a wind to rest the oarsmen. By mid-afternoon, the wind calmed to a breeze, and come evening, they dropped anchor to keep the captain's promise to rest shoulders.

A steady, hair-tussling wind blew throughout the next day, but when they reached a bend in the river, the trees grew thick on the banks and stole much of their wind. Men took to the oars without a grumble and proceeded easterly. They passed four larger towns that Pikarn had never seen, but the Broldun in the crew named them as they passed: Kibit, Enslak, Oriko, and Mesang. The sailors held fond memories of each one, even when the recollections were bar brawls or broken hearts, but the towns were empty of people and housed all manners of critters from raccoons to deer to bear. If there was a positive when staring at nature reclaiming the buildings, it was that Shadows and Taken were scarce. A lone Shadow followed them for half a day before disappearing, and they'd seen a pack of a half dozen Taken staring at them from shore, but this was the extent of their sightings. Which wasn't to say more hadn't sighted them and remained hidden.

They made good time the next day and reached Polgin Bend late in the morning, where the waters turned north before swinging west into a stretch of river known as Fekin's Doom. It sounded ominous, but the river was broad, slow, and plenty deep. It turned out the name came from Fekin Broldun, who died when challenged to swim its length to earn the hand of a woman.

They were five days out from Ulmun when the terrain changed enough for Pikarn to know where he was. Tall trees faded into shrubs, and the dirt-covered land turned to brown rock. They were either at the entrance to Sunset Canyon or a few horizons from it, opinions varied, but it meant they were closing in on the Harumin River, and it was those waters that would carry them to Berul Island.

They were horizons up the Sobuno when they anchored for the night, and Bour had men at the oars early enough that, when Pikarn cracked his eyes, it didn't look much like morning. But in flickers, the sun rose. He languished near the prow finishing off the last of the boiled eggs they'd gotten in Ulmun when Rikis settled by his side.

"We've a good wind; if it holds Bour says we should reach Berul in a couple of candles."

Pikarn grunted and belched; the latter wasn't an intentional assessment of the situation, but it could've been. "It'll be interestin', no godsdamned doubts." Rikis squinted, and Pikarn knew the question was coming, so he headed it off. "She's a Broldun and a woman, all you needs to know. I can hardly imagine yer blessed father never told you of her."

"He kept mum. A hundred tales of the Choerkin boys and their mentor, Pikarn—"

"Mentor, the hells. They taught *me* every bad thing I know except the cussin'."

"Who the Twelve Hells is Oldenu Broldun? I've heard the name, but nothing more."

Pikarn stuck his finger within a whisker of Rikis' nose. "You go repeatin' this to anyone, and I put a crick in your nose, ya got me?"

"The story will die with me."

Pikarn didn't trust the man's smirk. "Only reason I'm gonna tell you is I know for godsdamned sure, if the woman is alive, she'll give you her version. And somehow I can't imagine that tough as a rivet Broldun dyin' without her takin' me with her. You've heard of Hervud Broldun?"

"Heard of him, they called him the Dragon's Fire."

"Aye, but in some quarters, he were known as Dog Wind 'cause of the smell of his gas. That were my name fer him anyhow, no tellin' what that man ate." Rikis was chuckling, but Pikarn didn't let it slow his tale. "Hervud could make a vulture's eyes water with a fart, but by some mysterious twist of the heavens, the youngest sister in the brood was a comely lass whose only flaw was her last name."

"Oldenu."

"None other. It were a couple years before your uncle Lovar took the lead of the clan that the Lord Choerkin sent us boys east to get Lovar's nose frosted tryin' to negotiate somethin' or another with the Broldun. We were at Broldun Fost, and all the Choerkin were sparrin' all the Broldun, braggin' on whose balls were bigger, the usual horseshit, and toward evenin' Oldenu arrived. We sparred with sword and shield near sunset, and then we sparred all night at the *Whispering Raven*—"

"Whoa, whoa, whoa... you and a *Broldun*?"

"Me and Oldenu. So come about sunrise—"

"*You* and a Broldun."

"Me and a Oldenu Broldun. We ain't slept a wink—"

"You! and a Broldun."

"Me and a Broldun, godsdamnit. We ain't slept, and there comes a pounding—"

"You recall that you hate Brolduns? Or was that a ruse all these years?"

"You wanna hear the tale or not, you little shit?" Rikis pinched his lips. "We'd just dozed off when a pounding came on the door, then the head of a mace split the timbers."

"Hervud."

"None other, and his ire were rankled like I ain't ever seen." Pikarn grinned; at least once a year, he had dreams of that night. "I bolted out the window wearing little more than my sword belt and shield, the rest of my clothes in my arms, bouncing from the eave to the street. I ran nekid all the way out of the Fost before figurin' on hiding until the Choerkin rode out."

"Not so bad a tale. You and a Broldun?"

"So hard to believe?"

"A beautiful Broldun?"

"Now that is the less likely side o' the story." He grunted. "It was what came after that painted it dark. Within the week, Hervud was telling everyone who'd listen that I'd raped his little sister. There was a blood price put on the *Wolverine's* head. For years I couldn't go near Broldun territory alone, and I cracked more'n a dozen heads of those who came to collect on the lie. Istinjoln, all the holies, they'd sneer the name Wolverine every time I came near, and it reached the point I got tired of a name I'd earned with pride."

Rikis leaned back. "Neither of the Choerkin boys would ever give up why you turned against the name. Now I know."

"Now, you know. There's always a Broldun to blame."

"In this case, two of them."

"The only thing worse than a Broldun is two Brolduns. Never been a night I regretted more." That was a lie. Whether it'd been the thrill of Oldenu, the thrill of running naked for his life, or the thrill of pissing off the entire Clan Broldun (excepting Oldenu), it was a sliver of memory he savored.

"Did you ever see her again?"

"Oh ho! Gods no. The old man Broldun didn't take no pride in his niece beddin' a man who rode under the Choerkin banner. I can't say if he ever believed I raped her, but he helped make certain folks believed it. Way I hear, she denied it, but the word was already out. No, never seen her again and better off for it."

Rikis smiled, his brow over his left eye raising. "I guess we'll see about that."

"I'd rather fight a Shadow barehanded. Almost, anyhows." It was a peculiar terror roiling his gut. He feared she was dead, he feared she was alive and hated him, he feared she might have kin on Berul still anxious to kill him, but most of all he feared that she'd forgotten that night, that it hadn't been the same thrill for her as it was for him. "If she's alive, we should at least get a good chuckle over old times."

The flicker Oldenu Broldun saw Pikarn step from the *Singing Dolphin,* she stormed to stand right in front of him and she punched him in the gut. Of course, Pikarn didn't feel a thing. He was a thinking man who'd made sure to be wearing his mail when meeting an old lover.

"The godsdamned Wolverine."

"I'm pleased as all the hells to see you again." Her arm cocked, but this time he caught her fist. "Hit m' keg of ale all you like, my nose is off-limits."

She was his height and still carried a punch judging by the rattle his mail had made. She'd also retained her figure, and though her hair showed some gray, she was still the beautiful Oldenu from his dreams.

"What brings your grizzled beard here to turn my heaven into a hell?"

Pikarn glanced at the barren, rocky island around them, its walls and sparse crops. Berul sat a few hundred strides from the western shore on a broad patch of shallow water where the Sobuno River damned near looked like a lake. Berul was the southernmost of five small islands of granite protruding from the waters. From shore, he could see a dozen buildings built of stone with thatched roofs, and he wouldn't doubt it if several more stood over the rise. Her idea of heaven wasn't much, but so long as the waters didn't freeze, it was safe.

There was one thing he knew for sure about how to answer her questions; the truth wouldn't suffice. "I came to rescue you, princess."

She cracked a grin. "I know that for a load of shit, you didn't come to rescue me back when, why start now."

"So, you do remember."

"How could I forget the night you attacked me."

Pikarn's face burned red. "Now you just—"

"I let you win in the courtyard and the bedroom."

He grunted and chuckled. "That's how you're gonna play it, eh?"

She smiled and looked past him. "By the gods, it's like Kotin Choerkin never aged."

Pikarn turned as Rikis approached. "Rikis Choerkin, I'd like you to meet Oldenu Broldun."

He bowed. "*You* and Pikarn. You're far too pretty for his likes."

She turned a glare on Pikarn, and he sported a grin. "No respect for a lady's reputation, I see."

"Hells, way I tell it, you attacked me."

She grabbed his chin hair and tugged with a wink. "Not so far from the truth. Now tell me, what are you Choerkin boys doing here on a Broldun longship?"

Rikis said, "We come to put eyes on Istinjoln."

"What the Forges for? I've seen it. It's no place for the living."

"How long since you were there? Is the Celestial Gate still there?"

Her eyes flicked between them, and Pikarn said, "A beam of light into the sky, the Shadows of Man enter our world through the gods-damned thing."

"Ah, yes, it was there two months ago."

"So you can get there safely?"

"Aye, a smart girl can. Rains swelled the creeks, and we were hunting... We didn't mean to go so near the cursed place, but once close, we took a look. Now, why the hells do you want to get there?"

Rikis said, "Pikarn has a plan, half-boiled, but it's a plan."

"I do at that."

Oldenu gave Pikarn a cockeyed stare. "A plan better'n how you escaped the *Whispering Raven?*"

"If it works out half as well, I'd count it a win. Have you spoken to any Colok?"

Her eyes widened. "You're telling me them rumors are true?"

"Oh aye, them rumors are truer than I'd believe had I not heard 'em m'self."

"What the hells good are they?"

"They're the key to locking down Istinjoln and the gate." He smiled, hoping to instill confidence.

"That's the same smile you wore when we first met. You looked stupid then; you look stupid now. Come on. I'll feed you dumb bastards."

Rikis stood beside him, and they both watched the woman stride up the rocky hill toward its crown. "Memories of you turn the woman into a weeping puddle of joy, I see."

Pikarn snorted and followed the woman's trail. "I still got all the teeth I came with. Let's see if'n she learned to cook; still got my teeth after gnawin' my way through a meal, then you should be right impressed."

Seventeen

Ironwing's Pouch

In the Kingdom of Yunkîlêô did the master bard find her harp restrung with the sinews of her mistress. She wept and strummed the strings, and the lady's ghost sang whenever the bard would play, and with every stroke of the string, the bard's murderous husband suffered.

—*Oxeum Codex, from the Compilation of Pains*

Living and dead spent the night in a small stone tower Morik named Rejenhert, and in the morning, their escort to the Ironwing's court surged to over a hundred men, but the one who mattered to the Lady Choerkin remained behind, waiting for priests to come and take him to his funeral with the Ravinrin. Meliu had prayed for the man's soul, but prayer was a tricky thing when you cursed yourself as a failure. *If I arrived half a wick quicker... If I didn't split from the group... If I'd seen that horse coming... If I'd given myself to the Stars.* These and a dozen other ifs withered her concentration.

Meliu was alive, though sore as the hells, while good men lay dead because of her failure. Erginle, Kibole, and Januel had all been with her, and still, she'd failed. Or maybe she hadn't. Kinesee still lived, even if the girl might hate her for the rest of their lives. Hate her more. Meliu couldn't bring herself the courage to say a word to the girl, and

Kinesee seemed to want words from no one, riding surrounded by the five Silone warriors who survived the attack.

They traveled now as a war party ready for battle, but there wasn't the typical frivolity of soldiers on the march; in that respect, the mood was more of a funeral procession. They rode the winding trail with Morik barking orders to scouts, and riders arriving from gods knew where in the mountains. By the time they could see the gates of Molikîn in the distance, Meliu guessed the count of Kingdomer warriors riding with them was close to five hundred. The display of horsemen and heavy armor made her wonder, and not for the first time, if maybe the Tek had done the Silone people a favor by prodding a sleeping Helmveline bear.

They passed through the massive gates of the city by midafternoon, and while most Kingdomers dispersed into the thinly populated streets, Morik called her and Kinesee together.

"The Ironwing is honoring you at the First Throne and wishes to know whether you'd prefer to meet straight away or if you'd like to refresh yourselves first."

Meliu glanced at Kinesee. "The Lady Choerkin's decision."

The girl's hand wandered to clasp the pearl around her neck, the only sign of nerves as she sat straight and dignified in her saddle. "We came here for a purpose. We should see to it."

Morik nodded to a young girl, and she took off at a run before he turned back to them. "I reckon I wasted your time the other day when I spoke to you of our customs when meeting with the Ironwing. I'd assumed our visit would be the Third or Second Throne. There is no kneeling at the First Throne, bow when greeted, and an attendant will escort you to your seat at the table. The First Throne accepts its visitors closer to equals, more akin to dinner with the king than a show of humility."

Meliu couldn't help but think of food as her stomach grumbled, but resisted the urge to ask. "Our best manners, but no scraping our noses on the floor."

"Precisely. Follow me. Today we take the short route instead of the one meant to impress visitors."

They dismounted, handed their reins to youthful stablehands, and Morik led them to a narrow path wide enough for two men with high walls on either side. Meliu's best guess was it ran southwest before arriving at a single black-iron door. A lone guard greeted them, wearing plate armor like nothing she'd ever seen before, covering the warrior from head to toe to make him look more a sculpture than a person. He bowed and opened the portal for their entry.

The room they entered was unadorned and lit like a bright summer's day by four lanterns hanging on the walls. The white of their fire reminded her of Light, but they cast shadows. A man in linen trousers and a blousy silk shirt snapped to attention. His hair was long and black like most Kingdomers she'd met, but his face was shaved clean. This and his softer step meant he wasn't a warrior.

He spoke in impeccable Silone. "Welcome. I am Medîn Morkrin, the Ironwing's official interpreter for this meeting." He stepped to Kinesee and took her hand, bowing until his forehead touched her palm. "You are Kinesee Choerkin, daughter of Solineus Mikjehemlut. It is an honor."

She withdrew her hand and placed it on his head; a gesture Morik had taught her. "I pray you serve your king well."

He smiled and rose as her hand slid away, then he turned to face Meliu. With a single crisp step he stood in front of her, but there was no bow. "High Priestess Meliu. Word of your heroics has already spread into the city."

She strained to smile, his words bringing a burn to her gut. "I did what I could, but it was not enough."

"So rare to meet the valorous with modesty." His smile felt sincere. "The king and queen await our arrival. Follow me, please." Meliu glanced but didn't see any doors until Morik kneeled and stood, lifting a trapdoor.

They descended a spiral stair crafted from iron until they were at least two poles deep in the ground, then followed a passage with an arched ceiling tall enough for a Colok to walk without fear and lit by the same bright lanterns as the room above. It led straight as an arrow past two more spiral stairs, each rising higher than the last, but other than these ascents, there wasn't a side passage to be seen.

It was a five-pole climb to the surface, and instead of a trapdoor at the top, they strode from an arched entry into a room filled by the soft light of natural fires burning in two fireplaces. A thick rug covered the central floor while polished furniture, carved with griffons, clouds, and more abstract designs, were upholstered in rich burgundy and gold. Meliu half expected to stop here, but Medîn strode straight into a connected hall. The ensuing walk reminded her of the halls of Istinjoln, cornering, rising, and falling until a blindfolded person might wonder if they'd wandered a circle, but when a turn led into a vast hall with four armored guards standing stiff beside double doors, she knew they were close.

Medîn pushed the doors open with practiced grace, revealing a room warmed by four fireplaces, additional light from golden chandeliers sporting a hundred candles each, and six candelabras sitting on a long oak table carved with griffons and mountains along its edge. Every piece of decor impressed, but once Meliu's eyes landed on the woman standing at the head of the table they didn't leave. She stood draped in a snow-white rabbit-fur cloak pinned with a golden broach, and sitting atop her ruby-red hair was a golden crown streaked with violet hues and lit by the glow of the diamonds set in the points of the crown. *A red-headed queen, I knew I liked Helmveline.*

Queen Nîsenî spread her arms wide. Medîn translated as she spoke. "Welcome to the halls of Molikîn." She strode to stand in front of Kinesee and only a few feet from Meliu's nose. The queen was a floral bouquet with hints of honey, and it made her ponder how she smelled after days on horseback. "Kinesee, bride of the Warlord Choerkin, my apologies for missing your wedding. I offer this to celebrate your eternal vows."

She raised her hand, but her palm was empty. For a flicker only. A servant darted to her side and placed a wooden case in her outstretched fingers before opening its golden hinges. Meliu had promised to keep her calm, but she gasped. A delicate gold chain held twenty-two griffon-claw settings, and each of their grips secured translucent gems the color of pinks in a sunset. Not one was the same, but the center stone was lightest, and they grew darker as they approached the clasp. Breathtaking, but more so when the queen spoke again.

"My people call the stones Sundown Latcu."

I really, really should've married Ivin. Meliu glanced at Kinesee. Kinesee sat frozen in a stare, so Meliu took it upon herself to break the silence. Besides, if she didn't speak, she'd have to slap her hand to keep from touching it. "It is the most stunning gift. I've never seen latcu jewelry. Is the color natural?" Hells, she didn't even know what Latcu was not so long ago.

The servant took the necklace from the box and draped it around Kinesee's neck, the clasp closing with a click.

"Natural and very rare. These stones were collected over three centuries for their size and color. We have a collection room if you'd care for a tour."

"Oh, I would... if the Lady Choerkin would enjoy such a thing?"

"I'd be honored." Kinesee tucked her chin, her eyes pinned to the largest gem dangling between her breasts. "I will fear to lose it."

"The clasp will never fail, and the settings are not gold, even if they look it. It would take a smith of exceeding skill to remove them. But please, come. Sit."

As Nînesî turned, a servant strode to escort them to seats at the table. A young lady took Kinesee's hand and directed her to the seat of honor at the end of the table, and a handsome Kingdomer man took Meliu's arm and led her to sit to the left of Kinesee and across from Morik. The queen strode to the head of the table, where two massive thrones sat side by side. Their color was such that from this distance, she wasn't certain if they were carved wood or polished stone with onyx tones.

The queen sat with her hands in her lap, spine stiff, and eyes cool. "I will schedule a visit to the collection for tomorrow morning." Footfalls padded from behind the thrones, and Meliu saw the glow of the crown before the man.

King Sînhôlar arrived alone and sat beside his queen at the head of the table. "Pardon my tardiness." He was broad and powerful, and his jaw chiseled as the stone of these halls.

Nîsenî raised her left hand, little more than a flinch, and servants shuffled toward the kitchen with quick but dignified strides. "It gave us ladies time for small talk."

The Ironwing adjusted the crown on his head as his eyes settled on Kinesee. "Kinesee Choerkin, daughter of the honored Solineus Mikjehemlut of the Clan Emudar, I am pleased you grace our table. Unfortunate that your father couldn't be here."

The king bore a presence, a weight in his gaze that made Kinesee want to look down, but she managed to hold steady. She swallowed and cleared her throat. "I am honored by your words. My father's travels are in part why I am here."

Sînhôlar didn't flinch or blink. "I deemed the north and south your concern, not the distant west."

A caravan of servants entered with silver trays covered by golden domes. "I would choose to begin our conversation with a positive. My father is..." She noticed a serving girl standing to her side, so she stopped talking. Only then did the girl place the tray in front of her and remove the dome. Diced red and white potatoes, carrots, and a green, leafy stalk she didn't have a name for rested beside a pile of sliced beef, everything drizzled with a dark gravy. It was more than she ate in a typical day, but of a sudden, she realized she hadn't eaten breakfast. The king gestured, and she picked up a tri-tyned fork, poked a chunk of potato, and popped it into her mouth. Her eyes widened and her chew slowed as she smiled. The gravy tasted as if blended with a sweet wine, or maybe some sort of fruit. "Delicious."

"The beef is our chef's specialty... or maybe it's the sauce. Please, try it before continuing."

Juicy and tender, having soaked up the sauce, she stifled a moan before swallowing. She smiled. "The fare of the Ironwing makes it difficult to speak."

"We have the rest of the day to eat and speak."

She nodded. "I received a pigeon from Klondihîk. My father is seeking a trade route between Molikîn and Mulshahar, one to include the Helelindin." She skewered a piece of beef while judging his reaction. The queen's eyes raised, and her lips stopped in mid-bite, but the Ironwing's expression didn't change. Only the silence spoke to his surprise; it was several flickers before he spoke.

"By river from the south or by land from the east?"

"By river is his goal, the Gulf of Tomulok is at war, the Gorotan and the Boboru."

"War on those waters is not uncommon from what I hear. Kingdomers have attempted the route more than once. What makes him think he can open this passage?"

"He found his father in Mulshahar, who now leads the Clan Emudar. Many thousand Emudar now live on islands south of Kônu Bay. Opening a route will be the result of reconnecting our clans, a cause more vital than mere trade. He will not fail."

Nîsenî said, "I underestimated your father once. Give the man ships and an army, and he might achieve what our kin have desired for a century."

Sînhôlar stared to the sunny sky painted on the ceiling before his gaze fell back to Kinesee, time enough for several bites of beef and taters. "Expeditions have made it to what foreigners call the Monsoon Strait, but my people are not famed for their ability with sails and oars, nor boat-craft."

"My people plied rivers in trade and raids and war for the past five hundred years."

His emotionless stare showed its first crack as his right eye squinted. "The journey would still be long and dangerous, but the taxes we'd avoid would be lucrative. You wish to strike some sort of trade deal?"

"No. Our peoples are beyond treaties; our peoples are friends. Solineus will bring you this trade."

"I see. All of Helmvilîn thanks you. What is it that you *do* want?" A hint of grin flexed his lips.

Kinesee smiled and sipped her iced water. "My husband is sending four thousand men to the place known as Green Mountain to straighten out the troubles in the south. If you matched this number, it wouldn't drain our forces guarding the wall from whatever the Malstefnê have planned. And it might speed Solineus' return if we meet him partway."

The king breathed deep and exhaled. "I must divert our conversation to apologize. I fear I bear some responsibility for the attack on your party. I had word of Teks crossing the river in small groups but never imagined they gathered for such a bold endeavor."

Kinesee ducked her head and fought back sorrow. "There is already too much blame shared at this table. Past regrets are behind us to remember, but our eyes must settle on what lays ahead."

"Wise words. But I fear that Helmveline faces matters that might prevent our sending such a number of men. A faction known as the Black Waters has fomented violence across the Eight Kingdoms since your father retrieved the coin... and Morik lost half of it."

Morik's head tucked to his chest, and Kinesee wondered what part of the story she'd missed. "Any number is appreciated in helping rescue your people as well as ours. You received our pigeon requesting maps?"

The Ironwing raised his chin and nodded, but it wasn't to her. A woman with gray hair bound in a knot atop her head approached the table with bowed legs. Rolled parchments carried in a leather pack peered over her shoulder, and with a grunt, she placed them in front of Meliu. The priestess made busy stuffing her mouth to clean her plate.

"You can make study of them, copy what you need. Ask any questions of Humêl, our Lady of Histories."

Meliu mumbled through her food. "My many thanks."

Kinesee smiled, but her nerves tightened. "How many warriors might I tell my husband to count on?"

"Ôgrihîn raids and the Black Waters Cult would limit any response I desired, and now the Malstefnê riding boldly into our lands to attack us as well as our allies... And I ask myself, *why* attack your party?"

Morik spoke up, "We'd need to speak to the dead for that answer."

"You're incapable of speculation?"

"No, my king."

"Well then, why?"

Kinesee nodded to Morik and cleared her throat. "It could've been luck, happenstance. But, taking or killing the new bride of the Warlord Choerkin was, to my mind, their goal. Several split from the fight to give me chase."

The Ironwing leaned forward in his seat, resting elbows on the table, a pose less formal than he'd struck before. "To what gain?"

She blinked and stared. "I'm not sure I have an answer..."

"I have seen few battles, but my father taught me to think as a warlord. Would they seek ransom for capture?"

"No."

"Would your husband ride forth from his fortress-like a crazed fool to avenge your death?"

Kinesee blushed and ducked her head. "No."

"Would they force him to some tactical error in trying to rescue you?"

"Yes. Maybe."

"And how would they know you rode for my halls in Molikîn?"

Kinesee glanced at Morik and Meliu. "Not hard to imagine they'd have spies behind the wall. I don't know."

Meliu said, "This isn't the first time someone has tried to kill the Lady Choerkin, just the first time since she's *been* Lady Choerkin."

Kinesee's heart lurched and pounded in her chest. "You're suggesting..."

The Ironwing sat straight in his throne and put the weight of his stare on Meliu. "Suggesting what?"

"You spoke of a Black Waters Cult among your people. I know nothing of them except they are bringing you trouble. There are priests outside the Pantheon of Sol; we call them the Heretics of Rin. They tried to kill her almost three years ago."

"Why would these people do such a thing?"

Meliu raised a finger and drank water. Exhaled. "We don't know. But we believe it has something to do with a prophecy. Our best guess, they believe she is foretold in prophecy, and killing her will somehow defeat this destiny."

"My people say destiny is a cruel ax whose blade bears many curves."

Kinesee said, "If this is true, then one of our people told the Malstefnê of my travels."

Sînhôlar squinted at her, his gaze concerned. "I asked myself, why would a Malstefnê general order an attack in the mountains of Helmveline, and if this is true, I have my answer: They did not."

Kinesee cocked her head. "What do you mean?"

"Men paid gold care not for the boundaries they cross."

"Assassins? To kill me?"

Meliu said, "He's right. It fits."

"I may or may not be right. The answer could be one we will never guess. But to my mind, it is the most likely answer to a question with unknown variables."

Nîsenî turned to face the king. "You can spare two thousand to escort her back to the wall *and* to ride south."

The Ironwing didn't so much as turn his head. "Can I? A thousand, I say." Then he grinned. "But if I know my queen, by morning you will have the two thousand she suggests. But I cannot afford war with the Malstefnê, not with the storm clouds rising in the western mountains."

Kinesee drummed her fingers on the table even as Meliu handed her empty plate to a servant. The priestess unrolled a map and gazed on its markings. Kinesee couldn't let it distract from her cause. "Six thousand might suffice to the south, I am not a warrior nor leader of men, but can we hold the wall if the Malstefnê siege?"

"There can be no guarantees in war... what magics the Malstfne might have."

"I need guarantees."

"I have none for you."

Nîsenî stabbed a piece of meat on her plate in dainty fashion. "But he has an idea."

"Do I?"

"You do, but it hasn't finished rattling around in your head yet."

He chuckled and slumped in his seat, for the first time appearing a normal man. "The queen knows me too well. There is a possibility, but you'd need to prove you are related to your father to achieve the feat."

Kinesee straightened. "I am my father's daughter." Even if Solineus weren't her birth father, Iko's blood would suffice.

"War with the Malstefnê I cannot afford, but the Eight Kingdoms could. There is a mountain to the east—"

"You want me to climb a mountain?"

The Ironwing laughed. "No. Your people are friends with the Helelindin, yes?"

Kinesee sat perplexed, her mind turning over possibilities, but she remained uncertain of how to answer. "We are at peace. They sent archers to make a show for the Malstefnê once, but they're unwilling to go to war for our cause."

"I've little doubt their archers and magics would make for another guarantee, but... The Twenty-Second Foundation stands in mountains on the eastern side of the Roemhien, and the Helelindin claim its heights. Our peoples warred over the territory for three centuries, and they bar our pilgrims from prayer and sacrifice at its altar. If you could speak to the Helelindin, convince them to allow pilgrims to the Twenty-Second Foundation, it would gain you favor with all Eight Kingdoms."

"This would take time, time we may not have."

"The wall will not fall in a day. Even if they attack tomorrow, you will have time."

Kinesee's enthusiasm and confidence sank to her toes, and she slouched. It was a hope, but more fleeting than the promises of her dreams. She didn't know what to say, but Meliu saved her.

The high priestess tapped a map in frantic fashion. "This name here? What is it?"

The old woman shuffled to gaze over Meliu's shoulder, her voice scratchy and weak. "Endelêun. A city."

"What do you know of this city?"

"Very little. Big, powerful... a great enemy of the Foundationals."

"My map names these plains Tomarok."

The interpreter asked, "Tômôrôk?"

The old woman, Morik, and the royal couple shared glances, and Meliu stood with a queer smile on her face. "You know the name."

The Ironwing raised his hands to silence everyone. "It is a word we first heard very recently. What does it mean?"

Meliu laughed and collapsed into her seat. "I was hoping you knew. It is a place, a place someone told me to find, but I don't know why."

Kinesee stared at each one in turn. "Well, it's the first I've heard the word at all."

Nîsenî's face turned cold, and it wasn't some air she put on like when they first met. "The Black Waters speak of Tômôrôk."

Kinesee turned her stare to Meliu. "How... why would the Black Waters be speaking of a place you are looking for?"

"You would need to ask a dead man... Lord Priest Ulrikt. He's the one who told me to find it before I sailed to the continent."

Kinesee couldn't control the rising tone of her voice. "And what's this to do with the Heretics of Rin?"

"Nothing! Nothing I know of, I swear. Please believe me, if they are connected, I know nothing."

Kinesee fumed, and her hand wandered to the pearl. A warmth pulsed against her chest as she rubbed.

Nîsenî said, "Your priestess does not lie."

The Ironwing nodded. "She does not lie." His eyes turned back to Meliu. "But you will tell me all you know of Tômôrôk without a lie, lies are known before the crowns of Helmveline."

Meliu pulled a scroll from her haversack and spread it on the table. "I haven't a need to lie; I only wish I knew more." She pointed at the map, but from her vantage, Kinesee couldn't see. "These are ancient words in a tongue I can't read. A Trelelunin scholar told me they read 'The Plains of Tomarok'. My lord priest left instructions to find this place written in mystic ink, which glows beneath the stars of Skywatch. This is all I know."

Nîsenî said, "She does not lie."

The queen's words faded into an awkward silence; a silence Kinesee couldn't take with the hammering rhythm of her heart. She blurted, "I don't care if she lies. What does it mean?"

The Ironwing's eyes still studied Meliu, ignoring Kinesee for flickers, until he turned with a deep sigh. "You will have your four thousand and four thousand more. If we find this Tômôrôk, we will destroy it. But more than ever, Helmveline will not be able to afford war with Malstefnê."

Nîsenî's eyes were wide. "Eight thousand? If the Tek realize our weakness..."

The Ironwing raised his hand to curb her words. "I will send a pigeon to Tûrûrôt. They will match our four thousand or send warriors to assist us against the north. It is the way of the Foundations."

Kinesee's fists balled in victory and frustration, uncertain what good it would do to save their people in the south if everyone in the Roemhium lay dead. All the more painful that she'd failed after Maro and so many others gave their lives so she might succeed. But there wasn't a reason to make the best of a maddening situation. "This is most generous and noble of the Ironwing, and I thank you. It would be more generous and more noble if when your army rides, they travel the Bollybone Road and make a spectacle of passing through the gates of the wall."

Sînhôlar's placid lips turned to a grin, the grin shifted to a smile, and the smile brought a laugh and a waggling finger in her direction. "You are your father's daughter. Done."

EIGHTEEN

Slave's Understanding

A whipper of the will, teeth in the till,
what payment have you for the carving?
Where are your Wings?
Where are your Lights?
Where are your Dreams?
Where are... Ah, yes. The dream.
No better dream.
I sing a song unsung unknown unfounded,
Foundered and fat, the curling hoof is doom,
Weakened and wakened from the herd to
feed the Lone Wolf alone.

—*Tomes of the Touched*

Rinold figured the Histê spoke a language unrelated to the Wiirê tongue, which was more than enough to confuse him even further. Still, their new owner was serious about teaching the Silone. A wrinkled and bald yellow-eye arrived with several guards by his side every day to instruct the group in the language they called Histên.

They rode on an open-platform barge tethered between four other barges, the Silone with their wrists and ankles hobbled, but they weren't shoved into cages either. Or at least their cage was a moat instead of bamboo bars. Bound as they were, they'd drown in flickers or get eaten right quick if they tried to swim. Whether their lot had improved a little or a lot depended on whether a man considered the freedom to die when he chooses real freedom.

Rinold's grasp of the language improved markedly over the next five days as he not only studied but helped other Silone learn. He grew eager to test his words on someone who mattered, but the warrior-slave had so far only made brief appearances to stare at them from a neighboring barge.

Their tutor had just canoed back to the main barge when Edlmir put his meaty hand atop Rinold's head and squeezed. "We've put a lot of horizons between us and home; when we gonna do somethin' 'bout that?"

Rinold ducked from his grip and wandered to the fore of the barge, staring at the unending and ever-changing trees surrounding them, but it didn't keep the bastard from bugging him.

"How's that plan of yers goin', Squirrel?"

"I'm not sure it was even a plan. A hope at best."

Edlmir grunted. "Shoulda let me fight 'em when I had the chance."

Most days, he wouldn't agree, but Rinold grew fed up watching the horizons grow between him and Puxele as much as the others. "I'm starting to agree with you."

"The next time we have a chance, we take it."

"Your courage—"

"It ain't courage no more, I'm disgusted, and I'd prefer to go out on *my* terms instead of as some godsdamned entertainment for heathens."

"I hear you, but these people are cocky and disorganized. You saw how they charged our line. The time will come, and when it does, we'll take it."

"The men are impatient."

Rinold huffed. "I've got a wife and child waitin' for me back there, what the hells you got?"

"We all got someone, some more than you."

The barge rocked before Rinold could answer, and at first, he thought maybe they'd struck rocks or some beast in the river attacked, but truth was the river narrowed, and they gained speed on choppy waters. He grabbed a rail as his legs swayed with the lean of the barge's ups and downs.

The river ahead turned, the endless trees ended, and all he could see was water ahead. "A sea? The ocean?" There was no way they'd floated so far.

The waters slowed as the river widened, and trees appeared in the distance to reveal the truth. Their river was merging with another, one a half-horizon wide. It was glorious and beautiful, bigger than any on Kaludor by a good stretch, a river deserving of the name Puxele, but then his mind turned.

"How godsdamned big you think a critter could get in that there river?"

"Big enough to eat you without noticin', I'd wager."

Men plunged poles into the waters on the other four barges even as the steersman leaned on the rudders with all their weight, and it didn't take long to realize they were guiding them to the far shore. The forest ahead wasn't a twin to the woods they left behind, the trees were shorter and there was more bare ground between their trunks. It was a woodland that felt more familiar, more like the Dragonspans or Kaludor.

They were maybe a candle on this new river when they rounded a hard bend in the flow, and on the horizon, a small fortress appeared on a hill. The hill was a bald head of gray rock and the castle its hat or crown, even as its shape reminded Rinold of a face. When he squinted, he could see a man's gaping maw screaming.

Edlmir said, "Looks like maybe our lady's home?"

"Reasonable enough guess, I figure."

But guesses were guesses because they often proved wrong. They floated straight past for a half candle before the barges navigated into what Rinold figured was a man-made crescent of stone that jutted into the river with its inner curve fitted with a dock along its entire length. It created an awkward harbor with a slow vortex in the middle, but the Histê sailors maneuvered their train of barges with deft poles and ropes cast to men waiting on the dock. Ropes drew taut, and Wiirê slaves cranked pulleys, and they clunked against the pier with startling ease. Less surprising were the archers pointing arrows at them, making sure they didn't flee. As if they knew where the hells to run to.

Shackles clamped their wrists and ankles as they stepped to the dock, and Bossman led them west like an awkward band of baby ducks waddling along. Trees covered the trail for the first several hundred paces, but the forest cleared to fields of grain he couldn't name, where yellow-eye slaves labored under the watchful stare of Histê masters carrying rods and whips. The road here stretched another quarter-horizon before they passed through the gates of a small city, its stone walls formidable at thirty feet. Only a scattering of guards manned the watch, and the rusted iron portcullis and crumbling mortar in the stonework's joints suggested they didn't feel the need to upkeep their defenses. It was another strike against these people if it came to war with the Silone, and Rinold tucked it tight in his memory.

Mud bricks made up most of the town's construction, or so it appeared at first, but as they traversed the chaotic streets, he realized that often as not stone foundations lay beneath the bricks, and in some places, mud bricks were repairs for older and sturdier buildings. Their destination was one of these, a stadium with empty stands whose floor was a couple of hundred strides in diameter. The Silone marched to the center of town with their proud escort, and it took him half a wick to realize that hope had arrived.

The warrior-slave whistled to get everyone's attention. "We've two fists before nightfall. You will train, and then we will eat." Fists were the way the Wiirê gave a general measure of time, by stretching their clenched fist out and counting how many fit between the sun and the horizon.

A score of archers marched into the arena and fanned out around its edges, and a long-necked critter pulled a cart filled with wooden weapons, none of which were much like those the Silone were used to wielding. The warrior-slave made his way down the line, unlocking their shackles, and when he reached Rinold, he said, "You will sit there with me, and we will talk of how your people fight."

Rinold rubbed his wrists with a grin, winked at Edlmir, and wandered to where the man had pointed to wait. By the time the man got to him, Silone had swung and clacked their weapons. He motioned for Rinold to sit in the dirt and followed suit, facing the fighting only fingers from Rinold's shoulder. "You are their leader?"

Rinold shrugged. "They look to me, but none here is a true leader."

"But they look to you, that defines what a leader is."

He chuckled, never having thought himself in such a way. "I suppose so. My name is Rinold."

"I am Nehek. You are not powerful among your people?"

"No. But I know powerful people."

"Among the Histê, this makes you powerful."

Rinold chortled, chagrined that the man made good points. "Again, you're right, in a way. We have no kings, but I have ridden with the Warlord Choerkin. My people will come for me, men in steel will raze this city without mercy, tear it stone from stone. Help me escape, and they'll never need to make the journey."

Nehek watched as men beat at each other with sticks. "I am but a slave."

"You are a warrior. A fighter. I see it in your scars."

"My scars are greater than yours." He puffed with pride.

The number of scars the man bore up and down his body made him cringe. "Not even my twitch will argue that. What armor do you have to stop steel arrows? What spear point to puncture our steel rings?"

"This city is a drip in the river of the Histê Kingdom. The great cities are far to the west. You will not tear down their stones. I am a slave, to die is a gift."

"You would see all these people killed? Their crops burned?"

"Yes. It is why I spoke for you."

Rinold blinked as his eye twitched. "You plan to die here, fighting against my people?"

"I will fight poorly but die well."

"So, you brought us here hoping my people would come and destroy this place, but you will fight against them?" Nehek had a peculiar view of honor far as Rinold could tell, and it irked him. "Help me escape, and we can save people who needn't die. Wiirê need not die."

"They are slaves; death is a gift."

Rinold grunted. The man was a warrior, so it was that fire which needed stoking. "If death is a gift, it's like a punch in the nose on your birthday. Piss on that." The man glared; pissing seemed to get his attention. "*Freedom* is a gift. Piss on the Histê Kingdom. Piss on your Mistress Hukêlê. Piss on dying as a slave. Escape. Come with me."

"I am a slave."

"You were a child once and became a man."

"I became a slave."

"You were a child once, became a man, and someone stole from you what that *means.* What you are today isn't what you must be tomorrow. Piss on those soft-bellied Histê. Instead of bleeding for them, bloody them."

The man's eyes danced back and forth from Rinold to the fighting Silone. "How many men in steel rings are there?"

Rinold stifled his grin in case Histê eyes watched them. "Hundreds of hundreds. Five hundred hundreds. And more will follow." It might take every damned man, woman, and child to make that the truth, but with help from the Kingdomers, he figured it was only a big lie, not a giant one.

"Rinold of the Silone, this is many, but not enough to face the Histê."

"You want these toad biters dead... So piss in their mouths. We escape, reach my people, and we return to tear this cursed place down, send every last Histê to their ancestors. But with you with me, no Wiirê need to die."

The man's eyelids fluttered, but his expression otherwise remained stone. "When Histê war with Histê they take Wiirê slaves as their own."

"My people, the Silone, do not believe in slaves, our gods forbid it. We are a free people. You will be a free man. Your people will be free."

Nehek breathed deep, a rumble in his chest. After a wick of silence he said, "It is generous, but ill winds would blow for my kin. I am Tunotuwiirê. If I betray my mistress, their armies will stomp the men of my people into the mud, take the women to breed, and shackle the boys."

"Is it so different now?" He gave the man a plaintive stare, but Nehek wouldn't meet his eye. "Do this for me, and the Warlord

Choerkin will tip your people's spears and arrows with steel points and cover them in steel rings. We will fight and we will win. Together. Your sons will never be slaves."

"If I do this thing, they will feed me to a crocodile while you die in the pits, torn limb from limb by a great gorilla."

He wasn't sure what the hells a gorilla was, but it didn't sound pleasant. "Are you more afraid of dying or living free? Fight. Piss on their dead eyes."

"If you tear down the bricks of Tekekî, the Histê will not ignore your people."

Rinold cocked his head; he hadn't thought much about how the Histê would react. "Helping me is your chance, your people's chance to be free. Take it or don't, but we will escape by our own hands or when my Warlord comes. Whether the Wiirê die on our return is your choice."

Nehek spat in his hands and rubbed them together. "Steel tips and steel rings?"

"On my word."

The man stood and gazed down on him with luminescent yellow eyes. "I will think on your words. Mistress Hukêlê plans to sell you in Tononoholu, the great city ruled by the Histê Takuhêil. My decision will be swift. If I wake you in the night, you and your men must follow my every word."

The man turned and strode away without giving Rinold a chance to respond, snapping his fingers at several yellow-eye guards along his way. Rinold stood numb, not quite sure whether to believe his luck. Would the man betray him? He might gain favor with his mistress if he did. No. Rinold trusted Nehek for the same reason Nehek chose to trust Rinold; they were both slaves unwilling to accept this dismal fate.

He stared at the fighting for over a candle as the sun turned orange on the horizon. The Silone chugged water from barrels, and Edlmir strolled to his side, his clothes drenched in sweat, and a couple of bruises marred his face.

"So, what the hells did that bastard want? You two ladies swappin' secrets on darning a hem while the men fight?"

Rinold clapped him on the shoulder. "I think we just started a war."

NINETEEN

Hall of Glass

The cloaked anger in the closet of depravity
burrowed by moths and swallowed by the swallow,
the Swallow's Tail striking to kill from bent wood and bone,
Taste oh taste the slurry within the fury,
the streaking talon of triple feather flown true,
the pulse and spray to end you days.

—*Tomes of the Touched*

Kinesee sat sipping lemongrass tea after breakfast while praying for anyone's arrival to break the silence between her and Meliu. It didn't help that the priestess buried her nose in some book every candle for the past three days, worse still that the book held words Kinesee couldn't read. Just a few years ago, she couldn't read at all, so maybe it shouldn't irritate her to the point of childish fury, but it did.

She puffed steam from a fresh pour of tea and took an exaggerated sip. "So, what are you reading?"

Meliu's glance made her feel stupid. "You really want to know?"

"I may as well."

Meliu smiled. "I think I cracked the code to the Prophecy of the Twelfth Star."

Fury and stupidity faded to honest curiosity. "The Twelfth Star?" Kinesee wasn't a scholar, but she knew of this prophecy's connection to the Shadows of Man from the rumors bandied about by the lords of the clans. "Anything about the Heretics of Rin?"

"Nothing so useful, but it's interesting."

Kinesee stared at her. "We aren't busy."

"Has the Lady Ravinrin turned you into a budding scholar? The most famous line, at least the most rumored, while at Istinjoln was 'By the Light of the Sliver of Star will the king priest rise from eternity to unify Sol's people.' By my translation, this is wrong in its most literal sense, and almost without doubt, purposefully so. The question is, by whose purpose?"

The woman's cockiness grated on her. "You're so certain you're right?"

"In Canonic Silone, the word we translate as king priest is *îumôtar*, and the word for foreign kings is *polâl*. There's no confusing these. There is no word for king in Canonic Silone, but there is Warlord, *dêumôtar*."

"Which sounds a lot like *îumôtar*. So, the prophecy predicts the rise of a warlord?"

"No. It translates like this: 'Assassinated into dying eternal by foe turned friend turned savior, so by the Light of the Sliver of Star will rise the *lîumôtar* from eternity to unify Sol's people, taking the Pantheon's Crown upon the peak of Tomarok.' Not *îumôtar*, *lîumôtar*."

Kinesee squinted. "It's one letter."

"One letter that creates a word I haven't seen before."

She sipped her tea to give herself a contemplative pause. "A queen priest instead of a king?"

Meliu shook her head. "Canonic Silone doesn't distinguish between sexes with its word for priest."

"But does it with king and queen?"

Meliu straightened. "It does. *Selêl* is a foreign queen. It's useful to not always think like an adherent."

Kinesee puffed, pleased with herself. "Then I'm right?"

"Maybe. Texts I've read have mentioned the names of women who were *îumôtar*, but they were more recent texts, not written during the

God Wars. What you suggest makes sense, but it could be something else."

"Well, whatever it is, we know it isn't Lord Priest Ulrikt." Kinesee grinned, but the look on Meliu's face wasn't amused.

Meliu's next words felt as much spoken to herself as to Kinesee. "No, he didn't have the Sliver of Star. He knew he didn't have the Sliver, but he needed the other lord priests to believe. He faked his death, how? How many times can one man die?"

"What are you going on about? Faked his death?"

Nîsenî's voice came from the room's entry hall. "Five times if he is one of the Five Earls."

Meliu cocked her head. "Excuse me?"

Kinesee smiled at the queen. "You've learned Silone."

The Heart of the Ironwing strode into the hall in a gown so long its train swept the stone floor a stride behind her. "The king and I both do, but it would be improper to speak so in the Thrones."

Meliu said, "Five earls?"

"A story for children, but we've plenty of time for fireside tales later. If you wish to visit the Latcu collection, I've requested it opened for our tour."

Kinesee bounced to her feet. "I'd be delighted."

Meliu glanced at the book, then back to the queen. "These pages can't compete with beautiful stones."

Nîsenî led them on a long enough walk that Meliu weaseled the story of the Five Earls from the woman, but Kinesee didn't see the point of a fairy tale about some legendary king. She was far more interested in the sculptures, some built into the walls, that decorated their route. Mountains, griffons, axes, hammers, and swords were the most common themes, but there were also life-sized busts sitting on pedestals. Some were of men, ranging from handsome to scarred and ugly, others were of women, beautiful or homely, but the most fascinating were of horses. And all the horses were magnificent whether their pose was regal, stern, warlike, or wild. Surprising that a mountain people esteemed horses to such a degree.

After taking a stair that drilled them deep into the mountain, men in armor standing guard replaced the impressive decor. "Is latcu so valuable as all this?"

Double doors fashioned from some silvery alloy opened in front of them. Nîsenî waved her arms in a sweeping gesture as she entered the room and said, "As valuable as they are, no." She pointed to a marble shelf holding several discs. "The guards are for the coin—half a coin, I should say—that your father fetched for us."

Bins lined the walls, and the room sparkled in a dizzying array of colors that'd put a rainbow to shame. A single glowing globe hung in the middle of the hall, but nothing escaped its Light. The largest display was at the opposite end of the room, crystals so clear they were hard to see if not for their sparkle. Pinks, violets, and oranges were the most plentiful of the colored stones, but blues ranging from sky to deep water, and greens from soft pastel to deep emerald, and reds spanning shades from blushing coral to rose caught her eye as she turned in a slow, mesmerized circle.

"Any thief would surely become dazzled and forget what they came for."

Meliu said, "I haven't words."

Nîsenî stepped to a bin of pink latcu, reached in, and tossed one to Kinesee. The stone sparkled as it flew, and she caught it before considering that the legend of latcu was how it penetrated steel and flesh. But the stone was oblong like the caricature of an eye. "I'm happy it has no edge."

The queen sauntered to a bin of emerald green stones and tossed one to Meliu. "I imagine that will bring out your eyes and show off your beautiful hair. Stones suitable for arrowheads or some other function never make it here. What you see before you is a blinding fortune in stones useless to everyone but those with an eye for beauty."

"Useless!" The concept annoyed her, but function outweighed pretty. "Helmveline could flood the markets in Mulshahar with jewelry."

"I tempted the Ironwing with such a notion once, and he informed me, cordially, that my genius was something everyone must overcome on first stepping foot in this hall."

"If it's useless, why not?"

The queen turned to Meliu. "Have you the answer?"

The question startled the dazzled priestess. "I'm still imagining the setting I'd need for this stone."

"Imagine it, and it will be yours." The queen walked with her hand rummaging through bins, sparkles shining in a flurry. "Your father holds the answer, and so too does your husband."

There was one possession that the two men had in common, and before this moment, she'd never considered the coincidence of her father and husband bearing the only latcu weapons she'd ever heard of. "Latcu swords."

"Precisely. One day, what you see beautiful before you, smiths will hammer into tools of war more valuable than any necklace or ring."

"You could supply an army."

Nîsenî stood with a smile, her red hair framed by an aureole of violet. "It seems so, doesn't it? There is a reason why latcu was treasured even during the God Wars. Everything you see before you might make a hundred swords, a thousand spear points... I'm not a smith, so I can't say for certain, but its value would be immeasurable."

Kinesee wandered to a bin of light blue stones. "May I?" With a permissive nod, she stuck her hand in the Latcu. Cool, smooth, and round, she watched the play of light like a cat staring at the reflection of the sun off a silver spoon. "Not to be nosy, but how is that silly disc more valuable?"

"Because it *is* useful. This half can find the other half no matter where it goes in the world. But truth is, we don't know how badly the Dark Waters want it. Yet. But at some point, they will, and we must keep it from them."

Meliu said, "Tomarok. I wish we knew what it means."

"Far as the Ironwing is concerned, nothing good. And I agree."

Kinesee had no desire to dye the wool on this topic a second time. "Where does the latcu come from? I mean, it's mined, but where?"

The queen turned back to her with a smile. "It's scattered, but volcanic regions are most common."

"Volcanoes? Sleeping ones, I hope."

Meliu said, "It's like obsidian then?"

"Some have postulated as such. Many have guessed it a form of volcanic glass, but anyone who knows isn't saying."

Kinesee nodded and would've let the topic drop but for the phrasing. "Implying that someone does know?"

The queen's face passed from cordial to the cold stone of when they first met. "Gers'voresh-kûmjotu-kî."

"I don't recognize the Kingdomer word, I'm sorry."

"The swords your father bears spoke this name, and he asked us if we knew what it meant. It took a woman wiser than I in the lore of the ancients to find an answer. Gers'voresh-kûmjotu-kî is a Wisewoman named on the Cliffs of Knowledge."

"I thought the swords spoke in gibberish." Kinesee had heard of the cliffs, a place where men long dead carved history from times Forgotten into the mountain's face. "Why would the swords speak the name of some dead woman?"

"Gers'voresh-kûmjotu-kî is not one who dies, but the wise believed her gone from this world."

"You're saying this woman is still alive?"

Meliu stared, her precious stone loose in her fingers. "A god?"

Nîsenî's smile twitched at the corners. "No. But swords that speak this name... I fear for your father."

"Did you send him word? Warn him?"

"No, we dare not speak of such things by pigeon; the Dark Waters might use this knowledge. Until we know what it *means*, this should be a secret. Tell your father, your husband, no one else. Not even Morik." She turned to Meliu. "Only tell scholars you trust to keep the secret."

Meliu's brows bunched. "I trust no one but myself, but who the hells is this Wisewoman?"

Nîsenî's face softened, and her smile was fanciful and out of place. "Her name means 'She who was born in the flames of creation' but what that means, we do not know."

Kinesee muttered, "Born in the flames of creation." Nîsenî knew more than she was saying, but even in the castles of her childhood play, the lowborn knew not to press the queen for answers she was unwilling to give.

TWENTY

Four-Eyed Riddle

What do you see when bones wear flesh?
I see boiling eyes and ice-cold lies
in from the tongue breaking the bung
of the whiskey barrel's pour...
the store, the house, Fiddling Mouse
and its Crooning Whore...
Whiskey Barrel's pore over wisdom lost,
the melting freeze of all the days so unlike these.

—*Tomes of the Touched*

Helmveliner men delivered the table to his side room the day before, and Ivin sat admiring the inlays of semiprecious stones and exotic woods set in its top; the cut stones formed diamonds between rows of mahogany, maple, ebony, and cherry to contrast the oak. The craftsman was a cousin of Morik's, and she'd claimed it a gaming table of some sort, but no one had bothered to teach him to play.

His chair squawked on the floor as he shoved back, reaching for a plain maple box sitting above the fireplace. He flipped the latch and opened its lid to dump the dice on the table.

The four-eyed snake. All ones.

Every godsdamned time.

"Nice roll."

Kinesee's voice startled him; staring at the dice, he hadn't noticed the door open.

"You're back." He leaped to his feet and hugged her. "Gods, it's good to see you!"

She leaned into his hug. "I'm fine."

He kissed her forehead and held her at arm's length for a better look. "Beautiful as ever—" She unpinned her cloak, and pink stones dazzled his eyes and stole his words. He reached out, touching a stone and her warm, soft skin.

She smiled. "A gift from the king and queen."

"It seems things went better than the pigeon suggested."

"Better than we'd hoped, but imperfect. I arrived at the lead of two thousand Helmveliners, another two thousand will follow within two weeks."

"This is imperfect?"

She sighed. "I need to travel east to the Helelindin."

"There are others—"

"I promised the Ironwing I would see to it myself."

She was hiding something, but Meliu had taught him that a woman's secrets were hers to keep. He gestured to the table and the dice. "You know Hawk and Snake?"

She giggled. "A smidgen. Enough to know the four-eyed snake is a winning roll. Tedeu wouldn't allow me near dice, nor would Pa... Father."

Ivin tried to smile but Tokodin haunted his thoughts. He picked up the bones and rattled them in his hand. "Watch." He cast and they tumbled across the table until coming up ones.

Kinesee gasped then laughed. "Loaded! My word, the Warlord is a cheat."

"You remember the monk who killed my father?"

She sat across from him, spreading the fabric of her dress smooth as reflections from the necklace sparkled in a dance across the table. "I know the stories."

"Tokodin was a gambler, always carried his three days and one night in his robes. When I found him dead in the garderobe the night die rested on the floor, a one." He held it up. "The other three were missing."

She cocked her head and stared at him with a crooked grin. "You had four dice that day in the Roemhien."

"I did, and that was the first day that I did. Someone slipped them into my pocket."

They blinked at each other for several flickers. "I don't understand."

"Neither do I." He swept up the dice and threw them again with the same result. He exhaled and avoided saying a name. "Someone told me that he'd been gambling at the Crack of Burdenis where the Shadows first attacked, and the day it was overrun, he lost a huge pot when he rolled three ones and a two. Now they never not roll ones."

"Meliu told you this? You're aware that I can survive hearing her name."

Ivin blanched and ducked his head, searching for a quick change in topic. "Yes. Meliu. But whoever left the night die... whoever returned the rest, what mocking message were they sending?"

"So, his loaded dice failed him that day?" She picked up the dice and rolled all ones.

"No, his dice weren't loaded. Neither are these."

"They must be." She rolled again, all ones.

"No, there isn't a loaded die in the world this perfect. I examined them. The corners are exact. A craftsman who tinkered with them said there's no weight imbalance out of the ordinary. Then I noticed this." He picked up the night die, turned it to a three, set it on the table, and when he lifted his finger, it flipped to a single pip.

"That's a fine trick." Kinesee picked up the night die and held it up; Ivin chuckled and gave the days a toss. At first he didn't look, there wasn't a point, because the damned bones were perfect, but then came her whisper. "A two, four, and six."

And she wasn't toying with him. There the dice sat, taunting him. "The night die..."

She lowered her hand to throw the die, but before it left her fingers, the three days flipped to ones. "It controls the others. If cheating, you wouldn't even need to swap out all the dice. But..."

His memory of chatting with Meliu was clear but it confused him now. "Tokodin lost the pot when the days were ones and the night a two."

Kinesee held the black die far away as she could and turned the whites before drawing the night closer. The range was close to two feet. "A good cheat would have a different night die for every number... The four-eyed snake would grow suspicious over and over." She rolled the night die by itself, and it never strayed from the single pip staring at them. "A person might have a set of dice for *any* result."

Ivin rubbed his face. "Remind me to keep an eye on you, clever girl."

"I should hope you do, being married. But I'm not clever enough to answer *why* someone put them in your pocket."

He grimaced as he took a deep breath. "Meliu doesn't believe Tokodin killed Kotin. She pretended I convinced her, but not for a flicker did she believe it. Whoever put the night die by his body... hells, that person might've killed him and dropped the die on the floor for all the forges I know."

"And in your pocket?"

"To rub it in my face. Whoever killed my father is here. Somewhere. Close enough to get dice into my pocket. Close enough to kill you or me, which is why I got you a present." He stood and strode to a closet, proud of the grin he'd brought to her face.

"A surprise for me?"

The sword's blade was a hand over two feet long but narrower than the heavier swords most Silone warriors carried, more in the fashion of Helmveline. The hilt was forged from blued steel and the grip wrapped in titanium wire, a metal he'd never heard of until meeting the Kingdomers. "I asked Morik to have a sword made, beautiful but practical. It pales when compared to the Ironwing's gift—"

She snatched it from his hands. "No. It's beautiful. Truly."

"I meant to give it to you for our wedding, but some folks talked me out of it. Now I wish I had, with your being attacked."

She rolled her eyes with a smile. "If I'd had this sword and stayed to fight, I would probably be dead." The blade slipped from its polished sheath, and she pointed the tip at the window. "These Kingdomer etchings, what do they mean?"

"The Lady."

Her grin belonged more to a demon than the pretty girl she was. "Alu is going to so *jealous*."

"Aye, I suppose she will. But remember that she'll beat you around the yard if you practice with her."

"But my sword will be prettier."

Ivin wagged his finger and smiled. "No live steel."

She eyeballed him and exhaled, her gaze soft, and for a moment he forgot there were other women in the world.

"You Choerkin are an odd lot. No Ravinrin man would give his new bride a sword."

"Kotin always used to say the only thing mightier than the sword was the woman behind the man wielding it. I'm just changing it up a little."

She leaped to stand in front of him like a jubilant child and hugged him, sword and sheath clanging behind his back. "I love it. Thank you." There was nothing childlike in how the hug felt; he gripped her back and smelled her hair, fresh and windblown.

A knock rattled the door, and in an instant the world intruded. Worse, a woman's world.

Meliu's voice came through the door as she knocked again. "Are you two in there?"

"Oh by the gods—"

Kinesee laughed and whispered in his ear. "I invited her."

Kinesee bounced to the door and opened it. The two women hugged, leaving Ivin to stare and ponder whether things had gotten better, worse, or just godsdamned weirder. Either way, he found himself lacking breath.

Kinesee waved the sword in front of Meliu. "See what Ivin got me?" Not so long ago, Ivin would've been worried his bride would strike her with that blade.

"I do. I see it. Lovely. Lovelier in its sheath."

Meliu wore the robes of a high priestess, suggesting this was a formal visit, which would be far better than watching these women sit and discuss *him*. "Meliu. This is a surprise."

"For me as well. But there are things to talk about."

Ivin swept the dice from the table and stashed them in his pocket. "What do you wish to discuss?"

Kinesee took a seat at the table and Ivin followed her lead, but Meliu sat on a cushioned stool as far away from them as she could.

"I kept a secret from you. More than one, and seeing as I'll be traveling south... I should say these things and be done with them. Lord Priest Ulrikt sent me to find a place called Tomarok."

Ivin's heart chugged in his chest, and a spasm kinked his neck. "What the hells are you talking about? When?"

"Before I left Kaludor. The scroll he gave me, when read beneath the stars of Skywatch, told me to seek Tomarok."

"What, where?"

"Somewhere south of the Dragonspans. It's where king priests were crowned in the Age of God Wars."

His fingernails dug at the table, and he was happy for the thick lacquer lest he leave scratches. "Are you shittin' me? King priests!"

Kinesee's hand touched his. "Let her talk."

He nodded and took her hand in his. "Go on."

"The reason the Ironwing is sending twice the men you requested is that a group he calls the Dark Waters Cult is also interested in Tômôrôk, but if he knows why he isn't saying."

Ivin breathed deep, his thumb caressing Kinesee's hand. "Morik spoke of the cult. They seek to awaken some slumbering god... at Tômôrôk?"

"Hells if I know. But there's more. And worse."

"Please, every word you speak makes the rest of my day seem like sun and glory."

Her head bowed to stare at her toes, and he prepared for something horrible. "Lord Priest Ulrikt didn't give me the *Codex of Sol* until I was already in Inster... or at least, someone who looked like him. He—"

"Whoa! Stop there." Ivin clenched Kinesee's hand; he loosened his grip at her squeal. "Sorry. But you! What the forges are you talking about? Inster. Alive?"

"Well, he didn't give it to me dead! I know I should've told you. He made sure I went to save you in Bdein too."

"You needed that whoreson to tell you to come after me?"

"No! I would've... I was. I'm sorry, I know this is a surprise but listen to me. I don't know if it was Ulrikt."

Ivin's mouth wanted to explode in a string of incoherent curses to make his father proud, but he swallowed the fury. "How could you not know?"

"There's a legend in Istinjoln called the Lord Priest's Face. This person can change their appearance with prayer to look like anyone. A little like Lelishen did to look human, only... more perfect. A spy."

"An *assassin.*"

Meliu stared. "Could be. Could also be that Ulrikt has this ability himself, which I believe. Far as I can tell, he could look like anybody, man, woman, or child. That's why I gave you the necklaces, to know it was you."

Her eyes darted back and forth as if they wouldn't meet his gaze no matter how hard she tried. "What else?"

"I think Ulrikt was heating the war between the Malstefnê and the other Tek nations to keep us safe. The head they delivered the other day might've been his."

She was about to continue, but he held up a finger for silence, giving himself a wick to think and relax the knots in his shoulders. "So a man who may or may not be Lord Priest Ulrikt sent you to find a place where king priests were crowned, and oh yes! it might also house some slumbering god... and this same man who may or may not be Lord Priest Ulrikt who may or may not be dead... again, and he may or may not be wandering around wearing any godsdamned face he pleases?" He looked to Kinesee. "How much of this did you know?"

A nervous grin. "None of that, none at all."

"She only learned of Tomarok when we discussed it in Molikîn."

He wanted to be furious, to throw the woman from the room with a curse, but beneath the anger and frustration, a niggling worm squirmed with curiosity. *A man who could appear as anyone could go anywhere and kill anyone. Including me.* He glanced at Kinesee then set a hard stare on the priestess.

"It's fine, Meliu. Some secrets are harder to tell than others, and I appreciate the truth." Ivin let go of Kinesee and slipped his hand into his pocket to grab the dice. With his left hand, he grabbed a chair and slung it to sit in front of the table. "Come. Sit. I have a secret as well."

Meliu stood, walked his way with sheepish steps, and sat without meeting his eye.

"I have this secret—"he pushed the dice into her hand"—but I'll only tell if you roll the four-eyed snake."

Twenty-One

Mother Secrets

Beneath the pale sliver known as the Saddle Moon, the Kings of Setemekon convened to decide the fate of the treasonous survivor of the Battle of Mehedî. Refdel-ô argued for his head while the remaining nine kings spoke of mercy and banishment. So Takuhôtu the Blooded-Hand walked free into the Damned Lands only to return and take ten crowns for himself. Neither being wrong and merciful nor right and bloodthirsty, kept a kingly head on its shoulders.

—*Ôxêum Codex*

The *Isebulî* was an Edan ship, slender and long, with a single mast and three sails. It wasn't built for war or hauling cargo; speed was its sole mission. The vessel was forty feet long and split the waves like nothing Glimdrem had ever imagined, faster even than the *Entiyu Emoñyo* under the influence of Luxun Elemental powers. But it wasn't just the boat making the *Isebulî* fast.

The captain was an Edan current-tamer by the name of Nezeldun, which meant the ship slipped through waters as if downhill on a greased slide. Other than this lone Edan, seven Trelelunin crewed the ship, and they carried another dozen warriors along with Inslok and Limereu.

Three Edan were leaving the Eleris, and Glimdrem was a witness, but the impossible was becoming stale bread these days.

They arrived at Herald's Watch in a week at full sail, a mind-numbing speed. They dropped anchor and admired the roiling, steaming sea and the tower of Fire. Limereu's personality since returning from the Father Wood had shifted toward wooden, but she didn't hide her awe of the raging Fire.

"What force brought this into existence?"

Glimdrem didn't resist the temptation. "A young priestess."

Inslok didn't allow the answer to stand. "And an artifact called the Sliver of Star."

"Yes, I have ears to hear the stories. But what is the Sliver of Star?"

"The Edan libraries hold no known explanation."

Glimdrem added, "The trouble is that the name describes its appearance more so than providing clues of its origin. A thin crescent of energy. According to the Choerkin, the priestess was in Istinjoln and summoned its energies, but released them for fear it would consume the entire island of Kaludor."

Limereu glanced at him. "Was she right?"

"I would not say she was wrong. The energies here have not faded since the first time we passed."

The Edan stared at the Fire enveloped island until Glimdrem grew distracted, his eyes trailing out to sea.

Limereu sucked her breath. "There's something in the Fire. There." She pointed high above the cloud of steam.

Glimdrem stared, but all he saw was Fire. "Where?"

Limereu trained her eyes on the Fire, but the puzzled creases in her face spoke to her mind tumbling for an explanation. "It's gone. It was like a disembodied wing in the flames."

The Edan stared into the tower's inferno until dawn the next day, leaving Glimdrem to curse the patience these people possessed. Come morning, they raised anchor and departed without catching sight of anything in the Fire a second time.

They arrived at Choerkin Fost in the late afternoon of the same day, and instead of sneaking off to the side of the city, they sailed straight to a dock and disembarked. Edan and Trelunin alike geared for battle, slipping into lamellar armor and taking up shields to complement their arms. Glimdrem figured he looked enough like a warrior to impress a fool, but he wasn't fooling himself.

The *Isebulî* clunked the dock, a rope flipped over a post, and Nezeldun cinched the tether tight to keep them steady against the lapping waves. The Edan hopped to the pier without effort or sound, and the Trelelunin warriors followed, albeit without the grace. Glimdrem stared, then eased himself over the edge; he reached the planks with the silence of the Edan even if without the grace, and he smiled even if no one else understood his act of nonconformity. It wasn't as if anyone bothered to look at him, what, with a couple dozen Taken standing at the end of the dock.

He wasn't certain if Taken were capable of confusion, or if their facial expressions could even display such an emotion, but it seemed a reasonable interpretation as the possessed stood watching them from the wharf instead of attacking. He thought he saw Shadows hiding in dark places between buildings, but they were harmless.

Inslok turned to the ship. "Drop anchor in the harbor and wait for us. If it rains, feel free to hunt for fresh meat."

A warrior cast the ship off, and Nezeldun waved his hand; the *Isebulî* glided into the bay as if carried by a gentle breeze, but she was barepoled. As soon as it floated twenty strides away, Inslok strode toward the wharf with Limereu and Nezeldun at his sides. Inslok carried his Latcu scimitar while the other Edan wielded Ikoruv-bladed arming swords and shields. The Trelelunin warriors formed two six-abreast lines behind them with pikes and shields, and Glimdrem was more than content to follow them all. He was none too eager to demonstrate his meager skills in combat.

The Taken charged, and Glimdrem's heart sped. The creatures loped their way with bestial speed, their mangled bodies horrifying. Taken ducked, Taken leaped, Taken ran head-on, but in every crack and crevice was an Ikoruv pike to gore them, with steel bars along the hafts keeping them from rushing down the length of the weapon, much like a boar-hunting spear. Held at bay in this fashion, they were flailing target dummies for Edan blades. Taken were hewn and tossed into the waves of the bay, and in under a wick, the dock was clear of everything but their entrails and black blood.

Glimdrem sheathed his sword and slipped his shield over his shoulder without a spatter of gore on his clothes. "I see you gave the Taken thought since last time we were here."

"I did." Inslok stepped through the black-blooded mess, and as the Edan reached clean dock, Glimdrem realized that Inslok didn't leave blood-marked prints while the other Edan left faint traces.

Does he tread so light, or is it the boots? But he didn't voice the question lest he seem like a fool.

They reached the wharf, and Inslok paused to stare at Shadows skulking across the waterfront. "Nezeldun, send the Queen-Mother a message."

The Edan current-tamer nodded once before sheathing his sword. He stood stone still for a flicker then swiped his hand at the city streets; a sheet of rain slashed through the air as if carried by gale winds and slammed the waterfront. Shrieking Shadows shredded into vaporous wisps, and for the first time, Glimdrem understood why a current-tamer stepped from the boat.

"A message? You think the creature inside the Celestial Gate knows when her Shadows are killed?"

"Zwinfolkum knows."

Glimdrem froze his expression but had a feeling he was standing on the outside looking in. "You know more than you've told me."

Inslok turned, and instead of the expressionless gaze he'd come to expect, the Edan smirked. "We all have our secrets, don't we?"

"I suppose we do." He took a step, hoping to end this conversation before it turned more unpleasant.

"I know your secret, Limereu knows your secret, the Chancellor of Knowledge knows your secret, and no doubt the Volvrolan knows your secret. The question is, do you wish to share your secret with everyone else?"

Glimdrem swallowed hard, wondering if this journey was one he wasn't meant to return from. "So why am I here?"

"You lost the faith of the Volvrolan, and despite failing the Chancellor's first offer of redemption, she has given you a second chance. Perform well and all is forgiven."

First chance? He should have admitted to copying the Oxeum Codex. Or was it some other secret? "You said, Queen Mother."

The smirk disappeared into emotionless stone as he turned to walk. "Zwinfolkum was once mortal, a human. A queen. She was captured by a people known as the Dontopuor and their gods and priests twisted her, corrupted her... there is not a word for what they did to her. Her children were the Shadows of Man, demons capable of possessing only those related to their Queen Mother. Humans."

"How do you know this? The Chancellor couldn't have found this in the Oxeum Codex so quickly."

Limereu cast him an iron glance. "You will forgive us for not revealing the name of the book to one deemed untrustworthy."

"And yet here I am. But how do you know the Queen Mother knows?"

Inslok glanced at the Taken on the roofs and in the streets. "Do you see a Shadow?"

Glimdrem grunted, disgusted with himself. "But how did you know before?"

"It is believed that Zwinfolkum retains what you might call a spiritual umbilical cord with all her children. The tomes speak of a group awareness the Shadows share, it's weakened once the Shadow takes a body, but it's still there."

"What message were you trying to send?"

"An unfriendly hello." They reached the western gate and walked into open ground. He sheathed his sword. "When you are curious enough to admit your secret, I will tell you more. But now, we run."

Inslok slid into a jog that didn't leave a print in the snow, and the others followed him. Without humans along this time, travel wouldn't be a casual walk. The energy of Elemental Life flowed around him, no doubt a gift from one of the Edan, and Glimdrem kept pace without growing tired. They ate while they ran, they drank while they ran, and the only excuse not to run was to relieve themselves. They ran through the dark of night, through the next day, and through the dark again until they arrived at Istinjoln just past midday, a pace faster than any horse could have carried them without dying. If not for Edan magic, he too would have collapsed a day before, but instead, he stood on a high hill overlooking the road to Istinjoln.

Fresh snow covered the monastery, making the wandering Shadows and Taken stand out, but the Celestial Gate still rising into the sky drew everyone's eyes.

Limereu inhaled deep. "The Celestial Gate feels so familiar, like it's tugging a memory long lost."

Inslok said, "You were renowned for your way with infused gems in the art of defeating Xê and dark celestials. Over the ages, you likely saw numerous gates."

"It's spectacular."

Glimdrem scoffed. "It's demonic."

"Still beautiful."

Glimdrem refused to agree. "If it's so beautiful, what are we waiting for? Let's go inside Istinjoln and admire its wonder."

Inslok said, "Not yet."

Glimdrem shifted his weight and rubbed his face. Elemental Life got him this far, but he'd welcome a rest. "We wait for the Silone then."

"I doubt they're close to Istinjoln just yet. The one called Wolverine has a clever plan, but it will be some days or weeks before they arrive."

Glimdrem closed his eyes and stilled the beat of his aggravated heart. "Quit dancing around whatever it is, why are we here?"

Nezeldun said, "So that Limereu and I could see the Celestial Gate."

"Oh! Why, I'm so glad it was important." Somehow he didn't think the Edan got his sarcasm, and the Trelelunin warriors kept their faces blank.

Inslok said, "Now we run."

They ran, and Glimdrem swore the pace was faster, probably just to irritate him. "Where are we going?"

"You know where we're going."

Their route turned west along a road, and he recalled their last journey to Istinjoln, coming in from the north over the Oemindi Pass. Once the realization clicked, he was eager for the run, even if for no other reason than to listen to a skeleton insult an Edan again. "The Tomb of the Touched."

"Indeed."

Twenty-Two

Click Stick

Old king, new king, or old queen, new queen. The number of people who care can be counted by counting the heads of the noble and wealthy, for the common cares not a wit which one takes their crops to feed their horses.

—*Oxeum Codex, quoting Nebederth of Vulêz*

Ivin stepped to Alu's side as she stood with hands to knees, panting and nursing the latest strike to her ego. He shoved Nander from her side. "What the hells are you doing?"

Her answer came between gasps. "Sparring."

"And what spirit from the Forges prevents you from hitting him?"

"None! He's bigger. Stronger."

Ivin glanced at Mondlin Ulthar, a distant cousin of the Mulharths. He was over six feet tall and lean, muscled as a man who'd hewed thousands of cords of wood in his short life, but he relied on his reach and power more than he should. He pointed. "That there man talking to Mondlin trains the Mulharth boys; you know what he's saying right now? He's telling that man to forget who your husband is, forget your sister and who she's married to, and forget that the Warlord Choerkin is talking to you right now, and when he finishes his spiel, he's going to tell him to hit you and hit you hard. Sure as shits, he's got a foot's reach on you and can lift you above his head; you'll never be bigger, you'll never be stronger, you'll never weigh more, but if you step out there and hit him in the head, ring that steel cap like a bell, he and every godsdamned man here will respect you."

"Nander said not to go for the helm."

"Piss on Nander, that's a rule they made up in pity for you."

"In the head?"

"Straight to the face if he hands it to you."

She grinned and pulled her helm back over sweat-drenched hair. "You're the warlord."

A warm easterly wind blew across the top of the wall this afternoon, and there was no way to hide from the sun. Ivin wore a broad-rimmed hat to shade his eyes and long sleeves to keep himself from turning red as an ingot at the forge ready for the hammer, but whether the sweat drenching his shirt was from heat or nerves, he couldn't say. A Tek army marched in the valley below and grew closer by the candle. He guessed the mass of black crawling their way numbered thirty thousand men.

"Warlord Choerkin!"

The voice caught him off guard, and he turned even as wasters clacked, and Alu grunted with effort. "Morik, what brings you to our little war?"

"We got ourselves a problem."

Ivin ducked his head with a sigh then turned back to the friendly fight. Alu ducked under an overhead blow and shoved Mondlin in the back, but he was too big of a boy to push around. He spun and swung, but she caught his blade with the flat of her waster to redirect it over her head; he lunged to put an elbow into her chest, and Alu twisted, this time getting her leg scissored between his. Mondlin took one awkward step before the *clang* of her sword rattled his skull. Alu bounced away on the balls of her feet and kept her guard despite the fight being over.

Men roared, and Mondlin took a knee, pulling off his helm. "Shits, my ears are ringin'." He held out his hand to Alu, and when she took it to pull him to his feet, he said, "If you weren't married, I'd be proposing."

Alu thumped the man's chest with her mailed fist. "I'd say no."

More laughter and cheers.

Morik said, "You married the safer daughter."

"I gave Kinesee her gift the other day."

"A fine sword. Well, at least you have a couple of years before Kinesee's as dangerous as Alu."

Ivin strolled to lean against the parapet before eyeballing Morik. "So, what's this problem? I already got an army of Tek close enough I'll be able to pick out faces soon."

"We've got a second army that needs through."

Ivin's mind flashed first to Tek Malôbund, but the truth registered in a flicker. "The Tûrûrôt?"

"Yes, *Rûîrn* Frâbor Silverwheel has two thousand men ready to pass into the south."

"There isn't another route?"

"I reckon so, but he'll lose a week at least, more for a safer path. It's all goat trails leading into the Rôemhîen Pass from the west; any better route would mean a lot of backtracking."

Ivin noticed Alu standing beside him, and he smiled at her before speaking further. "So what's Frâbor thinking?"

"Tûrûrôt isn't at war with the Malstefnê, so he entreated for safe passage, and the Malstefnê leader has granted an audience."

Alu smirked. "There's an 'and' coming, I wager."

"Oh aye, a hells of a demand. He wants to talk to the Warlord Choerkin."

Ivin snorted. "Don't think I trust a Malstefnê."

Alu shrugged. "Send someone else. They don't know your face."

Morik said, "I'd say you make it an honest meeting or don't meet at all."

Ivin cast his gaze into the valley and on the black mass of men below. "I'll meet with them. Meeting the enemy eye to eye is the best way to gauge their worth."

They agreed to meet a half-horizon from the gates of Rôemhîik Wall that evening. Ivin rode with five Silone, and Morik brought five of his men with loaded arbalests on their backs. *Rûîrn* Frâbor arrived wicks after them with a dozen men covered in plates of steel and mail. He straddled a buckskin stallion whose coat shimmered as if rubbed down with wax, and he wore a blued steel breastplate filigreed with golden griffons. A gray beard stuck from beneath the face of his helm until he raised the visor to reveal a face wrinkled and leathery, his eyes all but hidden by his squint.

Frâbor snorted at them. "Gentlemen, you trust these northerners more than I do."

Morik rode close to the man and leaned in his saddle as he took the man's forearm in greeting. "I trust riding faster than you." The newcomer guffawed. "*Rûîrn* Frâbor Silverwheel, I present to you Ivin Choerkin, Warlord of the Silone people."

"A whelp barely off the mother's teat, aren't you? Unless you're woodkin, then you might be older than the trees. You woodkin, boy?"

Ivin grinned. "No, sir."

"Good. I heard you got married, a shame, I've a fine daughter—"

Morik said, "And a beautiful bride at that."

"So I hear. I also heard the Tek tried to kill her. Should they succeed next time, keep my girl in mind, the marriage would bring our people close."

Ivin wasn't sure if the man was serious or if he toyed with him. "I'll remember that if the unthinkable should happen."

The man grunted and pointed north. "Would you get a gander of that?"

A lone horseman on a rhone approached at a canter.

Morik said, "I think we're being insulted."

A yellow cape fluttered behind the Malstefnê, and he wore a cream-white silk shirt with matching pants and a bright red sash around his waist. A trimmed mustache sat on his lip, and his sideburns reached to his jaw, but they framed his face with razor-perfect lines. Ivin recalled the first time he'd seen a skunk as a boy on Kaludor. He'd asked Kotin why such a small critter walked in the open, and his father had said, "An animal who walks bold and alone knows it has little to fear."

Ivin said, "It's not an insult; it's a statement."

The Malstefnê reined in strides from their group, horse puffing from the ride; his smile was broad and his teeth white but crooked. He spoke in Kingdomer. "Frâbor of the Tûrûrôt. Morik of the Helmveline. And you must be the Choerkin. I am Ôlisbenar the Razer, Scepter of the King of the Malstefnê, Spear of the Fourth River, Partisan of the Night Sky, and Crown of the mighty city of Qwôhar."

Frâbor grunted and spat before answering. "I've plenty of names myself when of a mind to waste people's time. I'll be leading my men through yonder gates and want to make sure you aren't thinking of stepping in my path."

"I fear I must. If you intend to fight beside these northern dogs, then you may as well die here and now instead of later."

Ivin said, "They are passing through and moving south; this isn't their fight."

The man picked at his teeth with a finger as he observed them. Ivin had no idea what the gesture meant, but whatever the intent, it was intentional. "It *shouldn't* be their fight, yet here they are."

Morik said, "Helmveline has met an enemy in the south and has asked for aid from the Tûrôrôt. It is to the deep south that they travel."

"I know nothing of enemies nor the south, all I know is you seek to ride into my enemy's den. Prove to me that you do not fight with these dogs, and I will let you pass."

Frâbor's squint widened to reveal iron-gray eyes. "How would I prove such a thing?"

The Malstefnê scratched his head in theatrical fashion. "Did you bring children as hostages? I know you Kingdomers value your children. No? Then you see my problem. There is no way to prove this except to turn and leave."

"If we march and you attack, it will incur the wrath of all Eight Kingdoms."

Ôlisbenar laughed. "You mistake me for a weakling, a Malôbund. By the time the Eight Kingdoms would gather, this war will be over. Men's lives and supplies are expensive; I don't plan on being here long. Would your peoples ride through Malôbund and Loenfarar to reach me? What of their allies who would ride to their defense? Commanders as far away as Bdein speak of your reputation as a commander, so you aren't so foolish as to believe your words a threat."

Morik shook his head. "This wall will not fall in a fortnight nor months to come. Maybe never."

"Maybe yes. Maybe no. Who here speaks for the gods and the future they ordain?"

Ivin said, "There must be something we can offer."

"Your head?"

"If it would save my people."

"This youngster is bold and full of honor." Ôlisbenar smirked. "You are a sly leader, but not even your head will suffice. My people have a saying, 'Give a Kingdomer a fortress and your world will break before theirs.' The only way they pass your gates is if they earn their path through my cavalry." He looked at Frâbor. "My apologies for wasting your time, but I desired to meet the Warlord before I kill him."

Frâbor's eyes narrowed. "Never count skins by the number of traps you've set."

The Malstefnê stroked his mustache. "Good advice. I never take an enemy's defeat for granted." He turned back to Ivin. "Soon, I will carry your slippery head and present it to my king." He reined his horse through a full circle and smiled at Ivin. "They say that a sly man is slippery, but wise men also say a warrior's blood is slipperier than his sweat, and that a king's sweat is more slippery than his blood. Which are you, Choerkin?" He reined his horse into a turn and walked thirty strides with his back to them to show his lack of fear before breaking into a gallop.

Ivin looked to the Kingdomer commanders. "What the Earls was that?"

Morik scratched above his ear, snorted, then spat. "You might need the wits of the Five Earls to figure it out."

"I've had experience with cryptic talkers."

"Horseshit, if you ask me."

"No, he was saying there's a way out of this situation. If a man called the Touched spoke those words, I'd know it for sure."

Frâbor said, "Giving you hope for peace is a distraction. While you ponder falsehoods, he plots your defeat. Ignore it."

"I suspect you're right." Ivin stretched in his saddle then leaned back to puff a breath at the sky. "What do we know and what do we think?"

Frâbor said, "What I think, I know. If he attacks, that army will slaughter us."

"But will he? It's a risk to kill you."

"My king sent me to ride south, not to start a war. As much as I'd like to ride that preening bird down and strip his tail feathers, I'd need orders and a bigger army."

Morik nodded. "The Ironwing, too, has done what he can, built you a wall, it's up to you to hold it."

Ivin patted Nameless' neck. "I thank you men for what you've done. We'll hold this wall and gods willing kill that bastard. I would never ask you risk your men for such a thin hope."

"My Wayfinder will get me to the south by some route or another, goat trail or no. I will help the both of you the best I'm able."

Ivin bowed his head in respect. "Find those people and save them." Hope rested in the Malstefnê being weakened by years of war with the Malôbund, and if they still proved too strong, hope turned its eyes to his young bride. "And maybe Kinesee will have good news from the Helelindin."

Twenty-Three

Fresh Flesh

Why does the Unfettered Liar ask of the Dame of Fire?
What use have you for truth or truths,
the soothsayer to soothe,
the Happy Harpy's blood in the groove,
move and move to suck the udder utterly dry,
milk blinding the Eternal Eye tight,
shadow painting the Ephemeral Lie loose.

—*Tomes of the Touched*

"What am I missing?" Wandering around the island talking to herself was becoming a bad habit. Oh, it started out logical in its innocence; how better to attract some disappearing old woman than to walk the streets like the first and only time she'd seen the woman? Asking questions to the air, it seemed, might catch her curiosity. It was when she started answering her own questions that she first worried, but by now she knew everybody thought her batty.

"There's something in that shrine isn't there? Yes, and you've been there a dozen times. Same with the stars. You may as well lay down in the garden, grow old, and die. That would be foolish, and it probably wouldn't even work. Best I can tell, I don't age even when I'm in the garden."

She wasn't far from the garden, and though she wasn't hungry, she wasn't full either. She arrived to find the gate locked, an attempt by some folks to keep the free-eaters out. Free-eaters pretty much referred to every adherent in Skywatch. Every one of them was a priest and every one of them deemed working with their hands beneath them, unless the work was picking a fruit or vegetable and eating it. If they even bothered to cook a thing, they hid it.

She unlocked the gate and strolled into the grape rows first, plucked a couple and popped them into her mouth. A tad tart but approaching ripe. With several harvests per year, they'd be able to start bathing in wine soon enough, or simply eat more, which would be far more practical. She turned toward the strawberries, but a voice caught her ear.

She saw no one, and her first thought turned to the disappearing woman. Her second turned to garden thieves and free-eaters.

A grunt and a groan, but it sounded like two people. She hunched and skulked in her best sneak pose, taking a guess at the direction of the sound by heading for the tomato patch... which made no sense, they were green and a couple of weeks from edible. Soft breaths caught her ear and she leaped around the corner of a row expecting to stir up priests hiding from her with robes full of veggies.

What she got was Jinbin's bare ass and an eyeful of Deleu beneath him. The girl screamed, Jinbin screamed, and they both scrambled for clothes.

"What in the names of the Seven Heavens are you doing?"

Deleu clutched her dress to her bosom and ran, but the monk was feistier. He cinched his pants and glared. "What the hells are you doing here? The tomatoes are green!"

"Well, that poor girl's face was red enough. If this is how you guard against free-eaters I think we should unlock the gates again."

Jinbin scowled. He was one of the loudest voices condemning people who took food without taking a share of labor. "Deleu and I are in love."

"In case you haven't noticed, there are about a thousand empty buildings in this city, a whole lot of them with beds. If her father had caught you, he might well have killed you."

His shoulders slouched and he stared at the dirt. "She wants children."

It took several flickers for that to sink in. Nothing aged nor grew outside the garden, so they came here to conceive. Once the shock wore off her fury lost its humored edge. "Are you mad?"

"What? What would her father do? Really."

"Are you daft? This garden isn't the normal world... The Elemental energies here... And what was she going to do? Live in here while the child grows within her? We have no idea, none, of what the energies in this garden would do to a baby, let alone outside the garden."

"I... We—"

"The baby might not even grow outside the garden, inside it might twist into some monster! We have no idea."

"Or it could be a healthy, happy little person."

"Maybe. Either way, Deleu would age. And the baby, what? Would you all live in the garden until it's a teenager?"

"We could build a little house."

She stomped her foot. "Are you hearing yourself?"

"Why not?"

"Jinbin! Jinbin! Jinbin!" Deleu's scream sent both of them running. Eliles kicked off her sandals to better keep up with the monk, then she ran smack into his back on rounding a wall of vining green beans. Deleu stood over Wilu. The woman lay crumpled like a bug curled to hide or die, but her pallor and staring eyes left no doubt she was dead.

Jinbin grabbed Deleu and pulled the trembling girl away.

Eliles caught her breath, recovering from the shock before she kneeled and sighed. "Did you see anything? Anything at all?"

"I was over there getting dressed and then I just rounded this corner... No, I didn't see anyone."

It had been a stupid question; judging by the pool of blood she'd been dead a while, but how long was impossible to guess. Time existed in the garden, but the fact fruits were slow to rot suggested time's effects were uncertain. And the gate was locked when she arrived, Wilu always left it open when she visited.

"You two, go find her boys... and send Artus. Send Artus first." She didn't want to deal with Wilu's sons on her own.

Jinbin said, "We will... We never heard, saw anything when we were here. Just so you know."

She waved them away, staring. "Oh, Wilu. So much death; you didn't deserve this."

She glanced at the dirt around the body, the loose soil, pebbles, and sand. The only footprints looked to be Deleu's and Jinbin's, but they might've covered the killer's marks. A wooden handle stood at the end of the row, a rake, and when she looked again, she noted the sweeping scratches of tines in the dirt. She wanted to poke around, move things, but instead she relaxed the best she could and waited the wicks for Artus to arrive.

"Shittin' hells, I couldn't hardly believe it when Jinbin told me."

"I'm still having trouble wrapping my wits around it."

"She told folks she'd kill a free-eater one of these days. Maybe she caught someone?"

"She was angry and said something stupid. She wouldn't have killed no one."

"I dunno, you may be right, but the woman had a temper. If she flared a fury at the wrong person..."

"Who the hells would kill over vegetables?"

"A hungry person."

"Exactly. There isn't a soul going hungry on this island."

"Which brings us back to a spat over free-eaters."

"Do you imagine a priest so hot-headed as to kill her?"

"They're lazy, entitled rots, but no. Not unless she hit them or somethin'."

She pointed at the rake standing at the end of the row and the scratches in the dirt. "If the pieces fit together, we have a murderer calm and collected enough to kill and erase their tracks, then comfortable enough to put the tool back where it belongs."

"There's no way to know that for sure."

"See any of the neighboring rows freshly raked?"

"You know I don't." He stepped to Wilu's body and kneeled, lifted her hands to reveal dry, black blood on her fingers and palms. He felt her clothes and spread a hole. "Stab wound, I'd wager. It probably weren't a quick way to die. She could've run for help; why didn't she run for help?"

"Why's she dead at all?" She looked for anything unusual but saw nothing out of sorts until looking to Wilu's waist. A loop hung from her belt where she carried the key to the garden, but there was no key. "Her key is missing."

Artus snorted. "It's gotta be here somewheres; who the hells would steal a key when you can climb over the fence?"

The suggestion came like a whisper between her ears. "Where in the world did Wilu get the key to the garden gate? One day she just had it."

Artus folded the woman's hands. "Hells if I know."

Jinbin's voice came from behind them, startling her. "She found a key in the kitchens to open the salt room."

Artus grunted. "No. No. It wouldn't be the same key."

Jinbin shrugged and he voiced what was creeping into her brain. "Would it be so unusual? Wouldn't the cooks need to visit the gardens?"

She looked to Artus. "Don't tell me you weren't filching food from the kitchens in your day."

"Oh aye, I filched a serving lass as well. Beautiful, but she done broke my heart after her pa pert near split my head. But keys? I guess I dunno, could be."

Reinus stormed down the row, dropped to his knees, lifted his mother by the shoulders; his eyes clenched and tears flowed into his beard. "I'm gonna lynch me a free-eater for this."

Artus said, "Easy, lad. Which one of the sons of bitches do you suspect?"

"She and Niktir were having it out two days past."

It didn't jibe for Eliles; Niktir was a thorn more painful than most, but murder? "When was the last time you saw her?"

"That was it, the last time."

"Oh my, Wilu?" Temeru's voice.

Eliles turned to the High Oracle. "How did you hear?"

"I didn't, I was coming to speak with Wilu about Niktir and saw Reinus running."

Reinus glared at the priestess. "Your man Niktir, he did this."

"I assure you, if he did, I will scald the skin from his meat. But I came here hoping to settle their dispute."

"He seems to have settled it for you."

Eliles stood. "Enough. When we find who did this, they'll pay. Reinus, take care of your mother. Jinbin, you help him and his brothers with anything they need."

Jinbin nodded. "You can count on me."

"Good. Artus and I need to take a walk; Temeru, join us."

They strode toward the gate and the oracle's voice came huffy behind her. "I'm not one of your people to command."

Eliles stopped in stride and spun. "If I find one of your people did this, you won't need to scald them. Don't stand in my way; don't dare test me."

Temeru snorted with a smile. "There she is, the little queen of the island flexing her powers."

"I'm no queen, I'd rather folks left me alone, but I'll ask this one thing of you... for now. Wilu's key."

The woman flinched. "A key? You think this about a key?"

"The temple picked fresh foods from the garden same as the keep. The cook there, did she have a key to the garden?"

"Yes, of course. But it wasn't the master key, it wouldn't get them into the keep and its stores."

She glanced to Artus, who shrugged, then back. "A master key?"

"The key from the temple opened most doors there including the kitchens and the garden, but I imagine the Choerkin kept a skeleton key that opened them all." A chilling wave swept through Eliles and she strove to recall her conversation with the Touched. "I said something?"

"No, it's just that Wilu's garden key is missing."

"And you think it's the master key?"

Artus rumbled, cleared his throat. "What the hells would they be lookin' to unlock? I ain't seen a damned door we haven't knocked in if it didn't open."

"Well, nobody killed the woman over green beans, I guarantee that. Temeru, you should have Niktir stay scarce for a time." She turned and glanced back to the gate where Barold and Kavlin ran through the entry. "But don't go easy on him; if he has answers we need them."

The woman gave a smile that made fewer promises than her words. "I'll see what I can find out."

"Artus, you and I need to talk to Seden. She might know about keys."

She turned and strode downhill with long strides hasty enough to make Artus jog to catch up. "What the hells would Seden know about keys?"

"She's been on this island most or all her life and I've no doubt she dealt with the gardens." She waited until they rounded a corner far enough away that she figured a prayer for hearing wouldn't catch her whisper. "We're agreed that a skeleton key might be more worthy of killing than beans?"

"I'm a gullible fish; I'll take yer hook."

"Two murders on the island. What do they have in common? The boy was buried in salt so no one could tell when he died. The killer stabbed Wilu in the garden. We don't age outside the garden, but only in the garden is decay of dead things delayed."

"That there's something I hadn't given thought to."

"Most folks wouldn't know this quirk in the Elemental energies. I do. Wilu probably noticed, her being in and out of the garden most often, and her boys. Jinbin. Seden maybe."

"The holies?"

"They might've figured it out or guessed it." Her thoughts flipped to the Touched. "Skeleton key. Skeleton. Key."

"I ain't followin' your thinkin'."

"When I spoke to the Touched in the stars, I asked him about the Snakebite Skeleton and in his ramble he mentioned keys: 'in particular pitches and particular keys to play'."

"He's talking about music."

"If ever you're lucky or unlucky enough to meet the Touched, never take a single word he says at face value. The talk of music was disjointed from the rest of the conversation, it always felt out of place, but I didn't know what to look for or why. A skeleton and a key, there's one skeleton on the island, at least most of the time."

"The shrine? I think you're stretching for answers, but I'm the fool fish who took the hook. Lead on."

They took the usual route to the Salty Frog but then wove down to the docks and hopped on the trail toward the shrine. They found the entrance covered in brambles, and in the brush, a rag tied to a stick right where they'd left it.

She took a deep breath and dropped to the tunnel's floor before calling Fire to light their way. The tiny flicker arrived in an instant, giving comfort with its light.

They followed the gentle twists of the tunnel and reached the holy chamber. The glowing garnets ringing the wall, the sand-glass shaped shrine, and the fused skeletal bones in their pose. "Artus Choerkin, I'd like you to meet Elimwoth."

"That's the poor bastard's name?"

She followed the rounded walls of the room with her response on her tongue, but a silvery glint in the skeleton's mouth caught her eye. Two steps to kneel. A key sat clamped in the skeleton's bite.

"Holy hells." She plucked the key from the teeth. "Look for a keyhole. No. Don't bother." She stood and crouched behind Elimwoth but he stared straight at the middle of the shrine's dais. Beyond were glowing garnets, but she didn't see a hole. "Check the stones in the wall, where the skeleton would be staring if the shrine wasn't here. If not, then everywhere on the wall in that area."

"You tellin' me that because there's some curse or trap?"

"You are who you are, how could a curse best that?"

"You are a funny lass, ha ha."

"You should take note of that laughter." He stared at her. "Never mind, just check the stones."

Artus took a gander at the skeleton's gaze and followed it to a stone, gave it a twist. "Do I get to keep every one I can dig out?"

"If you can find a place to spend them."

He laughed and gave a tug and twist to another stone. It lifted from its setting with a grind of grit and he leaned into its glow. "That was so obvious I shoulda thought of it."

"It's only obvious and useful if you have a key." She strode to his side and stuck the key in the hole, turned the lock. The tumbler rolled, but something somewhere clunked.

"What the hells did we just open?"

"I don't know. Think like a sneaky priest."

He groaned to his feet. "I wouldn't put nothin' in the skeleton, so..." He gave the dais a shove and it pivoted from atop a dark, empty hole. "Well, so much fer my dreams of diamonds and gold and a damned old bottle of the finest whiskey."

"What was here worth killing for?"

"Diamonds, gold, and whiskey? But aside from whiskey not a one of those is worth the kiss from a fish's lips here on Herald's Watch."

"The killer had to be from the stars, but who? It doesn't make sense. If Meris were alive, I could believe her knowing, but most of the elders of Skywatch left the island."

"Someone stumbled onto something?"

"Or someone we don't know about is in the stars. And we're being played. They knew we'd find the body, they left the empty key loop, and sooner or later they knew we'd be back here."

"Right. So why bother making sure the body is in the garden, why would they care to hide when she died?"

Eliles couldn't believe she was going to say it aloud. "The Lord Priest's Face."

"That tale of Temeru's? You might as well slap shit on my back and call it wings."

"Think about it. Meliu and I saw Meris in Istinjoln, but Temeru and others saw her here. Joslin is dead, Joslin was there when Tokodin poisoned Kotin. The Face could've been Joslin for days. Weeks. Wilu..."

"Her body wouldn't have gone unfound for long, not there."

"Maybe she wasn't dead at all. Maybe he held her somewhere."

"Why?"

"I don't know. The Face is powerful. He didn't need to kill her to get that key. For some reason or another he needed to be her."

"Horseshit. One of those godsdamned priests killed her, took the key, and came here, and my money is on the same bitch who planted the idea of this cockamamie Lord Priest's Face."

His version of events was more believable, but it left unanswered questions. "You could be right, and Temeru did cast that seed of fear."

"Strike it to the Forges. Why the hells point us here either way?"

She stared at the empty hole in the ground. "To let us know they know more than we do. What's the fun of winning if your opponent doesn't know they lost?"

"Taunting us?" He scratched his beard. "Or is this an invitation to join the game?"

Both notions made sense. "You're a more clever man than you let on."

"Nah. My clever jest ain't about books or prayers, it's stayin' alive."

Three steps toward leaving and she turned to stare at the garnet lit room. "What if this wasn't the invitation? What if the body was the invitation?"

"Then I'd say we played the game well enough..." He studied her. "Except the game ain't over?"

"Step, step, step. We found the body, we realized the key was missing, a skeleton key, a secret lock, an empty container... What would be a great way to convince someone to stop looking?"

"To make them think they found it already."

"And in this case, we're hit twice because whatever the prize for winning was, it's gone." She returned to the skeleton and sat beside him, trying to level her eyes with his. "He's staring in line with the stones and that keyhole, but not at it. 'Some said he had such a lazy eye that he could stare at two things twice!' Check the next stone."

"That there is more wisdom from the skeleton in the stars?"

"He had flesh covering his bones this time, but yes."

"Usually I'm a person's strangest friend, but with you I ain't sure where I rank." He twisted the next stone and it popped out. "No keyhole. But they make perty eyes, aye?" He held them up to his face, the glow of the stones lending a creepy glow and shadows to his features.

"Quit goofin' around and stick them in the skull's sockets."

The stones fit Elimwoth's eyes but they did nothing but light up the bony face.

"Lazy eyes wander kinda like."

He fiddled with the stones, and she noticed a peculiar glow through the skull's teeth. She wiggled a finger inside and pried the jaw open. "It's hinged, most of the bones are fused. Stick the stones in his mouth."

He did and she clacked his teeth shut. Light shone through the eyes, strong enough to focus on a single spot on the wall. Eliles scrambled with the key in hand to a crack in the wall and after jamming it in three times it found a hole. She turned it clockwise and felt it catch and roll a tumbler, and something clacked near her knees.

For a flicker she feared a trap, but when she looked, her Fiery friend revealed a tiny nob of metal protruding from the stone. She took hold and lifted, and with a thought the Sliver of Star lent her strength. The stone broke free and she stared into a second hole, but this one wasn't empty.

"Forges be damned!" Artus laughed and whistled. "It ain't whiskey but it sure the hells is treasure."

The Fire illuminated a crown of gold with seven points, each tipped with a different precious jewel. She took a deep breath and lifted the crown, counting twelve sapphires for the Twelve Hells around the brim. "A crown of kings."

"The Silone ain't never had a king."

"No, but they once had king priests." All her doubt faded as she held the crown aloft; the Lord Priest's Face was real. But why did it lead her to a crown lost for more than five hundred years?

"Put it on! If you don't I will."

Artus laughed, but Eliles grimaced. She lowered the crown back in its hole. "No, we'll leave it here for the time being. Locked. Tell no one. Got it?"

"Gods, I woulda looked right handsome with a crown... but whatever you say. Super secret."

"From now on, anybody who wants this crown will have to kill me to get the key."

Twenty-Four

Slippery Thoughts

The Fairy Fox in the lion's den,
Whisker Tweaker,
hiked leg leaker,
territory marked and territory sparked.
A war. A treaty. A hare fat and meaty.
Be watchful of eating another's meal for them.

—*Tomes of the Touched*

The fox's coat was beautiful, a perfect red with streaks of black, but the animal laid on its side in the mud beside a gurgling creek with a steel trap clamping its leg. Ivin skidded down the creek's bank and approached with cautious steps. As he grew close, he crouched and held out his fingers for the creature to smell or bite. The animal neither sniffed nor gnashed its teeth, not even a snarl.

"Easy, Fox. I'll open the trap."

The fox's head cocked, and its tongue dangled from its mouth for a flicker before licking its nose. "Why should I trust a Choerkin?"

The notion of a fox speaking didn't shock him; Colok and Ilu could speak, so why not a fox? But the question knocked him off balance, or it was the mud sinking beneath his boot, and his fingers stuck in the mud to keep from falling. "Because I do not lie."

"Never? That seems peculiar; I lied to a hare just the other day so that I might eat her."

"That was rude."

"It was. But I was hungry."

"Will you bite me?"

"No."

"How do I know you aren't lying?"

"Because I'm not."

"And neither am I. Hold still." Ivin lifted the trap and pulled on its toothy mouth. "I don't think your leg is broke."

"I've the luck of that beaver I didn't get to eat yesterday before the hare. The beaver was a suspicious fellow. Safe from me today, but he might not be so lucky tomorrow."

Ivin strained and his muddy fingers slipped from the steel. He slapped and swiped his trousers to remove the mud the best he could. "You're obsessed with food, aren't you?"

"Foot first, food next. I could just chew my foot off like brother wolf." Fox glanced across the creek, and Ivin's eye followed.

A wolf with three feet stared at them. The beast was huge, the size of a small pony, and black as coal. "You didn't eat my foot, did you?"

Fox laughed. "No, I think the trapper wears it on his belt."

Ivin refocused on the trap, but its grip refused to budge. "Wolf is a warrior. No chewing your foot off today."

Fox reached out with a paw and touched his hand. In a blink and blur of tussling red fur, Ivin found himself on his side in the mud, small and breathing fast, his foot clamped in the trap at the ankle. No pain. Fox stood above him, free, a breeze ruffling his beautiful fur. "Help me, Fox."

"I can't help you, I'm a fox, not a man, and I am hungry." Fox shook his head. "Pressure makes a man sweat. Pressure confounds some men but brings out the best in others."

"Sweat is slippery."

"And so is blood. What is a warlord? A warrior or king?" Fox's feet planted, and he crouched to bolt, with his ears and eyes gazing across the stream.

Ivin expected to see Wolf but instead saw Iro Adinfin with his stubbed arm, and in his good hand he carried a sword. He hopped across the stream with a smile. "I told you I'd have my revenge. You and your people will die."

Ivin pulled on his leg until it ached, his skin slick with sweat, but it was too late to slip the trap.

The sword thrust, and Ivin awoke with his heart racing and a fading throb in his ankle. Wide eyes stared into the dim glow of embers near dead in the fireplace, and he wished Kinesee were here to share his dream with.

Kinesee, not Meliu.

This lone thought eased the beat of his heart and changed his mood. Had he recovered from the pain of Meliu? He wished this true, but the answer was still no.

He moved to the fireplace and stirred the embers before tossing a couple of logs on the grate then stared until flames licked the wood. If Wolf was a warrior, then Fox was a king who suckered a fool to trade places with him.

"Am I a warrior or a king?" The fox's question begged an answer he didn't have. He'd always thought himself as a warrior, never a king. The Silone didn't have kings, they had lords, and he was clan-blood. "I'm wasting my time on words when I need answers." The fire didn't hold answers, but for a flicker, he imagined Eliles' face in the flames. Strange that a girl he knew for scant few days could still haunt him.

He strode to the window to find the sky clear of clouds and filled with stars. Who the hells could he wake up in the middle of the night without rousing more bodies than intended? Roplin and Inisfer were a wick away but he'd awaken a dozen people. Tedeu Ravinrin was halfway to Foggy Vale by now, and Morik was at home or in Molikîn. He didn't know where the hells to find Sedut, nor did he know her moods this time of day.

He considered climbing back into bed but scratched the notion as futile, so instead, he donned a linen cloak and stepped into the hall. Kilk and Berün cast him glances from either side of the door.

"You men up for a walk?"

Kilk shrugged and Berün said, "Better'n standin' here another candle."

Ivin strode down the hall with his guards in tow. "I apologize, but everyone seems to think I need guards."

Kilk said, "An honor, m'lord."

Ivin didn't argue the point but figured there were more comfortable honors in life. He led them to a commons room where servants kept the fires burning all night, every night, and was surprised to find he wasn't alone in his late-night wanderings.

"Puxele? What are you doing up and about?"

The woman sat in a felt-lined chair with feet propped on a stool and hands resting on her swollen belly. "Leave it to Ratsmasher to have the comfiest chairs in the place, aye?"

Ivin sat across from her with a grin. "I'm sorry I haven't gotten to see you much."

"No worries, warlord. Pregnant gals aren't always the most pleasant talkers no how. I'm just waitin' to get Rinold's whelp out so I can hunt his ass down and slap him."

A young woman arrived with a steaming tray of food and set it beside Puxele. She grabbed a chicken leg and dipped it in a white sauce.

"If luck is with us, we'll get him home so you don't have to travel so far to beat him."

She nodded and pointed the leg at him. "I'd appreciate that. Now, what troubles our warlord so that he wanders these halls in the dead of night?"

"A better question might be how I sleep at all."

She laughed and patted her belly. "She's laughing too, methinks."

"A girl?"

"Aye, if for no other reason than to spite her pa. Tell me the truth, run out of rats?"

Ivin chuckled. "I've never known the world to run out of rats. No, the conversation I had with the Malstefnê commander has been eatin' at me. It's like he lay out a puzzle... a riddle is more apt. Tonight I had a dream about a fox and a wolf; the fox was in a trap. The way he spoke to me of warriors and kings, of sweat and blood, it reminded me of the way the Malstefnê spoke."

"Rinold loves a good riddle, but I swear he's worse at 'em than me. When he proposed to me he left a note on my bed, some piss poor riddle a child could solve, but it was sweet. By the time I tracked him through a half a dozen riddles, I was ablaze. But when I found him, did this idiot say what he wanted? Nope, he asked 'what will be a glow on your finger as sure as a glow in my heart' or some such godsdamned thing, and I told him to tell me *straight* or I was puttin' an arrow *straight* in his eye."

"You are a romantic."

"It'll be a good story for all his daughters."

Ivin smiled. "He don't give two shits whether it's a boy or girl."

"I hope he does, or my curse is worthless. I got a ring and a husband, what's the prize fer guessin' yer riddle right?"

"We get out of this trap." Chills struck and his shoulders goose-pimpled; just like Puxele, the person he needed to speak to was the one who composed the riddle. "Kilk, do you speak Tek or Kingdomer?"

The man stumbled over his words. "Aye, well, Kingdomer well enough. Just enough to haggle in Tek."

"Would you deliver a message for me?"

Kilk shifted his weight. "It'd be an honor."

This would be an honor worse than standing guard. "Come sunrise, I want you to ride to the Malstefnê army and tell their commander that the Warlord Choerkin wishes to speak to him at midday in the same place as before, and this time I will come alone."

Ivin popped the cork on a fresh bottle of Broldun whiskey as a warm breeze swirled around him. He took a swig from the bottle before holding it out for Ôlisbenar. The Malstefnê slipped from the saddle and took the bottle, sniffing before taking a sip.

"Not terrible." He sat on a chair Ivin had men bring for the occasion and took a longer drink. "Why are we here?"

Ivin sat in his chair, and it creaked with his weight. "Because it's what you wanted."

"Funny. I seem to recall claiming your head for my king."

"I seem to recall a man coming here alone and speaking in riddles, as a man with things he wanted known but refused to say."

He sipped from the bottle and handed it back. "Have you decided what you are?"

"I am warlord, neither a warrior nor a king, or either one on demand. Here and now I am a king, a slippery fox."

"Ah! Then you being so wise and sly, you must know there is nothing I could want from you."

Ivin wasn't sure whether it was a trick of semantics in translation, with Kingdomer being neither of their native tongues, or if the man was playing coy. "If you want nothing, then there is something I could do for you."

"No, I fear not. But you are right; I did want to speak further." The grin implied a lie. "For the past two years we've been at war with the Malobund because of the deception you pulled at the Dinsâng Bridge."

"In my defense, Lord Sevin was an arrogant cur set to betray us."

Ôlisbenar raised his hand to fend off further comment. "I don't doubt you. Lord Sevin was worse than a cur and I applaud his end, though I've no clue how you managed it. Decapitation in the man's bedroom? Impressive. The trouble is, he was second cousin to the queen, and my king didn't take kindly to his death even if he should've welcomed it. We already had one war in the north, and *you* brought us a war to the south."

Ivin drank from the bottle and plopped it on the table. "If you're laying out why you're here to kill us, there's no need and we can both ride away."

Ôlisbenar raised his hands to the sky and smiled. "It is a beautiful day! Why be in a hurry?"

"I understand your king being angered, but you must understand why we did what we did."

He nodded with a solemn smile. "I advised my king to forget the lot of you; you meant nothing compared to the war in the north. But General Kîgerê had already thrown a tantrum and was in pursuit... it might even be his horse you ride. The beast looks familiar. And when the general was dead—"he threw up his hands in disgust"—honor and pride were both wounded. More men, more dead, and then a war with the Malobund."

"Does this yarn have a destination?"

"The city of Qwôhar was sieged. My home. And my king commanded me to return to defend it. Three times I came close to defeating my Malobund enemy, and each time they seemed to know when the killing blow was coming. Four times I was within a hair of negotiating a peace with my enemy when some atrocity... Assassination. Arson. A lie spoken. Poisoned wells. Four chances for peace, four chances spoiled. I kick myself for a fool when I think of how long it took for me to realize that *you* had a spy, assassin, someone in our midst feeding the fire of our war."

Ivin stared, uncertain of how to react. Taking credit might strengthen his position or get his people flayed. "I don't know what you're talking about."

Ôlisbenar leaned in, then back, then in again, each time his face more bewildered. "I can't believe that. You are an exquisite liar."

"Because I'm telling the truth."

"Impossible. If not you, then someone in your camp." He rubbed his forehead with a grimacing smile. "I've a keen eye for faces, you see? One day a man from my command passed me twice in the same hall, and the second didn't remember passing me the first time. Think that strange?"

Lord Priest Ulrikt reared his changing face again; Ivin swallowed hard while trying to keep his thoughts straight. "I do. But what's it to do with me?"

"I had that man hunted down and questioned, he expired from the difficulty of the questions, but it was the *real* him. But that meant if I saw him again, I knew this other was false. The next time I saw him, I gazed through his disguise and saw a Silone man."

"You're certain?" Ivin grabbed the bottle for a drink, and this time he didn't put it back.

"I am. This man—if man he can be called—changed faces a dozen times as we gave chase and a dozen times we took prisoners who looked like him. Man or woman, it didn't matter. We were close, but he ran into a crowd. We surrounded them and I looked into all their eyes, but not one was a disguise. Then a guard brought me a note. Do you know what it said?"

Ivin's head was beginning to spin from whiskey and history. "I couldn't guess."

The man's fury snarled in his throat with every word. "It said, 'Your eyes aren't clear enough to see me again.' Everyone, everyone we had surrounded died by my hand that night."

Ivin breathed deep to settle his nerves. "A tragic story. I think he might have left me dice instead of a note. This same man may have murdered my father. Was he one you killed?"

Ôlisbenar blinked, then shrugged with a smile, his furious demeanor fading to calm in a matter of flickers. "There is no way to know, but the next time I had the Malobund under my ax, the head rolled and the war was over."

"And yet you don't think you killed the right guy."

"I don't. I hope not."

Ivin recoiled with his face scrunched. "Excuse me?"

"You hope not as well."

Ivin handed him the bottle. "You need to drink more, so you start making sense."

Ôlisbenar nabbed the bottle. "I will ask questions, you answer them. You are my king fighting a war to the north, do you start another war?"

"No."

"You win the war to the south, do you start another one or finish the war to your north?"

"I finish the northern war."

He took a swig from the jug, then another. "See how easy those are? How does a man not grasp those answers?"

Ivin waited several flickers before deciding the question wasn't rhetorical. "I don't... Because he's a warrior."

"Kingdoms need warriors to fight the battles, but it needs a king to pick them."

The way Ivin's gut roiled, he should've eaten lunch before taking this meeting with a bottle of the Broldun's best. It wasn't doing his head any good trying to piece this together, so he delayed. "I heard a legend of a priest who can change his face. A legend, a myth to scare postulants in the Church, I've been told. Except it turns out he's real. My people have seen him."

"How long ago?"

"Far as I know... a long time. But as you say, man, woman, child—"

"Child! You know this? A child could've slipped free easier." He rubbed his brow. "I never considered he could change so... No matter. If he is alive, he is the perfect assassin."

Ivin snorted. "If I had the perfect assassin, I could send him to kill you."

"Yes you could, but they would send another."

"And I'd kill him."

"And they'd send another."

"So, I'd send him to kill your king."

Ôlisbenar took a pull of his whiskey with a bottle distorted smile, and the conversation's destination flashed into view.

Ivin laughed. "Your king is a warrior, and you, his warrior, are a king."

"I am the hero and lord of Qwôhar in command of fifty thousand warriors, loyal to the crown and the Malstefnê throne."

"But not to the man sitting in it."

"I would never betray the throne."

"But if the throne sat empty, you would need to travel north to take the throne."

His brows knitted. "The warrior again sneaks into your thoughts. I would ride north to make certain the Litrâ don't take advantage of our weakness. I would win the war and return to a grateful court a victor for a second time, and the man who brought us peace. Who would the court choose to sit the throne next? Well, that isn't for me to decide, is it?"

It wasn't just the whiskey making him want to puke, it was the notion of needing Lord Priest Ulrikt to save the Silone from this war.

But he had to hand it to Ôlisbenar, the man was clever and ambitious. "You are a sly fox."

"And my king is a wolf who'd bite off a thousand legs to escape a trap he set for himself. His death by a northern assassin would force my hand."

Was this man in my dreams? A chill prickled Ivin's skin but he ignored it. "There's no way to know if I can do this thing."

Ôlisbenar smiled and nodded. "Excuse my crass behavior." He stood in a rage, throwing the table to the side as he kicked Ivin in the chest, toppling him in his chair. He pointed at Ivin with a peculiar smile and wink, then paced, waving his arms in a false fury. "I cannot stop my attack, so *if* you can do it, do it with haste. I will slow the attack as much as I can, neither of us wants to lose men, but people will die until I need to ride north."

Ivin leaped to his feet and drew his sword, cocked it his over his shoulder and screamed, "I'll do my best."

Ôlisbenar stepped back, hand at the sword riding on his belt. "That's a fine weapon."

"Thank you."

"I hope you get to keep it and your head, but if not, it would be a fine prize."

"It's sharper than it is beautiful."

The man laughed. "In his message, Iro Adinfin noted he liked you even if he wanted you dead. I know now why." He stuck a foot in a stirrup and swung into the saddle. "He'd be furious if he knew I passed a chance to kill you. It might be another war, except he's too many kingdoms away."

"If you ever meet him face to face, tell him this from me: tits."

Ôlisbenar blinked. "I will."

"Make sure he's too drunk to fight."

"If rumors are true, that'll be easy." The Malstefnê reined his mare and put spurs to her ribs, thundered down the slope. Ivin sheathed his sword, then picked up the bottle of whiskey and took a swig to find most of it gone. Within flickers, hooves beat the turf. He turned to see Roplin and a dozen Choerkin warriors in full armor. He waved as he stumbled to his horse and patted his neck. "A general's horse? You could've told me and we would've settled on a name a long time ago."

Roplin's horse rattled to a stop strides away. "You're drunk."

Ivin smirked. "And thank the gods for that."

"I thought for godsdamned sure you two were coming to blows."

"Not yet. He's a fox. I'm a fox... a wolf needs to die."

"I pray to the Seven Heavens you're gonna explain that."

Ivin puffed and took a drink before tossing the bottle to his brother. "I don't think I should."

Roplin tipped the whiskey. "Empty bottle and empty words. Do we have peace?"

"No. But there might be. Kinesee and the Helelindin aren't our only hope." Ivin eased his way into the saddle and his head spun with the change in altitude. "I need to eat. Then I need Sedut to help me find a dead man."

Twenty-Five

Mule Ears

Today, Yesterday, and Tomorrow.
Our lives' moments stolen by our need
to stare forward and back.
Flicker, wick, candle, day, month, year.
Berating or praising. Caring or cursing.
Mortals spend more Time
thinking outside their Now than living their now.
What a foolish game it is they play,
I once Played... oh, to be so naïve again,
as I live, relive, forever nows with
no Today, Yesterday, or Tomorrow.

—*Tomes of the Touched*

"Godsdamn, boy. You had to go and buy them boots, didn't you?"

Solineus glanced at his feet and wiggled his toes. He ordered them the week before, custom-fitted, and they were snug and comfortable on his feet like nothing he'd felt before. They were crafted from berôt skin, some sort of lizard-fish that hunted the waters of Kônu Bay. Folks claimed it had teeth long as a man's hand. "If I'd walked across the mountains wearing these, I would've made it a week sooner."

Adinvan snorted, and Hadin waggled his finger at the boots. "How'n the hells can you wear them damned things with those... those *things* flappin' on 'em?"

Straps a hand a half long dangled to either side of both boots, and they flapped as he walked. "Says the man who doesn't wear boots unless there's ice on the ground. They're called mule ears; they help to pull them on in the morning."

Adinvan said, "At least cover 'em with your pantlegs; you humiliate me."

"Anyone looking at my boots is scared to look me in the eye, what the hells else should I care about them for?"

"Berôt eat people, you know. It's like the damned things are chewing their way up your legs."

"They're comfortable."

"Your mother will disown you."

"They're already paid for."

"As lord of the Clan Emudar, I command you throw them into the bay."

"I'm buying the both of you a pair. Two pairs each."

"The hells, you say."

Hadin said, "Cut off the wings and I'll think on it."

"Ears, not wings." Solineus turned and walked down the dock. "Forget the boots, let's get to the *Lady Moon*."

"Can't forget them damned boots with their flap, flap, flappin' like that."

Solineus couldn't fight the smile any longer and was glad they walked behind him. "Got all our favorite beers loaded?"

"Aye, kegs and kegs. Best gold you spent, but they're aboard the cog."

"We're sailing on the wrong ship, then."

Hadin said, "I'm kind of gettin' m'self used to the rhythm of them there winged boots, I might needs me a pair after all."

"Don't you go encouragin' him, you oaf."

Solineus said, "Think I'm going to rename the lead longship *Mule Ears*." But even as the words hit the air, blue plumes and silver helmets rising above sailor heads caught his eye, and they were on the dock beside the *Lady Moon*. He was glad to know that Captain Edmordô's ship, as well as the Emudar cog and the other two longships, were clear of the docks and waiting for them. "Who the hells are those people?"

Adinvan said, "By those feathers I'd wager they're Mô'od's people from the Prâterêut."

Now he'd heard the words, familiarity returned. He recalled the gear from the search for the Guardian of Mulshahar. "Wishing us a safe voyage, you wager?"

"You're the one with coins to wager. I'm just happy to know if they wanted us dead we'd be that way already."

"Always the optimist."

Solineus didn't slow his strides nor bother to make eye contact with the guards before hopping aboard the *Lady Moon*. When his eyes settled on the frail form of Guardian Zerik Mô'od, he doubted that he hid his surprise well. He'd expected some underling. This man making the long walk with the canes leaning by his side boded ill, as he doubted his cause was to take up the oar he sat beside.

He bowed. "Guardian Zerik Mô'od, a pleasant surprise to see you again."

"I've never been aboard one of these vessels. It has a different feel than a cog or caravel. It promises sweat, sore muscles, and nights of deep and exhausted sleep with poor accommodations."

Solineus' head bobbed. "You've forgotten the sail?"

"On a good day, it will save shoulders and cast shade. It is built so that even if it takes on water it will not sink, am I right?"

"Aye, so they tell me. I've been on a ship that sank; I prefer it this way." He grinned. "What brings you here?"

"I've two messages, one bearing the seal of the Ironwing." He pulled an envelope from a small pouch that rested hidden beneath his arm and handed it to him. They stared at one another. "Will you be opening it?"

"It might be private."

"Then by all means, don't read it aloud."

Solineus licked his lips and smiled as he broke the seal. The handwriting made him smile. "It's from my daughter." But there was a second note beneath, and this one *was* from the Ironwing. He perused the parchment with dramatic grunts and nods. "All of Helmveline is pleased with my plan. In fact... it appears they're sending an expedition downriver to meet me." *And to rescue captured people.* "It seems my daughter will be heading to Helelindin territory to begin negotiations for further trade. Married now and a blossoming diplomat."

"An ambitious girl, much like her father."

"Indeed. And the second message?" He held out his hand.

"Is oral."

"Some piece of your wisdom?"

"A Smiling Man's wisdom."

"But not a Smiling Woman?"

The man's head cocked, and he clucked with a grin. "It's impossible to tell, and we don't name them such to their faces, it might make them frown."

"I look forward to meeting one of these *smilers* someday." The man's stare suggested his bemusement had died. "What did this Smiling Man say?"

"That you should not sail for seven days."

Solineus blinked. "We're ready now, and our other ships have left the docks. Seven days is specific. What the hells is that about?"

Zerik shrugged. "The number of days and everything else would be conjecture on my part. The Smiling Men, or at least some of them, have taken interest in your success or failure. The Smiling Man who spoke to me implied it would be safer to leave in seven days."

"Did he break bones? Sacrifice a goat? Or maybe he just sniffed the wind for pirates and rough seas."

"I'm certain this is an answer I can't give."

A twitch in the man's eye hinted at something more. "You're sure this person has my interests at heart? Maybe they want me here to kill or delay."

"The Smiling Men have strict rules regarding interference in trade as well as murder *in* Mulshahar and *on* the waters of Kônu Bay. This one desires no such thing."

Solineus leaned close. "*This one.* You're suggesting another might have different designs?"

Zerik grabbed his canes and stood, unsteady, and Solineus lent him a hand as he stepped up to the dock and turned. "He said you wouldn't listen, but he wanted you warned all the same. Sail safe and make Mulshahar all the richer." The man took a single step toward town and turned. "Communications with Molikîn are known to take six months or a year, might I enquire as to how yours moved so swiftly?"

"Depends on whether you want an answer."

The Guardian of Mulshahar nodded with a grin. "Fair enough."

Solineus bowed and watched the man shuffle down the dock with guards on his heels. It was impressive to witness a sea of hale men part for a cripple with such haste.

Adinvan spat into the bay. "What the hells you make of that? Honest warning or subtle threat?"

"So subtle I didn't see it? I don't think so. Soon as we're on open seas without a sail in sight, we change course and swing wide on the way to the islands. We'd be clinging to sticks if one of these larger ships caught us on open water."

"Might be better to hug the coast to take advantage of our depth of keel."

"Aye, and if there's someone waiting for us, they'll be expecting it."

Hadin flopped onto a seat. "Bastard might've been horseshittin' ta make us think he's a better friend than he is."

"I reckon not, or he would've spoken plainer. We castoff, raise sail, and keep a keen eye for anyone who might be following."

Adinvan said, "We'll need to get word to Captain Edmordô soon as we can."

Solineus grunted and plopped on a chest used as a rower's seat then broke the seal on Kinesee's letter. His heart jumped.

> *Maro is dead, killed on my way to visit the Ironwing. The attackers were Malstefnê, but Meliu has suggested the attack was meant to kill or capture me. The Heretics of Rin. But no one knows the truth. If not for Meliu, I would not be writing this today. But there is more news and worse.*

The war to our north has come to an end, and the Malstefnê have turned their eye on us. War is coming. The Silone have moved into the Roemhien and beyond, and the Helmveliner wall will stand between the Malstefnê and our extinction. The Ironwing will make a show of force in the north, but these men will march south to face a second threat, a people we call the Yellow-Eyes. They have captured hundreds of Silone and Helmveliners, including your friend Rinold. Ivin and the Ironwing are sending thousands of warriors south to free them.

I will be traveling to the Helelindin city of Holelorin in hopes of convincing these people to allow Kingdomer pilgrims to the Final Foundation. The Ironwing believes this would earn Kingdomer support for our war against the Malstefnê. I won't rely on this, and will also seek aid from the Helelindin themselves.

There is another message for me to deliver that I swore to deliver in person. Lelishên came to see me. I have a baby brother. You have a son. She asks you to find her where the Snow meets the Sun. If anyone finds out, your child's life is at stake, tell no one.

His name is Veldehar.

The letter ended without a signature nor a smart quip, and Solineus sat staring at the final words.

"The news is bad?" Adinvan sat beside him.

Solineus folded the note. "We've war to the north and south." He'd hold his son a secret until he wrapped his brain around it himself. "That's why she's heading to see the Helelindin, to gain their help."

Solineus jumped to his feet and tromped to the back of the ship.

His father was on his heels. "What the hells are you doing, boy?"

Solineus grabbed his sailor's chest and tossed it onto the dock. "I'm buying a horse. Buying a godsdamned army and riding east." He was a flicker from launching himself to the dock when Adinvan's hand caught his shoulder.

"I get it, by the gods, but that letter is over a month old. If she's half the woman you claim her to be, she might've already sealed the peace."

Solineus' heart drummed, and he fought the urge to strike his father's hand from his shoulder. "I can't take that chance."

"And where're you going to find this army, eh?"

"Tales abound of mercenaries—"

"All employed by locals."

He spun on his father with a glare. "Then I ride alone! I've done it once."

Adinvan exhaled. "Yes. You did. But where would you leave the Emudar? There is an army on these seas and it's yours; we just need to find the route for it to take."

Solineus closed his eyes and eased his breaths. "We?"

"I reckon I'll be making the journey with you. This isn't trade nor exploration. This is war. I won't be at the back of the fight again."

Solineus grabbed his chest from the dock and dropped it back to the bottom of the boat. "Well then, I reckon you'll get to meet your new grandson sooner rather than later."

Solineus didn't know why the words slipped from his tongue until he saw the blank expression on his father's face.

"Not a great-grandson?"

"Not yet."

The smile on Adinvan's face was part shock and part joy, then he laughed. "Good! That's godsdamned good. I don't wanna be that old yet. A boy! Congratulations. The mother?"

Solineus cocked his head, uncertain how far to let his words wander. "She is beautiful and well, but worried for me." How did one explain an impossible child from an improbable union?

Twenty-Six

Facing Deceptions

Somersaulting miracles are curses unworked,
awakened or sleeping and dreaming
of being awoke?
It is the cursed fool who thinks they know.

—*Tomes of the Touched*

Word of Sedut's reputed location reached Ivin's ears the next morning, and it came as a surprise. If the rumor was right, she made camp above East Quarry with a handful of priests and adherents, including Meliu's little friend, Deelee. He'd expected to find the high priestess amongst the larger holy site folks had taken to calling the Priest Moot because of the way they argued and nagged at each other, but when he arrived at the base of the quarry and looked up, he understood her choice. Ivin figured that with her prayers, she might see as far as the Gediswon from the vantage.

A green canopy sprouted above the boulders hundreds of feet above, and no doubt there were smaller tents hidden by his angle of view. The slope grew steep within a couple of hundred strides, so he didn't bother to make General carry him any farther. He dismounted and handed the reins to Kîlk before following the path by himself. He wound his way through prickly shrubs, trees, and boulders, breathing hard but enjoying the scent of cedar in the air. Before reaching the plateau, he already heard priests in prayer, and by the time he scrambled the final strides, he thought he recognized Sedut's voice leading the sermon.

His ears tracked the prayer to a bullhide yurt set back in the trees, and as he paused with hands to his knees to regain his breath, Sedut stepped into his peripheral vision from the green tent. "I heard you were looking for me."

Ivin lurched straight, gazing first at her, then the yurt with a smile. "You could've saved me a climb then."

"At the cost of my own legs? Please, come in."

She stepped through the flap, and as he ducked to enter the priestess tossed incense into a brazier before turning the knob on a lantern to give the space more light. Three cots lined the walls with chests for clothing at their feet, and a table with chairs to seat six sat in the middle. In moments the smell of lilac and mint filled the tent. She eased into a seat at the head of the table and stared at him.

Ivin grinned and took the opening to speak. "I suppose with your view of the valley, you know the Malstefnê movements better than I do." He sat as her stare didn't fade, and her mouth remained shut.

"You've come here to ask of the enemy?"

"No." Ivin exhaled and slapped his thighs. "Look, I'm not going to beat the rug clean nor blame anyone for the muddy prints, I don't have time to be angry or nice. Is Lord Priest Ulrikt alive? Or the Lord Priest's Face? I don't give two shits for which one."

Sedut's brows arched and her lips twisted to one side of her face. "You've heard of the Face?"

"I have, and I need use of him... her. Ulrikt, whoever the hells it is."

She rubbed her chin, staring at him for flickers without a breath before answering. "Lord Priest Ulrikt is dead, has been for some time. Does this please you?"

"That depends on whether his Face is still breathing."

She licked her lips with a grin. "Before I answer yay or nay, I must ask why you need this answer."

One thing confirmed, the Face was real, whether dead or not. "If a Malstefnê dies, their army will go away."

Her fingers drummed the table. "I've not known you to be a man of fanciful notions, but this? Killing their commander only forces them to grow another head, you know that as well as I."

"I do. Their king, not their commander."

Sedut leaned in her chair, fingers twined beneath her chin. "That is ambitious, but this animal will still grow another head."

"Ôlisbenar commands this army, but he'd rather sit a throne than a horse."

Her eyes fluttered and a creepy grin passed her lips. "King Trefifân is young and hale and with only a single heir. You have a promise from the Malstefnê's lips?"

Ivin didn't even know the king's name, let alone his heirs. *How much does she know that she hasn't shared?* "In not so many words, I do. He believes his king a fool to keep fighting two wars, and if the king dies, he can ride north to win that war and earn the throne."

"The plan has merit, and I wish I could assist, but I regret to say that the Face is dead, if ever he was real."

Ivin slumped in his chair, deflated. "You're certain?"

"Your Tek friend delivered his head to Meliu and Polus Broldun at the Gediswon Ford."

Ivin clenched his eyes shut. He'd heard of the battered head, a spy, but at the time hadn't a clue of the Face's existence. "We *need* that king dead. Is there any way you could get close enough?"

Her head rocked back, gaze intense, like a rooster ready to fight. "My dear warlord, you fancy me a burglar or some such? Meliu would be more suited but we sent her south."

Ivin nodded. Meliu's prayers would make more sense; Sedut was a poleax when a dagger was more useful. "We could—"

Sedut's voice came from the tent's flap. "What the Twelve Hells is going on?"

Ivin spun in his seat to see the high priestess with a horrified gaze on her face, and when he turned back around, it was in time to see the other Sedut's face melt. Or that was the first impression. It was more accurate to say it shifted and flowed like hot wax in a twisting current, for a flicker looking like a man or woman with the mumps or some stranger disease, before disfiguring itself again.

The lips shifted into a flowing smile, and the voice became deep, male, and on the verge of laughter. "Well, this is embarrassing."

Ivin stared at the thing that may have killed his father, his mouth gone dry. He didn't believe this creature was humiliated. In fact, he assumed it expected Sedut's arrival. He cleared his throat. "Shall I kill you so to make your words the truth?"

The Face laughed, waved to Sedut, and when it spoke, the voice was feminine while shifting between highs and lows. "Sit with us, please. The Warlord Choerkin was just speaking of a plan to murder the Malstefnê king."

Ivin said, "Murder is killing without a war. This king is our enemy."

"My boy, whether war has simmered unseen or boiled like Purdonis Bay does now, it has *always* been there. I'd rather say that murder is for a personal cause, while assassination has a broader political intent."

Is that how he justified murdering my father? Ivin bit back the question and instead asked, "Is Ulrikt dead?"

"Yes."

"But being his Face, what does that make you?"

"No different than any other priest of Istinjoln forced to do his bidding."

"Ulrikt was an evil son of a bitch."

The Face shrugged, and its features were unreadable, but the voice came as a hiss. "Ulrikt was a *monster*. What he achieved was only half of what he was capable of."

Ivin leaned in his chair and observed the creature, but he'd might as well seek meaning in the ripples of a wind-blown pond. There was no way to know if this Face meant the words, or if so, why. And it didn't matter. "What the hells are you if not a monster?"

For a flicker the flow of its lips smirked. "I am but a priest with a particular talent, not so unlike your Meliu. I'm also the one who kept the Tek nations fighting for the past two years to give you time."

"You want my thanks?" He clutched his head, hoping it didn't answer. The conversation drifted toward pointless; he needed to refocus. "As I said, I'm not here to beat a rug. Can you kill the king or not?"

Sedut leaned her elbows to the table. "What good is it to kill their king? Does he have sons who'd fight for the crown?"

"He has one son, and he is only twelve. No, it seems we have a man of ambition pushing toward our gates, and he would rather be killing Litrâ to take the throne from a dead man."

Ivin said, "That's the gist."

Sedut smiled, more sinister than attractive. "That's a good gist."

"I do love lilac." The Face sniffed the air. "Notôlhof is the capital of the Malstefnê, which isn't a short journey in itself. Passing through Malobund and Loenfarar makes it riskier and slower. It might take me two to three weeks to reach the city, and then I would need to find a way to reach the king. This is no small feat. A month at the minimum, more apt it'd be two unless this king is more a fool than I suspect. And still, no guarantee of success."

Ivin nodded with a grimace. "Ôlisbenar will delay the siege best he can while appearing not to delay. I've no doubt we can hold that long."

"At what cost? Our people are not so many that we can afford to throw lives away. You need to delay any way you can."

Ivin stretched his legs and stared at the ceiling. "If I sued for peace the message would travel to the king. That could be your ride to Notôlhof and it'd slow the attack."

The flesh-tone flow of the thing's skin congealed into the visage of a woman Ivin had never seen before, and this new woman smiled at him as she stood. The voice sounded like Polus only with a Tek accent. "I will make my way to the Malstefnê camp this evening, and come morning, you make your offer to Ôlisbenar."

Ivin followed the sensual sway of the woman's hips toward the tent's flap. "It'll be done."

The Face turned and spoke in sultry tones with perfect white teeth. "I know you must wonder... If it makes you feel any better, I didn't kill your father."

Ivin swallowed a brick and waited for it to hit his gut before speaking. It wasn't like he could believe a word from this thing's mouth, whether it was man, woman, or demon, but he could get something of an answer. "Then why leave me the night die?"

The disturbing part was how a creature so frightening could smile with such beauty and innocence. "The monk didn't have the courage to take his own life. I wanted you to know that someone had done you a favor."

She ducked from the tent before he could ask about the other dice, and Ivin rubbed his forehead before turning to Sedut. "Is Ulrikt truly dead?"

Sedut's laugh faded into a groan. "You know as well as I, but... I don't know."

Ivin felt as if she was about to say he was alive, but either way, it did him no good. "I'd just begun to trust you."

She sighed. "Meliu kept his secret as well, for longer than I did."

"But you never told me, she did." He stood and sauntered to the tent's flap. "But I don't trust her either."

"It's unfortunate when we can't trust those with whom we share love, but perhaps these are the people we should trust least because they are closest. Because their betrayal will hurt most."

"That's not the way I wish to live. When war comes, can I trust you to be there?"

"In that, you can put all your faith."

"That's all I need, I suppose." He ducked through the tent, greeted by a whipping wind that carried flakes of grit to pelt his skin. He squinted against the sun and swirl of dust. *At least it isn't cold. Everything hurts more in the cold.*

Twenty-Seven

Rising from Low

Walk the darkness,
speak the light not the ness,
Beholden to the holder,
the spoken and the told,
the unspoken but said,
when my words you understand
you will know you are dead.

—*Tomes of the Touched*

Rinold spent every candle of the next three nights expecting his new Wiirê friend, Nehek, to wake him so they could crack a few heads and take flight east. He and every enslaved Silone lost sleep in hope and expectation, but on the fourth day, Histê guards kicked the Silone awake and led them into the arena's bright sun, as they had every day before. Everything seemed as normal and unfortunate as ever with archers eyeing them as they entered, but Mistress Hukêlê was here today. She stood atop a two-wheeled cart of some sort, tethered to two critters about the size of a cow, but their front feet bore four toes and their faces were dominated by rounded snouts that hung low enough to reach their mouths. When Edlmir first saw one, he'd sniggered and called the poor thing a snake-nosed pig-cow, but those they saw in the forest were more the size of a burrow.

From the flicker he spotted the mistress, he knew the day was different. Nehek arrived at the lead of three wagons—one a cage and another bearing the crate of iron weapons and armor—pulled by great ox-like beasts with massive horns that curled like a mountain goat's. They bellowed and snorted goo from their flaring nostrils, and Rinold felt worse for the slaves leading them than he did for himself.

Nehek strode straight to him and grabbed the shackles at his wrist, leading him to a wagon, but a Histê guard stood too close to risk a word. He didn't want to believe it, but it seemed his ally had changed his mind on freedom.

"At least you didn't tell yer mistress, ya cowardly priss." He spoke in Silone so not a one of the bastards understood him, but Nehek backhanded him hard enough to make his jaw ache.

"Shut your mouth, worm." The warrior-slave led him aboard a wagon with wooden poles for prison bars and clacked a lock through his chain and a ring built into the wagon's side. Nehek slapped his hands twice, pointed at his eyes, and slapped his hands again before retreating from the back of the wagon.

Edlmir stood beside him with a smirk. "I think he's plannin' on eating yer eyeballs."

Witty retorts came to Rinold's mind as Nehek loaded the remaining Silone. But he kept his mouth shut, choosing to stare at Nehek until the bastard offered his neck to the mistress' chains. The wagon jerked beneath them, and the train lumbered from the arena and through the streets of the city. A half-dozen Histê guards walked to either side of their wagon with spears in hand and bows on their backs, but twice as many yellow-eye slaves. Histê and Wiirê alike stopped to stare at their passing, children pointing at the strange men in a cage.

"We're a right queer oddity, it seems. Too bad you didn't let me fight that first time."

Rinold grunted, not wanting to give Edlmir the satisfaction of words.

Once out of town, the road turned to grassy dirt that rode rougher than a storm at sea, slamming wheels to jar bones and make a man stumble, the bars and chains the only thing keeping him from tumbling out. On the bright side, it kept everyone's mouths shut for fear of biting off a tongue, so he didn't have to hear from Edlmir or any other. After several wicks, most men sacrificed their tailbones to save their knees by sitting, all except Rinold. He clutched the bars in front of him and suffered the ruts, bumps, and swales so he could stare at the back of Nehek's head while wishing him dead.

Wiirê slaves ran ahead of the train clearing branches fallen from the forest, their eyes always up and keen to spot any dangers, and more than once Rinold hoped for a giant serpent to attack the bastards. But no such luck, and as the sun approached midday, the forest thinned and he spotted critters more familiar, a herd of prong-horned deer, rabbits, and a flock of turkey-like birds too fat to fly far amongst others. It brought a strange ease to his soul, as if he'd arrived in a world he knew while leaving something evil behind.

The left wheel slammed. A *crack* came in an instant; Rinold was thrown against the bars, kissing a pole with a broken nose as the wagon flipped onto its side.

Rinold looked up at a world which appeared frozen, with everyone's eyes on them, then bedlam. His eyes locked on the lead chariot as Nehek rose and the mistress' throat sprayed red. Wiirê slaves plowed into Histê guards and struggled for weapons.

Rinold shrieked, "Stand! Fight!"

But the Silone were tumbled one on top of the other and chained. It took flickers for half of them to stand. They twisted and pulled, rattling their chains to no avail. He licked his lips of his own blood and stared at the bronze ring set in the wagon. "Edlmir! Shrîk! With me, grab my chain and pull." The three men yanked and leaned, and in a flicker, the bolt wiggled loose. They stumbled backward, saved from a fall by pressing bodies. "Work the rings!"

The Silone worked their way free of the wagon but were still chained together as the fight raged around them. A Histê with his back turned nocked an arrow and stretched the string, and Rinold charged, dragging Edlmir with him. Rinold went low and Edlmir high, and they crushed the man to the ground, and in a flicker, Edlmir had the flailing man's neck wrapped by chain. The struggle ended with a broken neck, while at the other end of the links, three Silone beat another Histê unconscious.

Rinold leaped to his feet and charged a third Histê whose spear was thrust through a yellow-eye chest... his wrists whipped and his feet flew from under him, and the only thing that kept him from landing flat on his back was Edlmir, but he was still on his knees. The Histê pulled his spear free and turned with a trilling scream, spearhead pointed straight at Rinold's eyes, plunging true until a bronze blade punched through the Histê's neck.

The guard dropped to his knees and tumbled to his face with Nehek standing behind him, a scowl stretching his face. The Wiirê screamed at him. "What are you doing?"

Rinold wiped his bloody face and shook his shackled hands. "The best I can with these cursed things on."

Nehek strode close with an exasperated glare in his eye. "I gave you a key."

"What key!"

The man slapped his hands and pointed to his eyes. "If you'd looked by your hands you would've found it."

Rinold glanced back at the tumbled wagon. The fighting around them was over but for finishing the wounded, and he sucked a deep breath before turning back to Nehek. "Well, that would've been too easy."

The Wiirê laughed, dropped his knife in the dirt, and grabbed Rinold by the face. He thought the man might kiss him, but then his nose crunched as Nehek twisted; a flash of pain flared through his face, into his eyes, and he teared up.

"Son of a whore's buck! You could've warned me."

Nehek only stared, as Rinold had screamed in Silone. Edlmir grinned. "I'm not too big a man to admit when I was wrong, even if you were a godsdamned idiot."

"Yeah, thanks."

Nehek trotted to the wagon and returned with a key to unlock their chains. "Freedom."

"Aye, freedom." Rinold rubbed his wrists and turned a circle, blinks clearing the tears from his eyes as he stared at his surroundings. "Where are we?"

Nehek rattled Edlmir's lock. "Far from where we need to be."

Rinold turned to face east. "Back into that infested forest."

"My home, yes. We will need supplies and to warn my people."

Edlmir said, "The real fun begins."

Rinold breathed deep and smiled. "With freedom comes the hard part."

Rinold's toe clipped a root and he stumbled for more than the tenth time; his exhausted body demanded to use all his energy on more important things after reaching double digits. His hand slid along the rain-slicked slime of a tree as he recaptured his balance and lumbered back into a trot.

Nehek glanced back and must not have liked the look on Rinold's face. He raised his hand and brought them to a stop.

When laying awake at night imagining their escape from the Histê slavers there was always a bloody fight, it only seemed right, but for whatever reason the stories his mind concocted never included what came between the glorious battle for freedom and hugging Puxele along with his newborn child.

Nehek and six Tunotuwiirê led the Silone, but the rest scattered to their own tribes. On the bright side, if they survived this thing, at least three Wiirê tribes would know of the offer of freedom.

"You're sure the Histê are after us?" Nehek's frown was somewhere between smirk and glare, naming Rinold an idiot without words. "All right then, how far behind do you think they are?"

"Hope for a day, but assume it's less. That's the trackers, but messengers will send fresh hunters from outposts as they reach them."

Edlmir wiped his brow of sweat and leaned against a tree panting. "I'm gonna be skinny as a squirrel by the time this' over."

"So long as you aren't skinny as bones in the dirt, count it a win."

Nehek pointed east. "Rest a wick. We shouldn't be far from the Yunsokutoi River."

Edlmir scrunched his lips. "The what a what river?"

Rinold said, "The big river, I think he means; the Puxele."

"You think naming that river after her is gonna save yer ass?"

"I'm a hopin', ain't sure my boyish smile is gonna do it this time 'round."

"That smile ain't saved you since you *were* a boy."

Silone laughed, but seeing as he didn't understand their words, Nehek ignored them, staring east. The Wiirê sighed and his lips pinched like a man who'd just realized something bad. Rinold cleared his throat. "Some bug just bite your butt?"

Nehek looked to the dirt before speaking. "We need to move. What we're really racing are tongues."

"Whoa. What do you mean?"

"The Yunsokutoi is mighty. Without a boat there are two bridges we could cross. If word of our *setokô*—"a word Rinold knew meant something akin to murder of the masters"—has reached the river the big bridge will be watched first."

"And this second bridge?"

"Is less known, little used and to the north... and it will take time to find, there are no roads made by man leading to it."

"There are roads by other than men?"

Nehek stared, shrugged. "Animal trails, washouts. The Wiirê keep it passable, but few Histê know of it. We call it Widow's Fall."

"Now that sounds right encouraging!"

"There is a famous story of a queen of the Wiirê. When the Histê first came and took her husband, she leaped from its heights instead of being captured."

"Oh, so it's a happy story."

Nehek laughed. "Few stories are happy. If we beat the Histê to Grand Bridge all is well, but if we don't, we're dead."

"So, we head for Widow's Fall."

"And if we waste time finding it, they'll beat us to both bridges, and we die."

Edlmir grunted. "That's a lot of dying."

Rinold asked, "Have you been to Widow's Fall?"

"Yes, once, but I came from the eastern side."

"We're in your hands, do what you think best."

Nehek gave a curt nod before leading them onward, and Rinold didn't ask which bridge he'd chosen, but noted their path bent more northerly than before. The sun glowed orange in the west by the time they caught sight of the Yunsokutoi. They stood perched on a rocky outcropping overlooking a sheer bluff, and below them, the mighty river spread like a flowing inland sea. At least to Rinold's mind.

They made a fireless camp, eating fruits and raw eggs that the Wiirê collected along the way, and in the morning, they turned away from the river and wheeled north. Wiirê scouts ran ahead and checked on the river throughout the day, but Nehek didn't want them following its shores for fear of boats or other patrols. The trek was slow climbing and winding, but after four days, a scout returned babbling so fast Rinold had trouble picking out his words.

Nehek turned to him. "White waters and he spotted the bridge to the north."

"What are we waiting for?"

Nehek rubbed his face and took his pack from his shoulder. "We wait because now is the difficulty." He pointed north to high hills. "We need to climb to find the bridge. I will stay here with you. My people will explore the trails ahead until they find the route to the bridge."

It sounded easy enough, but it was a day and a half before a scout found a passable trail, and he did that by scaling cliffs and backtracking to find them after reaching the bridge. Once the route was known, it took them three candles of scrambling up a goat trail to reach their destination.

Widow's Fall was a vine-strewn bridge of ropes and wood spanning a gorge that threatened to bring Rinold's breakfast from his belly. Fifty poles or more below the narrow span, the mighty Yunsokutoi narrowed to a thrashing whitewater rapid marked by jagged stones and boulders. Rinold swallowed hard. He'd be happier if the gorge was as narrow as the bridge, then he could jump it. The Yunsokutoi was a quarter horizon wide south of here, so narrow was a relative term.

The span of Widow's Fall was five hundred strides of weathered wood slicked by moss and dotted with ankle-biting holes. "Grand Bridge is sounding like a better way to die."

Nehek grinned. "The fall is far, but your death swift."

Edlmir slapped Rinold's back. "Squirrels ain't afraid of heights."

"I ain't speakin' for all squirrels, mind you, but this one would rather stick to trees."

Wind howled and ropes creaked as they approached, and the sound that promised rotting twine brought an ache to Rinold's knees. He crept to the edge and glanced over the edge: jagged stone descending to spraying and swirling waters. "Ah, hells."

Edlmir took two steps onto the boards, streaking the moss on the boards. "Slicker'n shit in the mud... but no more dangerous than packing thundersticks, I figure."

"I expected toting them damnable things around would be the dumbest damned thing I ever did."

Edlmir bounced, but his weight was nothing compared to the winds that already had it swinging.

Nehek said, "Let's move. We waste time and risk eyes in the open."

Edlmir turned and led the way, followed by several Silone and then Wiirê, before Rinold set his first ginger step to the planks, his fingers white-knuckled as they clutched the ropes. His eyes were so trained on his toes and the heels in front of him that it took flickers for the scream to register, and when he looked up, an arrow struck the side of one Silone's head. The man stumbled and tumbled over the ropes, falling into the gorge. But Rinold didn't follow the plummet with his eyes; his vision was pinned on a swarm of arrows humming into them from the southeast.

Everyone pulled shields and froze. He took two steps back and collided with Nehek.

The Wiirê bellowed, "Forward! West is death!"

Rinold's feet wanted to argue, but his brain recognized the truth. "Run! Charge!"

Edlmir's shield sported three arrows as he roared, rushing forward as two more points hit his mail before rattling to the bridge's boards. "Show these bastards what steel will do!"

An arrow struck Rinold's leg, less painful than a hornet's strike, and he followed the others with shield high. A Wiirê in front of him fell with an arrow in his thigh... from the northeast. "Archers to the north! Move on! Move fast!" He lifted the wounded Wiirê, and they stumbled forward struggling not to step on each other, and as they lagged behind they might've been deer to the slaughter if not for most of the arrows tracking the men in the lead. Rinold knew hope again when Edlmir and the remaining Silone hit the ground at a run. He'd feel even better if he could see the enemy, but they cowered among rocks and bushes to launch their attack.

"Come on! Come on!" He yelled in Wiirê, and once he had rock beneath his feet, he handed the wounded man his shield and slung his bow from his shoulder. "Keep that shield up."

Smoke. Unholy shits. His eyes tracked the source, but it disappeared in a rocky copse of trees... A Histê rose from behind a rock, bow bending, and Rinold loosed. The steel head split the wooden lamellar dead center to the sternum but not before the bastard's fingers twitched to release the arrow. A Silone dropped with an arrow through his throat, great shot or lucky, but there wasn't a way to know if it'd been the dead man's shot.

Nehek sprinted past, and by the time Rinold put an arrow in a second Histê, the warrior reached the fray, his spear punching through a Histê chest. His shield-bearer collapsed with fletching sticking from his chest, and Rinold spun north; of a sudden, he had multiple targets to pick from. Three warriors charged, but the archer took Rinold's arrow to the gut and dropped.

One more. He nocked, drew, and dropped the lead runner in a bloody tumble, then dropped his bow and snagged his shield in time to block a spear and roll backwards as the man crushed into him. They flailed and he could feel a knife stabbing at his mail. He drew his sword, and as they rolled, he draw cut the back of the man's neck before shoving the screaming man away.

He rolled away and a spear scuttled and scraped off rock near his head. On his back, he raised his shield, but in a flicker his attacker lacked a head, and in the next Edlmir appeared as the man fell. His shield sported seven arrows, six of the shafts broken, and the fletching of another dangled beneath his armpit.

Rinold grimaced as he struggled to his feet. "You've an arrow in your back."

"Am I dying?" The man bore a puzzled expression as he spun a circle, unable to see until Rinold put a hand to his chest to stop his turn. The head had forced the rivet on a ring just enough to reach his doublet and stick. He yanked it free.

"Not quite yet."

Nehek trotted up to them. "They've scattered, but the signal fire... others will come."

Two Wiirê were dead and one Silone, but he wasn't sure of injuries. "How battered are we? Who can run if need be?" No way Redhead could run even after they got the arrow out of his calf, and Bentnose, well, his nose and half his face looked broken, but the rest of the Silone looked hale enough for flight even if no one admitted to a wound.

Nehek said, "We run or we die."

"No. If you're wounded, slowed at all, stay behind and hide. If you're exhausted, stay. You run slow—"he eyeballed Edlmir"—find a cave, a nook, anything. I will run with Nehek and others to his home, draw the Histê behind us, and when we reach them we'll send Wiirê back to get you."

Edlmir snorted. "No way in hells I ain't runnin'."

Nehek squinted. "I will order two of my men to stay and guard your wounded. This way, only my people will send help."

Rinold nodded to both. "Nehek, with me."

Rinold trotted toward the smoke, scrambling up a rocky trail with shield and sword in hand, but didn't find an enemy, just the fire he'd hoped for. He stripped cloth from several nearby bodies, and they snagged two burning branches, wrapping each with a strip of fabric to burn better.

Then they ran, Rinold, Nehek, and Edlmir along with two Silone and two Wiirê. Half a horizon later, Rinold squirted a hollow log with oil and shoved his makeshift torch and half their cloth into its gut to catch a blaze, and later used the second to ignite a patch of dead brush, both sending satisfying trails of smoke into the sky. With luck, the pursuit wouldn't bother to look for the wounded left behind.

Twenty-Eight

Snow Blind Kin

A dark spark bright it ignite,
a King's Spade to dig a grave,
a Queen's heart to love a slave,
and a soul knotted into a braid.
All these to begin a war,
All these to end a war.
But what if the war is never fought?

—*Tomes of the Touched*

For three days, they spread word that the Lady Choerkin would ride south to Forest's Gate—not long ago a frontier town of a couple hundred, it had burgeoned to thousands—for her safety. They whispered stories of spies warning them of more Tek assassins hunting the warlord and his bride, and on the fourth day back from Molikîn she rode south from the wall amid four thousand warriors.

Polus commanded the Silone forces while a grumpy graybeard named Bîdorik Gorshtim headed the Kingdomer army. His men called him *Rûîrn,* which she translated herself as commander, but she didn't know the names of the Kingdomer hierarchy. Kinesee was officially third in command, but this was honorific. In reality, she suspected they'd listen to Meliu before her. The high priestess rode in the command group and pitched her tent beside Polus'.

But even if Meliu's words held more sway, Kinesee had won the battle that might prove decisive in winning the war for Ivin. Kinesee's plan to force Meliu's honesty had gone better than imagined with admissions of secrecy beyond her dreams, all of it driving a wedge between her and Ivin. She didn't hate Meliu, but Kinesee didn't trust her a lick around her husband, so it was good she didn't need to keep up the pretense of a strong friendship longer than two days' ride.

Scouts rode from the marching rows of men day and night, so it was that Kinesee departed the army with a handful of the most trusted Choerkin and Ravinrin men under a moonless night sky. Behind her she left another blonde girl to wear her gowns and ride with the command.

Once they reached a trail leading east into the mountains, they met up with two more bands of scouts to bring their count to twenty, and midday they found Tîmik Jôlvar, Ivin's second cousin, and his men holed up in a cave waiting for them. This brought their count to one hundred and twenty warriors.

They spent the night in this cave and rode a snaking trail east come dawn. The mountains here were low and covered in trees of all sorts, and aside from the snow resting on the highest peaks in the distance, there wasn't a hint of foul weather.

Their destination was the city of Holelorin, the Helelindin seat of power in the north, but Kinesee intended to get sidetracked. She'd convinced Ivin of the necessity to find Lelishen without trouble; it made sense, as the woman had served as a go-between before, but the man had sensed she wasn't telling the full truth, and it pained her not to let him in on the happy secret of a little brother. She managed to lie enough times that he surrendered, and she promised herself she'd make up for the deceit when she could.

They rode for ten days before stumbling onto the road they expected to find two days previous, or at least they hoped it was the road they were looking for. Tormîkul was their guide, a Ravinrin who'd been fortunate enough to visit the city *once*. The old coot swore up and down that he'd know the way when he spotted the right markers, but even when they found the road, he wasn't ready to declare he knew where they were. So they followed the road east for a day before reaching a trident in the road where an obelisk of black granite stuck from the dirt like a finger pointing straight to the sky.

Tormîkul hushed them as he perused the stone then announced the middle road led to their destination with a black-gapped smile. Holelorin was seven days distant, and he was jubilant to know they were on the right route, but when she asked where the other roads led, he stood staring and confused. The northern branch carried them to a village named Melôjer in under a day, and it was time to see if any of the Edan language she'd studied the past two years had stuck.

Kinesee changed into a black gown cut for riding and draped its trail over the flank of her horse. She sat straight and regal as she rode at the lead of the party as they approached, and she didn't forget to smile. The village was built from local stone and the roofs were shingled with split wood, more akin to human domiciles than she'd expected after hearing tales of the Eleris Edan, but Helelindin had visited the wall before, so their appearance wasn't a surprise. They were lean and tall, more or less human, except their eyes were too large and sparkled in the way of the Trelelunin and Edan. There wasn't a one you would call too skinny nor too fat, nor bulked with muscle. Their faces were long, and where the Silone had earlobes, the Helelindin's ears stretched in a piece of skin that arched in a ridge that reached the center of their jaw, and in a similar fashion, the tops of their ears never formed tips but grew into their hairline.

They weren't beautiful in the way of the Trelelunin, in many ways more worldly and human in presence, but at the moment a dozen men and women pointed arrows at her.

She reined her horse to a halt and raised her hand to stop the party behind her. "Greetings. I am Kinesee Choerkin of the Silone. I come as a friend seeking a Trelelunin woman named Lelishên Endûrân." Her Edan wasn't perfect, and she knew it, but she hoped it was good enough.

A woman with curly silver hair approached—she knew it a natural color and not a sign of age—with eyes shimmering gold in their green depths as she stared at Kinesee. "There are no Trelelunin here in Melôjer. Friends don't bring so many warriors."

Kinesee retained her smile. “By the Treaty of Simâm, one hundred and twenty Silone warriors may ride to Holelorin in a journey of diplomacy.”

“You make one hundred and twenty-one.”

“I am not a warrior. They are here to protect me.”

The woman nodded to the sword at her hip. “A huntress may carry a bow and not call herself a warrior, but who carries a sword that claims the same?”

“The sword was a gift from my husband, the Warlord Choerkin, but I know little of its use.”

“Warlord Choerkin? Who is it you said you seek?”

“Lelishen. She told my father to find her where the sun met the snows but didn’t give the place a name.”

The woman laughed, bowstrings creaked as muscles relaxed, and the tension in the air faded in a flicker. “In our cousin tongue, the word you seek is *perelôn.* It means snow blind from the reflection of the sun.” She pointed to the snow-capped peak of the mountain to their west. “The morning sun gave this mountain the name Perelôn.”

Kinesee gazed at the heights. Climbing a mountain hadn’t been in her plans. “Is there a road?”

She made a *shuck shuck* noise as she struck her right thumb over each of her shoulders; Helelindin laughed and most turned to walk toward town. “No road, only wilderness. You and your people are welcome to make camp outside of town. We will send word to Nosuperelôn to see if this Lelishen will come and speak to you.”

“I am in haste to reach Holelorin, but I need this woman’s aid.”

The woman huffed and wrinkled her nose. “Dismount and let me look into your eyes.”

Kinesee flung a leg over the saddle’s horn and slipped to the ground, her trailing cloak wiping her footprints behind her. She stopped strides in front of the woman. Kinesee was only fingers under six feet tall, but she was used to feeling short around her father, Ivin and other southern Silone men, but there were few women she didn’t look in the eye. She looked straight at this woman’s shoulder blades if she didn’t raise her eyes.

Slender fingers raised Kinesee's chin so that she did just that. Pine-needle green with flecks of gold, they were eerie and beautiful. "I see both humility and greatness in you, child."

Kinesee felt her cheeks redden. "Me? I don't think so."

"You prove my first observation. I see also honesty. My name is Sololu Felihol. Speak to me the name of the one you seek."

"Lelishen Endurane."

Sololu's eyes widened. "Speak to me the full truth and why."

"Veldehar Endurane, he is my baby brother."

The woman's fingers left her chin and settled on her face to slide her eyelids closed. Kinesee's heart beat faster, but she stood stone still despite her uncertainty. Lips kissed her forehead. "I will take you to Nosuperelôn, but only you."

Kinesee rode behind Sololu for three days, which was at least two days longer than she'd hoped the journey would take, and when she saw smoke billowing from a chimney she was relieved. She'd brought heavier clothes, but the nights at this altitude proved chilly.

Nosuperelôn sat at the edge of the mountain's snow line, but trails leading higher proved that something compelled folks to climb into the frosted evergreens above. Unlike the Trelelunin, who Kinesee knew to care little whether it was cold or not, Sololu donned heavier gear.

The village was a collection of a dozen stone buildings with slate roofs and oak doors. Like Melôjer below, it was utilitarian and bore few decorations to set one apart from another, except for the central building spewing smoke from its massive chimney. Blades and ax heads hung from hooks along a chain strung across the front of the building; the smell of coal smoke and the ring of hammers ended any question of this being a smithy.

Sololu greeted a Trelelunin man who poked his head from a nearby building. "Is Lelishen Endurane here?"

"Who's asking?" The man no longer looked to the guide; his eyes landed hard on Kinesee with glints of silver.

"The boy's half-sister."

He stepped outside and pointed. "Third home down on your left. If she's in."

"The rest of the journey is yours." Sololu dismounted and held her hand out to take Kinesee's reins, and in a flicker she was on the ground trying hard not to run, but when she reached the door, she hesitated. *What if I'm not welcome?* She needed to remember that her cause was more important than meeting her brother, and this hardened her will. She knocked and the door opened.

It was the first time she could recall seeing a Trelelunin startled. Lelishen's beautiful blue eyes grew so wide they went round. "Kinesee? What are you doing here?"

But she didn't get a chance to answer before her eye was drawn to the child toddling their way, and she ducked past Lelishen and dropped to her knees. "Veldehar?"

The boy looked at her with eyes not so large as his mothers, but they were the same deep blue with silver shimmers. Other than this single feature, he looked more Silone than Trelelunin. "Veldehar."

"By the gods! My little brother. He's the cutest thing I've ever seen!"

Lelishen laughed but her words came with a stern edge. "Kinesee, what are you doing here?"

Kinesee smiled at the boy as she spoke. "I need your help."

"Is it Solineus?"

She stuck her finger out and Veldehar nabbed it with a pincer grip and giggled; she struggled to break his grasp to stand. "How old is he?"

"A year and a half. Solineus?"

"He is sailing south on his way home, the last I knew, but I did send a note mentioning his son. "

"A note!" Panic struck the woman's voice.

"Don't worry, the Kingdomer pigeons are discreet and I didn't mention you. There are larger troubles."

"The Malstefnê. I heard rumors."

"An army prepares to cross the Gediswon. They might have already."

Lelishen sat in a fur-lined chair and the boy rushed to her lap. "What help could I be? The Helelindin won't go to war for the Silone."

"No, but if I can secure the privilege of pilgrimage to the Final Foundation, the Eight Kingdoms will... or they might. It's our hope."

Lelishen lifted Veldehar to her knee and stroked his blond hair. "On whose word?"

"The Ironwing and his Heart. He figures three to four kingdoms would send immediate aid if such a treaty were struck, maybe more because the best route to the Foundation is straight past the wall."

"The Treaty of Simâm was the first the Helelindin signed in memory."

Kinesee smiled with a shrug. "Perhaps it should become a habit? Solineus plans on opening trade between Helmveline and Mulshahar, would this interest the Helelindin king?"

"They are a people little interested in trinkets or wealth, and they remember the wars with the Kingdoms better than the Kingdoms do, as many fought in them."

It was tricky to wrap her head around people having fought in a war over four hundred years in the past, but it made for a seriously one-sided grudge. "Any trade at all to pin my hope on?"

"They trade spices with the Gorotan to the east, and the Trelelunin and Edan, of course. Useful supplies."

"Everybody wants something. Will you help me find it?" The way Lelishen gazed at her son Kinesee feared she would say no. "Please?"

The Trelelunin smiled, but she wasn't happy. "You are your father's daughter, even if not by blood. I will do my best even if our destiny is to fail."

"I *am* my father's daughter. He floated in Purdonis Bay for days and lived, slayed demons, took down a stone bridge, and fathered an impossibly adorable son... How much trouble could one little old king be?"

TWENTY-NINE

Pointed Message

Too often do those considered wise correlate knowledge with intelligence. A man who speaks six languages is not smarter than a man who speaks one. A woman steeped in the courts of Wedinholir is not smarter than a woman on the farm chopping wood and raising crops. The truly sage understand their intellectual superior may exist anywhere, and that the very act of believing oneself wise can make you more a fool than a simpleton.

—*Codex of Sol*

"You're lazy dung suckers, and that's why you ain't gettin' a bite of our food."

Artus' voice echoed down the street, and Eliles hastened her strides, turning a corner to find Artus and others blocking Temeru and six other priests at the gate to the gardens. Weeks had passed since Wilu's murder, and they were no closer to discovering who wielded the knife. Tensions between the two groups started out drawn taut, but the rope frayed with every passing day.

Temeru pointed. "There's more food than you can eat."

The woman had a point, but much of the garden grew wild without Wilu, and weeds made an impressive return. Despite the care lavished by some, no one had the will to spend so much time aging in the garden.

"No thanks to you and your worthless ilk. If'n there's food aplenty thank Wilu first, then me and her boys, but you ain't gettin' none."

Temeru huffed. "You think you can thwart me, old man?"

Eliles managed to step between them before they knew she was there, and she glared into Temeru's startled eyes. "I'll *thwart* you both."

"Oh look, the Fire Queen graces us with her threats."

"It's a simple agreement: If you work in the garden, you enjoy the crop of your labor."

"We are the holy—"

Jinbin shouted from behind, "Who murdered Wilu."

Eliles shot him a glare before turning back to Temeru. "The holy are as capable of pulling weeds, pruning, and watering as any other."

"This is the job of the common folk."

Artus puffed and surged a step. "And what the godsdamns is your job? Sittin' on your ass eating while we grow old?"

"We see to your souls—"

"My soul don't godsdamn need you, but I'll trade you a bushel of taters and onions if you turn Niktir over to us. Way I figure, that's a job you can handle."

Eliles raised her arms. "Enough! The rule is simple: You work; you eat. I've heard rumor that priests have offered to help in the gardens, and you denied their requests." Nefelêu, a priestess near Eliles' age, whispered this to her weeks back.

"Such work is beneath them."

"Since when have the tenants of Sol forbade labor?"

"The servants of Sol have no need to dirty their fingers. And it wouldn't be safe, not with your people being so belligerent."

"Safe? Was Wilu a priest killed by one of these people?"

"Unless you know more than you've said, there's no proof your people didn't kill her... maybe even one of her sons, gods forbid. As I know where your loyalties lie, perhaps this island needs a new queen."

"This island doesn't *have* a queen."

"Then who commands my people not to eat the food the gods provide?"

"It doesn't belong to a queen; it's a command of common courtesy." Eliles saw the priest coming before Temeru had a chance to know he was there. "What does Niktir think?"

Temeru turned on him. "I told you to stay in the stars."

Niktir strode close before stopping. "I grew tired of the night. Look, everyone! I didn't kill Wilu, and I'm happy to spend time tending the garden."

Kavlin, Wilu's youngest boy, stepped from the group. "You're the last bastard who'll eat from these gardens."

"Your mother and I had words, but I implore you—"

Blood showered from Niktir's skull and he fell in the street. Fletching sprouted from his head, but Eliles' eyes didn't linger as priests kneeled with prayers. The arrow came from the east, so she focused the energies of the Sliver in that direction even as priests and islanders gave chase to a fleeting shadow.

Artus came close to whisper. "A blunted bolt by the size of the hole in the boy's head. Teks make 'em, but I've seen clan-blood use them for hunting. Who the hells has a crossbow on the Watch?"

"No one I know." She felt someone running; Reinus, Wilu's eldest. She grimaced and dropped to a knee beside Niktir. "Will he live?"

Solumor answered, "He's dead; there's nothing my prayers can do for a wound like this."

Eliles understood the truth. The quarrel hit the man square in the one place most difficult to heal: the brain.

"It would require the gods themselves to bring this man back to our world." Temeru loomed above them. "Unless your Sliver of Star can heal him."

The sudden temptation gnawed at her, and she drew on the energies of the Sliver. Then she stopped, her mind flipping to the Prophecy that foretold that the Sliver of Star would raise the next king priest from the dead. She didn't know if it was even possible—she suspected it wasn't—but she wasn't about to try. "As you say, only the gods."

Shouts came from the east and she rose to see Reinus escorted their way. Jinbin and priests led while islanders hung back, solemn. When they arrived, Jinbin held up a crossbow of Tek make. "He didn't run far."

Reinus said, "I didn't mean to run at all. Not like he did. A coward to hide in the stars after murdering my ma."

Temeru said, "An admitted and unrepentant murderer. The Pantheon of Sol will deal with the life and soul of a man bold enough to slay a servant of Skywatch."

The notion of the man burning alive while Life forced his torment to endure made her skin crawl; being Thrown to the Thorns might be kinder if they had any. "Herald's Watch is clan territory subject to clan law." Denying the man's crime and punishment would be foolish, but whether by ax or sword, the man deserved better than burning.

"The gardens are on hallowed ground."

"And we are not inside the gardens." Eliles matched Temeru's glare until the woman smiled.

"Clan law it is, by Queen's Decree. If his execution isn't swift, we will come for him." She turned to her people. "Bring clean cloth so we might prepare his body."

Eliles turned to Artus. "Bind him."

Artus stared at her. "With what?"

"Be creative. Let's just get the hells out of here."

Artus stepped behind Reinus and ripped his shirt down over his shoulders, then twisted it around the man's wrists before leading him downhill. "What the shits were you thinkin', boy?"

"I waited for you two to do something... so I decided to wait for him to show his face."

Eliles stayed behind him. "I told you I didn't think he did it."

"You aren't one of them, but you are... He did it."

Artus said, "You showed a fool's courage, I grant you. Where'd you get a Thonian crossbow?"

"And how'd you know to hit him in the head?"

"Head? It was the shot I had. I found the bow months back, hidden in a shed not so far from Skywatch with a sheaf of quarrels."

Eliles huffed. "I wish you hadn't done it."

His laugh was weak. "Right about now, I'm agreeing with you. Damn, I mean... I half expected to miss him."

Artus said, "You understand we're gonna have to execute you?"

"I thought I'd come to grips with that... but now it's done I'm not certain I'm ready to die."

"Forges, boy! Forges be damned!"

Eliles slowed, letting the men walk ahead. They took Reinus to a small jail a street up from the docks. Its barred cages once held brawlers and drunks, and she imagined the occasional killer, but its cells stood empty until today.

When the door clanged closed, she stepped outside and headed for her fishing boulder to think. She plopped her butt down hard enough to hurt, planted her hand to her palm, and sulked.

"Holy hells! That's a big one!"

Eliles turned to see Barold holding up a black sea bass that stretched two feet from nose to tail if it was a finger, but it was the man screaming his congratulations that stopped her thoughts cold: Reinus.

She leaped to her feet and stormed his way. "Bless it, Artus! I leave you alone for a wick and you let the man go?" She tromped down the dock. "Reinus! What the Twelve Hells are you doing?"

The two men stared at her, and Reinus said, "Fishing?"

"Well, it is a nice fish, Barold." She grabbed Reinus' collar and hauled on him. "You come with me."

"All right, fine. Let go of me."

She let loose his shirt. "If you run, I'll turn you over to Temeru next time."

"What are you talking about?"

She led him through the front door of the jail and there sat Artus with his feet kicked up on a stool. Snoring. The jail cell stood wide open. She kicked his chair. "Artus!"

The Choerkin flew from his seat. "Reinus! What are you doing out of your cell, boy?"

"That's exactly what I was wondering when I found him fishing."

"Why would I be in a cell?"

Artus grabbed his shoulders and shook. "You put a quarrel through Niktir's head!"

Reinus' eyes flew wide. "I put a what? Is he dead?"

Eliles raised her hand. "Stop. Reinus, do you have a crossbow?"

"A crossbow? I haven't ever seen one except on a Tek ship."

"Do you know what a sheaf is? A sheaf of quarrels?" The look he bore was the answer she needed to erase any doubt that the Face of Ulrikt wasn't a myth and that it shared this little island with them. "How long were you with Barold?"

"Since this morning."

Eliles shared a glance with Artus before turning back to their prisoner. "Reinus, you're going to have to do me a favor and go sit in that cell for a while."

"Oh, hells no. I didn't kill no one, and I'm not gonna sit and rot for it."

"I didn't say rot. Just go and sit for a bit. I'll even have Seden cook up that fish for you."

"I know the punishment for murder... I'd like to keep my head."

"If you sit in your cell I'll make sure you do, and make sure you aren't burnt alive."

He was a smart man and took the offer, closing the cell's door behind him. "I want her to break out some of the good spices."

"Done."

Artus stepped close. "The Face is real?"

"I can't doubt it any longer. Worse, the Face wanted us to know."

"So what the hells is its game? It ain't like the holies in their stars, and the rest of us were all friendly like to begin with. What next?"

"I'll stay with Reinus and try to explain what we know. You need to find Temeru and send her to me. She and I need to talk."

Reinus and Barold sat through Eliles' tale with polite, albeit disbelieving, attention. She left out details of the shrine and crown because they raised more questions than she could begin to answer, but even simplified, the men found the whole hard to swallow. She couldn't blame them, but in the end, they needed to accept the unbelievable as true.

They ate dinner and were sitting around sipping Artus' whiskey by the time Temeru arrived. She strode through the door with the airs of superiority and righteousness typical of a high priest.

"This is how murderers are treated under clan law? Eating and drinking while the dead burn?"

After candles of waiting on the woman, Eliles wasn't of a temper to dance with words. "Reinus didn't kill Niktir."

"What game is the queen playing? I've a half dozen witnesses to his confession."

"The Face of Ulrikt killed Reinus. This man was fishing with his brother."

Temeru's brows rose. "An unassailable alibi! Brothers will never lie for one another. He was there, he admitted it, we have the crossbow—"

"All lies. You yourself suggested the Face might be on the Watch."

"Did I? Idle musings harkening to my youth as a barefoot postulant. No one believes in the Face except, apparently, you. And then only when it's convenient."

"The Face is trying to drive a wedge between the adherents of Sol and the islanders."

Temeru strolled to the window and gazed outside. It was the first time that Eliles noticed a gathering of the holy, more than thirty, more than she figured lived in the Stars. "They came for an execution, a way of seeing the murdered welcomed to the Stars, and you wish me to feed them some tall tale of the Face of Ulrikt murdering their comrade... And for what? To frame this worthless man?"

"What life is worthless in the eyes of Sol?"

"I am not Sol, and neither are my people. The King of Gods will judge his soul, but by his own confession, his body is guilty. He must pay for the crime."

"He will not die for a crime he didn't commit."

Temeru turned her gaze to Reinus. "It isn't the mythical Face who drives the wedge between our peoples; it is you. Show your devotion to harmony with the devout by offering this man's life to appease the aggrieved."

"You don't care whether the Face did this or not. You don't care about truth."

"Truth? Are you so arrogant that you believe you know the truth? A fact isn't truth, and truth isn't a fact; truth is whatever those people standing outside believe. They will have blood."

"You think I'll let your people serve holy justice?"

Temeru's face twisted with mock humility. "Gracious no. My people would never defy their beloved queen. And even if it were their will, you are the god of this island, and what hope do we mortals have against a god?"

"You aren't defying me. You're defying reason."

"Am I? If I presume the Face is real and that it killed Niktir, while under the guise of the man in your cell, I have nothing more than your word that this still isn't the Face, guilty of his crime."

Winning this argument wasn't possible; every word from the woman's mouth made that clear, but it was *why* that troubled Eliles. "Or maybe it's you who are the Face. Why else—"

"There is one truth you need to grasp: I am *not* your friend, Eliles of Istinjoln, and none of those people standing outside will be for so long as the murderer breathes." She smiled as she turned and strode through the door, and soon after, Eliles heard the priestess' voice speaking to her congregation. "There will be no execution today, by edict of the queen. Wait. No. There will be a trial by clan law, but until that day, we retreat to our stars and wait."

Artus whistled from his chair. "Aye, well, that went better than expected."

"I'm going to strike that woman straight to the hells."

"Whoa, girl. The Face would love that, now wouldn't he?"

She spun on him. "What the hells can I do that the Face wouldn't love? I execute an innocent man, appeasing Skywatch for a time, or I do what's right and keep him alive, and the holy hate us."

Reinus said, "My vote is for keeping me alive."

Eliles laughed. "You won't die by our hands."

Artus poured a shot and drank. "You could kill all of them. I wager the Face wouldn't like that at all."

For a flicker, the notion appealed to her. "No, what he'd hate more is my proving he's real to the entire island."

"Aye, and how the hells you thinkin' of doing that?"

She skulked to the whiskey but stopped short of the temptation. "I don't know."

The bottle disappeared from beneath her nose as the Choerkin poured again. "You know what the Face really wouldn't like? You killing him."

"Do all your solutions end with killing someone?"

He shrugged. "Old dog and all that."

"Killing isn't something I make a habit of."

Artus raised his glass in salute. "One does not a habit make. Ain't no one safe so long as the Face is on this island... maybe not even you."

His admonition rang true. Even if the Face couldn't kill her, she was vulnerable. "There's another way. I just have to find it."

"And if there ain't?"

She couldn't say the words aloud but forced herself to swallow the notion that she may have to kill the Face of Ulrikt. It was easy to justify his death; it was difficult to imagine herself killing in cold blood; it was impossible to conceive of a way to ensnare someone who could be anyone.

Thirty

Dry Rains

A seed, a weed, a deed,
where does the plant growing lead?
Vines and barbs prick the bird and stick the man,
but by what twist of nature is the root forgotten?
The foot, nibbled and eaten by mouse so lowly,
Vines and Spines killed by meager foe,
so low it's below,
who feeds its flesh to so many.
Your root, my root, two foot two by two,
Do and do what the thorny bush cannot see done,
Stomp and tromp to keep the Weak and Wily Killer away.

—*Tomes of the Touched*

For five days, they zigged and zagged through a forest only tolerable because it was a leg of the journey home. Rinold hated this place, its stench of festering pools, the mud sucking at his boots, the whipping plants with thorns, the snakes with their fangs, and the heat of the midday sun before clouds blackened the sky again. *Dear gods, more rain.* It wasn't even the rainy season yet.

He heard distant thunder in the early afternoon while a bright sky was still visible through the leaves, promising to make their ducking and dodging flight more brutal than it already was. Lightning streaked the sky and within flickers of the first spits of rain in his face, the drops grew heavy and numerous enough to blur the world. Nehek and Jitô were the only Wiirê still with the steel covered Silone, and Rinold couldn't blame those others one lick for outpacing them. Fatigue tempted him to strip his armor more than a few times, but the threat of whizzing arrows was a reminder of why he suffered the flopping weight.

When the rain grew so heavy that even Nehek had trouble seeing vines needing slapped from his face, Rinold grabbed his shoulder. "We need shelter! Rest."

Nehek ducked behind a tree whose trunk was broad enough to carve into a home. "It isn't safe to stop." Lightning struck the canopy a hill away as if to accentuate his point.

"It isn't safe to run. Do you know where we are?"

"We're past my village. We couldn't risk leading the Histê to them."

Rinold wiped his brow of rain. "Then you know the area, find us a cave or somethin'." The man's brow furled. "Come on. There must be somewhere."

"Ontotutusku. Forbidden ground. Evil gods. Demons."

"Demons. Evil gods, I don't give a shit nor piss for any godsdamned gods, whether the Histê run us to death or put holes in our backs we're dead if we don't find a place to hide."

They rested their lungs long enough for the rains to slow before setting out, but the mud-slicked terrain discouraged running as much as the fear of crossing the edge of exhaustion. A half candle into their slipping and sliding march, Nehek raised his hand, and as everyone stopped, he pointed to an arch of stone down a steep incline, barely visible through the downpour. "That is the entrance. It is a place mortals do not walk."

"These mortals will." He wanted to say that he'd faced worse in the Shadows of Man, but figured it best not to tempt the fates to prove him wrong.

"There's a winding path—"

Rinold's helm rang and something clacked off a tree to his right; it took a flicker to realize that it was an arrow that clattered into the woods after the ricochet. He clutched his targe and spun in time for two more arrows to strike his shield, but Rateyes took a point straight to his face. The man's arms flailed, his sword flung in the air, and he tumbled backward, sliding down the hill, bouncing off trees in a spray of rain and mud.

Nehek said, "Run!"

But the Histê were already charging, a dozen of them and coming fast.

Edlmir set his feet. "I'm dying here and now if the gods demand it. No more runnin' for me."

Rinold relaxed in a flicker of decision; damned if Edlmir didn't have it right. The running ended. He glanced at Rateyes' body as it spun to a stop at the bottom of the hill, and his mind slipped back to the bowl of the Touched and its icy slope. His calm spun into a pounding heart. He slapped Edlmir in the back of the head. "How do you feel about sliding?"

He didn't wait for an answer; he turned and leaped, sticking his legs out and letting the greasy mud do the rest. Turned out mud wasn't as fun as a sheet of ice, and as a stick rammed him in the thigh he tumbled, coming upright in time to put a shield between him and a tree. His shoulder crunched and the trunk beat the breath from his lungs before he could scream. He tumbled, croaking for air, scored the hill with his elbow as a rudder, and ducked beneath a fallen log a dead man didn't have trouble slipping beneath.

Thirty feet from the flat bottom he took to the air all of a horrible sudden, arms flailing as if a shield and sword could help him fly; he hadn't seen that drop-off from on high. Eyes wide, he landed flat on his back and was for the first time thankful for all the mud stuffed in his mail to break his fall.

He gasped for breath on hands and knees; his mud packed armor felt as if he had a soggy rider on his back. He planted his sword in the ground to stand just in time for Edlmir to take his legs clean from under him. The men tumbled in a jumble, and even as others arrived, Rinold came to his knees laughing.

Edlmir kicked from beneath him. "What the hells is so gods-damned funny, Squirrel?"

"Tokodin would be laughing his holy ass off about now. "

"The bloke who done murdered Kotin?"

"I'll explain later." He staggered to his feet as arrows splattered into the mud, and he lumbered three paces before reaching an overgrown stone path that kept his feet from sinking. He stood and stared, mud slopping from his back to splat behind his heels; at least he was a little lighter now.

The stone arch loomed ahead, a lonesome construction in the middle of the wilderness. Its columns stood thirty feet high, and its span bore a weathered scene displaying the busts of men and women, except someone had chiseled the faces flat. In the middle of whatever had been there was a carving that resembled the head of a lion. "What the shittin' hells..."

But he didn't have time to ponder further as Nehek shoved him through the entrance. "Find cover!"

They scrambled forward, but none of the stone paths appeared to lead anywhere. The best he could see was a row of thick bushes that grew along a trail, damned near like a hedge grown wild for decades. He put his shield in front of his face and plowed into the bushes, thorny vines whipping his skin and snagging links of mail.

Then he tumbled onto a pristine marble floor. The stone was dry, but a flicker before it'd been raining. He looked up at the sky, watched the rain fall, tumbling from the canopy of the forest above before striking with spatters ten feet above his head, collecting into neatly spaced streams before disappearing as if flowing into an invisible gutter. Nehek and the rest tripped and stumbled in after him as they penetrated the shrubbery.

Edlmir panted, fighting for breath to speak. "How safe are we?"

Nehek grunted. "The Histê won't follow, forbidden ground is forbidden."

"You're certain?"

"They aren't as desperate to kill us as we are to escape them. They won't enter."

Rinold ignored them, staring at the floor. "This stone, it's perfect. No dirt, no cracks, no weeds. I've seen this before."

"It is Ontotutusku. It is not a place of the living nor the dead."

Rinold looked to Edlmir and spoke in Silone. "It's like the Tomb of the Touched. Unmarred by time and nature."

Edlmir's lips pursed. "Let's hope no riddlin', dead bastard shows up."

"I don't know. The Touched might be handy about now."

Edlmir grunted at Rinold and spoke to Nehek. "What'll these Histê do now?"

"They will surround us until morning, then leave."

That sounded too damned optimistic for Rinold's taste. "Why the hells would they do that?"

"Because no one survives the night in Ontotutusku."

So much for optimistic. Rinold let his sword and shield drop to the floor to lean back on his elbows, then figured to hells with it and laid down, hands propped beneath his head. He stared at the rain that never reached his face. A sense of calm swept him, and he remembered the night spent in the Tomb. The silence had been so intense as to force him into slumber, and he'd slept like a babe who knew only swaddled warmth and a mother's milk, not a man hunted by Shadows of Man and Taken. No silence here, but the patter of rain over an impossibly dry marble floor was a different sort of comfort. He yawned.

"Well, leastwise, we have a few candles until dark. Wake me before we die." A funny thing that a place so unnatural could make him feel so safe.

Rinold awoke to Edlmir's toe in his ribs. "If'n we ain't about to die, I'm gonna kill you."

"We mightn't be dead yet, but you should see this."

He sat up in pitch black with a groan, his thoughts groggy. "Can't see a shittin' thing." Not true; a beam of moonlight shown through a window, illuminating the pale white floor. *There weren't windows... because there weren't any walls.* "Where the hells did you drag me?" It was ludicrous; a snapping twig would wake him from the deepest sleep.

"I didn't drag no one nowhere. I was sitting the watch as the sun fell... I look up—"

"Walls." He spat and reached for his canteen for a drink, a swallow for time to think. Before meeting the Touched, a building appearing from nowhere would've sent his feet to shaking in his boots, but now the rain made sense, it had been hitting a ceiling he couldn't see. He looked up, and sure enough, a roof hid his view of trees and stars and moon. "As the man said, it's Ontotutusku."

"Forges, you ain't seen nothin' yet." The big man crawled to the window and Rinold followed close.

The moon lit the outside world with haunting shadows, but other than the fact the overgrown hedge was pruned to perfect globes, he didn't see anything so unusual. "You've been gardening?"

"Shush them squirrel lips and watch."

A small yellow light hovered down the stone path, swinging hip-high as if it was a lantern along for someone's casual stroll, except there was no lantern, no one there at all. He ducked behind the wall. "Shits."

"Aye. A specter of some sort?"

"A ghost maybe. Solineus saw one in Istiinjoln, talked to the bastard."

Edlmir stared with slow blinks. "I should never have ridden with you whoresons; weird shit follows you both."

"The ghost was Eliles' Master of Fire at Istinjoln; Lord Priest Ulrikt Sundered his soul for murdering him."

"That's s'posed to make it pissin' normal?"

"No, but he helped us. Seein' ghosts don't mean they're out to tear your eyes out and stuff them in yer ears like some children's story."

"What the hells kind of children's story is that?"

"The Wolverine's." He rose to look out the window as the light passed, and another floated down a path more distant. "We see the flames of the lanterns but nothing else, how does that make sense?"

"Yer shittin' me, right? I don't see nothin' that makes sense."

"Good point. Wake Nehek and get him over here." Rinold stared out the window while he waited, watching another fire wander past.

Nehek's breath sucked next to Rinold's ear. "Demons."

"I've seen demons... These are spirits of the dead carrying fires."

"They look like men... demons."

"You see them?"

"Yes."

"All we see are fires." But as a light approached it turned a darker yellow by a couple of shades, and Rinold's heart thudded when he saw the vague outline of a man in robes. When this person turned toward their building, his bladder filled. "Forges. Hide." The room was empty except for them. "Sit stone still. Do nothing."

He cursed himself for letting the others sleep, but waking them now might be a disaster. The door opened and Rinold pressed his back against the wall beside Edlmir. Nehek knelt with hands splayed and his face against the floor. An oppressive silence descended, and he feared that if his gut grumbled it'd give them away.

The apparition strode through the door with strides like a man, the impression of eyes in his spectral face glancing around the room. He twisted the nob on his lantern and raised the hood, a silver plate casting a beam of light straight across the sleeping men, but the ghost didn't react to their presence, not even a pause in the light's movement. Might be the ghost couldn't see them.

The being stepped deeper into the room, its transparent feet disappearing inside Snortspittle. Rinold grinned. *They can't see us.* But then the ghost looked down at its feet, raising and lowering them, and his free hand pulled a short, heavy-bladed sword from beneath his robes.

Rinold's skin chilled with sweat as the figure turned his lantern around the room. Its light landed upon Nehek and lingered. Slow strides brought him closer, his lantern lowering, his sword pointing straight at the man. The Wiirê trembled.

Don't do it. Don't run. Don't move. But Rinold didn't dare speak aloud.

Trembles turned into fidgets, and in a burst, Nehek rose and fell back into his prostrated pose, a drone of prayer from his lips. The ghost leaped backward, battle-ready, his lips moving, screaming, but he didn't make a sound Rinold could hear. The ghost of the fire master in Istinjoln could hear Solineus, but no one heard him.

"Nehek! Quiet! Shut your mouth!" In the light of the lantern the Wiirê's yellow-eyes glowed. "Cover your eyes! Shut them!"

But Nehek's bowing prayers with wide eyes went on, and the haunt drew closer, screaming in silence and prodding forward with his sword step by step. He was within a stride of striking the Wiirê's skull when Rinold's will snapped. He rose and lurched between them, shield raised. "No!"

He expected the ghost's sword to pass through him, killing him or not, but against expectations the apparition stopped. Rinold stared straight through translucent eyes. He would've preferred the ghost more opaque, as then he wouldn't be able to see three more apparitions gathered in the building's entry. Two women and a man, all carrying lights, and all armed. "No."

The spirit in front pointed his sword at him, but waved his light to those behind him, his mouth moving as he stepped back.

"Edlmir! Get Nehek to shut up."

"I can knock his ass out."

"I'd rather you didn't." Edlmir shook Nehek, and at least the prayers ceased, but the ghost side-stepped to gaze at the kneeling man. "I think he sees his eyes."

The spirit circled them with his lantern focused on Nehek or Rinold, his strides slow, his face puzzled as if observing some curiosity.

"This yellow-eye is my friend." The ghost's gaze jerked to face him, proof the ghost heard his words, but the spirit's ears weren't the only ones to hear him.

The sleeping men awoke, Jitô's eyes shining in the light. The spirits leaped, striking in a fury, and the Wiirê screamed in more than panic. Rinold could see the world through the blades of the weapons, but they bit flesh as sure as any other, driving the man to the ground in spatters of blood. He stood transfixed, unable to scream in time to save the man.

"No! Friend!" The three ghosts turned on him, and he stayed between them and Nehek, ready to test whether his shield and sword would do a spit's worth of good. "Godsdamned bastards! Let us sleep the night! We'll be gone come morning!" They pressed forward and he snarled. "Come on then! Forges take your Sundered souls, you sons of bitches."

A spectral arm appeared before his eyes, short blade in hand, and the three stopped. Stopped and glared, none too happy judging from the twist of their lips as they spoke. But the first ghost sheathed his sword, held his lantern high, and pointed toward the door; the three backed to the entrance, not quite leaving as the first ghost turned to Rinold.

His mouth moved and he tapped his left ear. "No, I can't hear you."

The ghost rubbed his chin and specks of light flickered. The stubble of a day-old shave? "Do you know the Touched?"

The ghost's gaze was a blank. He pointed to the ground, raised a hand to his ear, and leaned his head.

"You want us to sleep? You won't harm us?" A spectral nod was all Rinold needed. He sheathed his sword and leaned his shield against the wall. "Thank you. And I swear on the Seven Heavens we'll be gone after first light."

The ghost's gaze shimmered as the light of the fire in his lantern flickered a shade darker. He gave a single nod before walking to the door, directing his fellow spooks to vacate. He closed the door and lowered the hood of his lantern to darken the room before setting it on the floor.

Edlmir stood. "That there had me pissin' straight to the hells. That was courage like I ain't seen afore."

"That was stupidity I ain't done before. I was wagerin' fifty-fifty they wouldn't be able to hurt us. I lost that one."

"Least yer alive, Squirrel. You ain't a pelt on no one's wall just yet."

Rinold glanced at Nehek as the man turned Jitô's body to his back, laying his hands clasped on his bloodied belly. The other Silone crept from the corners of the room, eyes on the dead man in the dim light of moon and hooded lantern.

"Worked out better for us than another."

"We've slept beside more dead than we can count. We make it to morning just like we always do, or we die tryin'. Now tell me about Tokodin, I could use a laugh about now."

Rinold slumped and plopped to the ground, crossed his legs. "We were on our way to see the Touched. This bastard holy, Tokodin, his ass is so tight I doubt he shits..."

THIRTY-ONE

Mother's Paradise

Monemolar claimed that demons always lie, but confessed that truths aren't always facts. Therefore a demon's lie could accidentally speak a truth.

—*Oxeum Codex*

The *Lady Moon's* prow struck glistening black beach on the island of Pôn twenty-seven days after setting sail from Mulshahar. It took five days to get out of Kônu Bay with weak winds, but much of the extra time was from their circuitous route to avoid any ambush. The island was small, two mountain peaks connected by a forested ridge, and Solineus figured a person could circle the island's coast in a day. The glossy beach with pristine waters and perfect blue sky over emerald greens woods suggested why his father said folks would hesitate to leave, but he only had flickers to appreciate the beauty before his attention was ripped away.

Solineus' eyes bugged as men rushed ashore to hug loved ones, but it was the young ladies running for the beach that unerringly drew his stare. Dark-haired, dark-eyed, and with a deeper tan than he imagined a Silone could achieve, they were naked except for short skirts.

A hand thumped his shoulder. "You'll get used to it."

He glanced back to his father. "I hope so... or not. I reckon I'm not sure."

"They're a kind people who welcomed us."

"And attractive." He tried not to stare. "They welcomed us just like that?"

Adinvan chuckled. "Not *just like that.* They were plum terrified when first we arrived and we had no idea why. We traded a few trinkets for fresh water at first while we dropped anchor beside smaller islands with no one on 'em, just over the horizon there. Then one day we show up to find galleys in the harbor and some bastards dragging men and women from the island."

"And you saw a way to make friends."

"Aye. Sol never shined his light on them who take slaves. Those ships are sittin' beneath the waves as we speak, and every damned Histê aboard fed the sharks." He vaulted onto the beach, and Solineus followed as he led them along a path rising toward trees in the distance. "All the islands hereabouts are terrorized by Histê."

"The Kingdomers spoke of the Histê. They had a low opinion of them."

"For good reason. Their cities are huge yet primitive. Their ships are floating turds with oars, and their weapons and armor are inferior steel, if steel at all, but there's a godsdamn lot of them. And their priests are wicked bastards from all I hear. A Luxun trader told us that any ghost ship we see is because of their priests."

"But you defeated them?"

A proud smile. "We attack 'em before they get close enough to work any witchery, and their boats are too damned slow to catch us. If we had Wyvern's Flash, we'd really torch 'em right. The big island of Chitorâ is south of us, that's where we did the most damage and made the most friends. The bulk of the Emudar who've made it this far south are on Chitorâ and its sister island to the west, Tebôhûu. There're islands between we haven't protected as well as these."

"You don't fear reprisal?"

"The hells we don't. And it was comin'. A Sedeswên trader spoke of a buildup of galleys in the harbor at Rôqwu, so we raided several villages horizons north of that hive, took one of their temples, and when they came for us we torched their shipyards at Rôqwu, sinking or scorching a hundred galleys or more. No major threats since, but we're building for the day they come back."

The Sedeswên he'd never heard of. "But no mention of yellow-eyed men?"

Adinvan shook his head. "Gods know what lives in them forests. Heard rumors ranging from dragons to trolls to boar-faced men with tusks. Might be every damned story is true."

A scream broke the calm and his fingers unlatched the Twins to fall to his hips, but then he saw the woman running toward them. It wasn't terror; it was joy.

She was blonde and in her mid-forties, he guessed, and though she wore a dress her breasts were covered only by her hair... but her skin was too light for a native of Pôn.

Adinvan leaned toward his ear. "That's your mother."

Solineus raised his arms at the last flicker, and he stumbled to keep his feet in the squealing hug. For a flicker, he forgot her name again. "Mother! Suseru! Great to see you again. So much of you!" He'd tried to avert his eyes, but it'd been too late. Naked strangers were awkward enough. This was something other.

"My boy is back! Your sister will be thrilled."

I hope she's wearing more clothes. "And I'll be thrilled to see her. Erênu is here if father spoke true." She was the youngest but twenty by now.

"She is, she is. Kulloru is on Chitorâ."

Adinvan grabbed her arm and pulled her into his own hug. "I reckon our boy isn't used to seeing his mother bared to nature."

Solineus didn't even try to meet her eye; he stared right over her head.

She spoke from beneath his chin. "I reckon he's seen breasts before."

"Oh aye, we're grandparents now... two girls and a boy."

"I'd be surprised by so few."

"Whoa! Whoa. The girls are adopted, and the boy is on the surprising order, I admit. Let's walk. I want to see this island father here's been bragging about."

Suseru took the lead and Solineus discovered how barely her skirt covered her cheeks. He coughed but didn't say a word.

"The people built up the mountain a bit like Herald's Watch, only warm and beautiful instead of cold and ugly." She pointed to an odd plant with long green stems edged with hook-like barbs. "The natives call this *ilbolu,* we harvest and mash the stems, and the juice can be spread on the skin to keep the sun from burning your hide, and it helps heal as well."

He already knew the plant's oils smelled of pungent ginger from Adinvan's insistence on having him smear the stuff on his face while at sea. "Looks dangerous."

"The barbs aren't as hard nor sharp as they look."

They walked without a hurry as Solineus took in the lush trees with branches drooping with long frilly leaves, flowers of more colors than he'd imagined possible, and birds with displays of plumage so bright they made him wonder how they survived without being eaten. As they walked, Adinvan recounted the harrowing tale of the Silone's migration south for his wife while Solineus shut out the depressing stories and focused on the dewy humidity and tranquility of the island.

The trail snaked and wound through dense trees and small clearings. Birds sang and chirped in a hundred different voices, and the breezes across the mountain cooled his skin when their path led out of the shade. When a large beetle buzzed his head, he ducked, and a flicker later, realized how few bugs he'd seen and that none had tried to bite him.

When the trees cleared, he found himself staring at a plateau with thirty or so thatched-roof buildings, the walls of which were covered in a cream-white stucco of some sort. But the walls weren't plain, the eaves and window frames were painted in swirling patterns of pastels ranging from violets and reds to blues, greens, and oranges. The native men, women, and children smiled as they worked or played—not a one covering their chests—and the place wasn't lacking for laughter. It was dizzying in its foreignness and yet idyllic enough to make him stop and ponder.

"I see why nobody wants to leave this place."

Suseru turned and Solineus raised his eyes over her head again. "Yet you will be leaving."

"There are pressing matters to see to."

Adinvan said, "And I'll be going with him."

She eyed them both, turned with a huff, and strode toward a building. "Men are fools. Erênu, come out and say high to your fool of a brother."

They stood for a wick, then a young woman with blonde hair down to her waist stepped from the door. She was beautiful, a perfect picture of his mother younger, but as she ran to him, he smiled to note she covered herself better. She leaped high and plowed into him with a draping hug, and he struggled to keep his feet as he laughed.

"Good to see you too, sis."

She unwrapped her legs and dropped to her feet, but her hands still rested on his shoulders. "We all thought you dead!"

"Turns out I'm not so easy to get rid of. Good to see you still wear more clothes than some of us."

"You *are* my brother... But when there are only ladies about?"

"No, not you too."

Suseru said, "Your brother's grown squeamish."

Erênu cast him a playful grin. "I'm pretty sure all us kids ate from—"

"That's it!" Solineus laughed. "Enough. Find a quiet place and a wrap for mother's... mother's nakedness, and we'll tell our tales proper like."

The story of the Silone's trail of pyres leading south struck everyone who listened like a knife to the heart. They ate a lunch of roast hog and pineapple with a thick, sweet Edinberry sauce after, and no one spoke a word.

But as soon as the food disappeared, Suseru lit Adinvan's ass on fire. "If you think you're traipsing off on some Forges-cursed, gods-damned, years-long journey, you aren't going to have a wife when you get back."

"I—"

"No! You set sail for Mulshahar and don't come back for six months."

Adinvan stewed before a controlled growl. "I brought our boy home."

"And home you should both stay. But you aren't a young man no more."

"I'm the Lord of the Emudar now. I need to meet with the other lords, the Warlord Choerkin."

"Yes. You are the Lord of the Emudar, which is why you need to *stay* with the Emudar. The threats here are as real as they are inland. The Hive is buzzing."

Solineus knew enough to understand she spoke of a Histê city, and The Hive was a shortened nickname. "What do you mean?"

Adinvan said, "Some months after we sacked the shipyards at Rôqwu, we got wind of building farther to the south in Hîvukûqwunowu. It's upriver several horizons; no way we reach it without more blood than we can afford."

Suseru glared at the both of them. "Neither of you is trying for The Hive. I forbid it."

"We can't let some Histê fleet hit Chitorâ."

"You said yourself it isn't possible."

Solineus knew he missed something. "Raiding up rivers is nothing the Silone haven't done."

Adinvan nodded. "We've got more deepwater ships than longboats these days and built for trade mostly. The river is plenty wide and plenty deep, mind you, but there's a fortress just inside its mouth. I'm not so certain we'd make it past, and they'd be ready for us at The Hive."

Suseru chimed in. "Which is why you must stay, to defend the clan."

Solineus reached into his jacket pocket and pulled out a map he'd scribbled. It was a rough mess, but it gave him the gist of where things were. "How far south is this river?"

Adinvan tapped the map not far from where the waters turned into the Monsoon Strait. "That's my guess, anyways. Your map is about as perfect as my knowledge of the area. What I know is what I've been told."

"Captain Edmordô will know better, but I reckon precise isn't what I need. Any towns or cities to its north? Close enough horsemen can carry a message quick."

Adinvan chuckled. "The Histê don't have horsemen to speak of, least not I've ever seen. Oxen in the fields, sheep and goats. I don't know of any cities or towns, but I haven't sailed so far south. They've villages and such scattered all along the coast I've seen."

Horses were rare and expensive on Kaludor, but no horses at all boggled his mind. "Mother is right; you stay here. When sailing south we'll raid villages above the river, and then farther down south. We'll raid all the way down and keep raiding as we enter the Strait. They'll send ships after us, forgetting Chitorâ."

Erênu said, "We've led them on more than a few chases; they aren't going to forget Chitorâ without a better reason."

"We give them a better reason then."

His sister's pretty smile was just annoying now. "Like?"

"Hells if I know. I don't know the region. I'm just slingin' shit at the wall. I'll be sailing south, and when I see it, I'll know it."

Suseru enjoyed a smug smile. "It isn't a plan at all, and not one worth your father leaving us."

"I don't want him along."

"I'm going."

Solineus snorted. "The hells you are, your place is here."

"Your son has spoken."

"I'm going, godsdamnit! "

Then Erênu, "I'm going as well."

That shut the bickering down in a snap, and they all stared.

Suseru broke the silence. "My youngest isn't going off to war... or whatever the hells these foolish men think they'll conjure."

"I'm old enough to decide—"

"Your father isn't old enough to make a sound decision!"

"Because he doesn't agree with you?"

The two women glared, and Solineus leaned back in his seat, not wanting in the middle. His eye wandered to the map and landed on a speck of land. "What's on this island here?"

Adinvan said, "Lîopu? Bare rock more than anything else."

"What about these islands just inside the Strait?"

"I haven't the faintest idea. None of our ships run so far south."

Solineus groaned and leaned back in his seat. "We need something big, something they can't ignore. Something that takes them south."

Suseru said, "We don't know these people so well to even say what that'd be."

"But we do know their ships are shit. It's their weak spot."

Adinvan said, "And the lack of quality iron."

Erênu said, "We've hit their ships over and over. It's like kicking 'em in the shins, they've grown used it. We need to kick them in the jollies; no man grows accustomed to that."

Suseru gave her girl an arch-browed gaze. "Erênu, really."

"My little sister is right. We just need to find their crotch and put our boot there." If he wanted to start a war with the Tek, how would he do it? That was too easy. All he needed to do was show his face. But Helmveline? Stealing the Shrine Coins would work, maybe. Better, destroying one of the twenty-two shrines. They'd hunt him for an eternity. "What gods do the Histê worship?"

His kin met his gaze without offering an answer; it was a young islander girl named Sîu who spoke. "Môgôdûu, the great serpent. They commune with her through sacrifice and the worship of their ancestors."

"Sacrifice?"

"Not all who the Histê take become slaves. Some are offered to Môgôdûu. The souls of children are fed to the great serpent four times a year."

Human sacrifice made him cringe, but it didn't feel like a weak point. "What times?"

"The equinoxes and the solstices. Ninety twelve-year-olds, one for every tooth of Môgôdûu's maw."

"Twelve? Why twelve?"

"I do not know. We Sikotô worship the Bolêwoz, our ancestor gods. These children are taken as infants, raised to die on the altars of the Great Serpent. It is the holiest right of the Histê."

"Where could we find these children?"

The girl's brow furled. "Many sites, I've heard, but many Sikotô children are bled atop the Temple Mount of Yungilêtunu, outside the city of Rôqwu."

Solineus grinned. "Well, there you go. Simple."

Adinvan stared. "What the hells are you talking about?"

Solineus smiled, ignoring his father. "Sîu, what would the Histê do if someone stole their sacrifice?"

Thirty-Two

Final Foundation

Nose Licker! ha ha! an impressive proboscis for an agile tongue,
oh, the hound he bounds
he licks and bites, flees the thickets, eats the rickets doomed boy,
toddling and wobbling and hobbling
The snicker of the blood-thirsty nose licker,
the hound to bound to bay into the fray.

—*Tomes of the Touched*

Lelishen leaned into Kinesee's ear to whisper. "King Sebedil will be curt and straight to the point, a trait he learned from the Volvrolan of Eleris Edan. You won't have much time to figure out what, if anything, he wants. For the Helelindin, wasting another person's time with trivialities—pleasantries you might say—is rude. Bear that in mind when is he is short with you."

Kinesee gazed at the living walls of vines draping from the trees around them, their pristine pink and purple flowers, not a one with a petal turned brown. They called it the chamber of waiting, and the name was accurate. They'd been here at least two candles without so much as a stool, and Lelishen wouldn't let her risk her gown by sitting on the lush green grass.

"Everybody wants something—a chair, for instance." She'd been cocksure of the former for the entire journey, but now that she was within strides of meeting the king, she grew nervous. She'd seen Sebedil from a distance, at the ceremonial signing of the treaty between the Silone and the Helelindin, but didn't speak a word to the man, or for that matter, any of his people.

"Whatever he might want could dissolve in a blink after hearing what the Kingdomers desire. Sebedil was king during the wars and his memory is keen."

"More keen than yours or the Edan's?"

"The Edan were untouched by the war... but either way, the Helelindin bear angry memories in ways as fierce as humans, with far more heat than the Trelelunin or Edan."

More human could be a positive or a negative, from what she knew of the Edan. "The worst I can do is fail."

A voice spoke from beyond the curtain of vines, and they parted wide enough to walk through shoulder to shoulder. Two Helelindin men bowed as they strode through the opening, and Kinesee strove to keep her gaze steady and her eyes narrow rather than awed.

The court of King Sebedil the Third was a garden of trees, shrubs, and flowers, or this was Kinesee's first thought, but garden wasn't the proper word. Every rose, tulip, lilac, barberry, juniper, cedar, bur oak, and a hundred other varieties of plant stood placed and pruned with a precision she'd expect to require an artist's brush. Perhaps even more precise. It was perfect to the point of taking her breath away, of making her question its reality.

Figures passed through arches high in the canopy, glimpses of Helelindin nobility, and only then did she realize that the living wonder hid a framework of stone pillars and walkways.

She wasn't in a garden. She stood in a palace where the sun could shine and the rains fall, a palace that felt much like the city of Holelorin itself, where trees grew through the roofs of buildings and the roads were turf instead of stone. Pools of water to catch rain, while appearing to have a slow western current, lined both sides of the courtyard for the final fifty paces to the throne. The seat was the stump of a massive tree sitting atop a hillock with two seats carved into its face, the backs of which rose at least six feet above the seated king's head. A griffon with sweeping wings rose above royalty, its chiseled feathers stained light to dark as they moved from the body to the edges of the wings.

King Sebedil sat alone this day, his back straight and his nose aloft as he looked down from high. He wore brown robes threaded with glinting silver, but it wasn't a dirty brown; the color was rich and reflected the light with shimmers of supple movement. On his head, he wore a crown of gold set with white stones that held a silvery luster. From what Kinesee understood, there were four Helelindin kings, but they all swore fealty to Eleris Edan, so she comforted her jittery nerves by telling herself he wasn't a *great* king, just a little king. She'd been nervous to meet the Ironwing in Molikîn, but he was a man, a human-like her, but this king was something other, and it brought fidgets to her fingers.

Helelindin nobility lined the far sides of the streams, men and women with stern gazes, but without a hint of hostility. The women wore gowns fashioned from layers of supple silks and velvets, the colors subtle and soft, mimicking nature's less flowery hues, but the jewels they wore were brilliant and bright and every color of the rainbow. It was as if they adorned themselves as flowering plants, basic on the stalks and stems but flowering and gorgeous in radiant splashes. If the women were flowering trees, the men were more oaks and maples. They stood straight, garbed in greens and browns, and only gold and silver adorned a few fingers and throats.

Kinesee had brought only one of her gowns for this meeting, and she was happy now that she'd chosen an elegant dress of understated gray and silver. Its train swept the ground behind her as she strode with a stiff posture beaten into her by the Lady Tedeu, and when she reached the end of the walk and bowed, she unclipped her white rabbit-skin stole to reveal the latcu necklace gifted to her by the Ironwing. Its sparkles from the sun danced on the ground and leaves around them, and she knew it had its desired effect by the widened eyes of those staring at her.

The Helelindin weren't Edan, nor even Trelelunin, when it came to stone faces. Even Sebedil's eyes widened at the sight, and she took advantage of his hesitation to speak. "I am Kinesee Choerkin, bride of the Warlord Choerkin. I thank you for seeing me this day."

The king's voice was deep and solemn, and though unstrained, it was powerful and loud. "It is both an honor and a surprise to meet with you. What brings the Lady of War to our court?"

Kinesee was uncertain whether he toyed with the warlord title in a mocking gesture or if he was serious. "I prefer to think of myself as a lady of peace." She was happy that she'd left her sword hanging on her saddle. "There is an urgent matter which needs fixing."

"I assume you mean the Malstefnê army my scouts have been braying about for the past month. Your people and mine signed a treaty for trade and peace, but the Malstefnê are a trouble of yours, not mine. My scouts also proclaim your wall stout."

"Rôemhîik, the Choerkin Wall, is stout and the enemy is ours alone."

He nodded and raised a hand in a dismissive gesture. "If you fear your enemy circling your wall by an eastern road in great number, do not. They will not dare to raise our ire. Small bands could pass unseen, perhaps, but no army will flank you from the Somenor Eler."

Kinesee curtsied with a flourish. "And for this my warlord is eternally grateful, but there is another favor you might extend to the Silone people. If you allowed pilgrims from the Eight Kingdoms to journey to pray at the Final Foundation—"

"Why would I do such a thing?" His words were curt, his tone sharp, and his throat full of sand. The snarl on his face made Kinesee wish the Helelindin hid their emotions as well as the Edan. "Signing a treaty with a friend of the Eight Kingdoms was a knife to swallow, but I did so at the behest of the Trelelunin beside you and with the sanction—nay! The command of the Volvrolan of Eleris Edan. Kingdomers will never set foot on Fedeletêun without fear."

Lelishen stepped forward. "Fedeletêun, the Final Foundation, is sovereign land and yours to do with as you will. It's been more than four hundred years since your wars, not a Kingdomer is alive who was your enemy."

"The descendants of my enemy are still my enemy. I will not trust them. You will not dissuade me on this."

Kinesee remained calm. She'd expected refusal from the offset, albeit in not so blunt a fashion. "My father plans to open trade between the Silone and Mulshahar down the great rivers to the Monsoon Strait. If you did us this favor, we'd be pleased to carry any goods you have—"

"I spit on Mulshahar. They have nothing we want nor need, even if I'd deign to send them a worthless trinket for their crown jewels."

Lelishen said, "The Trelelunin might be more eager to trade. By assisting in establishing this route you could curry favor in the courts of Nenaree Eler."

The king paused and for a flicker Kinesee held hope, but while the words held less growl, the bite was the same. "*No* Kingdomer will set foot on Fedeletêun."

Kinesee sucked her breath and held it, her mind whirling. Her hand reached for the still hidden pearl, but her hand found the Irongwing's gift. Kinesee unhooked her necklace and held it high, glints of pink sparkle dancing all around. "Latcu."

Sebedil's attention refocused on her and she felt small. "It is a beautiful necklace worth many suns and moons and stars, but it is not worth a mountain and the memory of those dead at Kingdomer hands."

"This was a gift from the Ironwing of Helmveline, I will not trade it away, but deep in a mountain of Helmveline are rooms filled with latcu."

The king's face softened as he paused this time, but the response was little different. "No Kingdomer will set foot on Fedeletêun and no Helelindin hand would accept food from a Kingdomer hand even if starving, even if in fair trade."

"But if I gave you this necklace, you would accept it?"

From his furrowed brow, Sebedil questioned whether to step into the obvious trap being set for him. "I would."

"And if I promised you a hundred latcu gems, you would agree to a fair trade even if you knew I purchased the gems from Helmveline?"

"We have signed a treaty with the Silone. Where the latcu comes from is not a concern."

She glanced at Lelishen. "Other than the Final Foundation, do you have any idea what the Kingdomers might want?"

"Nothing so valuable as latcu, but there's no way to know for sure."

Kinesee groaned and turned back to the king, hesitating. Then she realized she was smarter than she thought. The Clans signed the treaty of Simâm on the slope in front of where the wall now stood, where war would soon begin. Whether negotiations succeeded or failed, the presence of the Helelindin and Helmveliners might slow its arrival. "If you will send a negotiator to the Choerkin Wall four days behind my departure, I will arrange a meeting with the Helmveline at the same place we signed our treaty. Neutral ground."

The king frowned and shook his head. "We will not meet with a Kingdomer."

"I misstated. Your people will meet with the Silone, while the Silone will meet with Helmveline. The Silone will carve the deals; the Helelindin just need to be there to agree to terms."

"The Volvrolan would need to sanction any such agreement."

Lelishen said, "I will speak for the Edan and make certain the Volvrolan knows of any bargain struck, and that he approves."

Sebedil's back straightened and his chest puffed. "Three hundred bricks of latcu, or it is not worth our arriving."

Kinesee sighed, then smiled and batted her eyelashes. "I am the queen of no one and can guarantee nothing, but they have much more than that."

He nodded. "My Minister of Trade will arrive at the Choerkin Wall in twelve days." He stood and turned his back on them before striding away with a train of nobility behind him.

Kinesee turned to Lelishen as the room emptied except for guards and spoke in Silone. "That went well!"

The woman's scrunched brow foreshadowed the response. "Too well."

"How can something go too well?"

Lelishen turned and walked toward the exit. "Why would they want gem-grade latcu?"

"Because it's beautiful."

"The Helelindin do not lack for beautiful things. If we were trading points for arrowheads, it would make sense. There's a specific reason."

Kinesee snorted and shook her head. "I don't give a blink why they're coming to the table, all I care is that they take a seat and that the seat is between Rôemhîik and the Tek army."

Lelishen grinned. "You're as clever as your father. You're certain you aren't of his blood?"

"Solineus is my father, but my pa was no fool neither."

"I've no doubt. And you are right. Winning is the point, not how you won."

Kinesee grinned. "But you'll look into it anyhow." The lack of an answer was everything she needed to know.

Thirty-Three

Empty Climb

Snapping jaws and razor teeth flattened,
I walk the merry jaunt,
flaunt the walk merry I, eye, in my eye, your eye
to spit, a flicker and a flash, grinding teeth to gnash.
Oh the Fury! Oh the Fear! Oh the Fever!
I digress to impress no one but me;
the Wolves howl, but the army marches on.

—*Tomes of the Touched*

The Southern Forest they rode through bore no name more interesting, at least not so far as Meliu knew. It was a horrible name to give such a place, as once they'd traveled into the extensive woodlands, a portion of the Southern Forest was to their north; this innocent fact bugged her more than it should. A name on one map was Lîsinômê, a single word all alone seeming to indicate nothing, so it might well be the name of a forested region. It was hundreds of horizons farther south, however, which would make the forest too big for easy reference.

Four thousand warriors moved through the woods at a snail's pace on foot, which gave her mind three weeks' too much time to think on trivialities. "We need a better name for this forest."

A steady drizzle pattered through the leafy canopy the entire morning, keeping the Broldun's beard soaked and his mood sour. "What the hells're you yappin' about?"

"It doesn't seem right to point north and call something the Southern Forest."

Polus swatted a mosquito on his neck, leaving a bloody patch. "Rain and critters eatin' on us day and night, and this's the horseshit you're learned self is thinkin' on?"

Her eyes darted back and forth while failing to compose an excuse. "Yes. It is. And I haven't thought of a good name."

"Twelve Hells and a Hammer from the Forge, you're serious?"

She puffed her chest. "I am. Things need names, especially on maps."

He eyeballed her. "Yer sure you got smarts? I'm thinkin' the Choerkin's headboard clunked the wits right out of yer skull."

She blushed after making it two days without an Ivin joke. "Gods know the whiskey rotted your brain to mash long ago."

"Roemhien Forest."

She took three strides as she searched for a retort. "Too obvious."

He laughed. "Too right, you mean. Keeps things godsdamned simple. You ride from the Roemhien Pass into the Roemhien Forest and back the same way."

A dozen more strides, and all she had were petty curses for a comeback. The big bastard was right. "Roemhien Forest it is. Until I come up with something better."

"Clunk, clunk, clunk."

Meliu punched his arm. "You shut up."

His smirk let her know this line would be revisited. "Whatever you come up with, keep it simple." He raised his arm and pointed to the horizon where a squared top of brown and green rose from the forest. "Green Mountain."

Meliu squinted and muttered a prayer for vision as she reined her horse to a stop. The Broldun was right again. There was no doubt she stared at the right pyramid; the three highest tiers bore a phalanx of sharpened trees for a wall, lashed together by vines and rope, angled to make a climbing attack more formidable than the steps would've made it already. She prayed and her ears sharpened. She sucked her breath. "I don't see a single soul, nor do I hear a thing except birds and bugs." No hint of movement except some gigantic bird flying overhead.

"Mmmm, you're sure of this?"

"If there's a soul up there, they're hiding or they're a ghost."

Polus licked his lips before rising and turning in the saddle. "Bîdorik! A word."

Rûîrn Bîdorik, commander of the warriors of Helmveline, trotted his mount to their side as the men kept marching past. He nodded to them both, rain beading on his cheeks and dripping from his beard. "We've reached the Green Mountain, almost."

"Aye, hmm, but this li'l lady says there ain't no one up there."

Bîdorik leaned and tugged his beard, wringing water to stream to the ground. "We were told at least sixty manned the peak."

Meliu said, "That's the word we had."

"The wall still stands?"

"Yes. They could be hiding, or they could all be on the south side..."

"South was the stairs, I heard tell. Could be they're fighting off an attack."

"I'd expect to hear a battle. Voices I might miss, but not a battle."

The Helmveliner eyed the pyramid and slipped his helm onto his head, the rain pattering on steel. "If somebody or something's up there, we're four thousand strong and they know we're coming. If we don't find our people, I expect to find no one, but we should prepare as if one of your hells is waiting."

Polus nodded and stood in his saddle. "Helms! Shields! Arms!"

Cries of those three words traveled north and south as they spurred forward. The Green Mountain was close, but getting there was slowed by men walking with their eyes trained to the woods rather than on the heads of their comrades in front of them.

Within a candle, Meliu saw a wall of stone half-covered in vines and moss; it stood out more now than it had for decades as warriors marched on every hiding place to make sure no one spied or lay in wait, tearing at vines and bushes to see what lay beneath. They followed the remains of stone roads with giant blocks upturned to clip toes and hooves as they passed, and at one point rode beneath an arch at least three poles high at its zenith. In this way, the force of four thousand wheeled far around Green Mountain to come straight at the stairs.

A wall of shields and spears formed in front and to all their sides, and down the middle, a path opened as the three of them rode to the stairs.

"Mmm, you see anythin', girl?"

"I see nor hear nothing of our people."

Bîdorik said, "The gate stands wide open, is it sound?"

Meliu squinted, focusing her eyes and prayer. "Seems so."

They reached the fore of the army and dismounted. Polus gave the command. "You six lead the way, a dozen follow us." He glanced at her and winked. "Pray for our souls."

She grinned and prayed for Light as her foot hit the first stair, then prayed for Dark by the fifth step in the climb. The energies came and the twisted tension fled from her gut; it was good to feel Elinwe's touch again. They climbed every step with slow and purposeful strides, as if stalking prey, but without a clue of what they might find. Part of her expected carnage to rival the Crack of Burdenis—but that should have attracted carrion birds—and some piece of her even touched on the horror of seeing the Shadows of Man at the summit—beings who would, no doubt, have no fear of her Dark—but it was her strongest fear that came true.

Nothing.

No sign of anything living nor dead.

She squirmed between spearmen at the peak and released the powers of the gods with an exasperated breath. "Hells."

Bîdorik strode to the remnants of a campfire beneath a sturdy lean-to as warriors fanned out, searching every nook, cranny, and shadow with the tips of their spears. "Rains and wind make it difficult, but I'd sooner wager against the Five Earls than say this fire burned in the last five days."

"Mmm, we knew we might find 'em all dead, or captured, who the hells knows. It was a long time to hold this ground even if it is high."

Meliu meandered as much with her feet as her wits. She flipped open a trunk full of arrows and held one up. "Trouble being we can't say what the hells happened. Doesn't look like a fight, though the rains could've washed away blood." She pointed to crude tables and chairs and stools. "They godsdamned took the time to build things, and not a one is knocked over. It's like they picked up and walked out."

Polus hefted a skin full of liquid from the ground, popped its wax seal and sniffed. "Whale oil from Kaludor. Mmm, nobody just picked up and *left* without arrows and oil."

Bîdorik said, "Surrounded into a surrender, maybe?"

"Mmm, maybe."

Meliu said, "We've all the time in the world to figure it out; we brought a lot of axes, I suggest we put them to use. And send riders back to the Bluffs to let the north know we're here."

Meliu surveyed the region from the peak of Green Mountain; what four thousand hale men could achieve in ten days didn't fail to impress. The four roads entering the ruins were cleared, and not a tree stood within two thousand strides of the pyramid. The foundations and remaining walls of buildings throughout the city were cleared of growth, and they'd discovered seven more arches spanning roads. From her vantage, she could see the remnants of a building, inside which lay massive millstones for whatever grains the residents once grew here.

Best guess was this city housed maybe ten thousand souls in its day, leaving her people with plenty of space to stretch their legs and plenty of stones precut to start construction of low walls. A ring of wall five feet high already stretched four hundred strides, giving archers and crossbowmen cover as they watched the forest for signs of an enemy. But no enemies, no friends, not even the monsters Kingdomer tales promised, showed their faces; maybe it shouldn't surprise her that so many warriors would frighten foreigners and beasts away, but it did. The only creatures they'd found were bugs and animals too stupid to slither away.

Poisonous snakes bit a dozen men over the past week, but with the prayers of the holy combined with poultices of local plants, not a man died nor lost a leg. A Silone man crushed his hand while moving a massive stone and ended up burying his finger in the hole he'd been trying to fill, but it was a trifle compared to the horrors she'd feared they would face. Whenever she allowed her mind to wander to their luck, an unease grew ill within her, promising that the lives she'd feared to lose would bleed too soon, and so she turned her thoughts north.

The riders escorting the Wayfinder would reach the Bluffs soon enough, and the next phase in the Helmveliner plan would commence; road construction crept along with Silone clearing the forest and Helmveliners bringing in pave-stones and gravel, too slow to help at Green Mountain, maybe, but knowing something good was coming their way helped assuage her fears.

No matter where her thoughts went, she worked hard to veer them away from the *Codex of Sol* riding in her pack; it was this struggle that led her out the gate of the pyramid. She turned east once on the fourth tier from the top, figuring she'd get an overview of the men working to clear and build without descending to the ground where snakes tended to hide from laborers. The building most intact, not including the pyramid, lay to their northeast. It had been shaded by so many trees and overgrown with so many vines and lichens that they didn't know it was there until the third day of clearing. The empty pools and pipes that once must've held water suggested it was a bathhouse. A public bathhouse. As bad as she might stink right now, her only baths coming from rain, she didn't know what to think of baths that showed no sign of separating men from women.

She sighed, the scent of roses and chocolate from her last hot bath in Bdein bringing a smile, before she pondered the fate of the Ar-Bdein and her traitorous mind turned to Ivin and—

"Agh! Damn that son of a bitch."

She glanced about, happy to see no one was near enough to take notice. Then her eye caught a gash in the bark of the fortification. *A stray blow from an ax,* but the explanation didn't satisfy her. It convinced her less when she noticed another, and afterward, she couldn't keep her eyes off of more and more peculiar marks in bark and wood. A Silone stood watch not forty paces and three lower tiers away. "Erud! Fetch Polus Broldun and send him this way."

"Aye, high priestess."

She contemplated climbing a tier to stand beside the palisade but without a handhold in sight, being short damned her again. She could wait for Polus to lift her, which begged some sort of humor, so she walked back to the stairs to ascend a flight; the embarrassment saved was worth the extra walk.

She'd taken twenty strides alongside the wall when she heard the Broldun. "You wanted something?"

She turned, watching the big man jog up the weather-worn steps. "I just wanted you to sweat."

"That what attracted you to the Choerkin? How he sweated?"

Her head rolled back. "Are you ever going to stop?"

He reached her, standing with hands on his knees, panting with a smile. "Once we're married."

"You're already married."

"And I've a habit of outliving m'wives."

"This one will see you to your grave."

He laughed and stood straight, stretching his back. "So, what the hells did you really want?"

"Come on." She led him east, her eyes plying the wall up and down as they walked, and it was only after they rounded the corner to the northern face that she found a scar.

"What the hells of it? A notch from an ax."

"No."

"A scar from dragging it, then."

"I don't think so. There's nothing like it along the eastern side, but all along this northern side... a hundred marks if you look close enough. An ax would score the bark and wood, not this." She worked her finger into the crack, and it slipped into a hole. "Something scratched the bark before puncturing the wood a knuckle deep."

Polus rubbed his beard and his eyes squinted. "Shadows did shit like that to stone."

A shiver passed between her shoulder blades. "They did."

He licked his lips. "Gods damn us to the Forges, not again."

"It's a leap too far without proof. Way I heard, Shadows left dimples and it wasn't in wood. Some kind of animal?"

Polus meandered to another score in the palisade, unsheathed a dagger, and cleared bark before picking at the hole and sticking a pinky in. "Mmm, supposin' it tapers a bit like a claw. And there're marks to either side... but godsdamned thing would be climbin' damned near upside down. Like them monkey kinda critters we seen?"

"Sloths, and they've claws no doubt, but they move too slow to be a threat. And they seem to eat leaves." She'd seen plenty of monkeys in the trees, but they all kept to the tops of branches and didn't tear into trunks and branches like this.

"The yellow-eyes?"

"Are just people, far as word we have. Best bet, whatever this was came from the north."

"Yer suggestin' some *animal* climbed over the wall and took our people, dragging them back over these spikes without leaving a spot of blood nor scrap of cloth? Sixty men?"

She peered north. "I could be wrong... I'm suggesting some *thing* climbed the wall, then opened the gates to drag or carry them out."

"Improbable."

"But not impossible."

"Demons?"

The notion couldn't be discarded; what she knew of demons was limited to running from the Shadows of Man. "Start spreading the word; I want to know of anything... everything that looks or feels odd out there. Scratches, smells... I don't care how shit-brained it sounds. We need to look into it."

"We got some devil dragging people away we'll want more fires at night. If you're thinkin' is right, these things are godsdamned sneaky, so more guards on the rounds."

"Yes. And it's time for a priest or two to lose sleep as well, particularly during rain or fog. Too bad..." She stared at the palisade, hands to her hips. "Did we burn all of that dagger-vine?" The thorny bastards slowed down clearing the city with needles at least as long the brambles at the base of Istinjoln's southern wall.

Polus grimaced. "I see what you're sayin', but aye, mmm. I think most of it was burned."

"I suggest tacking what we got to these walls and send folks out to collect more. If it's a living thing, it'll think twice before climbing through those knives."

"Have your priests ready to heal a thousand bloody pricks and worse."

She giggled, but it wasn't funny. Men had put the barbs straight through their boot and out the top of their foot. "That just guards us on the top of the pyramid."

"Mmm, true that. And anything nimble enough to climb this barricade won't think twice about our little wall yonder. Some of the goat herders used simple crosses of wood and stretched branches, brambles, and vines to make a fence."

She blinked, then smiled at the man. "You lowlander Broldun aren't as thick as people say."

"Nah, we're thicker'n Choerkin, where it counts."

She groaned. "If someday I catch you taking a piss and your manhood is a shriveled leech, I'm gonna be saddened."

He laughed, then winked. "Two leeches at least, even on a cold morn."

"Just get folks on that fence, you oaf." She stared beyond the ruins and sweating men as Polus strode west. She hoped that whatever was out there was an animal, animals could be understood, dissuaded, and killed; if it were demons or something other, their performance against the Shadows of Man boded ill for their prospects.

Thirty-Four

Seeking the Mountain

Insipid Dreamer and Harried Weaver,
what magnificent lies have you told
the Loving Believer?
Love is strong but vulnerable to trust,
Hate is strong but vulnerable to distrust,
while Reason is vulnerable to Love and Hate.

—*Tomes of the Touched*

Rinold awoke in the morning to see leaves swaying in the breeze overhead and glimpses of a clear sky. No roof, no walls, but Jitô still lay dead. They didn't leave at dawn as promised. Instead, they waited for high sun to make sure no Histê waited for them.

At Nehek's insistence, they left Jitô's body in Ontotutusku. The Wiirê explained that dragging a body from a cursed place risked spreading the evil beyond its borders. That being the case, there was no way in the hells anyone was going to move him or dare to dig dirt damned by demons and ghosts.

They backtracked to the west, hoping to reach Nehek's village, but as they cowered behind bushes atop a high overlook to watch a Histê patrol pass, Rinold swore he could hear Nehek's teeth grinding. It was the second group of warriors, which meant it wasn't some coincidence to ignore.

"We should head east. We'll come back after reaching my people."

Nehek grimaced. "No."

"They're watching the area; if they catch us returning, they might slaughter your family." Rinold had no idea of the odds of such brutality. "Or take them all as slaves. In a month, they won't be watching so close."

"The Histê will kill them if I don't warn them."

"Could you go alone?"

"Too risky."

"We wait then. But if more hunters pass..." Rinold decided on a change of subject before coming back to his goal. He sat and crossed his legs. "You could see the ghosts in Ontotutusku? I couldn't until they entered the room."

"It is the vision of the Montoqûu."

"Any relation to the *monto*?" *Monto* was a fruit about the size of Rinold's fists side by side, its skin patched in reds and greens that faded together when it was ripe enough to eat. They ate plenty of it every day since crossing the bridge, as the bushes were commonplace in this forest.

"The *qûu* is the seed, cooked and crushed into a powder."

"A yellow powder? The color of your eyes, the powder causes it?"

Nehek squinted at him as if maybe giving up some secret. "Yes. We eat the powder from the time we are children so that we can see things others cannot."

"Ghosts?"

"No, this was the first time I ever saw a ghost."

"Those giant snake-things?"

"Yes. And other predators. It is difficult to explain. A jaguar who blends into shadows and trees for you, I see his spots as another color that does not hide."

"If I walk into the woods?"

"You stand out as bright blue in a world of yellow."

"That's useful." How handy would it be to see a hidden foe before you were in arrow range? "So, if I eat this powder?"

"It takes years as a child to gain the sight, and it destroys our bodies."

"What do you mean?"

"In the days before the Wiirê came, only a few of a village's hunters gained the vision. It is poison. Few with the sight live beyond forty years."

It made a twisted sense. "The Wiirê force the vision on you to serve them better."

"Yes. Some tribes, far distant from here, they live as in the Free Days with nature's eyes. But it is hard for them to hide when the Histê use our eyes to find them."

Rinold nodded, not wanting to push farther as the man's answers carried him to a darker mood. "Could you hear the ghosts?"

"No."

Rinold expected the answer; Solineus said the Fire Master's ghost could only hear him. But, Solineus saw the details of the ghost's face, enough to recognize him. "Their faces were glowing outlines for me."

Nehek turned to face him, a squint to his eye. "They looked like you. Your people."

Rinold smacked his lips; it was the answer he feared. He spoke in Silone as he turned to Edlmir. "Like us. You saw the lion head carved in the arch?"

"I did. Not the only place, neither."

"What the shittin' hells would Silone ghosts be doin' this far south?"

"I'm supposin' ghosts don't go growin' old to die... from the Age of God Wars?"

"With weapons that could kill us. What the hells sense does that make?"

"Before meetin' you, I'd say it makes no sense at all, but yer the one who has seen more impossible shit than I ever thought on. Maybe our gods are the evil gods."

"Or they defeated the evil gods and ruined their carvings. Their lanterns... they changed color, telling time. I've heard tell that the holies in their holes do the same." A click in his brain, and he turned to Nehek. "That ghost about to kill you, I don't think he saw me until he saw your eyes behind me... through me."

The Wiirê blinked his bright eyes. "I'd say that's right. Tsst!" Nehek froze, his eyes staring at something Rinold couldn't see. The good news was that he stared down near the road, not behind them.

A wick later skulking Histê with painted bodies slipped from the woods, following the road a hundred paces before disappearing again.

Rinold sighed. "You might make it past these bastards, but we're meat without you. And if they have Wiirê eyes?" He shook his head.

Nehek shook his head as well, his eyes trained hard on the road. "Those were hunters... Those coming are not."

Rinold waited without questioning the man; he trusted Nehek's eyes as much as he trusted a Wayfinder's sense of direction. Within a wick of being hushed, Rinold spotted the first row of men walking the road five abreast. The Histê bore slender shields only a foot shorter than they were tall and carried long leaf-bladed spears. Rinold counted twenty-five rows of men.

Nehek stood, chest puffed long after the enemy was out of earshot. "Warriors from Kentesuhô."

"If that's supposed to mean something to me, it doesn't."

"A Histê fortress far from here. If they are here, it's to destroy my village. Kill you. But they couldn't have marched here this fast; they had another reason to be traveling east."

It took a flicker for it to kick him in the head. "My people. The Histê sent an army to meet the Silone."

Nehek nodded once and scooted through the brush, dropping down the steep hill leaps at a time before reaching the road.

Edlmir said, "There went our guide."

Rinold glanced down at the man, his yellow eyes staring up at them, waiting. "He's going to get us killed."

"Way I see it, we're dead without him anyhow."

"Since when did you start using godsdamned logic on me? Come on." Rinold ducked through and descended, following Nehek's lead by leaping and planting his feet in the dirt and sliding before hopping again. It was a quick way down, but when leaves shifted on his fifth hop, he lost his balance and was thankful to reach bottom on his feet. Edlmir and the others took a more reserved and traditional approach to reach the road, and the moment they found bottom, Nehek darted into the northern woods and disappeared down another slope.

"I guess this is the short cut."

Edlmir chuckled, but it was the last sound other than panting and cussing that he heard from anybody for several candles as Nehek wound through valleys, jumped streams, and climbed hills. Just as Rinold figured Edlmir and the other men might collapse, they burst into a clearing. They slid to a stop, gasping with hands to knees.

Two dozen huts capped with stick and leaf cones stood out, but the fire pits were cold. They were the only living souls in sight. Nehek dashed to a hut and threw the door open; his eyes said it all, no one was here. "My parents lived here. They forbade me to visit for the past three years."

Of the homes, it was the largest, so Rinold figured they were important people. Rinold wandered to a fire-pit and glanced at the coals. It was a rare day without rain so far, but there was no sign of yesterday's rain on the charcoal. "This is a good thing, right? They got out."

"Hunters must have warned them of the Histê warriors."

"Perfect. They're safe, now let's make ourselves safe and scarce. Get out of here."

"No. My people do not understand... They will have hidden, but they'll believe these are slave hunters coming. Slave hunters move on easy; these warriors are coming for slaughter, and they will track them."

"If you know where they are, go. We don't have time to waste."

"I remember hiding once when a child..." He turned and took off at a trot, and of course it was uphill.

Edlmir stepped to Rinold's side and stared. "You little bastards got too much energy if you ask me."

"Look at it this way... saving a Wiirê village will look good when we try to make friends with other Wiirê."

"If we don't roll over and die in the brush somewhere."

"Quit grousing and run."

They spent the night in the middle of a deep thicket of thorny bushes, none too fun crawling into, but they figured nothing in its right mind would come hunting them there. At least nothing with bare skin. Come morning, the pricks and pokes on the way out were good to make sure they were awake. Rinold crunched into an edible root Nehek called *enjïs*, bitter and fibrous, but the Wiirê claimed it was full of energy; the kindest he could claim was that it filled his stomach.

"How far do you think?"

Nehek itched for the Silone to finish eating so they could move. "Two to three horizons if I have my bearings."

"How far behind do you think the Histê are?"

"No way to know. Any route of theirs will twist as much as ours, but there's no telling how many search parties might be out here. If slave-hunters... They might never find them, or my people may be dead already."

Rinold stood with a huff and threw his root into the woods, then kicked Edlmir in the ass to inspire him to fall in behind Nehek. This morning he took it easy on them, walking up the hills and only running on slopes not covered in deadfalls. The steps dragged and the horizons passed, and Rinold was half convinced Nehek didn't know where the hells he was going, then Nehek disappeared.

Rinold ducked behind a tree and stared, uncertain of what had happened. Brush and trees and rocks were all he saw, but winded and sore after all they'd been through, he hadn't been paying close attention.

Edlmir crept to a nearby tree, the big man so drenched in sweat it looked like he might've just climbed from a river. "What do you think?"

A creak caught his ear—he'd heard the sound of a bowstring too many times to mistake it—and he raised his empty hands palms up. "I'm thinking we move godsdamned slow and smile big." At least one yellow-eye archer sat in the canopy above, but he had the sensation of a lot more eyes watching. "Peace."

Nehek burst from the bushes ahead, waving his arms and shouting so fast that Rinold didn't understand a word. All that mattered was the bowstring's tension easing so that his heart could stop fluttering.

Several men and women strode from the bushes—Rinold figured there was a cave tucked away—and listened to Nehek tell his tale.

Edlmir said, "I hope this shit was worth it. What're your ears pickin' up? I don't understand nothin'."

"Hells. I caught somethin' about Untûgu, other bits about us, an army, armor... four-legged beasts. Guess he's meanin' horses. But I think he's trying to convince them to flee."

"I dunno, seems like a fine hiding place."

"I'll wager three shits to two that he knows better than we do."

Nehek turned to them on cue. "I've convinced them to run. The women and children will move to another location. We will wait for them to leave, then the men will cover their tracks. Once we know they're gone, we'll leave while making tracks they can follow."

"We'll travel with your people?"

"No, they don't trust you. But we will leave a trail for the Histê to track us. With luck it will split our pursuit."

Rinold nodded. "You mentioned Ungûtu, where the Histê might hold some of my people. You said it was too far away, but we've headed south anyhow. How far away are we?"

"We're closer to Tômôrôk now... Ungûtu, too many Histê. Too many Wiirê thralls and slaves."

Edlmir said, "You said the priestess spoke of Tomarok. What do you think the chances of her havin' made it there?"

"I did, and I don't know. Nehek, how long to Green Mountain from here, straightest route?" Calling it Green Mountain instead of Stone-Claw made him feel better.

"A month? One can never know these things."

"If we go to Tomarok then Green Mountain, how long?"

"Closer to forty days. Over twenty days, but under a month to reach Tomarok, but it takes us more south."

Edlmir sighed. "We know we got people at Green Mountain... or damned well hope we do."

"Aye. Tomarok is rolling dice in the dark. Green Mountain is the safe choice."

Thirty-Five

Island on Island

The shit shitter and the shit eater!
Ha ha!
Vile and Liberated Bile,
Toil the Fettered Foil.
Oh, he dreams, she dreams, I dream. Do you?
I do indeed, perhaps I dream now
of you, Warrior Naked riding into battle
with a wooden spoon for a spear
a flat cake for a shield,
and a noodle for a crown.
Beware the saddle horn with a sudden stop.
Ha Ha!

—*Tomes of the Touched*

The islanders gathered at the Salty Frog three days after Reinus' arrest and had spent their nights in its rooms since. For two weeks Reinus volunteered to stay in jail, awaiting trial to help keep the peace, but after that, he only spent the nights in his cell and joined the others to fish and socialize during the day. No one wandered the town alone, and, except for visiting the gardens for food, they stayed close to the docks.

Eliles found trying to explain the Face a chore, seeing as she didn't understand how prayers could achieve such a power. It didn't help that her grasp of prayer was theoretical.

She stood in the garden this morning while Seden and Artus picked their way through overgrown plants and weeds. The priests had unfettered access to the gardens, but as far as Eliles could tell, they spent no time tending or picking, and she wondered if the whole spitting match over the gardens was just a wedge to keep the island split into two camps.

Seden wandered the rows of beans muttering while Artus wandered amid the grapes cussing. Artus and Jinbin alternated days of tending the vines, but it wasn't enough to keep them and the weeds under control.

"Your garden is chaos, my dear."

Eliles' spine bolted straight, and she glanced to her right side. The white-haired woman stood with hands on her hips with a judgmental grimace on her face. She wore holy robes, as she had before, stitched with silver. "Seden! Seden!"

The woman turned to look. "What is it?"

"Do you see this woman?"

"Yes. Leave it to the priests to send their eldest into the garden to age."

Eliles turned back to the woman, pleased that at the least somebody saw her. "Are you, by chance, Fedenu of Ulmor?"

"No, dear, but you could rephrase that to make it true."

Seden returned to work without a second thought, and Artus raised an eyebrow at the woman's presence, but nobody gave two carrots for the woman's appearance. *Rephrase.* Her heart thudded; did she stand beside the Face? "Do you look like Fedenu of Ulmor?"

"Yes."

"Are you the Face of Ulrikt?"

"No. But I assure you, this body saves a great deal of fuss."

Eliles' blood slowed. "Who are you?"

"Some names are unsafe to speak, for some names can be used. Some would like for me to utter who I am, so I will not."

"Fedenu lived a long time ago."

"I spoke once of relativity. I recognize the years that have passed since Fedenu walked Choerkist, as this castle was once known, but to me, time is a lazy river compared to the whitewaters of the mortal journey."

"Who are you?"

"Call me Fedenu if you need a name."

"Fedenu, you sound oddly like another person I see now and again in the stars."

"The Touched? Oh, he is a charmer, the charmed and the cursed." She grinned and Eliles laughed despite herself.

"Why are you here, Fedenu?"

"You invited me." She gestured to the Tower of Fire.

"To check on your grapes?" This detail registered in her head; it was Temeru who wasn't Temeru who mentioned Fedenu and grapes. "Did you talk to me in the stars as Temeru?"

"No."

Eliles fluttered her lips with an exasperated sigh. "If you won't tell me who you are, at least tell me why you're here."

The woman strolled, and Eliles followed. "Which crop do you miss most?"

"I miss red meat. I'm sick of fish."

"In your garden, my dear."

"Potatoes. They're so weedy nobody has bothered to dig for two weeks."

Fedenu strode straight to a patch overgrown by jagged-leafed weeds standing six feet tall. Whatever name the weed might bear, it thrived here with the Elemental Life. The woman kneeled and pinched a leaf low on the weed's stalk. "Sometimes, you need to starve a thing to kill it. Sometimes you need to give it too much of what it desires most."

The weed grew as she stood, but its stems twisted and its new leaves curled with crooked veins. It browned, withered, wilted, shriveled, and within a wick it drooped to the ground black. The death spread and weeds spiraled to their doom in fits of growth. It wasn't long before the potato plants got light again.

Eliles didn't bother to ask who she was. "You're hired."

"It is a little thing."

"No, you are an amazing gardener."

"Fedenu was a finer gardener than I. Hard work and a love for the soil counts for more than Elemental trickery."

"So, you knew Fedenu?"

"I did. She was a fine woman, as interested in pleasing her plants as her gods. I spent hundreds of candles with her in this very garden."

Eliles gazed into her eyes; a power resided there that she couldn't fathom. "Did she know your name?"

"No. Names are words and words are without power unless power is given to them. But sometimes names can be used, in particular when a name is never heard."

Eliles puzzled this. If the Face had a real name, and she spoke it, the person might react and give itself away. "What is the Face's name?"

"Ah! Now you've found your red meat."

"Do you know?"

"Nooo, I wasn't invited, but sometimes false names are more useful than real names. But if the Face is your game, you know already everything you need to know, you just need to understand it and yourself."

"Why not just tell me?"

Fedenu smirked. "There are games within games within games in this universe, and with games come rules. Words are without power, but knowledge too soon may be as devastating as knowledge too late. The Touched came close to speaking too much—" The woman straightened with a start. "You must excuse me. A friend of yours has invited me by name."

"A friend of mine?"

"Yes. I spoke to him once before he became who he is now, but he does not remember."

Eliles didn't even blink, where Fedenu had stood was empty air. As peculiar as it seemed, she was growing used to people disappearing.

Artus, on the other hand, was not. He coughed, and chunks of grapes flew from his mouth. "Friend or foe?"

"Friend, I think. She said that she spoke to a friend, but he doesn't remember. It must be Solineus."

"You're just confusing more and more hells out me, girl. Who was she?"

"You can call her Fedenu, but it isn't who she is."

"Fedenu. The one who planted the grapes?"

"That's who she looked like anyhow."

"You're confusing hell number four out of me, I figure. If she's a friend, she isn't the Face. Who is she?"

Eliles stretched her memory to her last conversation with the Touched; there was only one being she knew of privy to that conversation. "I'm not sure, but I think the great eye and the wing in the Fire are this Fedenu."

"I always figured it a demon, but others say a dragon."

Eliles' mind spun like a dozen tops, picking words and phrases from the Touched's crazy conversations. "A dragon." Poetry and riddles and gibberish, but she knew now she had another needle with which to stitch together more of the Touched's meanings. "Finish picking. I need to find a quiet place to think."

"My baskets are by the gates..." His eye caught the dead weeds and thriving potato plants. "Unless you want me to dig some taters."

"We can come back to—" Smoke rose in the distance. From here, she couldn't tell its source, but it billowed from the direction of the docks. "Fire!" She bolted through the garden gate, stumbled over a cockeyed cobblestone, but righted herself before driving her face into the street.

Many of the buildings were stone, but the closer you got to the docks, the more wooden structures. Her first fear was the jailhouse, but it was stone and iron. She wound down the streets, sometimes feeling like her legs outpaced her body on the slopes, but by the time she reached the gate to the docks, she figured she knew what burned, and by the time she rounded the turn, she was horrified to realize she'd been right.

Flames engulfed the Salty Frog, and islanders formed a bucket brigade to try and save it. She stopped and stood straight, the power of the Sliver not allowing fatigue. Most of her life she'd been setting fires, but in the trials at Istinjoln, she also learned to put them out. She closed her eyes and felt the heat of a hundred little friends dancing in the Salty Frog's flames. *My friends, rise and feed on the fire.*

She opened her eyes to see nothing changed, but she felt the movement of energy. The tongues of flames rising from burning wood rose higher, spinning and twining into balls of Fire and fire. A wick later the Salty Frog stood blackened, but without a single burning flame, not even red embers, and the fires that had spread to other buildings were extinguished. Her little friends danced in the air by the thousands, relishing their game. *Disperse.*

Streaks of Fire shot into the sky, most heading straight for the flaming tower.

Artus rounded the corner with Seden on his heels. He raged through labored breaths. "Those dirty sons of bitches."

Seden collapsed to her knees, struggling to sob after a long run. Eliles walked to her side and put a hand on her shoulder. "We'll rebuild even if we have to claim lumber from other buildings."

Artus snorted. "Something more needs done. This fire wasn't some confounded accident."

Eliles understood what he meant and agreed: The Face needed to die.

Thirty-Six

Sacrificial Souls

When war is the natural expression of survival it is a thing pure in its brutality. A war for land, a war for gold, a war for food, a war for freedom, and others are understood. When a people wars for lies, it is a tragedy. When a people wars to subjugate themselves to the tyranny of others, they are unwitting slaves and fools.

—*Codex of Sol*

Captain Edmordô wanted nothing to do with striking a Histê temple, and Solineus didn't hold it against him for a flicker. They decided that the captain would sail south to the island of Toltûk with several Silone longships to reload provisions and wait. Silone cogs, along with two dozen longships, would execute the raid itself.

Solineus stood in the crow's nest with a fareye to get a better view of Rôqwu. The city was big, its walls several horizons around, with brown-stone towers standing tall, but the waters leading into its harbor bore the colorful glint of a slick of oil, and broken crates cluttered docks already filthy with fish guts and half-naked sailors. The city lowered Solineus' opinion of cities right quick, even from this distance. Mulshahar and Molikîn had spoiled him into almost appreciating the people-packed clusters of buildings. Almost.

But it wasn't the city he'd climbed the mast to find. What his eye searched for was the Temple Mount of Yungilêtunu, even if he didn't know what the hells he was looking for. Finding a mountain and a temple close to shore should be easy. That assumption seemed sound until they reached the region and there wasn't a mountain in sight. Rôqwu sat on a flat plain surrounding the mouth of a river, and the tallest thing he spotted inland were trees. Yet, when they rounded the Trâqûu peninsula, he knew they'd found the temple.

The step pyramid sat like a mountain atop sheer two-hundred-foot cliffs overlooking the ocean. He turned to the sailor with him. "Signal the other ships that we found Temple Hill." The man smirked as he grabbed a mirror and adjusted another to send flashes of sunlight to the northwest where more ships sat on the horizon. The answer came within flickers. Solineus and his team would hide and wait for the ships to strike, distracting the warriors and priests at the temple so they could free the children and race them back to the boat. Simple in its simplicity but complicated by its lack of details.

Solineus scaled down the mast and jumped aboard a longship soon as it arrived. There was no delaying the initial foray. If the Histê spotted their ship and raised the alarm, time would run short fast. Within a candle of first laying eye on the pyramid, he, Adinvan, Sîu, and two dozen men set foot to the rocky shore a horizon from the temple, following a stone-paved road several hundred strides before moving into brush and boulders.

Sîu knew no more than they did about the place, which meant they didn't know how to get where they were going, nor did they know how long it'd be before the ships reached shore, but at least they couldn't get lost. The pyramid on the cliff was impossible to lose unless it splashed into the sea with an earthquake. They followed the road close as they could, but the barren washout they followed through the brush and stone led them inland. The water-worn trail led them on a winding route until reaching the end of their climb, a ravine strewn with head-sized rocks. It was a broken ankle or clattering fall waiting to happen, but it was a hells of a lot better than the cliffs in either direction.

Solineus glanced out to sea; they had maybe a half candle before the Silone longships landed and struck. A gong sounded from over the top of the rise, so he reckoned he wasn't the only one who'd seen the Silone coming. Or maybe the Histê had seen him and they were about to attack. He preferred to think it was a peaceful call to prayer.

He checked the clasp on the Twins and gave his father a nod before trying his luck at the climb. Within four strides, he was scrambling on all fours and wishing he was some sort of giant spider. Stones wiggled loose and clattered, and once he had to stop to wait for Adinvan to free his foot or risk sending several larger stones thundering toward those who followed, but within five wicks he hunkered beside a boulder with Adinvan and Sîu. Their view wasn't ideal, the plateau was flat as the glimpse from the crow's nest promised, but they were three hundred strides from a sprawling temple compound they couldn't see from below.

While the pyramid dominated the view, buildings and streets formed what could pass for a town on its northeastern side. It wasn't a cluster like so many villages. It had more in common with farm communities on Kaludor with buildings scattered enough to march armies through. It was easy to imagine that the design roots lay in a camp of workers who'd needed to move and raise massive stones.

Adinvan picked loose skin on bloodied knuckles, a gift from the climb. "So, where the hells are we gonna find these children?"

"Feel free to go ask someone." Solineus pulled a fareye from his belt and extended the tube to get a better view. He counted fifteen Histê carrying spears and shields and wearing light lamellar armor. A handful of half-naked folks wandered the area as well, their golden raiment suggesting they might be priests or some sort of holy. As the gong sounded again, every face he could see turned to face the pyramid.

He ignored the noise and scanned the buildings with his fareye until landing on a stretch of spiked fence between two buildings. "There's a fence of bronze rods back yonder, the only damned thing that looks built to keep anyone in or out."

"See anyone inside?"

"Not a soul."

"Slave pens?"

Sîu snagged the fareye from his grip. "They could hold them there. I've heard they're led from beneath the mountain on the day of sacrifice."

"Let's hope they're out for a breath of air." He took the fareye back and perused the field as the gong sounded three times.

Solineus' eye followed a warrior trotting toward the pyramid, and the man wasn't alone. "Our ships have their attention; most're heading for the temple. Two guards I can see are holding pat." He handed the fareye back to Sîu.

The girl peered across the yard. "As soon as they're darted, you come to me. Only you. I'll wave you in." She handed him the fareye and slid out of her linen blouse. All she wore was the necklace her father had given her—which drew his eyes right where he tried not to stare—and a sash with strips of linen to cover herself, but a bamboo tube hugged the length of her forearm. The belt held darts that looked more like decorative feathers and a vial of inky poison to transform pretty into death.

"We had an agreement."

"If those guards see a young slave girl clothed, what are they going to think?"

She had him and he didn't like it, so Solineus got his revenge with a smirk. "They're going to think she's wearing a pricey necklace."

She rubbed the central stone and stared. The gem looked like onyx to his eye, but she called it a soul-catcher. If she died on this journey while wearing the necklace, the stone would make certain her soul wouldn't depart her body, and they could return her body to her people for funerary rites. Solineus didn't know if it was true, but he understood her hesitation to remove it.

She unlatched it and handed it to him. "If I die, get this around my neck. Promise?"

"I swear it, but try not to die. Go."

Sîu trotted east a couple dozen strides before slowing to a saunter that turned sensual with a sway of hips.

"That Sîu is right pretty, perky. If I were unmarried and a couple of decades younger—"

"We've bigger problems."

"I'm just warnin' you, bed the girl and that's as good as married with the Sikotô peoples."

Married, just what he needed to confound his life further. "Gods no, I've got two daughters and a—"*what the hells is Lelishen?*"—a beautiful woman. Mother of my son. Beautiful."

"You're repeating yourself. You're in love."

"I don't know what the hells I am, but I reckon I don't need another woman no matter how perky. Now pay attention."

Sîu turned south for a stretch before rounding in behind the first guard, the man's attention focused on the pyramid to the west. She raised her arm, and Solineus imagined he heard the puff of her breath, but there was no need to imagine her accuracy and the efficacy of the poison. The poor bastard clutched the back of his neck and didn't even get the pretty red feather pulled from his throat before his face seized and his head jerked back. In a flicker, his knees buckled and he dropped to the ground. Sîu plucked a dart from her belt and dipped it in the vial before reloading her blowgun, and in flickers, she passed the dead man without giving him a second look.

"Shits. Don't piss this one off."

"Aye. It's been ten years since they took her brother, and from what she says, she's blamed herself every day after. The Histê won't earn her tears."

The second guard turned as Sîu approached, but he smiled when she gave a flirtatious wave. Five strides later, his eyes were wide and his lips rigid. She moseyed a dozen more steps and waved.

Of a sudden, Solineus didn't know what to do. Walk? Run? Skulk? He dropped the fareye and leaped to his feet, breaking into a trot while unclasping the Twins. A hand wandered to the Sister, and her murmur suggested no immediate danger. Sîu smiled at him as he arrived, and damned if he didn't smile back. She was beautiful. More beautiful than before now that he'd seen her kill men with the grace of a predator bird. *Gods, there's something wrong with me.*

"Follow me, but not too close."

She turned south, the linen at her hips swaying to reveal strips of skin. *There's something wrong with me. Eyes up, man.*

A holy stepped from behind a corner and his mouth twitched open at the sight of the girl, but it was the last reaction he had; his fingers were locking into clutching claws of paralysis by the time Solineus passed his staring eyes. They didn't see another soul before reaching the bronze fence, and they still didn't see a soul. The pen was empty, but the chains attached to posts scattered about suggested the temple kept slaves here. "Godsdamn it."

Sîu's eyes turned to the pyramid. "He's here, I can feel him."

Solineus admired her optimism even if he didn't share it. "You said there's a way beneath that mountain."

"A ramp into a tunnel."

The gong sounded, and this time it didn't stop booming. Warriors poured out of a building, a barracks he surmised, and ran west. Other doors opened with a blend of warriors, holies, and slaves rushing to the alarm. Solineus froze beside Sîu, and they stood staring as people passed them. One or a dozen, twenty paces away or a hundred strides, not a soul took notice of them.

"Follow me." She broke into a trot toward the pyramid, matching the pace of other slaves, and Solineus fell in behind. They were on the fringe of the herd now, and if anyone glanced their way, they didn't note the foreign giant rattling along in mail so much as to raise the alarm.

"Shits, you're crazy as I am."

"Crazy and determined look a lot alike."

Sîu veered southwest and away from other people, heading for the center of the western base of the pyramid. He didn't hold a clue of where she thought she was going as she zigged and zagged between buildings that grew closer together, and from the way her head turned back and forth, he reckoned she didn't know more than he did.

He caught sight of a shadow on the ground to the southwest, but there was nothing around to cast its darkness. He grabbed her shoulder, pointed, and she moved on the balls of her feet until a woman's head emerged from the shadow. Her blowgun puffed and the woman fell in silence, but the two men behind charged with spears and shields.

The Twins surged into his head with eager screams as he stepped in front of the girl. The men hesitated a flicker, and he guessed that a steel-clad Silone had been the last thing they expected. He clipped the head from one man's spear before the bastard thought to jab, and as the other lunged, he shaved the spear's length to redirect its strike, then stepped in with a sweep, taking off his right shoulder. The headless spear rattled the lobster tail of his helm, and he turned with a grin. The Brother cleaved into the man's shield to reveal his hiding face, and the Sister swept under to catch his armpit, sheering upward to drop his head and shoulder together on the stone ramp.

He glanced at Sîu, her blowgun at her lips and staring at him. "I'm a little messier than you are. Come on." He avoided the blood slicking the ramp as he trotted into the depths of the hole, pleased to see lanterns lighting the hall, but it annoyed him to find it splitting in two directions.

"Which way?"

Sîu glanced to and fro. "I haven't a clue."

The Twins rumbled in his ears, but he thought he heard something more; he sheathed the blades and listened. Sniffed the air. His ear caught a high-pitched voice echoing. "I hear a child's voice, I think."

"Which way?"

"I can't tell; there's an echo." He sniffed again. Left held a putrid acidic odor; piss, shit, death, or all and more. "This way."

Sîu retook the lead, but she kept the blowgun to her lips and didn't bother with a sexy sway for distraction. They came to another "T" and followed the acrid stench to the right, and after twenty paces there were no more lanterns.

The girl gazed into the shadows. "We should turn back."

"No. I hear breathing."

"I hear nothing. See nothing."

"Say something in your tongue."

"*Onolu*?"

He'd picked up enough of their language to know she said hello. A rattle of young voices came so fast he hadn't a prayer to understand what they said, but he ran back down the tunnel, grabbed a lantern, and walked with its light and the Sister leading the way. In twenty paces, a brick-lined hole opened in the ground and the source of the reek saw light. He sheathed the Twin. "Twelve Hells."

Four filthy islander children stared up at him, shading their eyes, and a dozen or more bodies lay scattered around their feet. They were too young to be this year's sacrifice, but they might know where the others were. He rested the lantern on the ground and dropped to his knees, reaching his hand out, but it was nowhere close. He flopped to his chest, but not a child would take his hand.

Sîu spoke in gentle tones. "*Esêtu nbû. Esêtu nbû.*"

The tallest girl in the group reached, but fingers still came up short. "Godsdamnit." He crawled forward but the extra reach failed him. He eyed a lad stouter than the others. "That boy there, tell him to give this girl a lift."

The boy was too weak to lift, but he made a fine step stool, and the other three were free in a matter of flickers and chatting in hushed tones with Sîu. That left this heroic boy to die, and that didn't suffice. He considered jumping down and lifting the child to the edge, but there was no guarantee he'd get back out. He jumped to his feet and drew the Brother, then severed the stitches of a mule ear from his boot, careful not to slice his leg or ruin his pricey favorites. He dropped back to the ground and leaned as far as he could without falling into the pit, but even with the ear, it wasn't enough. "Sîu, sit on my legs."

The girl perched on the backs of his knees and he slithered farther, the boy's fingers slapping the leather before finding a grip. But the leverage was horrible and his shoulder stretched to its limit. Sîu grabbed hold of his mail and pulled, and he wriggled backward, the boy dangling. Solineus heaved with his right arm and reached with his left, nabbing the child's wrist, and a dozen grunts and groans later he settled the boy onto the ground. He panted with a smile as he lay on his back. Sîu leaned over him.

"The twelve-year-olds and others are in cages not far from here."

"No more pits? Excellent." He stood and stuffed the mule ear into a boot. "Let's go."

The tall girl led them back from where they came, but instead of turning, she took them straight, out from beneath the pyramid if Solineus' directions weren't all spun around. It was maybe a hundred paces before the tunnel turned then split in three directions, but they stopped to stare. Cages lined all three halls, and the lantern's dim flame lit dirty faces staring out at them.

"Nêkulû!" Sîu cried.

"Damn it, girl, there might be guards." But a glance said he was wrong. Either the distraction worked, or no one bothered to worry about a breakout. "Where're the keys?"

Sîu wasn't paying him no mind as she trotted down the center tunnel screaming. He looked to the children. "Keys? Keys?" He mimed unlocking the doors, but their stares told him he was a fool. "To the hells with keys." He drew the Twins and skulked to a bronze door, waving for a child to step back.

The thin bronze of the lockbox on the cage split like butter for the Twins, and he walked down the row opening every cell, then back down the other side. Along the way, he found Sîu hugging a boy through the bars. He stopped to stare and smile at this small victory. The boy was her blood, and his mind wandered to seeing his son. He shook his head of the wishful thought and tapped her on the shoulder. "Stand back, we've a lot of cages left."

Sîu let go of the boy but spun to hug him, and he reached over her shoulder to slice the lock. He kissed her head, and she smiled up at him before letting go. "I know, lots of cages."

He turned his back on the reunion and finished the row before heading into the next hall, and by the time he met Sîu again, children surrounded them in a swarm that trailed into the dark. He grimaced at the number of mouths to feed and how they'd fill the ships. "Well, hells, let's go, girl. Reckon we got enough to piss them Histê off."

She giggled, but it was hard as hell for her to move with her brother squeezing her legs. Sîu took his hand, and Solineus led them back to the exit, and as the sun blinded their climb to the surface, the sound of the gong assaulted their ears. Nobody stood in their way and he ran in the lead.

A single priestess stepped in front of them, but her eyes went wide and she ducked from their path before he could kill her. He reckoned there was no cause to give chase. So it was they reached Adinvan without further bloodshed. Solineus laughed when he reached his father, but his old man bore a serious gaze.

"When you mentioned hiring yerself some mercenaries, I didn't expect it to be an army of children. What the hells you thinkin', boy?"

Solineus turned and his arms flapped to his side. "Son of a shits." When he'd been opening cages he didn't bother to take a headcount nor even guess. He'd known there was more than ninety, but there had to be four hundred heads milling behind him and another hundred still streaming in. "I never do nothin' small. Except these, but what they lack in height they make up for in numbers."

Solineus thought he was funnier than his old man did, and Adinvan's voice was gruff. "Hells. We can't go shoving all of them down this godsdamned ravine. We'd break a dozen arms and legs and a head or two!"

"We take the road, then."

"The road, he says. The road." Adinvan turned west, slung his shield from his shoulder and drew his sword. "The road it is. Spread out boys, like we're herding godsdamned goats. See a Histê, kill 'em."

They trotted forward, but stragglers kept them to a gut-eating walk. Sîu held her brother's hand, but her eyes were on Solineus. "This is a wonderful thing you do."

"Tell me about it when we're alive and on a ship." A man called Ilstin shouted words he couldn't discern over the noise of children, but the sword he pointed toward the pyramid he understood before looking. Histê warriors trotted in rows, ten abreast, chanting and thrusting spears into the sky before banging their shields in unison, and there was only one road down to the shore. They could beat them to the road easy enough, but if they wanted to make it alive, they needed more than a snail's pace. "Get these whelps movin'! Everyone who *can* run, run."

Sîu nodded and screamed orders and those who were able followed her command. Solineus watched the mass of filthy bodies swarm by, spotted the tall girl from the pit crawling in the dirt, struggling to regain her feet as others pushed and shoved and stepped on her legs in the effort to pass. For a flicker, his mind teased that the weakest in the herd sometimes had to die. She wasn't even a part of his herd.

"Forges be damned!" Children bounced off his legs as he bound to her side and lifted her; bloody lips leaned into his shoulder and she weighed nothing, little more than bones beneath the swath of fabric she wore. Five strides later, he grabbed a boy no older than six and hugged tight, striding until reaching the downhill.

A trail of youngsters surged ahead, but seaside there was fighting not far from the dozen longships beached on the shore. Around him, the Silone warriors herded the children the best they could, but the Histê would catch stragglers before they reached halfway down the slope. He slipped the children from his arms and patted their shoulders to send them onward.

Adinvan stepped to his side as Solineus turned to contemplate the enemy, and the Silone warriors formed a line to either side of them ready for a fight. Turned out father and son thought alike. "Well, boy. They've got shit for armor, but there's a hells of a lot of them."

"Soon, there'll be a whole lot less." Solineus slung his shield from his back and drew the Sister, but a thought crept into his head. He glanced to the pack of youngsters stretching the length of the road, the fastest already reaching the rocky beach. "We've got it wrong. They won't kill their sacrifices; they're too valuable."

Adinvan sucked his teeth and smacked his lips. "If you're wrong—"

He didn't have time to debate with himself or his father. "They're countering the ships. They'll let the children be. Run! Reach the shore and fight 'em there." He banged his Kingdomer shield; it chimed with a sonorous note that broke the warriors from their staring at the enemy. "To the ships!"

Men turned and moved from a jog to a run like an awkward flock of geese and Solineus sprinted ahead into the point of their "V", but he veered on reaching Sîu. The other men pulled up to stop but he waved them on.

"They won't harm these young'ns, but they'll kill you."

"What?"

"Tell them to move to the side, if they aren't in the way, those warriors will run right past them."

She stared at him horrified, but for a flicker only. "I won't leave Nêkulû."

Solineus sheathed the Sister and lifted the boy, covering him with the shield in his other hand. "Tell them."

Sîu turned and screamed, waving her arms east, and the chaotic swarm veered. It was far from military precision, but most would be out of the Histê path.

They trotted downhill with Sîu yelling for people to form a line and as he reached the bottom of the hill, he turned to find himself proven right. The Histê passed the children without a second look; more troubling was they were only a few hundred strides behind him. He handed the boy to Sîu and shook the cramp from his arm as the chanting army drew close. He sprinted for the shielded row of Silone warriors, fatigue and aches fading. A hum of arrows passed over his head to guarantee the enemy would come for them.

When he reached Adinvan he turned in time to see bodies falling, some with arrows in them, others tripping over the dead and dying. There was no fear; the Histê burst into a screaming run.

Adinvan puffed and stomped his feet. "Well, boy! That was a fine trot to warm us up."

Solineus drew the Sister, and she hissed *Gers'voresh-kûmjotukî* between his ears. He stomped his boot with mule ears flapping and slammed the Sister's hilt on his shield to the beat of his foot and screamed, "Gers'voresh-kûmjotukî!" He didn't know what he was saying and he didn't care, nor did anyone else, but the cry traveled down the line until hundreds of Silone warriors chanted, pounding shields and stomping feet.

The Sister hissed and Solineus repeated her cry. "Gers'voresh-kûmjotukî!"

He raised his shield and, in a flicker, the Histê struck like a tidal wave against boulders. Spears sailed, men leaped, some dove low, but the bastard straight in front of Solineus ran head-on into his shield with a trilling scream. The shield sang and the Sister darted, giving the warrior an excess hole in the middle of the forehead, but the press of the man's weight didn't go away; a crush of scrambling bodies trying to reach Solineus held the dead aloft.

He braced his legs in the dirt and the Sister slashed and sliced, severing, killing, maiming men he never saw, and he could only pray some Silone hadn't gotten out in front of him. Adinvan bellowed beside him, and for a flicker, they pressed shoulder-to-shoulder, the better to fight the weight of men throwing their lives away. A blade slashed low beneath his shield, but if it pierced his armor he couldn't tell.

Arrows dove into the Histê ranks ahead of him, and by now he saw gaps forming in the Silone line, Histê pressing through. The Sister took a head from in front of him, and his feet slipped in the blood-soaked gravel of the beach. The press of battle didn't allow the dead man to fall; Histê crushed the body into his shield. He took a knee, thrust the Twin through a Histê thigh, then swept the blade to remove the man's other leg.

And still he slid backward until his foot caught a stone and he drove forward with his shield. A spear rang the crown of his helm and he surged back to his feet. "Kûmjoto-kî!" He swept a man from his path with his shield and let go of the treasure, his left hand drawing the Brother. A fury of voices. A fury of hate. A fury of survival instinct.

The Twin blades weaved through arms and legs and heads like severing needles in a cross-stitch. In flickers, he'd opened a hole in the enemy ranks and not a damned one wanted to get near him. He flicked a spear from its arch and lunged to reach a Histê, putting a blade through his sternum. He raised both swords, challenging any who dared to face him amid the carnage. "Kûmjoto-kî!"

The pyramid exploded in a blaze of fire that reminded him of Eliles' tower, but this wasn't a defensive wall, it was volcanic obliteration. Flames rose hundreds of feet into the air, and smoke billowed before a quiver of earthquake shook their feet. He crouched low out of instinct, sheathed the Brother, and retrieved his shield. *What the hells are those? Shits. A*rching shadows flipped through the sky, massive fragments of pyramid; if those reached this far, his shield might survive the hit better than he would.

The fighting all but stopped, both sides of the battle staring at the eruption from the cliff, flames spouting from a roof of smoke and debris. The flames rose and kept rising until he realized they were no longer flames, but a being on fire, its great serpentine body curving like the blade of a flamberge sword streaking higher until it slowed to a stop; massive wings unfurled, jaws filled with rows of jagged teeth opened, and an explosion of fire arched through the sky. The creature was greater than any living thing he'd ever imagined, greater than the pyramid it destroyed, greater than the Foundations, and then it disappeared.

As if never there.

Except for the fire, smoke, and destruction it left behind.

When Solineus' eyes returned from the heavens of destruction, he saw the Histê on their knees, praying in a chant that named the creature their god, Môgôdûu. Then the rain of stones came.

"To the ships!" None of the stones landed near them, but he didn't want to wait to see if there was a 'yet' needing attached to this fact as the ground quivered. He gave his father a shove. "Move!"

"Forges! What the hells was that?"

"You can ask Sol after it eats you! Now run." He turned, spotting Sîu and her brother, and rushed to her aid in guiding the children to the boats.

"No crying, the great serpent came to save us. To the boats, to the boats."

Children stared at him, some crying and fleeing at his sight, and he glanced at his sword, shield, and blood-spattered armor. "Take your brother to the ship; we'll make certain they all get aboard."

"No."

He turned his back to her, eyes peeled for an attack, but the Histê were locked in their prayerful routine, rising at the waist and slithering into a stretch that kissed the ground while chanting Môgôdûu over and over. Some part of him reckoned he'd be a safer man if he started killing them all before they lost their faith and attacked him, but it didn't feel right.

"By the heavens, get yourself aboard that ship before these bastards decide they want us dead again."

"You first."

"Godsdamn! Why are women such trouble?"

She laughed but stayed by his side as they ushered children aboard the longships, shoving them off as they grew heavy.

Fifteen wicks later, the Silone had all the children loaded, they even took the time to pull their dead on board, and not a single Histê stood or said a word to stop them. The *Lady Moon* was the last ship shoved from shore, and Solineus stood at her prow staring at an empty cliff where a man-made mountain once stood. Sîu stepped to stand beside him.

"We witnessed a wonder today."

Solineus allowed himself to sit, and in this moment, knew his body would ache for a week. "A god, Môgôdûu."

"Môgôdûu is a great serpent, but it is said she wears eight wings of eagles, and her head is that of a lizard with goat's horns."

"Then what the shits do you name that thing?"

"You named her. You called her. The great dragon, Kûmjoto-Kî."

It took a flicker to settle in, and he glanced at the Twins. "I didn't call her."

"You called her name and she listened."

A cry rang out, and he was saved from further discussion, "Sails to the north!"

Solineus jumped to his feet and stared. Not just a few sails. A fleet.

Adinvan pressed through children but got stuck paces away. "Some of them ships fly the flag of Boboru."

The Boboru were pirates and slavers whose home was through the Monsoon Strait, not far from the Gorotan. "They might not be after us, then?"

"I reckon the Histê thought like you and hired them on."

They'd counted on being able to outpace Histê ships; the Boboru were an island people born to decks and sails. "Damned to the Forges. I reckon it's a good thing we were headin' south already."

THIRTY-SEVEN

Wasted Negotiations

Balance the wire walking,
a thread of steel, a steal to dread,
Balance your words walking.
Free the deed. The written or the action?
Only you can decide what I mean to you,
Freed deed bleeds, but is that possible?
I say so. You say no.
The Deed says go low in tow.

—*Tomes of the Touched*

Ôlisbenar remained true to his word. The Malstefnê army crept across the river while the supplies rolled in slow and took days to settle in. They built bulwarks of dirt and topped them with spiked logs, pure nonsense unless the Tek anticipated Helmveline or the Helelindin attacking.

Puxele strolled to his side, her belly swollen and her strides awkward, but she managed to walk the wall every day. She pulled her Edan recurve from a sheath at her belt, the tooled leather doubling as a quiver. She nocked an arrow and drew the bow. It was awkward as the hells watching her stance as she balanced and kept the bow from hitting her baby-belly.

"You should head south." It was the hundredth time he'd made the suggestion, so it was more running joke than serious.

"I ain't runnin' from no fight, in particular when I can't run anyhow."

"A good point."

She stretched the string several times before she huffed and stuck the weapon back in its sheath. "What do you think they're doin' out yonder behind all that dirt?"

Ivin pointed. "It isn't all dirt. There's stone in their wall. That means they're tunneling their way here to undermine the wall if they have their way." It was also the slowest method to attack a position without making it obvious you were moving slow.

"How do we stop 'em?"

"Morik assures me it won't work. The Kingdomers dug the wall to rest on bedrock and put down a series of steel rods in the dirt to make tunneling more work."

"Why the hells don't he up and attack then? That's what I'd do."

Ivin kept the secret of Ôlisbenar from most folks, fearing a tongue would wag, plus he didn't want to get hopes too high. "They've got a war to the north to fight still; they want minimum losses here. But they've been up to other no good. We've found Malstefnê scouts headless and hanging by their ankles in the trees to the east, bled out like a deer."

"Ôgrihîn?"

"Helelindin. Rumor is they rolled the heads back down into the valley."

Puxele rubbed her belly. "And you sent yer new bride to entreat with them. I don't know as I trust our neighbors any more'n I trusted them Edan up north. You and me ain't so smart with our spouses."

"She's safe as a treaty can make her, maybe safer than here. And stopping Rinold would've been like keeping a squirrel from an acorn, what happened isn't your fault."

"Just how long you think they're gonna hold off their attack?"

She pointed, and when he turned a boulder soared their way. It landed well short, denting the soil and rolling within strides of the base. The arms of the trebuchets in the distance still stood straight in the air.

They'd launched ten stones per day, no more, no less, for three days straight. "Bastards just wanna keep us on edge."

Puxele's mouth opened, but she stopped to stare past him to the gatehouse. "Yer bride beat my no-account husband back. The first attacks will come sooner than I'd hoped."

Ivin spun to see Kinesee walking their way. She still wore buckskin riding trousers and a loose linen blouse that reached the middle of her thighs. The necklace around her neck sent shimmering sparkles to dance on the stone of the wall as it bounced on her puffing chest.

"We need pigeons sent to the Ironwing and Morik."

Ivin admired the way she carried herself, the confident smile, and the ease with which she issued her demand. "Morik is here for a visit."

"His wife, whoever commands then, though the Ironwing is most important."

"Why? What happened with the Helelindin?"

"I failed, but not so utterly as Lelishen expected."

"Lelishen? She's here?"

She hesitated. "No. She had something of importance to attend, but she'll arrive with King Sebedil's negotiators."

The more she said the more confused he became. "I thought you said you failed."

"More like I think I *will* fail, but... The Malstefnê wouldn't dare attack with Helmveline and Helelindin in their path, am I right?"

Ivin snorted. "I believe Ôlisbenar to be a smart man. No."

Puxele glanced between the two of them. "You two are confusin' the hells outa me."

Kinesee smiled at her. "How long until the baby?"

"A week late, by the Seven Heavens, which is more on time than her daddy. Good thing he ain't a big man with a big baby, or I'd be cussin' him all the more."

Ivin raised his hands. "Whoa, whoa. Don't change the subject. Helelindin are doing what?"

Kinesee turned and gazed north to the enemy. "You signed the treaty right down there, between the army and the wall. Now you're going to negotiate another. You will work with Helmveline to attain Latcu, and with the Helelindin to gain access to the Final Foundation."

"What the hells do you mean, me?"

"The Helelindin refuse to speak or trade with Helmveline, but they will trade with you. And they *won't* let Kingdomers onto their mountain."

Just when things started to make sense... "You're saying I have to convince them to allow Kingdomers on the Final Foundation when they flat refuse the notion?" He leaned on the wall. "Sounds plenty easy."

"I didn't say you'd succeed, but it could give us more time, for—"

"You're right." The pain in her voice clutched his heart, but it was the word *time* that brought his brain back to the right path. He stepped to her and put his fingers beneath her chin so that she looked him in the eye. Instead of speaking he kissed her, perhaps the first real kiss they'd shared since their wedding. "You succeeded. We don't need a treaty; all we need is time."

Her face softened, and for a flicker, he felt like a man she hadn't been forced to marry. "You're pleased?"

"By the gods, girl, you've gone a long way toward saving us from war. How long we got until they arrive?" A stone crushed into the wall several hundred strides away. "Hopefully before they rain a mountain down on us."

"We had a delay getting back... two days at the most."

"Forges be... It'll be easier to stop the mountain before it starts. Drumun." Kinesee's guard snapped his heels when addressed. "Find Morik and tell him we're throwing a party for the Kingdomers and Helelindin. Kinesee, will you ride to make sure the pigeons are sent?"

The girl... the Lady Choerkin beamed. "I'd love to."

"Good. Puxele, you and that daughter of yours bored or busy?"

She laughed. "Hells! I'll do anythin' that might help push the brat out."

Kinesee said, "You're a tougher woman than I ever seen."

"I've plucked three arrows out of me over the years and survived a mountain lion; no heavens blessed baby is gonna stop me."

Ivin said, "Go to the kitchens, make sure we got quality enough supplies to feed honored guests. Get some hogs on spits. Whatever it takes."

"Yer sending me to the kitchens? You know the way to this pregnant lady's heart."

He grinned. "I do."

"Maybe if I eat enough, it'll shove my darling out of me." She looked at Kinesee. "You married a good man."

Ivin paced. "Everyone get going. Lots to do. I'll see to tables and tents."

The main gates of the Rôemhîik opened and Ivin followed six wagons laden with supplies through the portal. It closed hard enough behind them that he felt the rattle of the iron portcullis in his teeth as it ground into place.

"You didn't need to come along."

Morik rode beside Ivin while gnawing an unlit pipe, and one of his dozen men carried a black flag sewn with a golden griffon, the mark of his mountain, Shuntiskâ. "The way I reckon, the Malstefnê are less likely to get frisky with a Helmveline banner out here. This is a godsdamned bold move."

"Maybe so, maybe not." The wagons didn't stop until they were within the outermost range of archers, and as they looked on, not a single arrow arched their way. "But I guarantee you we have Ôlisbenar's attention."

Morik laughed. "I'd feel better if you let me in on the little plan you're hiding."

"I can't give details. All you need to know is I have a spy and this war may never get started."

"We haven't sprouted turkey feathers; so far so good."

They sat their horses and watched men unload the wagons, set up tables, and prop pavilion tents with colorful silk banners. They were the same they used during the previous treaty negotiation.

A dozen wicks after the first tent was staked, a prancing horse appeared on the rise of the bulwark, and it didn't take long to recognize Ôlisbenar's gleaming white smile. Unlike their previous meetings, this time he brought three guards.

Morik leaned in his saddle. "Speaking of bold."

Ivin swung from the saddle with a bottle of whiskey and moseyed to a table to wait for the man's arrival, and Morik followed him.

The gaited horse crossed the barren ground in flickers with its high steps, and the dapper Malstefnê leader leaped from the saddle, landed on the balls of his feet without a sound, and tossed the reins to a man who'd been pounding stakes a flicker before as if he were a Tek servant. "My friends! You throw me a party." His three guards dismounted in more traditional fashion and stood behind him.

Ivin gestured to the table and the three men sat. Ivin popped the bottle open and took a swig before offering it to Ôlisbenar. "The glasses aren't here yet."

"Glasses are a formality." He took a drink before handing it to Morik. "My birthday is months away."

"We have other guests in mind. We will be discussing a trade deal between Helmveline and the Helelindin."

The man's playful, cocky smile twisted into a smirk, and he stuck his hand out for the bottle. "This is a thin ploy to delay the deaths of your people by mere days."

"The plan runs deeper."

"No doubt it does, don't all plans? If I attack now, the negotiations will move."

"Have you met King Sebedil the Third? I suspect your scouts have met his people in the mountains. Sebedil himself insisted on this meeting place to honor the deal we struck before. You know how the woodkin deal with mortals who interfere in their affairs in unbidden ways."

"They're gutted and strung up like slaughtered boars. But is it worthy of war? I think not."

"Ask Overseer Iro if the Edan need to go to war to win. A single Edan adorned his bed with the heads of his commanders while he slept, never waking him. He left the Eleris to do so."

The Malstefnê paused, eyes staring straight through Ivin for a flicker, then he shrugged. "I heard such a rumor."

"No rumor, I witnessed the heads."

"Still! My friends, the Helelindin are not Edan."

"You are right; they're easier to anger and don't fear to leave their woods."

Ôlisbenar took a drink and leaned over the table, handing the bottle to Ivin. "What is your downriver play?"

Ivin wiped whiskey from his lips. "A true fox wouldn't need to ask."

"Even a skilled fox cannot always know the mind of another skilled fox. But I do love games." He leaned back in his seat, eyes flicking between Ivin and Morik. "A trade route guarded by the parties on either side of the Roemhien... but if we didn't interfere in the travel of merchants..." He smiled and laughed, fingers flicking so that Ivin would pass the bottle back. He drank and stared, then pointed at Morik. "Your Ironwing has something the Helelindin want, but by all the Known Names, the Helelindin hold a bloody grudge. They won't trade with a Kingdomer to save their lives." He pointed at Ivin. "You are trying to be the invaluable middleman, untouchable."

Ivin kept his face steady despite being impressed by the man's quick wits. "Maybe so, maybe it runs deeper and farther downriver than that."

Morik said, "He's a man smart enough to be a danger to himself."

Ôlisbenar laughed and kissed the whiskey bottle, but spoke before taking a drink. "You sound like my father. It turned out I was smart enough to be dangerous to him."

"Patricide?"

"Self-preservation. But I ask myself, what is it the Kingdoms have that the Helelindin do not? Some ore I'd wager. But something so rare, so valuable, what could the Helelindin have to pry greedy Helmveliner fingers open? Hmm?"

Ivin shrugged. "The tail of a wise fox doesn't give away the head's direction."

The Tek drummed his fingers on the bottle. "You have given me a fun game to play, fellow fox, when I'd thought the game was closing for the kill."

"Another fox may take the grand goose's head anytime."

"All the grand gooses are in danger all the time, as are the wolves." He raised his arms then folded in a mocking bow. "You win, Warlord

Choerkin. I will delay the siege, but I warn you, if I find this was a ruse and no parties arrive... I recommend you die in battle; our torturers are bored of late. I admire a quality foe, but I loathe liars." He snapped his fingers and rose. "Farewell, until the table is set for another game."

"Don't go falling off your horse and dying. I don't want to be accused of poisoning you."

He laughed as he swung into his saddle. "That wicked liquid might burn my tongue of taste for a week, but it'll take more than that to knock me from my saddle."

Ivin watched the Malstefnê ride away, but he felt Morik's stare. "What the shittin' hells was that then? Fox this, fox that. Gooses and wolves."

Ivin glanced around to make sure no one listened, then corrected his Silone before leaning in close. "Geese. The delay was a given. He doesn't want to fight us."

"The hells, you say."

"He knows it'd be smarter to be fighting the Litrâ in the north. He's waiting for... his people to convince the king of this wisdom."

Morik took the bottle, his hand big enough that his grip touched thumb to finger around its girth. He snorted before taking a drink. "Folks trap foxes, you know."

Morik seethed, and Kinesee was glad the man's boiling eyes stared at Ivin instead of her. He growled low so the other tents wouldn't hear him. "I came into this knowing it was a stall tactic more apt to fail than win the Final Foundation, but a man might only endure so many insults before he bleeds or draws blood."

Ivin sat with his hands buried in his face, and she mused to herself if the man might not prefer war to this. "Is there anything else the Kingdoms might entice the high-nosed bastards?"

"Far as I can tell, not one shittin' thing. Reparations! Reparations for a war four hundred years old. If not for my respect for you, I'd have walked on over and shoved a mace up his ass that first day."

The Helelindin ambassador had arrived in poor faith to begin. Instead of talking trade, he demanded three hundred bricks of Latcu to forgive the war over the Final Foundation. The trouble was, many of the Helelindin were still alive and fought in the war. Hundreds of years between didn't soothe their grudge so much as the generations of long-dead Kingdomers. Once they'd managed to get to the discussion of trade, the Helelindin offered up many things for the Silone to "purchase" and exchange for Latcu, but not one of them spoke of the Foundation the Helelindin named Feteledêun. It didn't help that Lelishen had never arrived. In fact, that might be the driving factor in the abrasive behavior of the Woodkin.

Kinesee stood, huffed, and turned her back on the table. "Ivin, speak with me, please."

He arrived with an exasperated smile on his face. "There's no way in the hells these two parties will ever sit beneath a single tent. The Helelindin came to humiliate an old enemy."

"We're missing something. Lelishen needed to be here."

"Well, she isn't. If what we're missing is her, we're treading stormy waters. We came here for a delay to avoid war; if these two keep at it, we're going to be in the middle of another war."

War was hyperbole, she hoped, but tensions would be on the rise unless this meeting bore some small fruit. She glanced at Ivin and smiled. "What we're missing is trust."

"Aye, what of it?"

"The stakes in this game are too high, latcu and right of passage to the Final Foundation. We need to lower the ante, so to speak. If they leave here happy, it doesn't necessarily matter that neither got what they came for."

"You're saying we make a deal, any deal."

"The Helelindin offered rare woods. Did you miss the gleam in Morik's eye?"

"That was a fire, not a gleam. Wood isn't worth latcu."

"No, he wanted the wood, just not at that price. Let me try something?"

He nodded and she strode back to Morik, planting her palms on the table. "The Ironwing would trade for Elemental woods?"

"Not at the price laid out."

"Elemental ore? Ikoruv and others?"

"A bargain could be struck."

She smiled and pranced from the tent with Ivin on her heels. She bowed on entering the Helelindin domain and walked straight to Deseter, Sebedil's lead negotiator. He was arrogant and bore a haughty grin. The woodkin's brows arched. "Yes?"

"If we brought you Ikoruv and other infused ores, would you trade me infused woods?"

"The exchange would need to be fair, but of course we would."

In the distance she heard the chime of the gates of the wall opening, but she ignored the distraction. "I propose this: We table the latcu and access to the Final Foundation. Forget them for the time being. We establish a rate of exchange between various ores and woods and carry out trade. When this proves beneficial to both the Ironwing and Sebedil, we'll discuss the greater deal. The Warlord Choerkin—"

Thunder roared and the ground shook. Flickers later clods of dirt and tiny rocks pattered on the tent's roof.

Smoke and dust rose fifty strides to the north, and where once there had been solid ground, there was a hole. As Ivin stood outside the tent and stared, the sound of cheers reached his ear. Hundreds of Teks stood on the bulwark, arms in the air, hooting and hollering and whistling. Ivin wagered that the man out in front of it all was Ôlisbenar.

Ivin didn't bother to have General saddled, he walked straight downhill toward the man with long strides, and he didn't slow until within paces of the man's cocksure smile.

"My friend! What brings you north?"

"You know damned well."

"That? Oh, my apologies, it was an accident. On the Hearts of the Named, I swear it."

"Horseshit."

"You've outwitted me. I admit to our crime. We were testing the efficacy of the Wyvern's Flash for use on your wall."

It made more sense, but Ivin needed sugar water to wash it down. "Nope."

Ôlisbenar sighed and shook his head. "I was bored! My men were bored. We needed something to give the day a little fire. Admit it, no one is bored now, yes?"

"Oddly enough, I believe that."

"Also, I needed words with you."

"You might've sent a messenger."

His grin was a skunk's after sucking an egg dry. "That *would* be boring. My king is growing impatient. He wonders why his army eats through supplies while they are not fighting. My position is tenuous, albeit not so tenuous as yours."

"The negotiations are ongoing—"

"My king will care little for your negotiations, and he has eyes and ears in this camp."

Which was why he'd made an explosive show of gaining a conversation with the enemy warlord. "I can no more hurry the Wraith than I can a negotiation."

"Word will not have reached my king about this delay of yours, but be forewarned, if my king isn't dead before your treaty fails, a war begins. And if I receive orders to ignore the Helelindin presence..."

"The war begins."

Ôlisbenar shoved him, and when he stumbled, the man put a boot to his ass, driving him to the ground. "Begone, barbarian! Your days alive are counted on my fingers."

Ivin brushed himself off and strode south without a word, the walk longer and slower not only because of the rising slope. Kinesee met him twenty strides away from the tents, a stern look on her face. "What were you thinking, heading down there like that?"

"Ôlisbenar is a crazy son of a bitch."

Hands went to her hips. "And what does that make you? I know you two got that fool's plan cobbled together, but walking alone to the enemy?"

Funny to think of how crazy she'd think he was if he hadn't let her in on the play using the Face. "He and I are in the middle of a game; he isn't going to kill me before it's over."

"And the explosion is part of this game?"

"If the king isn't dead soon... he's concerned that the king will order the attack, Helelindin or no."

"So, what do we do?"

"Unless you've got a better idea, I suppose we negotiate this deal, then we find out if this wall is tough as Morik swears it is."

Kinesee put on a brave face that he couldn't help but admire. "It will be more than he says. Let them come."

Thirty-Eight

Bone Fingers

To lose in battle is a sin, but the greater sin is to not learn from your loss, for winning isn't simply a thing done; it is a thing learned, and once learned, it is a thing willed.

—*Codex of Sol*

Shouts awakened Meliu as the first hint of sun glowed a hazy orange on the horizon. She scrambled to her feet and stumbled to the tower—more a scaffold—she'd commanded built. Her boots slipped on dew-slicked rungs, banging her shin as she climbed, and by the time she reached the top, the shrill shouts ceased.

A knee-high fog covered the ground, but it was easy to see where the shouts had come from; a brace of men with weapons drawn surged to an area due north of the pyramid.

Polus shouted from below, "What do you see?"

No need to waste a prayer. "Nothing, too many men are blocking my view." She hurried down the ladder and to the gate with Polus on her heels, stopping short of the stair. Scurrying and half-asleep men blocked her route in every direction; as many men as could fit on the pyramid slept here off the ground.

Polus bellowed, "Out of the way! Let the High Priestess through."

A single voice was no use with so many in their path. Meliu prayed for Light, then unleashed the power overhead in a steady flow. The pyramid grew bright and without shadow, and dozens of men shaded their eyes and backed away.

Cries followed Polus' lead: "Let the High Priestess through! Make way!"

She descended faster than she'd dare during the day, as the dangerous stairs were safer with their edges delineated in shadowless Light, and when she reached the street below, they took off at a trot. Confused men cleared a foggy path, and within three wicks, they reached the cluster of armed men.

"What the hells happened here?"

No one answered, but they parted like grass until she reached a body lying atop a crumbling wall. The man's arms and legs were stiff as if rigor had set in.

"What the hells happened?"

The man standing nearest the body turned to her. "I ain't right sure, high priestess."

She strode to the man sprawled on the wall; there wasn't a drop of blood, and closer now, she saw that his chest rose and fell with shallow breaths. "What the godsdamns do you know?"

"I... I was having a fitful sleep and sat up, heard somethin', and went to shake Adrin... but he weren't there... heard him being dragged through the fog. I yelled, drew my sword, and something damned well hissed at me. I ran for Adrin, and when I saw his foot rise above the fog, I done lurched and swung, hit some Forge-born somethin'! Three times before the son-a-bitch let go."

Polus asked, "Kill it?"

"Hells no, not so I can tell. I took Adrin's arms and dragged him here thinking he was dead."

A sharp scream from the north; Polus surged into the throng of men, bulling his way until they stood facing an empty and long-dead city covered in fog. Sticks and scattered stones protruded from the haze, but nothing else caught Meliu's eye.

"Mmm, anyone know what happened?"

The few men standing with swords and spears at the ready shrugged or shook their heads. Meliu stared at the fog and prayed for Life, her eyes intense and hearing acute; *scrit-scratch,* then a deeper sound as something dragged across the ground. She closed her eyes, focused her ears, and the *scrit-scratch* came again. Her eyes flicked open in time to see a bony knob rise above the fog, then another rise as the first fell: *elbows, knees? What the hells is that?* Pale green eyes, beady and unblinking, rose above the fog for a flicker, met her gaze, then disappeared.

Meliu's feet moved before her tongue as she ran. "There!" She released her prayer for Life and prayed for Light. The swirl in the fog from the movement was evident even without her eyes enhanced, but as she and Polus grew close, everything went still.

A grumbling sound cocked her head for a better listen, but she had no idea what she was hearing. A man's feet rose into the air, statue-stiff, and her eyes widened in confusion. Fear struck like a hammer to her gut and she lunged, grasping for the man's feet. "Underground!" He was stiff as a log. "Polus! Help me!" She unleashed Light, and though its energy didn't cut the fog, it revealed a hazy truth: the man was headfirst and thigh high in dirt.

"Godsdamn!" Polus plunged his sword into the turf, crouched, grabbed the man's ankles, and pulled with all his strength, but the man's trousers slipped, and so did Polus' grip.

Meliu dropped to her knees and scratched at the dirt. Men followed her lead. "Pull harder!" She heard cracks.

"I'm breaking his godsdamned bones as it is!"

Polus dropped to his knees to keep his grip, and the disappearing man's ankles crunched, his toes straightened to point to the sky, the big man's grip slipped, and in a flicker the poor bastard disappeared into the ground leaving only his pants and boots behind.

The Broldun roared, taking up his sword to strike into the soil, but Meliu grabbed his wrist. "More likely you hit our man. Back to the wounded man, let's go."

They sprinted a hundred strides to the downed man on the wall. She collected herself with several deep breaths, prayed for Life, then laid hands on the unconscious man, but the energies of the prayer didn't feel eager to enter his body. Perplexing. "We need a healer. I can't do a thing." She turned to the swordsman they'd spoken to earlier. "Did you see it? Did anyone see it?"

"Might've seen an elbow. A knee? Somethin' boney stickin' up, but I guarantee, when it let go, it were gone faster 'n spit jumpin' on a hot stove."

"Yes, I saw similar... and green eyes."

Another man spoke. "I was on watch. I mighta seen eyes." Mutters of agreement, and the man spoke with more confidence. "Green glows in the light of my torch."

"How long's this fog been around?"

The torchman answered. "Rolled in, oh, three candles back? Right about."

"Dancing Bastards... three candles. Everyone! Check on everyone you slept beside! Everywhere! If we've got men missing, we need to know!"

Polus echoed her, his powerful voice followed by others in the distance before he turned back to her. "What're you thinkin' this is? Lizard?"

"I don't know. Elbows, knees? The way its eyes peered above the fog... Lizard doesn't sound right."

"If'n they saw what they think they saw. Fog's maybe two feet deep... Giant rat, panther?"

"That man struck it thrice before it let go... hit a head or mouth, wouldn't it let go fast?"

"Godsdamned more monkeys around these parts than a man can count."

"Monkey, you might be onto something." She shook her head and shrugged as she spun a circle staring at the ground. "This fog's thick as stew, we won't know more until the sun burns it off."

High Priest Gilimo arrived a handful of wicks later. He laid his hands on the man, prayed, and the scrunch of his brow told her something was wrong, that her impression had been right. "What's the matter with him?"

The priest shook his head. "I've never seen the like." He grabbed the man's arms and lifted; stiff as a board, Adrin damned near tumbled from his stone bed, then the priest leaned to listen at the man's chest. "His heart is beating, his breathing is weak, but his limbs are stiff as a man dead for candles."

"My prayer for Life... it was like the body rejected the healing."

"Yes, in Redjin's Monastery we healed wounds on the dead... Prayers for this man feels much like healing the dead." The priest rubbed the man's hand. "He's cool, but not the cold flesh of the dead."

"But you still healed the wounds?"

"Yes. It can make seeing the deceased... easier for kin. But this man isn't dead."

The exasperated sigh she'd been biting back escaped, and her fists clenched. "So?" He stared at her as if she was an idiot and her teeth ground. "What the Twelves Hells is the problem?"

"The living... Life can find the wound and heal it, strengthen the body to fight poison or disease, but Life and the dead? I need to *know* the wound to heal it."

"But he isn't dead."

"As far as the gods are concerned... he is."

Meliu's head turned to Adrin on the wall, but Polus spoke her mind. "He's the Wakened Dead?" His sword clicked as he loosened it in his sheath.

Meliu said, "The Wakened don't breathe, don't have a heartbeat."

"Mmm, then he's godsdamned Taken."

The healer said, "I don't know what he is... has become."

Meliu took a deep breath. "You need a wound, let's find a wound. The creature dragging him had the poor bastard by the leg or ankle." She looked to the man's bare feet and raised the legs of his trousers. Not a thing to see until she crouched and looked up. Two holes in his leg about a foot apart, one at the ankle and the other mid-calf; no blood but blackened as if by necrosis. "Here. I've seen wounds like this from a spider bite."

The priest ducked in beside her, sucked his breath. "The Eclipse Spider, yes. Extremely rare. Could be some kind of poison." He prayed and touched the man's leg. "There is hope."

Polus said, "If that's a spider bite... godsdamned big bug."

Meliu stood. "Not a spider, it's our climber from the palisade. Angles of the punctures, the spacing..." She glanced at the rising sun and the fading fog as two Helmveliner healers arrived to help, and she stepped aside to give them room to work.

The man's bedroll appeared as the fog faded, and her eyes guessed the route the creature dragged him as north. If her guess was right, it was straight towards the ground where the other man disappeared. She spotted the shadow within a dozen strides, too small to be their beast, but still a strange shape. She unsheathed the dagger she'd kept in her robes since Inster and took a tentative poke, catching and lifting a bony hand cut off just above the wrist, but it wasn't human. She wasn't even sure it was from something alive.

"Mmm, what bedamned thing would leave that behind?" Polus kissed two fingers and put them to his forehead. "You be careful with that thing, girl."

Meliu's heart raced and her fingers tingled as she drew the thing close. The palm wasn't no bigger than Polus,' and it sported five fingers, but the middle finger and what she figured was a thumb were as long as her dagger and directly opposed to each other. Together they created a freakish pincer grip not so unlike tongs she'd seen men use to pull ice from a lake. And the skin—*Can I call it skin?*—was like calcified grit, as if the thing had rested beneath a drip in a cave where stalagmites form. She stood without taking her eyes off the thing. "That's our climber. No doubt, these are the creatures who took the others."

A man came running to Polus and bowed, panting and near out of breath as he spoke. "Lord Broldun, at least a dozen men are missing."

"Shittin' hells. Sound the horns. I want every man in their armor. Make sure Bîdorik knows what's happened. Make it known; no one pisses or shits alone. Mmm, search parties, no less than twenty souls in each, got it?"

"Aye, m'lord."

Meliu set the hand on a crumbled pillar a couple of strides north of Adrin's feet before sheathing her dagger. She changed her mind, pulling the blade with a shrug. "Can't hurt." She pointed with its tip as the last trails of fog disappeared. "Looks like he was being dragged to..." Hole didn't feel quite right. "Where ground swallowed the man."

Polus drew his sword and motioned to men around him. "Every curious man with a sword, ax, bow... hells, a club, is welcome to join us." Within twenty strides, they had half a hundred armed and angry men milling behind them.

Meliu kneeled; marks in the ground might be a sign of feet, but... "No blood trail."

"Mmm, aye, I wish the Squirrel were here to find these nuts."

She stood and strode forward but didn't see another sign of anything as they reached the man's pants and boots sitting by their lonesome. "Spread out, look for other spots of loose dirt. If they took a dozen men, there're probably more."

Warriors fanned out with eyes plying the turf, but fresh dirt was too easy to find with all the work they'd been doing moving stones and tearing out young trees. Men cleared this area days before the last rain, but the dirt here wasn't caked.

Polus stood beside her. "Mmm, slavers to the south and some undead devil beneath us. Not sure I like these woods."

Meliu kicked the pants and boots to the side. "It's not a proper hole, like a cave. Put your sword to it."

The sword's blade hissed from its sheath and he rammed it into the dirt, a foot or more deep. "Don't seem so unusual."

"But it must be, a man doesn't get sucked through solid ground. Again, put that big Broldun belly into it this time."

He snorted, raised the sword above his head, drove it two-handed—the blade disappeared, and the hilt hit the dirt just before the Broldun did as he collapsed off balance and tumbled. He scrambled to his feet. "Holy hells!" He glanced at the grip of his sword and the patch of dirt as if one or the other might bite him. With ginger steps he closed, then wrenched his sword from the ground and hopped back like a dainty girl. "Shovels and picks!"

A dozen archers surrounded three men digging, but it didn't take long before the forest floor collapsed into a tunnel eight-feet deep at its bottom. Meliu prayed for Light and lit the hole; her head bonked

Polus' as they peered into a tunnel that traveled north and southwest, its ceiling and walls just big enough for a man to crawl, or get dragged, through. "How the hells was it sealed so good? So, Broldun, you like tight spaces?"

"No, hells no. I wouldn't send a Choerkin into that hole."

Meliu reached high to pat his shoulder. "Let Bîdorik and everyone know that the search parties should look for a cave."

The voice in her ear made her jump. "Hand them picks and shovels to my boys, more than a few have worked mines."

Meliu turned to Bîdorik; as a child in the mountains, her father had always said that miners were a different breed, and he didn't always mean it as a compliment. She smiled at the Kingdomer's offer. "I'm sure you and your men will put this Broldun's cowardice to shame."

Thirty-Nine

Tinder Emotions

Whether man or woman, love is a tragedy in the making as few loves end in joy. The question becomes is this love to be your tragic tale or the other's? Try to never let it be both.

—*Codex of Sol*

The Histê and Boboru fleet must've stopped to inspect the desolation of the Yungilêtunu temple; the spotters in the crow's nest didn't see enemy sails to the north for five days, and when they did, the flags were the angled red and white stripes of the Boboru. They reckoned the Boboru had already left the Histê ships in their wake, so at least if it came down to a fight, there'd be fewer to kill.

Day by day the sails grew closer, but after ten days of chase, the winds died, the sails drooped low, and the only thing carrying the cogs south was the current. It was the break they'd needed; Boborun ships had plenty of sails, but not a single oar.

They shuffled the children onto a dozen longships, and by current and oar they headed south until out of sight. By their reckoning, the island of Imukel rested seven days to a week away, so those ships would veer southwest and disappear from Boboru line of sight, while Solineus' command would draw the bastards deeper south, all the way to Toltûk.

They spent three days without a wind to speak of, and fresh water was growing scarce after keeping so many extra bodies alive. Then the winds came with a vengeance, sending them south at a pace their pursuit matched for three days before disappearing behind them. Another day they caught sight of a Luxun flag coming up from the south and they sailed close for news. Solineus introduced himself and named the Entîyu Êmoño and Captain Intoeño before asking that they make sure the Boboru giving them chase would learn that ships full of children sailed south.

The days grew hot and men hid beneath makeshift lean-tos the best they could. So it was that Solineus found himself sitting beneath a shirt from his trunk, the linen stretched between two spears, when the shout of land came from the crow's nest.

Sîu sat up beside him, awakened by the cry, but her brother still snoozed between them. He'd tried to convince both of them to go with the other ships, but it'd been a short discussion that ended with him staring at the back of her head.

"Toltûk?"

He smiled at her. "I reckon so."

"There are people there who I trust to take Nêkulû home. It will be sad to say goodbye, but he will be safe."

"Goodbye? You're going with him."

"Lord Mikjemelût"—it was always funny how she mispronounced his last name—"I am bound to you."

"The hells you are. I asked, there ain't a damned thing in your culture—"

"I am bound because I choose to be. You saved my brother... not just my brother. Hundreds of my people."

"No way in the hells am I gonna let you tag along into every Forge-born death trap I'm bound to find on this journey. Hells, a dragon could've eaten you already and that was our first stop."

"The dragon was there to help. And Adinvan already said I could sail with you. He is *chief* of the Emudar."

Solineus reckoned Adinvan was as much a matchmaker as his mother. "Ask Suseru, and you'd find that the Lord of the Emudar doesn't even have permission to sail with me. We're not done here." He stood and strolled back to Adinvan. The unsuspecting man stood with his back turned while speaking to a sailor. Solineus pulled the mule ear he'd cut loose from inside his boot and thwacked him in the back of the head. "That's two uses for these mule ears that I've found."

Adinvan turned with a scowl. "What the Forges was that for?"

"You told Sîu she could come with us."

"I did." He snorted, snatched the mule ear, and slapped him on the top of his head. "The girl makes wicked poison, right? She also makes salves for sunburn. Salves to keep from burning. Salves to keep bugs away. Salves to heal the bites from the bugs the other salve fails to keep away. That and your mother thinks you and she would make beautiful grandbabies."

All witty retorts he'd been working on vanished. "You shittin' me?"

"Yes, on the last one. At least halfway." He grinned and handed him the mule ear. "Now, if you'd just smarten up and cut all these damned things off."

"It gets stitched back on the flicker I find a cobbler. About this girl—"

"She's going with us. There ain't no stoppin' her, considerin' you're as good at telling women no as I am, so my permission gives you an easy out in the argument. You should thank me for all the time I'm saving you."

Solineus grumbled every step of the way back to his flapping shirt-tent and slipped beneath. At least the girl was kind enough not to smirk. Nêkulû stood at the rail staring at the island on the horizon. The boy had cleaned up well, the sun and fresh air brought color back to his skin, and he already added a little weight.

Her tone hinted at her victory without being smug. "I'll keep covered for so long as you want me covered."

"That's some small victory."

"Normally I'd be worried about being a woman aboard a ship full of men, but I don't think I need worry about that with you around."

"I reckon not. Any man who touches you without your say-so loses everything he touches you with, in the order that kills slowest."

If she was shocked by his answer, she didn't portray it. "I saw you fighting before Kûmjotu-kî came. Histê feared to even throw a spear at you. It terrified me, the children... your anger."

"I wasn't angry. I was just... surviving."

"Gods have mercy on the enemy who angers you, then."

Masts became visible on the horizon, the first sign of harbor to his eye. "Do you fear me?"

She giggled, a delightful sound. "I fear where you take me, but fear you? No. You may be the deadliest man I ever met, yet I... Your aura is complex, but you are a protector, and you have taken me inside your aura. There are others there with me."

"My aura?"

"All people emit an energy; only the *enesutilu* can see it."

"And understand it?"

She laughed. "Understanding a person's aura is little different than understanding a person; it's tricky and uncertain. For me, the vision comes and goes, but yours is strong."

He grinned, time to turn the table. "Can you see your own aura?"

"No, I never have."

"If you could, what would it say?"

She smiled at him as Nêkulû snuck up behind her and draped his arms over her shoulders in a hug. She laughed at her brother but kept her eyes on Solineus. "It would say things I won't admit to."

"A woman of mystery."

"Only to the unwilling to see."

Solineus snorted and jumped to his feet; he caught her grinning as if he'd proved her point. "It won't be long until we reach one of those dangerous places I'm taking you."

"Toltûk? I've heard it a place of trade and peace."

He turned north and pointed to sails and red-white flags on the horizon. "The Boboru will have something to say about that."

The island of Toltûk was a small chain of mountains rising from the sea, but it was the deep harbor on its northern shore that made it special. That and its location on the eastern end of the Monsoon

Strait. A dozen ships sat at anchor, in addition to the *Fefemor* and the Silone longships. The crown and moons of the Luxuns adorned three ships. Sîu informed him that four more were from the Gorotan, all flying the banners of their home cities, and the remainder were various kingdoms of the Korômun. He knew nothing of the Korô except that they were from the continent of Southern Vandunez.

Captain Edmordô and the *Fefemor* sat smack dab in the middle of the bay, and he welcomed Solineus and Sîu aboard, giving them each a personal hand to the deck from the rope ladder.

"It is well to see you, friend! I'd begun to fear you drowned before you make me rich... richer."

"I can't say things went as planned, but they went well."

"You live and breathe and bring the lovely girl with you. I see no children, and you're missing ships."

"It's a story for several beers, but they should be on Emukel by now. Safe."

"Ah! Children safe, ships safe, and you made new friends, I see. Or it is coincidence the sea vipers follow you."

"The Boboru? That's what happens when a dragon destroys a temple and you get blamed for it."

He blinked. "You are a joking man."

"He isn't," said Sîu. "Kûmjotu-kî destroyed Yungilêtunu."

"The Kî?"

Solineus thought the man might drop to his knees in prayer on the spot. It annoyed him to no end that everybody seemed to know the name he'd been puzzling on for two years. "If she were so great, she'd burn them ships to ash."

"Do not taunt the Kî." His words were brash, but he calmed. "The Boboru are of little threat to us here."

"Twenty ships sounds right dangerous to me."

"Oh, aye. But not here. The sea vipers are dangerous, but every ship here has paid the Boborun Right of Trade or intends to if passing their way. To attack you here... bad business."

"And what if their business with the Histê pays better?"

"Inconceivable." He turned to Sîu. "The pyramid is gone? It was an excellent marker for my maps. I will have to note it's destruction."

Solineus grumbled. "The Boboru."

"Are dropping anchor."

Solineus glanced, despite not doubting his word. Their sails had gone to bare poles and they bobbed on the waves. "So, they wait us out?"

"I doubt the Boboru think in siege tactics. No, if I were you, I'd sail to shore. No matter who they send, they will be more uncomfortable on land, in particular with so many from the Gorôtan here. Mention you sail for the Ôlfindarâ Islands and offer to pay for Right of Trade."

"They'll believe that story?"

"No. But it will speak to the fact you have no qualms lying to them."

"And that's a good thing?"

"Yes. Anger the Boboru if possible. He will be impotent to do anything here, and he will seethe and plot against you."

He chuckled. "And that's a good thing, how?"

Sîu said, "It's suicidal."

"No, no. The Gorô have a saying: A Boborun on fire will jump in kerosene to put it out."

Solineus squinted. "An angry Boborun will do stupid things."

"Precisely."

"What if he tries to kill me right there?"

"Well... That would be the stupidest thing possible, wouldn't it? Now go, have your men row you to shore."

Solineus, Sîu, and every man who worked the oars enjoyed a meal and a pint of ale and were nibbling fruit beneath a palm tree when a man from the docks came to whisper. He was old and gray and missing half of his teeth, but not from poverty, judging by the gold adorning his neck and wrists.

Sîu translated for them. "Lord Captain Ushtrûôk of the Boboru wishes to speak to the thieving captain of the longships."

Solineus popped a chunk of juicy nectarine in his mouth and bit, deciding that if lying to them was good, disrespecting them would be the first step to setting them on fire. "Bring him over."

"I..." the man stared. "Hmm."

Sîu said something and the man turned, loping away.

"What'd you say?"

"I told him the lord captain could enjoy the stones of our fruit if he hurried."

"I didn't think you were keen on angering the Boboru."

"If you're going to do something, do it well."

He laughed and handed her a wedge of fruit as he watched a beast of a man approach. He was six and a half feet tall with shoulders broader than Polus Broldun's, and royal blue silks sewn with gold draped over his body, pinned by a yellow-diamond broach at the neck and cinched by a golden belt. He had green eyes the color of moss and didn't have a hint of hair on his head; irregular pentagons patterned every piece of visible skin, almost as if tattooed, but their texture reminded him more of a snake's skin.

Three Boborun guards followed him, pikes in their hands, and a human with a chain around his neck walked in front, tethered to his master's wrist, his face decorated with gemstones sunk into the flesh of his cheeks to mimic tears.

The lord captain revealed rows of tiny, but razor-pointed, teeth as he spoke in a guttural tongue that didn't even sound like words to Solineus' ear. The slave spoke in the islander tongue, and Siû translated. "Lord Captain Ushtrûôk wishes to know who the thieving captain is."

Solineus picked a random person walking by and pointed. "That one! I'm certain that's the bastard, gut him for sure." And he laughed.

"You will stand when you address his holiness," the slave said.

"When I see someone worth standing for, I will."

The guards bristled, but the lord captain's cold stare didn't change. "Where are the Histê slaves? If you hand them over, my lord may be persuaded to merely kill you instead of harnessing your soul."

Solineus sliced a nectarine, removed the stone, and handed half to Sîu while gazing into her eyes with a smirk. "This man believes I have a soul."

"Big mistake," she said before biting into the fruit, juice dripping down her chin.

Solineus tossed the pit to the lord captain and it bounced off his chest before hitting the ground. "It's more than you deserve, but thank you for visiting. We will sail for the Ôlfindarâs and pay your Right of Trade, but I don't have to be friendly about it."

"Impotent sea wretch, you will not reach the Gulf of Tomulok alive. My master will chain you, burn tears into your bones, and harness your soul before eating your heart."

"Oh my, that does sound gruesome." Solineus leaped to his feet and put his hands to the Twins, soothed by the soft purr of their murmurs. The son of a bitch was huge; he didn't realize just how big until he stood to face him. "Let's finish this thing here. Now. To the best of my recollection, I never once killed a lord captain nor a Boboru shit."

"His holiness will not bloody his hands with the like of a barbarian thief."

"I will reach the Gulf, and when I do, I'll leave his holiness alive. But his hands will rest bloody on the deck of his ship."

The man's guards ground their teeth, spoiling for a fight, and maybe the lord captain would've given it to them if not for forty or more people, sailors and islanders alike, gathering to watch and stare, and more than a few held their hands to weapons. Edmordô was right; everybody disliked the sea vipers.

"My master will see you again, soon, and for your last breath."

Solineus gave a curt nod with a smile. "I look forward to sundering his soul."

The four Boboru hissed on translation; he'd hit a nerve he didn't expect to find. *They know the Pantheon of Sol, and they fear him.*

The slave snarled, "You will not die; you will suffer as no mortal should survive."

And with those words the group turned, the lord captain snapping the slave's chain so hard the man stumbled and ground his precious tears on the street. He stumbled regaining his feet, bleeding, crouching to skulk behind his master.

Solineus' only fear was that his little show might've gotten the slave killed. The people around them dispersed until all that remained was them, the Silone sailors, a bottle of wine, and a tree.

Sîu glowed. "That was so much fun! I could dart him. He's still in range. Right in that bald pate."

Solineus sat and rocked back to his elbow to stare. "I've spawned a demon." He laughed. "Your heart will slow soon and you'll realize how godsdamned crazy that was."

"You're probably right."

"Mmhmm, I reckon so. What'd you see in that bastard's aura?"

"Evil."

"Aye. With any luck, he'll be waiting for us in the gulf."

"Boboru spies are likely all over this island, even if not, someone will look to earn their wealth with our destination."

Solineus bit his nectarine, enjoying the twang and sweet before speaking his thoughts. "Which is why we start throwing gold around and whispering of... Pick a city beyond the Strait."

"The Free City of Mostul Ûbar." She grinned.

"Mostul Ûbar. It has a ring to it. Any particular reason?"

She shrugged. "I always thought it sounded pretty, regal, and they've trade with the Ôlfindarâs as I hear it told."

"Perfect." Solineus relaxed in the shade of the palm leaves and freshened his glass of wine, but before taking a sip, he dug into his pouch and handed one of the sailors a handful of gold coins. "Yorin, my good man. You and Hîdim should go to buy us a dozen bottles of wine. Buy glasses for all your fine men and be sure to whisper among yourselves about the fortune you'll be making in Mostul Ûbar. Not too obvious."

"Aye m'lord."

The two men trotted off with springs in their steps and Sîu grimaced. "My heart has calmed. We've spat on the shoes of one of the most powerful men on these waters."

Solineus raised his glass in toast. "All the more reason to live well today."

Forty

Wide Skies and Tight Spaces

Your sentence is a pittance for your unequaled lie.
Your sentence is the pity of the Unblinking Eye.
Aha! No.
Shower me with flowers me oh wanton lover
so spry.
Spread your bosom and show me your heart.
Does it beat? Does it drum?
Does it heat or does it run?
The beat of a Craven Raven heart is surprising
and Dull.

—*Tomes of the Touched*

The Helmveliners who took to the picks and shovels tore through rain dampened turf like kids playing in sand, but so far, their search turned up more drain pipes than monsters. It didn't help that there were fewer tools than miners to use them, but when they'd set out on this trip, digging wasn't their focus. It wasn't more than four candles after Bîdorik announced that an aqueduct once fed the city's water supply that a patrol reported finding such a thing collapsed a horizon to the east, hidden amid dense trees and vines.

Meliu's first thought was to repair it and flood the tunnels under their feet, but the Kingdomers had a good laugh at the idea after tracking the aqueduct to its source and noting the repairs required. Still, if they made a permanent home of Green Mountain, the aqueduct would be a boon during the dry season... if there was a dry season.

For a week now, miners had chunked holes in the ground deep enough to peer through the tunnels, then struck another hole from point to point. The result revealed a wild maze of tunnels leading in drunken circles traversing the world beneath the dilapidated streets of the city from the pyramid's foundation to the outskirts of town, but so far, not a single one led into the forest nor hinted at a den where these things lived. However, whether it was their being alert for attack or the hundreds of holes in the streets, none of the critters showed themselves.

When Polus stepped to her side and cleared his throat, it was a welcome break from the monotonous tension of staring at a fresh hole being explored. "What now?"

"A search party—"

"A cave?" Her heart pattered.

"No, a yellow-eye camp four or five days southwest along a river. They didn't spot none of our people, but them slaver bastards were there."

"Shits." Her thoughts were so focused on the tunneling creatures that the news disappointed her; it shouldn't. "Yes, yes. Good." The men dragged into tunnels were dead, or so she'd convinced herself to keep her sanity, but those nabbed by the yellow-eyes were still alive, or so she'd convinced herself to keep her sanity. *What won't I talk myself into to stay sane?*

"The searchers say it's a camp of twenty to thirty. Bîdorik is sending thirty Kingdomers, so I figure to match the number. Mmm, I'll lead it m'self to get godsdamn away from this Green Mountain hell for a few days."

Meliu watched as a Helmveliner climbed from the latest hole and, with a frustrated shrug, paced off the distance to his next dig. She turned back to Polus. "I'll be coming along, and I want High Priest Dondolus with us."

"That your Choerkin replacement?" A smirk raised the corners of otherwise serious lips.

"Sir prim and proper, you shittin' me?" If there was a man here who missed a scented bath as much as she did, it was Dondolus. "I'm done with men."

But she realized that she should've qualified that declaration, as for the next five days she was surrounded by them; thank the gods for the rains that at least eased the smell of so much sweat, in particular when lying next to a dozen of them on a grassy hillock overlooking a crooked stretch of river. The waters flowed dirty green with swirling patches and what she figured were logs, until one of the logs headed upstream.

"What the hells you think that is?"

Kosef, who had led a dozen excursions into the woods, replied. "Lizard big enough to swallow this Broldun whole. Gotta watch for 'em anywhere there's slow or still waters."

Polus grinned at her and said, "Best not to use yer dainty soaps hereabouts, I'm a-thinkin'."

"Noted." Her eyes trained back on the camp. "I've seen only six yellow-eyes at once, but from this distance I can't pick out individuals." The yellow-eyes were skinny and not much taller than her, and that was the men; by appearances alone, she figured her pa could've walked into the camp and slapped a handful of the bastards around if they weren't armed. But as with her petite frame, appearances could be deceiving.

Kosef said, "We saw a party of at least a dozen enter the other day, eight more in camp, plus who the hells knows how many in huts."

What he called huts were more lean-tos, and they did little to convince her this was a permanent camp. "Mostly men, best I can tell, and no children. A hunter's camp."

Polus scoffed. "Hunting people."

"Who would they be hunting? There isn't nobody else living in the region we know of, and there's no way they could've known we'd be coming. They're simple hunters who lucked into capturing our people, turning a profit with the Histê I'd wager."

"Mmm, they won't see it as luck when we're done guttin' 'em."

Kosef said, "First, we need to follow some to another camp, find where they took our people, then we gut them."

Meliu ran fingers through her mussed hair as she ignored gut talk. "We need to get that aqueduct flowing for fresh water." She noted the confused looks from the menfolk. "Sorry, distracted a flicker. You boys gut as many as you like, soon as we get one or two alive."

"Mmm, alive? Ain't no way you can talk to one."

"Not right off, no, but if we're going to find our people... they're probably downriver a couple hundred horizons or more by now. We need information."

Polus licked his lips. "I assume you got yerself a plan?"

"Ehhh... How fast can you run?"

"Faster'n yer average Migo Tortoise."

She glanced to Kosef. "Who's the fastest man here?"

He glanced around and scratched his neck. "Ain't no squirrel who could keep up with me in the woods back home, so long as I weren't forced into the branches, but that's a damned lie and the Broldun is faster than I am if I don't like yer plan."

Come midmorning of the next day, Meliu was hiding behind a tree on the path Kosef would take from the river, proud of her plan and its simplicity. The Helmveliner, Kosef, would come running up the river's bank, looking behind him as if chased, and when he gained the attention of the yellow-eyes, he'd sprint away to lure them into the ambush. The evil slavers would give chase. The Silone would wait, capture a couple, and kill the rest.

Simple.

Simple, except the yellow-eyes stared after Kosef's sprinting feet without making a move toward the river, let alone crossing and giving chase. Either they were suspicious, the river was too dangerous to cross, or they just didn't give a damn, but the cause didn't matter. The fact was that simplicity had failed her, and trying a second time to draw them across the river would seem even more suspicious.

So they sat for two days hoping to spot a group of them heading to cross the river on their own; Fortune smiles on the patient hunter, or so the ancient wisdom went. But fortune frowned on Meliu and rained on her every damned day to boot, and that drove the patience right out of her.

"We need to nab one of them bastards and get back to Green Mountain."

Polus nodded as he scratched his bearded cheek. "Mmm. Ready for the direct route?"

"There isn't a good crossing without boats for horizons, north or south. Unless you want to swim with them toothy lizards."

"They got the boats to cross."

"You ain't got no other plan than pissing them off?"

"Angry men are stupid men, most times."

She couldn't argue that logic. They'd hammered out a plan to do just that the day before, but she'd snuffed the idea with her paranoia. Angry men were also dangerous, and not knowing what powers their priests wielded, she preferred surprise. The notion of trading lives for a captured man felt like a losing proposition; she needed to remember that in war people died to win.

"Gods bless us. Fine, if everyone agrees, we'll punch them in the face and see what happens." Every man here itched for a fight since finding the camp, so the decision was swift and predictable.

Polus took thirty men and prepared the ambush some several hundred strides over the hill overlooking the river while Kosef prepared the assault meant to entice the enemy to cross the river. Meliu and Dondolus stood to the side, the healer less comfortable with battle than she was.

The man paced with petite steps to clear a patch in the leaves without ever walking more than five feet from her side.

Meliu said, "Relax. We've got numbers."

Dondolus stopped to stare at her nose. "Relax? We haven't a clue what we're getting into."

He was nervous but still smelled better than her; she envied the man his secret. "Their weapons and armor are no match for our steel."

"And yet, they captured the others without a fight."

It was the big question no one wanted to ask aloud and no one had an answer for: How the hells did these yellow-eyes drop men in mid-stride? "Life witchery, maybe Spirit. That's why you're here. But with my prayers, we may not need much steel."

"And if I fail?"

"The gods will heed your prayers, Elinwe will not fail you."

Kosef trotted to their position. "We're ready."

Meliu nodded and slapped Dondolus on a shoulder. "You stay clear but close; I'll be at the ready when you pull them close."

Dondolus followed after the Helmveliner, leaving Meliu by her lonesome. She waved to Polus, and the big man raised his shield before she trotted to the top of the rise. The birds and insects went silent as men with bows skulked through the woods towards the river in a broad line, then Kosef and a dozen Kingdomers sprinted ahead, dropping to their knees at the river's bank.

Quarrels flew from their crossbows and into the encampment; two yellow-eyes screamed in pain even as the Kingdomers couched their shields to form a line. Next came the Silone archers, standing behind the shields and launching arrows. The camp was chaos as more yellow-eyes than she expected raced from tents and lean-tos, and they organized faster than she'd hoped. Six of the bastards lay on the ground writhing, but a couple dozen of them pushed to the river and leaped into their canoes with Silone arrows thudding their body-tall shields.

Oars splashed and not long after arrows came from the opposing shore; several thwacked Kingdomer shields and stuck in the dirt like feathered weeds, but not a one found a living target. When the boats reached halfway across the river, Kingdomers stood and stepped back, paced and in control until reaching the woods, then archers scattered behind trees to continue the attack.

When the first boat reached shore, four men jumped to the bank, forming a shield wall that grew with every canoe to reach shore, and in no time, the wall formed a roof of additional shields. Another yellow-eye fell from a lucky shot, but his gap in the wall filled, and the horseshoe of shields stood stone still. Arrows and quarrels rained, sticking in shields, ricocheting, but the yellow-eyes didn't push forward nor return volley.

Meliu prayed for vision and stared, trying to glean a sign of anything, but it was a flash of movement in her peripheral that alerted her; she was looking to the wrong place. Her head spun to see a Helmveliner fall; she saw no wound, no attacker, nothing. He crumpled as if struck to the backs of his knees, limp as a strand of dropped rope, and others followed.

Her mind flashed to Choerkin Fost where the great Shadow stood on the dock. The yellow-eyes shielded a priest or some power; maybe they even prayed to empower the witch. Dondolus burst from the woods running straight toward the enemy then stopped to raise his arms in prayer, but men slumped or tumbled to the ground, falling one after the other until the priest was the only man standing.

"Run, you dumb son of a bitch, run." Dondolus ran, but the wrong godsdamned way. Meliu would've considered the man a coward before, but instead of showing the smarts to flee, he dashed to a fallen man, dropped to his knees, and prayed.

Meliu's hands quivered with fury as she prayed for Light and then Dark, but the distance was too great to attack or defend. To charge was suicide against an unknown power. Her gaze shifted to the yellow-eyes, where the shield wall opened and an old woman strode into view, her long, gray hair the only thing covering her sagging breasts, and her arms and legs painted in yellow tiger stripes as vibrant in color as her eyes. Her bowlegged stride carried her to the kneeling high priest with shield bearers to her either side. She stood over Dondolus with a yellow-toothed smile that flickered silver glints.

Dondolus' hands never left the man lying on the ground, even as he looked up to face his enemy. "Not Life! Nor Spirit!"

The crone's hand flicked with uncanny speed; blood erupted from Dondolus' throat as a bone blade exited near the base of his skull. The word escaped her lips without a thought: "No!" It took all her will not to run forward, not to try to destroy these people, but some piece of sanity kept her feet rooted.

Dondolus crumpled face-first at the crone's feet, but the yellow-eye no longer paid him any mind; her bright eyes surveyed the woods around and in a flicker lit on Meliu.

She gasped at the intensity of the stare; she could feel the hate, the malignancy, the confidence, the power, all before her hair lifted as if with a breeze and her head spun. *Not Life. Not Spirit.*

Meliu whirled on her toe and scrambled into a run, her breath short before hitting her second stride; she inhaled deep as she could and held it for twenty strides before the air exploded from her lungs. Men stared at her. "Run! Get the hells out here! Spread out!"

Polus wasn't a man to turn tail, but even he didn't question her. Silone and Kingdomer alike broke from their hiding spots and ran in wild lines, no two together. Meliu veered toward thick brush and slid downhill with her forearms blocking branches, leaves, and vines, then scrambled on elbows and knees into the deepest shadows she could find. She turned until she faced uphill. She laid still, catching her breath until she saw the first yellow-eye crowning the rise; she prayed for Light and Dark, then the world disappeared in an envelope of impenetrable Dark.

Her mind scrambled to make sense of sounds and smells, but this strengthened the fear the Dark tried to drive into the base of her skull. She refocused, clenching her eyes shut. *Not Life. Not Spirit. Dondolus died to tell me. But the witch couldn't drop him? Her witchery came for my lungs, my breath.* The *Codex of Sol* leaped into her mind. *The Battle of Erunovôlis: Breath Stealers.* The Silone hadn't met a witch like this crone in over five-hundred years, and this yellow-eye was powerful, reaching to steal her breath from a hundred strides or more, Meliu's Dark wouldn't reach half that before destroying her mind.

Twigs and leaves crunched as someone ran by, then the footfalls of another, slower. Hunted and hunter? It didn't matter, the flow of Dark was tranquil and managed now that her heart had stilled, she could lay here until nightfall if need be. Silence. A forest at rest.

Then, *she* came.

No sound nor scent gave the crone away; Meliu could feel the woman's intensity without seeing her wicked eyes. She inhaled deep and held her breath; her skin crawled, toes tingled, and her nose itched, but she forced herself still, forced herself not to breathe. The presence disappeared, and in an instant the itches and tingles faded;

Meliu waited another dozen flickers before allowing herself a breath. A relief to breathe; a relief there was air *to* breathe.

But she made certain not to twitch, to disturb a single leaf.

Half a candle later, footfalls came again, this time from the opposite direction. This time dragging something behind them. Laughter. Voices. A language she didn't understand. The vowels and consonants ran together *so* fast, and they spoke with nasal tones that made it sound like they had head-colds. The voices disappeared, but she heard others farther away four more times; it grated her nerves to hear how pleased with themselves they sounded.

A candle passed before she released the Dark hiding her, then prayed for Life to see and hear better. Nothing. No one. Friend nor foe.

She crawled knees and elbows from the prickly brush, swiped at mud dried to her clothes. She cast about with her eyes and ears a second time, then released the prayer for Life. She bowed her head, but kept her eyes open and prayed for Light and Dark. The powers flowed, instilling confidence, and she strode up the hill, ducking only near the top, castigating herself for letting Light's confidence overtake her need for stealth.

She skulked to a tree trunk and glanced across the river. Yellow-eyes settled around a fire, and one struck the first rhythms on a drum. Singing came next—a celebration.

A twig snapped and she spun—bright yellow eyes. Hands reaching. She twisted and ducked, and the man ricocheted from her ribs, keeping his feet with a hand to the turf. He looked at her and smiled, ferocious eyes fit more for a tiger than a man, but he didn't have a literal or figurative prayer.

Meliu slid down the hill on wet leaves until a foot planted against a root, and she smiled back; the man's yellow eyes disappeared in Dark, a torrent of demons and devils, whatever this man feared most, and she didn't stop until his bare feet stuck from the Dark, twitching instead of flailing.

She released her prayer from the man and looked around the area; far as she could tell, he was the only yellow-eye on this side of the river, or at least if there was another, he was smart enough to stay clear. She strode to stand over the man; yellow foam bubbled with bloody froth from his lips as he sputtered gibberish, fingers scratching the dirt, chest convulsing in spasms. She kneeled, putting a hand to hold his head still as she pulled the dagger at her hip. Light eased the edge of her horror as she slipped the blade into his throat to release his life. A calm overtook her as she watched his blood slick the ground.

She wiped blood from the dagger and onto the man's bare chest as his suffering faded into weak breaths; she stood with a sigh and sheathed the blade, taking a look around to assure herself the area was clear. She glanced back to the yellow-eye, his mouth sagging as his heart beat its last. "I never met a woman like your crone, but I guarantee she hasn't met no one like me either."

Forty-One

Impassable Waters

What am I hiding? I hide nothing.
An answer I give to every question asked,
if you don't understand the answer,
how should this worry me?
What answers have you hidden?
Liar.
You cannot hide lies from me,
but oh how well you hide them from yourself.
Unbound, Unfound, and unWelcome
Craven with a Raven for half a soul.

—*Tomes of the Touched*

Captain Edmordô called the Monsoon Strait the swiftest trade route in the world for half the year, in both directions, but also the deadliest. Solineus didn't know about the latter, but the former seemed true enough as the current carried them even when bare poles and against the wind. The storms they encountered the captain called gentle, torrents of warm rain that arrived in the afternoon on a near-daily basis, but they threatened no lives.

The more formidable issue was navigating the northern passage and its islands, big and small, as well as all the shallows capable of punching a hole in the hull. The center of the strait was safe from this threat, but the way the captain and crew spoke, they'd be more apt to face the Boboru on open waters and no one wanted that confrontation.

So they wound and weaved through islands and reefs and threats unseen until reaching a scratch on the captain's charts that he entitled "safe harbor," seeing as the island didn't have a name anyone knew. The island was no bigger than many they'd passed, but it had a deep cove on its west-northwest side and a high mountain to help block stormy winds rolling in from the east.

Solineus gazed through the fareye and spat into the sea. The Mûulbon Delta was wide and welcoming, and the ruins surrounding its waters were there as Captain Edmordô promised, but the Histê had arrived first. He wagered there were forty ships moored to stone piers, some stretching up the distant banks of the Mûulbon, and the bastards swarmed the ruins like bees hard at work to repair their hive. He turned to Edmordô. "You said this place was deserted."

The captain streaked wax along his mustache and twisted. "Was but isn't. I don't know what to tell you."

"You can tell me how the forges I'm going to make it up that river alive."

"I admit, I expected you to die much later in your journey. The good news is they don't know how badly they'd like to kill you."

"There's no way they're here because of us?" Solineus asked.

"Gracious no. Whatever the Histê are doing here, it started months ago."

Adinvan grumbled and kicked the rail. "I'd wager this has somethin' to do with our people up the river."

True or not, there wasn't much Solineus imagined they could achieve here to thwart their unknown plans. "No doubt that's possible, but not a damned thing we can do."

"We could maybe feint an attack, draw them off?" Adinvan asked.

Edmordô quipped, "We aren't enough to achieve such a thing. They know we're here and they don't care, but if we sit long enough, they will grow curious."

Sîu said, "Is north by land an option?"

"The river is dangerous, and from what I hear, dry ground is worse. That isn't counting the Histê and their Wiirê hunters."

Solineus collapsed the fareye and handed it to Edmordô. "We need to sail for the Gulf of Tomulok."

"I told you there is war. We could take a southern route to the Strait of Boboru, but I guarantee your Silone ships will draw the admiral's eyes. This means staying north into the Gulf itself, where the Boboru assume every ship is an enemy."

"What of the Gorô? The captains we met at Toltûk were friendly enough."

"You angered and threatened the admiral; this does the traders the favor of keeping his eye off them. The Gorôtan is losing the war at sea while it's impossible to lose on land, but they would not attack you without cause."

Solineus snorted. "We sail for the Gulf of Tomulok; we don't have a choice."

"You could turn back and live, but seeing as you're determined to die... You need to reach Nudoru Bay and pray the Gorô still control its waters. Getting there should be safe enough. Most traders will sail the southern route, and so the Boboru patrol those waters most. It rests where the Monsoon Strait meets the gulf. Nodoru is a city of thieving pirates if you ask the Boboru, or free captains if you ask the Gorô. Either way, it's a dangerous place where you can make dangerous friends. The right Gorô might see you north safely."

"I've been running to and from battles for years. This is no different. Raise anchor, captain."

Edmordô laughed and slapped his back. "You are the child of demons!" He whistled to his sailors and they scurried to the anchor-wheel and cranked. "Of course, this changes our agreement."

The Silone Armada, as Edmordô had taken to calling their longships, followed the captain and the *Fefemor* south into the Monsoon Straits, but only so far as to escape the chain of islands. Once in safer waters, the Silone sailed due east while the *Fefemor* sailed for the Strait of Boboru and the Free Cities to the south. Edmordô promised that he'd return and wait for them at the safe harbor on his map, but only until mid to late Beldrên in summer, the beginning of storm season. This gave them three months to return.

The Silone sailed night and day with a copy of the captain's charts, heading straight for Nudoru Bay with all the speed favorable currents afforded them. They ran their longships ashore seventeen days later with one brave (or greedy) soul from the *Fefemor* joining them as a translator.

Benelê hailed from the Gorôtan, a wiry man with wild eyes whose words flowed with a roll from his tongue, and he swore up and down that he'd find the Gorô they needed to get them through the Gulf alive. He'd been saying that for two days, and just this morning, he claimed he had a man for Solineus to meet.

"No, no, no, I don't know Captain Galortêu personal like at all, but he's a reputation, you bet. A stalwart from the *Izdelê* Oltumênu."

Solineus knew enough of the Gorô tongue to understand that Izdelê referred to an independent city-state, but he didn't know the first thing about the one mentioned. They could be slavers enthralled to the Boboru for all he knew. "This is good, I reckon."

Adinvan stood rigid beside him. "This city curdles the blood like a scream in the night. The sort of place I avoid when sailing."

Benelê laughed. "It *is* a place to avoid. This is why you have me. To make it safe."

Nodoru was a dark place in the middle of the day, the wood of its structures unpainted and weathered by sun and the salty spray of the sea into dark grays and browns. Only a handful of buildings rose more than a single story, and straying from the docks took you into a cluttered maze of leaning buildings where the rats were thick enough to battle the cats.

A dog barked through the bars of a window with broken glass as they turned from the docks and down one of the many unnamed streets. The tavern they entered didn't bear a shingle over its door, but Benelê called it the Hissing Mink. A man crashed into a round table—well built, as it didn't even quiver with a man's weight—as they entered in the midst of a brawl, a dozen or more sailors throwing haymakers and jabs and breaking every bottle in their path. Those not fighting sat as if it were nothing out of the ordinary, guarding their drinks and moving only when the melee got close.

Benelê barred Solineus from striding forward. "Give it a flicker. It'll calm down for sure. No weapons are drawn, likely as not these blokes are buddies from the same crew." They stepped to the side to watch, and within a wick, the men were righting their chairs, laughing, slapping backs, and rubbing jaws. As peace broke out the room swarmed with people, as if they'd come down from the rafters and out of hidey holes. Four young men swept the floor with straw brooms, while two serving wenches, in brown dresses to hide beer stains, made sure the men had full cups.

Brass kerosene chandeliers hung from the ceiling, and the bar sat in the corner to the right like a low tower protecting the workers from the crowd. A dozen tables sat scattered across the hall, all surrounded by sailors and townsfolk, and when he stood on tiptoes, he could see a small dance floor in the back where men and women twirled to the songs of musicians he could see but not hear over the din of the chatter around him.

Benelê said, "You men stay here, I'll look around and see if the captain is here."

The little man disappeared in the crowd, leaving him with his father. Adinvan snorted. "Might be my kind of place after all. I'll head for the bar and grab us a couple of ales."

Solineus nodded as his eyes scanned the crowd until they lit on a woman standing not far from the end of the bar. Her hair was long, black, and wavy, and her skin darker than Sîu's, but her eyes shone as they met his.

He needed to know what color they were.

He walked without thinking, unaware of anybody in his path, and she strode his way as well, their eyes never breaking contact as she weaved through mingling drunks. Her eyes were the color of polished walnut, and her fingers slipped into his palms without him knowing whether he took her hands, or she took his.

"Solineus Mikjehemlut."

"Polênu Juvilêus." The name carried the roll and trill of the Gorô tongue.

Her blouse was light blue and sewn with intricate flowers, making her a splash of color in this dim place. "I know you." He spoke in Edan and her eyes widened.

She licked her lips and wiggled them as if trying something new. "What language are you speaking?"

The warmth of her hands in his made his fingers tingle. "Edan, you speak it too."

"I don't speak Edan," she laughed at her own words. "How do I speak Edan?"

A hand gripped his shoulder and tugged. "Come on, lover boy. Benelê found our captain."

Solineus didn't let go of her hands, and she squeezed his. "I... I have to go. I'll be back."

Her grin was as curious as it was flirtatious. "You better."

He let go of her hands and followed his father with a groan. "Januel alive, boy, we need to get you settled down before you've got bastards all over the world."

"I haven't bedded a woman in over two years."

"That isn't no excuse to go chasing the hems of the most dangerous gal you can find."

"I know her."

"You know her?" He laughed. "You *know* the Contessa of Mostul Ûbar? Or at least that's what them who like her call the lady."

"You know her?"

"Of her. The Half-Breed Contessa."

"What the hells does that mean?"

"Her mother is of the Gorotan, but her father was the Count of Mostul Ûbar, a black-skinned man of one free city or another."

The Free Cities of Nomnuvar were legendary for their wealth and sat on the east coast of Southern Vanduzez. "What's she doing here?"

"A damned fine question, but we got business."

Benelê's shrill voice caught his ear and he looked up. The Gorô stood beside a table with three men in their seats. "Solineus and Adinvan Mikjehemlut, Lords of the Emudar, this here is Captain Galortêu."

The man didn't stand but motioned for them to sit. "The way I hear it, you men seek passage to the Helelindin woods."

"The mouth of the Mâbuhon River to be precise."

"Mouth of the Mâbuhon. That there's a problem. That there river sits west of the Emulên Isles, which are held by *Izdelê* Kôlechâ and her allied cities."

"What's the trouble?"

The man laughed before chugging from his mug. "You aren't from around these parts. The Boboru Armada has blockaded the islands the past two years and they patrol the region. Nobody gets past."

Solineus shrugged. "If nobody can get us through, we won't be needing your help."

The man pounded his chest with pride in his voice. "Captain Galortêu will see you to the mouth of the Mâbuhon! I will—"

Slender fingers gripped the sides of the man's head from behind, and a flicker later Solineus stared at the back of the captain's head. He fell dead from his chair to reveal the murderer; beautiful brown eyes met his. Polênu smiled with a wink, and with a whisper a rapier was in her hand.

Solineus leaped from his stool, but the blade pointed at Galortêu's men. "Damn it, woman, you just killed the man I'm trying to hire."

"He would have *sold* you to the Boboru." One of the sailors made a move, and she pricked his shoulder with a jab so swift it was hard to see. "*Telelê Jîu. Jîu.*" The man clutched his shoulder and sat with a furious gaze.

Six more men rushed the table and the Twins dropped to Solineus' side, but these sailors babbled Gorô at the Contessa of Mostul Ûbar rather than attack. She turned to him and offered her hand, and he took it. But men grabbed her shoulder and yanked on her, pulling her toward the door. "*Bolivêsu nôdol,*" they repeated as he followed her gripping hand, gazing into her eyes. He wouldn't let go, and neither would she.

"Meet me on the *Silver Willow* in the morning."

He released her hand and watched in a stupor as the men escorted the contessa through the door, and she called out one last time. "The *Silver Willow.*"

Solineus stood with what he didn't doubt was a dumbfounded gaze on his face. If there were doubt, it was erased when Adinvan tromped to stare at him. "Your taste in women is dubious, boy. Shittin' killed our guide. I'm not sayin' I ain't impressed with how quick and clean... but forges!"

Benelê circled to them in a grovel. "My lord, the Contessa of Mostul Ûbar, she lies... The captain could be trusted. It's her you can't—"

"If I see your face again, I'll skin it from your skull." He glowered at the slack-jawed man. "Say aye, m'lord."

"Aye, my lord."

"Be gone before I cut the ugly out of your stare."

Benelê bolted and his father grumbled. "I hope to the Seven Heavens you know your business, boy. He was the only man we had who speaks Gorô, and I don't know the contessa's name because she's the sweetheart of the seas."

"I don't know one hell from another, but I know her." He glanced around at the eyes staring fire at them. "We better get out of here."

Forty-Two

Dents and Holes

Treasure Seekers and Treasure Leakers
turning staring outside in at the word,
priceless and unheard.
The jingle and the jangle,
the treasure and the bangle,
which do you carry in your mouth
and which in your purse?

—*Tomes of the Touched*

Ivin ordered the tents packed and loaded before the ink dried on what Morik titled the Trade Treaty of the Rôemhîik Three—a mouthful, but Ivin wasn't in a mood to argue—and the gates of the wall were closed well before the Helelindin delegation left the field. The deal itself was equitable so far as Ivin could tell, but his knowledge of infused ores and woods and their values was limited to what he'd learned over the past two days. Much of the valuation was as contradictory as you'd expect during a negotiation. The Silone would purchase a load of ore from the Helmveliners and sell that to the Helelindin and, in turn purchase infused woods and sell them to Helmveline while turning a small profit. With no direct exchange of goods or coin between the two kingdoms, the trade was welcome.

It didn't make a lick of sense to Ivin, but he had more significant concerns with the trebuchets groaning in the distance as their ropes were wound taut and their towering arms cranked low to load with stones or whatever the Malstefnê chose to heave their way. Ôlisbenar and his king weren't waiting any longer.

Ivin and Morik reached the heights of the tallest tower to gaze down on the enemy just as the first boulders crashed into the walls. The nearest one shattered as it struck and Morik cheered and laughed.

"Whoresons brought soft rocks!"

Ivin grinned but wasn't as excited. "What do you think, Kesup? Are you having fun yet?"

Kesup was a distant cousin and the hornsman of High Tower, and of the ten men up here, the only one Ivin knew by name. "Not a lick."

Another stone struck the wall. "That one didn't fall apart."

Morik winked. "Aye, we'll sneak out at night, roll her inside, and send that one back at the bastards."

"Unless you're stronger than you look, we don't have a trebuchet."

"Not yet, you don't. I put a few folks to work on that a few days back. What? You think we only work with stone?"

"I didn't say a word."

"The Malstefnê will need to bring their rocks in from a distance to sustain an attack worthy of this wall. Now out yonder, that's where they'll find the present we left their sappers, you'll see steel rods sticking up."

Morik handed him a fareye, and it didn't take long to find a dozen rods protruding a couple of feet from the ground. "They're lifting the rods you put down to block them. How much are they going to slow them?"

"I reckon you'll see in the next few wicks." He leaned against the wall but kept his eye north. "I apologize for not doing better with the Helelindin. There just wasn't a way to make a deal without our being able to reach the Final Foundation."

"It was spittin' at the moon from beginning to end. They had no intention without... Without giving them something they wouldn't even name. But you got something out of it."

"And so did you, assuming these walls stay in one piece."

A deep rumble resounded, and for a flicker Ivin suspected the Malstefnê had thrown Wyvern's Flash at the wall, but dirt and rock flew in a cloud of smoke and dust where the rods had protruded from the ground.

Morik thumped his shoulder and whooped. "That'll put some new thinkin' to their noggins. I do love the *boom*."

Ivin's eyes widened with his first experience of a thunderstick. The clearing smoke revealed a rounded pit with five steel poles twisted by the explosion jutting from its bowl. If there were bodies, he didn't see them from here. "So, that's what took the bridge down."

"Aye, beautiful wasn't it?"

"I thought those things were dangerous as the hells."

"Oh, they are. There aren't a lot of them out there, but enough to make it bloody to reach the wall unless they want to go through bedrock."

Ivin peered through the fareye, arms of siege engines bending and releasing carved boulders up and down the line. "Rocks and nothing more. It worries me."

"You think Ôlisbenar changed his mind on a war? You expected more?"

"Even if I trusted the whoreson, which I don't, I think he'd need to make a better show to please any royal advisors."

"He wouldn't be fool enough to waste lives against the wall so early."

An explosion, and this time the tower quivered beneath his feet as if a small quake shook the world around them. The glass left his eye and he looked for flying dirt and smoke.

Morik confirmed his fears. "That wasn't no thunderstick."

Kesup's voice came full of terror. "West!"

Brilliant white flames caught Ivin's eye before the man's scream faded. "Where the hells—" Another explosion, this time to the east. Men screamed, and he turned in time to see a blazing man plummet to his death while another ran toward the central gate, a white streak that collapsed flickers later in a fiery heap.

Morik said, "They brought more than stones."

Ivin turned to Kesup. "Four short. Repeat. I want everyone inside the wall and the towers—"

The horn blew, echoing, but its call was drowned out a by a flash of white flame no more than a hundred strides away. The wall shook, and liquid flames showered from where it struck the top of the parapet; the fire splashed and ran over the back of the wall, and Ivin watched in horror as the buildings tucked against the wall caught fire.

"Blow that horn! Blow!"

Morik coughed. "We should follow your orders as well. The Ironwing didn't give me permission to die here."

"Aye. Blow that horn until you see no one on the wall... you see anything coming this way you join us inside."

"Aye, Warlord."

The other men roosted in the level below the roof, but Ivin stormed down the stairs with Morik on his heels. "That son of a bitch wasn't kidding when he said he'd attack. He's starting to piss me off."

"In the end he's a soldier with a king. At some point, you follow orders or they gut you."

The tromp made his feet sore by the time he reached the Grand Hall of the gate, and Kinesee ran to embrace him. He hugged her and kissed her forehead.

"What's happening out there?"

Ivin looked around the room. Puxele sat in the cushiest seat with her feet propped on a stool, and two dozen men and women of clanblood stared at him for an answer. There wasn't a tear or a hint of panic, only faces hardened by the dark times of the Trail of Pyres. There was no reason to paint his story with honey. "Wyvern's Flash from the Trebuchets. It's scary as the hells. Killed a few... burning supplies behind the wall in places. But if we hunker in our hole we shouldn't worry much."

"Then hunker with me," Kinesee said, taking his hand and leading him to a cushioned bench. He sat beside her, arm over her shoulder as the floor quivered.

Perin Mulharth rolled dice on the dining table. "Anyone up for a game of Hawk and Snake?"

Ivin laughed. "No."

Several folks meandered to the table and the jingle of coins followed, but others remained glued to him. Tellês Lôldon, Polus' cousin whose husband and sons manned the gate, strolled to look him in the eye.

"It sounds worse than you're sayin'."

"It might be. It might be less. There's no way to know, but they won't rush the walls when they're on fire any more than we'll stand there waiting to burn."

"You hope."

"Horns will sound if they come. We've had enough go wrong today; the gods won't feed us another shame."

Puxele screamed, her face anguished. "I just broke water!"

Ivin and Kinesee both leaped to their feet, and Ivin blurted, "You shittin' me?"

The woman smiled and put her hands to her hips with a laugh before settling back in her seat. "Sure am, though I wish I weren't."

Ivin fell back in his seat with a roll of his eyes. "Don't be doing that again, Little Sister. I don't think my soul will take that twice." The room shared a chuckle before falling back into a stale mood.

The explosions slowed by evening while boulders hammered the walls until the sun set orange in the west, but even as he lay beside Kinesee trying to sleep, he knew bright fires still burned along the wall. Some might burn until morning. He refused to ignite the fireplace for this simple reason, but it was plenty warm beneath the blankets with Kinesee snuggled into his chest.

Her eyes were closed, but he could feel her heart beating fast. "Ôlisbenar won't take this wall tonight."

"I know."

He stared at the ceiling for a wick, but her heart still fluttered. He craned his neck to kiss her on the head. "Something's troubling you."

"I was just thinking... thinking maybe we should earn our silks untethered."

Ivin froze even as her lips brushed his neck with a tentative kiss. "If you think it might help you sleep."

She didn't answer until her lips were on his. "Mmhmm."

Ivin awoke the next morning beside a woman for the first time since Meliu... and, Forges be damned, if that wasn't the first thing he thought of, and he cursed himself as a fool. But his heart's folly was forgotten as the day brought more boulders and flaming attacks, and the night brought Kinesee and he together. By the fourth morning, he awoke without a whisper of the priestess' name in his head, not even so much as to be thankful for not thinking of her like he did the morning before.

He kissed Kinesee on the forehead and swung his legs over the edge of the bed and stared at the dark fireplace. He wasn't sure there was a good reason to get out of bed; every day seemed much the same as the one before. Terrifying, and yet nothing of consequence happening.

A knock boomed at his door and he leaped to his feet, scrambling for trousers and a shirt.

Kinesee watched his awkward dance. "The warlord will be a flicker."

Morik's voice came. "We need to take a look at somethin'."

Ivin grunted, hop-stumbled, and opened the door to find Morik in full armor. "Shits, it's that kind of look at something?"

"Aye, it is at that. Good morning to you, little lady."

Kinesee smiled, blankets pulled to her neck as she sat up. "Excuse my lack of attire."

Morik laughed as Ivin slipped into his armor and grabbed his black shield. "My eldest sprung to life during a war with the Tek... My youngest as well, matter of fact. A fine time for makin' babies I always found."

"Worse things have happened this week."

"And we need to be worryin' about even worse, I reckon."

Ivin strapped his shield and Eredin's Glass to his back and snagged his helmet. "Ready, now what the hells is this about?" He blew Kinesee a kiss as they entered the hall and closed the door. Two guards followed him, and three remained behind to guard Kinesee's door.

"A foot messenger arrived from the Ironwing this morning... And no, this isn't what concerns us. It's what he noticed along the wall."

"He was out front?"

"No, the backside."

They descended to ground level and exited through a door near where the buildings had burned the first day of the attack. Morik eyeballed the blackened cinders the lean-to left behind.

"What the Forges are we looking for?"

Morik strode to the wall even as an explosion resounded from somewhere to the west, and he wiped his hand along the soot. He held his palm up; it was black and gray. "The demon fire is eating at the stone, making it brittle and powdery, even here where it ran down the back of the wall... Can you imagine where the fires burn all night and with impacts?"

Ivin's brain wasn't groggy no more. "Unholy hells. Are you saying they could burn a hole through thirty feet of wall?"

"All I'm saying is your Malstefnê friend has a plan. We'll have to walk the walls and try to get a view to know if it has a chance of working."

Ivin slid Eredin's Glass from its wooden sheath, strode to the wall where Morik had wiped his hand, and pricked the stone with the sword's tip. A flake the size his palm chipped with a puff of dust and tumbled to the ground. "This is hells-shittin' bad." Ivin paced before jabbing the wall, much harder this second time, and the blade sunk three fingers into stone; not even latcu should puncture stone like that.

"A man can hardly tell the damage unless you look close."

"If that son of a bitch blows a hole in the wall, you'll need to get away from here or ask the Ironwing for permission to die." He walked west with his eyes pinned on the wall looking for fire marks. "Ôlisbenar is no fool. Would you say he's concentrated Wyvern's Flash in any one area?"

"None of the reports I've seen mentioned it, but no one was looking for it neither."

"A guess."

"A guess you say? Pains me as it does, I'd wager he avoids the Helelindin as well as the central gatehouse and towers—"

An explosion of white raged up against the wall in the distance, and they spoke at the same time. "West."

They sprinted to the stable and mounted horses kept saddled for messengers. They spurred the animals toward the inferno at a dead run. By the time they arrived, men had formed a bucket brigade to douse the fire, but throwing water on Wyvern's Flash just made the flames angry, hissing and popping but growing no less intense.

Ivin feared he knew the answer but asked anyhow. "What the hells happened here?"

A sweating man with a bucket stepped to his stirrup. "I saw the son of a bitch! He came riding a horse down from the mountain... Figured he was a messenger until too late. Our arrows bounced off him until he ran his horse straight up to the wall and the Twelve Hells thundered."

Ivin glanced back to the fire as the man ran for more water; flames licked over the wall from the other side. "Shits. They're coming. Right here."

"I need to get a pigeon to the Ironwing."

Morik heeled his horse farther west, but Ivin reined east, making for a stair built into the back of the wall. He flung himself from the saddle and hit the steps at a run with his guards close behind. He crowned the top of the stair just in time to see a projectile arching through the air, and he watched it strike the white blaze on the front of the wall. Stone shattered and flew, but it was the wall this time, not the boulder. He leaned out over the parapet as far as he could; even from here he could see the damage to the wall, but there was no way to know its depth.

He turned to his guards but spoke to no one in particular. "Today, tomorrow, three days, a week."

Ilumnost said, "M'Lord?"

He looked the man in the eye. "This is where our fight will be. We just don't know when."

They rode back to the central gate, passed the news down the wall, and sent the call to those warriors who'd retreated to prepare to reinforce the western flank.

Kinesee cried and Puxele cussed up a storm, but in the end both of them traveled south into the Roemhien. That night Ivin slept even less than normal, awaiting the morning with a dread he hadn't felt since the morning of Eredin's funeral. He crawled from bed and slipped into his armor without a thought of food and strode into the hall, making his way to High Tower to get a view of the enemy at dawn.

Kesup greeted him as he climbed the ladder to the roof. "You ain't gonna believe this shit."

Ivin closed his eyes and didn't want to open them to see, but he turned north. No one. Not a soul. Not a horse. Not a single trebuchet arm.

"I was gonna send word, M'Lord, but I wanted the sun higher to believe my own eyes."

Ivin wasn't sure he believed it himself. If the Malstefnê had opened that hole through the wall, it would have sent thousands to the walk the Starry Road. Maybe ended the Silone as a people. He wasn't sure whether to bless the Seven Heavens or damn the Twelve Hells.

Or to praise the Face of Ulrikt.

Forty-Three

A Name Unearned

The Wiley Weasel and Feinting Fawn,
oh where will they be come the raging red dawn,
will they fish or will they fly?
will they live or will they cry?
will they weep dour tears?
will they spread unfounded fears?
Fear is the enemy of reason.
Guilt is the weapon of treason.

—*Tomes of the Touched*

"Almost! I didn't see you coming until you left. It is a rare rarity of delights for an Edan to surprise anyone, most especially themselves."

Glimdrem counted the journey worth it already, just to hear the Touched's opening salvo on the Edan. They ran for four days and four nights to get here from Istinjoln; it was a demonstration of both Edan endurance and Edan power to instill him and the other Trelelunin with the energy to match their pace for so long, but their ability was limited. When he'd asked why they didn't do this with the humans, Inslok informed him that a human's heart would explode.

He didn't bother to ask if he meant this literally or not, preferring to imagine humans dropping dead with holes in their chests.

Inslok smiled at the Skeleton, but it looked as forced as it was. "You are speaking to me this time?"

"An eternity of temerity gives way to an infinity of you not liking my words, the spoilt curds tumbling from my tongue from beyond my long rotted lung. What brings Almost to my humble library with so many friends? Snake! So good to see you again. You weren't gone long."

"I missed you."

"Venomous words and kind." He strolled with his bony fingers clutched behind his back and stared with empty eye sockets. "Limereu, it has been never since I saw you last as you or whoever you may be this time."

"We have spoken before?"

"Before, during, after, oh the laughter! Have you forgotten how to laugh, the gaff in the gap between the Mother and the Father gone?"

She blinked and stared like a true Edan, so Glimdrem answered for her. "She knew how to laugh when last we spoke in your tomb."

"Tis a pity she's a bore. What entertainment have you brought for me, orphaned Edan with your bow?"

Limereu said, "If I had my memories, would I be able to close the Celestial Gate in Istinjoln?"

"Questions questioned questioning, are inquisitions everybody's idea of fun? Let me see, let me feel, let me seed, let me feed. A deed. A gate of Celestial bound for hell. Would Limereu know how to slam the gate ba-bam! If she were Limereu before visiting the father. Yes."

Glimdrem blinked and stammered from shock at getting a straight answer. "What happened to your riddles?"

"What point to riddling on a point moot, obtuse Snake with pointy fangs and a vine for a body?"

"So, I could have closed it?"

"Did I say that? Did I? What did I say again? I said you would know how, not that you could. Such big ears and yet you don't listen!"

"Could I have done so?"

"Maybe, but you are not the Limereu of before the Father, you are the Limereu of now. Something less and something more, less entertaining and more a bore."

"If I understood, could I do it now?"

"No, the opening has passed, and so the opening remains, a portal; a disproportionate contortionist will it take to defeat the gate now."

"It can't be closed?"

"It will be closed."

"By me?"

"Toss a coin into the Well Wisher and see if he chokes."

Glimdrem couldn't help but ask. "Who is the Well Wisher?"

And the Touched and Glimdrem said in unison, "A name unearned!"

The two of them laughed, but Inslok wasn't amused. "You wish to make a mockery of our speaking?"

Glimdrem gasped. "Me? He doesn't need my help."

"Then cease your assistance. Touched, if she knew now how to close the gate and had the help of Eleris Edan, could it be closed?"

The Touched leaned over the two Edan. "Come close and listen. Shhhh. The Listeners don't need to hear with their noses so high. It is easy, simple, like a kitten being cute... how could it not be, it's a kitten? I am right. I know I am because I am wrong not often to soften the blow of simplicity's charge."

Silence for a wick, then the Touched winked his dark socket at Limereu. Winking bone... unfortunate he didn't have time to ponder that oddity.

Limereu said, "You did not say anything."

"I did not? I didn't? I swear I did, but maybe that was you yesterday or tomorrow or the day next. It is simple to close a Celestial gate when no mortal on this side works to keep it open."

"If it's so simple, tell me."

"I didn't, did I? That's right. It's simple: Convince the gate it no longer wishes to be open. Poof! It will close."

Inslok said, "Celestial Gates need a hold on both sides to exist."

"Almost almost sounds like he almost knows something. Almost. Ha ha! Was that me being clever or repetitive, sometimes I've trouble telling. The queen grew strong and not only in her anger. With one hand she holds our world, in the other she holds her own."

"Can we convince her to let go?"

"I know not the mind of the queen any more than I know the mind of the one who created her. I see the gate closed one day, but which day and how I do not know."

Glimdrem wanted to laugh. What a peculiar notion, convincing a demon queen to give up her own Celestial Gate. "How would anyone motivate her to defy her self-interest?"

"Such simple questions today. You make it in her best interest. Ha ha!"

Inslok spoke in a tone approaching a growl. "What does she want outside of the power to enter our world?"

"Think and think, and you will find answers and more than one. But what does she want that you can give? Nothing, Almost."

"Then how do we close the gate?"

"Did I say you close the gate? I hate repeating myself about your ears... No, no, I don't hate repeating myself about your ears. Someone closes the gate, and the simplest answer is the queen herself, but the simplest answer may pose and posit the most difficult questions. Who is the queen, your dream corrupted to nightmare?"

Inslok said, "Zwinfolkum."

"There's no shame in the game of names, but little power. Words only have power when you know their meaning, unless confusion is power, and names only have power when you know their future, present, and past."

"She was human once but became the Queen Mother when the Dontupûor captured her."

The vine said, *Fascinating, don't you think?* Glimdrem agreed, but he was more curious as to why the Touched was being so helpful today.

"The Dontupûor, indeed, to feed, to seed, into Shadow and deeds. Does every queen need a king? Does every child need a father?"

"It depends on the species and the culture."

"Almost thinks too much without thinking right, but you'll get there."

"Who were the Dontupûor?"

"You mean who are the Dontupûor."

"They still exist?" Inslok asked.

The Touched hopped to sit atop his tomb, and he pulled a black shield filled with arrowheads from its bottom. "Did, do, will, these things are all so similar to memories. If not yet, then soon, though they have kin reviled on the island of Ritikôn."

The name was familiar from the bits of the Oxeum Codex he'd managed to read, but it wasn't an island. Glimdrem muttered, "Ritikôn was a city." Edan eyes turned on him, but he didn't care.

The Touched said, "This shield fought against the Dontupûor in the city that is now an island."

There weren't many cities that dominated islands that he knew of. "The Boboru are Dontupûor?"

"Clever Snake. Yes and no and sort of. When the Dontupûor introduce themselves, you will know them."

"But they aren't known?"

"Evidently not. Ha ha!"

Inslok said, "They aren't on Northern or Southern Vandunez. Anduran is unlikely, as is Molo. Are they on Sutan, Kutu, or Demmen?"

"Yes! Ha ha!"

Glimdrem said, "I'd wager Sutan or Kutu; was Uvin Lo... Wait. Did the Dontupûor write the *Oxeum Codex*?" The Codex referred to them as an observer, but then, nothing he'd read indicated whose perspective the book was written from.

"The Codex, please, the Oxeum *Codices*. It is not an answer as simple as one. Many hands of many peoples inked those pages."

The question sizzled into his mind with the vine's hiss, and he uttered the words. "Was Oxeum destroyed?"

"Snake? Snake? Is that you or the lying vine's asking? I can answer yes, and I can answer no, yet I lie neither time. This is turning into so much fun! Nezeldun, join the fun, fun, fun and climb the rung with your tongue."

Nezeldun intoned, "Could you close the gate?"

"Oh, ho ho!" He dropped the shield back into the coffin and skulked to loom over the Edan. "Could I? It depends on how you frame reality, the disparity, the cart of tea... Sugar, next time bring sugar. And cream."

"Could you or not?"

"In the right time and place it would've been a yawn, a snap of the fingers, or a tap of the toes who knew too much until they turned black and fell off my feet. In this time and place, I'd be more apt to break an anvil with my head. Ha ha! Have you an anvil?"

"So, not even you could close it? I figured you were powerful."

"I'm dead, or haven't you noticed? Big eyes, big ears, so blind and so deaf. I am stuck here, but still if you framed the question... I could."

"How?"

"She would need to do it for me?"

Inslok said, "The Queen Mother?"

"No, someone who could eat the Queen Mother while having her for tea, you see? To the sea? But she will not listen; she does not interfere unless the whim strikes."

"Marukane, what do you know about this Shadow?"

"Marukane, Maru and Kane. What did you wish to know?"

"It's one Shadow. It entered Istinjoln. Or so the Colok named it."

"The Colok remember things others do not, but still forgot so much. A shame, a shame, the Dame, the Dame, in her Fire with a liar... I digress and repress under duress. Maru and Kane were the human born children of Zwinfolkum."

"How is that possible?"

"Oh, Almost! You half a being, Almost! You knew them and knew them well, you and you and you alone condemned to the fate they died to live! Oh, Almost. But in this case, you did not *almost* them; you did them all the way. Ha ha!"

"I have no idea what you are speaking of."

An edge struck from his voice, a breach in Edan normality, and the Touched loved it. He danced to stand in front of Inslok, tickling his chin with a bony finger like he might a baby. "Of course not! And yet you do, that's the cause of the blade in your throat. Guilt spilt in blood and lies to sever the ties of living and dead and Shadow. On which side did you fight, guilt-ridden and unbidden, Almost. Screaming babe, thumb sucking knave, tool of tools not quite whole."

Inslok's sword left its sheath in a flicker and swung for the Touched's looming head. The Touched didn't flinch and the blade stopped a hair from his cheek. For a flicker, Glimdrem figured the Edan pulled his attack, but then he realized none of the Edan moved except to breathe. He glanced around; the Trelelunin were frozen as well.

"Almost was always a slow learner, a flat cake turner, a half-flamed burner. What do you think, Snake?"

"Is Snake my earned name?"

"Ha ha! I like you, Snake, don't ever let it be said otherwise even if I kill you one day."

Glimdrem swallowed hard. "Kill me?"

"Oh, not now. No. I will kill you, or you will kill yourself, or maybe another, or maybe you will be shredded to live forever, a twisted sort of kin of mine. Snake is not your name earned. It is but a moniker I enjoy."

"What name have I earned?"

"None. Not yet, but you will. Tell me, Snake, how does it feel to wriggle snuggled between Edan toes? Is it comforting? Is it cozy? Trelelunin, half an Edan at best. Tell me how that feels? They can't hear you."

Glimdrem grinned. "They are condescending shits, to borrow a Silone term. But what is there to do about it?"

"You could die. But no, that is beyond your courage. The Father might hold answers, but you remember not what the Father is and what the father means, let alone who the Father is. A father, a bother, you the fodder as you dodder, but why ask what can be done when it has already begun?"

"I don't know what you mean."

"Of course you don't, that's what makes it so fun. But I am done. I have other conversations." He turned and strode away, and still the Edan didn't move.

"Should we leave?"

"That seems impossible, now doesn't it? Stay awhile. I'll wake your Edan and Trelelunin friends when the time comes." He pointed to nothing and shouted. "You! Away from that Tome, you snipe!" After that, he spoke a language Glimdrem didn't understand.

After three candles of gibberish to his ear whispered and shouted, Glimdrem grew bored. None of his group so much as twitched, so he wandered to the antechamber where skeletal guards watched over him. It felt like they stared, but it was difficult to tell since they didn't have eyes. He removed his pack and reached his hand to the bottom to pull out his copy of the Oxeum Codex.

Glimdrem wandered the tunnels of the Touched's Tomb twice a day as the Edan stared at the antics of the Touched as if they were a crowd watching a most powerful performance. Most of the time Glimdrem didn't understand the language the Touched spoke, and the Edan weren't of a mind to reveal what they understood, seeing as they hadn't moved in three weeks. Not even a blink, so far as he could tell.

Instead of letting the situation aggravate him, Glimdrem accepted this as the perfect opportunity to study the codex. While he couldn't claim to have learned any world-shattering wisdom, he picked up on a few intriguing points.

A traditional Edan story of wisdom taught that what a person sees wandering the forest on the darkest of nights is not so unlike what that same person sees beneath the full light of day, the difference being that during the day, the wanderer *believes* they see everything. Edan, Trelelunin, and Helelindin had this truth woven into their being to enforce that confidence in a perceived truth would never overtake a healthy skepticism of all things you believe you see.

After his forced sojourn with the codex, Glimdrem realized he had been wandering in the dark, that he always had been. This wasn't so shocking, no. What brought excited gasps and glee to break his meditations was the realization that the Edan were no more than wanderers during the day.

How much didn't they know behind those smug, expressionless gazes? How much did they know while feigning ignorance?

The wise man in the Edan story was named White Eye; this was ignorance or obfuscation. It was a sliver of reality pulled from the misconceptions in his mind: The White Eyes were a people, not an individual. The Codex presented this truth in unequivocal fashion, but every word he'd heard from Edan lore and scholars stated the name as an individual.

People feared them, and the gods coveted them, but nothing he'd read so far explained *why*. The codex spoke of them in terms approaching reverential; they were chosen by the gods, but being chosen wasn't enviable. The White Eyes didn't always have white eyes, from what he gathered. The gods discovered that these people were special, and so several pantheons captured all they could and sewed their eyes shut, branded their eyes shut, and even one reference to gouging their eyes out so they could see better.

The Oxeum Codex didn't speak well of the Pantheon of Sol often, but it did credit Sol with birthing the next generation of those he captured without pupils, no eye color at all, in fact. And so the White Eyes entered the vernacular of the time. Within a few generations, every pantheon had their pet White Eyes. The tome danced around the why with such precision that it must've been decreed that it not be written. Some secret so powerful... *the ability to forge Latcu and Ikoruv?*

Possible, but then how would Uvin have found the answer?

The vine said, *You are half an Edan.*

"Half an Edan at best."

You see how the gods twisted a people, blinding them. You see how the Dontupûor and their gods twisted a human and demon into the Queen Mother. What are you but a broken Edan?

"I am Trelelunin," Glimdrem said.

What were you before?

Glimdrem laughed. "I was a life-sculptor, several times."

And whose vine stood in the Father Wood?

He hesitated at the memory of his dying of the Fever Snake's bite and how he saw a vine with his life-sculpting signature in the Father Wood. "It was a delusion. I was feverish, delusional."

The vine said no more, but Glimdrem understood that it disagreed.

"Time to check on Inslok anyhow."

He buried the codex in the bottom of his pack and strolled to the Tomb of the Touched with the skeleton guards parting so he could pass, a creepy but polite gesture he grew accustomed to. The skeleton ranted at no one he could see, and after fifteen wicks his patience grew thin. "Touched, might I ask a question?"

The Touched froze with his mouth agape and finger waggling at someone unseen, or air, or perhaps at his imagination. "One question and make it quick. I'm in the middle of a fine debate with Doom Seeker."

"Ah, well. The White Eyes, what made them so special that the gods turned their eyes white, blinding them?"

"Would you appreciate it if I answered without a riddle?"

Glimdrem chuckled. "Yes."

"First, a correction. The White Eyes were only blinded in the traditional sense you would understand. Second, I will not answer that question; it is an answer too dangerous." He waved his bony hand to dismiss him. "You all may leave now. It is time." He strolled away and barked at someone Glimdrem presumed was Doom Seeker.

He stared for a flicker then turned to find the Edan and Trelelunin blinking and moving. Inslok stared at the blade still in front of his face. "What happened?"

Glimdrem stretched a smile as far as he could across his face. "You lost your temper, so the Touched froze all of you in place."

"Froze. For how long?"

"Almost a month, Almost." He'd hoped to irritate the Edan, but his words didn't crack the Edan like the Touched's barbs did.

"But not you? Why?"

"So that I could tell you how long you were frozen, I suspect. He said it was time to leave."

Limereu said, "A month. The Silone could be close to Istinjoln by now."

The Touched yelled from across the room, "They are."

Glimdrem couldn't stretch his smile farther, but tried. "It seems we should be leaving."

Forty-Four

This for That

Tiny Wings who buzzes my ear,
voice so dear and unclear,
what is it you say?
Do you curse, question, jest, or demand?
An out of hand reprimand.
You drown your meaning with your drone,
like a child with whine, a drunk with whiskey,
the crazy man with gibberish.
the Dark-Infested feasting on your low-born kin,
skittering, crawling, tickling between his cheeks
makes more sense.
If when tick tock should unlock,
unbury the treasure and speak your pleasure.

—*Tomes of the Touched*

Solineus awoke at dawn's first rays the morning after meeting the Contessa Polênu Juvilêus with a kink in his neck, thanks to Adinvan convincing him that there wasn't an inn in the city safe for them. He might've been right or he might've been wrong, but not even the throbbing ache pounding into his forehead mattered.

"The *Silver Willow.*"

Sîu sat up, fingers from his side. "Your father doesn't think you should go to see this woman."

"Adinvan is a yellow-bellied sapsucker."

The girl stared. "I don't know what that is... a bee?"

He groaned to his knees before finding a seat on the rail. "A bird, but it means a flittering coward."

"Coward, is it?"

Solineus turned. "You're up earlier than I hoped."

Sîu crossed her arms. "I suspect she's pretty."

Adinvan said, "And you'd suspect right, but she can kill a man quicker than your poison."

She huffed. "I can kill a man faster than my poison."

"I didn't mean it as a compliment, my girl."

"I reckon the last thing we damned well need is a bicker over who can kill a man faster." Solineus pulled on his mule-eared boots, grabbed a chunk of jerky, and tossed on the Twins and his shield. "Ain't a soul who should be complaining, seeing as this woman can get us to the mouth of the river."

"Did she say that?"

Truth was always a thorn in a justification's ass. He climbed onto the dock. "I'm gonna go take a look for the *Silver Willow*."

"You aren't going alone, boy."

Adinvan and Sîu stepped onto the dock behind him. They wandered the wharf for a candle looking for the ship when the answer struck him: Polênu gave him the name in Edan. He turned to his shadows. "I don't reckon either of you know what *Silver Willow* is in Gorô?"

"Are you shittin' me?" Adinvan asked.

"No, I'm not shittin' you."

"You threatened the life of the only man in this gods-be-damned city we could speak to, and you don't even know the name of the boat?"

"I know the name of the boat. Just not the Gorô name."

"So just how do we find this boat then? Not thinkin' things through, you get that from yer mother's side."

"It's a damned good thing I lost my memories or I might recall you bein' a—"

Sîu let loose a shrill whistle and Solineus turned. "What?" But she hadn't whistled at them.

She called out to a sailor aboard the ship, "Contessa of Mostul Ûbar?" She pointed in both directions and smiled while in a stance that accentuated the curve of her hips.

The man waved his hat west and held up five fingers twice.

Solineus snorted. "And what was that supposed to mean? Ten ships? Ten docks?"

"It means west, which is more than we learned from you men grousing."

Solineus and Adinvan fell in behind her and let her do the talking to men along the wharf, and within five wicks, they found the *Silver Willow,* or the *Nesurô Walindolu,* which he assumed meant the same thing. The ship was a beautiful triple-masted caravel painted in deep reds and yellows that reminded him of sunrises and sunsets he'd seen at sea. He did not doubt that such a vessel could outrun and outmaneuver most ships on open waters, but by the number of ballista onboard—some only a little larger than a Kingdomer arbalest and swivel-mounted along the rails, while others looked as if taken from a siege—he wondered if the ship didn't do more chasing than fleeing.

He approached three guards who stood at the gangplank and stood tall. "Solineus Mikjehemlut, the Contessa invited me."

The man understood enough to call out, "Contessa *sefenenî trûôldolê.*"

The woman appeared after a short wait, more beautiful in the light of the sun than in the cloying smoke of the tavern. The face was unknown to him outside of the night before; how could he have ever seen her before? And yet something about her called a forgotten memory that refused to stir from the depths of his mind.

Her voice was cheerful and lilting as she spoke in Edan. "You found me. I recall the old man from last night... the girl, she is your slave?"

Solineus coughed, thankful that neither of them spoke Edan. "Polênu Juvilêus, this is my father Adinvan Mikjehemlut, and this is Sîu, *not* my slave. She is a friend of the family and a skilled herbalist."

The lady's brow wrinkled. "Is she? My mother was famed for her healing prowess."

"We have things to discuss."

"We do." She smiled and walked to the cabin doors; the four of them followed close behind. "Do they speak Edan?"

"No."

"That is good." She sauntered to stand in front of him, so close he could smell the lilac in her perfumed hair. Only fingers shorter than he was, he could've kissed her with a lean. "How did you know I speak Edan?"

"I didn't. Why did you kill the captain?"

She laughed and glided to sit behind the desk as the door opened. A broad-shouldered man with dark eyes and dark skin, but white hair, stalked into the room. He didn't say a word as he made his way to stand at Polênu's shoulder. "This is my man, Âvorê. Âvorê, this is Solineus; he thinks he knows me."

The man's gaze shifted to a glare. "You are a bold man to say—"

"I don't think he meant in that way."

"Yes, Contessa." His face relaxed, but he still stared at Solineus.

"Here is what I do know. Every man in the Hissing Mink knew there's a price on your head, a fleet of longships crewed by tall, white-skinned men, and you were led to the *one* Gorô who'd take that gold with a kitten's joyful leap."

"You could've warned me instead of breaking his neck."

She shrugged as her fingers toyed the plume of a quill sitting beside a bottle of ink. "I've this bad habit... When I take a dislike to a man, my ire sets fire and I snap! Or, I suppose he snaps."

"Seems you owe me a guide to the Mâbuhon River."

"I saved your lives, yes? You owe me. The pretty slave girl, perhaps?"

"She's not a slave."

She grinned. "I know, but you're cute when you defend her. Tell me again, how did you knew I spoke Edan when I did not?"

He gazed into the depths of her brown eyes seeking something to trigger a hidden memory. "I know you. We've met before."

"Then tell me when and where."

"I can't. I have no memories before... I was on a ship and it sank, and by some miracle I survived, but my memories were gone. Do you remember me?"

"No. Not at all. And I'd remember a man like you. The swords in particular."

"I didn't have those... But you didn't know you spoke Edan, explain that?"

"I speak seven, now eight, languages thanks to my mother and the life I've led. I knew words but not which tongue I spoke by saying them."

"Is there a gap in your memories?"

She flinched, as if hiding something, but he couldn't detect a lie in her words. "I remember bouncing on my father's knee when I was five and crying at his funeral at six. I recall a thousand herbal remedies my mother taught me from the age of seven on. My remembrances are keen; sometimes I can still smell the flowers outside my childhood home."

"You walked straight to me at the tavern—"

"You were staring at me."

"And held hands—"

"You're good looking in a pasty, northern manner." She shrugged.

"Tell me you didn't feel something."

"I didn't." And that was the first time he knew she lied, with the glance away and the flutter of her eyelids. "If you think to bed me with this tale, it's growing tedious."

He was more determined than ever to have the woman lead them, if for no other reason than to maybe trigger a memory. "The river's mouth then."

"As I recall, you owe me, but we'll call our debts level. Which means what price can you pay?"

"Can you get us past the Boboru?"

"Unlike your dead captain friend, I'm not going to lie to you. Not six, not even one, longship is going to make it to the Mâbuhon with anything less than the luck of the gods. But I can get you there with as many men as you like aboard the *Silver Willow*."

"Confident or cocky?"

"Reasoned. I fly the silver-bear flag of Seraru harbored here but sailing north I fly the colors of Mostol Ûbar. The Willow may be stopped, but in the end the Willow sails free."

Leaving his ships and much of the crews behind chewed at his gut, but if the woman spoke the truth, it might be his safest bet for reaching the Dragonspans alive. "Let us say this is amenable. What do you wish in return?"

"By happy circumstance I could use an outsider. A foreigner. A man hunted by the Boboru. Though there are many of the latter, you fill all my needs."

Solineus smiled, but doubts washed over him. What if the woman walked to him because she'd found her perfect mark and nothing more? What if he'd played into her game instead of her into his? "My cause is rushed. If this thing may be done with haste, fine, if not, I can pay."

"You mistake me for a poor woman. I trade in deeds and causes."

"A hundred thousand Smedên guaranteed by Mulshahar writ."

She coughed and cleared her throat. "I won't bother to ask—"

"My people. I need to get back to them. It isn't complicated. Or it is, but it's simple as well."

She stared at him. "I may be the only captain in these waters who would turn that offer down. I need a deed, not gold."

Solineus sighed and ran his fingers through his hair. So much for old fashioned greed working in his favor. "What is this deed you require of me?"

She opened the drawer of her desk and lifted a silver-lidded canister engraved with rose vines. "Have you ever heard of Honêsh?" She popped the lid to reveal gray shavings of some plant, a bit like tobacco.

"No."

"Honêsh is a rare herb, difficult to grow and cultivate. Chew its leaf and it will make your tongue tingle, little more. But when seasoned and crumbled, it may be stored and later made into a paste that prevents infections and speeds the healing of open wounds. My mother dealt in the herb often."

"What's this to do with me?"

He picked up the container and brought it toward his nose for a sniff, but Sîu blocked his hand. "Don't do that."

He blinked and put it back on the desk. "You didn't lie about this girl. This is Donu-Honêsh, the fumes make some vomit, but if smoked in a pipe they cause euphoria, hallucinations... differing effects on different people. It is potent, dangerous, and precious. I need to know where it's grown; you will find it for me." She capped the canister and stared at him.

"So you can get rich?" This notion didn't jibe with his gut feeling of the woman. He hoped he was wrong.

"I am already rich. My cause is no more your concern than yours is mine. You claim yours is a simple tale. Mine is not."

"You need to know the source, ask no questions. I get it."

"You may ask, but I won't answer until you can tell me how it is you think you know me."

"I'll have to discuss this with my people."

She shrugged and tilted back in her seat. "As you like. My cause is in no hurry."

Solineus nodded and turned to Adinvan and Sîu. "She claims the Boboru have a price on my head and our ships... She can get us there, but the longships stay behind."

Sîu nodded at the canister on the desk. "We call it *Dûfoldu.* It will heal wounds, but its true gift is killing."

"She mentioned visions, making you feel good."

"If you swallow or fire it in a pipe, but this will bring you three breaths from death."

"She wants us to find the source of the Honêsh... Dûfoldu."

"Shits, boy, I don't like her connivings one lick. Do you still trust this woman?"

"I believe what she says about the longships; they'll stand out to any eye in a crow's nest or along the shore. We can leave them here, and later they can sail to Safe Harbor to wait for us, or all the way to Toltûk."

"But do you trust her?"

Trust was optional and a luxury. "She's like the wind at sea: you have to set your sails and lean on the rudder to make sure she gets you where you're going."

Forty-Five

The Gulf Between

Lady of Fur and Lady of Steel,
are you one and the same?
Do you know why your wounded soul is lame?
It limps and it gimps,
it bubbles and burps,
it loses its footing in galloping stirrups.
But I digress. Who are you to know my name?
Who are you burdened by two names earned?

—*Tomes of the Touched*

The Contessa of Mostul Ûbar was as slippery as her ship and twice as deadly, or so Adinvan's rumor mill reported, so when she sent them sailing without her, Adinvan smiled all morning. Smiled enough it grew irritating. It turned out that the *Silver Willow* was one of seven ships the lady owned or employed, and that Polênu was a cautious soul.

Solineus, Adinvan, and Sîu rowed from port the next morning on the *Lady Moon* but left their other longships behind. Their route would carry them east until rounding Seahawk's Horn, a peninsula of rock said to have taken more than its share of ships during storms, where they'd swing north northwest while hugging the coast.

Avoiding the Boboru relied on two factors, taking advantage of their depth of keel by sticking close to shore, and three of the Contessa's ships staggered in front of them and three behind them, all farther out to sea, to draw the attention of any Boboru patrols. The *Silver Willow* was their distant shadow, out to sea, but within view from the top of the mast with a fareye.

They rounded Seahawk's Horn that evening with favorable winds. They arrived at their destination, a town called Montôltok, in the afternoon of their third day at sea without spotting a single Boboru flag. Montôltok was nothing out of the ordinary to the naked eye, a fishing village with thirty or so buildings and a few small boats tethered along the shore while others plied the Gulf of Tomulok's waters for the day's catch. There were only two peculiarities to disturb its image of innocence that Solineus noted as their keel ground onto the rocky shore.

"A foreign ship approaches shore and not a soul gives us a second glance. Don't see no children, either."

Adinvan grinned. "We aren't here for no pleasantries."

Sîu touched his cheek and directed his gaze her way. "May I come along?"

Solineus shrugged. "You might as well. The place looks calm enough."

Solineus hopped over the rail of the *Lady Moon*, landed in the surf, and lifted Sîu to a dry piece of shore with a smile. Adinvan splashed along with him, along with Nôkid and Dûzden. Both had picked up snippets of Gorô in their travels, but if they had to rely on their knowledge of Gorô, they were in sorry shape. At best, Solineus figured the two men combined knew enough to get them to the man they needed to find.

Solineus strolled to the nearest townsman, an old man with a fishing pole seated on a boulder broad enough to crush a house, but only four feet tall. He looked a hells of a lot less busy than the younger men with their nets. "We're looking for a man folks name Infoduhû, the Crying Man."

The man spat and jabbered. Nôkid translated: "Go, you scare the piss away."

Dûzden said, "Fish, scare the fish away, you idiot."

Solineus took a deep breath. "Infoduhû."

Dûzden translated this time. "He says something about a village in the rear, never heard the name."

Solineus glanced at the trees rising behind the town. "Village in the rear? What the hells are you talking about?"

Nôkid chuckled. "He said maybe the one you seek is in a village to the north."

Solineus glared at the both of them. "Are you two shittin' me?"

"You people should hire better translators." The voice came from nowhere, speaking in the trade tongue of Mulshahar. It wasn't the old man, this he knew for sure.

"What did he say then?" It was his first use of the language outside practice with Adinvan, and father gave him a nod and grin for his effort.

"He said the one you seek sits behind the rock." A man with the whitest skin Solineus had ever seen stood, and on catching his pink eyes knew him as an albino, but his hair was black as pitch and trimmed close to his head. His face was pocked with scars, like tears, resembling the gems on the Boboru slaves' faces.

"You are Infudohû?"

"I am! And you men have a mighty price on your heads if I'm not mistaken."

"We do. Offered by the same people who gave you those tearful scars, if I'm not mistaken."

He chuckled and strode around the rock. "Indeed. Why do you seek a humble fisherman like myself? A man who only wishes to live out his days in peace."

"I heard a rumor you do a little farming."

His brows raised as if surprised. "I dabble in the garden, but wouldn't go so far as to compare myself to those of such a noble profession."

"A big garden."

"A tiny garden. Full of weeds."

"And beneath the weeds grows Honêsh."

"Why... I do not know. I am a frail man, too poor to hire the weeds cleared."

Solineus reached into a pouch at his hip and pulled out a gold Smedên, held it so the sun reflected in the man's eyes. Infoduhû blinked and grinned.

"The sun has grown scorching hot on my frail skin. Come, we shall talk inside."

He led to the middle of town, a lone stone building amid log structures. Inside was a wide-open space with four desks and shelves full of books. The room was neat and tidy, a place of business rather than a home. Infoduhû pointed to a table in the center with a dozen chairs. "Sit, please. Mokên!"

Solineus startled at the shrill call, but in a flicker a young man entered the room. "Yes, sir?"

"A pitcher of Okwên for our guests."

The youth bowed and departed through the same door he'd entered from.

Solineus sat straight and propped his elbows on the table. "I need Donu-Honêsh, as much as I can haul, and I hear you're the man to talk to." He untied the pouch at his waist and tossed it across the table with a heavy thud and jangle. "Yours just for hearing me out."

His hand crept to the bag as if it might hold a snake, and he opened it enough to take a glance inside. "That is a high price for words. This is a perilous thing you seek."

"It can kill—"

"Not what I mean, no indeed. My buyers pay well and leave me only a brick or two to share with my friends."

"The Compunêu Trade Consortium." The Consortium was a group of merchants who took their name from the city of Compunêu, a once-powerful Gorô city that an army razed stone by stone centuries ago, and its lands salted to make sure it never rose again.

The man's eyes widened as his smile shrank. "You've heard of them, and yet still here you sit asking for their promised crop."

"I'm an ill-mannered barbarian who cares little for the hurt feelings of some Gorô shits."

Mokên returned with a pitcher of golden liquid, but most surprising were the pieces of chipped ice in the glasses. He poured and served everyone a drink, but no one put a glass to their lips before their host did. Okwên tasted of lemons, oranges, and coconut on top of a healthy dose of alcohol.

"Those Gorô shits, as you so vulgarly put it, purchase my every harvest four times a year, and if I had more they would buy that as well. I can spare a brick..."

"I want a harvest."

"Friend... Your gold spends as well as theirs, but there is an agreement in place."

"A ship sinks, some mishap... A quarter of the harvest."

"In a normal time, maybe... They lost half the last harvest when the ship blew into a Gorô-Boboru battle in the Gulf. If I am short again... It cannot be."

It was time to improvise before weaving in the details of the Contessa's lies. "You've heard of the Smiling Men?"

The man blinked before sipping from his glass. "I am not an untraveled man. They do not allow Donu-Honêsh in their cities."

"I didn't stumble my way through the Monsoon Strait, and I didn't stumble my way to you, and angering the Boboru along the way was intentional. The Smiling Men want the Boborun city of Enepal flooded with Donu-Honêsh... I say this to you, a man who bears their scars on your face, and I say the Smiling Men will pay a market premium."

The man rubbed his chin, no doubt wanting to nibble, but he wasn't ready to take the bait. "This is a proposal with ramifications reaching beyond our warring gulf, both large and small and unpredictable. But it can't be done."

"The Smiling Men show wisdom in all things; they are not in a hurry. The next harvest will suffice."

Infoduhû's hands kneaded and his brows scrunched. "It isn't possible—"he sighed in melodramatic fashion"—unless your smiling friends pay me upfront. For the harvest after this one."

Solineus blew bubbles in his drink as he snorted and laughed, plunked the glass on the table. "Upfront three months out isn't going to happen."

"Then it won't happen at all. The Gorô must receive their shipment."

"If they *must*, then how do you supply both of us?"

He leaned back in his seat then stood with a lurch. "Let us walk, away from ears." He made straight for the door and Solineus followed him. Outside he noted a dozen men strolling the street with eyes trained away from them. Too much so. They looked like fisherfolk, but no doubt they were guards.

"You trust your people?"

"I do. It's not like they'll go telling the Gorô anything, you see how well they speak the tongue."

Infoduhû laughed. "Their Gorô is atrocious, but still, word of this cannot spread. And I'd need two hundred Smedên per brick of Donu-Honêsh."

"That's twice what I heard whispered. How many bricks are you talking?"

"A thousand bricks. Enough to kill every Boboru in Enepal, the fates willing. And this way, it would not starve the Gorô of their trade."

"It's expensive."

"I'm the only supplier in the world and your employers can afford it."

"They can at that, but how are you going to meet this demand?"

"There is a sugarcane field I've been preparing, it isn't ready to seed with Honêsh, but with the gold from the Smiling Men it could be. Four months and you'd have the equivalent of a full harvest. No one can know about it, yes?"

And yet the Contessa knew about the field already, even if she hadn't a clue where it was. "The Consortium will notice when Donu-Honêsh hits Enepal."

"And the Gorô will blame it on Boboru pirating during the war... the ship believed sunk was instead boarded and seized. All explained away."

Solineus stopped and planted his feet, giving the man an amused glare. "It's too gods be damned convenient. You had me going, I admit. But my people have a saying: you don't scratch a lead bar to find gold."

Infoduhû tapped his gesture. "It's all true. I swear on it."

"Near a quarter-million smedên on a promise... I'm not sure what the Smiling Men would do to me, but I wager you'd live long and in agony if you failed them. No pirates, no storm, no infestation of insects would make for an excuse."

"It's no risk at all. The sugar cane will guard the Honêsh against the weather—"

"What you claim isn't what I know. I need proof."

"What proof have I?"

Solineus reached into his pack and pulled out a writ from the bank in Mulshahar. "A blank writ, up to half a million smedên, but of course I'd need to sign it and supply the coded stamp."

Infoduhû leaned close, squinting and reading. "It seems I am undercharging."

"They were prepared to purchase more. Now, my proof."

"All right. All right. Kûlkuk! You and your men join us." A dozen toughs in piecemeal armor appeared from around a corner and fell in behind them as they walked. "If you'd prefer to leave the Smiling Men out, I'm sure those swords are worth more than enough to cover my expenses. Or we could split that writ between us?"

"I've seen enough of the Smiling Men to know their reach is as long as the grudges they keep. And get any ideas about these swords or that writ, and you'll learn how long it takes for twelve men in shit armor to die. Then I find out how long it takes you to go visiting your gods from a poke to your navel."

"Gracious. Not what I was saying."

Solineus wasn't so certain what the man meant, but the men on his heels fell back several paces. He reckoned it was time for a subject change. "How does a Boborun slave come to such influence and riches?"

Infoduhû laughed and patted his gut, maybe to make a tingling in his belly button go away. "Pain and knowledge, my friend. You could argue which is more important, but pain and knowledge. I put two and two and two and two together and made sixteen instead of eight."

Solineus puzzled the man's words. Multiplication instead of adding, but it seemed there was a deeper meaning. Or maybe it was a saying he wasn't aware of. "You figured out something anyone could figure out, but hadn't thought of in the right way?"

"Mmm! Sort of. Sort of not. Few folks will ever suffer enough to see the truth I found."

They walked inland maybe half a horizon along a winding trail through broad-leafed trees before climbing a hill to walk its ridge. Another half horizon later, they descended a steep slope that opened to the sky above, and in the valley stood a field of blowing grass higher than his waist and topped with bushy pink flowers. Men and women wandered the field, tying the grasses into tall bundles.

The man stopped at the edge of the field and stripped a leaf from a plant. "Sugarcane, sweet and tasty. We approach the harvest, as you see. Enough to make a man a bed of silver in itself." He stuck the leaf in his mouth and chewed before reaching to sweep the grasses to the side. "Sugarcane grows tall, Honêsh grows about half the height. Any strong winds, hail... they damage the sugarcane. Insects? Insects love the sugarcane and ignore the Honêsh."

"And it gets enough sun?"

"Ah! Honêsh in nature grows in forests, even in areas with dense canopies to block sun and rain."

"You harvest the sugarcane then the Honêsh. Maybe I should invest with you instead of the banks of Mulshahar."

Infoduhû laughed. "I am an honest man. You are more apt to die in doing business with me than the banks."

Solineus reckoned his claim to honesty a flat lie and didn't doubt the latter might be a subtle threat. "And the new field?"

"This way." He led Solineus over the western rise and down to another field where the sugarcane was being bundled yet. Instead of stripping a leaf, he kneeled and stuck his fingers in the soil. "The soil is beautiful in these parts, holding water but not too much, and below is sand. No matter how much rain, it never becomes a bog. That is a key."

"A hundred and fifty thousand smedên for the crop. Two hundred if you sell me the harvest coming in."

"My life is worth more to me than the whole of your writ. One ninety, yes? It isn't your treasure."

In fact, it *was* Solineus' gold. "But I earn more with a better deal."

"One seventy-five and the pretty islander girl."

"Minus the girl and you have yourself a deal."

Infoduhû spat and ground it into the soil with the toe of his boot and Solineus followed suit. It was a peculiar way to sign a contract, so it was fortunate that the Contessa had forewarned him. Otherwise, he would've stood dumbfounded and staring. "I suppose we should head back to your friends before they suspect I killed you."

"They might suspect you tried."

He led Solineus up the hill with a pleasant enough laugh. "You are an arrogant barbarian. I like that."

"And you are a very expensive yet free slave; I like that." Solineus suspected Infoduhû didn't believe him and knew for damned well he didn't believe Infoduhû.

They arrived at Montôltok with both of them wearing smiles on their faces, and while Adinvan gave him a grin and wink, Sîu frowned. "He wanted you as part of the deal; you should be happy it took so long."

Adinvan grinned. "So, you struck a deal? A good one, I hope."

"Not as good as I'd hoped, but it'll suffice." He pulled out the Mulshahar writ and sat, speaking to Infoduhû in the trade tongue. "If you've ink and quill?"

"Of course."

Solineus signed the writ for the agreed amount then pressed his seal over the signature and the number. He slid the parchment across the table. "Don't lose that."

"I've the stickiest fingers in the Gulf, rest assured. And you realize, if for some reason this writ isn't honored, then the Consortium is greeted with a happy surprise at the next harvest. And the price on your head will double and come from two directions."

"And if for any reason you fail the Smiling Men, you will find yourself a crying man again; the tears will be blood, and they will flow for years."

His nod was solemn. "So long as we understand each other."

"Then it was excellent doing business with you, but you'll forgive our abrupt departure." He stood, spat on the floor, ground it beneath his toe, and Infoduhû did the same.

"May the waters calm your sleep, and your sails fill come morning, no matter where you travel next."

Solineus turned and strode through the door, nodding to the guards with a grin. The sun approached the western horizon and Solineus' steps hastened. "I'd prefer to be a few horizons from here when night comes."

"Aye, the bugger's got your gold, he don't need us anymore."

"Fear of the Smiling Men might temper his greed." He glanced at the Silone down the beach by the *Lady Moon.* "Ready her to shove off."

Sîu said, "Could've sold me again?"

"I'm waiting for a better price."

"There's no pile of gold worthy."

He put his hands to her ribs and lifted her to climb over the ship's rail without getting her feet wet. "You're an arrogant islander; I like that."

Adinvan held out his arms. "Me next?"

"You're too fat... and ugly."

They sailed due east as soon as their oars carried their keel from shore, and as the sun set they spotted the *Silver Willow.* They dropped their sail and rowed toward a single lantern until reaching the caravel's side. They tied off, and rope ladders swung to their deck for an easier climb.

The moon crested the horizon behind the Contessa in a halo when he set eyes on her, and his gut clenched. *I know you.*

"Success?"

"I'd appreciate getting my writ back."

"Would it be honored?"

"Aye, and it would hurt."

"Mmm—"she purred and stroked his chin"—maybe I should pretend to remember you."

He batted her hand away as Sîu strolled close. "His crop is close, but the valley is a little tricky to find."

She strolled to the rail and leaned over the edge as more Silone climbed aboard. "I've sent people to look, but few of them ever came back. I wasn't sure you would."

"I told him the money came from the Smiling Men. I think he feared them."

She laughed as she turned her back to the shore, eyes catching the moon. "Tell me where the fields are."

He scrawled a reasonable map on parchment and she hovered over it with a lantern in hand. "This is good."

"The Hoshên grows in fields of sugarcane. A sweet grass of some sort."

"Sugarcane? Clever. You've earned your journey north, Silone."

Solineus turned to his people. "I reckon we'll be sailing north tomorrow. We'll take thirty volunteers with us."

Adinvan said, "Thank the gods! It'll be good to give Lady Tedeu shit again after all these years, assuming she still lives."

"You should captain the *Lady Moon*. Get back to mother."

"You shittin' me, boy? I come this far, I might as well earn the thrashin' she's got waiting for me."

"You see to the volunteers then." He turned back to the Contessa, pointed to shore. "What's your plan?"

"The plan? Well... over yonder there's going to be a little fire."

Solineus arched his brow; he'd misread this woman. "That's burning a king's ransom into ash."

"Oh, yes. And when his seeds burn up as well, how much do you wager the lost cargo of Donu-Honêsh will be worth then?"

He'd misread her again. "You have..." But even in the dark, her smile suggested he was still misreading her. "Will you kill him?"

"Would you have me show mercy? Why do you think he let you leave, Smiling Men? Infoduhû didn't escape the Boboru; they still own him. They'd own you and all your men within days, and the Crying Man would be weeping on the gold collected from the price on your head. He will die, but the moment hasn't been decided yet."

Solineus leaned on the rail and stared toward a shore he couldn't see. He refused to admit it aloud, but her explanation made a hells of a lot more sense than his.

"Just get me my writ back."

By midmorning the next day, plumes of black smoke rose to the west, and by the time they took lunch, he'd already shredded the sealed writ and scattered it in the gulf. She didn't tell him what became of the Crying Man, and he didn't ask.

FORTY-SIX

Bear Talk

The pitter the patter,
the bubbling of the batter.
Beat the fire and heat the soul,
leech the healthy and lance the boil.
Drain the refrain to find the truth,
refrain the brain to starve the Uncouth,
the master, the ham and the hammer,
ride the boar, handle the tusks,
and hide your nose from the Musks.

—*Tomes of the Touched*

Pikarn never imagined that he could forget the cold of Kaludor, but when they left Berul in the middle of a rainstorm, he knew he'd grown soft. Not that he was going to let Oldenu see this truth, though. The woman was still northern tough, and no doubt surviving the past few years had tempered her. Adding to the misery was that although he was mighty used to hard work, he wasn't accustomed to traveling afoot for long distances. Hells, most of his horizons traveled on Kaludor were on horseback. His fingers froze, his feet hurt, and his heart wondered what might've been as he watched Oldenu lead the way down animal trails he no longer knew.

She assured them that the biggest danger was leaving Berul. The Shadows and Taken watched the island but hid when wet snow or rain fell, and once a few horizons out, the wilderness was just the wilds. Pikarn wondered if the wilds weren't in part wild because the Colok kept them that way. He didn't know what life and death meant to a Shadow, but they seemed inclined to avoid the rending paws and claws of the Colok.

They were eight Silone versus the wilds. They were six days out from Berul and four days into the foothills when Oldenu's favorite tracker, Nîdol, spotted the first signs of Colok. The tracks were of wolves and sled runners and a day old, but they followed anyhow, just in case the Colok came back the way they went. It wasn't long after that they came across the remnants of battle, with Taken bodies and black blood spattered through trees and not yet frozen.

Rikis said, "It don't look like the Colok are idle."

"Aye, damned handy for them clear the path for us. How often do you find sites like this?"

Oldenu shrugged. "They aren't rare, but most times it's hard to tell how old they are. This here is pretty fresh."

"Shadows fightin' Colok is like us trying to fight our own shadows: Pointless. If the Colok kill off all the Taken on the island, Kaludor is theirs. Unless the Queen gets through. There are only so many Silone left alive for the Shadows to take."

She scanned the area. "Might be these Colok are headed for Snow's Eye."

Rikis froze. "I don't want to give no one any worries, but something just moved in the woods yonder."

Pikarn squinted and stared. "I don't see nothin'."

Oldenu said, "Let's be walkin'. There's a Shadow up there."

He took two steps and glanced back; something flittered from the trunk of one tree to another. "Shits. I suppose we shouldn't have hung out by the slaughtered Taken."

Rikis said, "If we're lucky, they'll think we did it."

Oldenu reached beneath the furs of her cloak, pulled out a wineskin, and gave it a shake. "Water's our only weapon. Of course, you boys might be able to take a piss at 'em."

Pikarn laughed. "Now there's standoff worth seeing." A Shadow streaked by and Pikarn got his wineskins out, one in each hand.

A Shadow darted at the party from behind a boulder, but Nîdol squeezed and sent a stream of water at it. It screeched and fled, but another came from the rear. Water flew, the creature howled, and they kept walking.

"This ain't the way to win no battle. Rikis, get to the middle and blow your horn."

Oldenu said, "You'll attract every Taken and Shadow for a horizon."

"Aye, maybe, but do you think our wineskins will hold out until snow or rain flies?" They packed as many as they could, and they were oversized just for this, but they wouldn't last forever. A Shadow swooped close, and Pikarn squeezed with his left arm against his ribs. Water flew and it hissed in pain and darted away. "There's a band of Colok somewhere around here, and there ain't no way they don't check out a horn's call."

She nodded and Rikis blew until his cheeks turned purple. The number of Shadows grew to three he could see at any one time, and one followed straight behind them. It matched their pace but never got close enough to be hit by water.

Pikarn spat at the thing and smiled but got no reaction. "You ever seen one do this?"

Oldenu said, "No, but this whole godsdamned thing is new to me, or I'd prolly be dead before now."

"Another Shadow, maybe two more. At some point they'll rush us."

"Or they'll toy with us until we're out of water."

"Or that."

Pikarn glanced back and their stalking Shadow was there; a flicker later he was gone. "Be careful; our tail has gone missing."

A bellow shattered the still air and a dozen Shadows streaked in random directions, but they were running, not attacking. Colok came from the rocks all around them, leaping, running, swiping, tearing strips of Shadow. Pikarn charged one and squirted with both skins, making the thing howl even as a Colok ripped at the fabric of its being.

Pikarn howled with the Colok. "Gods! That felt good. Lousy sons of bitches."

Instead of surrounded by Shadows they were surrounded by Colok. Pikarn said, "Don't nobody pull a weapon." He looked to one Colok who seemed might be in charge of the hunting party. She was over eight feet tall and had pieced together a nice set of mail to cover her torso. "We are Choerkin. Peace with Colok."

The beast huffed, leaned, and sniffed him. She growled once, then cleared her throat and growled again. This time he heard the words. "Choerkin good bait."

"Yes! Well, ain't that lovely. You used us as bait."

Rikis said, "I would've felt a lot better knowing we were part of a trap."

Oldenu said, "I think that makes eight of us."

Pikarn held his smile, hoping the beasts didn't hold a grudge after decades of his hunting them. "Zjin. We need to speak to Zjin or Grolkan."

The Colok grunted. "Zjin. Snow's Eye."

Pikarn sat at a fire with Zjin at Snow's Eye. The old tower stood much as it did the last time he was here, stepping inside this time brought on painful memories of Modan's agonizing end. But now, as then, there were more pressing matters.

"You've more people here than last time." He'd seen at least fifty different Colok, or so he guessed. It wasn't always easy telling them apart.

"Three tribes. Watch Istinjoln."

"The Edan haven't found a way to close the Queen's gate, not yet, but they want to get close to study it."

"Saw Edan go north."

Pikarn puzzled over this one for a flicker. "When?"

"Twenty-three days."

He glanced at Rikis, and the boy shrugged. "I know nothing you don't. The Edan are keeping us in the dark."

Pikarn nodded. "North. I'd wager they headed for the Steaming Lakes. There is an Edan who may know how to close the gate. We need your help to make sure she gets the chance."

Zjin growled, "Edan three."

Pikarn grinned. "Three Edan left their blessed woods? They might know more than they're letting on. The way I figure it, it doesn't matter if the Edan close the gate or not, Choerkin and Colok should work together on Kaludor starting today."

"Work?"

"The five islands in the Sobuno River, Oldenu here already has people there. We settle all those islands, a few hundred Silone, maybe more with your help. We start sweeping the island, an army with Colok focused on Shadows, while we both fight the Taken. They can't go making more Taken without people to Take. If we cut them numbers, eliminate them, all they've got is Shadows and Shadows can't touch Colok.'

"Marukane."

Pikarn shook his head. "I admit to not knowin' a damned thing. I only heard the tales of that one. But I wager Inslok and the Edan have a beef with that demon. But it don't matter none. What I want to know most is if the Colok will work with Choerkin at Berul Island. Like your friend said, Choerkin are good bait."

Zjin rumbled with laughter. "Zjin go Istinjoln. Zjin speak Grolkan. Grolkan speak tribes."

Pikarn slapped his knees and smiled at them. "That's all I ask."

Oldenu said, "You and that stupid smile."

Forty-Seven

Dead Eyes Alive

The highest art of deceit comes in making an enemy believe the impossible, but even then, it is best to begin with the expected and believable.

—*Codex of Sol*

Binôtu Kodûl was born and raised in a small village called Rî-Hemer deep in the bosom of Malstefnê Nation. His parents were farmers with a quarter lock of ground to plant seeds and raise chickens alongside a handful of goats. He was the fifth son of eight children, and because all his siblings survived, he became an excess mouth to feed. As he sat his saddle, weary from a long day's ride, he wondered how life would've been different if, like on so many neighboring farms, a couple of brothers and sisters had died within their first couple years of screaming and crying.

Would he still have wound up fighting in battles he didn't give a rip-snort about? His father wouldn't have sent him to Camp Gîgîol after locusts wiped out half their crop, of that he could be sure, but war had come to the Malstefnê a year after and conscription gangs struck the small towns and farmers to bolster the army. Odds were good that his father's sending him away had saved him the "knock and knot" on his head that so many green soldiers awakened to find.

Perhaps he was lucky then, being a scout and messenger. It kept him from charging walls where arrows and stones were the day's weather.

Instead of facing death fighting foreigners in the south, he approached the city of Notôlhof, seat of King Trefifân, on a gorgeous day without a cloud in the sky, a day when the sun warmed the skin when the gentle breezes died, and the gentle breezes cooled the cozy heat of the sun on their return.

"Never complain; worse days are a-comin'."

Captain Yorvul glanced at him. "What the blazes was that?"

Binôtu didn't realize at first that he'd spoken aloud. He coughed. "Somethin' my father always told me." He'd only been to the city of Notôlhof twice in his life and both times it had been an unnerving honor. As a farmer's son who'd grown up able to count all the folks at a town gathering on fingers and toes, he figured he would never get used to the crowded streets.

They approached the gates that led into the city's military quarter ready for the journey to end and to celebrate with a pint of ale or three. The city walls stood a modest twenty-feet high with square towers maybe thirty at their peaks framing the gates, but they were twenty strides wide and had impressed the demons from his soul the first time he saw them. That was before reaching the fortress walls that surrounded the king. The base stones of that wall seemed as big as the inn back home.

A bulky man whose gut bulged around his belt stepped from the shadows of the gatehouse with four guards at his side. The first iron portcullis was open, but the second, which allowed passage into the city proper, was closed. In times of peace they would both be open until nightfall.

"In the name of King Trefifân, state your business in the city of Notôlhof."

Yorvul said, "Sir, we've a message from Lord Ôlisbenar for the King. It is urgent." He held forth two sealed envelopes, and the fat man nabbed them, breaking the seal on one to gaze at its contents.

His face was an unreadable blank as he perused the note, but then he cleared his throat and smiled. "This is wonderful news. The king himself... Well, all of you should deliver this to him in person." He turned to the guards around him. "A glorious day! You men, take their horses to the stable."

Binôtu swung from the saddle with a smile and a puffed chest. He didn't know what news they'd carried from the Dragonspan Mountains, but it was monumental if the king would wish to honor them.

Binôtu followed Yorvul and the rest of the messenger party into the dark passage. They all wore jovial smiles when they reached the second portcullis.

Until it didn't raise.

Until the one behind them fell. They turned, confused, then an oily splash wet his skin and weighted his clothes.

He looked up at the murder holes above and the dripping slick. Only Yorvul had the wits to scream before a guttering torch fell from above. The world burst into searing heat and his voice joined the growing chorus around him.

Fulmor didn't know why he poured oil through the murder holes or why those men needed to die, but he thanked the Hokandît and the Fields of Tomenor that he wasn't the one ordered to drop the torch. He knew Binôtu just well enough to believe he could pick his scream from the other voices in the rush of flames, but the sound had died in flickers; it was the stench of oil fire mingled with burning flesh that lingered in the gatehouse halls, lingered in his nostrils and the back of his throat. The fifth mug of ale had yet to wash away the greasy memory, and he stared at the bottom of the mug pondering whether six would be the magic number.

He glanced around the main hall of the *Rusty Spear*, a tavern squatting on Mutton Street, the unofficial border between the Military Quarter and the seedier Spice Quarter, which was a generous name for a place where moneyed folks carried incense in their pockets to hide the odors wafting from the drains. Most times he decided to waste a silver sinin on a night of drinking he kept to pubs popular with soldiers, but tonight he wanted his drink cheap, and the off chance of getting killed by a street thug when stumbling back to the barracks appealed to him.

"Wench! I burned men to death today; another ale to put out my fire."

Men covered in as much grease and dirt as hair stared at him, but when he didn't jabber on with his story, they turned away. He dropped a nel-sinin on the table and eyeballed the bottom of his mug again, but still didn't find any answers.

"I burned a man I knew today and didn't even have the courage to ask why."

A hand slapped him between the shoulder blades. "There you are."

The trouble was, when he turned, he didn't know the man's name. The face was familiar, and the streetsword at his waist suggested he was a soldier. "Do I know you, friend?"

"Not without my beard and armor. Nah, Worlt was locked into the watch tonight and he wanted me to make sure you didn't end up swimmin' in the cess. I'm Kornik, from the fourth regiment."

"How the Holy Names did he know where I was? That whoreson has trouble finding his boots."

Kornik pulled up a stool and sat, dropped coins on the bar. "Worlt said you had a cursed day of it on the wall." He looked to the barkeep. "A helm of ale for my friend and me."

Fulmor shrugged then leaned his elbows to the bar. "I'm most of the way to a hangover already. You're out to get me killed by my captain."

Kornik chuckled. "Long nights make for longer days, my pa always said."

"He wasn't bullshittin' about that one."

The barkeep slid a bowl full of ale down the bar and nabbed the coins as he strolled past. The bowl resembled the traditional flat-topped helmet of the Malstefnê guard and was popular in all quarters where men drank to forget their day. Kornik lifted it with both hands and chugged several swallows before sliding it to Fulmor. He wiped his mouth of foam. "I heard there was a fire at the Gatehouse."

"I don't wanna talk about it."

"Yeah, you do, and you know why you do?"

Fulmor glared. "Speak easy. I knew one of them men." He lifted the helm and drank.

"I knew three of them, not my mates or nothin', but I knew them. I want to talk about it for the same reason you do: Why'd they meet the torch, that's what we both want to know."

"I'll be cursed if I know." He lifted and drank, belched. "Cap'n Hûlm, that fat bastard, never gave me the first word on why."

Kornik leaned in. "You know where they rode from?"

"The Dragonspans is what I heard."

"Oh aye, and you know what the whisper faeries say? They say one of them was a spy."

If he wasn't drunk Fulmor might've been more surprised, but he shrugged the words away. "A spy, one of our own a spy?"

"I heard they didn't know which one it was, and that's why they lit 'em all."

Fulmor's gut rumbled and he stifled a belch. "Burnt 'em all to get one? Sounds like my captain." He snorted then lifted the helm for another drink.

"Sounds more like our king. Just what I heard, anyhow." Kornik took the helm and drank until ale ran down his chin to his chest, then he slammed it to the bar.

Fulmor stood and the bar spun. "I need to piss."

Kornik grinned and punched his shoulder. "You do that, and then we'll head back to the barracks before we're forced to bang the drum in the morning."

Fulmor laughed, but the threat was serious. The men who returned latest and drunkest were often forced to beat the sunrise drums that announced a change in the guard along the wall. The drums were concussive enough on a hangover from a hundred strides; he didn't want to imagine them so close.

A half candle later his bladder was as empty as the helm, and he wobbled from the tavern with his new drinking chum by his side. The odors of smoke and sweat faded to rot and excrement as they exited the Rusty Spear and stepped onto Mutton Street. The city of Notôlhof needed a good rain to wash it clean, but the season had been dryer than usual.

Fulmor strode toward an unnamed alley and Kornik caught his shoulder. "Where're you goin'?"

"Short cut."

"You sure about that? It's late to be alley walkin' in the Spices."

Fulmor scoffed and slapped the hilt of his streetsword. The weapon's blade was short for fighting in close quarters and crafted from quality steel. "Street creeps are a cowardly lot in the Spices."

Kornik grinned. "As much as you've drunk, I fear you'll fall into a sewer."

"I've made my way home so drunk I thought I had four feet." He leaned on the corner of the Rusty Spear as he rounded the corner and stumbled. "Don't worry none. This alley gets narrow enough it's hard to fall down."

It wasn't much of an exaggeration; within fifty strides the leaning walls were close enough that he could stretch his arms and touch the rough bricks on either side. A song jumped into his head. "Ohhh!"—the song leaped back to the nether—"I need to piss."

"Again?"

He turned and leaned against the wall, but shadows appeared ahead. In the dim light of the moon he thought he saw a knife in one man's hand. "Gods, just what I need. A fight!" He spun, drew his sword, and damned near fell against the opposite wall. "Only three of you? Come on, you daisy cutters."

The man in the middle spoke. "If you drunken twats drop yer coin purses you can walk away, all safe like and back to yer holes in the wall."

"You hear that, Kornik? This rat wants our coins."

"I heard." Kornik stepped past him, and at that moment he realized how big and intimidating his new friend was. The man pulled his sword and faced the thugs.

"You boys don't wanna mess with my pal, here."

Boy was he wrong; these boys were more than ready to die. The thugs rushed them, blurry shadows wielding weapons in the alley's dark. Kornik put his blade through one man's chest and spun him, putting the man between Kornik and a club's blow from another robber. He threw the dying to the ground as he flicked his blade at an incoming knife and steel rattled on the cobbled street. A quick slash opened the man's throat, and he struck the third square in the face with the hilt of his sword. The man hit the street with a bounce before the tip of the blade punctured his lungs with three rapid jabs.

Fulmor stood laughing and waving his blade. "Haha! Take that, drunken twats indeed." The tip of his sword struck the wall and he fumbled his grip before sheathing the weapon. "You're Death's Angel with a sword, friend! Death's Angel."

Kornik wiped the blade of his sword on the dying man's jacket as he wheezed toward his final breath. "I keep myself alive."

"You are a modest whoreson. I damned near couldn't see 'em in this dark, and you... Good work."

His friend sheathed his sword. "You're drunk. It makes me seem deadlier than I am."

Fulmor snorted and stumbled to a body. "I'm wonderin' if they got a coin purse or two themselves."

Kornik's shadow loomed over his shoulder, but Fulmor paid his friend no mind until he felt the garrote seize his throat. He reached and pulled, flopped to the ground, flailed and kicked, but all his effort didn't land more than a glancing blow. His muscles seized. He couldn't scream. He couldn't breathe. His fingers wouldn't so much as twitch. He was a board being strangled to death. The little strength remaining faded from his body, and all he could do was listen.

"First you answer some questions, then I'll let you nap."

Captain Hûlm patted his ample gut and adjusted his broad belt after a heavy meal of stewed pork and greens that he washed down with goat's milk. His first twenty years in the army had kept him fit and lean, but the past ten sitting atop the wall had brought on more of an appetite than his meager workload sweated off of him. Sometimes he'd boast how young and strong he once was, and for a flicker even believe his boastful words about wishing he'd taken command in the cavalry instead of his cushy position in the city guard. But truth be told, fat and happy went together like cherries and chocolate.

A servant collected his plate and shuffled away in a hurry, but he stopped her. "Ôlgret."

"Yes, sir?"

"Fetch me a tankard of mead."

"Make it two, if you'd be so kind." A man's voice came from the entry and it took a flicker for his eyes to adjust.

"Fulmor?"

"Yes, sir. Might I come in?"

"Of course. Two meads, Ôlgret. Have a seat."

Fulmor strolled into the room like the nervous ninny he was. The man was big enough to look the part of a soldier, but Hûlm had him figured as a coward from the flicker he'd spotted him arriving at the wall. But cowards had their uses, being afraid to die often made a man amenable to doing things a courageous man might refuse.

"Please excuse my intrudin' like this."

"Not at all, boy. What you come for?"

"Well, I... It's damned awkward to ask. We burned those men the other day—"

"Yes, a horrible thing, but horrible things sometimes gotta be done." *Even if we don't know why.* He'd turned his back on the portcullis when the screams began, and three days later no amount of mead purged the memories from his head. It irritated him that this weakling would remind him of such a horror. "What of it?"

"Why? Why'd you make me do it?"

Hûlm bristled as a silver tankard clunked in front of him. "I ordered you to do it because the orders came from on high."

Fulmor bowed his head. "Sorry, sorry. I understand that. I do. Why'd they make you do it? I'm trying to wrap my wits around it, the nightmares. Those men were, one was a friend."

Hûlm leaned back in his seat and quaffed his mead, his anger soothing as he stared at this pathetic man. "I don't know, and I wish I did. The message said to give them a flaming welcome, and that's what I did." He shrugged. "Every gate captain along the wall knows what those words mean. It was just our piss poor luck to be on duty that day."

"Luck, no doubt, but why?"

Hûlm rubbed his nose and snuffled. "Last time the guard set men ablaze was a year or so before you they assigned you to the city. A Litrâ diplomat and her men. I didn't know why then, I don't know now, except to say someone important wanted them dead."

"Forgive me, sir, but who?"

He held the mead in his mouth as he swirled his tongue through syrupy sweet before swallowing. It was dangerous to speak of things soldiers shouldn't hear. "I don't see how that's any of your concern."

The man ducked his head like a scolded dog. "I just need someone to blame, a name to curse in my prayers each morning."

Hûlm didn't often take pity on men, but in this instance, there was a sadness and anger in this man that ate at his will. And by The Names, it wasn't like this weak bastard could touch the one who signed the message, it'd be like a gnat chasing a dragon. "You never heard this from me. One peep and the cat-o-nine will take your hide. Understood?"

"Yes, sir. I do."

"Ôlisbenar commanded the men killed in the name of the king. His message was brief and direct; men like him don't need to explain their decisions to men like us."

Fulmor's head remained tucked to his chest as he nodded. "I thank you, sir. Most kindly, I do." He took a drink of his mead and set it back on the table. "I'll trouble you no further."

"Boy, go ahead and take the mead with you."

Fulmor raised his head and smiled. "Most generous. I think I'll walk the river to ease my soul." He grabbed the tankard and slunk from the room. Hûlm had his peace again.

But that would end the moment he got back home. His wife would nag, and his son would no doubt cry and moan about something petty. He stood and drained his mead with a smack of his lips. By the time he stepped outside the sun was creeping behind the western wall and cast long shadows. The notion of home didn't feel so pleasant; maybe a simple soldier like Fulmor had the right of it. A walk by the river might do a man some good.

A cool breeze chilled the sweat on his jowls as he walked, and he forgot all about men burning and a wife waiting to ambush him with her daily complaints at home. The sound of the water washed away the city's noise, except for the yap of the common folk in earshot, and he enjoyed the peace.

Until he spotted Fulmor sitting against a wall sipping at the same tankard of mead he'd given him. One thing for sure, if he heard from Ôlgret tomorrow about how a mug had gone missing, the bastard would hear it from Hûlm.

Fulmor's eyes raised to catch his with a creepy squint and scowl. Hûlm glanced away, then back again as the soldier stood and wandered into the alley. He scratched the back of his neck, pondering what by The Names made the soldier look at him that way, and why he'd wandered into an alley that led to the warehouse district.

He smacked his lips as curiosity and irritation grew, and his legs carried him north despite his sore feet. The alley was dark and shadowy and he didn't see a soul at first glance, but not ten paces down stood the tankard atop a crate. "Damn it, soldier! Where are you? Mugs cost as much as the mead in them."

Not a sound from the alley except the scratch of what he suspected was a rat trying to work its way inside a wooden box. He snorted and strode toward the tankard, but when he came just within reach, he froze. Not from fear nor nothing else he understood. His muscles locked to stand him in the middle of the dark lane like some statue. His eyes glanced at his hand, but his head couldn't move, then he saw a faint shadow pass before his eyes and a rope cinched his neck.

"Ful—" was the only sound he made. He wanted to fight, to kick, to struggle. He wasn't the lean man he was twenty years ago, but he was still powerful enough to throw men around when pressed. But in this moment when his size might've saved his life, every muscle failed him. His legs tingled with weakness, but he couldn't even fall.

The rope burned around his neck, and Fulmor's voice whispered in his ear before Hûlm passed into the unconscious black. "Nothing personal, mind you, but I will find you useful. And sincerely, thank you for the mead. It was pleasant."

Most folks assumed that Lady was a nickname, but Lady Serilu was in truth a lady despite her profession. Forty-two years ago, she'd been born to an aging Lord Dervit Hôlgwîr and his shapely young wife, Julêl. Her parents raised her in what many people called a castle—but it was more a manor house surrounded by a wall—until her father died when she was ten. In the wake of his death came the chaos of four sons all older and more entitled to his wealth than the new bride and their half-sister.

Brothers and uncles murdered each other in defiance of the King's Law until King Remreth put an end to the whole affair by having all remaining male heirs put to the ax. His highness then bequeathed the old lord's lands to a new lord while soldiers carted Julêl and Serilu back to Notôlhof with promises of generosity from the king, but that kindness only extended to her mother after she found a new and aging lord to bed. Her mother sold Serilu to another wrinkled lord to warm his bed, but not in the official capacity as a bride. She lived vaulted away in a room high aloft in *The Singing Spire*, a house of ladies so exclusive that use of the word whore resulted in a whipping, castration, or one last swim in the river, depending on who the insult was aimed at. Serilu was a concubine for a decade, until her patron died in battle somewhere to the west, but even after his demise her beauty and breeding earned her high regard and few suitors to afford her.

While her looks faded little, and she still had a devoted following of men, the Lady of the Singing Spire had noted Serilu's keen wits and ways and took her under her wing. At thirty-five, Serilu earned the title of Lady that she'd lost so many years ago, even if it was a different sort of Lady than who ran a manor house or castle. In her capacity as overseer of The Spire she rubbed elbows with the cream of Malstefnê society, even if it was in the shadows.

That's why the appearance of a lowly captain of the guard outside her door confounded her. He was rotund for a soldier and homely in an ordinary way, his body jiggling as he took a seat, but he couldn't have reached her without having a purse of coins fuller than a captain should have. Either he'd made booty of some smuggler's wealth, not unheard of, or another capable of buying his way this far sent him, so politeness was in order.

She sauntered behind her desk with a sway of her hips while fanning her face with feathers. "My dear captain, what brings you to The Spire?"

He cleared his throat and wiped the sweat from his dangling jowls. "My name's Hûlm, m' lady. I was wondering if you had the time to answer a few questions for me."

Serilu straightened her dress and smiled. "Most men don't come here to pay for pleasantries; words are often more expensive. One of our solemn tasks is to carry secrets, many without price." The Singing Spire was an ever-growing collection of secrets, and Serilu figured she'd killed more men than any soldier on the watch with her whispers to the king, but if it didn't concern the king or his highest court, secrets remained secrets.

The fat man wiped his brow with his sleeve. "My business today is another's, not my own."

She breathed easier and understood why the man sat drenched in sweat. Someone forced him to make the inquiry. "Do go on."

"Thank you, ma'am. I'm just a hound sniffing for a lowly rat, ma'am. No way I'd be here without a knife at my spine, you know what I mean. There was a fire at the Military Quarter gatehouse about a week back, you heard about it?"

"An unpleasant accident, the Whisper Faeries say."

"Indeed, and I'm the one who ordered the accident, as it were."

She clutched her hands in front of her chest and leaned forward. "So, you're the man to squeeze juice from the peach."

He coughed and blushed. "I wouldn't go so far, but my peach *did* get squeezed. I gave up the name on the letter who ordered me to ignite the gate."

"I see. Tsk. I'm guessing that's how you found your way to my abode?"

"It is indeed."

"And what's it to do with me and The Spire?"

"Everyone knows men spill their secrets best in bed."

She leaned back in her chair with a sigh. "If you want to squeeze this peach, you need to give up some juice. Who ordered the fire?"

Hûlm reached beneath his coat then tossed a heavy bag of coins on the desk. "You don't need that answer."

Serilu reached and dragged the pouch close, and a glance inside showed nothing but gold. "I still need a name."

Hûlm smiled and threw up his hands in defeat; she'd underestimated the man, that much she realized now. She was being played, and she didn't know the game. "One name and one name only, then my benefactor needs his answer. Ôlisbenar."

Serilu swallowed hard and took her hand from the pouch of coins. Games with secrets and gold involved were always dangerous, but this was a name high on the list of people not to cross. And worse, whoever paid this lowly captain was no doubt in the same rarified altitudes. "I'm not a woman who has survived this long by taking lordly risks." His cocksure smile told her that she'd more than underestimated this man, and she patted the dagger hidden in the waist of her dress to reassure herself it was there.

"You'll find it's a simple answer. Who is Lord Kervik's favorite woman at The Singing Spire?"

Her mind scrambled for any answer that wasn't the truth, but he'd caught her off guard. Kervik was Lord of Merchants to the crown and sat daily at the king's table, and Serilu had been his favorite since her twenty-second birthday. "Heredên, a young and insidiously beautiful creature."

Hûlm smiled with a nod and stood. "I'm certain she is, no doubt as beautiful as you once were."

She laughed but feared it came out more nervous than humored. "Me? Gracious, I was never the beauty she is."

He didn't take a step to leave no matter how hard she willed it. "Your hesitation spoke more truth than your words. Go ahead and pronounce the name."

"It would seem I don't need to say my name because you already know it. Lord Kervik is a tight-lipped man even when he sleeps. I don't have a secret to tell."

"You were the only secret I needed."

He strode around her desk, and she stood, backing away while pulling her dagger with a shaky hand. "Get back, I warn you."

"Your knife has no point."

She glanced at her dagger; the tip indeed appeared round, but in a blink its piercing head returned. "I assure you it does, and it's bloodied more than a few men."

The fat man's smile became beautiful and innocent, reminding her of a young noble she once loved, even if he looked at her only as entertainment. She jabbed at the air as he drew closer, then her muscles froze.

She stood stone still except for her thudding heart, and he peeled the dagger from her hand with a casual grace before slipping it back into the sheath at her waist. "Tell me about you and this Lord."

She tried to scream, but to her horror, all that came out were soft words. "He's always been good to me..." The words kept coming, and she couldn't stop or change them.

Until he whispered, "Sleep." His fat fingers gripped her neck and squeezed, thumbs driving hard to block her air. She gasped and stared in horror, but his calm smile never changed. "Honestly, I have never liked causing pain. I never enjoy hurting a woman, in particular one so beautiful. I do apologize." She didn't believe him.

Her head slumped, and her vision of his smile turned black.

Long days turned into long weeks and long months for Lord Kervik in times of peace, such was the lot in life for the man tasked with the taxes and finances of a kingdom, but his reward was a life of luxury with the finest foods and women that gold could buy. It was a fair trade, and he knew a thing or two about fair trades. War with the Litrâ challenged his wits to an indebted end, but two wars allowed him no chance to enjoy the fruits of the debt.

It'd been more than a month since his last visit to The Singing Spire, and his fifty-year-old knees held a spring they'd lacked for a decade or more. He entered the back gate into the rose garden and his bodyguards took positions beside a dozen other guards left behind as their betters enjoyed the ladies of The Spire. Leaving his guards behind was an elation, a freedom to breathe as a man instead of a powerful prisoner to politics. This was going to be a good night and he wouldn't leave until morning. Maybe he'd even eat breakfast off of Serilu's belly.

He smiled at the fantasy of sucking egg yolk from her navel and stepped into the red hall. Not a soul greeted him, as was typical, for this wasn't the entry for ordinary men of wealth and influence, but for those of the heralded king's court. He took a deep breath and listened to the voices of the ladies laughing and drinking with men in the main hall. The Hokandite had their Fields of Tenor, but for Kervik, this building with its perfumes, garish velvet decor, and bold flowers everywhere was heaven for mortal man, a place where his gut could relax, and his mind slip free of worry.

He took dignified steps up the carpeted stairs—in case other eyes from the court saw him—instead of running like the randy bastard he felt like inside. He took four flights of stairs this evening by special instruction from Serilu, and they'd meet in the highest room that gave The Spire its name. He took the final flight two steps at a time before gathering himself at the door, catching his breath before knocking. But he didn't wait for an invitation.

The chamber carried a light chill as the windows stood open and a breeze fluttered the gauzy curtains. Soft lantern light lit the room, and on a round table sat a bowl of pears and grapes beside a wheel of cheese and bottle of wine.

Her perfect voice came from behind a dressing curtain. "You've been away too long." She stepped into the light wearing a golden silk gown that hugged her curves. It amazed him that the woman he'd met twenty years ago still aroused him so.

"These are trying days."

Serilu sauntered to stand so close he felt her breath on his face, and her hand rubbed beneath his chin before kissing him. "So I've heard." She spun on a heel and sat at the table, plucking a grape and popping it in her mouth.

She always said that fruit was her favorite foreplay. It was one of the things that frustrated him, but kept his will too weak to not come back. He slid a chair back and poured wine after sitting. "You are as beautiful as ever."

"Am I? You know I always fret these things; the years pass me by like they do everyone."

He shook his head. "Not like they do everyone. No, time seems to forget you now and again." He sipped the red wine, enjoying the notes of black currant and cherry.

"Tell me your troubles, dearest. You'll feel better."

"Mmm, I'd forgotten how to feel better until I stepped into this room."

She smiled, her teeth white and perfect. "The first time we... met, was in this room."

It was an afternoon he would never forget. "If I could enshrine that day in the heavens to live in forever, I would."

Her brow scrunched. "You've always been one to lavish me with sweet words." She sliced two chunks of cheese and handed him a sliver before taking a nibble. "I know when something troubles my lover."

He sighed. "We've known one another too long and too well, except I can never tell when you're troubled."

"Dearest, that's because I have no worries except pleasing you."

He chuckled into his glass. "I know better than that."

"There was an incident at the Military Quarter Gate. When was that? About a month back?"

He grimaced, grabbed a pear, and sliced. "Heard about that, did you?"

"I have a lot of ears. All of them lovely, mind you."

"Whisper faeries?"

"My ears are mortal and hear best while laying on pillows. I heard it had something to do Ôlisbenar?"

He stopped in the middle of crunching a wedge of pear. "Your ears are keen." He chewed and swallowed. The Spire was famous for knowing things and feeding them to the king, well, famous at least in the loyal court. But it was just as prone to expose men who let their tongues wag too much as it was to reveal a traitor. He stared into her soft brown eyes and decided there was no harm in a few words. She already knew he wasn't fond of Ôlisbenar. The gods knew, and for that matter so did the king and Ôlisbenar himself. "Yes, the whoreson commanded the fire."

"I've been in Notôlhof thirty years and only heard of such thing a few times. Why'd he do such a *horrible* thing?"

Now she pushed too far, and he smiled. "I don't know."

"I heard he believed one of them a spy for the foreigners in the south."

He pursed his lips before they shifted into a cockeyed grin. In a way he was proud of the woman, and maybe what she angled for was giving him the name of the man who let slip this information. Whomever it was had to be tight with the court. "Who told you this?"

"A pretty little gal named Heredên, men just have a way with words around her. You'd like her if you weren't so smitten with me."

She grinned and winked, disarming him enough that he took another drink. "I don't think she divined this on her own. Who spoke the words?"

"Tsk-tsk!" She popped three grapes into her mouth one by one and juice trickled onto her lips as she spoke. "Tell me who he wanted dead and I'll name the courtier."

He blinked. "So close to the king?" Her smile answered the question. "I didn't come here to dig into court intrigue."

She stood and sauntered around him, a finger and nail rubbing his cheek before her hands pressed into his shoulders. Tension faded and he topped off his wine.

Her breath came hot in his ear. "Ôlisbenar begs for power at every turn; it'll be his undoing. I won't tell a soul."

He laughed. "You know the man better than most in the court. By the Names, it's all a fairy tale he's built in his head. The Wraith of Qwôhar."

She purred in his ear. "Sounds exciting."

The woman knew him better than he knew himself. He released the remnants of stress in a single breath and unleashed pent anxieties. "Four months after our *grand* king sent that braggart to Qwôhar to fight the Malôbund, he began claiming a wraith haunted the city, some sort of curse. It took the faces of men and women and spun war from peace. It stuck daggers in hearts, it did whatever it took to foment war. He believed the barbarians sent this thing and he slaughtered dozens trying to kill this beast of his fancy."

"Did he succeed? He won the war."

"A real enemy is easier to kill than a nightmare. Despite winning, he claimed the wraith survived. That's why he had those messengers killed. He was convinced the Wraith of Qwôhar was one of those men. That's why they *needed* to die." It felt good to say it aloud, even if it didn't soothe his disgust.

Serilu squeezed his shoulders a last time and rounded the table to sit. "Not all fantasies are unreal."

He smiled as he bit into a grape, hoping this was the beginning of a more pleasant conversation. "This room has made many come true."

"Did he say why this Wraith was coming?"

He sighed, exasperated and dying to end this. "To kill the king, why else?"

She smiled, but it wasn't a smile quite the same as he'd ever seen on her face before. "When and where do you meet with the king? Are these meetings regular?"

He meant to say that she'd crossed the line of decorum and that it was time to think of wine and sheets, but instead he said, "We used to meet every couple of days, but of late I only see him when the council gathers every first of the month, unless he commands an audience." His words droned on, and his eyes sagged.

"Stay awake," a man's voice said.

When he opened them again, he was speaking of Ôlisbenar. The Lady of the Spire whom he loved had turned into an old, blue-eyed man with a barbarian's face and smile, but he passed it off as some dream as his head lulled.

"There will be plenty of time to sleep. Awake," a boy's voice said. What was Mered, his son, doing here?

His head jerked straight with a start as if he'd nodded off, and he spoke of the queen, telling his son of Queen Elunid's habits and how she and the king got on in public and private. He needed to sleep. A slumber so deep.

"Thank you. You may die now." This voice was his own, but it didn't come from his mouth or mind, and Kervik didn't bother to open his eyes. There was a pain in his gut, maybe from the wine, but the overriding sensation was tranquility.

King Trefifân didn't hate his father. Indeed, Trefifân appreciated that Remreth died before his fortieth birthday so that Trefifân could take the crown before his brothers were old enough to give him an argument. The twins died in their sleep without a fuss soon after the crown rested on his young brow. No, the man he hated was his namesake and grandfather, King Trefifân the Third.

This great king died in battle before the Fourth held memories of his grandfather, so it wasn't that the Third had done anything to him. No, it was living up to the man's reputation that fueled the Fourth's fits of hatred, and on the first of every month, everyone took their shot to remind him of the heralded deeds his blood had once achieved.

Trefifân the Fourth sat at the head of a table capable of seating seven advisors, but Kervik and Morên were the only ones not traveling or at war. Oh, if only he'd been able to conjure an excuse for these prickly thorns to leave as well. This morning his emotions rested somewhere between bored and furious. Lady Morên, Voice of the Ladies, was a prissy old gal who took her title with a seriousness that drove him to drink so often that he preferred to take these meetings drunk. The Third had instated the advisory position to keep the peace after beheading the old queen and wedding a voluptuous new bride. The people heralded the move, while the Fourth—and he suspected The Third as well—suffered from it.

Her nasal voice drove nails into his ears. "Litrâ dogs stole a dozen girls from their homes on the border. We're *weak*, and our neighbors know it. Your grandfather would never have allowed such thing."

A finger idly twirled the dark locks dangling over Trefifân's right ear. "Send a writ demanding reparations in gold."

Lady Morên snorted and tossed her gray hair. "And they'll ignore us or send a pittance as they have the past four times they braved our borders."

"I assure you when these wars are over, Litrâ will regret their impertinence."

"One war was over—"

"No! Not another word. One enemy fell defeated, but another stands proud having run roughshod over our sovereign ground."

"Your Highness—"

"Ôlisbenar will hold the barbarian warlord's head soon; the Wraith of Qwôhar is dead." Trefifân grunted in satisfaction as she bowed her head, but the next voice was as sure to annoy him.

Kervik said, "You pin victory on destroying a haunt from a child's dream?"

Trefifân glared down his nose. "By the Names, are the both of you out to stoke my fires?"

"Men died, indeed, but what proof the Wraith died or existed at all?"

"What proof? I have the word of Ôlisbenar."

"The Wraith of Qwôhar is real. I'll accept the premise. This thing murdered and fueled a war for two years. It defeated Ôlisbenar once, twice, three times, why do you assume it dead?"

Trefifân stifled a laugh, but his smirk he let shine. "Because my life was the perfect bait for the trap of peace."

"Ôlisbenar is a brilliant mind loved by his soldiers, loved by you, but the creature fooled him more than once. Who is to say the Wraith didn't anticipate his play?"

"Something happened the third night out, it was too dark to see well, but the Wraith moved into the messenger's camp that night."

Morên laughed. "If you men are going to speak of fairy wings and demon kisses, I'd as soon adjourn."

"So would I, but we haven't discussed how poorly Kervik is managing the realms fortunes. No doubt, he's spent a handsome sum trying to track down the one who killed the Lady of the Singing Spire." Trefifân was gladdened to see that his jab didn't go ignored; Lord Kervik turned a deeper shade of red and seethed.

"As the Voice of the Ladies, despite her profession, I declare Serilu's death a stain on the court."

Kervik's voice rasped. "She is *missing*, not dead."

"Is it your brain or cock that holds out hope, sir? Or perhaps you murdered her?"

Trefifân laughed. He'd never heard such wickedness from the woman's lips before. "Yap, yap, yap." The king waved his hand. "Do me the favor of leaving, woman, so Kervik may say something I might have his head for. The one attached to his neck. As the Voice of Treasure, what say you? How much is your head worth?"

Morên stood and curtsied before leaving but didn't say a word.

"Down to we men. What word on our treasury?"

"Empty but for what we borrow. But I'd rather speak of the Wraith. I believe it's real, and I believe it's in the city."

Trefifân blinked. "If you're mocking me, I might decide to end you."

"I didn't wish to speak in front of Lady Morên, though it seems my secret was less a secret than I hoped. Even your guards. You see, I visited the Lady of the Spire a week back—"

"To ease your burdens?"

Kervik squirmed in his chair. "She was a spectacular woman. She disappeared sometime after I left."

"You believe the Wraith killed her?"

Kervik stood, his face flush. He strode too close for Trefifân's comfort and leaned to whisper. "We need to speak in private. The Chamber of Muzod?"

The Chamber of Muzod was beneath them, a secret hall with seven entries so that kings, queens, generals, advisors, and spies could gather and disperse without being seen. "This had better be worth my time." He stood and spoke to the guards. "We will be reading in the library, make certain no one disturbs us."

Trefifân did his best to keep from stomping his way to the antechamber that served as a small library and an entrance to the Chamber. Several hundred books sat on shelves, and here the walls wore panels of worm-maple to warm and soften a place otherwise walled by stone. Then it came to him of a sudden: *What if this man is the Wraith?* He sauntered to the side. "Lead the way, Kervik."

"As you say, my king." The Lord slid his fingers behind a shelf, and a lever clicked. He reached high, pulling on a kerosene chandelier so that it lowered a finger or two. He grabbed a seat built into the paneled wall, and it swung open.

Kervik grabbed a small lantern for light, and Trefifân smiled as he followed the man down a spiraling stair. "So, what do you know?"

"When we reach the bottom and know we are alone."

Trefifân huffed with relief to find the room empty except for a rectangular oaken table with eight chairs and a lamp sitting in the middle. Kervik set his lantern on the table and raised the glass. He lit a tinder and then the table lamp.

Kervik glanced around like some sort of spy before nodding with satisfaction. "You and Ôlisbenar had eyes on the messenger's party?"

"We did."

Kervik pulled a scroll from beneath his jacket and held it up. "I have reason to believe the Wraith killed one of those men and entered the city. When I visited Serilu, she asked unusual questions about the fire at the gate and Ôlisbenar... you. I didn't answer, and she didn't press. I didn't think much of it until she gave me this name." He unrolled the parchment and gestured to its face.

Trefifân leaned to look, but the page was blank. "There isn't a name." And when he looked up, he stared into his own eyes as if looking into a perfect mirror, except the mirror smiled. His hand jerked to the streetsword at his waist, but the blade wouldn't leave its sheath. He realized the sword wasn't stuck; his muscles no longer obeyed his commands.

His mirror spoke in his voice. "I need you to write two letters for me." He opened a box on the table with jars of ink, held forth a quill. Trefifân's horrified hand gripped it between his fingers and scrawled the words dictated. "On this day, Merrân the Twentieth in the five hundred and sixth Year of Remembrance, I Trefifân the Fourth, pass along the illest tidings of my reign. My wife and child are murdered by a Litrâ assassin, and only by the Grace of The Named did I avoid his blade..."

Trefifân's hand swept and swayed with pristine letters even as his mind came to grips with staring at the Wraith of Qwôhar and that Trefifân the Fourth would be the last of his line.

Ôlisbenar stood watching as trebuchets lobbed stones at the barbarian wall. The effort was impressive and fruitless against the Kingdomer-built wall, but he hoped it lulled the enemy into a false sense of security. The towers and kegs of Wyvern's Flash were ready, but sneaking adequate men behind the wall without starting an additional war took time. He'd received the message of the Wraith's demise weeks ago, but he forced himself to keep calm and play the dice tight no matter his inner desires.

When a second messenger arrived from Notôlhof, he was excited to break the seal and read, hoping the king demanded swift action, any excuse to escalate the fight. What he read crushed his soul into the nether. *My wife and child are murdered...*

His first thought was to curse Litrâ and every conniving soul who'd ever been and would be born in that devil's country, but the real pain came when his mind turned to the Wraith of Qwôhar. It was a coincidence beyond reason. If the Wraith had followed the Choerkin's orders, the queen and her boy would've needed to die as well. Trefifân somehow escaped with his life and would be under so heavy a guard that killing him would be nigh impossible.

The second half of the letter confused him as well: *Bring your army home, we march on Litrâ to end them for all time, in the name of my sweet Honeybell.* Honeybell. Ôlisbenar figured he'd have to cut a couple of fingers off to match how many people knew the king's nickname for his wife. This letter was a royal declaration and a personal cry for his help. There was no choice but to follow orders, both duty and friendship demanded it.

He summoned his second and relayed the command: Stop everything, destroy the siege engines, and return to Notôlhof at once. Within half a candle, he and a hundred men rode for the king's city. It took two weeks to reach the main gates, slowed by storms and other bad luck. Once at the palace, he stormed through the halls until Lord Trêtun horse-collared him.

"Whoa, slow down."

Trêtun wasn't a match for Ôlisbenar with a sword, but if you stuck horns on his head, he'd pass for a minotaur, and his grip was steel.

Ôlisbenar shook his shoulders but couldn't break the grip. "Where is he? What happened?"

The man's barrel-deep voice rumbled. "The king found his son's throat slit in bed, and not ten paces away, the queen. A poisoned quarrel took him in the shoulder, and he ran far enough to reach his guards, but the assassin vanished. We thought the king dead for sure. His left shoulder was busted up good and the poison... He sweated and turned mushroom white, but the healers pulled him through."

"Litrâ? You're certain?"

"Certain as we can be. The crossbow's trigger is their peculiar design, and the king said the bastard looked like one."

Appearances meant nothing, but what the king believed did. "Where is he?"

"Only the Named know, but someplace safe. Nobody I know has seen him."

"Thank you." Ôlisbenar trod with measured steps, but he knew where the king hid: The Chamber of Muzod.

He passed one hall that held a secret entry, but a cluster of nobility meandered too close for him to use. Wandering down to the Council Hall might draw suspicion even with his being on the King's Council, so instead of heading for the closest doors, he skulked to the Gardens of the Named, which was a veritable labyrinth of shrubs, bushes, and flowers, until he came to the Indôl Mausoleum.

The building was an octagon, each side fifteen paces, and honored a married couple. Everyone assumed they were influential people in their day, yet nobody but The Named knew their names or why they earned a majestic tomb outside the palace. The garden was pristine, but trumpet vines overgrew the mausoleum with orange and yellow flowers that gardeners trimmed only once a year.

A statue of a man stood on the backside of the tomb, a hulking fellow carrying a head by its hair in each hand. The warrior was as unknown as the tomb's occupants, but some folks still came to pray and whisper in his ear. It wasn't the man's ear Ôlisbenar was interested in; it was the ear of the head in the right hand. He stuck a finger deep to tickle a stone eardrum until it shoved with a click, then he glanced around to make sure no one watched him. He braced his shoulder against the statue and spun it on its base.

A narrow hole dropped into a dark world lit by a single stone ensconced in the wall and glowing a soft orange. If he were a large man, he wouldn't fit. His feet found rungs as he lowered himself, and once inside, he cranked a bar that moved the statue back to its home with the help of a counterweight. The climb was damp and smelled of a root cellar, but despite bricks having shifted over the centuries, there wasn't a rat nor worm, nothing that skittered or crawled, to be seen.

He settled his feet on the floor and glanced down the black hall. Thirty strides of abject darkness lay between him and the next glowing stone where the route intersected into two choices. A left turn led to death—though he knew not what form the trap took—as did four more wrong turns, but Ôlisbenar knew the correct turns as well as any king's spy who entered from the garden.

His quick steps brought him to his goal in under three wicks, and he spotted the king hunched over a plate of food and rubbing his temples. He strode through the door, and swords rang from their sheaths around him. Six guards pointed their blades at him, and he held his hands high.

"My king."

Trefifân stood with a smile of pure delight on his face, as when they were boys and Ôlisbenar had come to play in the courtyard. "Sheath your swords. It is you, isn't it?"

"As surely as I know the first girl you desired was sweet Frelê."

"Sheath your weapons, indeed! My friend, please sit." Ôlisbenar breathed easy and sat, and the king shoved the plate of food in front of him. "I haven't been able to eat. Someone might as well." The guards returned to their stations and stood rigid.

He ignored the food. "I came as fast as I could."

"How far behind is your army?"

"There's no way to be certain. A few days, seven at the outmost."

"Good, good. You will ride north to Egremest tomorrow to oversee preparations."

Ôlisbenar hesitated but couldn't let his mind stay silent. "Are you so certain the killer was Litrâ?"

The king laughed. "I know my own eyes as well as you know your own; there was no mistaking the killer."

Ôlisbenar snorted and rubbed at his neck as he paused. He'd been certain that Trefifân believed him when he spoke of the face-changing Wraith, but wasn't so sure now. "My king, the Wraith of Qwôhar... We can't trust our eyes."

Trefifân lowered his eyes and a smirk threatened to laugh again. "Ah, my old friend, tongues and eyes are both tools for lies."

Ôlisbenar glanced at the plate of food and back to the king to find the man's eyes had turned a brilliant blue. He tried to stand, but his body didn't budge; only his head remained mobile. "Guards! Slay this man! He is not the king!" His heart fell when not one of them moved; they didn't even appear to hear him.

The king stood and meandered to stand in front of a guard, his arms outraised. "I am the Wraith of Qwôhar. I command you to kill me." He waited for several flickers as the man stood still as a boulder, then turned with a shrug for Ôlisbenar. "I tried."

His mind raged, his thoughts cluttered as the sound of a hundred horses on the race. "What have you done?"

The Wraith sat with a sigh. "Why, I did as you set me out to do. I murdered the king and left him without an heir. I even gave you peace in the south to pursue war in the north by the king's writ."

Ôlisbenar tried to interrupt, but his tongue only made clucking noises.

"You should be proud. I consider our game to be my greatest victory to date, winning by giving you precisely what you asked for. But I will have plenty of time to gloat over your failure. What I need is an answer from you. My offer is simple. Lead the Malstefnê to victory against Litrâ and become the king you pretended you wanted to be. You have three broad choices. You may refuse me outright, and I kill you here and now, a noble end for certain. You may pretend to accept my offer and betray my trust at a later date, but honestly, we have seen how well your play acting turns out. Yes? Personally, I think you should swallow the immense pride and honor that swells your throat and lead your people to victory and peace; forget about the Silone people, forget any bruise they have given your ego, forget how I defeated you, but *do not* forget about me, because I won't forget about *you*."

Ôlisbenar didn't notice the guard behind him until he felt the tip of a sword pressing against his lower back. With a single shove, his years of service to the king would end with a gut wound. His throat loosened and he cleared his throat. "The sword suggests my answer is urgent."

"Indeed, if you wish to die now, now is the best time for an answer. Whether you betray me later is an answer for later."

"I will live."

The Wraith clapped his hands, and the sword pointed at Ôlisbenar's kidney went away. "Good! Here is what will happen. I will name you Lord General, making you the obvious heir to the throne. You will ride north to take command and the southern army will follow; you will catch the Litrâ flat-footed. In a week or two, poor King Trefifân will disappear and the kingdom will be yours to rescue."

The Wraith's plan secured the crown for Ôlisbenar with near certainty, and he swore to himself that he *would* have his revenge. But he also understood that the Wraith knew his vow. "I understand."

"Do you? After the king disappears, I don't. I could be anywhere at any time. Confess your desire to strike south to your most trusted advisor, and it might be my ear. Forget the south, and it will forget the Malstefnê."

"I understand." It galled him, but revenge might not be worth his life or a war. The kingdom would be frail and vulnerable to outsiders and civil war.

Trefifân stood and turned for the hall with his guards flanking him. "Good. I will prepare royal writs and proclamations."

But he couldn't let him walk away without a flicker of defiance. "What sort of demon are you?"

The king turned, but he was no longer Trefifân, nor was he human at all. His face was a swirl of shifting flesh, the shape and color of his eyes ever-shifting. "I am the worst kind of demon, a lowly man." His chuckle followed him down the hall, but it wasn't a sound the king had made before.

Ôlisbenar sat in the Chamber of Mozud staring after the Wraith long after the sound of footsteps disappeared. He glanced at the plate of beef and greens, then forked a bite, gazing at the pink in the middle. In truth, even as a boy, he'd never dreamed of being king. It wasn't his place. But this didn't mean he'd make a bad king.

He stuck the meat between his teeth and chewed.

Forty-Eight

Faithless Facing

If you wish to convince a righteous man he is evil when he is not, and knows it, begin with some past evil, a truth or believable lie, by his kin past. The righteous by nature, if weak, will strip the bones of their backs bare in penance.

—*Codex of Sol*

Ivin stood atop the wall, staring south instead of north, thanks to the departure of the Malstefnê army. It had been four weeks since boulders and Wyvern's Flash stopped slamming the walls, and though he assumed this was the work of the Face, there was no confirmation of any sort. Men filled sapper tunnels and the craters the thundersticks left behind, and they did their best with the damage to the wall, but a couple of sections needed stones replaced, and that would fall on Helmveliner shoulders. Kingdomers were already cutting stone, but it'd take time to see the repairs finished.

No matter his confident words, folks didn't feel secure to travel back to the valley to reclaim the land, and no one who had fled south had returned. In fact, more moved south in a trickle, heading for a land plentiful with game, rivers full of fish, and trees filled with nuts and fruits.

Ivin grew bored of standing around waiting, and his patience ran thin. He planned on traveling to Foggy Vale within the week in order to strike south to Green Mountain with an army, but he'd prefer to do so knowing what happened in Notôlhof. He could've left a week prior if he'd assumed the north secure and pushed warriors to the march. Or maybe it was a boon to rest the anxieties of men before rushing them onward to another war.

Leto Ravinrin stepped to his side, startling him.

"For a warrior, you're light of foot." The Ravinrin was a good man, even if he was poor at hiding his affection for Kinesee. The marriage strained the comradery and friendship that burgeoned after the Battle of Tarmujon, but Leto grew comfortable around him, at least when Kinesee wasn't nearby. He'd turned from a boy into a strong man the past couple of couple years, but he kept his face shaved.

Leto chuckled then breathed deep of the morning air with a smile. "Every dawn is beautiful when you aren't staring at an army."

"Aye, no lie there."

"How in the hells did you manage it? What made the Tek turn tail?"

Ivin wanted nothing more than to deflect that conversation. "I didn't see them running, did you?"

"No, no I did not. But they weren't moving slow neither. Was it some threat from the Helelindin? The Kingdomers? How?"

"There's no way to know. I'd wager the war to their north grew grave, realigning their priorities."

"All the clan lords nod and smile when you say that, but not Morik. Not Kinesee. Not Roplin. They know the truth. Hells, more than half the clan lords don't believe the story."

This was the first that Ivin heard his story wasn't being swallowed whole. It wasn't like he knew the full truth himself. "They're welcome to their theories."

"All that time in those tents negotiating... Most assume you struck a deal under the table with one or both of our neighbors. Why not admit it?"

He turned to face Leto. "Because it isn't true."

"True or not, there're rumbles of making you king of the Silone."

Ivin choked and coughed, turned to face south again. "King? Forges, I don't want to be Warlord, it was a better name for my horse."

Leto laughed and leaned beside him. "It's the talk, even if they won't let you hear it."

"The Silone don't need a king. If you hear that bandied about again, you stomp on it."

"Oh, I will. I promise. You claimed the title Warlord—"

"They foisted it on me."

"Like they foisted a bride?"

Now they'd touched on the heart of the matter. Ivin turned toward him, but the Ravinrin kept his eyes facing south. He felt for the man; denied love wasn't a knife easy to swallow. It was something they shared. "I know you loved her—"

"I did and you don't. But I'm not here because of Kinesee."

Ivin wasn't sure anymore of his own feelings. What he felt was different than with Meliu, but it wasn't less. "I care for her deeply. We will—"

"I came here to let you know one thing: If the clans seek to name you king, I... the Ravinrin will not support the move."

He spun on his heel and strode away with long, heavy strides. Ivin muttered to himself, "Good." The world around him fell back into tranquility, but his mind whirled. The clans dropped the title of Warlord on him without warning, or he might've declined the honor. King? No way in the Forges did he want such a thing.

A girl's voice broke his thoughts. "Warlord Choerkin."

Ivin turned to see Deelee striding his way with the bright eyes of a child at play. She wore the white holy robes of a postulant, and guards glanced her way but didn't bar her. "What is it, Deelee?"

The girl bounced to his side. He'd seen Sedut stalking the walls once or twice before the fires raged but didn't know any postulants remained with her. "Missing Meliu? I am."

He groaned. "No. I've bigger worries."

"The sparkle in her eyes, the curve of her lips... I might be the only man alive who knows her lips better than you."

Ivin's gut cinched, and he turned to the girl. The child's body stared up at him, but the face was Meliu's, and she winked. Shivers ran his spine. He turned to gaze south rather than give Ulrikt's Face the satisfaction of a greater reaction. "I assume things went as planned in Notôlhof?"

Lord Priest Ulrikt's voice replied. "As *we* planned, not as Ôlisbenar planned."

Ivin turned back, but he was no longer a child. He raised his eyes to meet Ulrikt's face. He balked at his next words, startled that none of the guards reacted to the man. "What does that mean?"

"A trap set will snare a coyote or a hare and can as easily kill a king as make one—words you would do well to remember. The Malstefnê will ride to victory in the north with the combined might of their armies; I imagine you have at least a year before you need to worry about them again, if then."

"Tek Malobund? Others?"

"Malôbund is a kingdom broken, devastated by their defeat. It will take time before they threaten our borders with more than raids."

"Raids won't be much of an issue with folks staying behind the wall and moving south. I guess nothing is keeping me from killing you."

Ulrikt laughed as he turned his back to the parapet and leaned, relaxed as an old friend waiting to share a keg of ale. "You could try, and if you fail, I disappear. Difficult to use a man you can't find."

Ivin matched his relaxed pose. "Me use you? A man might as well stick a hot coal in his teeth to light a fire." But something else caught his attention; the man didn't threaten him. "You wouldn't try to kill me if I attacked?"

"No. If I wanted you dead, you would've been. Long ago."

"On the Watch? Like my father?"

Ulrikt groaned with a theatrical roll of his head. "I told you, I did not kill Kotin. If the monk had tried to poison *you,* your father might be alive now."

Ivin puzzled the pieces. "Because you would've stopped him from killing me. Why me? Am I in the *Codex of Sol*, some piece of prophecy, some part of its bloody destiny?"

Ulrikt's voice changed, and the tone brought bile to Ivin's gut, a tear to his eye, and it took all his strength not to punch the bastard in the nose. Kotin's voice. "Oh, my boy. You've grown confused. Destiny is written in history books, not the stars, and prophecy is a map to a dozen destinations. And you, who's the right spittin' image of your beautiful mother, are a waypoint on that map."

Meris' prophecy sure the hells felt like more, but he was in no mood to thrash that history. "So, you won't kill a waypoint?"

Ulrikt's voice shifted into the nasal drone of Lord Oracle Meris, and for the first time, Ivin wondered if the man wasn't inside his head. "It is so much more, my child. You are *needed.* You are the Warlord Choerkin. I will not kill you for the same reason you won't try to kill me; the people need the both of us. You are the face of the clans, and I am..." His smile was broad and toothy, inviting a fist.

But all Ivin gave him was words. "The Face."

Ulrikt straightened and rolled his shoulders. "Indeed. I must take my leave, and you have much to attend. We will speak again."

Ivin watched the Lord Priest's back pass down the wall, and still, not a single guard reacted to a man thought dead, a man in lord priest's robes, a man they hated. But his thoughts slithered back to Tokodin and Kotin, the poison and the dice. He didn't take the Face's word on Tokodin's guilt, but one thing was clear. "You were there. Who were you?"

Ivin awoke in the deep of night, all the darker because of the lack of fire, a moonless sky, and his mood. He stared at a ceiling he couldn't see, his heart racing. Kinesee's breaths deepened, and a hand stroked his chest.

"What is it?"

"Nothing. A dream. Go back to sleep."

"You first."

He laughed and sat up. "If we're going to sit awake, we may as well have a fire." He slipped bare feet to the cool stone floor and lit the fireplace with a Kingdomer firestick. "I dreamed of my father dying."

"We've got a fire, now come back to bed."

He sat motionless, hunched on the balls of his feet. "The Face of Ulrikt was there when my Father died. Do you know what that means?"

"Come back to bed and tell me."

He stood but made his way to the door, opened it a crack. "Harlik. Wake Roplin and the Lady Choerkin. We need to talk."

By the time the door closed, Kinesee was already slipping into a gown. "Should we call for food?"

Berries and cheese arrived a wick before a groggy-eyed Roplin and Inisfer, but they weren't more than flickers into Ivin's tale of the Face and the Malstefnê war before his brother was wide-eyed, and it wasn't much longer before he bore a sustained glare.

"It'd be unseemly to kick the shit out of the Warlord in front of his beautiful bride, but I'm considering it."

Inisfer stared. "The tales of the Face have whispered through Istinjoln for more than a century."

"A demon."

"No, a priest dedicated to guarding the Church and Lord Priest from treason."

The ramifications of this statement made Ivin prefer it was a demon. "If generations of Faces served the Lord Priests, there's nothing to say there isn't more than one. Ulrikt could be the Face, one of gods knows how many."

Inisfer shook her head. "The traditional tale was that every Lord Priest had only one."

"Even then... There'd be the Face from the previous Lord Priest, and another in training for the successor. With my modest math skills, I suggest there could be three."

She bowed her head. "Ulrikt ruled for decades, the Face of Sadevu could well have died. Being able to change your appearance is a gift from the gods I can't imagine, the skill and power of the prayers... the gift would have to be rare."

Roplin tugged his beard and grunted. "One, two, three... a hundred. You're dancing around the real reason we're here."

Ivin stood and paced in front of the fire. "Who was there when Kotin died? Kotin and Tokodin are dead."

"Rikis, Pikarn, you, Eliles, me... Inisfer."

"She arrived after he was poisoned."

"Servants."

"Joslin." It felt good to name the darkness in his dream aloud. "Name another."

Roplin sputtered. "I... Well... I'd say a dozen on the periphery—"

"The day I left for the Fost, Joslin served breakfast. He was there to listen to the fight we had."

"Proves nothing."

"He showed Tokodin to the garderobe, and the monk turns up dead."

"Holy hells."

"And who was serving us drinks at every godsdamned meeting we had outside the town of Inster? He was privy to every word we spoke. Then, when was the last time you saw the boy?"

Roplin sat in silence, staring at his hands. "Winterhome is the last time I recall, and with the chaos of them days... I don't even remember. I just assumed the boy's parents took him away when the shit turned to blood."

"Aye. I never gave him a thought, not once."

"The Face would kill a child?"

"He murdered a king, Tokodin, maybe our father... There's untold blood on the bastard's hands. There is nothing beyond a person who unleashes demons."

Roplin glanced at Inisfer and back to Ivin. "And you used this demon to kill a king, what does that make you, brother?"

Ivin licked his lips, uncomfortable with any answer. "Pragmatic." He breathed deep and weighed his words. Inisfer was his brother's wife, the woman who saved Rikis and tried to save Kotin, but she was also a priestess. "He's useful to us, and I'm useful to him for the time being, but at some point the coin will flip. We need to be ready to kill him when it does."

He looked to each of their faces as they shared awkward glances, and Kinesee spoke first. "How in the world do you kill someone who can be anybody?"

Inisfer said, "Whoever the Face is, they wield the prayers of the gods in a way I wouldn't have believed. Even if you know who they are..."

Roplin pressed his palms to his eyes and groaned. "We've faced longer odds before, and yet here we sit. When the day comes, we find the demon and kill him."

Ivin smiled at his brother's optimism, but his thoughts trailed to his conversation with Meliu and how so many of the prophecies ended with the Lord Choerkin dead. "Either we kill him, or he kills me, that's the short of it. But until that time, we need to move south."

Kinesee said, "I'll have my things prepared to travel."

"You can go so far as Forest's Gate, stay there with Alu and Tudwan."

Her piercing stare suggested this hadn't been her plan, but she didn't argue... yet. "Situations change."

"Some remain set in stone."

He smiled. She smiled.

They sat in silence for a wick before Roplin stood and laughed. "Hells, brother! Look on the sunny side. If you're headin' for Green Mountain, you might not live long enough for Ulrikt's Face to kill you."

Forty-Nine

Shifty-Eyed Answer

The fool's wisdom is to understand the jester that they are. The jester's gift is to point out the fools around them. The greatest fool is one who believes they are above being mocked, for a fool incapable of laughing at themself is lost.

—*Codex of Sol*

Jinbin stared with a blank face. "You want me to pray?"

"You weren't far from the priesthood."

"Sixty scars prove how far. I walked away before Sixty-one without attempting the trial."

Eliles tried to imagine the pain others suffered in the trials, but as difficult as imagining the pain was, understanding how they endured the torture was nigh on impossible. Part of her still believed she was weak for having suffered only one lash. "Pray for Light."

"Why?"

"I need to see if I can end your prayer. I'd ask our friends in the stars, but not a one has shown their face since the Frog burned." Eliles figured if she could interfere with the Face's prayer that the face they wore might shift, shimmer, or end to reveal the person's true self.

"You're chasing the Face. What if I'm him?"

"Her."

"How do you know that?"

"I don't, not really. But Fedenu of Ulmor intimated it. She is an old priestess from Skywatch. A friend." She grinned, not wanting to explain any further. "Fewer questions, more prayers."

He bowed his head and a flicker later a ball of Light appeared above his head. Eliles drew on the Sliver of Star as she learned when manipulating the Elements around the garden, then willed a vacuum of Light. When the Light above Jinbin's head persisted, she willed a vacuum of all Elemental Energy. She sensed the lack of energy around him, but it didn't affect his prayer in the least. This confirmed that the power of his prayer came directed from the gods, not his surroundings.

Sometimes you need to give it too much of what it desires most. She released the vacuum and focused Elemental Light on Jinbin. Nothing happened at first, but when she pushed—

Jinbin collapsed to his knees, and the Light disappeared with a flash. "What the hells did you do?"

"Did it hurt?"

"No. It was more like... If I was carrying something heavy and you dropped more weight on it. Except weight isn't the right word. Fatigue isn't right, either."

"I sent a surge of Light into your body."

"If it's so easy to stop a prayer..."

"It's easy because of the Sliver of Star." But the notion of overpowering prayers in this manner did raise questions. "Do you remember how often an adherent did well in practice but struggled in the trials?"

"Are you suggesting high priests stifled prayers to make sure we were lashed?"

"No, I'm just… I don't know. But the main thing is it worked. How are you with prayers of Life?"

Jinbin laughed as he stood. "I wouldn't have made it past bare feet."

"The answer is in my eyes. Come here and look at my eyes." She'd tried with a mirror earlier in the week, but no matter what she did, she couldn't get her eye color to change. Her eyes and features changed of their own accord in the past without her knowing it, but creating the effect proved difficult.

She stood statue-still and focused Life, imagining her eyes green. "Are my eyes green? Any different at all?"

"No."

She drew more Life and strove for a change more extreme, the picture of herself in her mind with red eyes. A pressure built in her sockets that bordered on pain. "Anything?"

"You've got a violet tint."

"I was trying for blood-red." She sighed and released the energy.

Jinbin shrugged. "Well, at least you changed."

"If I understood how and what the Face does, I might counter it. Technique. Decades of training. Or maybe without the assistance of the gods, it isn't possible."

"Maybe it isn't Life."

She mastered Fire, but Spirit remained a strength throughout her training. She focused on her eyes with Spirit and Jinbin's head tilted back. "Red?"

"Like pools of blood."

She released the energy. "It doesn't make sense. Not a lick." She prayed for Life and Spirit and focused on her nose, aiming for bigger. If it worked, she hoped it didn't stay that way. "Anything?"

"Where?"

"My nose."

He stared for flickers and the pressure built like it did in her eyes, but it was beginning to ache.

His eyes widened. "Stop! Stop."

She released the Elements in a panic, and her voice carried sharp nasal tones. "Is it huge?"

"No, but it was turning red and swelling like it might pop."

She grabbed a hand mirror; her nose was beet red and swollen, but the inflammation was shrinking. "I'm not doing that again."

He sighed, eyes wandering. "Might the Face have an artifact like the Sliver of Star?"

This was a possibility Eliles hadn't gotten around to considering. "Perhaps, but I think I would notice a source of power like that. The Face's change is so perfect that it fools my senses. If you walk up behind me and I hear you coming, I can reach out and feel you. Know it's you. The Face feels like whoever they look like... and they sound like them. How is that possible?"

"Prayers of air can mimic voices. When they shift their face, they shift the vocal cords?"

"Have you ever heard someone so good with prayers that they can do that with Air?"

"Dekore of Pinth could mimic most every instructor. He was in trouble every other day until they whipped the comedian out of him. But that was a few words here and there, not some long speech."

"So, Air, Spirit, Life... All of them at the same time. Possible?"

"You're asking a man who made it to his tenth year; how the Twelve Hells would I know? You'd be better off asking an elder, Fedenu of Ulmor, you said?"

Eliles pinched her lips tight, uncertain of what to say. "She is hiding in the stars with the others."

His hand went to his hip. "You lied just now."

"I didn't. Not exactly. You must swear two things, tell no one, and don't laugh."

"Can I promise not to laugh until I'm drunk? Once I've been drinking, sometimes I can't help it."

"So long as you keep your yap shut." She inhaled a deep breath. "The gray-haired priestess, I think she's a dragon."

He blinked once, but the second didn't come for several flickers. He leaped in the air. "Ha! I told that Choerkin it wasn't a demon in the Fire! Haha! That bastard owes me a lot of grapes! Woo!"

Eliles smirked. Given a hundred guesses, this reaction wouldn't have been one. "I said, think. Now settle it down."

"You talked to a godsdamned dragon! Gods, girl!"

"I think the tower of Fire *invited* her."

His smile and voice remained giddy. "So ask her how the Face does it."

"I did. She told me I needed to figure it out."

"Just like a dragon, I suppose. All cryptic and scary."

"She's sweet, albeit a bit cryptic. Come on. We need to talk to folks. I think I know enough to expose the Face."

They strode through the door and headed straight to the Salty Frog. Everybody was back and working on repairs, from Feru and her husband Voelim tuckpointing the mortar in the stonework to Poluk and Markile heading up the effort to finish pulling out damaged wood while others gathered planks from sacrificial buildings. She sauntered over to Artus and Reinus, the men standing next to a barrel of drinking water.

"Gentlemen, we're going to have ourselves a trial."

Both men stared at her. "You been hittin' my whiskey, girl?"

Reinus said, "There's no lord for a judge."

Eliles nodded and figured she may as well break the worse news. "It'll be a public trial."

Artus' eyes were wide. "Set me as the lord with Choerkin blood."

"No, they wouldn't believe there was going to be a trial in that case."

"A public trial makes a jury out of everyone. There're more priests than us islanders. There's no way we win. Do you even know what you're asking for?"

"I read up on what I could find. There's an arbiter, a neutral party; the ax, who prosecutes the charges; the shield, who defends the accused; and witnesses, none of whom get a vote on the charge of guilt or innocence."

"Aye, so you know the ending: Reinus loses."

Eliles focused energies and hammered both men with them; neither flinched, and neither showed a sign of being the Face. "We invite Temeru as the Ax, and she brings her witnesses. More priests will testify than our people, which will bring the numbers close. She may not realize that, as the Church doesn't hold court in this manner."

"So your idea is to find him innocent by trickery?"

"No, my idea is to expose the Face. Whether it's pride, arrogance, or curiosity, there's no way in the Twelve Hells the Face doesn't show up for this trial. Right in front of everyone, I reveal the deception."

"Jinbin's part of this?"

"Only in so much that she proved she could disrupt my prayer for Light."

Reinus poured a glass of water from the tap and drank. "And if it turns out you can't reveal the Face?"

Artus said, "You're found guilty or not, dependin' on how many votes we got. And if guilty, it's a choice 'tween loppin' yer head off or Eliles here defying the court to spare you. It'd look bad to defy your own court."

Jinbin said, "Not a soul on this island could touch her unless the dragon is on the Face's side."

Artus' eyes bugged, and his face turned red through his beard. "You told this beer-swiller about the dragon?"

"I didn't know I wasn't supposed to, but we've more important issues."

"Like my head," said Reinus.

"Like your head. Reinus, I'm not going to force you into the trial, it's up to you. But it's the only way we could get everyone together to witness the Face. But not for a few weeks. I want to practice and see if maybe I can glean more hints and clues from... from conversations I've had."

"So long as you swear to me that you won't let 'em have me, I'll play along."

Artus said, "You're talkin' all but a civil war on this tiny island if it doesn't work."

Eliles planted her feet. "It'll work."

"And if it does, what then? Kill her?"

"If there isn't another way, yes."

Silence as they eyed one another, until Reinus blurted, "Dragon?"

Eliles smiled. "I was really hoping you missed that."

Fifty

Leaving Memories Behind

A sedentary mind and sedentary soul
wanders the world ensnared in body active,
reflexive, decisive, and defective.
Sediment, soil, or smoke rider,
The Fighter, the Runner, and the Hider
Bound to follow the eyes white without sight.
Who Falls, who Flies, who lives and dies.
Are but
The perspective of a fisherman on his dock,
Gauging whether the waters lap or he floats away.

—*Tomes of the Touched*

The Nebuhol Pinch was a short stretch of water between the disputed Emulên Isles and the western shores of the Gulf of Tomulok. Sailors didn't name it Pinch because there wasn't plenty of water between the masses of land; it was the number of Boborun sails in this region of the gulf. Anyone smuggling goods around the Emulên Isles was subject to being boarded, cargo seized, ship commandeered, captain executed, crew enslaved, and often all of the above. To make the Pinch more exciting, far as the Boboru were concerned, anyone who hadn't paid the proper taxes was a smuggler no matter the ship's port of departure nor its heading.

The Contessa's fleet gathered within half a horizon of one another on the first day of sailing north, and on the second day, the pennant of Mostul Ûbar rose on every mast: a field of blue with nine stars, eight white and the third star from the mast red. The stars represented the Free Cities, and Mostul Ûbar was the third city along the coast when sailing south from the equator.

Solineus stood on the aft deck much of the first day staring at the horizon with a fareye, nervous as the Twelfth Hell that one of the Boboru ships would come for them. They never did. By the second day, he didn't pay attention to enemy sails and wondered whether his benefactor was friendly with the Boboru after all.

The Contessa had two rules for his men, stay quiet and stay out of sight, and to make sure of this Polênu sequestered them below deck. Even Adinvan, which didn't please his father one lick. Solineus and Sîu were the only ones allowed on deck during the day, and if a Boborun ship grew close, the Contessa ushered Sîu into the captain's cabin and shoved him down below so his father could gripe at him. The Boboru hailed them once but never boarded, so whatever Polênu's relationship with the Boboru was, it didn't include turning them in for a reward.

Late in the second day, he stood staring at a row of Boborun flags to their east when Polênu arrived at his side. Siû stood and joined them a flicker later, unwilling to let them speak without hearing the conversation, even if she didn't understand the words. It was awkward. More awkward considering one of his goals on this journey was to meet his young son and his mother.

The Contessa kept arm's length from his side, whether out of respect for Sîu's jealousy or some other motive he'd yet to glean. "You're looking the wrong direction."

"Which way should I be looking?"

"Northwest. The mouth of the Mâbuhon River will be visible before nightfall. It would be best for you to row for shore as soon as possible, so our stopping doesn't raise suspicions."

"This was a mighty easy journey."

She laughed. "You understand so little of these waters."

"The flag of Mostul Ûbar is so potent?"

"Take a look around the deck, Silone. What do you see?"

He saw sailors. He saw ropes. He saw sails. "I don't see anything outside the usual on a ship."

"You don't, do you?"

He blinked, wondering what sort of fool he was making of himself. "I wish I knew."

"Every man on deck is black, from the Free Cities or the Ôlfindarâ Islands. If I had even a half dozen of you white northerners prancing around out here, the Boboru would swarm our ship no matter what flag I flew. They'd assume you were pale-skinned Gorô and we'd be running or in a fight."

Her point was obvious once she stated it. "Black, white, blue. Guess I never bothered to consider it. Sailing with Luxuns maybe prepared me for damned near anything."

"A rare privilege to sail with Luxuns."

"Captain Intœño of the Entiyu Emoño, a fine man."

"I've heard the name and seen the ship. You are an interesting barbarian, Solineus Mikjehemlut."

"If you're impressed by Luxuns, I've tales of demons, gods, and even a dragon."

She cocked her head and stared. "I'm sorry that those stories will go untold. Get your people together. You'll be heading for shore within a candle."

The Contessa turned and strode away, leaving him to Sîu's glare. "She is an admirable woman."

That wasn't close to what he'd expected to hear, and he searched for sarcasm in the tones of her voice but didn't find any. "She is something."

"You still think you know her? From before?"

"I don't think, I know. She either lies well or she's forgotten me."

"I know she lies well, so it could be both."

"Fair enough."

They rousted the men below deck, and everyone was armored and packed by the time the sun slipped into a red horizon of silhouetted trees. The anchor splashed, the chain rattled, and within wicks, a dinghy bobbed in the bay. Four of the Contessa's sailors climbed down a rope ladder to take the oars and a dozen Silone warriors followed with Adinvan and Sîu shimmying down right before Solineus swung his leg over the rail.

His legs swayed on the rung as his fingers clutched the rail, and Polênu propped herself above him, hands close to his as she leaned close. "Someday the both of us won't be so busy."

Her face was beautiful even in the dim light of the fading day, tinted red. "Is that an invitation?"

"No." She stood straight and turned, taking five strides before turning back with a wink. "I *do* know you. That's your invitation."

Solineus watched the woman until she disappeared through her cabin's door, then climbed to the dinghy to sit beside Sîu. He sat silent as sailors shoved them from the *Silver Willow* before putting oars to water. But his tongue couldn't stay quiet for long. "Now that's an evil woman."

Adinvan snorted. "Damned glad you're comin' around to seein' things my way—or you meant that as a compliment."

"She got us where we needed to go."

Adinvan snorted a second time, and Sîu sulked or glowered, it was hard to tell in the light. Either way, it was a hushed trip to shore.

Solineus slumbered on rolling waves, a peculiar irony since he knew he slept on land for the first time since the island of Toltûk. He opened his eyes to the expectation of a blue-gray world to find himself wrong. Not that he wasn't where he expected, but the blues were faded and the grays were closer to white.

"Hello, my love."

"Can't you let a man sleep? I'm on a warm beach beneath the stars!"

"Hush. There isn't time." The tone in her voice clamped his mouth more than her words. So much for levity.

"What is it? Kinesee?"

"Come tomorrow, you will find a Helelindin man who captains a riverboat."

"Aye, a riverboat heading west against the current?"

"East."

"East!"

"Tell him his wife is with child and the baby is not his. Tell him, *Nedarô*."

His mind pondered her conniving ways. "The hells, you say. I'm going to see my son."

"I didn't say otherwise. We must hurry. You must hurry. The White Lion is coming."

There wasn't time for a question nor witty comeback, not even a burning kiss on his brow. He awoke staring at the stars with Adinvan snoring paces away, and Sîu curled beside him. He may or may not have dozed after, but it sure the hells wasn't the good night's sleep he'd hoped.

The dawn cast its golden rays before he would've preferred, and he rolled to his hands and knees with a groan. "White Lion." He rubbed his crusted, burning eyes half expecting to see some great feline loping from the forest to eat him, but there were only trees and birds. And Sîu staring at him.

"You didn't sleep well."

"No. Father, what color is Sôl?"

Adinvan stoked a small fire with driftwood. "I can't say as I've ever heard. I've seen his image depicted with red gold before in some shrine somewhere. He's Sol; folks have cast his image in every metal, I reckon."

"Ever hear of him being white?"

"Not once, but I didn't sit through so many prayer sessions as to know for sure."

Sîu said, "Why do you ask of your king of gods?"

He wasn't in the mood to share the tale of the Lady in front of a group. "I had a dream. A White Lion is coming and with him a sense of foreboding."

"You got me, boy. I haven't even seen a real lion, like them with manes?"

"Only ones I've seen walk on two legs. And talk." Solineus jumped to his feet, but the burst of energy was more for show than a demonstration of his vigor. "We need to hurry. We've got a man to meet."

Adinvan glanced from his fire and a fish stuck on a stick. "A man. What happened to a lion? And I'm eating my fish either way."

"We eat, then we head for the river."

A malaise had come over the group, not just him; he could see it in the way everyone moved, slow and measured as if their bones creaked with rust. Ships were uncomfortable, and the food oft times terrible, but what lay in front of them was a long godsdamned walk. The only one with a bounce in their stride was Sîu, and he reckoned that was because the Contessa of Mostul Ûbar was horizons away by now.

They ate a breakfast of bread and a variety of fish, whatever they could set spear to, and they reached the edge of the river well before midday. It was then that he felt the pull of Kinesee's pearl, and he feared for her, that the White Lion might be after her instead of him, but she was just checking on him. It also felt like she was due west of his location, and from his recollection of maps that didn't make much sense. And that made him nervous; what if his memory or the maps were wrong? By his reckoning, the Sebedil Helelindin should control the Mâbuhon River, the same folks the Silone had a treaty with, the same folks Kinesee had just met. If his reckoning was wrong, arrows might skewer them before getting a chance to speak. Hope rested with a fisherman's boat going the wrong way and a philandering wife, but there was nothing to do for his lingering doubts except to keep walking.

A couple of times during the day, their route took turns, and they couldn't see the river; these were nervous wicks spent hurrying to regain a view. He didn't know the Lady's game, but if he'd missed Ilpen and the Ears team years ago, things might've gone even worse than they did. Then night came without seeing a soul. Every watch had one man whose job was to keep his eyes on the river, but the only thing that arrived was frogs. Boisterous, croaking, sleep-depriving frogs and their songs to make him realize how quiet the ships had been.

Come morning they were eating fish again, a trout of some sort with speckled skin and too cursed many bones, but it tasted well enough when filling an empty gut. Solineus was picking his teeth with one of the ribs when the nose of a boat rounded a bend in the river. He leaped to his feet and tossed the bone as he trotted to shore and hailed the steersman in Edan. "A blessed morning, friend."

The man's Edan held a peculiar accent, but Solineus understood his every word. "Blessed are the waters to feed our families. What brings a foreign man to our river?"

The boat was flat bottomed and fifty feet long, set with a single sail, and had half a dozen oars to either side. A cabin stood on either end of the vessel, and long arms on either side held rolled nets. At least twenty Helelindin crewed the vessel, but he couldn't pick a single one as the captain.

Solineus figured a little fibbing wouldn't hurt. "We are Silone needing to reach Holelorin to see King Sebedil as set out in the Treaty of Simâm. Are you the captain?"

A lanky man with his hair pulled into a knot atop his head stepped from the aft cabin. He covered his eyes from the morning sun as he stared at them. "I am captain Jebuhûk."

"I've a message for you..." He stopped to stare at his toes; what the hells had the Lady gotten him into this time? "Your wife is pregnant?"

The man's head cocked and his chest puffed. "Yes. Who are you?"

"I've a message. The child isn't yours. Nedarô."

Fishers glanced at one another as the captain's face went blank. The boat floated downriver unabated without another word, rounding the bend and disappearing with the captain staring daggers.

Adinvan strode to his side. "What the hells was that?"

"I told him his wife carried another man's baby."

"The hells, you say."

"That's exactly what I said."

"Is it true?"

Solineus shrugged. "I reckon so, but no idea..."

Rhythmic shouts came from around the bend, and the fishing boats rear now came up the river as its nose until it sat offshore. Jebuhûk fumed. "That demon's son, Nedarô! I knew his intentions, but she denied... How do you know this, foreign man? How?"

"For passage west, I'll tell you a tale of dream visions."

The captain bellowed orders, and oarsmen turned the boat to bring them straight at the shore. Sîu stepped to his side. "If your dreams of a man and his wife are true, what of the White Lion?"

"I've little doubt they're true; the question is what the hells it all means."

Fifty-One

Reunion at the Gate

The Bevedâis Confederacy first battled the Dontupûor in 472 E.C. under the reign of Exendâhok the Third. The arrogant king eschewed the aid of the Pantheon of Sol, and by 475 E.C. half their gods were defeated and the king dead. This victory began the Dontupûor ascension.

—*Oxeum Codex*

Forest's Gate wasn't so much a village or city as it was a sprawling encampment spread thin across several square horizons of cleared land. If you asked anyone where you were, they'd all answer the same, but the region had dispersed into small communities with different gathering places and personalities. Farmers, hunters, fishers, trappers, and some folks took their hand at panning for gold in the multitude of streams coming down from the Dragonspans.

Ivin visited ten months earlier when it was a village of only a couple thousand souls, so he knew where to find the founders of Forest's Gate. Danwek Bulubar and his people had hewn and split the first logs of the first buildings along the banks of a stream glorified by naming it the Renwerk River, which meant Southern Werk River, blending the old tongue with new. Forget that the Werk River was thousands of horizons north.

Ivin didn't need to find Danwek, all he needed to do was get close, and every clan-blood in the area sought him out. Every horizon of the journey, he faced questions of why the Warlord Choerkin departed the north for the south with an army on his heels, and Danwek was no different.

Ivin slid from his saddle and clasped the Bulubar in a hug, then pushed him back to appraise him. "Hairier than ever, and your hand never did grow back. Life down south is treating you fine."

The man snorted and glanced at the stub of his right hand. "I see the Malstefnê didn't manage to kill ya. When the hells are they gonna get a damned thing right? If'n you ain't careful, you'll have crown pressed on your head one of these days."

Leto groaned behind him, but Ivin ignored the latter comment. "Events unfolded better than expected, I admit."

Danwek bowed to Ivin's entourage. "Lady Kinesee, Lord Leto, Mountain Lord Morik, it is good to see you all hale and well." He turned back to Ivin. "Every word from the north was of an inevitable war. Then they tell me the Malstefnê fled the field... What, in truth, happened up there?"

"In truth, someone assassinated the Malstefnê king, and we became an afterthought. And my beautiful bride managed to open trade between Helmveline and the Helelindin." No lies, just not the full story. Hells, he didn't know the whole story.

"Trade! I'd heard the rumor... that's a fine thing, Lady Kinesee. You do your father proud."

"Thank you, my lord. I look forward to telling him soon."

Danwek blinked and coughed. "We've word from him?"

"He sent a pigeon some time ago and planned to come up a river to find us, but he's in that direction now." She pointed east toward the Gorotan, and Danwek pursed his lips.

"How the hells do you know that?"

Morik said, "She knows."

Ivin said, "She just does. Trust it. Any word from Green Mountain?"

"Lord Polus, Bîdorik, and High Priestess Meliu made it safe, but you likely knew that. We got conflicting words after.

Disappearances. Last I heard their scouts were searching for Yellow-Eye camps, but it's been a week or two since I've had a trustworthy word. Things have been beehive crazy around here, and that might be generous, so I might've missed some news. Any word from Foggy Vale?"

"We rode straight past them; our route is south, and the detour would've cost us a day."

"You still believe them folks are alive?"

"With slavers, they're worth more alive than dead... which is an unsettling reason for hope." Ivin licked his lips, none too thrilled to be giving orders. "Look, I know things are busier than a blacksmith before a war, but Roplin has plenty on his hands at the wall, and the clans overrun Foggy Vale as well, but I'm going to put it on you to keep communications between these three regions fresh as can be. Daily riders, even if there's godsdamned nothing to say. I'm going to try to get riders moving from Green Mountain to her weekly and word needs passed on. Got me?"

He grunted. "Aye, it'll be done."

"Good. If the Forges set a fire, it burns hot and fast."

Ivin turned to Kinesee and Leto. "You two go find Alu and Tudwan."

Kinesee eyeballed him. "I'm not staying here, I'm going with you."

"Green Mountain is no place for the Warlord's wife."

"And just where do you think I'm safer from the... Them. In the middle of this camp or the middle of your army?"

He sighed and bowed his head. "Just go find your sister." He hoped that Alu would talk some sense into Kinesee's head. "I need to speak with Danwek and other clan-blood, no need to bore you with them details."

Kinesee reined her horse, but Ivin wasn't sure whether the cluck was a command for her horse or Leto. Either way, they both followed her lead as if chained to her will.

Danwek grinned. "She's changed and stayed the same."

Ivin snorted. "She spits the hells like an angel. Now, has anybody down here dug in, worked on a fortification?"

"Speakin' of someone who doesn't change—no, nothin' of the sort. Folks aren't settling. The Kingdomers started laying down road the flicker they arrived, and lots of folks make Forest's Gate a stopover, not a home. Villages are sprouting like weeds along the road already."

"How far have they gotten?"

"Depends on what you mean. Way I hear, Kingdomers following Polus down made the initial clear with axes and fire. Several thousand Tûrûrôt Kingdomers followed, and combined there's maybe ten to fifteen horizons of finished road, which impresses me."

"The Kingdomers are skilled and don't fear hard work."

"Aye, but why are they working so hard for us?"

Ivin grinned. "They're mum on the details, but I fear ours may not be the only war on the horizon. Now, let's go speak to others about working some defensible terrain."

Kinesee rode ahead of Leto, not wanting to talk to the man any more than she wanted to talk to the boy years ago, but he was persistent.

"You've taken on a glow for the Warlord."

She wanted to tell him to shut his yap. "He is a good man."

"But, you don't want him near Meliu without you around."

"You're out of line, Ravinrin." Her gut snarled, but she relaxed her face.

Leto snorted and rode in silence several flickers before saying, "A high priestess may not marry, but it doesn't mean they don't bed other women's husbands."

Kinesee reined her horse to a stop and turned with the full intent to tear into him. He still had fish lips, but he was a handsome enough man. He was also one of her oldest friends, even if they hadn't seen much of each other since the wedding. "Meliu and I... Let's just say that the Warlord knows where her loyalties stand, and mine." She softened. "I know you had a notion of our betrothal that day in the Bickering Tent... I did as well. Horrifying as that would've been. Those notions are dead and must remain that way."

She spun her horse and rode toward plumes of smoke downriver where folks had told her Tudwan's tent sat. Leto followed close.

"Forgive me for wishing things had gone as they should have."

"There is no *should* any more than there is fate. History only has a direction when you look backward."

"So you're going to stay in Forest's Gate as he commands?"

Her aggravation grew. "He made no such command. He gave me a decision to make and hopes I make the one he desires."

"Oh, seems to me the Warlord makes demands—"

"Not of me!"

"Kinesee!" Ilpen's booming voice broke the rhythm of their growing spat, and they both turned to look. "Get this confounded goat away from my mules before I kill her."

Kinesee slid from the saddle and ran. "Ilpen!" She clamped her arms around him the best she could. "You are a sight."

"So are you, my girl. I'd heard there was peace in the north."

"There is, the south is another matter."

"I heard that too. When are you taking Tengkur back? She's making a habit of riding Ears the Elder around, and the Younger done kicks and bites at her 'cause of it."

"She'll have to stay with you a little longer. Ivin and I are heading for Green Mountain."

He blinked and fidgeted. "The hells, you say. Does your husband know this?"

"He still thinks it's up for debate."

Two horses trotted down the hill, and Alu jumped from her saddle to hug Kinesee before admiring her. "You're wearing your sword."

"It's little more than decor, but I like it."

Ilpen snorted. "She'll be needin' it if she travels south with the Warlord."

Leto said, "She should be staying here."

Alu gave her the same scolding look with a raised brow that papa used to give. Gods, how she missed that withering gaze. "He's right."

"Nooo, he's wrong. What I need is a sword instructor to come with me."

Tudwan said, "I know several fine warriors—"

Alu cut him short with a laugh. "I think she meant me."

"I see." Alu's eyes didn't leave her husband's, and Kinesee joined in on the stare with a playful smile. "Well, the yellow-eyes took Daksin in the south, and I've been itching to find him. Lady Tedeu did say to keep an eye out for good territory to claim in the Ravinrin name."

Leto shook his head and glared. "She didn't mean Green Mountain and the monsters of the forest. And you, you're a fool for holding out hope."

"And you are a weak child to give up your brother's life with such haste."

"Thousands of horizons—"

Kinesee stepped between their horses. "Boys! Keep it up, and Alu and I will be traveling without either of you."

Alu's eyes were wide. "Whoa, whoa. I didn't say I was going... not exactly."

Kinesee turned on her sister and Ilpen whistled. "It's a day for sibling feuds, I see!"

Kinesee grunted, relaxed. "Men have me on edge. I haven't been married long, but I know my Ivin well enough. He's counting on you talking me into staying."

"And if I agree to go, you've tanned his hide." She clutched Kinesee in her arms and didn't let go. "You can count on me, sis. Have you heard from father?"

"He's east of us now."

She shoved Kinesee back with a smile. "East!"

"He's kind of circling Green Mountain. It's a little peculiar when you think about it. But I'm sure he'll catch up with us soon enough." She turned to Tudwan. "Are you coming or staying?"

The Eldest Ravinrin brother glanced at his younger brother before he shrugged. "I'm going."

"Ivin will love that."

Leto rolled his eyes. "Tedeu will have your hide."

Kinesee pouted her mouth. "Po' Fish Lips is a scaredy-white."

The Ravinrin scowled. "I have to go, no way I'm going to be the one who informs the lady her eldest and favorite grandson just rode to Green Mountain."

Ilpen cleared his throat. "You thinkin' they might be needin' a smith down there?"

Kinesee darted to hug the man. "Dederu and your girl would kill you before you made it out of camp. You stay here and watch my baby."

"Tengkur ain't so young no more, though still spry as a grasshopper."

"Watch my old baby then. If ever it gets safe, you and the family will be the first I invite."

He patted his still ample gut. "Farther south we go, the less of me there is, and the wife is liking it."

Kinesee laughed as she stepped back and looked to Alu. "Ivin isn't wasting time in Forest's Gate. We'll be riding out come morning. Be ready."

Alu smiled. "Do you need any help breaking the news?"

"One of Tedeu's wedding night lessons was that beds were for breaking bad news." She winked and caught Leto's scowl from the corner of her eye. A part of her felt for him, but the Ravinrin just needed to get over his childish crush.

Fifty-Two

Talker Taken

The Dastard, the Bastard,
the onrushing disaster
the tongue of the howling licker and its flicker,
Tasting the distasteful, the blood and the bowels,
the bowels in the blood,
the piss in the spit,
the venom in the sweet sauce.
Which king falls faster, skewered or poached?
Poisoned or pushed?
Or he loved too much.

—*Tomes of the Touched*

Meliu sat beside the dead yellow-eye with her back against a tree, wondering what the hells to do next. Polus and the others would've reached the rendezvous point by now and would be circling back in her direction. The first plan had gone piss poor, and the backup had been for her to hide and pick off a straggler by surrounding him with Dark. The Crone and her powers popped that idea like a bloated bull on a hot day, and then Meliu had gone and turned this poor bastard into a bug-eater.

Her one shot; she let anger and surprise take it from her.

She stared at the stiffening dead man. "What would Solineus do?" The question sent a chill down her spine and brought a giggle; she turned to glance at the river, making sure no one had crossed. "You don't know Solineus, but I'd wager he'd nab one of them damned river lizards and ride it across before butchering your whole camp." The dead man's stare mocked her. "Fine, maybe not, but close."

Solineus was a handsome son of a bitch as lucky playing dice with the Fates as he was in the eyes his parents gave him. He'd swim across unscathed, while some river monster would eat her within five strides, considering her luck. Getting them to this side was the lock; killing the Crone was the key.

"Be a gentleman and tell me what powers she wields?"

The man's intense yellow stare was fading to green, peculiar as a block of ice in the Forges, far as she could figure. *And the yellow spittle? Something they eat?* It made sense.

She shook her head. "Distractions. The Crone. How do I kill her?"

A breath stealer. Maybe. Prayers of Air smothered flames in the Trials, but she'd never heard of them smothering a man until reading the *Codex of Sol*. The Codex gave her no details of its use, just descriptions of armies falling limp. If the woman could drop her at a hundred strides, Meliu needed to get close without the woman knowing. Twenty strides, closer, the better. Something.

Solineus' dual at the river.

She stood, straightened, and puffed her chest. "What would Solineus do? No lizard-riding horseshit."

She grabbed the yellow-eye by his cold, stiff hands and dragged him over the crest of the hill and down toward the river until stopping twenty strides short of the nearest yellow-eye arrow marking their range. She planted her feet and stood tall over the corpse, daring the bastards to come for her.

Not a one noticed.

She waited.

"You shittin' me? Hey! Yellow-eyed pig-pokers!" She slouched with a huff. No way in the hells was she going to embarrass herself by jumping up and down waving her arms. "Them yellow eyes make them deaf or what? Hrrm. Solineus couldn't do this." She prayed for Light and unleashed the energies in front of her in brilliant white scattered with green, red, and blue streaks.

Her display drew the eyes of every yellow-eye in camp, and while most stopped where they were, sitting or standing, one trotted to a tent.

Meliu propped her hands to her hips and waited with a smile. "There you are."

The Crone ducked through the tent's flap and faced Meliu with a bowlegged stance to challenge her.

Meliu raised her hands and gestured, summoning the woman to her side of the river. The Crone studied her, but best she could tell, the old gal was unimpressed. Meliu eyeballed the dead man, dropped to a knee, pulled her dagger with one hand, and yanked his hair with another; with a breath, she sliced the crown of his head until his scalp tore from his skull. *He's dead already. He's dead already. No worse than skinnin' a possum.*

She stood with the man's hair held high, pointed her dagger at the woman, but still, not a one made a move toward the river. She dropped the scalp and stomped on it. Spat. The only reaction was that confounded stare. "What the hells is with you people? Scared of one little girl? What the hells do you bastards consider the ultimate insult?"

She kicked the man, stabbed him, then prayed for Fire, burning his feet to cinders: Nothing. She glanced behind herself a dozen times to make sure some yellow-eye wasn't about to jump on her; by now, she'd welcome the fool's attack, but no one came from anywhere. *What would really rage my goat?* "The hells if I'm going to take a bite of the bastard. What the hells." She grinned, dropped her trousers, squatted, and pissed on the dead man's head. The fact was she just needed to pee and didn't expect a reaction, but men clamored and grabbed weapons, shouting at the Crone, waving spears and bows.

Meliu tied her pants and smiled. She had no idea whether it was a woman pissing on a man that got them riled, or just pissing on him in general, but it sure worked. Now, she needed to survive whatever assault was coming for her, and what was coming for her was every damned one of them, Crone and all.

She waited for them to reach halfway across the river before she turned and strutted up the slope, and their oars were still strides from shore when she crested the hill. She glanced to make sure they couldn't see her before lurching into a downhill run, diving and sliding back into the bushes, turning to face the hill, and praying for Light and Dark.

The first yellow-eyes crowned the hill at a dead sprint with shields hiding their bodies, fools if they hadn't expected an ambush, but they stopped dead in their tracks as they stood over an empty valley. One turned and yelled, and a couple of wicks later, two dozen men with shields and spears stood atop the rise. Flickers later, the Crone filled a gap in the middle.

Meliu prayed for Life to take a closer look; the woman's wrinkled brow was brown and weathered like the rest of her skin exposed between yellow stripes, and... Meliu blinked. The woman's breasts didn't sag from age alone. The ribs of some rabbit-sized animal pierced her nipples, and dangling from gold chains set on their ends were four small animal skulls, as if each head hung from a scale to weigh them. It made her breasts ache and her mind question the symbolism. Each skull was a different animal: Hanging from the woman's left breast were the skulls of two birds, one a predator, judging by the hooked beak, and from the right, two mammal skulls, one with yellowed buck teeth, the other something fanged. Predator and prey weighed on a scale?

She shook her head to refocus. *I need to kill this witch, not understand her.*

The Crone swept her arms, pointing, yapping in her manic tongue, and two groups of six yellow-eyes skulked down the hill with shields raised, separating, spreading out as they walked. Life prayer faded and she closed her eyes, praying for Light, then she spoke to Kibole: *Fill me with the terror of the Forges so I might show these people your true might.*

The men looked up into trees and jabbed spears into bushes as they searched, but she let one group draw close before she settled her eyes and will on the group farther north. She felt the invisible demons in her breath as she exhaled, and in an instant, screams erupted from within a twenty-pace circle of utter blackness. Arrows flew in random arcs from the Dark, and the other party of six yellow-eyes charged, spears brandished and shields in hand, or bows at the ready, but they stopped when a man sprinted from the Dark, a spear rammed through his gut. He fell strides from the other group's feet, propped to his side by the shaft of wood, and bled out with no one daring to touch him.

When the screams stopped, she released the Dark hiding them; three lay curled on the ground shaking, and two more were dead, though Meliu couldn't tell whether from their hearts seizing or wounds. The second group edged forward, one shouting at the Crone, but the old woman remained silent with a sour gaze.

Meliu relaxed her soul into the Light. Killing these other men would be no more complicated than the first, but if she spooked the Crone and they fled across the river, she was back to throwing the ante into the pot; she needed to end the game.

The Crone wasn't about to do her any favors, standing there on her hill like some sort of queen. The witch was alert, and so were the men by her side.

The Crone barked words in an audible blur, and archers put arrows into the writhing men. Mercy, or did it speak to their value of life?

Shits if I care... I need a rabbit for these hounds to chase.

She steeled herself to a test of her will, body, and soul. *Erginle, Kibole, lend me your combined prayers.* She closed her eyes, focusing on a point between her eyes. *Kibole, bring me your Dark so that fear will blind my enemies, Erginle lend me your Light so my enemies might see, and so too bring me Life so I might stand instead of fall.* With a final thought, she giggled to herself: *Empower and embolden me; my Solineus time has come.*

In the vision of her closed eyes, Dark surrounded her as the night sky, and her Light was a star, but the core pulsed with the energy of her heart's rhythm. Serenity and eternity nestled amid horror.

But when her eyes opened, the world was the same as it ever was, until her heart fluttered and Dark enveloped the second group of men. Screams and shouts, but Meliu watched the Crone and her people, their keen eyes. She blinked and sent Light fifty strides to her south. The Crone pointed with a shout, and the men from atop the hill sprinted toward her display. As they passed, Meliu crawled from her hiding spot, clinging to the energies of Light and Dark to hold them in place. She ran toward the witch; every step hitting the ground shook her grip on the energies of the gods, and when the Crone's eyes turned on her, she held her breath.

A wave of energy passed over her, a thousand chills like a breeze carrying tiny flakes of snow, and she stumbled over a root. Her grip on the manifestations of Dark and Light loosened and released, but Kibole and Erginle were still strong in her soul. She ran without tiring, ran without the need for breath; she felt the arrow when it passed through her left thigh, felt the arrow break as her right leg scissored its shaft. Arrows struck around her, splitting the bark of trees and piercing the dirt's crust, and the Crone's eyes widened with the first hints of fear.

Erginle's Light and Life carried her within twenty strides, and her fingers shook to release Dark, but Life and Light shunted the power of Kibole to the side and overwhelmed the Dark; she needed to get closer.

The witch raised her arms, and Meliu felt her energy tingle every stretch of her body; there was no escape for either of them. Meliu collided with the woman, tackling her into mud-slicked soil and leaves, sliding down the hill.

"Kibole!"

Light and Life fled her, and the universe went black.

A shrill scream pierced her ear; hands pounded her back; legs flailed, kicking her shins and kneeing her thighs; teeth latched onto her jaw, ripping her cheek. She was cave-blind, but felt the witch's fears: Serpents with feathered wings, a man with fangs whose mouth hinged wide like a snake to eat a hare, a massive ape with blood-streaked fur tearing at her soul, a beautiful white lion with serene, blood-red eyes... only this fear stared straight at Meliu. And her soul calmed despite the horrors around her.

The beast strode to her on silent paws bigger than her head, lips twitching as it sniffed her soul. The voice came as a rumble. *Who are you?* Demons and devils unthinkable and unnamed swirled around the creature, but it paid them no mind.

Without considering the implications, her mind answered: *Meliu, Daughter of Kibole.*

She felt the Crone's pounding heart heavy in her own breast and knew when at last her will burst. The Crone's body relaxed as Dark drove her into death's embrace. Meliu smiled at the white lion.

Then screamed.

Piercing pain erupted in her right shoulder, and her arm flailed weak and limp in an instant. She rolled with the dead woman, bringing her corpse on top of her. "Kibole!"

Dark erupted in all directions, a torrent from the depths of her soul, and the screams of men engorged her rage. She came to her feet, blind, except for the vision of the lion by her side, so huge her head only came to its shoulder.

She released the core of Dark and sent a blinding ripple of Light in its wake. As the Dark disappeared, she was pleased to see that the only men alive were blinded. Only the serenity of Erginle's might kept her calm when she realized the lion still stood by her side.

Meliu, the lion's voice said, *Daughter of Erginle.*

I'm going crazy. She blinked, and the great cat no longer stood beside her.

But enemies remained.

The rush of fletchings buzzed her head. She turned, her heart pulsing in a slumbering rhythm as Life tickled the wound in her shoulder, itching as her body and bones healed around the arrow's shaft. *Six men standing.*

Dark snaked through the air in six weaving trails, and to a man, the yellow-eyes dropped their weapons and turned tail. Her laughter at the futility caught her off-guard, but as the first fell writhing with Dark swallowing his head, tears streamed from her eyes with body shaking guffaws of joy. Another fell, and another, sprinting, ducking, diving, it didn't matter; Dark overtook and felled them until one remained.

Meliu wiped her face and stifled her humor, willing Dark to pass the man, to surround him. The yellow-eye collapsed into a ball, covering his head with his arms, and he whimpered and cried by the time she strode through the lasso of Dark to tie his wrists behind his back and hobble his ankles.

She strolled to stand in front of him. "I know it might be hard to believe, but you're the lucky one. Yes, your name is Lucky."

She gazed around the woods. Whimpers and moans drifted to her ears from several directions, but not a single yellow-eye stood in opposition. She released the Dark from her soul but didn't dare relinquish her grip on Life. She wobbled at the release of the energy and exhaled to steady her head. "Thank you, Kibole. Thank you, Erginle." *Of which am I the child?*

She glanced at the broken shaft in her leg, tore cloth for a better look; dried blood and scars. *And Zarhôt's wounds healed as he ran...* The words came to her from the *Codex of Sol*. She hadn't known what those words meant until now; she'd never heard of such a thing before. And while praying for Light and Dark? Favored by the gods, indeed.

She yanked the rope until the yellow-eye stood, refusing to make eye contact, but following her with the shuffling strides her knots allowed. She reached the top of the hill, gazed to the river and the camp beyond, and her eyes flew wide at the sight of men, then she realized she knew them by name.

Halfway down the hill and with her prisoner close behind, she yelled. "You're late, Broldun."

Polus' head spun on a swivel as he cut the bindings of a captured Silone. The big man licked his lips and stood, strolling to the river's bank. "Where the hells are all the yellow-eyes?"

She waved her good arm back at the hilltop. "What are you doing on that side of the river?"

"We met a band of yellow-eyes up north, probably coming to flank us. We took their boat and one of them bastards alive."

Meliu turned to her prisoner. "If I'd known that... You really are Lucky."

Polus pointed at her. "You all right, girl?"

About damned time he noticed. "Now you mention it, I've been better." She moseyed to a dugout canoe and tied the yellow-eye tight before taking a seat out of his reach.

"Don't suppose you wanna row one of them boats over?"

She fell to her back and laughed at the sky. "I don't think I can do that."

"Don't you fall asleep before we get over there, don't want nothin' eatin' on my future bride."

"Don't you worry about me; no way I could sleep." But when her eyes closed, she dreamed of a white lion with blood-red eyes.

Fifty-Three

Son in the Blinding

The heat of love, the pressure of hate,
the end of beginning and the beginning of the end,
A loop to loop to loop,
Time eating its own tail until consuming the head.

—*Tomes of the Touched*

Wind and Helelindin magic carried Solineus and his party upriver faster than he had imagined, depositing them in the town of Nevaruherin. It was a peculiar place built of stone but covered in vines, and the Helelindin here served King Sebedil. When he mentioned trade and treaty Solineus found himself treated to horses, a guide, and friendly smiles.

It took two weeks of hard riding to reach the town of Melôjer. Here they found Sololu Felihol, a Helelindin woman who had guided Kinesee to Nosuperelôn. Their guide from Nevaruherin remained in Melôjer with the Silone warriors.

Solineus, Sîu, and Adinvan rode behind Sololu for three days before reaching Nosuperelôn. The woman scoffed at his offer of gold for her service, and she left them at the gate to the village without stepping a foot inside.

The village sat on the edge of the mountain's snowline. A dozen squat buildings stood in view, but it was a cone-roofed building spewing smoke from its great chimney dominating the view. A powerful Helelindin stood beneath the smithy's eave pounding red hot ingots while two other men pumped the bellows. "I'm looking for Lelishen Endurane."

The man looked at him as if unsurprised to see a human speaking Edan. "You the boy's father?" Solineus blinked and stuttered, and the smith saved him the question. "How many humans you think we get here who speak Edan? Your daughter came for a visit some months back; I figured you'd show up down the road. If that weren't a give-away, there are the swords on your back."

"The swords are more famous than the man." Solineus offered his hand. "Solineus Mikjehemlut."

"Bedîuho, Third Smith of the Round Fire." The man's fingers were long and thin, but his grip was iron when they shook hands. "You'll find Lelishen down the road, there." He pointed.

"Many thanks."

Adinvan spoke as they walked. "Looks like some fine steel they hammer in these parts."

Solineus ignored his father, his eyes pinned on the door, and when it opened, he stopped dead in his tracks, Sîu colliding with him.

Lelishen glanced up and froze. Their eyes locked, but words didn't come despite his mouth opening.

He cleared his throat and said, "Good to see you."

She fidgeted, an unusual show of emotion or nerves. "Come inside. Leave *them*."

The woman disappeared through the door, leaving it open. He turned to his companions. "Maybe I'm not so welcome as I expected."

"Godsdamns, boy, get your ass in there ."

He accepted the wisdom without hesitation and trotted to the door, ducked his head inside. The home was cozy with a fireplace to the north while heavy furs covered the other walls where there weren't windows. A single bed sat against the western wall, and a table with four chairs stood in the middle of the room, while the eastern wall held cabinets filled with books. A red velvet lounging sofa for reading sat nearby. When Lelishen turned to face him, she held a child. He was blond and could damned near pass for human if not for the eyes with flecks of silver in the blue.

"His name is Veldehar."

"I heard." Solineus stepped into the home with tentative steps, thrilled and terrified. He had so many questions, but so many were inappropriate for meeting his child the first time. He slung the Twins from his shoulders and hung them on the back of a chair before walking closer. "He's beautiful."

"You brought a woman to meet your son. And who is that man? If word gets out—"

Solineus straightened and planted his feet as if under attack. "Whoa, whoa. First things first, that *man* is Adinvan Mikjehemlut, my father. Veldehar's grandfather. The girl is Sîu. She's a friend, nothing more."

"She thinks she is more."

"She doesn't."

"She does."

Solineus sighed. "I'm here to marry you if you'll have me." He grimaced and looked to his toes. "My apologies, I meant that to be more romantic."

Lelishen stared, then laughed. "Forgive me."

"For what? Your laughter or your answer?"

"For everything. Veldehar, my sweet. Meet your father." She stood the boy up and pointed him at Solineus, and Solineus smiled as he went to his knees.

"It's wonderful to meet you." But the boy hugged his mother's leg. "I can be a little scary."

"He'll warm up. He isn't frightened of much. And don't let him fool you into thinking he can't talk, he's full of jabber when he wants to be."

Solineus sat cross-legged and gazed at her beauty. "Marry me."

Lelishen joined him on the floor, propping Veldehar in her lap. She put her hands to Solineus' face, kissed him. "We can never marry. The Edan—"

"No one needs to know. Hells, it doesn't even need to be official. Just say, yes."

"If they discover our child, I fear they'll kill him."

The Edan were peculiar and brutal, but this was difficult to believe. "Why?"

"He's an impossibility. He's impure—"

"He's a child, how can he be impossible when he sits right in front of you?"

"Humans and Trelelunin coupled throughout the Age of God Wars, but the books make a point of there being no children. Not even the pairing of Helelindin and Trelelunin will bring a child. You and me? This child?"

Solineus scoffed and reached out, running a finger through the boy's hair. "He's here. He's ours. I can't believe they'd kill an innocent."

"They might send him to the Father Wood for judgment, but either way, they'd take him from me—us. Our marriage would be an invitation to another impossible and impure child. They wouldn't tolerate that threat." She propped Veldehar on his feet in front of him before heading for the door. "I'll invite your father and friend."

Solineus heard her words, but they didn't register in his consciousness as he stared into the child's eyes. So like him, and so not. "Hello."

"Greetings."

Solineus grinned. "That's a big word for a little boy."

"Your eyes are funny."

"They are, aren't they? Yours are far prettier than mine."

"Yes, they are."

He felt Adinvan's looming presence before he heard the man's breaths close to his ear, leaning to gain a view of his grandson. "By the gods... He got his good looks from his mother."

"And now I know where Solineus gets his flirt from. Please, make yourselves at home. I apologize for earlier; your arrival startled me."

Sîu took a seat at the table as far from everybody as she could get. "No worries. And I know not to mention the child. I won't breathe a word."

"I appreciate this. Someday the world may know of him, but not now." Lelishen pointed at the girl's necklace. "That is a beautiful stone. A soul-catcher?"

Sîu smiled, disarmed at least a little by the Trelelunin's charms. "It is. A gift from my father for this journey."

"It is exquisite."

Adinvan tickled the boy's chin. "If you and the boy need a warmer place to stay, you're always welcome on my island, no Edan will find you there."

Lelishen smiled. "The cold of the mountain doesn't bother me."

"And my grandson?"

"He is part Silone, snow and ice are in his blood. But he will shiver if it's cold enough. He wandered into a storm, and I chased after him, worried... We ended up playing in the snow when he wore no more than he does now."

Solineus hadn't considered how many traits the boy picked up from his ancestry, outside of his eyes and nose and hair. "A tough lad, then. Does he have a way with the Elements, like Trelelunin?"

"Even full-blood children rarely show the affinity so young... but his cuts and bruises appear to heal faster than most humans."

Adinvan chuckled. "A lucky tike, he'll need that if he's like his father... Solineus here was always tripping and stumbling, his mother cussin' and worryin' on about him."

"I wasn't so bad." Solineus squinted, wondering why he bothered to defend himself when he had no idea of the truth.

Lelishen patted Veldehar's head. "He has only fallen twice since he learned to walk, and he took his first steps at four months. That's unheard of for a Trelelunin child, let alone Silone. He is an impossible and gifted child."

Solineus offered his finger and Veldehar grabbed hold, shaking it as if shaking his hand. "How have you kept him secret?"

"I claimed to be working on relations between the Silone and the Helelindin and declared a break in my service to the Edan. I've traveled back to the Eleris twice. The master smith here, he might be my father... No one dares cross him, and Veldehar is a favorite with everyone. They help care for him and make sure he remains a secret."

"Might be your father?" She gazed on him with her don't be a foolish mortal smile, and he pieced it together. "The Great Forgetting."

"He remembers me as his daughter. I am uncertain."

Solineus knew the sensation all too well. "Last I heard from Kinesee war brewed in the north."

"No longer. Litrâ assassins murdered the Malstefnê king's family, and soon after, the king disappeared, so war rages farther north."

"This is good news, but I've a feeling all isn't well." He smiled and wiggled the finger still clamped in the boy's playful grip. Veldehar let go and ran with a giggle.

"This is so. The bad news rests in the opposite direction. Whispers from the king's court suggest Ivin and Kinesee ride south with two armies."

Solineus rubbed his eyes. "Twelve Hells. I forgot all about Rinold. Two armies, what do you know?"

"Morik of Shuntiskâ rides with an army from Helmveline as well as a force from Tûrûrôt; the Helelindin have eyes on any passing Kingdomer army, I assure you. I've only rumors, but a hornet's nest may be erupting to the south."

He watched Veldehar stalk Sîu, and the young woman covered her eyes to play peekaboo. "The Lady spoke to me again, what do you know of a White Lion?"

"In Silone lore, nothing. What else did she say?"

"Outside of giving us the fuel to fire up a marriage... No. She said we were in a hurry because the White Lion was coming."

"There are two lions in your people's tale of Creation."

"Sol and Rin."

"It could be Rin. There is much lore in the Pantheon of Sol that I don't know, and more remains lost to scholars. Whether you trust the Lady is your decision."

"Trust... I believe what she says, but can I trust her motivations? I would like to stay a few days."

"Now you're speaking a grandfather's language!" Adinvan chuckled. "Your mother will kill me already for having met him first, may as well make the best of it."

"You said the Helelindin have eyes on the Kingdomers, might they be able to escort us south faster than returning to the Roemhien?"

Lelishen took a breath then sighed. "Maybe, but I'd have to travel with you."

Solineus shook his head. "Stay with Veldehar—"

"He'll be fine with his other grandfather. He's been without his mother before."

"We'll stay a while then. That is, if we're welcome."

Lelishen's smile warmed Solineus' soul. "Absolutely. Your father might enjoy hunting in the mountain, the smithy."

Solineus listened in utter contentment, the warmth of love and kin easing his spirit into tranquility, so when Veldehar wandered to the Twins hanging on the chair, it took flickers to register. The child's fingers stretched, and Solineus' heart stuttered in panic. He twisted and reached, but the boy was too far from his grasp. "No!"

Fingertips touched Ikoruv, and his little fingers wrapped the hilt of the Sister the best they could. Solineus stared, his breath gone, and Lelishen's scream was nonsensical in his ear.

But Veldehar giggled and his left hand wrapped the hilt of the Brother. He made babbling noises as if mimicking their language before Lelishen swept him away from the weapons. "Are you all right?"

"I'm fine, mommy. The voices are funny." He cocked his head. "The swords grandpa makes don't talk."

"No honey, grandpa's swords don't talk." She hugged against his squirm and carried him back to sit in her lap.

Solineus rose to his feet as his heart slowed, plucked the swords from the chair, then hung them from a peg on the wall far from Veldehar's reach. No one who touched the Twins before had so little reaction. "No pain? No fear? They didn't try to make you do something?"

He shrugged with his face full of childish innocence. "No. They spoke to me is all."

"You understood them?"

"First they babbled like. Then the girl said 'hello untold,' and the boy said 'blessing'."

Veldehar glanced at Lelishen and she grinned, but it was with nervous lips. "It's his name. Veldehar means *untold blessing.*"

Solineus sat in front of him. "Did they say anything else? Gers'voresh-kûmjotukî?"

Lelishen's eyes widened. "Kûmjotu-Kî?"

Solineus spoke to her before looking back at his son. "We've things to discuss. Did they say that name?"

"No."

"Don't touch them again, you hear?"

He nodded, staring at the ground with pouting eyes. "Am I in trouble?"

Lelishen nuzzled his hair. "No, sweets, you aren't in trouble. No trouble."

Solineus glanced at Sîu and Adinvan. "I wouldn't speak of this."

Adinvan grunted. "I don't even know what the hells I saw." Sîu shook her head without a word.

Veldehar reached and took Solineus' hand. "Father—"Solineus turned to him, smiling, soul melted by this single word"—they said they wanted to play with me."

Solineus' gut twisted, but he held his smile despite the terror in Lelishen's eyes.

Solineus strolled beside Lelishen, keeping his eyes on the terrain to avoid annoying her with his stare. The evergreens stood frosted with glints of snow, and the valley stretching below snaked for rolling horizons of verdant woods and grassy vales where last night's snow melted away, but the rising slope strained his thighs and burned away any sense of leisure. "Been a while since I climbed so high."

"I heard you climbed far higher."

"Oh, aye. God-high. I loved the view, but if I never step foot so high again, the blessed I'll be for it." On this, the second day after his arrival, it was their first time alone, as Veldehar gave his Silone grandfather a tour of his other grandfather's smithy and town.

She pointed to a sharp rise of dirt and shale. "Here."

"The hells you say." Solineus grinned as he clutched a narrow tree and dragged himself up several steep steps to a stone shelf. When he turned to take Lelishen's hand, her eyes caught his, and the words blurted out unbidden. "You won't reconsider?" It was this sort of foolishness he'd hoped to avoid by not looking at her. "I reckon I should apologize for that."

She grinned, eyes twinkling in the sun. "Do you think Veldehar and his grandfather have driven the town crazy yet?"

He pulled her to stand beside him, faces close. "It's in the blood from both sides."

Playful eyes. "That topic is already at rest."

"Put to bed, as it were?"

"We're not here for that either. A second impossible child would prove my insanity."

He released her hands and strolled to lean against a juniper grown crooked from mountain winds. His eyes wandered across the wilds below, finding the smoke from the smithy before turning back to her glittering eyes. "Then why are we here?"

"It's my favorite place to sit and think."

"It's a vision of a wide and beautiful world. So, what are we thinking about today?"

"A couple things, like you having a son. I can't raise him here forever. The Edan will question what I'm doing. Time passes like a soft breeze for them, barely noticed, but one day they will raise the question."

"If you fear for his life, you can take him to—"

"No."

"You don't want him with his people?"

"He has no people. He only has who he knows. I don't fear for his life yet, because so few know of him, but I won't always be able to be here."

"I will return as much as possible. Help as I can."

"That is well. But I wouldn't want to see him taken from these mountains unless need be."

He turned his eyes back to the distant smoke. "The journey would be dangerous anyhow. I've no idea what I'm walking into. But I reckon it's been that way since I crawled out of the waters on Kaludor. My father told me I was on my way to Choerkin Fost to warn them the Church, Lord Priest Ulrikt, was planning something."

"And you wonder what if you'd reached them?"

"It don't make sense, but I do. It wouldn't have changed a thing."

"You would never have met Kinesee and Alu, their family. Where would you be without those girls? Where would they be without you?"

Hands rested on his shoulders, and he leaned into her. "Hells if I know. I'm not so sure where I'm at right now."

She spun him by the shoulders and pressed her lips to his, but stirring romance wasn't so easy now. He shrugged from her grip. "We didn't come here for that."

Lelishen stepped back, eyes sad over her smile. "Kûmjotu-Kî."

"Gers'voresh-kûmjotukî. Is that what we're here to speak of, in truth?"

"It's a conversation that shouldn't be overheard. The swords spoke this name? The histories I'm aware of only named her Kûmjotu-Kî, or simply, the Kî."

Solineus snorted and moved to lean against the tree again. "All I know is what the Twins said. The first time they spoke the name was before I used stone-breakers on the bridge. Peculiar, yes, but nothing came of it. When we went to the Temple Mount of Yungilêtunu to rescue islander children, well, we were being overrun by the enemy. The swords chanted the name into my mind. I screamed the words without knowing why, over and over like a battle cry. Others picked up the call, and the next damned thing I knew, a great beast rose from the world, destroying the pyramid. Thousand-weight blocks of stone rained from the sky."

"The Kî came when you called."

"That's what I've been told, but what shittin' sense does that make? The swords called her, not me."

"No spirit harnessed in a weapon would have such power. They are minor beings, even if dangerous. They told you to call her."

He chortled and rubbed his forehead before sighing and casting his eyes to the wilderness. "I am a minor being. The Kî erupted from that temple with a brute power I never imagined in a single creature.

It wasn't the Elements as with Eliles' tower; it was strength, pure and simple."

"I wish I had borne witness. Few living people can recall seeing the Kî. But I assure you, if all she did was destroy a pyramid, it was a fraction of what she is capable."

He didn't mean to stare at her as if she was insane but reckoned his face didn't hide his confusion. "I've heard tales of men fighting dragons—"

"There are dragons, and there are dragons. You've heard of the First Dragons?"

"Aye, the Touched mentioned them. Creators of the world or some such."

"Some legends say so, but other texts, including the Tome of the Touched, speak of them as arriving at the creation of the world. That they bred or spawned in the energies of Creation. The First Dragons left their children behind, disappearing into the stars. The writings of the Touched are hard to decipher, but they suggest every generation of dragon hatches lesser than their parents. The Kî… We don't really know, but in some ancient texts, even your gods paid her deference."

"She lived during the Gods Wars?"

"No doubt she did, as did the Touched, I suspect."

"How could he claim to have seen these First Dragons?"

"I don't know. He seems to have memories of a deep past and future."

"He's a knack for jabbing Inslok in the eye, that I know." Solineus chuckled. "Hells, it might make sense if the Touched called the Kî, but me? Why?" A blank stare; he couldn't tell if she was thinking or stumped mute. "How? Why?"

"She chose to, and her reasoning is hers alone. Great powers interfere in the lives of mortals and aren't required to answer questions. Could she be the woman in your dreams?"

Solineus' head rocked, more from not having considered it before than any revelation. "No. It doesn't feel right. But if she chose to help me, it means the Twins could've had a hand in it. More than just giving me a name."

She shrugged and ducked her head. "I don't want that to be true. Legends of such weapons speak of a raw consciousness trapped by the blade; their awareness of who holds them is surprising enough. That they spoke to Veldehar… I would've been more pleased if they had frightened him."

A sentiment Solineus understood, even if he disagreed. Solineus didn't know what kind of terror the Twins might put in a boy's heart and didn't want his son to find out. "The Ironwing spoke of the swords as more of a connection to another being rather than a prison. That they reside in the Celestial. The blades are a fire in the night guiding them to the wielder, so to speak."

Her lips pursed. "If true… Keep them far, far from Veldehar."

Solineus' brows arched, and he grinned. "But I've nothing to fear?"

"You survived traveling to and from Eliles' island, and you entered the Eleris without growing sick. You fathered our child. I don't claim to know what all this means about you, but it proves one thing for sure: You aren't normal."

The tone of voice and expression were bland; she meant no insult, but his gut twinged anyway. He kicked peevish retorts from his tongue, and a notion struck him. "Assume the Ironwing is right. I'm here, and the spirits of the Twins are in the Celestial. The swords are the connection. I touch them, and I hear their voices even if I can't understand them most of the time. For argument's sake, let us say that the woman in my dreams is also from the Celestial."

"Reasonable assumption."

"She's poked and prodded me while conscious, but she can only speak to me when I'm asleep or near death. How does she do it?"

"How do you speak to Kinesee?"

Frustrating to not know how something he crafted worked. "I don't know. A spiritual connection of some sort, I reckon. The pearl."

"And you speak to the spirits of the Twins via the swords."

"So what the hells is my connection to the Lady?"

They stared at one another until Lelishen broke a wick of silence. "A dream. Near-death. Dying. Some say the soul can slip from the body."

"And like a moth, I'm drawn to where? A blue universe of energy. Not any heaven I ever heard of."

"Nor any hell. I do not know. Someplace you can both reach."

He ran his hand through his hair and chuckled. Preposterous was the word that came to mind, yet it was hard to deny even an irrational reality. "So, the Lady and I might have our own pearl or sword out there somewhere."

"It makes as much sense as any other idea. But I couldn't feel you with Kinesee's pearl. Nothing at all. The Twins can reach anyone who touches their hilts. Force their wills upon the wielder."

"Could you expect some tiny pearl to be as strong as God Wars forged weapons? After all, I made the pearl and don't even know how I did it. The swords never control me. They warn me, suggest actions..."

"Be wary of them. Always. We don't know who the Twins are."

"Aye." Solineus turned to face the twisted juniper and propped himself against it to gaze over the valley. "It might be better we don't know." Movement caught his eye; two trees swaying while the canopy around remained still, almost as if they danced in a crowd. They were a couple hundred feet below and at least that far east. He pointed as they moved again. "Do you have walking trees?"

She giggled but caught her breath when she looked. "No."

The trees stopped, and everything went still for several flickers, then thirty strides southwest trees swayed. "Those are damned big trees for something to be moving them like that."

Lelishen nodded. "Watch that clearing ahead. Whatever it is follows an animal trail we crossed, if I guess right."

He stared at a patch of grass and rocks maybe a couple hundred feet wide, and a wick later, a lumbering beast strode from the woods, then another and another. Spiral horns caught his eye first, polished and glinting in the sun, above necks so thick an executioner's ax wouldn't lift their massive heads from their bodies. He knew what they were. "Ôgrêt." He'd reckoned folks exaggerated when comparing them to bison, but if anything, it might've been an understatement. They stood fifteen feet tall despite their hunched shoulders. Shoulders more than capable of leaning trees from their path. Covered in heavy furs and brandishing iron staves longer than Solineus was tall, he wasn't eager to pick a fight with one. "They make Colok look like babes. The village?"

"Stay out of their way, and they'll stay out of yours. Most times."

"That's damned good to hear."

A half dozen more of the creatures entered the clearing, three with a deer slung over both shoulders, the weight not even an inconvenience. Grunts, growls, and hand signals; a wick of discussion later, they shuffled into the woods.

"If that's the trail we crossed, they're heading our way."

She exhaled, a rare sign of nerves. "I hope you're wrong."

"Should we leave or stick to the high ground? I want an army before fighting those."

Trees moved, headed their way. "We're better off here than the woods. If it comes to running, we're faster and fit through tight spaces."

"Any point to hiding?"

"To hide would show fear. If they come, we greet them."

She grinned, and he smiled despite his misgivings. "You don't think they'll attack."

"I don't, but neither do I want to be proved a fool."

He took her hand and kissed her. "Just in case it's our last chance."

"You're sure you didn't invite them, just for that kiss?"

He smirked and turned his eyes to the woods. Time crawled as he questioned whether leaves shook every time he blinked. Right until the motion became undeniable. Imagining a line between the clearing, the movement, and where they began their steeper ascent left no doubt. "They're tracking us."

"They are."

He wasn't sure whether to find comfort in her calm answer or not. "Folks always spoke of them being dumb brutes."

"Which is the way of people when speaking of things bigger and slower than they are, in particular when frightened of them. They are primitive but far from stupid."

"With the carcasses they're packin', at least they won't be looking to eat us. Unless they've a hankerin' for something other than deer, I reckon."

"I think my mood would lighten if you stopped talking. Stand tall and don't flinch."

Mighty beasts stepped from the cover of woods below, and narrow, pitch-black eyes gazed up at them. An Ôgrêt broader of shoulder than the rest stepped forward with an iron staff in hand. He splayed his arms and gaped his fanged maw, large enough to fit a man's head, and howled, a low, rolling bellow. He stomped three times, then lifted his staff over his head and slammed the turf three times. "Ûlf dwo nô! Ûf dwo kâ! Ûf dwo zîk! Nôwonê!" He stomped a circle, slamming his staff with every stride, and on facing them heaved. The iron bar sailed past their heads, slamming into the stone behind them with a crunch, ring, and clatter. The beast flexed its arms and snarled as the others grunted in rhythm with his stomps.

Solineus dropped the Twins to his hips and glanced at Lelishen. "I don't reckon you know what the hells he said?"

"He may have been cursing our ancestors and us or just saying hello."

"Useful insight." He turned and picked up the iron bar, making damned certain it didn't look like as much effort to lift it as it was. "Holy Sôl, this thing is heavy." He raised it above his head twice, then let its butt slam to the ground in his left hand as he drew the Sister. Her murmurs came soft, but there was an edge suggesting she was ready for blood. He swiped once, twice, three times, chopping the bar into four sections and dropping the last to the ground for emphasis.

"That's thick iron to cut without effort, even for latcu."

"Poor steel." He picked up the quarters and threw them back down the hill one at a time, then removed his shield, slamming the hilt of the Sister into its face. The Singing Shield of the Kingdomers chimed, echoing from rocks around and carrying with an unnatural volume. "Gers'voresh-kûmjotukî!" He banged the shield three more times, then planted his feet. Stared.

The leader snagged a staff from another ôgrêt and hammered the severed pieces on the ground one by one before tossing the weapon back to its compatriot. Then, he hiked his loincloth and a great stream of piss wetted the cut pieces of iron. He grunted when finished and stomped another circle, snorting and roaring in rhythm with the others' grunting. At the last, he spat up the hill before turning and walking into the woods.

Solineus said, "Well, at least I have an idea what the pissing meant."

The ôgrêt grunted in unison as they marched into the woods.

"I don't think he liked you cutting up his rod. The Kî was a nice touch."

"I reckon it sounded impressive, even if they didn't know the name."

She grinned. "I reckon we shouldn't climb down for a while."

"You are wise as you are beautiful." He stepped closer. "Have we something else to speak of, or do we need to find a better way to pass our time?"

"Mmm. You could tell me about the Smiling Men of Mulshahar and this trade plan of yours. Or maybe, tell me all about that sweet young girl with her eye on you?"

He rolled his eyes and laughed as he stepped away. "Well, hells. You know how to ruin a moment."

FIFTY-FOUR

Silent Talker Screaming

A flicker to breathe, a flicker to leave,
A flicker to play, a flicker to pray.
Every chancing step in a flicker may cross
the fine line between vinegar and wine.

—*Tomes of the Touched*

Meliu slept until the middle of the next day and hadn't a clue when Polus and the others arrived on her side of the river. She ate like a starved dog and gulped water before they marched for a couple of candles. When her body couldn't take it anymore, Polus claimed a swale for camp.

Her prayers were more potent the next morning, but they still traveled as slow as a man skulking toward the gallows because Meliu wasn't capable of fast.

Her prayers grew strong by the third day, but Lucky and the other yellow-eye, who they named Grunt for the only noise he made, proved willing to take blows before they'd pick up the pace. Adding to her frustration, blank stares rebuffed every attempt she made to speak to them, and it took everything she had to keep the Broldun from pounding them into the dirt the first time she wiped spittle from her cheek.

No one ever said learning a new language was easy.

Lucky and Grunt awakened the camp with howling screams on their fifth day together, and she had to jump between them and Polus a second time. The two men screeched, and words rattled from their tongues, an insanity of syllables to her.

Polus stood with sword drawn. "Godsdamned bastards are hollerin' for their kin."

"We didn't go through three hells to catch these men to split their skulls the first time they speak." She smiled at the men and gestured for calm, her voice even and mellow like talking to an angry dog. "Quiet. Easy. Quiet."

But there was no quiet. They jumped up and down with hands bound behind their backs, and she picked up a repeated sound. *Tehemeto? What the hell might that mean?* But she'd have a better chance of understanding the *Codex of Sol*'s code.

Meliu grimaced, almost afraid to ask. "*Tehemeto?*"

"*Tehemeto! Tehemeto!*"

Polus snorted as the men bounced. "Springy little bastards. What the Twelve Hells does that mean?"

"I can't even guess." Then she realized they were staring straight over their heads when they jumped. She turned to stare. Nothing. "I think they're looking at something, but I see..."

Trees smashed flat and disappeared, but nothing was there. Her mouth opened, but she couldn't put words to whatever she was seeing, and a vague "rrr" rattled in her throat. Men closer to the trees turned to look.

It appeared in a mind-blurring blink that flashed the word *dragon* into her mind for a flicker, but this was no legend; it was a horror. Lustrous green-gold scales cast a halo of light reflecting the sun, and on its crown, it wore two wobbly horn-like protrusions. "Run!"

But a half dozen men disappeared beneath its crushing bulk before they'd a chance to obey her. Men ran. Men froze. Men drew weapons and charged.

Polus swept up a pike from the ground. "Spears and bows!"

"You keep these yellow-eyed bastards alive! I'm going to see what I can do." The beast turned north and disappeared, but she could tell where its tail ended by the brush rising back from the ground. She prayed for Light and Dark without knowing what one or the other could do to stop a creature thirty feet long, then charged.

She'd heard the stories of the attack on Rinold's group, and if true, she figured they were lucky this one wasn't as big as the other. A peculiar notion, seeing as this thing was big as a whale. She sprinted at an angle to its maws; her prayers weren't what they would've been before her battle, but the gods were with her. She slid to a stop twenty paces to its side and unleashed everything the gods gave her. Trails of Dark whipped and slithered. She could feel the cold kiss of devils as its monstrous face disappeared in an energy that would've driven a dozen men to madness... If step one to killing this thing was getting its attention, she succeeded. "Shits!"

The *tehemeto* turned with a speed and tighter angle than she'd ever imagined. She ran, veering left behind a boulder, then a right to leap over a fallen log; the boulder ripped from the dirt and rolled a hundred strides and the log half her height ground into a half-rotted mess. The sound of crushing death grew closer, branches breaking and puddles sucking under its weight, and she looked back in time to dive to the side, skidding through greasy dirt before regaining her feet. She prayed to Erginle alone now; it was her only hope as the beast turned to follow.

Polus and his pike darted into her peripheral. He planted his feet and lunged as the monster grew close. The haft was fifteen feet long, and the steel shank on its end embedded into the roof of the creature's mouth. He roared as the thing's weight drove him backward, and she watched as in a flicker he planted the pike's butt against the base of a boulder and dove from its path. It might've been a stroke of killing genius, except the haft snapped in half, leaving the creature flailing the ground and biting at the weapon jammed in its mouth.

Polus reached her side. "Climb a tree! A big one!"

"Didn't work for Rinold!" But she was running for the biggest tree she saw anyhow.

"I don't run like a squirrel... do you?"

She didn't waste her breath on an answer and beat him to the trunk by a dozen strides. She jumped for the lowest branch and missed twice before Polus slid to a stop beside her. He stirruped his hands, and she put her boot between his palms; as she straightened, he launched her into the air, damned near slinging her over the branch. She dangled with the branch knocking the air from her gut, scrambling to not flip over head first.

Flickers later, Polus pulled himself onto the branch, his mail laying in the dirt below. "Higher, girl!" He scrambled on up past her as she balanced on her gut and looked at the world upside down, at the giant serpent coming at them. She scrambled to the trunk and climbed after the Broldun. The *tehemeto* rammed the tree; branches shook and leaves fell, but they clung tight. Its maws opened, thick blood pooling in its lower mouth from the pike dangling in its mouth.

Meliu caught her breath, prayed to Erginle for Light, and unleashed the energy straight into its eyes. It shifted its head, she directed the Light to follow, and it backed from the tree. "That's something, at least."

"Godsdamned things got tougher eyes than I got."

"It might have poor vision... it could hunt by smell or even heat." She glanced around the area, spotting several Silone in a tree a hundred strides away, and the yellow-eyes were with them. The *tehemeto* slithered toward the bodies. "At least we didn't lose our prisoners."

"Yet. Ain't no way I see to make the damned thing leave, and hells... How do we even know it has left if it can go invisible like that?"

She sighed as the beast's mouth opened wide, its lower lip scraping the ground to shovel the crushed corpses into its maw. With a flip of its lip, it tossed the meal deeper in its mouth and swallowed. "When the yellow-eyes climb out of the tree, we know it's safe."

Meliu learned several important things in the past day. First, the giant serpents bore the name *tehemeto*. Second, the yellow-eyes could see the serpents even when they were invisible to her. Third, *tehemeto* were patient hunters. Four, a result of number three, was how to sleep in a tree without falling out to get eaten and doing so without rope.

The morning sun lit the canopy of trees with the first candle of daylight, and the yellow-eyes were on the ground with other Silone munching on fruit and dried meat. Nobody was running or dying, so Meliu and Polus eased into their tree clutching descent.

"Mmm, I always told ya we'd end up sleepin' in the same bed."

Meliu stared at him with groggy eyes and considered kicking him from the tree, but figured she might miss and lose her grip. They reached the ground and moseyed to the others as she prayed to heal her muscles while her eyes plied the woods.

Polus bit into his jerked boar with a grimace. "This meat is getting tougher by the day, and not a drop of whiskey to wash it down."

"Better to eat shit than to be eaten and shat."

The Broldun laughed and took a second helping with a salute. "Yer a woman of wise words."

They packed their bellies full enough and with a new confidence that at least they'd understand the warning if a *tehemeto* was in the area this time around, they set out. It was half a day before they were in the trees again, but this time she never saw the creature. They wasted a candle in the branches before moving on and decided to sleep in the trees again, but this time she had rope to make sure she didn't fall out.

The next day's walk, they spent half the damned day sitting in various trees, and she began to wonder if the yellow-eyes were slowing them on purpose, hoping for kin to rescue them. But near sundown, she spotted a trail of brush crushing to their east, and instead of cussing the heathens, she decided to thank them. The next day they wound through valleys and climbed rises without a single cry of *tehemeto,* and she recognized a pillar of stone standing beside a stream.

"We're close, thank the gods. I could stand to see some different faces."

"Mmm, I second that. Yer right ugly to look at day in and day out."

She ignored him, and a dark thought crept into her head. *What if the creatures took them all? Or they fled? Or gave chase?* Silly paranoia, she chided herself, but her gut fluttered until the smoke of campfires appeared over the trees, and not more than a candle later, they reached the top of a rise and could see Green Mountain with men wandering to and fro along its steps.

The final leg of the journey was winding and wet with afternoon rain, but joyous and full of relief. Men smiled and laughed for the first time in days, and even their prisoners seemed in a lighter mood, twittering in their peculiar tongue back and forth.

When they broke from the trees to see a pyramid surrounded by a wall far more sturdy than when they'd left, she raised her arms in victory.

Then she damned near jumped from her skin as Lucky and Grunt shrieked and ran, striking the ends of their tethers to flail and pull and wail. She ran back to them.

"*Tehemeto*? *Tehemeto*?" They nodded, but she'd already learned that this meant no to the Yellow-Eyes.

Polus lumbered to their sides with his head knocking smile in place. "I'll shut the bastards up, mmm."

"No, something frightened them."

"Oh, aye! Thousands of men'll do that."

She glared at him, even if he might be right, then she took Lucky's hand and dragged the whimpering man back to the edge of the clearing. "What is it?"

He pointed at the camp, and Polus guffawed. "Told ya."

Lucky shuddered and dropped to his knees, clutching his face. "*Dulûmbolis.*" He pointed again, eyes closed to whatever he feared.

Meliu stood straight, a horrifying thought snaking down her spine. "I don't think so."

"What the forges is it then?"

"The pyramid. The godsdamned pyramid."

"Mmm, why fear a pile of rocks?"

"Be my favorite Broldun and fetch the critter's hand we found."

He nodded and set off at a walk faster than she would jog. Meliu turned to look Lucky in the eye. "I am Meliu." She pointed to her chest.

Grunt grunted and the two men shared heated words before Lucky stood, straightening his back. "Tugorunê."

"Togorunê." She pointed at a bird in the sky, then at a horse. "Bird. Horse." She kneeled and scratched a triangle in the dirt, then pointed. "*Dulûmbolis*? Pyramid."

The man nodded to mean *no.* "Tet, tet, tet. Dulûmbolis..." He scanned the woods around them and huffed, then squatted with his arms extended, knuckles on the ground; he hopped and made a *woot woot* with a trill.

The sound she recognized in an instant, the call of a breed of monkeys she'd heard throughout the journey. They were black with ruddy red glints in the sun, and the elder males in the family groups bore tufts of silver hair sprouting from their heads. Powerful frames and fangs half as long as her finger, but she'd never seen them attack anything. "Woot, woot... a monkey."

"*Bolis.*"

It made sense, the hand severed from a creature could be a monkey's. "Monkeys. *Bolis.* A type of *bolis. Dulûm?*"

Grunt and Lucky babbled to one another, and then Lucky stared at her. "*Dulûm.*" He hunched his shoulders, rolled his eyes, and made garbled growling noises.

She shrugged and nodded. "I don't have a godsdamned clue what you're trying to say."

He snorted, pondered a flicker, then ran a finger across his throat and made a gurgling noise. "*Dulûm.*"

No way to mistake that. "They're killers, I got it, you're scared."

Polus arrived just as Lucky slit his own throat again, and this time he dropped to the ground and flailed like a dying fish. "What the shittin' hells you got him doin'?"

Lucky stopped moving, feigning death, and Meliu kicked his foot. "Come on, get up." But the man remained curled for a flicker, then unwound to all fours, grunting, snarling, *woot woot,* and a trill.

"The bugger's gone mad."

Meliu spotted the severed hand in Polus' massive grip, and she took it from him to hold up. If she was right, it explained everything but the calcification. The man leaped from the thing, hollered as if it would attack him. "*Dulûmbolis?* Dead monkey?"

"*Nê! Nê.*"

Polus turned on her. "You shittin' me? Necromancy on monkeys?"

She turned to stare at the pyramid. "Could be, but there are places in nature where the Unlife will force the dead to rise, and I'm wagering strong odds that the godsdamned pyramid is one of them. And I'll put gold against your whiskey they live beneath it."

"Ah now, forges woman! I was looking forward to a better night's sleep on that damned thing."

"Taking my bet?"

"What do we need to do to get my night's sleep, that's all I'm askin'."

She plopped the monkey's paw in his hand. "We find and kill them before they feast on any more of us."

Fifty-Five

Monkey Moles

You rig the game as you sink the boat
forgetting that gold does not float.
Ones are ones and twos are twos,
says you.
Ones are twos or they may be threes,
and two may be five or twelve,
says I.
If you comprehend my new math,
well then, I have hidden nothing.

—*Tomes of the Touched*

"What the Twelve Hells do you think it is?" Meliu stood outside the perimeter of the wall around Green Mountain, so far outside that she was in the forest. In front of her lay a field of stones and rubble, ten by fifteen paces in a rough rectangle.

Rûîrn Bîdorik pointed at the jagged and broken rocks. "My man stumbled on it literally, caught his toe and fell. Leaves and sticks and other debris turned it into a trap. Once we cleared this much, if you look close, you'll see where someone poured a mortar over the area, using the rubble as a crude aggregate, so to speak."

Meliu knelt for a better look, and indeed, gray-brown mortar held the rocks together beneath the surface stones. "What's it mean?"

He pointed to the pyramid. "The edges run straight to the middle of the eastern side of the pyramid. If I was a wagerin' kind of man, I'd say this is... or was the entrance to the under-pyramid. Someone packed it full and set the mortar to keep your dead monkeys in."

Even with the notion of the monkeys hiding under the pyramid, it'd been a month of digging without finding a damned thing. Bîdorik even ordered holes dug at the base of the thing. They excavated twenty feet down before reaching the base, and when the hole filled with water, they surrendered. "Dead monkeys won't die from lack of air, and they scratched their way out... but from where? Can we bust our way through?"

"This may be crude, but it's set and harder than Polus' head. If we had Thundersticks or even latcu-tipped picks, we could make good work of it. If that there's a slope, it's a lot of fill, and we don't know how far it goes."

She eyeballed the rubble and the pyramid. "If we assume the tunnel runs straight, we could dig down to it."

"Sure, but how deep is it? After ten feet a hole begins to seep, and by fifteen, we start filling with water, plus the rains... And if I were building a tunnel in this soil and climate, I would've dug a trench, put down floors and walls of cut stone, sealed the cracks, then dropped a sloping roof of stone on top before covering it with soil. Could be an arched ceiling as well, but the way I figure it this pyramid stood before the rest of these buildings, and those older peoples liked big stones."

"Which means if we dig down to it, we'll need to chip through solid rock to get in." The troubles piled up fast. "How the hells did the monkeys get out then? If we find their way in, no digging needed."

"Might be we haven't been digging deep enough. Might be that the entry *dead* monkeys take is flooded with water. They won't drown. I'd say that's why we haven't a source tunnel... its waterlogged."

"Shits. Could we get Thundersticks or latcu tipped picks?"

Rûîrn Bîdorik stifled a laugh. "No one's crazy enough to carry thundersticks so far, and latcu picks... they're heirlooms. Possible, but unlikely."

Meliu scratched her head, squishing some bug that had gotten too friendly. *Gods, I need a bath.* "There ain't no way they filled a tunnel that stretches so far as the pyramid, and the longer we wait, the more apt these bastards take more people." They'd lost twenty-seven warriors and workers since the first attack. "We've never explored this far out... Stretch a straight line between here and the pyramid. Let's dig a hole right down the middle, just outside our wall there, see if we find a roof."

"It's the best bet we got. Get your people together in case we dig our way into a fight."

"We'll be ready before you get through any rock."

Meliu sent Polus to gather warriors and rounded up three priests she trusted not to panic in a pinch. Shinôu, Nilik, and Gamber didn't look like priests any longer, covered in mail and wearing helms, but they were all adept in prayers of Fire. She didn't know much about the Wakened Dead, but she knew they burned well enough. She and the priests arrived at the dig site as a Helmveliner shovel struck stone a little more than ten feet deep.

Meliu shrugged a dozen times, unaccustomed to the mail dragging her shoulders toward her hips, then adjusted her helm. Even the smallest man's armor made her feel like a runt; two of her could fit in the damned outfit.

Polus whistled at her and wiggled his brows with a growl. "Never more beautiful."

"Shut up, you oaf."

Bîdorik spoke to his men. "There she lays, boys. Looks like sloped rock... Let's clear it out to the sides, give us some space and maybe room to drain."

Within wicks, several Helmveliners stood in what had transformed from a hole to a pit to a trench with a sloped entry. Men climbed out and fresh bodies climbed in, and they chose a seam between the stones to assault with picks.

Polus stepped to her side and glanced around. Several hundred armed and armored men, Silone and Helmveliner alike, followed behind him. "Just how big do you think this tunnel is?"

"I ain't ever heard of no battle where someone brought too many warriors."

She sure hadn't read of that complaint in the *Codex of Sol*, and the armies in those wars ran into the hundreds of thousands in the greater battles. "I'm guessin' you're right enough, but you and Bîdorik both pick five men for our initial foray."

"Mmm, any number I can count on my fingers and toes ain't gonna make me happy."

"If we hit the shit down there, we don't want a pile of men blocking our escape."

"A pile of men might keep us from hitting the shit."

"Not if there's a choke in the passage."

He stalled and stared at her. "You've been readin' too much of that damned book. As you say, five men, but I want men in the tunnel entrance in case we're tails tucked and screamin' our way back."

"Agreed."

Shift after shift of picks climbed in and out of the hole, and Meliu went to sit beneath a tree and wait. She bowed her head to her chest and rested her eyes until she dozed to the rhythm of chipping stone. She stared into the blood-red eyes of a white lion until she heard the call from Bîdorik, and her head snapped to attention. The lion vanished.

"Meliu!"

She jumped to her feet and trotted to the circle of smiling men. A black hole in gray stone. "You might want to enlarge that a bit, make sure the Broldun's big ass fits."

"All muscle and whiskey, girl, I'll fit."

"Nothing came out?"

Bîdorik said, "Not even a hint of anything moving, but we've only lost people during the nights and foggy mornings. These dead monkeys of yours are shy."

"What the hells are we waiting for? Everyone ready yourselves, I'm going to light that hole to the heavens."

She prayed to Erginle and welcomed a soothing surge of energy into her body and soul, and when she opened her eyes, she willed Light to enter the tunnel below. Light lit the chamber below, but despite its intensity, it didn't blind them. The floor reflected the Light with a green glisten; she figured it was slimy, moldy water. Anything with eyes would see the Light for so far as the tunnel traveled straight. It was time now to wait and see if anything accepted her invitation.

They stood there a quarter candle staring until nerves eased and fingers loosened their grips on swords. Shinôu slipped to her side for a better view. "How long can you hold this prayer with such intensity?"

Meliu blinked, it hadn't occurred to her that something which seemed so simple to her now would raise questions with others. "For so long as Erginle allows." She turned to Bîdorik. "Who's going down first? Don't look like anything alive or dead is coming."

Bîdorik glanced to Polus, and both men shrugged.

"Seein' as my ass will fit..." He slid more than walked down the path to the bottom with his shield and sword at the ready, then dropped to hands and jammed his sword through the hole, rattling it back and forth before sticking his head in for a glance. His second look, he left his head in longer. "I don't see nothin'. Tunnel runs a long-damned ways west. East looks like it collapsed."

Bîdorik handed a ladder down, and Polus slipped it through the hole. Four men joined him beside the entry.

"You be careful down there, you oaf."

Polus grinned. "Let the histories read that I was the first fool to drop beneath Green Mountain."

With that, he turned and stepped onto the ladder, disappearing into the Light with four men close behind. The lack of screams was gratifying, but it was unnerving when all four of them stepped to the east and out of view.

She walked down the slope into the pit and kneeled, taking a look for herself. The men were looking at rubble and collapsed stones, and to the west, the tunnel traveled hundreds of strides. "Priests and warriors to me, no need to waste time."

She set foot to the ladder and descended into the Light, and when her feet reached the floor, she slipped despite anticipating it being slick. She grabbed the ladder, noting the floor crowned in the middle to shed water to the guttered edges. The slope heading for the pyramid wasn't severe, but it was designed to drain to the sides that provided an awkward ridge to walk. Feet passed her head as someone descended. "Watch your footing."

She turned west and stared, her nose wrinkling at the musty odor assaulting her nostrils. Within flickers, Polus returned. "For once, you smell better than our surroundings."

"I knew you'd warm up to me eventually. Nothin' will be comin' at us from the east if those damned things are here at all."

She took a deep whiff of the air; a hint of rot lingered behind the usual stench of a wet cave. "Oh, they're here, I know they are. Question is, do they know we're here yet?"

"If they do, I'd rather hope they come straight as us." He glanced around him. "We're all here."

"You and me in front with a line of warriors across. I want you priests ready with the Fires of Sol in the second row."

She strode forward as folks situated themselves around her, and Polus cleared his throat. "Might be a foolish time to ask, but will Light or Dark do anything to the Wakened Dead?"

She grimaced. "Sometimes. Light is more effective."

"You know how to make a man feel all cozy inside."

The tunnel ran straight for a hundred strides before side passages split north and south, perpendicular to the main tunnel. They stopped, and Meliu's gut burned. "We'll want men with torches watching these passages."

"Shigin, run on back and have Bîdorik send more men down. Fifty or so, just in case this godsdamned place turns into a maze."

The notion of a maze spooked her until she recalled the uncanny directional senses of the Kingdomers. So long as a Helmveliner lived, they wouldn't get lost. So long as she lived, they'd have Light.

They moved forward only when reinforcements arrived, but they needed to leave the safety of numbers behind. In a hundred strides they met more side tunnels, and they waited for men to arrive to watch them before moving forward.

The floor leveled and turned dry as a bone as they crossed a grated drain and twenty strides ahead their straight tunnel ended, branching north and south. She glanced at Jîkôlk, the only Helmveliner whose name she knew. "About where do you think we are?"

"I'd put us beneath the second tier of the pyramid, about twenty-five feet below."

With the sloping grade, it made sense. "I was hoping to just walk in, find the bastards, burn 'em all to the Forges, and get our asses out."

Polus cocked his head north and south. "You and me both, darlin'. Which way?"

She grinned at Jîkôlk. "Any suggestions?"

The man closed his eyes and breathed deep. "The echoing drips suggest both passages lead to the same place. My gut tells me it's beneath the middle of the pyramid."

She trusted his ears more than his gut but figured they both might be right. More guards brought up the rear, and Meliu turned north, in a hundred strides west, and in another hundred strides south. The idea of standing beneath so many massive stones cramped her gut despite the fact it had stood here for centuries without crashing these tunnels, but as Light illuminated the room ahead, her heart drummed this irrational fear from her head, and she stopped in her tracks.

Vines dangled from the ceiling, but they weren't growing and alive, and scattered debris covered the floor in lumps and jagged points; she feared some of the shapes were bones. Drips of water fell from the ceiling, splashing in small puddles, their echo lending music to the chill spreading through her. "Dancing Bastards, what do you think of them vines?"

Polus rolled his shoulders and settled his shield. "Every monkey I have seen likes to climb. And that's the first water we've seen since going beneath the pyramid."

Jîkôlk said, "Clogged drain system? We're beneath the waterline or damned close to it. It's impressive we aren't drowning as it is. Or them vines... Maybe a recreation of the forest outside for some holy rite?"

Meliu said, "We won't learn nothin' standing here. Shinôu, Polus, Jîkôlk. With me." She crept forward with dainty steps, and as more of the chamber entered her view, she pulled up. "There's something sitting against the wall back there. A monkey, I think. Pray for vision and tell me what you see." Despite the Light brightening the room, the thing didn't move.

Shinôu said, "It's dead dead, I think. Ripped open, the blood is old, flesh rotting."

"The Wakened stop decaying and clean off the rot. That's what I've read."

Polus grunted. "Mmm, eat off the rot I heard."

They moved to the edge of the room's entry and peered in. Dead monkeys sat propped against the walls, almost as if posed to appear sleeping. Their bodies were in various states of decay and showed wounds ranging from gashes to missing limbs. They all looked to be of the same breed, with the tufts of hair on their crowns, and they were all wet from water running down the walls or dropping from the ceiling.

The calcified monkey paw made sense when she recalled the formation of stalagmites and stalactites in the Chanting Caverns where the Crack of Burdenis hid.

Meliu plied her memory of all the monkeys she'd seen on the way here and to the south, then recalled she hadn't seen more than a couple in the pyramid's vicinity. "What the Twelve Hells is this?"

Polus pointed. "Those skeletons out there, some of them are human."

Shinôu looked and grimaced. "Some of these bones are our people, looks like other breeds of monkeys too. They're all eaten on."

"Mmm, I ain't one for runnin' from a fight, but I think we should get the hells out of here. Whoever sealed this place knew what they were doing."

A part of her agreed, but Meliu's feet didn't budge. "We need to understand what we're looking at."

"I know we're lookin' at our doom if we fight 'em down in this hole. You're supposed to be the smart one here. We got tufted monkeys dead, and we got tufted monkeys Wakened, this here is the breeding ground for more godsdamned *Dulûmbolis.*"

"Holy hells, you're right." The *Dulûmbolis* killed their living kin and brought them here, waiting for the Unlife to waken them. The dead monkeys posed the carcasses like living things asleep, not dead, and they feasted on their other kills until there wasn't enough to Awaken. "No necromancy necessary. This is fascinating and vile. Evil."

"We learned something; time to get out of here so we live to use it."

"You're right—"

Woot woot trill.

Meliu froze. The echoes confused her, but when Jîkôlk's head turned, she knew it came from behind them. The word was coming from her mouth before she saw the enemy, and the will of Erginle flooded her soul with Light, and she unleashed it in a blinding torrent she hoped the Wakened would fear. "Fire!"

The purity of her Light shone with an intensity that would've sent men diving to cover their eyes, but a score of calcified, mutilated monkeys swarmed down the hall with unblinking eyes until Fire engulfed the hall. For flickers, flame was all she saw, but from the heat of Sol's Fire screamed a dozen beasts with their fur and flesh burning.

Warriors braced and struck the onslaught with swords, axes, and spears, but it was the shields and armor that would save lives. Scratching, biting, and blazing monkeys leaped into their midst with horrific screams, and men fell to the ground beating at the things with sword pommels and ax hafts. Polus bulled past her and sent a head as a burning ball down the hall.

Meliu stared on, useless as the fighting raged. Her dagger was in her hand out of instinct, but it felt as useless as her prayers about now.

Hoot hoot trill. It wasn't a single call. It was three that turned into a dozen, that turned into a number she couldn't fathom with the echoes.

"Shits!" She turned to see *Dulûmbolis* sliding down the vines while others dropped straight from the ceiling, hitting the floor to run their way. "Behind us!"

She prayed for Dark and yanked the energy of Light from the room. The temptation was to flood the area in Dark, but instead, she put a wall of Dark in the hall's entry. She heard their scrambling and scratching paws coming, but after three breaths, not a one came through the Dark. They feared it, or it confused them. She turned back to the battle and on seeing Shinôu on the ground wrestling a flaming monkey, she kicked the thing in the head, sending sparks flying, but it turned to her with a hiss, one eye missing. She stabbed with her dagger and put it through its forehead.

The thing collapsed, and Shinôu threw it off of himself, kicking it farther. The fighting persisted, but most of the monkeys were dead... again. She prayed to Erginle and put a wall of Dark at the other end of the hall, and within flickers, they stood staring at the bloodless carnage.

"Mmm, by the heavens and hells, that's a stink." Polus stood unharmed, far as she could tell, but his gear bore scorch marks.

Hoots and trills came from both directions.

Shinôu looked at her. "They fear the Dark?"

"I don't know. I think it confused them more than anything else. They're leery, but..."

Polus loomed over her. "So, yer sayin' we jumped into the shit pit, and we can't wait for someone to come and pull our asses out."

"Dead on."

"We've got what, a coupla hundred strides back to the main passage? I say we flame them up and make a push for it. Waiting ain't gonna do us no good."

"There must be a better idea."

Polus eyeballed her. "Two directions, Wakened monkeys in both of them... the way we came is the shortest route. These things have been making more of each other for how many years? We need to get the hells out of here."

Meliu recalled a passage from the *Codex of Sol: If all you have is your fist, you use it.* But it didn't refer to weapons. What it meant was when you have only one chance, you take it. "You're right. I'll keep the Dark behind us, and we'll beat our way to the main passage. With armor and shields and Fire, we've got a chance."

"Hold up," Jîkôlk said. He and the other Kingdomers reached into their packs and pulled out glowing stones dangling from chains and put them around their necks. "No offense, priestess, but if you die, I don't want to be down here blind."

"No offense taken." She led them to within a dozen strides of the northern wall of dark and breathed deep, trying to convince herself there was no way there were as many *Dulûmbolis* in this direction as she'd seen back in the central chamber. "Nilik, Gamber... Set that hall ablaze, see what happens. Shinôu and everyone else, get ready for... one hell or another."

There was nothing to see through the barrier of Dark, but they felt the heat of the flames and heard the screeches of monkeys once dead dying a second time. Three monkeys on fire burst through the patch of dark, eyes wide in a fury, and they were struck down in flickers. The prayers of Fire ended, and they heard nothing.

"Go!" As they approached the Dark, she dropped her prayer. A half dozen burning Dulûmbolis writhed on the ground, and they trotted past without a second thought, turning right.

Woot woot trill. The cry came from behind them, and everyone burst into a sprint down the empty hall. Her mail jangled, awkward as the hells to run in, and her helmet squirmed and bounced on her head until the cheek guard obscured her vision. She ran into the back of a warrior, ricocheted, and clipped her toe on someone's boot. She splayed onto the floor, her helm jamming over her nose with the impact. "Dancing bastards!"

She scrambled into a crouched run, one hand on the ground, the other righting her helm, when clawed feet dug into the mail on her back, driving her to the ground. She rose to her knees and curled into a ball, slinking like a turtle into her oversized mail. Claws and teeth slashed and gnashed, but in flickers, the first attacker disappeared, driven away by a stampeding frenzy of *Dulûmbolis.* Dozens raced past her to either side and more lit on her back, launching from her shoulders in the chase.

She huddled until the sound of scraping claws disappeared, and not long after, she heard hoots, screeches, shouts, and the ring of steel blades. Still, she didn't move. She'd heard stories of warriors in battle bearing mortal wounds, laying down to die wicks after the fight. *Am I dying? I should be dying.*

After a wick, she was still alive and decided to stand. Fighting raged, but it was farther away. A small passage led northwest, but with no clue where it led, she had to go against every instinct and run to the fight. She took three steps toward battle when a *dulûmbolis* rounded the corner with a screech.

Northwest it was. She spun and ran, dodged into another tunnel. This one turned to dirt without stone walls, but it was tall enough to run through, but narrowing, so when she spotted a bigger tunnel of stone, she turned back into it. But she wasn't losing the thing on her heels, she spun and planted her feet with dagger in hand. One monkey against armor and a dagger, she'd faced worse odds.

The thing leaped, and she sacrificed her left shoulder. It bit the rings of mail, and with her right hand she struck, stabbing through both its lungs... a killing hit if the thing needed to breathe. The next blow went into its ear, and it fell with a screech.

She didn't waste time; she turned and ran, and in flickers, she heard more clawed feet giving chase. Meliu ducked into a narrow passage and, in twenty strides stumbled to a stop in front of a pool of inky water, lucky not to have slid on the mud and straight into the pools depths. She glanced back and set a wall of Dark as she heard scrambling claws coming. She crouched with her dagger and waited. The feet slowed and the creature snuffled somewhere near the edge of the Dark. Silence. But the tingling creep crawling her skin promised the damned thing was there.

The pool was the end of the tunnel. Escape lay behind her, unless... *Drowned tunnels could lead out of this hell. The way the creatures get out.* But the bastard things didn't need to breathe. Scratching claws loped down the tunnel toward her, and they too stopped to sniff. The *Dulûlmbolis* croaked to each other like speaking a primitive language. A dagger wasn't going to fight her way out of this, and no one knew where to find her if they even made it out alive.

She glanced at the pool and recalled swimming from the docks of Choerkin Fost, the prayer to Sol and the strength it brought her. Praying to Erginle and Kibole was a beautiful thing, but in this pinch, she figured it best to beseech the king himself.

She kicked off her boots and slipped from her mail, dropping them in a heap atop her helm. She felt naked without the armor, then realized this was closer to the truth than she liked, with only her smallclothes covering her. *Wet clothes are heavy and drag. And if I die, why the hell would I care what I'm wearing? But if I live and stumble into Polus like this, I'll never hear the end of it.*

She sighed and stared at the wall of Dark as another set of feet echoed in the distance. "Sol, King of the Pantheon of Sol, give me strength, give me breath." Energy flooded her soul as it did in Purdonis Bay, but there wasn't heat, just a lightness in being and power lacing the fibers of her muscles. She pushed what remained of Dark into the wall, hoping the residual energy would retain the wall long enough for her to disappear

It didn't matter. As her knees pushed, she saw a beast careening through the dark with yellow fangs.

She splashed into the water, arms stroking and feet kicking, and a claw raked her left foot. She feared she bled but didn't look back—kick and stroke and kick. *Erginle light my way.* The gray murk glowed around her, particles sweeping by as she swam, and she dared to glance back.

Dead monkeys couldn't drown, but they didn't swim very well either. The closest beast scraped its claws against the slick walls of the tunnel for propulsion, and it lagged behind. She turned her eyes ahead and kicked forward, bubbles leaving her mouth and nose, but against everything she knew as reality, her lungs never lost air. She exhaled, closed her mouth, and her lungs filled without breathing. A high—a giddy rush to the head, and she swam, powerful and confident and without fear of dying.

The tunnel wound down and curved before bottoming out, and she rose in a swift stretch before leveling into more winding curves. She lost all track of distance and wondered if the unholy critters who dug these tunnels had any sense of direction at all. Tunnels sprouted to her left and right, and fear bit her again. She couldn't swim forever, and there was no way to tell which would take her to the surface. A side tunnel went up, so she took it.

The tunnel curved then climbed near straight up, and Light wavered on a surface. She lunged from the water, the power of Sol putting her halfway from the water, but she was still underground. She shimmied from the water, and when she took her first real breath a peculiar exhaustion swept over her, and the high turned to a queazy that threatened to black her out.

Sol, give the will.

Her spinning head righted itself, and with a few controlled breaths she lumbered forward, ducking through the low tunnel. If she were a Kingdomer she would know how far from the surface she stood, and she might be able to dig herself out.

Her bare foot struck mud and slipped, falling to her back with a splash, and when she looked up, Light revealed a thin stream of water. *If it's raining.. This could be the loose dirt of an exit hole.* Like the one Polus plunged his sword into.

She jammed her dagger straight up, pried dirt; her reward was damp dirt and muck splattering her body. She stabbed and twisted over and over until a slide of dirt the size of her chest fell from the hole. If it was like so many other holes they'd found, she had about five feet to the light of the sun. She leaped and plunged the dagger into the side of the angled shaft and scrambled inside. She dug with a fury, carving holes and scrunching to jam her knees into them before stabbing upward.

Woot woot trill.

"Kibole, give me Dark to hide." The energies of Sol and Erginle filled her, and the Dark didn't come. She wriggled in her tight tunnel, facing down, in time to see a *Dulûmbolis* with half its skull missing staring up at her with a single fang left in its mouth. It hissed, and she stabbed, putting the tip of the dagger through its one good eye.

She didn't know if the Wakened saw in the way of the living, but either way, it didn't appreciate its eye popping. It screamed and fell backward, writhing on the floor. She wagered the thing would die from the wound, but the way it screamed, others would come. She wormed her way upright and plunged the dagger over and over, dislodging the soft dirt and shoveling it between her legs to press onward.

The hole pressed tighter as she climbed, and the wetter the ground became, the more it refused to fall away without a struggle. Her dagger punched to its hilt easier than ever before, and her heart stopped before beating into a flurry. The surface; it must be. She pried and sunlight swept into her hole.

Trill hoot hoot trill hoot.

There was more than one below her. Her arm plunged and plunged and plunged, and the hole grew, but not fast enough to make her feel better. Greasy mud slicked her face, forcing her eyes closed, and she could feel the fresh rain even as she heard snuffling behind her.

She stabbed and a hand grabbed her wrist, pulling with great strength. The fit was tight, but with the greasy wet, her slender body popped from the soil. She swiped in a fruitless attempt to clear her eyes of mud. "Don't stop! Drag me! It's coming." The hand jerked and pulled, and she let out an insane laugh when she felt her feet dragged free, but it died on her lips when she looked up. The mud could be blinding her, or... "Morik?"

A screech by her feet and she curled, but with a glance, she saw a clear latcu blade cleave the creature in two. She pinched her lips and took a better look around. Took a deep breath before saying, "Ivin. Kinesee. How lovely to see you both." She closed her eyes, tempted to curse the fates, but decided not to tempt them. She lay stretched on the turf three-quarters naked, but at least mud covered every embarrassing bit.

Fifty-Six

Whistling Woods

A shiver to deliver
the finest fear to the most sullen soul,
running the hill, running the hill,
running the mill and crushed.
A kernel of corn fine buried beneath its husk.

—*Tomes of the Touched*

Nehek swore to Rinold he wouldn't become some monster's meal. The Wiirê were born here and knew the sights and smells and sounds of predators, even ones that eluded their vision, and they understood how to avoid the threats or what would drive these creatures away.

Six days after warning Nehek's family, the Wiirê grabbed Rinold's shoulder and pushed him into a cave where they hid. For three days they sat cooped up hiding from something Nehek called a *begîk,* some sort of burrowing critter. Like most beasts he bothered to speak of, it ate people. Nehek trekked from the cave every day to gather food but made sure they knew to stay quiet, still, and in the rocky cave. On the fourth day, he returned with an ugly gray fruit with a look of pride, and Rinold figured it was something tastier to eat than roots.

Nehek crushed the fruit and seeds on the floor of the cave, and then he slathered everyone with the resulting gray paste. It got them out of the cave, safe from *begîk*, but the muck smelled somewhere between shit and a week dead possum. With a hint of lemon. Best yet, the stuff was greasy as the hells, so the rain didn't touch it, and every time he glanced at a river with hopes of a bath, Nehek shook his head and clapped his hands together to mimic snapping jaws.

For two weeks, they traveled at a snail's pace that would've been restful if not for the threat of being eaten or stumbling on a Histê patrol, and as far as he could tell, they kept veering south to avoid the enemy. Some days he felt as if they might be getting farther from their destination. It was about that time that the odor faded, and Rinold never found out what a *begîk* looked like, so he chose to call that a victory. They stalked through dense underbrush up and down steep rises to avoid rivers Nehek calculated as too risky.

Edlmir said, "Hells and damnation, Squirrel, it's gonna be the rainy season before we get back to Green Mountain at this rate."

They stood at the edge of a clearing to rest, and Rinold took Edlmir's observation to heart. "Nehek, where the hells are we? How far from the pyramid?"

Yellow-eyes stared at him, and Rinold knew he wasn't going to like Nehek's answer. "I do not know."

Edlmir flailed. "Oh, whore and hells. We're lost?"

"Not lost. We head east we'll find the Mûulbon River—"

"The Puxelê River."

Edlmir laughed. "You've been gone long enough you might start thinkin' about a South Puxelê, a North Puxelê—"

Nehek snorted. "Mûulbon! We can't miss something so huge. Once there, north will take us to the Shedetûk River."

"That's if the godsdamned Histê let us go east for more than a day."

Nehek shook his head. "I cannot explain it. They don't have this many patrols so far east."

Edlmir said, "You think they're here because of us? I don't mean *us*, but the Silone?"

Nehek said, "Reasonable guess."

Rinold sighed and walked. "Piss on 'em. We won't get there standin' around."

They trudged east half a day before seeing smoke rising on the horizon, and Rinold cursed. Even if it were a Wiirê village, they wouldn't be able to trust them to keep their secret, let alone not to attack them outright.

Nehek said, "We can skirt them to the northeast."

Rinold scrunched his nose as his eye twitched. The smoke billowed into the sky now, and the breeze brought its acrid odor to his nostrils. "That's more smoke than a patrol camp. What the hells is it?"

Edlmir snorted. "These woods are too wet for a forest fire. And this isn't the rainy season."

"Let's move in, might be somethin' we should know about if all these patrols are here lookin' for Silone."

"Have you lost your mind, Squirrel?"

"That isn't some cookfire or smithy. It might be crazier to try gettin' around it without knowing what it is."

They skulked over a couple of hills, and the fire ahead became a wall of black smoke, but thinning as it rose, Rinold could see a tower through the gray haze. "A town, city, castle?"

"Ungûtu."

Rinold sucked his breath. "You said more Silone and Kingdomers were being held there."

"I said it was a possible place. But if I'm right, we aren't far from the Mûulbon."

"I don't care where we are if our people are here. Even if we can't get them out, it'd be good to know they're here. I'll go alone."

"There will be Wiirê eyes. It isn't safe."

"The last time we were safe, we were slaves. I'll be back." Rinold slipped through the underbrush, and within flickers, Nehek was by his side.

"Come. You won't learn anything by staring at smoke."

The Wiirê turned south, flanking the fire, and within wicks, they had a view of the town and its lone tower. Ungûtu's walls were no more than fifteen feet high, and though there were wider squared shapes where towers might be, they were level with the wall. The ground was charred and cleared for three hundred paces to the south, toward them, but Wiirê slaves stood out front of the blaze, tending the fire and felling trees.

Nehek stared, eyes squinting. "Why would they burn? I've never seen the Histê plant crops."

"Clearing the field so they can see an enemy better." But Rinold's eyes drifted from the fire even as he answered. Outside the city's gate sat a dozen wooden cages with skeletons inside, and they wore too many clothes to be Wiirê or Histê. "At least some of my people were here."

"It is rare to kill slaves. They fought back or tried to escape."

Rinold glanced around the walls. Maybe half a dozen Histê walked the watch. Add those to them overseeing the slaves, and there were only fifteen. "Not a lot of Histê."

"Most are on patrols or...Tsst! Look." He pointed toward the blaze, and it took a flicker for Rinold to pick them out. They wore ragged clothes, and dirt and soot hid who they were, but a string of chained slaves walking the line of the fire were northerners, both Silone and Kingdomer. One was a stocky woman.

"Holy hells, I think that's Kurin. She's a Wayfinder."

"We are not lost."

"Nope, and we wouldn't be again with her."

Nehek exhaled. "There is no way."

"When this town sported a full garrison, there was no way. Look out there. There are more than a dozen men in chains hankerin' to free themselves. Those Wiirê, on whose side would they fight?"

"The Histê."

"People want to be free. You wanted to be free, and you made it. You've done it once. Convince them to fight or at least stay out of our way." Nehek groaned and Rinold kept on. "Fourteen northern warriors and double that in Wiirê. Every Histê guard carries a spear and ax; kill one and we arm two of ours. They—"

"*Sedûlu!*" Rinold didn't know the word, but he quieted. "What is your idea?"

"See that Histê half snoozin' with his spear? I'm going to put an arrow through his chest—"

"That is a long way, Fluffy Tail."

"That's why I said through his chest instead of through his eye. He'll make a racket before he dies and all them other guards will come runnin'. Edlmir, Snortspittle, and Monkeynose will run in from behind to kill them before they even reach me while you make sure the Wiirê don't attack us."

"We should wait, watch their movements."

"If they get my people behind them walls, how long until they're out again? And waiting means patrols returning. We strike fast before anybody notices us. It's our best hope."

"Edlmir will agree?"

"It's a fight; he'll agree. I'll give you men a half candle to get in position or call it off."

Nehek nodded before bounding away, moving fast despite the skulking hunch to his back. Rinold watched until he disappeared in the woods, then removed his quiver and leaned back on the hill. He had eight arrows remaining, all broad-heads for game, but unarmored men often fell easier than deer, let alone a hundred brick boar. He took them out one by one, checking their balance, the fletching, and the shafts to see if the humidity and rain had warped them. He enjoyed a moment of pride as he admired his handiwork. The wood was from south of the Dragonspans, but the turkey feathers from the north.

Which reminded him of another promise he made, pretty feathers for Puxele's next batch of arrows. He glanced into the trees expecting the usual selection of bright feathers and beaks flitting above, but there was a peculiar lack of birds. Peculiar until Rinold saw the griffon-eagle sitting in a branch that bent under the creature's weight.

"Godsdamn, Hirk, it's good to see you again. Are you here for luck or to see me die?" Feathers ruffled, and it stared at him. "I'll tell you what. You just let me know if you see any Histê a-comin'."

He relaxed for a spell then rose to a knee to take a gander at the enemy. The man with the spear had moseyed about some as he watched over the Wiirê tending the fire. The fire and smoke would make it difficult for guards on the wall to see the attack at first, or that was his hope. He jammed seven arrows in the dirt and nocked the eighth, stretched the string, and breathed deep. The Histê leaned, giving him a broad target, and his fingers slipped the string. He was nocking a second arrow when the first struck from its arch.

It was a beautiful shot straight through the bastard's heart, he wagered; the man stood straight then crumpled without taking a step. If he'd taken a deer at this range without tracking a blood trail, he would've been giddy and telling the story over beers for years, but Rinold meant for the bastard to run, make noise. He had a plan for failure, but he didn't for being too successful.

"Well, ain't that the shits."

He snagged one arrow from the dirt and trotted to another tree, not even bothering with stealth, but no one paid a lick of attention to anything around them. The guards guarded the slaves and didn't bother to think of guarding themselves. He strolled within twenty-five strides of the next Histê guard, close enough he could put the arrow through his head, but instead, he picked a bigger target.

The arrow struck his ass cheek and passed clean through, likely shattering the pelvis. The Histê screamed and collapsed, dying like the other, only slower and louder. He nocked the other arrow and loosed at the next nearest Histê before the man ran more than three strides. The Histê's hide-covered shield caught the tip and the arrow tumbled to the ground.

Rinold turned and ran toward his other arrows, long strides carrying him to the trees for cover. He grabbed an arrow and nocked as he spun. He found his target; the man ran with rhythm, his arms swinging, shield covering and uncovering. Rinold loosed, and the arrow buried in his chest to the fletching. He plucked another arrow from the dirt and loosed. The next Histê caught the arrow with his shield and this time with a better angle to send it ricocheting high, but when he raised his arm to throw a spear, he exposed his chest. The next arrow took him clean in the sternum; he dropped to his knees, dying while propped against his shield.

Rinold watched as three more Histê ran his way. He stood, nabbed his arrows, and smiled at them. The bastards had no idea they were about to die. Edlmir hewed and dropped one from behind while Nehek hamstrung another with his spear before leaping on his back for the kill. The third heard the screams and turned just in time for Snortspittle to sweep the Histê's head from his shoulders.

The northerners ran toward them the best they could in shackles, but the Wiirê slaves stood in dumbfounded shock. "Get them chains broke! Nehek, speak to your people." He ran to the nearest bodies, grabbing a spear and throwing it toward the closest slave. Rinold screamed in Wiirê, "Fight your masters!"

The Wiirê bent to take the spear, a tentative grip at first, but Nehek grabbed the man and shook his shoulders; his face changed, and Rinold knew that whether this man lived or died in the next few wicks, he did so as a free man.

Edlmir's heavy blows busted bronze chains, and in no time, his little army had grown. Kirun trotted to his side. "You took your time getting here."

"What can I say? I lost my Wayfinder." He stared at the gate through the fire, vague shapes running their way. "How far are we from Green Mountain?"

"If we had wings, a hundred and five horizons, give or take a few steps. No wings? I don't know, but I'll get us there."

"You want my sword and shield or my bow?"

She laughed. "I don't think I could draw your bow. Besides, this is personal."

Rinold slid his shield from his shoulder and handed her his sword. "Don't go gettin' yerself killed."

Rinold watched with an arrow nocked as the Histê arrived. Fools jumping through the fire one, two, or three at a time to die, and as each died another Wiirê gained a weapon. Within wicks, they strode to the gates of Ungûtu with Rinold in the rear, for the first time in his life feeling a little bit like a clan lord. Within a quarter-candle, Ungûtu was theirs, and the Histê lay dead without the Wiirê taking a single prisoner.

Indeed, he had himself an army now, seventeen Silone, nine Kingdomers, and as many as forty-seven Wiirê, depending on how many scattered for the forest the first chance they got. They were poorly trained, ill equipped, and most of them couldn't speak to more than half their allies, but by the gods, they were victorious.

Edlmir stood by his side outside the gate as folks rummaged through Histê supplies to make a meal. "That was my kind of plan, Squirrel. Straightforward and bloody."

Kirun trotted to them with Nehek by her side. "Do you want the bad news now?"

Rinold deflated. "How bad're we talkin'?"

Nehek answered for her. "There is a Histê army coming."

Rinold closed his eyes and didn't bother to open them as he talked. "Just what do you mean by an army?"

"One slave overheard that a *tutûlê* is on its way. Four to five thousand men."

Kirun said, "I picked up some of the tongue, and I heard that two more *tutûlês* are on their way."

Rinold rubbed his eyes. "Nehek. Friend. You mentioned nothing about armies."

"The only reason they'd be sending armies here is to cross the Mûulbon at the Far-Horizon Bridge across from the city of ghosts near Tômôrôk. It's the only place I know that an army could cross the river without approaching the mountains."

"More ghosts, that's wonderful."

"The only thing that makes sense is they plan to march on Stone-Claw... Green Mountain."

"How far out are we from this bridge?"

"Three days by road. Four to five over land.

"When are these bastards due?"

"The first army, two days. A week or more on the others."

Rinold looked to Kirun. "Are your weapons and armor here?"

"I'm pretty sure the Wiirê sold them to some Histê merchant."

He strolled to a dead Histê and shook arrows from his quiver. They were longer than he was used to and fitted with bronze points;

cutting them down might suffice, considering their shafts and fletching were quality, but their balance and weight would throw him off. He wouldn't win no archery contest, but he'd hit a man at a reasonable range. "If the road is clear, we get to the bridge before this *tutûlê* plenty easy, but we risk being seen."

Kirun said, "It isn't a risk; they *would* see us. Histê patrols with yellow-eye scouts have been in and out along the roads every other day."

"I guess the second thing our little army gets to do is retreat. A two-day head start, and we should outpace them even while avoiding the road, so long as they don't know we're in front of them. We'll need to cross the Mûulbon at some point. We may as well make for this bridge."

Edlmir grinned. "If nothing else, an army on our asses should inspire us to move faster."

"Everyone eat, rest up, bandage any wounds. Scavenge weapons and armor, food and water. We'll march soon as we're able." Rinold sighed, but instead of mulling the negatives, he reached for a kernel of positivity. "You see, Nehek? I told you it was a good idea to attack sooner rather than later."

Fifty-Seven

Mother's Dream

A dollop of fear is what separates the courageous from the fool-hardy, but there is no greater fool who dies faster than a coward in battle.

—*Codex of Sol*

The notion that Choerkin, or Silone as the case may be, made for great bait bore fruit on their trip to Istinjoln. The Colok shredded seventeen Shadows on their journey, including three Taken they managed to run down. They were eight Silone from three clans and thirty Colok from five tribes, arriving outside Istinjoln with what could well be a fool's confidence.

It was midday and the Celestial Gate appeared weak in the sun, but when they felt the Shadow birthing pulse, Pikarn knew it as an illusion. They sat huddled in furs on Colok sleds overlooking the monastery's lone gate at a position the Edan would find if traveling from the Oemindi Pass.

Rikis scanned north to west while Pikarn stared at their target through a fareye and chewed jerked pork. "How many Shadows do you think are down there? I catch sight of one here and there. Plenty of Taken tracks in the snow."

"I wanna know if the Edan are dead or still comin'." Pikarn collapsed his fareye with a snap. It'd been twenty-five days since the Colok saw the Edan travel north, so the question held merit. "From what Rinold said, Daevu could kill 'em. It were Solineus who killed one of those demons. But outside of that? It'd take somethin' Forges wicked to kill Inslok, and with two other Edan with him... I won't believe it."

It was two candles later that they first spotted the Edan party running along the western road, and they didn't slow down even as they made their way up the rise. "Them sons of bitches run like horses."

Rikis said, "I don't know if they're friends, but I'm damned happy not to call them enemies."

"Allies for a time. And we still have nine hundred and ninety-seven years at New Fost." He stood and stepped from the sled. "Inslok! Good to see you."

The Edan stopped, unwinded by his run. "How long have you been here?"

"Not long. Midday."

"Good. We were delayed at the Steaming Lakes."

"Did you learn anything?"

"Not so much as we hoped. It is up to Limereu to contrive an answer to the Celestial Gate, but the Touched suggested it will be some time before the answer."

"Which means maybe long after I'm dead by an immortal skeleton's reckoning of time."

"It is impossible to guess."

Pikarn turned to stare at the Gate as its pulse washed energy over him. "What good is it to keep on pumping Shadows onto an island without humans?"

Limereu said, "It could help reinforce the connection between worlds."

Pikarn snorted. "Is it worth goin' in?"

"Getting closer to the Gate might help stir memories, and the more I contemplate the Touched's words, the more I think we need to speak with Marukane."

Rikis said, "I don't wanna die for nothing, but part of me wants to see that thing up close."

Pikarn swallowed his jerky. "Fine. Do we head in now or wait fer mornin' light?"

Zjin growled, "Wait."

Inslok said, "We should be safe for the night. We will ignite campfires, so Marukane knows we are here."

Glimdrem asked, "Is that wise? Marukane didn't seem fond of you, and Solineus isn't here."

If Pikarn had ever seen Inslok pricked by a jab, this was it. Inslok turned on Glimdrem. "The human was irrelevant."

"Ha! Tell that to the *mokotu-xe* who was a flicker from turning you into powdered ice."

"The Volvrolan will hear of your insolence."

Pikarn stepped between them. "Whoa yer horses, boys. No need to go killin' Glimdrem when he might die tomorrow anyhow."

Glimdrem laughed but wandered off to speak to the Trelelunin warriors.

"Excuse him. He has become a problem over the last couple of years."

"Your problems are yours; they ain't two pisses to me. Our problem is Istinjoln."

"Agreed."

Limereu strode to stand in front of Zjin. "Inslok said it was you who knew the name of Marukane. How did you know?"

The Colok took a deep breath, but it took three to get the words out. "Legend of Queen's sons. Dark battles. Whips and slaves in the Evil Years."

"From your legends, do you have any idea what the Queen Mother would want?"

"To kill. To conquer."

"That was for the Dontupûor, her masters. What would she want for herself?"

Zjin cast an emotionless stare and shrugged.

Inslok said, "What are you considering?"

"The Touched said that Zwinfolkum could close the gate. If we can't close the gate ourselves, maybe she'll do it for us."

Pikarn gave a snort and sat back on the sled convinced that the lady Edan might be crazier than Glimdrem. "I'll let my betters go on speculatin' about such things. Wake me when there's a good fire and food." He leaned back and covered his face with his fur hood. The sled rocked, and he peeked to find Oldenu crawling in beside him.

She smiled. "Two is warmer than one."

It was cramped, but he liked it. "Aye, it is at that."

Istinjoln was a wasteland of blowing snow when they entered the gates, and this time Glimdrem hopped aboard a sled, letting the wolves do the work. The Edan and the remaining Trelelunin ran behind them. The Tundra Wolves took the turning streets slow compared to straights and did a marvelous job of not slamming them into any walls.

He wasn't surprised by the lack of Shadows of Man or Taken at first, so much the better to let them walk into a trap, but when the courtyard where the Celestial Gate stood proved empty, he found his curiosity growing. He leaped from the sled and raised his arms as a conquering hero.

"Success! We have rid Istinjoln of its invaders."

No one laughed, not even the fool humans, but most of the Trelelunin grinned. The Edan might hate him, so much as an Edan could hate, but he'd managed to make friends of his kin.

Humans and Colok piled from the sleds and milled about, uncertain what to do in the face of nothing. Limereu, however, strode straight for the Celestial Gate, and Glimdrem joined her. "Any memories?"

"It is tantalizing. I get flashes of glowing gems—sprinkling powders. But any knowledge is distant, like a scent in my nose that I cannot name. That a human achieved this is stunning."

"It is said that Lord Priest Ulrikt was the most gifted priest of the Pantheon since the Forgettings."

"Still, it is uncanny. It is an achievement not quite on par with the girl's flaming tower, but he did it without the Sliver of Star."

"She was an Instinctive, she didn't source her powers from prayer."

"I am aware. What if Ulrikt was an Instinctive who managed to build a connection to the gods?"

Glimdrem's head rocked back. "An Instinctive and Channeler?"

Inslok's voice came from right beside his ear. "It is a feat, but it would explain his power."

Limereu stopped within strides of the Gate, and waves of energy prickled his skin. "Yes and no." She held out a hand and her fingers glowed. "This Celestial Gate is powerful and stable; I doubt its like has been seen since the Age of God Wars."

She had a point that Glimdrem couldn't deny. Uvin's success at the Vale of Resting Winds, if it could be called such, had lasted flickers and killed him. "What are you suggesting?"

"I think he had help from the other side."

A shiver danced along Glimdrem's spine, but not from any revelation. Something watched them. He turned in unison with the Edan to see Marukane resting on his great, frog-like legs, and massive body of roiling, smoky shadow. His tentacled eyes stared at them.

Inslok spun on his heel. "Maru and Kane."

The creature's tentacles stretched, one slithering through the air to gaze on Inslok, the other on Limereu. "You know my names. Do you now know how to destroy us as promised?"

"No. Not yet."

"I assumed as much. Oathbreaker. And you, Edan woman, is your wisdom so vast that you know how to slay me?"

"I am not here to kill anyone. I am here to learn."

"Funny, as you were once an accomplished killer."

"You know me too?"

"I know you better than you know you. I admit to finding that amusing. And you, Nezeldun." The tentacle stretched to the third Edan. "Do you think your waters will harm me?"

"No, I don't."

"You are all wiser than I thought, and yet here you are." An eye stretched to gaze down on Glimdrem. "I'm surprised they brought you a second time, the fallen so low."

Glimdrem swallowed and didn't answer, and Limereu saved him from the continued stare.

"Zwinfolkum could close this gate."

"My Queen Mother is the Celestial Gate."

"What could we do to convince her to close it forever?"

The beast smiled and its tentacles rose high. "You could bring her through."

Inslok stepped forward, paces from the thing's body. "That we cannot allow. Something else."

"My Queen Mother has been betrayed more than once by mortal hand. *You* betrayed us once, and have yet to pay, but pay you will."

Limereu said, "Did Ulrikt betray your mother?"

"Someone betrayed my mother, but betrayal was always a part of our lives." Marukane sat with tentacles wrapped so that he stared at Inslok from both sides. "You were a fool to return."

Inslok's sword whipped from its sheath, and the Edan screamed as he hewed at the beast. The blade struck over and over, and Marukane bellowed with laughter like a man taunting a child who pounded on their leg with tiny fists.

Limereu stepped forward, but Glimdrem put a hand to her shoulder. "You are powerless to stop this with anything but words. Marukane has fouled his mind."

She screamed. "Marukane! Let him go. Let us forge an agreement with your Queen Mother."

Some part of him admonished himself for the joy he took in watching the Edan toyed with like a marionette. But Glimdrem ignored the whisper and smiled inside.

Dareun had learned a few strange things since the Face of Ulrikt Sundered his soul and executed him. One was that Taken ignored him, or maybe didn't see him at all, and a second was that Shadows didn't like his presence. He wasn't sure if they saw him, but if he got close, they moved away. Even if he teleported to try to get close, they weren't there when he arrived. The game proved entertaining for a month.

When Marukane arrived at Istinjoln, Dareun learned that not only did the beast see him, but they could also speak to each other. The demon wasn't much for talking, but he enjoyed listening. He loved stories of all sorts, whether history, religious canon, or ribald tales Dareun heard in his youth while sitting around the hearth.

The last time mortals arrived in Istinjoln he'd managed to calm Marukane's anger and get everyone out alive with a single promise: to tell stories. Today, however, Marukane wasn't listening.

Dark energies flowed through the Edan's body as he swung his weapon at the laughing demon. Dareun stood beside Inslok, waving his arms and screaming. Tears streamed down the Edan's cheeks and dripped from his chin as he screamed. There was nothing he could think of to do, except...

He stepped inside of Inslok. The demon's laughter ended, and Inslok stopped, his body matching Dareun's pose. Dareun spoke and for the first time in what seemed an eternity heard his voice with mortal tones. "Stop this."

"Little Spirit, why have you ended my fun?"

"This is torment."

"This Edan brought my torment."

"Release him, or I will tell you no more stories."

"I will release him when you do."

Dareun didn't know whether to trust a demon or not. "Tell these people what your Queen Mother wants."

"When they know what all mother's want, they will have their answer. But they must leave."

He sensed a familiar presence and turned. No one was there, but somehow she watched him. Ghosts couldn't cry, so he smiled.

"Little Spirit, at what do you stare?"

"Hello, sweet girl."

"Who is sweet girl?"

He didn't answer. He stared into the sky, praying to catch a glimpse of Eliles, but there was nothing more than a hint of her being. He stared for a time, patted his hand above his heart, winked, and then mouthed goodbye.

He turned back to Marukane. "I will release him. You do the same." Dareun stepped free from the body and the Edan collapsed behind him. He spun to face the demon. "What have you done?"

Marukane laughed. "Little Spirit, he is free. I have done nothing more than what you asked. Ask yourself what *you* have done."

"All I did was leave."

Marukane ignored him, turning his tentacled eyes back to the woodkin. "Take your broken Edan and go home."

The demon disappeared, but Dareun felt his presence deep beneath the monastery. He turned to gaze upon the crumpled Edan. Despite the demon's words, Dareun knew he had saved Inslok's life.

Glimdrem dropped beside the crumpled Edan. "Inslok, what happened?"

"I am... I am... I am..."

Pikarn rushed close, the grimy human showing real concern. "That's some deep thinkin', woodkin, come on! What happened?"

"I am Almost."

Pikarn stood straight and stared. "Almost, what the hells does he mean? Are his wits ruint?"

Glimdrem kneeled beside the Edan, cocking his head as the memory of the Touched in a tomb full of books dominated his vision. "The Touched named him Almost."

"What are you talking about? The dead guy in the tomb?"

"Yes, the dead guy in the tomb." He looked to Limereu, and in the background Shadows of Man appeared in the streets and Taken lined the roofs of buildings in numbers they couldn't defeat. "We need to load him on a sled and get out of here."

"Agreed."

Glimdrem put his shoulder beneath Inslok's arm, but the Edan lifted into the air. Glimdrem's heart lurched until he realized Zjin lifted him with one hand to put him on a sled.

The Silone woman, Oldenu, who smelled little better than the Wolverine, stepped to the sled. "We should head for Berul. If we reach the island, we'll be safe."

Shadows rushed from the eastern side of the courtyard, their exit, but windswept rain sent them shrieking. Glimdrem had almost forgotten about Nezeldun. Everyone clung to the sleds, and Tundra Wolves howled and pulled. In three wicks, the runners glided over ice and snow outside the monastery walls and swung in a southern arch to skirt the walls of Istinjoln.

Glimdrem didn't know if they'd learned anything that would close the gate, at least without bowing to the whims of the Queen Mother, but as he stared at Inslok's shivering form, an Edan maybe dying, he saw that Inslok in a pathetic state wasn't so different from himself.

The vine said, *He was what you were, and now he is what you are.*

Glimdrem didn't believe the words; the vine needed more proof. "We'll see." He glanced around, happy that no one caught him speaking.

Fifty-Eight

River of Ghosts

Black bones on white sands,
a message across time written with death.
What do you see? What do you read?
What won't you find? What don't you need?
I see you. Do you see me? Is my nose black
or alcoholic red? The dead unsaid and unspeakable
the benighted words and the Killing Joke.
Sneak on your heels and march on your toes,
dance with me, Pearl Dolphin, before the
Whale Hole blows.

—*Tomes of the Touched*

The view from atop Green Mountain impressed Ivin, even the crude wall improvised around the pyramid, but his arrival with so many warriors had already strained the region's ability to feed them. If Wakened monkeys were edible, they might've had meat for a month, but instead, they burned the carcasses in a clearing to the east. The only good news was that the repairs to the water reservoirs caught ample rain for fresh water.

He glanced at Morik as he topped the pyramid stair with a huff; Meliu and Tudwan accompanied the Kingdomer, and Lucky and Grunt weren't far behind. The two Wiirê no longer wore ropes around their wrists, but they followed the high priestess as if she pulled some invisible chain. Morik eased into a seat beside him with a grin and said, "Today's the first morning we didn't find any monkeys. Polus is still sweeping a few tunnels, but remaining monkeys are scattered and few."

"Excellent news. We've established our toehold in this land."

"Trouble is we brought an army where there ain't no war to fight, and we still need to feed them. We've cleared the region of every edible plant worth tasting, and we're starting in on stuff that'll wear a man's teeth to nubs."

He recognized the words as hyperbole, but they made Morik's point. "How long until supply trains arrive from the north?"

"I'd figure on a few days. The road should be pushing to half-way here by now, but that's still a lot of rough horizons for wagons."

"We'll make do." Ivin turned to Meliu. "You mentioned something about other ruins to the south. Have you gotten anything out of your little tagalongs?"

"The maps are more useful than these boys so far." She unrolled a scroll. "By my thinking, this pyramid and the surrounding holy site are known as Setemêz. At scale, I'd wager this circle here, Mekelên, is a good fifteen horizons to the southeast. Jûmjôlu is twenty horizons due south."

The names were written in fresh ink, and he guessed by Meliu's hand. "Where'd you get the names from?"

"A map from Istinjoln. Bear with me."

"Fine. Mekelên doesn't offer us much. This Jûmjôlu, what is it?"

"A ruined city. Lucky here knows the location, but I don't understand much of what he says."

"A walled city?"

She pulled a second scroll from her pack. It was larger and bore an aged patina to its bronze knobs. "This is a much older map, the paths of the rivers have changed, and the scale is different, but these symbols match up pretty well."

Morik leaned over the map and tapped what would be Jûmjôlu on the older map. "I reckon they do. The symbols are plain circles; I'd say no wall."

Ivin stood and put his palms to the table, staring at the selection of symbols. "Circle a city, triangle a pyramid. We need a fortress or a walled city, something readily defended. And I'd prefer one that didn't breed the Wakened."

Morik pointed southwest on the map. "Down here, we've got a double circle right next to a pyramid, along this stretch of mountains where they meet a major river. That's a walled city."

Meliu said, "The city is Endelêun, the pyramid is Tomarok."

Ivin and Morik both pulled back from the map while glancing at one another. "I reckon that's where the Ironwing wants us."

Meliu nodded. "It is."

Ivin put his hands to his hips and stared. "The Ironwing isn't the only one. Tomarok is the reason Lord Priest Ulrikt sent you south with the *Codex of Sol*. Have you uncovered why?"

"I've broken the code and translated much of the Eight Lights Prophecy. It references Tomarok, but as with every mention of the name, there's no detail. I'm beginning to think Ulrikt didn't know either, but it's mentioned so often it must be important."

"It's possible, but I don't believe it for a flicker of a flash. That whoreson played us. We thought we were fighting him every step of the godsdamned way, and here we are heading straight for where the bastard wanted us."

"And if the Dark Waters Cult thinks to free Hîmr from the same place?" Morik lifted a canteen from his hip, opened it, and took a swig before offering it to Ivin. "Don't worry, none; it isn't water."

Ivin laughed and took a drink. The flavor wasn't much different than water, but he knew full well the concoction could lay him out on his ass. He offered the canteen to Meliu but didn't let go when she grabbed it. "You're suggesting we head there, aren't you?"

"If I understand Lucky, there're four or five villages they would've taken our people, depending on which tribe caught them, and Endelêun gets us closer to them all. All signs point its way."

"It'd be a hells of a lot easier if they pointed to a cleared road as well. I don't like it, not a lick."

Morik said, "I can't say as anyone here does. But the Dark Waters can't be honey coated or ignored."

Ivin stretched and tugged at his nose before turning a hard gaze on Meliu. "Tell me one thing. Does the Warlord Choerkin die in the Eight Lights Prophecy?" Her hesitation spoke the truth. "No point in lying."

"At least this time, it doesn't give grisly details."

He laughed. "Well, by the gods then! I'm in. So, how the hells do we reach my funeral pyre?"

She glared at him. "Conflicting prophecies speak to an unknown end."

He'd heard enough of that line. "Nine of ten say I die, but it doesn't mean I mean to comply. What's our route? Any suggestions from the maps?"

"A road leads south from Green Mountain; it matches the general direction of Jûmjôlu. Or we could follow this river."

Ivin gazed at the map. "Clearing the ancient roads might prove easier if for no other reason than folks build to the terrain. And no doubt you stirred up Wiirê taking your yellow-eyes there. Even with an army, it might be better not to reveal our numbers. What say we head due south, with these maps in the hands of a Wayfinder, we might do well enough finding the old routes."

Morik stamped a foot and held his hand out for his canteen. "Agreed. Sooner we get this thing done the sooner the Ironwing lets me sit at Shuntiskâ in peace for a spell."

Meliu took a drink before returning Morik's alcohol. "When do we leave?"

He wanted to say now, or tomorrow morning, but reason won out. "We'll clear forest south until the supplies arrive, then we march. I suggest we take five hundred armored horse and three thousand on foot. That leaves a hundred or so horsemen here but two thousand footmen. When the road crew reaches Green Mountain that number will double, but the supply hauls will move faster."

Morik nodded. "The numbers sound good. I'll ride with you and leave Bîdorik and *Rûîrn* Frâbor in command of the Kingdomers."

"Polus will stay behind here."

Meliu's eyes widened. "He'll be piss'n fire."

"That's what he gets for playing with monkeys while we make decisions. Any word from the holies up north?"

"Sedut and a half dozen other high priests should be on their way any day."

This news was a blessing and a curse. "She anticipated our riding for Tomarok.'

"I doubt she's the only one. She'll be handy when the war comes. She can handle Breath Stealers better than I can."

Ivin grimaced at the memory of her story and the pains she'd suffered. "It's settled then—"

"What the hells is settled, mmm?"

Ivin raised his eyes to meet Polus' stare. "Broldun! Have a seat and some whiskey. We've got a plan you won't like."

Kinesee buckled her sword belt around her waist while knowing little more than how to draw the hunk of steel, poke a straw-stuffed dummy, and maybe clip the head off a sunflower with its polished blade. Nobody made the time to teach her, and this brought on painful memories, for she knew if Maro were still alive, she would be tormenting him with her lack of skill, and the sunflowers would be terrified of her by now.

Not that she could blame anybody, there were more pressing needs all around her. Alu meant well and was the only reason Kinesee managed to get a dummy to hit in the first place. The mature Lady Choerkin in her understood this, but the child grew peevish. It didn't help that everyone wanted to leave her behind somewhere or another. Morik would just as soon see her stowed in Castle Choerkin, sealed safe behind solid Kingdomer walls; Ivin wouldn't disagree with Morik, but he'd feel better with her at Forest's Gate; Leto would have her travel to Foggy Vale to live with the Lady Tedêu and the other Ravinrin clanblood. In the end, she believed Ivin respected her choice to ride with them, even if he preferred her somewhere else. Or at least that's what she hoped his smile meant the morning they set out.

They caught the small army clearing the terrain three days out at the ruins Meliu's map named Jûmjôlu. They didn't need a Wayfinder to tell them where they were, as broken walls and towers marked the location well enough, but Rendetu confirmed the distance as scaled on the map was dead-on accurate. If there'd been a lingering doubt whether Kingdomers had inked the ancient map or not, this ended the notion.

It was difficult to judge ancient Jûmjôlu by what was visible now. The forest consumed evidence of how many people lived there and what their lives were like centuries before, and even how long since folks lived in what was now little more than the foundations of civilization was a mystery. Were the people here after the Great Forgetting, or were they a culture that disappeared in a blink of time like legends spoke of?

They spent the night but didn't bother exploring beyond finding ways out. Five roads led from the city, but one pointed straight to Endelêun, making their decision easy. They rode at a casual gait surrounded by thousands of men on foot. Riding a horse should never get boring, but by golly, after a month in the saddle without breaking from a walk, it did.

After candles of riding in silence, Ivin's voice broke her idle ruminations. "These were a warrior people who built these roads."

"Why do you say that?"

"We've curved only a handful of times down this road since leaving Jûmjôlu, and those have been gentle. Instead of turning, they cut through hills and did whatever it took to keep them straight."

She pondered this, hoping to impress Ivin with some tidbit of wisdom, but her brain did her no favors. "Everybody likes straight roads."

"Ah, but the extra time and effort it took suggests they wanted to move their military as quickly as possible in times of war. Not just the armies, but supply trains. I've no doubt outposts and towns once lined these roads. The real irony is that the roads have been so straight that we managed to keep on going when it turned without our realizing it."

"We what?" She looked ahead and back and at the ground around here. Most times the road was difficult to see, but there had been a stray paver here and there uncovered. "When did that happen?"

"Hard as the hells to say. Half a day?"

"So, we're lost in this forest?"

"I wouldn't say lost. Instead of doubling back, we'll move on until we find a river. Follow that, and we'll find something, hells, it might lead us straight to Endelêun for all we know."

"I guess we didn't really know where we were anyhow." Strange to be lost and unlost at the same time. "These roads, were they built by an older culture or the last to rule here?"

Ivin's brow raised and his lips curved. "A fine question. Were the original roads laid by the pyramid builders or those who built after them? And perhaps the later people built over the foundations the others made."

She was proud of her question, but she wasn't allowed to savor it as Meliu and Leto trotted to ride beside them. Leto had attached himself to the high priestess, aggravating to watch him fawn over the woman, but satisfying to watch her not give him a single word for every twenty of his. Whether he was attracted to her cold beauty or he simply wanted to make Kinesee jealous, she couldn't decide, but it was a little pathetic.

"I've been meaning to speak to you about the *Codex of Sol*, but getting you alone is right impossible."

Kinesee smiled instead of snarling. "Anything you have to say to my husband, you can say in front of me."

"My lady speaks true. Did you get another one translated?"

"Another piece of the Dark Sword Prophecy. A piece I've been interested to find. I mentioned before how Lord Priest Ulrikt figured on the Sliver of Star to raise him from the dead, that was common lore amongst the gossips of Istinjoln."

"Aye, you did."

Kinesee couldn't resist. "Shouldn't that mean we can ignore this Doom Sword Prophecy?"

"Dark Sword, and no, we shouldn't. I've cracked four ciphers to get as far as I have, and I'm only half-way. The prophecy was considered vital by whoever put the codex together. We believed that Ulrikt sought to be raised by the Sliver of Star in order to claim the *Erikô Vôlkî,* the Crown of the King Priest. It seems his probable goal, but at some point, he realized he didn't have the Sliver. He was prepared for the possibility and didn't miss a note in the prophetic song. The Dark Sword Prophecy is why. Or at least it's one reason why."

Kinesee snorted. "You're managing to make a long boring ride not only more boring, but confusing."

"There are several key figures in the Dark Sword Prophecy. The Warlord Choerkin, first warlord of a New Age, and it's reasonable to wager that's Ivin here. The man raised by the Sliver of Star, who becomes the first King Priest of a New Age is another. But there is another, and he or she is vital. The *Êomulô Turgin ret Bontorê,* translated it means the bender of Bontore's will."

Ivin asked, "Who could bend a god's will?"

"Not everything is so literal, in fact, much seems to *not* be literal. I think it means a person who makes the futures Bontore sees come true. I think this is who Ulrikt sees himself as in the prophecies."

They rode in silence, and when Kinesee glanced back, Lucky and Grunt's luminescent yellow eyes startled her. They creeped her out every time she saw them, and it didn't help that they were almost naked. "So, you're saying he's doing Bontore's bidding?"

"Bontore speaks to oracles of possible futures, possible routes to desired ends. Ulrikt believes he is the figure to make one of those futures come true."

Ivin groaned and stretched in the saddle. "How noble of the bastard."

"I'm sure he sees it that way. He doesn't see himself as a follower of some prophetic vision, but its trailblazer. The one responsible for making certain a desirable prophecy comes true. And that brings me to you." Meliu smiled straight at her with a smirk. "Or at least maybe. The Lady of the Lion."

Kinesee blinked, and her hands tightened on the reins and saddle horn. "Lady of the Lion? I've nothing to do with Sol... his Fire. Eliles, in her tower of Fire, would be the Lady of the Lion."

"The lion conjures imaginings of Sol and his Fire, and that's what I thought for some time. But there is another lion."

Kinesee's stomach fluttered. "Rin. The Heretics of Rin." She wasn't bored any longer.

Ivin sat straight and glared at Meliu. "You should've started with *those* words. What the forges does it say?"

"I fear it was a single reference and vague. But it did suggest you will be a young mother."

Kinesee found her mouth lacking words at this revelation, and both Leto and Ivin stared at her. It was Lucky and Grunt who rescued her from their eyes.

"*Zimpotû utûê unô*!" Both men babbled the words over and over and pointed to the horizon, but trees blocked their view.

Ivin said, "Meliu, what're you yellow-eyes going on about? Some creature?"

Meliu calmed them with words and a soothing tone. She turned and scanned the trees. "Dancing Bastards, they're right. If you look close, there are mountains in the distance... or at least higher hills."

Kinesee squinted and nodded as if she could see them. They might be there, but all that green blended. "Why are they so excited about some hills? We see plenty of them."

"What they're saying is Ghost River... I think."

Leto said, "Pray, what is a Ghost River? Just a name, or should we be... spooked?"

Ivin chuckled but said, "Leto. Call us to a stop for the day, and we'll find out what we're getting into."

The Ravinrin sounded his horn with three short blasts, and men stopped marching all around, some removing their packs before taking a seat, others seeing straight away to making camp.

Kinesee sat her saddle while growing grumpier by the flicker. If there was anything more boring than riding in the middle of an army, it was sitting in the midst of one. "I want to know what a ghost river looks like." She eyeballed Ivin until he couldn't ignore her stare.

Tudwan, Alu, and Morik joined them for the ride, along with twenty warriors mounted on Tek warhorses with Tek armor. Meliu also joined them, to Kinesee's chagrin, but there was no way to argue that they weren't safer with Lucky and Grunt watching the woods around them.

Despite the dense canopy of trees, there was a carpet of vines and scattered underbrush, enough to irritate the legs of the horses. Kinesee hadn't appreciated the work being done to clear their route before now and promised kinder words for those men now that she'd witnessed it.

They moseyed through the woods for a horizon before her view changed. It was subtle at first, the trees in the foreground and the background blending, but in between, "A clearing."

One flicker, centuries-old trees surrounded them, and the next, the sun blinded their eyes as it beat down on a lush field of grass. No one was more excited than the horses, who pulled at their reins to take a bite. Everyone stopped and let their horses eat, as their eyes took in a sweeping river of green grass swaying in the wind with patches of pink and purple wildflowers. But not a single tree. It ran as far as the eye could see in both directions, and straight down its middle was a stone structure like Kinesee had never seen before, with low arches maybe four feet from the ground.

Morik stood in his stirrups. "An aqueduct."

Kinesee had heard the word before; Kingdomers had bantered on about water supplies when constructing Rôemhîik. "What is an aqueduct?"

"It carries water to a city or a fortress."

Ivin said, "Someone keeps the area cleared... Meticulously cleared."

Grunt said, "*Zimpotû utûê unô.*"

Meliu looked at him. "*Ne utûê?*"

"*Ne, ne.*"

"He doesn't see any ghosts."

"Good enough for me!" Kinesee reined her horse and squeezed her legs while loosening her grip on the reins. The horse broke into a trot. Open ground with a breeze would've livened the beat of her heart alone, but the role of the horse's gait brought joy.

It wasn't long before Ivin was by her side. "If I didn't know better, I'd say you were your father's daughter."

She laughed, running the fingers of her free hand through her hair, angling her horse toward the aqueduct to lengthen the run, but when she reined in, she was underwhelmed. The aqueduct was over three feet wide but covered in stone. "Well, pooh. That isn't much of a river."

Ivin slid from his horse, rifled through a saddlebag, then turned to wedge a hoof pick into a seam in the stone. He slipped his fingers into the crease and lifted, throwing the arching stone over the edge with a thud on the soft turf as the others arrived.

The sun caught the water with a shine so bright she covered her eyes and blinked. As she shifted her angle of vision, she realized the shine wasn't water alone. "Goodness." The aqueduct was dark stone, but silvery metal lined the channel.

Morik bounded from his saddle and splashed his hand in the steady flow, his face aglow from the light.

Ivin asked, "Plain water?"

Morik sipped. "Clean and pure as rainfall. Maybe more pure. That explains much."

Kinesee smirked and cast the Kingdomer a glance. "So explain it."

Morik pointed west. "Endelêun is yonder about forty horizons southwest if Wayfinder Rendetu is right. That's a long way to run an aqueduct without a good cause. Water this pure is a worthy cause, sure the hells cleaner than any river I've seen."

Ivin said, "So it's not the metal lining purifying it."

"Not of dirt or sediment. The source is clean as I've ever heard of. I'd wager this is some sort of Ofdôlus alloy, Infused Silver. The Ironwing and other kings drink from cups fashioned from the metal. It'll neutralize poison, a man can't even get drunk drinking from one. There are holding tanks in Molikîn coated with Ofdôlus, no algae will grow in them, and the water stays fresh, but on this scale? It's a dream."

Kinesee eased from her saddle, stepped to the side of the flow, and cupped her hands. The water was cold even in the heat of the day, and when she drank it chilled her teeth, but she'd never tasted water quite like it. "Gods. It's cold."

Meliu said, "So much for my dream of jumping in for a bath."

The mere thought sent a chill through Kinesee's body. "That's a lot of water."

"Aye, Endelêun must be a city on a grand scale." Morik untied his canteen and poured it on the ground. "I suggest filling up. You won't drink finer water than this."

Ivin didn't budge. "We've only heard of ruins until you move farther west, how could we not have heard some rumor of a *grand city?*"

Kinesee watered her horse with hands. "Why don't we ask Lucky and Grunt?"

Ivin glanced at her, then Meliu. The High Priestess grimaced as she turned to the men. "Endelêun? I don't even know the word for city..."

Lucky stared at her, and Grunt grunted with a shrug. Meliu hopped from the saddle and reached into her bags, pulled out a scroll. She pointed to the city's mark and said, "*Zimpotû utûê unô*. Endelêun."

Both men backed from her, eyes on the ground, hands waving as if to shoo away flies. "*Nonkonu utûê*!"

The men trembled, and Kinesee said, "Roll the scroll back up."

Meliu did, and the men calmed. "Whatever they said had something to do with ghosts."

"Why would they fear the map?"

"Superstition of some sort or another. The bigger question is what *nonkonu* means." Meliu stashed the scroll and approached the men. She held her arms in front of her in a loop. "*Tubûlê, yusnono lô wiir.*" She unlocked her fingers and widened her arms. "*Nonkonu, mônesu lô wiir?*"

Lucky nodded and held his arms out. "*Mônesu. Mônesu lô utûê. Nonkonu lô utûê.*"

Meliu stared, her face stone, but Kinesee knew her well enough to recognize the facade. The priestess had understood the yellow-eye. "What did he say?"

"Endelêun is a city of ghosts."

Fifty-Nine

Message to the Stars

Which is more valuable, a bushel of wheat or a pound of gold? Only one has absolute value, and yet mortals covet the other more until hungry. Which is more valuable, a pound of iron or a pound of gold? Neither has absolute value, but one is coveted more until the other is needed to break ground or spill blood.

—*Codex of Sol*

Eliles stood beneath the stars of Skywatch with her mind tossing from confidence to insecurity every few wicks. Weeks of study and practice proved nothing except that she couldn't shift her face, let alone her entire body, to look like another. In all this time, they'd heard nothing from the holy and seen not a soul, but there was always the possibility the Face had visited without being caught by one of her Elemental surges she tried on everyone she met.

She came to the stars to announce the trial but hesitated as she stood beneath the peaceful glints of light and figured on a way to calm her nerves. She sat cross-legged on the chiming floor of the bright sky. "Elinwe, show me Ivin."

Her vision spun south, and how far the sky traveled caught her by surprise. When the journey ended, she looked down upon a colossal city straddling two rivers where they joined, with a forest to the north and east and plains to the southwest. Several aqueducts fed the city despite being so near rivers, and the streets teemed with people, horses, carts, chariots, and wagons. The city's four gates stood open with traffic crossing in and out in steady flows, and from each gate, four pristine roads traveled. To the northwest, the road led to a massive stone bridge standing on a series of arches, a construction like she'd never imagined; the stones crossed a half-horizon from bank to bank.

To the east, rising from the forest, stood low mountains, and on the ridge of one stood a pyramid like she'd seen in ancient books. Here too, people bustled, but they were holy folk judging by the robes.

But the image focused on the city, and so she assumed Ivin was there. The center of focus was a great fortress in the southwest where the two rivers came together to form one. She smiled. "It would make sense if you are there. Elinwe, show me Solineus."

The vision of the city blurred and pulled north, but no more than a hundred horizons; it was hard to tell. When focus returned, she stared at a different pyramid, this one in the middle of a ruined city. It was smaller and uglier than the one to the south. People milled about on the thing's massive steps, but she wasn't close enough for details. "Elinwe, show me Lelishen." The view didn't shift; the last time she'd checked a few months back, all she got was a view of a mountain. "That's interesting. Elinwe, show me Meliu."

The view shifted south, and this time focused on the great pyramid in the mountains. "The pyramid is a holy site, then." She sighed. Who to ask after next? "Elinwe, show me Pikarn."

Her view blurred and spun; she was glad she had taken a seat, or she might have fallen over. But when she regained focus, her eyes flew wide: Istinjoln. "What the Seven Heavens are you doing there?"

The stars chimed with footsteps, but Eliles didn't turn. She already knew who it was. Or at least, who it looked like. Temeru's voice echoed across the heavens. "How are you doing that?"

"You can't?" She turned to face the oracle and hammered her with Elemental energies, but nothing happened. "I just ask, and the sky shows me."

"So, the Wolverine is in Istinjoln? Did he die there?"

"He sailed south with the clans. If he's back in Istinjoln... The stars won't show me the dead unless they're a ghost."

"What if someone is Taken?"

"I don't know."

The priestess knelt beside her. "Ask of Tuluth of Ilnoe."

"I don't know if it'll work for someone I haven't met."

"Just try. She's my mother."

Eliles grimaced, but at least if it didn't work, there wasn't proof of her being dead. "Elinwe, show me Tuluth of Ilnoe."

The vision spun and slid southeast across the Parapet Strait until landing on a bay with several ships floating in a harbor, and a village appeared with dozens of wooden buildings. Eliles glanced at Temeru and her swollen eyes.

"She's alive. On the coast near the Eleris Edan, if I guess right. Thank you."

"The Wolverine was here the last time I looked. Shall I find your father?"

The woman hesitated. "He died before I reached the priesthood."

They sat staring at the village, the faceless people going about their day's work. Eliles allowed her these peaceful moments, to let the woman's mind wander to which person might be her mother. Eliles enjoyed it as well. It soothed the soul to watch people go about their normal lives, to know that normal still existed, but it also brought a longing.

After several wicks, Temeru broke the silence. "She didn't travel south like the others; she stayed north along with these folks. No doubt, she dreams of reaching me."

"You love your mother."

"I do. She doted on me, especially after father died. She is a priestess as well, and my father was a priest. Offering their only daughter to Istinjoln to taste the Maimer's anguish was a bitter and proud day for them both."

"Rare parents, both having spoken priestly vows."

"Rare in so many ways." She breathed deep and smiled. "Why are you here, Eliles?"

"Reinus will face trial, high sun, two weeks from today. We both need time to prepare."

"With the hairy Choerkin as judge? That isn't anyone's idea of a trial."

"No, a public trial. Jinbin will be the arbiter, you the ax, and I will act as the shield."

"I don't need time to prepare; he confessed in front of all of us." Temeru studied her with steady eyes. "What game are you playing?"

"No more games than any trial. I intend to prove Reinus' innocence."

Her pause demonstrated less confidence than her words. "It's foolish. You can't win."

"I've translated a text I found hidden that describes a Face-like being during the Age of God Wars. The odd events on the island. I will turn the opinions of enough of your people, the ones who *didn't* hear his confession, to win the jury."

"This is all you have?"

"There is more. It's a matter of lining up the toy soldiers and knocking them over to win this battle."

"And if we don't show up?"

"Reinus will be found innocent and you a coward for not facing an unlosable trial."

Temeru bore a cocky, but crooked with doubt, smile as she stood. "If you wish to put on a show, I will join in the farce. But when you lose, if his head doesn't leave his shoulders, the holy people's opinion of their queen will never recover."

"Never is a very long time these days. Will you tell me who started the fire at the Salty Frog?"

"There was a fire? How dreadful. I suggest looking to your cook, or maybe the Choerkin lit the place ablaze while drunk."

"'No' would've sufficed."

Temeru grinned. "Thanks again for showing me my mother." She turned and strode into the infinite dark with her feet playing a solemn melody.

Eliles breathed deep and exhaled, relieved to be done with the invitation, but wondering if she shouldn't have set the date a month out. It wasn't like time mattered here. She started to stand but sat back down. It was a formality, seeing as the sky already showed her Istinjoln, but seeing as she'd shown Temeru her mother... "Elinwe, show me Dareun."

The sky's vision swung to Istinjoln as normal, but then it drew closer, swooping between buildings until coming upon a man's back. Dareun turned, and his eyebrows bunched before he smiled. His mouth opened, and she swore he said, "Hello, sweet girl."

Tears came to her eyes, but a smile shaped her lips. Then it struck her: She wasn't staring through a ghost, she was staring at a man with a physical body. "You're alive. Or it's a trick of Skywatch. It must be a trick."

But what a beautiful lie.

They stared at one another for wicks before he patted his hand above his heart, winked, and said goodbye. He turned and walked away, and she didn't ask the stars to follow, just in case they refused. She stood, the stars returned to normal, and she departed Skywatch with a rare smile to sustain her for days.

Sixty

City of Ghosts

There is more than one way to wage war and claim victory; all should be tried before the most famous sort of war, where tens of thousands die.

—*Codex of Sol*

Meliu wasn't sure what to think of the notion of a city full of ghosts. The Church taught that ghosts were real, souls that didn't Walk the Road of Living Stars for one reason or another. Sundered souls. Cursed souls. Broken souls. Souls with a hunger for revenge upon the living. Souls too attached to the suffering of their final moments. There were plenty of explanations for a rare encounter, none of them pleasant, but the best explanation she had for a city full of apparitions was a mass Sundering.

On the other hand, the Wiirê could be superstitious fools, and the city might turn out to be ruins not so unlike others. This was too optimistic to even bring a smile.

The army cleared forest and hunkered down for the night, and in the morning, Ivin strode from his tent a defeated man; Meliu knew this by the fact Kinesee wore her riding britches and boots.

Meliu spread a gracious smile. "Kinesee, wouldn't it be safer to stay here?"

The girl glared. "For me, maybe, but I'll kill him if he leaves me behind."

While Meliu admired the strong-willed woman in herself, she sometimes found it was an annoying trait in others. "I see."

Ivin said, "She'll ride with us, but the first sign of trouble she and her guard return."

"Mmhmm."

"And she stays with the host until I say otherwise."

"Yes, yes."

Meliu glanced at him. "The host?"

"We'll lead five hundred horsemen to this city of ghosts."

"So, the plan with a small scout party?"

Ivin glared at her and tromped by.

Kinesee looked at her with a grin. "He'll get over it."

"He won't if you die." Meliu stalked past her even as she heard Ivin shouting commands for riders to throw saddles on their mounts. It wasn't the first time she wished they had waited for Sedut to ride south. The priestess was a butcher of men and a holy voice to speak to about Meliu's unease.

Not that Sedut would be useful against ghosts. Meliu had already discovered how wonderful Light and Dark fared with Wakened monkeys, what good would a whirlwind of blades do against haunts? With a snort, grunt, and stomp of her foot, she sought out any holy soul she could find, which turned out to be Shinôu. The poor bastard had three fingers bit off beneath Green Mountain and singed his hair in the battle, but he proved uncowed.

He was slipping into mail when she found him. "Are you riding for Endelêun?"

"Aye. Shouldn't you be putting on armor?"

"Ivin's taking five hundred horse and his bride... I'm not expecting a fight. And what good would armor do against ghosts?"

The priest glanced at his heavy rings. "I'll take safe over sorry today. Sorry over safe is for hangovers."

His love for whiskey was one of the few things she'd heard about the man. "Walk and talk with me on the way to the horses?"

He eyeballed her. No doubt the man was suspicious of her, she'd spoken fewer than a hundred words to him since they met. "Not sure what I've to offer, but fine."

"I just need some perspective." And she figured the odds of this man being the Face in hiding were as low as finding gold in the piss of the Dancing Bastards. "Have you ever met someone who... damaged themselves with prayers of Dark?"

"Met might be over-stating the facts, but I've seen a few. It is an ugly affliction. Prayers of Fire are gentle in killing you fast."

She led him at a slow pace toward the Choerkin tent, meandering through folks preparing meals or getting ready to ride. "My prayers, I've done things... Horrible things, but that isn't the point. I've had trembles and shakes and somehow recovered—"

"Blessed indeed."

She wasn't about to mention Lord Priest Ulrikt or his Face healing her. "I was, or I am. In the fight against the Wiirê witch, I summoned so much Dark... my body and soul were weak for days. In the Dark there are demons, devils, whatever might be your worst horror, but in the middle of this battle, I saw a white lion."

"That's your greatest fear?"

"No. It wasn't even terrifying. But when the prayer of Dark left, the lion was still there. It spoke to me, called me the Daughter of Erginle."

Shinôu strode beside her with his lips pinched. "And?"

"When I started to doze outside Green Mountain, before our foolish journey to chase monkeys... I think I saw him again. Am I going mad? Has the Dark damaged me?"

"So you're asking a priest of Fire about this?"

"I'm the closest thing to a follower of Kibole's Dark here. And I don't trust my opinion."

He laughed. "Are you madder than a Shadow in a rainstorm? Is that what you want to know?"

"I think I needed to say it aloud more than anything."

"My opinion... Dark causes fear, yes? In the Citadel, I heard of a woman who ran into a wall a dozen times before she died. In Istinjoln, there's a man who crawls from corner to corner eating bugs. Another

I heard of ran screaming until he jumped from a tower. The two I've seen, one rocked back and forth praying in gibberish, and the other wandered the halls, running into people like he couldn't see them, and he never spoke a word. They're all escaping, either through killing their bodies so the soul can flee or by freeing their souls, leaving the body behind as a pathetic shell. You are not escaping. You are here, all here. I don't know what this white lion might be, a figment or a message from the gods, but it isn't the madness of Dark as I see it."

"Thank you for that." The idea that people went mad when their souls lost their tether to the body wasn't unusual, even if Meliu didn't necessarily believe it. "Do me a favor and don't mention the white lion to anyone." Whispers about being the Choerkin's Mistress of Dark were bad enough without being crazy to boot.

"Consider me muzzled."

They arrived at the Choerkin tent as men were putting boots to stirrup, and it didn't take long to find Ivin holding a horse for her, but Shinôu would have to find his own ride.

She turned to the priest. "I'll see you at Endelêun."

Shinôu smiled and held up his left hand with only its pinky and thumb remaining. "First Wakened monkeys, now ghosts. You couldn't keep me away!"

Ivin tried hard not to look at Kinesee as they rode, and for her part, she stayed mute even if she wouldn't leave his side at the front of the cavalry. It seemed only an instant from the moment their ride began to reach the clearing where the aqueduct ran. The aisle of grass was empty as ever of living things, but the instant they broke from the line of trees, he noticed the change.

He leaned and pointed. "Morik, you see that?"

"I do. Rendetu, with us."

Ivin heeled General into a trot, and they arrived at the place Ivin had removed the piece of aqueduct, except today the piece nestled right where it had started. He perused the ground but saw nothing out of the ordinary. Crushed grass still lay flat where the stone landed, and there remained a dent in the ground. There were horse tracks and footprints, he figured they made them, but no sign of anyone coming or going along the aqueduct.

The Wayfinder slid to the ground and circled. "I see our tracks over here, but no way in the hells anyone's been on this side to pick that up. There isn't a mark. No one is that stealthy."

Morik eyeballed Ivin. "What do you reckon that hunk of stone weighs? Thirty bricks? Forty?"

"The wind didn't come by and put it back, that I know."

"So we're sayin' a ghost did this? Why in the name of the Foundations would a ghost give a damn about a water supply?"

Meliu shrugged and quipped, "Maybe they like baths as badly as I need one. That goes for you too, Kingdomer. And the warlord as well."

Kinesee laughed, but Ivin refused to look at either of the ladies. "Dareun's ghost in Istinjoln couldn't touch anything... Solineus said he walked right through walls."

"Dareun was Sundered... we've all heard legends of ghosts doing things. Could be different types of ghosts. Nothing I've ever read offers us clues."

"Then our answers lie horizons away down this aisle of green." Ivin reined General and nudged him into a trot until rejoining the mass of riders as those trailing in the back exited the woods. Kinesee and the others wheeled in beside him, and they headed southwest at a leisurely pace with forests rising on either flank. It was peculiar to feel surrounded while riding in the middle of open pasture, but the trees presented cover for any enemy so stealthy as to not leave tracks.

The hills in the southern woods rose higher the farther they traveled, high enough to force the debate of whether to call them mountains, but the trail sloped downward despite a few rises and falls that affected the height of the aqueduct's base. As the sun set in the distance, they stopped to make camp and let the horses graze. He plucked a stem and stuck it between his teeth to chew; it tasted better raw than the gutgrinder they survived on along the Trail of Pyres, but he wasn't going to eat enough to find out what it'd do to his belly.

The land was lush and fertile, but most of the game they spotted stuck to the forest. The question was whether the animals in the trees stayed hidden from the horsemen, or if they never ventured near the strange stone structure in an open field. He assumed the latter, as neither he nor Rendetu noted any animal trails.

They awoke before dawn and were in the saddle as the sun rose, and by the time it was at its highest in the sky, the aqueduct turned southerly, and the world in front of them changed. A forest still arose to their north, but to the south rolling plains swept in front of them, the hills surging like waves of soil until reaching mountains covered in green. If they'd been on foot, he would've had to stop and stare. Even in the kingdoms of the Teks, he didn't recall seeing such a perfect landscape. Sweeping grasses and flowers swaying in a southern breeze.

"We've reached one of the heavens."

Kinesee responded first. "It's gorgeous. I never dreamed..."

Meliu grinned at them both, and Ivin knew something darker was coming from those lips. "None of the Seven Heavens are depicted in such a way, so the question becomes, whose heaven are we in?"

Morik laughed and slapped his saddle-horn. "There are places in the Foundations to rival this beauty, but I admit they aren't so expansive."

The horses nibbled as they walked, and as the sun fell into evening, they dipped into a deep valley a half horizon across. Stone arches stacked atop each other until they reached fifty feet high, carrying the aqueduct across the valley. The stonework was impeccable, as if built in the last decade, and not the hundreds of years ago they assumed.

Ivin rode while staring up at its grandeur until his neck ached, and he planned on calling a halt to the day's ride at the top of the valley's southern rise, but when they arrived his mouth clamped shut and his horse moseyed forward until he remembered to pull on the reins.

The plains swept onward and downhill to the gleaming white walls and tall towers of a massive city. It stretched too far to see its end even from this height, and inside the city, more walls rose in the western quarter, a castle, a palace, a... He didn't have the right word. His gut sank, and his mouth dried.

Morik whistled as he stopped his horse beside Ivin. "I reckon that's Endelêun."

Ivin chuckled and rubbed his face until he regained feeling in his cheeks. "If we were figuring on a siege, we got another thing comin'."

Ivin heard the escape of Kinesee's shuddering breath. "It's like a dream."

"Except it's very real." But as he gazed longer, it did seem more like a dream. He pulled a fareye from his saddlebag. "There's a gate wide open, but I don't see a godsdamned road. The aqueduct heads into the city yonder, and it looks like another aqueduct or two on the western side there by the palace."

Rendetu also peered through a glass. "You're right about the road, the grasses go straight to the gate far as I can tell, and I don't see a soul walking them walls."

Kinesee muttered, "They told us it was a city of ghosts."

Ivin scanned the walls and peered into the city streets the best he could. "Meliu, can your prayers see anybody?"

She stared into the distance, and Ivin wasn't so sure which answer he hoped for. "No. I see nothing. A hawk perched on a tower. No people, not even in the square there."

She pointed, but no matter where Ivin looked, he saw no one. "Camp for the night or ride for the gate?"

Morik laughed. "If there're people in there, they've seen us, and not going to the gate makes us suspicious. If it's full of ghosts, well, I'm not so superstitious a fellow, but riding into a city of ghosts coming on dark feels a fool's move."

"Bannermen! Affix your flags." He turned to Morik. "I'll lead a small group to the gate. You're welcome to ride along." He flashed his gaze to Kinesee. "You are staying here."

She stared at him, and he could almost see her swallowing the words she wanted to say. "As you wish."

"If your father were here, he'd already be inside." He winked and earned her smile.

Meliu said, "I'll stay here with Kinesee. My prayers would be worthless against ghosts."

Morik grunted and pounded his chest with bravado. "I'll remain here to make certain the ladies are safe."

Ivin smirked, unsure how serious to take the Kingdomer. "Ghosts have you all pissin' your britches? More apt we find men, alive and hale."

Meliu shook her head. "You won't find the living behind those walls. I can feel it."

Ivin glanced amid the horses looking for Lucky and Grunt, confused as they never strayed far from Meliu. Then he realized they hid behind her horse. "I don't think your yellow-eyed friends are going to volunteer."

Meliu shook her head. "Not even at the point of a spear, I'd wager."

"You shamed me into it! I cannot be so cowardly as a yellow-eye." Morik laughed and reined his horse to face the men. "Not a Kingdomer here is afraid of spooks... at least until we see one."

They departed with two bannermen each and a half dozen warriors covered in mail with shields couched, but their spears pointed to the sky, butts in their stirrups. The wind picked up as they galloped across the open plane, the ground as level as a perfect field, and it spawned visions of wheat or oats or whatever crop would grow well.

"There must be somebody here. The region is too perfect not to—" His eyes drifted east into the mountains and their peaks, but one stood a little too uniform. A pyramid arose from the side of a mountain, below it other buildings, and his heart skipped a beat. "Tomarok."

Morik followed his gaze. "Foundations, that's a huge pyramid. Let's hope the Dark Water shits got stuck and drowned in their hole."

"I second that with a prayer." Ivin turned his attention back to the gates and walls, still open, still empty, and no road. The seams of the blocks in the wall rested with Kingdomer perfection, but they stood polished to a sheen that defied logic for a defensive structure. The candles of work and upkeep required staggered him. When they reined to a stop, not a visible soul greeted them. No ghosts either.

They sat their saddles and stared. "Hail Endelêun!"

Morik stood in his stirrups, peering through the gates before dropping to the ground, strolling in a broad circle before returning to swing back into the saddle. "There isn't even a sign of a stone road. Not a brick. Either they sunk into the turf an age ago or there never was one."

The streets just inside the gate were dark gray cobbles, their edges pinched so tight there wasn't a sign of weed or grass. "How the hells does this make sense? Tell me that."

Ivin gave General's ribs a squeeze and the horse sauntered through the gate. The road ran in five directions, straight ahead, following the wall to either side, and two more paths splitting the angles these made. The buildings weren't as pristine as the outer walls. Most were fashioned from gray stone like the road, only some were painted white, blue, or green. Here and there the paint even showed chipping. Gazing farther, he noticed stone foundations with nothing on top of them. No ruins, no rubble, no nothing. It felt random.

"Your priestess is right; the living stay away from this place."

Ivin chuckled. "They did, but we're here now. And I don't see no ghosts either."

Morik nodded and pointed a finger to the western horizon. The sun already disappeared behind the city's wall. "It isn't dark yet."

Ivin wanted to laugh, to puff his chest, and defy the creeping fear the coming night brought to his spine. "Mornings are better for exploring."

They turned and rode back at a gallop, and despite trying not to, he looked back for pursuit more than a handful of times. When they dismounted, the two yellow-eyes rushed them, dropped to their knees, bowed before Ivin and Morik with arms and fingers stretching as if they wished to touch their toes.

Morik hopped back as the men babbled. "What the hells is this, now?"

Meliu shrugged as she stared. "I'm not sure, something about fearless men, ghosts... walking through... not the gate. Through you."

Ivin said, "We didn't see a thing, man nor ghost, not even a bunny."

Meliu smiled and pointed to her eyes. It took a flicker, and then he turned to Morik who already stared at him. "I'm damned glad we didn't stay 'til dark. How about you?"

"I am at that." The Kingdomer pointed back to the city's gates, and they were closed.

Sixty-One

Whispering Streets

Seven Heavens and only one life to get there.
Where lies the verisimilitude in an unfair proposition,
where rests in latitude the lie of a restless generation,
where dangles the attitude over hypocritical assassination,
the noose around the killer's own neck owned,
the crack and fall of a neck incapable of breaking,
faking and taking and slaking and snaking
to slither tail tickling tongue into your own mouth.
Bite Venomous
to die, to die, to die, but you're immune to your own poison.

—*Tomes of the Touched*

Lucky and Grunt sat their asses down in the grass and didn't budge. Meliu gave it her damnedest shot to cuss them into going with them, but her ability to curse and cajole in Wiirê was lacking. In the end, she waved her arms in defeat and convinced herself that if the ghosts were harmless, it was better not to know where they were anyhow.

Peppered full of false confidence was how she found herself sitting horseback with Ivin, Kinesee, Leto, Morik, Shinôu, and twenty warriors at Endelêun's northern gate. The sun was a candle high from dawn's first light as they passed through the yawning gates that had reopened sometime just before dawn.

She tensed while passing through the gate, expecting a tingle, a shiver, a sense of foreboding or dread, but it was like entering any other city or monastery gate, dark and hollow with the ring of iron-shod hooves until passing into the light of day. The difference was that instead of being greeted by the chatter of people, all they heard was distant birds and the chirp of insects.

Her constricted gut relaxed without an apparition in sight but managed to leave behind mild nausea. She hiccupped, the only human sound since they'd entered. "Sorry."

Ivin grinned at her. "We ride straight down this road to the center of the city, and don't no one go wandering off."

Hooves clopped in a prancing cadence as the horses grew nervous, but she couldn't say whether it was the riders or ghosts giving them the jitters. Everyone kept their mouths shut, unwilling to say a word lest they miss some subtle sound. Chirping birds swooped from above, but instead of bringing a sense of the ordinary, it pointed out the lack of animal life. Birds were scarce, but she didn't see a single rat or mouse or lizard... nothing that walked, crawled, or slithered.

A statue arose ahead of them, and as she approached, she realized it was of a man on a rearing horse, the ax in his right hand held high, standing in the middle of a fountain with eight griffons surrounding him, water streaming from their mouths to splash in the pool. On an ordinary day, it would be beautiful and relaxing, but today it rubbed her nerves raw. Then another incongruity struck her. "From all we know, neither the Wiirê nor Histê have horses."

Morik said, "Best I know, this is so. But I didn't even know the yellow-eyes were here until now."

Ivin slid from his saddle, and General put his lips to the water for a drink. "We know the city is older than those maps. Does the one date to the God Wars?"

"It would make the most sense. Building a city this size during the in-between years, I don't see it. The horse is big but isn't out of scale, I'd imagine. That would put the rider at what? Six feet tall?"

Morik nodded and gave her an appreciative smile. “Good eyes, priestess. Not many Kingdomers touch six feet, though it happens. He sure as shits isn’t Wiirê.”

“His face is worn by the years. Any runes around the fountain here are worn as well, but what I can see I don’t recognize.”

Ivin cupped a hand and sipped water. “Cold and clear. I wager folks came here for drinking water.”

“Public water from the aqueducts. These were a civilized people who appreciated water.” *And that means bathhouses!* All her fears faded with a burst of curiosity. “I say we split up and explore. If there are ghosts hereabouts, they aren’t bugging no one. I’ll take Kinesee with me.”

Ivin stared at her, suspicious as all the Twelve Hells, but she’d keep her plan to herself. To that end, she just grinned.

“Groups of five then, and the plus one is with you ladies. Shinôu as well.”

Leto said, “I’ll ride with the women as well; I’m feeling a little religious of late.”

Meliu grimaced. The boy was begging for a splash of Dark to end his flirtations, but she didn’t argue. “Kinesee?”

The girl pinched her lips. “I could do with some feminine company.”

Meliu glanced at her party as Ivin and the other rode away: Kinesee, Shinôu, Leto, Harlik, and Budôê. The latter two were distant Choerkin blood and often found themselves watching over the Lady. “We’re going to ride east. What we’re looking for is a big stone building... maybe pillars out front. Probably two doors as entries. The sound of running water.”

Kinesee laughed, but if the men understood what she was looking for, they didn’t show it. The eastern road ran straight and took them into an area she wagered used to be full of merchants. The buildings were larger, with double doors, and one impressive section looked like it could house a hundred small merchants without leaving them to the sun on the street to hawk their wares. And she noted for the first time hitching posts made from stone, with iron rings to hold reins of horses. Horses weren’t just known; they were common.

She spotted an odd square tower not much taller than the other buildings, and it took a flicker to register: a cistern. She nodded and led them down a side street, turning three times before spotting what she figured was her destination. A row of twelve pillars held a tile roof aloft, and two double doors stood wide open for entry on either end. It was larger than the ruins around Green Mountain, but she didn't doubt it had the same purpose. She poked Kinesee in the shoulder and nudged her horse into a gallop, reining in and jumping from the saddle with the girl close behind. She tethered the horse's reins and ran through a door.

She heard the water and turned left, then right, then froze in triumph. Three pools of water with steps down. Kinesee gasped.

"Are you joking?"

"A bath never jokes."

She leaned and whispered, "It's wide open."

"Women's and men's... I'm not real sure what side we're on, but what's it matter?"

Shinôu's voice came from the doorway. "I can't believe you two."

Meliu glared as she pulled a tiny vial from her haversack. "I stink! But not for much longer."

Leto scoffed and folded his arms. "You're wasting our time."

Kinesee leaned and stuck her finger into the nearest pool. "Gods, it's hot."

Meliu's brow cocked, and in a flicker of wisdom, she slipped her boots off. Her shoulders slumped. "And the floor is *warm.* You men get the hells out of her. It's lady time."

Kinesee said, "Doesn't it bug you that the water is heated? Who is heating it?"

"Take your boots off and tell me you care."

Leto stared, but the corner of his lips curled. "I came to guard you both, and I aim to see to that."

"What face do you figure the warlord is going to make when he hears you saw his wife naked?"

"Safety is paramount."

She smiled, prayed, and waved goodbye. An instant later a wall of dark stood between them. She was half-naked by the time Leto's screams faded down the hall.

Shinôu said, "I appreciate your sparing me. I'll keep watch outside with the Choerkin men."

"We appreciate it."

Kinesee turned on her, hands to hips. "That wasn't very nice."

Meliu slipped out of her riding britches and dabbed her toes in the hot water. Hot, but comfortable. "He deserved it."

"You get used to him."

Meliu mused for a flicker, then shook her head. "I think not. But *we*... We deserve this." She popped the top from the perfume and poured it in the water. The scent of roses bloomed, and her eyes rolled into the back of her head as she eased into the water. "Ohhhh, Seven Heavens come for me."

The girl kicked her boots off and tossed her clothes to the corner, but even as water covered her feet, she wasn't convinced. When the water covered her waist—Meliu was jealous of having so much leg to stick in the water—that's when Meliu knew she had a convert. "Gods, I didn't know my rear was so stiff from the saddle."

"Ass. You can say ass around me."

The reply came with a playful tone. "Ass. But doing that to Leto still wasn't nice."

"You liked the boy, didn't you? Gods know he was infatuated with you."

"I like the smell of roses better."

Meliu watched Kinesee's head lull and eyes close, then she did the same, allowing calm to penetrate her soul with the heat from the water. She breathed deep, arms spreading along the edge of the pool, and the concept of time and worry faded.

But her mind wandered to her companion. The first time she'd met the girl, she wasn't even twelve, an immature eleven, and now she was fifteen and a warlord's bride meeting with kings. "You turned fifteen not far back... I missed the celebration. Happy birthday."

There was silence, and she thought maybe the girl nodded off. "I try to forget birthdays."

"Why would a lady so young wish to forget her birthday?"

"All birthdays. I also try to forget why I want to forget birthdays."

Meliu exhaled, happy for the bath. "I suppose we all have a lot of things we'd like to forget these days. I used to want to forget people in my past, but now I've done things that make their pains afterthoughts."

"Regrets?"

"It was survival. Mostly." She wished she knew if she'd been the cause of the Rot striking the Tek, but she chose to believe Ulrikt, or at the least, to accept her role as an innocent dupe. "But most times, for most things, I just try to forget just like you. Hot water and perfume are great for forgetting."

Meliu soaked and breathed. And breathed, the pressure of the water on her chest forcing life's other pressures from her soul.

"Meliu." Kinesee's voice came in a whisper, and it took a flicker to register the nerves in her voice. "Meliu, I don't think we're alone."

She opened her eyes, and a question reached her tongue but was never uttered. The water at the edges of the pool rippled.

Kinesee stared in terror as the water rippled by her side, one foot then another, then a body slipping through the surface, or so she imagined, because there was no one there. Worse, there were at least seven ripples.

"Sit. Sit still. When did they show up?"

"I don't know. When I opened my eyes, they were just here."

A faint whisper inches from her ear; the voice wasn't loud enough to understand, and she suspected she wouldn't have understood the words anyhow. There was a distant rumble of chuckles, so soft it was as if they came from another room or through pillows, and it made one thing clear.

"Meliu. We're in the men's bath."

"How? Do you see one of their—"

"No! The whispers. You don't hear them?"

"I don't. Can they see us?"

"I don't think so."

"Our bath is over."

Kinesee put her palms to the edge and lifted, slinking from the water with as little ripple as she could manage. She lay on the floor for a flicker before slithering toward her clothes like a slippery snake. She appreciated the heated floor on her feet earlier, but as she crept across the floor, covering her breasts and pinching her knees, she thanked every god for the boon of warmth.

She slipped into her smallclothes as Meliu arrived crawling like a modest lizard. "Did they see?"

"I don't think so."

"I ain't never seen a man who won't react to boobs."

She had a point. "The voices are too soft. I've no idea. Let's just get dressed and get out of here."

She stood and was cinching the belt on her britches when she heard a new sound. A distant bellow, deep, resonating, not so different than Kingdomer horns echoing from mountains away. "Do you hear that? A horn. I think."

"I don't hear a thing."

The wall of Dark dropped away, and Shinôu's face appeared in a flicker, his mouth open, but Meliu shushed him. They skulked into the hall.

"What the hells is with you ladies?"

Kinesee said, "Ghosts in the water, and I heard whispers."

"Blessed Sol! I didn't see a thing."

Kinesee didn't pause long, heading for the street where Harlik and Budôê guarded the door waiting for her. The sound of the horn grew louder in the open air. "Nobody hears that?"

Everybody stared, and Meliu said, "More whispers?"

"The horn!" Her eyes danced, and her ears drew her attention to the southwest, the direction of the fortress. A screech. She ducked. "A child's voice!" She spun, but there was nobody there.

"They can't hurt us..."

The child screamed within feet of her; she stumbled backward and fell to the stones of the street. Harlik and Budôê's blades swiped from their sheaths, but the sounds bled into the rush of whispers surging around her, and she felt a surge of Fire and saw the glow in Shinôu's hands. The voices reached her ears muted and with a sense of rushing motion that swiped at her consciousness, spinning her into dizzy without ever moving her body; she put her hands to the stone, struggled to her feet, wavered and fell to her knees as her head spun. "They're inside of me!" Her heart raced with the inconsistent rhythm of the hooves of two horses at different gaits, and her breakfast spilled in the street. She scrambled on hands and knees. She felt hands but could no longer understand the voices of those she figured friends.

The child's scream faded, and she felt her body lifted, floating. Pavers passed swirling and gray in front of her eyes as her head lulled, hair flopping in her face. The whispers faded, and her heart rediscovered its rhythm, but her head and thoughts still spun.

"Get her to the corner. Into the room, away from the street."

She felt drool from her lip and spit bile from her tongue. "I'm fine. Fine."

Shinôu leaned beside her. "What the hells happened? I didn't see anything, or I would've burned it to the Forges."

Kinesee shook her arms from Harlik's grip. "I didn't see them either, but I heard them. Felt them running, it spun my head."

Meliu said, "You said they were inside of you."

"Running through me... I think."

Shinôu said, "Why didn't we experience any of it?"

"You're welcome to it." She took a deep breath and spit. "Water."

Budôê popped his canteen. "M'lady."

She spat warm water, rinsing her mouth twice, but on the third drink, she stopped with the canteen to her lips. A horn blew, distant but clear. "Gods, tell me you can hear this one." She didn't need more of an answer than to see their necks crane. The horn bleated out four short calls, paused, and repeated.

Harlik said, "That there's Letô's horn... Calling the heavy horse."

Ivin and Morik rounded the fountain and continued south for a long stretch, taking in every building, every turn, every nook where a threat might hide, but nothing caught their eyes. When the road split,

Ivin chose southeast for no particular reason. While most buildings stood as if touched by mere years of time, some of the stone foundations rested without a structure atop them.

"What do you think of these barren foundations?"

Morik shrugged as if he'd given it nary a thought, but Ivin knew better. "Thinking on it, we haven't seen no wood in this city. No sign of fire nowhere. My guess is it all rotted away."

"Without a scrap left behind?"

"Termites. Ambitious termites who value cleanliness." He laughed. "Until I know better, that's my story."

"And the paint?"

"Paint?"

"What paint have you ever seen that lasts hundreds of years? Some areas are chipped and faded, but others look as if they could've been brushed on last week."

"Artistic termites."

Ivin cracked a grin but managed not to laugh. "I've seen something similar before, at the Tomb of the Touched."

"So, you're expecting a giant skeleton to appear?"

"No. But the tomb was untouched by time."

"This isn't untouched. As you say, chips in the paint, fading..."

"Conceded. But it makes me wonder if they don't share a cause."

They came to a stone bridge spanning a river a quarter horizon wide. It was nothing short of a masterwork. Its pillars plunged in massive arches to the river below on islands of rubble to cut the current. The arches were the gray stone of the city, but the road and walls were polished white, and along the edges, silvery poles stood every ten paces with a lantern hanging from them.

Morik dismounted and walked to the edges to gain a better view. "This is staggering. The skill... the materials. They didn't even bother to take the shortest route across the river; they kept the road straight as if to show off."

"Builders are as prone to pride as any other man."

Morik swung back into his saddle with a chuckle. "Aye, they are. Least we don't have to worry about it falling from beneath us."

Ivin raised his head from the view and realized that for the first time, he had a good view of his destination: the tallest point in the city. The bridge led to a peninsula between two rivers before reaching another bridge, and to the west on that strip of land was a tower. "That isn't going to be as easy as I'd hoped."

The tower rose from the middle of a fortress, a sprawling mass of a stone structure. Finding the entrance might take the rest of the day.

Morik spurred his horse onto the bridge; the Kingdomer was engrossed with the span. "Hardly a crack to see. Impressive."

Ivin followed but opened his fareye to gaze west, trusting General not to jump into the river below. A massive gate led into what he figured was a compound for the fortress, and it appeared open. The ground from there rose until meeting the fortress walls, and farther out, the outer wall squared toward the west. "We'll see if we can get atop that wall, see what we see."

Once across the bridge, they veered onto a road leading straight to the gate, and indeed, it stood open. If it didn't, there was no way in the hells they were getting inside. The gatehouse tunnel was forty feet wide, and his nerves bunched in the cool shade as he looked up at murder holes above. But no flaming oil nor arrows nor rocks were forthcoming. Inside was an open courtyard with a road leading straight to the fortress, but Ivin led them to a set of stairs, dismounted, and slung his reins over a hitching post.

A stiff breeze hit his face as he stepped to the top of the wall, and he removed his helm, letting the wind chill the sweat on his brow. To the east, a grand view of the mountains, as well as the pyramid of Tomarok, with glimpses of its surroundings, from trees to small pyramids and more traditional buildings. The Mûulbon River ran from the northwest to meet the Temirân River's flow from the east, forming the fork of rivers the city of Endelûen overlooked. To the south, across the Temirân River, sat buildings in rows so straight he imagined they might be barracks for a long-missing military.

"I see a rider."

Ivin spun with his fareye and followed Morik's pointing finger. "Leto." For an instant, concern overtook him, but the man wasn't riding as if in a major hurry. When he cleared the side of the bridge, Ivin bellowed his name, getting the man's attention after several shouts.

"So, we're up here. Now what?"

Ivin sighed. "Hells, I don't know. Look for anything interesting, get a lay of the city."

"It's huge, sprawling. What do you figure, a million people could live here, and instead there are none?"

"Aye. And south, that entire district looks military. Barracks, open fields for training, a quick exit southeast or southwest through them gates, and bridges wide enough to march an army into the city right quick."

"A God Wars people. They put the Teks to shame, from what I've seen." He pointed to the northern river. "A dozen waterwheels are dipping that river there beside the building. Not wood, rustless-steel or nickeled... I can't say from here, and they're still running. How much you willing to wager the grindstones inside are still running and aren't worn to nubs? And that's just one grind-house."

Ivin clutched his head; it was impossible to take in all the details and incongruities. They stood and stared, eyes roving every direction for wicks.

"I've the fearful feeling someone wanted us here."

Morik eyed him. "What do you—"

Leto's voice interrupted. "Holy hells, did you men find a view!"

"Why aren't you with the ladies?"

"I got the distinct impression I wasn't welcome." Ivin glared. "Meliu found a bathhouse... the water and stone floor are even warm! But standing around while women soak in perfume?"

"You were lucky to find us."

"Nah, I looked for the highest point and knew you'd be somewhere round about. Damn! Damn! Look at this place."

Ivin appreciated that someone was excited, but the horrifying notion of Lord Priest Ulrikt and the *Codex of Sol* leading them here didn't fade. The Dark Waters Cult led Morik here. But for what?

"Let's head west and see what the view brings."

The walk was a constant climb, and the northern river fell farther and farther beneath their footsteps. It was dotted with grindhouses, their gleaming wheels spilling water, and the city spread deep beyond to the outer wall, but when they reached the tower at the corner and turned south, looking west brought a sensation of flight, the world falling away.

The wall stood atop a sheer cliff, as if the tip of the peninsula had been sheared away, and the river was at least three hundred feet below, a jumble of whitewater where the two rivers met. To the west spread a sea of treeless green, lush, tall grasses waving in the wind for as far as the eye could see. He squinted. "By the Forges, people." They crested a hill, running, then disappeared behind the next rise.

Morik said, "Yellow-eyes?"

Ivin gazed through the fareye, and sure enough, a half-naked man ran atop the hill. "One yellow-eye." But the others who followed wore clothes. He wondered if they were chasing the Wiirê. "And others. They're running together, but I don't see anything chasing them." The group was running toward the city's northwestern gate.

They stood and stared, dumbfounded, until he saw a hundred men with spears and shields chasing them over the plains. He shifted his view back to the folks running in front. Most of the men in clothes and armor were tall... one was short. "Holy hells... Leto! Sound your horn. I want our people at the gate."

The horn blew even as he fitted his helm to his head and sprinted along the wall. Morik fell in beside him. "What is it?"

"Rinold! Godsdamnit, it's Rinold."

Sixty-Two

Green Mountain

Scores of men died for the honor to carry
tattered rags and tattered flags,
Rat nests now, tucked in corners and holes,
gnawed into comfortable little homes.
prideful Dead rest tucked in crates and holes,
what honor resides in their comfortable bones?

—*Tomes of the Touched*

Rinold tried his damnedest to justify following the road to Far-Horizon Bridge; it ran straight for as far as his eye could see, and despite the grass, weeds, and small trees growing from the cracks, the route was in remarkable shape considering its age. Nehek informed him that while old roads streaked across the forest, connecting hundreds of ruins, the Histê kept only a few open.

It stretched in front of him like an invitation written in gold but being the prey instead of the hunter brought on a fear of open spaces. For the first three candles, they tried to mirror the road's path, but the terrain kept trying to direct them to or farther from the road; when faced with a hill so rocky and jagged that not even the forest covered its head, Rinold surrendered to caution and Nehek's alternate way.

They wound north from the road for several horizons before coming on a stream twice as wide as Rinold would want to try and jump. Nehek called it the Gerbolê-to Creek and claimed it flowed into the Mûulbon River just north of the Far-Horizon Bridge. It was a winding, thicket infested trail to follow, and lizards with bulging eyes peered at them from the stream's lazy waters, but so long as it got them where they needed to be, Rinold wasn't going to complain.

The Gerbolê-to widened as creeks joined its waters, and on the third day of travel, the ankle snagging vines and grasses thinned, but so too did the trees giving them cover. At midday, Nehek called them to a stop, and Rinold figured it was an ordinary break until the Wiirê sought him out.

"This stream will wander a little north before turning south again. The fastest path is southeast." He pointed to a high ridge covered in blowing grasses instead of trees.

"We're on the edge of the forest?"

"Yes, southeast is the Green Ocean."

"How far from the Mûulbon are we?"

He fidgeted. "A horizon or two. We will see it from the top of the hill, but it'll be farther away than it looks."

A thrill tingled through his soul, but he checked his enthusiasm. "It seems the obvious choice, so why are you hesitating?"

"We won't have any cover except to crawl through grass. I don't like crawling."

"Can't say I blame you." His eye twitched, and he found it hard not to bounce on his toes. "The time for safe is over."

The hill was steeper than it looked, but it felt good to have solid ground beneath his feet instead of the squish of the creek's banks, and when they crested the hill, a warm wind washed over him, and he removed his helm to appreciate the view. A rolling plain of grass led to the Mûulbon, and the river's broad waters stretched to the horizon. Rinold imagined that anywhere else, this mighty river would dominate, focusing the eye on the wonder of nature, but the Far-Horizon Bridge captured his gaze with the majesty of mortal creation.

Polished white stone stretched gleaming over dark waters, wide enough for three wagons and held aloft by a series of arches plunging into the water. Forty arches or more, each spanning more than a hundred feet of water. The builders crafted the bridge's entry from the same white stone, a massive arched structure that swallowed the incoming road and anyone who traveled it.

Rinold cleared his throat. "I never saw the Grand Bridge you spoke of before... but this—"

"The Grand Bridge may as well be sticks compared to Far-Horizon."

Kirun said, "I am honored to be the first Kingdomer to lay eyes on this."

Edlmir let loose a sharp whistle. "I ain't never seen nor heard of anything like it. A dozen far cries from that damned rope thing you had us on."

Rinold chuckled as his eye wandered back toward the forest. The Green Ocean flowed in grassy waves, concealing much of the road until ocean met forest. The delineation between the two jarred his senses with its stark contrast; from a distance, it looked as if the gods had stitched together two pieces of the world without a care for whether they matched.

He squinted and his heart jumped. "Histê." A row of heads and spears appeared above the grass no more than a few hundred paces from the forest's edge. "Vanguard or patrol?

Nehek hissed. "A patrol, likely as not, but there's no way to know."

Rinold glanced to the bridge, then back to the men. They were closer to the bridge by a long stretch and had a downhill start. "This ghost city of yours, will the Histê enter it?"

"No, but neither will the Wiirê."

"It's daylight, and I saved you before. If we make a run for it, we can beat them."

Nehek turned and spoke to his people. Their eyes widened, but they stood firm.

Kirun said, "If this is a patrol, we could wait for them to leave."

"And if it's the *Tutûlê*, we're stuck on the western side." He didn't wait for more dissent. He slipped his helmet over his head and took off at a trot straight for the bridge. He didn't look back but heard footfalls and breaths close. It felt as if he was a quarter of the way to the bridge by the time the land flattened, but he could no longer see anything but grass.

He slowed to a stop, catching his breath as the others arrived; there were stragglers, but it looked like everyone had followed. "Any idea if they saw us?"

Nehek said, "I do not know."

"We'll assume they did. Keep a solid pace, but we don't wanna tucker ourselves out in case we have a fight waiting for us at the other end. Let's go."

He walked with the longest strides he could manage, catching himself and slowing every time he slipped into a trot. His feet moved, but distance was harder to judge with a thudding heart and a sea of unchanging grass.

"Godsdamnit, we should be able to see the bridge's arch by now. Shouldn't we?"

Kirun said, "Over the next rise if my guesses aren't failing me."

She was right, and everyone broke into a jog without a word spoken, like a flock of birds in formation. The arch would've been beautiful any other day, gleaming white, standing a hundred feet high, its pillars carved with a perfect spiral of vine on both sides until reaching the top and its carvings of griffons' heads, but with an army in their rears, the gate might as well have led to the heavens. Only he hoped he would be alive when he got to this gate. He gazed west once atop the next small rise.

"Shits." He veered to let others pass. Histê in the distance, but across the blowing fields of grass, it was hard to get a measure of how far away they stood. He squinted and took a deep breath; from the way their heads and spears bobbed, they were running.

"Arms and armor to the rear! At pace! At pace! Get across this damned bridge. Straight to the city."

Nehek echoed his call in Wiirê, and Rinold fell in at the back of the group beside him. The Silone in mail held the rear, but two dozen others had scavenged wooden armor and Histê weapons. If it came down to a fight against a patrol, they had a chance.

Edlmir loped beside him, panting. "You know, Squirrel. It's a good... a good godsdamned thing we did all that runnin' afore. I'm in shape now."

The bridge looked a half-horizon wide, and he assumed a road led to the city rising in the distance with white walls and towers—a gatehouse. A flash of horror tingled his skin. "Let's just pray ghosts keep their gates open."

"Aye."

It was the last they spoke, conserving their breaths, and Rinold refused to look back until he reached the end of the bridge or he heard footsteps. He pinned his eyes on the stones passing beneath his feet and focused his breaths, controlled, shook his hands. *Do I die with a bow or sword in my hand?*

He caught an invigorated wind halfway across at a pace that made him feel like he could run forever. He made his decision and drew his sword, and a couple of wicks later reached the edge of the bridge. The group turned but there wasn't a road, just a flat plain of grass capable of feeding a thousand horses, but from here he could see that the gate was open. He glanced back; the Histê were gaining, no more than a quarter horizon away. And it wasn't a patrol. There were a hundred spears or more strung behind the lead runners.

"Run! Run!" He followed his own command, grasses whipping at his legs as he shrugged his shield from his shoulder. "They're fresher. We ain't gonna make it."

A horn echoed across the plain, faint over the pounding of his feet and heart, but it was real. He looked to the city gate, imagining he might see a hoard of spectral warriors, but all he saw was empty air.

Edlmir said, "Gods, if we were behind those walls..."

The horn sounded again, four sharp calls. "Did you hear that?"

Edlmir shrugged. "All I hear is footsteps."

Rinold risked a peek behind and wished he hadn't. "Ready to fight! Arms and armor turn!"

He trotted to a stop and turned, set his shield side by side with Edlmir, Monkeynose, and two dozen others. Fifty strides and closing. A familiar thunder shook the ground. *Thunder?* And to a man, the Histê turned, as if just now hearing the noise as well. The Histê warriors stared in confusion and awe before they turned to run, casting their spears and shields to the ground in terror instead of standing to fight. But they couldn't outpace the thunder of steel-shod hooves.

Horses trampled, swords hewed, axes split; men cried in triumph and anguish; it was a slaughter, and by the gods! Rinold wasn't on the receiving end. He leaped, cheered, and banged his shield with his sword before he and Edlmir shared a howl to the sky above.

Within a wick there wasn't a Histê standing, and they didn't lose a single Silone or Kingdomer in the lopsided combat. He turned as a second, smaller group of horses approached from the city's northwestern gate. He sheathed his sword and threw his shield over his shoulder before raising his arms in the air. "Ratsmasher! I love you!"

Rinold stared at the walls of Endelêun with a smirk. "I don't think I've ever been happier to see a city."

Ivin chuckled as he sat in a folding chair, the fabric and sticks not so much more comfortable than a saddle than they were different. They sat three hundred strides from the northwestern gate of Endelêun, as close as their yellow-eye guests would get to the city without an army chasing them. Nehek was the only one who came this far to sit with them. "I suspect you have a story to tell."

"Stories can wait. Those Histê were the vanguard of a *tutûlê,* which is something like four to five thousand men, and there are probably two *tutûlê* behind them. We don't know for certain, but it'd make sense that they're marching on Green Mountain."

Rinold translated back and forth with Nehek. "The Histê aren't a single people. There are five kingdoms along the west coast, and they expand east. The Histê chasing us were the Onsotuhistê. North is the Yuzilûhistê and the south the Repônoduhistê. Nehek here suspects we'll be greetin' a *Tutûlê* from all three. The Histê nations will come together against us."

"Any way to turn them against each other?"

"He doesn't think so. They've a treaty and... I don't know what the hells he is sayin'. Some sorta judge system to settles arguments between them. They've been at peace for over two hundred years."

"That's inconvenient. What about the Wiirê? It seems they're no friends of the Histê."

"This'll vary from tribe to tribe. Nehek and the people we brought along will fight, but until we prove ourselves, we shouldn't expect more help than staying out of our way."

"Prove ourselves?"

"In battle, and in not taking slaves or killing Wiirê."

"Leto, when our next messenger rides, make sure he spreads the word to harm no Wiirê except to defend ourselves." Ivin paused as the Ravinrin made a note. "So, we could have an army here within a day? Two days?"

The sound of hooves from behind distracted him, and he turned to see Kinesee, Meliu, Shinôu, Harlik, and Budôê riding from the gates, but it was Kinesee's slouch in the saddle that brought him to his feet. He ran to her side.

"What the hells happened?"

"I'm fine. I'll be fine. The city is full of ghosts."

"We didn't see a thing."

"I didn't either, but I felt them. A horn blew—"

"That was Leto."

"No, before Leto's horn."

Rinold's voice came from behind him. "Ghosts are real, I've seen them. A little bit anyhow. They butchered a Wiirê in front of me."

By the time Rinold finished his story, Ivin had a different view of the city gate he stood beside. "So, this ghost saw you once Nehek's eyes were behind you?"

"I can only guess they were seein' through me like I was them. The horns of the ghosts may have sounded because they saw Wiirê scouts rushing the gate."

"Can he see them now?"

"Oh, aye. They line the walls, armed."

Kinesee said, "There was screaming as if they feared attack... or maybe some were heading to the walls to defend them. I don't know, but I felt them in me, their emotions tearing at me."

"Do we know if they see the Histê?"

Rinold said, "No one seems sure, but the Histê don't risk haunted places."

Ivin turned to the gate. "If they can't see us, don't hurt us... We can use these walls." He helped Kinesee from her horse and led her to take his chair. "There's no way to win a war against the Histê in drawn-out fashion. We need to crush them here, then bloody them elsewhere, while taking our people back from them. We're on their frontier, and if we make it hurt bad enough, they won't be so eager to send their armies our way."

"Nehek has mentioned an encampment somewhere to the north-west. Any chance of finding our people is there, but he figures plenty of others are scattered and sold by now."

Ivin turned to Morik. "Are you ready for a fight?"

"I prefer a bed of feathers to a bed of swords, but I'd wager my people are tired enough of digging holes and building roads."

"Good. Leto, my friend, I want you to ride back to our footmen in the woods and lead them back here. Send a rider to Green Mountain and deliver word to Polus. I want all but a couple of hundred men here as soon as they're able. And remember, kindness for the Wiirê. The Histê are our enemy. Send riders to Foggy Vale and Forest's Gate. We want able-bodied warriors, and make sure they're told that we may have found a fortified city for their families, but we need to make it safe first."

"No mention of ghosts?"

"Aye, let's save that for a later discussion."

Leto laughed. "I'll take a score of men and ride immediately."

Ivin grabbed his shoulders and stared him in the eye with a smile. "Ride hard and ride safe."

Leto walked away, calling for his horse, as Morik stepped closer. "We've got five hundred horsemen against five thousand."

"We got a bridge, wider than I'd like, but it'll neck them down. We've got steel; they don't. And worst case, we have a city full of ghosts at our back."

Rinold piped up. "Their armor is shit, aye, but layers of hardened hide cover their shields; they'll stop arrows and blades well enough.

Don't be expecting a slaughter unless you bust their ranks as you did here."

Morik said, "We could hole up and wait for Leto to return."

"It'll take Leto a day to reach them, three days to get back, and the march will leave them fatigued. If we let them pass, there's no telling what route they take to Green Mountain. The only chance that Histê army has is a fight in the forest. If we hold them to this open plain, they're meat to our grinder when Leto arrives."

"And if they just sit and wait for their other armies?"

"We want them stalled, but we won't let them be that patient. I want all the Histê bodies propped on poles by the western arch. Not the Wiirê. Nehek and the others can perform rites for their dead, but I want the Histê spooked. Might be they'll think the ghosts did this."

"I don't reckon a commander is going to let his men sit."

Ivin grinned. "You're right, but we'll give them more reason to fear this bridge."

Sixty-Three

Stacked Mountains

The germination of evil is in the free will of mortals. Humble submission is the only route to righteousness.

—*The Codex of Sol*

While several hundred men slept—or more likely stood without sleeping all night—in Endelêun, Meliu made camp outside the gates. She kept herself plenty close to see a ghost, if any appeared, and close to Lucky and Grunt in case she didn't see them coming, but still well outside of the northeastern gate. Come morning, Ivin and Morik called Leto and other clan-blood and Kingdomer commanders—as well as priests and Wayfinders—to their side to discuss the impending battle. They invited Meliu, but she excused herself with a polite smile and the excuse of needing to work on translating the *Codex of Sol*. Not only did she escape the men with this, but Kinesee as well, seeing as the mere mention of the tome brought cringes of boredom.

Her true plan and destination she kept to herself and her two Wiirê tagalongs. She strode straight east from camp, passing the incoming aqueduct and heading for a tiny mark on the ancient map that may or may not mean a thing after hundreds or thousands of years, but judging by the construction prowess of whoever built the aqueduct and city she held out hope.

She approached a small stone bridge that crossed a narrow neck of river, and she was happy to see that it appeared intact. She pointed to the Pyramid atop a mountain in the distance. "Ghosts?"

Neither Lucky nor Grunt seemed eager to answer, or they didn't know. From this vantage, she saw trees and vines growing uncontrolled, one looking as if it had split the great stones of the road a hundred years ago. If there were ghosts, they weren't tending the area like they were in Endelêun.

Without an answer from her escort, she strode onto the bridge, and she figured it was a good sign that the two Wiirê didn't prostrate themselves or run screaming back to Nehek and the other yellow-eyes. She didn't quite understand why these two followed her as they did, she'd even grown fearful that they might think she owned them, which would be a frightful sin in the eyes of Sol. When she asked Nehek about it, she'd received a two-part answer. One, she'd freed them from their tethers and hadn't beaten them. For this they felt in her debt. The second was more perplexing. He told her that she was pretty—well enough, they were men—but it was her magical red hair that sealed their devotion.

Someday she would need a better explanation for that one, but, for now, she accepted it as a compliment and moved on.

The trail past the bridge wound into the mountains with sharp rocky inclines that were more friendly to people and goats than horses, and in some ways she felt she was reentering the forest as they climbed. Trees became numerous, though not the behemoths that grew to the north, and vines overtook most everything with their clinging, hairy tentacles. Halfway up she found a suitable walking stick, but it didn't save her from needing two rest breaks before her path crested on a sweeping plateau.

"Tomarok. Ghosts?"

Lucky answered, which she'd grown used to. He was much more chatty than Grunt. "Tômôrôk. No ghosts."

The response improved her mood, but she still felt an obligatory *yet* dangling and unspoken. But when she'd taken the time to absorb what she saw, she realized she wasn't yet inside Tomarok proper. She strode to stand beneath a stone gate cruder than she was accustomed to. In Endelêun and other sites, arches were the norm, but here the gate was two monstrous, rectangular pillars of stone bridged by another gigantic block. Sturdy and straightforward, and at some point in the distant past carved with figurines and symbols important to somebody, but rain and wind had worn them to faint bumps and grooves.

She realized then that neither Lucky nor Grunt followed her, and her goal certainly wasn't to get them killed. "Do you see ghosts?"

Both nodded, and her heart raced for a flicker before she remembered that nodding and shaking were opposite in meaning for the Wiirê. She walked through the gate and cast her eyes about. Crude stone buildings ringed the plateau, their construction showing not a flicker of the skill required to build Endelêun. Instead of walking to these cloistered areas, she headed straight for the stairs of a structure—the base of a pyramid with only two steps before opening to a broad, flat top. The Wiirê stayed behind to guard the gate, or so she convinced herself.

Her view revealed three more short pyramids running to the northern side of a flat plain overgrown with weeds and vines and on the opposite end another low pyramid that stood at the feet of Tomarok itself, guarding the path that led to the great pyramid, perhaps. Tomarok was only four steps, but the steps were monumental, and to her chagrin, the path leading up to its heights entered the pyramid instead of heading straight for the top. There was no way in the hells she was going to walk inside there without people by her side, so the journey to the top would have to wait.

She took out the *Codex of Sol* and sat on the top step, figuring she had a great view of any mortal creature coming to attack, and from here, Lucky and Grunt could still see her. She opened the tome to the Ailing Stars Prophecy, one often confused with the Twelfth Star Prophecy in rumors she'd heard in the halls of Istinjoln. She shifted the letters to the new code in her notes and read.

Mountain on mountain waiting for the will of the pantheon, Tomarok high where King Priests ascended to find the Sôshen Crown on their brow. The long lost Larumis Crown—

Meliu raised her eyes. This was the third time she'd seen reference to the Sôshen Crown, and she'd assumed it the same as the Crown of the King Priests, but she'd not heard of the Larumis Crown until now.

The long lost Laramis Crown will be found by the skeleton's eye before, but rise after the Sôshen reveals itself at the summit of Tomarok, but it takes a king priest not. The hidden is found where the Warlord Choerkin falls in victory, but on no legitimate head will it rest until He Who is Raised by the Sliver of Star walks the Fires and rides the Winds to claim its gems in blood and war.

Dancing Bastards be damned. The prophecies witnessed Ivin dead more often than they foresaw the rise of a king priest. But interesting too was the mention of the Sôshen Crown being hidden and the mention of the Sliver of Star raising from the dead he who is destined to wear the crown.

"Meliu! White *Imvôltâ!* White *Imvôltâ!*"

Lucky was yelling at the top of his lungs, and she leaped to her feet despite not knowing what *Imvôltâ* meant. She expected to see nothing, or perhaps to see a ghost; what she saw was a White Lion sauntering up the stairs toward her, silent and casual on paws twice the size of her head.

She calmed her breaths and picked up the *Codex of Sol*, stuffing it in her pack without dropping the massive beast's gaze. At least she wasn't the only one seeing a white lion this time. She could see Lucky and Grunt through the animal's body, and they stared at her in terror. Maybe she was seeing ghosts after all. "Who are you?"

"Who are you to stand beneath the gaze of mighty Tômôrôk?"

"I am Meliu. We've met before."

"Daughter of Erginle, I did not recognize you, smelling of flowers as you do."

"You know me, now who are you?"

A rumbling laugh as the cat topped the stairs and took a seat. He held up a paw and licked the pads, claws twice the length of her index finger retracting as his tongue passed. "If I had a thorn in my paw, would you pull it?"

So much for straight answers. "I would. Tomarok is a place. It has no gaze."

"Tômôrôk is an idea with a thousand eyes. A place never dead and never alive, but always with a heart beating with meaning."

"Are you Rin, brother of Sol?"

"I haven't a name I care to recall, but it is a short name for one with a tail so long." His tail swished the stone.

"This is the third time I've seen you. Why do you seek me out?"

"Do I? No, it is you trying to find me."

"I sought Tomarok... Tômôrôk and I found it. I sought the keys to ciphers in the *Codex of Sol*, and I found them. Why would I seek you when I do not know your name?"

A purr rumbled from the beast's chest and throat. "Why did you seek Tômôrôk, and why did you seek the ciphers? When you can answer these questions, I will tell you why you sought me."

"I sought them both for truths."

Languid eyes blinked once. Twice. "You can't even answer one."

"The codex gives clues to the past and the future." Why the hells had she been looking for Tômôrôk? "This place I sought because I was told to seek it."

"Of what use are potential pasts and possible futures when you live in the certainty of now?"

She laughed and dropped to her butt with a thump. "I don't know. I'm no more than a dancing bastard to another's tune."

The White Lion looked down on her with grave eyes. "You are the daughter of Erginle; the children of the gods are never bastards."

"I wasn't speaking literally."

"Neither was I."

"So, I might literally be a Dancing Bastard?"

"Why do you seek the prophecies? Why do you seek Tômôrôk?"

"Oh, hells, you tell me."

The White Lion stood and sauntered to the middle of the pyramid's platform before turning to gaze upon her. "People seek Tômôrôk for two reasons, to find the crown or to wear the crown, but for you, this is not the final answer. Once you've discovered the answers to these two questions outside yourself, you will have the answer to the third inside yourself. But still, you will seek me out, and maybe you will find me."

The lion turned and strolled away, leaping from the eastern edge of the pyramid. She jumped to her feet and ran after him, but as she suspected, he'd disappeared. She stared over the edge for a flicker before turning to descend to Lucky and Grunt.

The Wiirê stood wide-eyed as she approached. "You did see that, didn't you?" Someday she'd get them to speak enough Silone to vouch for her sanity. Instead of answering, they dropped to their knees and folded in prayer with fingers stretched for her toes as they kissed the ground. "Oh, hells."

She jumped back and strode around the simpering fools. If there were anything that Sol frowned on more than taking slaves, it would be to have some fool worship you as some sort of god. But then again, if she'd been speaking with Rin... "I'm going straight to the Forges. The only question is whether my soul pumps the bellows or is hammered into a weapon." Her mind wandered to what sort of weapon she'd like to be; she laughed and wondered if the Dark hadn't driven her mad after all.

Sixty-Four

Island Chain

The Erendotê were a free and prosperous people with wise rulers who believed that true evil was the desire to control others. They were untouchable in military might until they fell under the sway of False Righteousness: the desire to control others for their own good. In four generations they fell, and the Duntupûor swept their memory away.

—*Oxeum Codex*

The Wolverine was the Wolverine again the morning he awoke on the island of Berul and in Oldenu's bed. He slipped from the blankets wondering if this was the day the Edan chose to leave, but he'd been wondering that every day for weeks. If not today, then one day soon,they would.

He took his stand beside a window, throwing back the furs covering its hole, and savored the cold breeze. When first he returned to Kaludor, the cold shocked and disturbed him; now he realized it was the chill of home. He gazed northwest toward Istinjoln before moving to stick logs in the embers of last night's fire, and within wicks, he had a crackling fire. Oldenu wrapped her arms around his shoulders.

"You always were good at starting fires."

"So good I had to run from them now and again." He turned to face her and plied his lips to hers. "I've been thinking."

She smacked him in the side of the head. "Godsdamned man, I told you to stop that foolishness."

"I'm staying here when the Edan leave." Now that he said it aloud, he knew he would keep the courage to follow through. Unless Oldenu chose to leave.

She smiled and swept tangled hair from her face. "I was eager to leave this place once, but with the Colok on our side, things have changed."

"Aye, this cursed island is home."

"And the Wolverine doesn't abandon his den so easy."

His nickname sounded so different when she said it; it meant again what it was meant to mean. He was a man determined not to die, and he would fight any comers to save himself and others. "Someday, I will tell you how I earned that name the first time."

"I'd be honored." She let loose her grip and meandered to the bed to slip into furs.

Knuckles rapped the door, and Pikarn slipped into his bearskin cloak before answering. Rikis stepped inside. "Inslok is coherent this morning. They're talking about leaving in the next couple of days."

Pikarn stared and questioned his courage. He grabbed his axes and slipped them into their hangers at his belt. "Let's share words with this Edan."

They trod outside with Oldenu at Pikarn's side. "So, if you two get married, will you become Pikarn Broldun?"

It was tradition to take the name of clan-blood if marrying into the family, but... "I'll bite your ear off, Choerkin; don't think I won't." He caught Oldenu's glare. "Not that I wouldn't marry... I owe you one, boy. Maybe two fer that."

Rikis laughed and still sniggered by the time they found Inslok sitting on a rock beside Limereu. Pikarn eyed the woodkin and said, "I hear yer feelin' well, Edan." He might be better, but the fact he sat instead of stood told him that Inslok wasn't whole.

Inslok's head turned on a swivel. "I am ready to travel."

"What the godsdamns happened in Istinjoln?"

"Marukane took sway of me, brought me to a rage until a mortal entered my body."

Pikarn glanced at Rikis and Oldenu before his eyes landed on Limereu. "A mortal soul?"

Limereu said, "He claims a man named Dareun entered him."

The name was plenty familiar. "The Sundered Priest."

"Yes. It was Dareun who saved us from Marukane the last time in Istinjoln. He tells the demon stories."

"Like stories for children?"

"I don't know. Histories, maybe."

The Wolverine wasn't so sure. Zwinfolkum was a queen mother, and Maru and Kane were her children. Nobody ever said how old they were when turned into a demon. "So what about what all mothers want?"

"I suspect it is a reference to the Mother Wood."

Pikarn guffawed. "You might be overthinkin' things, Edan. She is the Queen Mother, after all. What did your mother want?"

He blinked once. "The only mother I have known is the Eleris."

Pikarn opened his mouth but then recalled something Solineus had mentioned: There were no Edan children. "You might be askin' yerself what a human mother wants."

Inslok looked to Oldenu. "What do human mother's want?"

"I'm no mother, mind, but my ma always told me she wanted me to find a good man and settle down. It didn't turn out so good for her notions."

"I do not think this would work with Marukane."

"I'm supposin' not."

The Wolverine said, "My ma just told me to go and be happy." He glanced at Oldenu then back to Inslok. "Marukane was once two mortals. Humans. How happy you think they are as some demon?"

"You suggest that the Queen Mother would have us bring them back to their mortal forms?"

"Aye, it sounds crazy aloud, but if you found a way... Zwinfolkum wouldn't be able to hold the gate as a human."

Inslok turned to Limereu. "Does this sound easier or more difficult than closing the gate in a more traditional way?"

"We don't even understand how the Dontupûor blended mortals with demonic beings, but if we understood, it is conceivable we might reverse the effect."

Pikarn said, "It's just my knucklehead idea. No way to know if I'm even right."

Inslok said, "We will study it after we reach the Eleris."

"Aye, you do that. I'll be staying here to fight the Taken with the Colok."

Oldenu punched his shoulder, the closest thing to public affection she showed. "I'll be with him."

Rikis eyed him. "You're sure on that?"

"Aye. With the Colok helping, we'll bring enough wood and stone, to connect these islands and settle them all. We can house a thousand here during the warmer months and five hundred other times. We'll start clearing the island of every damned Taken we can find."

"I'll send men and supplies from New Fost. We'll take Kaludor back, one day."

Inslok said, "You may never free Kaludor from Shadows."

Pikarn snorted. "I may not live to see it, but even if it takes us more than a thousand years, we will succeed."

Inslok nodded. "I will speak to the Volvrolan of an extension on your time."

The Wolverine laughed along with the other Silone. "You do that."

Glimdrem sat on a jagged peninsula off the northern point of Berul watching hogs rut in their pen, then stared at wild boars wandering the banks of the river. The amazing thing that he'd learned was that the feral pigs were once like the hogs. Domestication changed them. They were still huge, powerful, and hairy, but they didn't bear the tusks of their wild kin and ignored people. Yet, if you freed them, their hair grew thick and coarse, razor tusks sprouted from their jaws, and they became aggressive, attacking men at the slightest provocation.

You are the hog, domesticated and weak; the Edan are what nature intended you to be.

The vine's argument remained silly on its face, and he tried to ignore it by noting errors in the details. But the vine's intent was not to argue apples to apples, but to prove that such changes exist.

"You are wrong."

Am I? Did the Edan caught outside the Eleris lose their glow? That which, in essence, makes an Edan, Edan?

"Yes. It is well known. All those who returned to the Eleris departed for the Father Wood to heal."

Or they became the Trelelunin.

"That can't be."

And Edan cannot return from the Father, but one did.

Glimdrem stared at a sow and her piglets, most destined to be food for people. Did they envy their free kin, or did a pig care? A Trelelunin's children lived in service to the Edan, and not a one seemed to envy the Edan, nor did they care. "I was Edan once." The words struck him as ludicrous, but this sense faded.

You were. You've been misused, abused. Instead of honoring you for your sacrifice, they turned you into their servant.

"A pampered slave."

Maybe other Trelelunin would like to know the truth.

Glimdrem laughed, then looked around to make sure no one watched him. "It's an opinion without proof."

The vine remained silent, so he stood and meandered along the banks of the island, until finding six of the Trelelunin warriors.

Neoburo, the ranking officer, hailed him with a wave. "Glimdrem, we have word that Inslok has regained his wits."

Glimdrem didn't smile. "This is good. We will depart this cursed land soon. Speaking of Inslok, did any of you notice how much like a Trelelunin he looked when weakened?"

Warriors glanced from one to another. Sezwin said, "Perhaps. Yes."

"For a time he lost his *glow* or whatever you wish to name his aura, and he looked like us, do any of you not find that strange?"

Neoboru said, "Why would it be strange?"

Glimdrem laughed and smiled as if about to retell a joke he'd just heard. "I'm just throwing this out there, but, if an Edan who loses their innate Edan-ness and looks like us, might we not be Edan who lost their glow? I don't remember who I was before the Forgettings. Do any of you?" He knew they didn't, no one did.

None of them laughed with him, and he feared that he'd stepped over a boundary, but then Neoboru said, "On its face it seems unlikely, the Edan claim all who faded left for the Father Wood."

"How would they know? Stories passed down? They don't remember *any* of the faded leaving the Eleris. There is no record of a single faded departing after the last Forgetting."

They stared at him with nervous grins. Sezwin said, "Even if true, there is nothing to be done for it."

"But if true, we Trelelunin should be treated as their equals, not their puppets to march into the world where they fear to go. We should be honored for having sacrificed and faded." The pause was long enough that he knew his words penetrated the Edan stories they had been told for five hundred years or more.

Inslok's voice was placid as ever. "These are dangerous lies you broach, Glimdrem."

He turned to see Inslok and Limereu standing atop a cliff overlooking the shore. "What lies? It was nothing more than idle banter and speculation. Or maybe it was a truth you don't want known."

"It is foolishness."

"How foolish is it, Limereu? You've been to the Father Wood, tell us."

"I do not remember the Father Wood. The idea feels wrong."

Inslok said, "It is wrong and seditious."

Glimdrem turned to the warriors. "See? See how they do not want you to even *consider* anything that they don't teach? If it is not true, where does the harm lie in pondering the question? No, it's true, that is why they want you to stop thinking. Thinking men are harder to control."

"The Volvrolan will hear of this along with your other indiscretions."

Glimdrem spun with a snarl on his lips. "Go ahead. I no longer care what the Volvrolan thinks. What you think. What Limereu or her sister thinks. If you love these humans so much that you've done more for them than you've ever done for the Trelelunin, then I damn you to their hells."

Inslok's calm stare didn't flinch, but Glimdrem thought maybe he'd pricked his anger. "This is your choice. You had your chances. I will recommend a trial for the theft and copying of the *Oxeum Codex;* instead of remorse or humility for the crime committed, you foster lies and sedition. This will not go unpunished."

Glimdrem guffawed as Inslok and Limereu departed. He locked eyes with Neoboru and flashed a confident smile. "Revealing a lie earns the swiftest justice." He couldn't tell how much a chord he'd struck with these warriors, but they didn't laugh at him. He considered it a win.

Sixty-Five

Far Horizon

One hand steals while the other gives,
the lips kiss with passion while the tongue lies.
Different methods, different directions,
different roads, different skies.
Same destination.
Power.

—*Tomes of the Touched*

The city of Endelêun was built to withstand a siege, or perhaps it was constructed so well to discourage anyone from ever trying. But then again, in the Age of God Wars was any fortress impervious, let alone a city with walls stretching horizons? Either way, Ivin was grateful that the builders hadn't neglected the bridge's defenses.

The western end of Far-Horizon Bridge was a welcoming arch, but the eastern side had crenelated walls stretching to either side and gave a clear view of the crossing while it provided cover for archers. The bridge had two-foot-high rails to keep wagon wheels from spilling over the edge, but they wouldn't give cover to an army. He stood staring down the middle with Morik and Shinôu trying to gain a grasp of a strategy for when the commanders met in a candle. So far, Ivin thoughts chased figments in hope of finding reason.

He sighed, then cocked his head. "Is it just me, or does the bridge grow wider on the western end?"

Shinôu said, "Just a trick of the eyes."

Morik laughed. "No, no. Our Choerkin is right! The western side is narrower by five paces or close to it."

Shinôu clucked. "Why would the builders do such a thing?"

Ivin gazed at the priest. "Think on it."

"I'm a priest, not a warrior. After candles of prattle over tactics, I'm done thinking."

"You've got an army on the western side facing its entrenched enemy here. It doesn't matter if you send your men in a mad rush or line them up nice and neat in shielded turtle formation that's a perfect fit for the western end. By the time you're fighting in the east, you're pressed for space. A chaotic charge is more chaotic, probably sending more than a few for a drowning drink in the river, while most formations will press tight or crack, throwing off the defense and attack."

Shinôu's head bobbed. "I think I see your point."

"From what we know, I'd expect a bullrush from the Histê."

"Oh aye, it'll take them some time to learn if they're used to fighting in forests."

Shinôu said, "I leave it to you men, just let me know when you want a fire."

Ivin said, "Our biggest worry is if this first group of Histê sit tight on yonder shore and wait for the other armies. Five thousand half-naked men don't worry me much. Fifteen thousand or more gives me the jitters."

Morik stepped to the first stones of the bridge. "If we had time, we could build ourselves a wall."

"If we make it too formidable, they might reroute and come at us from some other direction. The southwestern bridge leads straight to the city gates, so if Nehek is right, they won't even consider that."

"Rider coming."

Ivin spotted the horseman on the road to the west, and he was coming fast. "Looks like we mightn't have as much time to plan as we'd hoped. Shinôu, raise a Fire to get everyone's attention."

The priest raised his arms and muttered a prayer; a burst of Fire roared twenty feet above his head, and within wicks Ivin figured every commander would be by his side.

The rider arrived with his mount blowing foam from her huffing mouth. "Warlord Choerkin. I spotted ten columns of Histê coming down the road."

"How many?"

"I waited for twenty rows and didn't see no sign of an end."

"Did they see you?"

"I don't think so, my lord."

The boy was no more than fifteen but an excellent rider and light in the saddle. "What's your name, boy?"

"Erdon Hoshkin, my lord."

With the Hoshkin name, he was guaranteed to be some distant cousin. "I commend you for a job well done. Ride on and let the others know; have them saddle General and send a hundred horse with bows."

The boy bowed from his saddle, and with a nudge, his horse thundered east.

Morik said, "We reckon the road leaves the forest about four horizons away. His riding time, I'd wager the tip of the *Tutûlê* is three candles out. What're you thinking?"

"First, I'm going to take a look at this army."

"Want me to ride along?"

"You're free to do as you will, but if you'd rather see to the defenses here, I'd appreciate it."

"That's more to my liking—"

"Scratch all that. Take the wagons, supplies... everyone but the Wiirê into the city. Soon as we hunker down, we lose our greatest asset: our horses. How many men stand true in the face of a cavalry charge?"

"Not many, I reckon. Damned near none if they haven't seen it before, been trained for it. That'd be fine with a thousand, but it's five thousand, the flanks would swallow a charge."

"Not if they don't have flanks. I want four hundred and fifty horsemen at the southwest gate, the rest will remain up here, inside the northwest gate. We'll welcome them to cross the bridge."

Shinôu stared at him. "If you're hitting both sides of the bridge... why so few here?"

Ivin glanced east, where Erdon returned with General in tow. Not far behind were horsemen. "Morik, you take command here. I need to ride to Tomarok and talk to Meliu. If we do this right, the Histê might not try to cross this bridge again for a hundred years."

Kinesee stood hiding behind a crenellation of the high wall overlooking the merger of the Mûulbon and Temirân Rivers, but she cast her eyes to the northwest where an army of Histê marched down the road. She heard horns blowing—they belonged to the ghosts of Endelêun—and felt the presence of ghosts all around her, but they weren't running through her, tearing at her soul. Harlik and Budôê hid as well, not that the Histê would think much of a few figures on a wall in the distance, but Ivin wanted the enemy to believe the city was empty. She stretched a fareye's tube and peered through the glass as the army drew close to the river.

They were maybe a thousand paces from Far-Horizon Bridge when they stopped. The dead Histê from the day before sat posed. She imagined the men stared at their dead comrades—bloodied and strapped to posts—and pondered whether mortals or ghosts slaughtered their kin. She scanned the rows of men, spotted one running west, and followed him to a Histê wearing a headdress of bright plumes sticking from a helmet fashioned from the bones of some animal. While most of the men wore bands of leather or copper with feathers, this was the only one wearing a skull. A priest or general, she figured, but there was no way to know.

This man and a group of four others broke ranks and marched the length of the column until reaching the bridge and bodies. They stood and stared, their lips moving and hands gyrating. Their eyes stared across the bridge at the field and the city walls. She was too distant to get a feel for their expressions, but bone-helm turned and waved, and five yellow-eyed Wiirê trotted onto the bridge.

They crossed and skulked around the trampled grasses where the Histê fell in battle then stared at the city walls and gates; they nudged one another and pointed at the empty walls before running back across the bridge.

Mumbling ghosts passed her ear, but she couldn't understand a word; their voices were unclear even if by chance she knew the language, but they held the sharp cadence of commanders barking orders or maybe encouragement. She turned and spoke in a moment of courage. "My lords, speak to me."

The voices passed without pause and she shrugged.

Harlik looked at her. "Are we lords now, or are you speaking to ghosts?"

"Ghosts, and they don't seem to hear me."

"I'm right glad to hear they don't hear you. Fact is, I'd prefer you didn't hear them either."

For a flicker she agreed, but in the end she wasn't sure. "I don't know... If I didn't hear them, I wouldn't know they are real. Now I know they are real, and they've still done us no harm."

Budôê said, "So far there ain't nothing to fear from what we can't see. Squirrel said they killed a Wiirê, that might come in handy if they rush the city. Quite a sight to see an army killed by ghosts we can't even see."

Kinesee's thoughts shifted. "What happened for there to be a city of ghosts? War, plague, the Great Forgetting? And they see the enemy, blow their horns as if readying for battle."

Harlik said, "Maybe they all died in a siege, killed by yellow-eyes and their Histê masters."

"Look at this city. Endelêun could house a million people, maybe more. With these walls, can you imagine what it would take to conquer this place?"

"The gods or disease. Or an army impossible to imagine in size. A flying enemy."

"Somehow, I think if we knew this answer, we'd understand so much more." She raised her fareye and pointed it at the bridge. "Whatever the Wiirê may have seen atop these walls, it isn't going to stop them."

Bone-helm stood to the side of the arch watching as columns of men marched onto the bridge, their shields forming walls to their front, sides, and over their heads. They marched in formation to cross the bridge with a steady tromp and rhythm she could see but not hear. A seeming eternity passed before the entire army marched on the bridge with Bone-helm in the rear.

Kinesee smiled. She didn't know every detail of the strategy to defeat this army, nor did she claim to know how it would play out, but she was certain that the apparent safety of being in back was wrong-headed.

Her stomach tensed as the head of the army approached the eastern edge of the bridge, her breath held, and she lowered the fareye. She forced a shuddering breath and stared. The lead formation scattered like drops of water sent sailing by a rock thrown into a pond. The screams in the distance were faint as the horns of the ghosts, and she couldn't yet see their cause, but she knew the woman responsible.

She turned to Harlik. "Command the fires lit."

The man grinned and banged a gong that hung on the wall two times. Fires blazed from atop four towers, flames licking high amid black smoke, but those who made the fires kept hidden.

"Men who are fearful and confused easily lose their way; it's as true in the dark woods and caves as it is in war." She spoke Ivin's words and prayed they were true, and as she brought the glass to her eye, she realized that darkness wasn't reserved for woods and caves.

Meliu didn't often wish she was someone else, at least not since she was a child dealing with a heavy-fisted father and drunkard mother, but being High Priestess Sedut about now would be handy as the hells. Oh, how convenient it would be to hold some artifact and teleport straight into battle in a blur of death. She could walk down the length of the bridge while feeding the fish and toothy lizards the bodies of her enemy in a grizzly show.

No, not me. Not little ol' Meliu. I get scrunched in some dark hole. The dark hole was less a hole than a shelf of stone nestled beneath the eastern end of Far-Horizon Bridge. She had three days of food and water, just in case, and she'd made damned sure the vittles were the best she could expect to keep while hiding under a bridge like some sort of monster from a children's story.

She was worse than any of those monsters, albeit far prettier—only hideous monsters hid under bridges and beds as far as she knew from tales her mother told—and all those monsters lost in the end, even if they did eat or flay a few children before dying. No, Meliu was determined not to die. In fact, she would make it a goal to change the reputation of monsters living beneath bridges. There should be at least one story about a monster who lends a hand to destroy a vile enemy, and this time the monster would be gorgeous, an epic beauty comparable to Januel, the Goddess of Love and War. A destroyer of men's bodies as well as hearts.

But all of these plans relied on her not going mad while waiting for the enemy to arrive.

She peeled a banana and chomped, quaffed a gulp of warm water, and stared at the river's waters rolling by in languid waves and swirls. She caught sight of a lizard's eyes popping above the water as it floated by, noted its tail swishing at least twenty-five feet upriver—a tremendous beast.

The creature's gaze turned west for a flicker, and she prayed to improve her hearing. The faint echoes of shouts came from the west, meaning the enemy had at least arrived. With any luck, they wouldn't waste too much time before marching across.

She waited and listened. Men ran over her on the bridge, their footfalls loud as drums with her prayer, and they returned after a couple of wicks on the eastern ground. There was a buzz of voices from the west soon after, but she couldn't make out their words, then the world roared in her ears, overpowering the rumble of the river. It was the beat of thousands of soles crossing stone.

She inhaled, closing her eyes while keeping her ears open. *Am I the daughter of Erginle or the daughter of Kibole? Today let me be the will of Kibole with the heart of Erginle. The burning strength of Sol with Elinwe's patience.*

Deep breaths only seemed to reinforce that time wasn't passing fast enough. Her heart told her it had been a candle since the army began its march; her mind told her it had only been flickers. Neither could be right. Under the influence of prayer, the marching army shook the universe like an earthquake, and she released its power. She could hear men above her.

She panicked. How much of the army had already crossed? Or were they just arriving? Maybe they weren't even here yet; was it just vibrations fooling her senses?

She tucked her head, clenched her eyelids shut, and prayed to Erginle for Light and blended a prayer to Kibole. The powers struck her soul in a simultaneous rush. She was the beautiful monster beneath the bridge; a monster who could know no defeat; a monster who could stand, lifting the stones of the bridge to face her enemy; a monster who no mortal wouldn't admire and fear even as they died.

Her eyes flashed open, and her head swayed to and fro with an intoxication it could no longer hold. Her mouth gaped as if to scream, but it was Dark, not sound, that poured into the world. Fists of Dark burrowed through the stone of the bridge above. Whatever her plan had been, it was no longer hers; it belonged to the monster.

Screams and shrieks from above and a flicker later flailing men tumbled from either side of the bridge, some bouncing down the rocky bank, others splashing straight into the river. The great lizard rose from the water, its jaws clamping, breaking a man before flipping its neck to swallow the Histê whole. In a flicker, it held another screeching man, and Meliu imagined that the beast turned to her in thanks, worshipping its patron above.

The river's currents were broken by a hundred or more men throwing their shields and struggling to swim, and more joined them in splashes. The toothy lizard paused, stared, then disappeared beneath the surface. The water erupted in frothing fury. Men screamed and the white water turned red. Snapping-jawed fish leaped and thrashed, mouths broad enough to swallow both her fists at once, jaws hinged wide like a snake, teeth as long as her pinky. She watched in fascination as much as horror. She understood she should be sickened, but the power of Light and Dark consumed any sense of guilt.

The monster beneath the bridge thrilled in its power.

The southwest gate to Endelêun opened straight onto a bridge, and Ivin sat atop General in full war regalia taken from the Teks. The barding was polished steel and more difficult to put an arrow through than his double mail, and General's shod hooves could send a man's soul to the stars, but he hoped the Histê would break like a flock of terrified birds.

He glanced at the high walls of Endelêun and saw a man waving a flag, meaning the Histê army started its march onto the bridge. His black shield sat ready on his left arm, but he left Eredin's Glass in its sheath and drew an arming sword. He nudged General's ribs, and the powerful animal clopped onto the bridge's stones with other horses following, their hooves drumming a beautiful if chaotic song that drove his blood through his veins with a surge. General rolled into a canter, and the strides passed beneath Ivin in a rush that defied time.

They swung hard to the northeast to follow the river as soon as hooves left the bridge, but the rises and falls of their vantage wouldn't give them a view of their destination until they climbed to the plain above. He peeled back to let the horsemen with bows in hand pass and kept his eyes on the walls of Endelêun even as Erdon reined in by his side.

When smoke rose from the wall the boy raised a horn to his lips and blew, and the horsemen spurred their horses into a gallop. Ivin glanced at Erdon. "Are you ready?"

"Aye, warlord."

"Aye will suffice. You keep yourself back out of the fighting; your horn has a job to do." He leaned, and General surged into a gallop alongside other riders and when they thundered over the rise, he knew his plan was working.

A dark cloud swallowed the eastern end of Far-Horizon, dark spots littered the river water, and men scrambled in a chaotic western retreat, tripping and trampling one another to escape, losing all semblance of an army as they approached the western side. A string of archers barreled toward the fleeing enemy, and Ivin reined General to a stop, holding his breath to watch what the Tek had done to them in reverse. He laid his sword across his lap and pulled his fareye for a better view.

Arrows flew; Histê fled; Histê charged; Histê died. The archers veered their horses west before the enemy had a chance to fight back.

But men poured from the bridge and organized in the direction of a man wearing a skull. Histê and Wiirê rallied around the man.

"Blow your horn three times."

Erdon blew, and the sound echoed down the valley; swordsmen leaned into full gallops behind the trail of archers. Five hundred Histê at most huddled with their shields on this side of the river, and arrows rained onto their shields as archers passed and veered. The enemy would expect the next horsemen to do the same.

Ivin watched through his glass as a wall of horsemen thundered north. The Histê held their ground. "Break. Break."

"They aren't breaking."

"The bastards have never faced this before. Soon as they figure out these men aren't turning, they'll break." But with the monsters of the forest, maybe they'd faced worse. His gut ratcheted with every moment they held their ground. The first shield fell and the bristling line quivered. Ivin knew the feeling of staring down charging horsemen and the fear thundering hooves pounded into a man's bowels. "Break, damn you!"

The quivering line fell apart on the eastern flank first, but a dam cracked is soon destroyed. Pieces of the line held for a flicker, but piece by piece, it shattered into men running for their lives; by the time the heavy horse careened into the Histê, the defense was no more than scurrying insects without holes to hide in. Hooves pounded, swords fell, axes hewed, spears plunged, and men fell by the tens then hundreds.

Ivin turned his eye to the bridge where Histê stood dumbfounded, uncertain whether to charge forward or back across the river. "Time to give them a place to run. One long, two short, one long."

Half the horsemen swerved while archers swung in beside the fleeing Histê to prick them with arrows. The Dark at the eastern end of the bridge faded away, opening an escape. The horsemen no longer in pursuit wheeled to the bridge's arch. The Histê faced horrible choices that ranged from charging, standing their ground, diving into the river, to running east, and they did them all as hooves thundered through the arch.

Histê in the middle of the bridge running west ran smack into men running east with steel-barded horses hammering into the stragglers. On the eastern end, Histê spilled onto the plain where a string of fifty horsemen thundered through the grass, skirting the Histê flank and casting arrows into the throng.

Ivin sheathed his sword and hung his shield on a saddle hook. By the time he brought the glass back to his eye, mounted archers in the west were riding down runners while the heavy cavalry rerouted for the arch.

Erdon said, "Impressive. Do all battles go so well?"

Ivin laughed. "No. This is a rare surprise. So far."

They sat atop their horses and watched as Wiirê lay down their arms, but the Histê fought on. Within five wicks not an enemy stood alive or uncaptured on the western shore, and to the east, the last vestiges of the Histê army bunched for a final stand, and if he wasn't mistaken, Meliu stood at the bridge making sure no Histê would make the journey to tell the tale of their defeat.

Sixty-Six

Steel Gambit

Submission is admission of everything unholy,
and the goal of every devotion.
Ah, but we disagree to agree you and me.
You believe that someone who doesn't lie states a fact,
while I understand that truth is perception at best,
or an opinion founded on misconceptions and or lies,
a festering in the mind that eats reason.
A self-flagellating beast to devour every season.

—*Tomes of the Touched*

Polus arrived at Endelêun at the head of an army swollen by Kingdomers, but Kinesee's eyes fell straight on Solineus riding beside Lelishen. She would be the only one not surprised by his arrival as the pearl promised that he drew closer every passing day, but expecting him or not, tears trickled down her cheeks.

She wiped her face and sat atop her horse determined not to make a spectacle of herself. Sitting and staring as the rows of warriors arrived, she realized just how slow footmen traveled, but like a boat on a lazy stream, they eventually arrived. Solineus bound from his horse, ran to her, lifted her from the saddle, and spun her around three times before setting her on her feet for a hug. "Gods, girl! It seems forever."

At least *she* didn't make a spectacle of herself. "More than forever, but you look well."

"You. You've changed."

"It's been over two years, so I should hope so."

A horseman rode close and dismounted, and with him standing beside Solineus, she did a double-take before staring. "You *must* be my grandfather."

The man took her hand and bowed, then stepped back to appraise her. "You're more beautiful and commanding than my boy let on. A fine sword as well."

Solineus said, "Alu must've worn off on her."

"You can blame Ivin for the sword, but Alu did give me lessons."

Adinvan nodded his approval. "A woman who can fight is all the more beautiful... sadly, your grandmother only spars with me."

Solineus grinned. "I can't get over how tall she's grown." A shorter girl with tanned skin, dark eyes, and black hair peeked from around Solineus and jabbed him in the ribs. "Ah! I am remiss. This is a friend from the island of Pôn, in the region many of the Emudar have settled."

Kinesee curtsied, but the woman hugged her. "Any friend of my father is like family."

"Pleased to meet you."

The young woman was gorgeous, and she wondered just what kind of friend she was, but she wasn't about to inquire with Lelishen so close. She was saved from her own curiosity by Ivin and Polus.

"Mmm, we came all this way and the fightin' is already over. I hate to miss all the fun."

Ivin said, "We've gotten lucky so far. We've enjoyed surprise with battles at Far-Horizon and only lost seventeen riders."

Solineus blinked. "I heard you had an army of thousands bearing down on you."

"Aye, we did. But they were all afoot, and we caught their commander in the rear... They fell to chaos then to the ground dead. We've got three hundred Histê prisoners we don't know what to do with, but on a brighter note, we've double that in Wiirê willing to fight with us."

"The Wiirê are the yellow eyes?"

"Aye. They're none too fond of them who take them as slaves."

Kinesee felt left out and blurted, "The Wiirê can see the ghosts."

Solineus turned to her. "Ghosts?"

"The city is full of them, but they're harmless... mostly anyhow. But Rinold told us that the ghosts will kill Wiirê."

"Rinold's safe then." He scratched his chin. "Show me this city; might be I can see the ghosts as well."

Ivin said, "Aye, take a look at Endelêun, eat and relax. Steam bath if you like. Come evening, we will gather and discuss our next step."

Adinvan said, "In the meantime, I can tell the Warlord Choerkin the Emudar tale. My condolences on the loss of your father, by the way. Kotin was a great man."

Ivin and Adinvan fell into a conversation as Kinesee turned and walked for the gate. Solineus, Lelishen, and Sîu followed close. "When the Histê attacked, I could feel the ghosts. Sometimes I hear muffled whispers."

Sîu walked beside her. "You are what my people call a *Notuhou*, a Spirit-Ear, I can see it in your aura."

"My aura? What is that?"

"A glow around you, layers of colors which speak to who you are. Among others, you have a band of white with shifting waves. You are sensitive to wandering souls and spirits... ghosts."

Kinesee didn't know what to think of the notion. "The ghosts don't seem to hurt anyone."

Solineus eyeballed the gates as they drew close. "Except for the Wiirê."

"And maybe Histê."

"I don't see any ghosts. I saw Dareun's soul in Istinjoln, but... I don't know. I can't explain that any more than not seeing ghosts now. Lelishen?"

The Trelelunin had been quiet, and she looked surprised to be asked. "Ghosts are not my expertise, but I do feel something."

Kinesee said, "They're here; I guarantee that much."

"Explorers from the Eleris avoid this city. It's pristine, do you know why?"

"Nobody knows. The bathhouse has hot water, the mill wheels at the river run day and night, the aqueducts and fountains are maintained, and yet there are pieces of the city, buildings, that appear to have vanished."

Lelishen stepped through the gate and gazed at the buildings. "It is a creation of the God Wars and a victim of the Great Forgetting... or perhaps the ghosts were the victims and city itself the beneficiary. Either way, it's astounding."

Solineus said, "And defensible. It's a lot of wall to guard, but a siege would have a hells of a time taking the city."

Kinesee caught Sîu staring at her. "What is it?"

"I'm not sure if you want to know."

She spun. "What? A ghost?"

The islander smiled. "No. Your aura. You're pregnant. Twins, I believe."

Kinesee needed to sit, and from the looks of it, so did Solineus. "Twins?"

"A boy and a girl, but that is less certain."

"You're sure?" Kinesee stared at her belly, seeing nothing out of the ordinary. "Don't tell Ivin, I want to surprise him."

Solineus crouched to look her in the eye. "Are you happy about this?"

Leave it to her father to ask the question that thrust straight to the point. "The timing could be better... like in five years, but yes. I guess I am. I'll let you know for sure when the numb goes away."

Solineus gave her a wry grin. "This will pain your grandfather; I'm certain he won't want to admit to being old enough to have great-grandchildren."

Kinesee strode out of the gate, moving so that she couldn't see everyone staring. "I'm hungry, is anybody else hungry?"

Ivin sat beneath a canopy large enough to shelter fifty, but only a handful of people were here. Morik, Polus, Lelishen, Meliu, Adinvan, Nehek, Rinold, Sedut, and Bîdorik and Frâbor all seemed ordinary enough, but Solineus held a peculiar look to his gaze; Ivin wasn't sure what to make of it, but Kinesee was missing with the islander girl. Whatever was going on, it was best to press forward.

"We meet outside the city of Endelêun so that our new friend Nehek could join us. From what I gather, his yellow eyes give him the ability to see the city's ghosts but also makes him visible and vulnerable to the ghosts. Over six hundred Wiirê surrendered at the battle of Far-Horizon the other day, many fought with us. It is from them that we think we know where many Silone and Kingdomers are held prisoner."

Rinold said, "Don't get yer hopes too high. While we know there are many still in the northeast, there's no doubt others have already been sold to the Histê."

"Aye, but there is a holding camp at the city of Fôlgumhîêr two weeks march onto the plains. Our Wiirê friends place our people there. The wall is low, but the armies that were on the march here rerouted after their scouts saw their dead at the river."

Polus grunted. "How many Histê are we talking?"

"Best estimate is eight thousand plus any regiments housed at the city to begin with."

Solineus said, "You're being polite; you've been sitting on the information for days. What're you thinking? Then I'll tell you what I need."

Ivin chuckled. "You're still Solineus. I want to raze the city to the ground, every godsdamned block. We sent a message at the bridge; we need to send a more poignant message. We take our people, free the Wiirê."

"What of these Wiirê? What help will they be?"

"Long term more than short. When we fight in the forests, they will be our greatest allies, but a siege on the plains is our fight."

Morik said, "I reckon you'll be wanting Kingdomers at the siege."

"No one knows stone walls like you and your people. Whether we sap beneath or scale them."

"Our primary worry is the city of Endelêun and the Black Water Cult."

"From what I know, they might be drowned by now. The Kingdomers headed for slavery are waiting."

Morik glanced to *Rûîrn* Frâbor. "What were your orders?"

"My king gave me much leeway, but the prisoners are of Helmveline. Endelêun was our objective and we're here, for whatever good it does, but we don't know this enemy well."

Adinvan cleared his throat. "The Histê kingdoms are big, lots of people, but they're as backward to us as we Silone are to you Kingdomers. Maybe more so. And it will take a year or more to organize a force between the Histê kingdoms to challenge Endelêun's walls. With the proper messages, we can keep them away longer."

"What're you thinking?"

Adinvan pulled a parchment from his pack and rolled it out for all to see. It showed the western, eastern, and southern coasts of Northern Vandunêz, but like many sailing maps, it lacked details beyond the coast. He pointed. "This here is the mouth of the Mûulbon River, which we straddle right now if I've been told right. The Histê are reclaiming a ruined fortress there as we speak, and Captain Edmordô believes it's because of you folks up north here. They won't sit idle in the east unless we make them."

"So, you're suggesting a third message here at the mouth?"

"Aye, sort of. We've got longships waiting for us, but they won't stay into storm season, so my boy and I need to get there fast as we can and safe as we can. That means sending us downriver with an army. We scrub the ruins of Histê to get the southern king's attention, and then we sail back to send the real message: Their western shore is in peril."

Ivin's brain clicked. "The Emudar raid the western cities?"

"We've already pissed on their heads a few times, stolen their sacrificial children, and a dragon destroyed their temple."

"A what?"

Solineus said, "I'll explain it later, but what he says is true."

Adinvan continued. "We've burned ships and raided ports afore. If we threaten their cities and trade hubs, they won't be looking east for a while, especially after you've poked 'em in the eyeballs a few times."

Ivin turned to Solineus. "You've a better idea of the Histê than I do."

"They're right pissed off at us as it is, I reckon. And they're hotheaded; it'll probably work. Marching to the Mûulbon is a long hike when you've enemy threatening your western gate. What of our Wiirê friend here? He knows them better than anybody."

Rinold spoke to Nehek, and after a wick of banter between the two, the Squirrel turned to them. "My speakin' ain't perfect in any tongue, but it makes sense to him." Nehek said something and Rinold nodded. "I was gettin' to that. Nehek thinks we should send a few of the Wiirê scouts to Fôlgumhiêr, feed them the lie of our marching on Tunefâmu to the north. They might split their army. He also wants us to free all the Wiirê, send them back to their villages to announce our defiance of the Histê kings."

"How many tribes?"

"As many as sixty, but there are hundreds of tribes hiding from the Histê in the forests. He's thinkin' that word spreads like a blaze on the plains."

"I hadn't gotten that far in my thinking, but aye. Let's go one step farther and invite the leaders of the tribes to visit with us. See if we can hammer out some agreements."

Nehek smiled and spoke in Silone. "Thank you."

Ivin said, "I thank you, Nehek. And your people. How many Wiirê are we talking about in these forests?"

"No know."

Rinold said, "Many tribes only know how to find their neighbors, and not always then. There's no way to guess how many are hiding out there."

"Fôlgumhiêr is our main concern. Lord Adinvan, how many warriors to take the mouth of the Mûulbon?"

"Unless they've worked wonders with the walls, five hundred might handle them, but a thousand would minimize losses and make it easy."

Frâbor said, "In my judgment, both Fôlgumhiêr and the mouth of the Mûulbon are threats to Endelêun, and the city is the key to holding Tômôrôk against the Dark Water Cult. The Tûrûrôt will fight at one or the other, but half my forces stay in Endelêun to watch for the Dark Waters."

Morik said, "With the backing of the Tûrûrôt's judgment, Helmveline will fight at Fôlgumhîêr as well. We'll send two Wayfinders south to assist at the mouth."

Ivin turned to Adinvan. "Will five hundred Silone suffice?"

"Aye, but if there are losses, it'll be a more dangerous trek back for them."

"Seven-fifty then. Tudwan, will you lead our warriors south and back?"

The Ravinrin eyed him. "I'd planned on saving Daksin, but yes, I will see to it."

"You've a longer journey ahead than we do, I suggest you, Adinvan, and Solineus prepare."

Solineus said, "I'll be staying here. My place, for now, is Endelêun."

"Your mother will rage like a bear."

"You and Sîu belong there, but I'll be back in time. When you reach Pôn and Mulshahar, you and Edmordô start making the trade connections on top of raiding the Histê."

Adinvan laughed. "You won't be riddin' yourself of that girl so easy."

Ivin fidgeted, knowing he had to be forgetting some detail. "Let's everyone get an idea of how fast we can move. We'll delay the scouts' false message for a day, and march in three if we're able, both to Fôlgumhîêr and the mouth." A chorus of agreement. "We'll meet back here in the morning after we have a better feel for the future."

The tent broke into muffled conversations as folks dispersed, but Meliu sat staring at him. Ivin said, "You were impressive at the bridge."

"You've done well yourself. *And the Warlord Choerkin will strike terror into his enemy when but a piece of his army shall defeat a foe greater in number, and with but seventeen Silone lost.*"

He'd never heard the line before, but its detail startled him. He chose not to let words scare him. "If you include horses, the prophecy was way off. And three of them were Kingdomers."

"It's from the Prophecy of the Red Bridge."

"That's the first you've mentioned it."

"For lack of a better term, it's a branch of the Twelfth Star."

He scoffed. "I assume the Warlord Choerkin dies in this one too?"

"You die and die soon, but it gets confusing. It states some will not be able to bear your living while others will not bear your dying, as if both *could* be achieved, but *both* would choose not to intervene."

"Poppycock and gibberish."

"How did your last meeting with High Oracle Meris go? How far off was she?"

"It isn't that I don't believe in something, but how many prophecies are in that book? What are you, a quarter of the way through it?"

"A fifth."

"So we have four-fifths remaining, and only the gods know what they say, or which one is right. If any."

"Not *only* the gods, Lord Priest Ulrikt or his Face. He's read all of these, and that number seventeen is going to shine like a beacon to his eye."

Ivin feared where her thoughts took her. "What are you suggesting?"

"The Face is here, somewhere, and he's watching. The number seventeen, a ridiculously small number for such a battle. Red bridge; Far-Horizon. It could be blood, or that horizons are painted red by the sun. Sedut has told me that the whispers of naming you the first king of the Silone are spoken aloud, and even Tedeu Ravinrin is leaning this way. If the Face interprets the *Codex of Sol* as I do, and sees himself as its facilitator, you need to die soon."

Ivin thought on it every night he laid sleepless beside Kinesee. The Face crumbled a kingdom and killed its king; try as he might, he couldn't conceive of how to keep the Face from killing him if the man decided to try. "If he comes for me, there's no way to stop him. He could be anybody. He could be you, Solineus, Sedut, Morik, or a child I've never seen before."

"What if the Wiirê eyes can see his disguise?"

Ivin shifted in his seat and stared. "I'm listening."

"They see things we don't. It's possible."

"What're we talking about?" Solineus stepped beneath the tent, and this time Sîu was with him. But not Lelishen.

"Whether the Wiirê eyes can see the Face."

"What the hells is the Face?"

"I forget you've not been around." Ivin explained and told the tale of the Malstefnê king.

The only look of surprise came from Sîu. "There are legends of shapeshifters among my people, but this is evil."

Meliu laughed. "He doesn't think so."

Solineus said, "It makes sense of one thing... the night I arrived at New Fost I rescued Kinesee from Sedut, but at the same time you claimed she saved Meliu's life. I assumed we were just... off in our timing."

Ivin leaned back in his chair. "I'd forgotten about that. We also think he impersonated Joslin."

"The servant boy?"

"Aye. But which of us then saw the real Sedut? We need to know which one was real."

"I reckon the Face was with Kinesee, asking about the Heretics of Rin."

"That would make sense."

Sîu said, "I see people's auras, I might be able to spot a false person if I know their aura."

Ivin looked at the islander. "Auras?"

Solineus grinned. "You'll learn all about auras soon enough. It might work."

"So we have two mights; that isn't going to cut it if the Face comes to kill me. First, I need to survive the next few weeks, but after that we've got one option: Kill the Face before he kills me."

Meliu grimaced. "To follow prophecy, he can't kill you himself."

"Then how the hells do you think—"

"Do you honestly put anything beyond his ability?"

Ivin regretted the momentary optimism. "No. In the Red Bridge prophecy, how do I die?"

Meliu's face went blank and she breathed deep before answering. "At the hands of a friend."

"Well shits, I guess I better keep my enemies close, it'll be safer."

Sixty-Seven

Ghost Home

Black wings beat the air,
feeding the red-throated call of the Craven Raven,
the deluded screams rifling through denuded reams,
what angst is left unretained?
what hope is left unclaimed?
what love is left unblamed?
A prayerless soul because a soul can't pray to itself.

—*Tomes of the Touched*

Kinesee wandered halls deep beneath the fortress of Endelêun. The tunnels were lit but without a source of light, and it was this phenomenon that proved to her consciousness that she dreamed. The halls were empty of people and ghosts, but portraits hung on the walls every few strides. They depicted men and women with blurred faces framed by detailed strokes depicting hair and jewelry. They sat in sumptuous rooms with bejeweled furniture and golden candlesticks, all in perfect focus, but her eyes landed without fail on blurry eyes stretched across blurry noses. A golden medallion with a name etched in its precious metal hung beneath them, but there wasn't a one she could read.

She heard the beat of a heart echoing through a door, and she turned, following a spiral stair deeper and deeper. It appeared to go forever down when she looked, but it ended in an instant that left her head spinning. She stood on a landing open to the world, a sky full of stars opened all around her, as if she stood on top of the world, but a wall stood in the middle of this expanse. Bleak, white, plain, and maybe forty strides wide and twenty high, it made her feel lonely and small.

She strolled to gaze upon its vast emptiness as the wall grew into infinity, and a mural painted itself before her eyes. A tawny red lion battled a white lion, massive paws swiping at one another. The wet paint of the white lion turned to look at her. Its lips didn't move, but she heard a voice: *Who are you, sleeping in my bed?*

She awoke with a start, sitting up, heart beating, eyes fluttering to focus on the room in the dim light of the moon peeking through the windows. She exhaled in relief, but a chill passed through her shoulders. She turned, and a translucent woman sat in a chair staring at her. She was insubstantial, visible but muted, faded like a painting left in the sun.

The apparition's lips moved, and the voice came faint as if carried on a distant wind, the words rustling leaves. "*Nesemê râ putolum enoi?*"

Kinesee's brow furrowed as she stared. "I don't know what you're saying."

The door flew open and Light erupted into the room, but it didn't blind her eyes as ordinary light would have. Meliu stood in a gown with Harlik and Budôê behind her, their weapons drawn.

"What's wrong? You screamed."

"I did?"

Sîu slipped around the frame of the door; she was naked and not even trying to hide. Kinesee wasn't sure whether she or the guards were more startled by her lack of clothes. "Yes, you did."

Having Meliu and Sîu living to either side of her was proving interesting. "I dreamed. A voice asked me who I was. That I was sleeping in their bed."

The Light faded in intensity, and Meliu noticed Sîu's lack of attire. "You might want to throw some clothes before you embarrass these two men to happy tears."

The woman huffed and turned away. "I don't understand you Silone."

Kinesee said, "You two may leave; there's nothing here to hurt me."

Both sheathed swords and turned, Harlik jabbing Budôê in the ribs, and they chuckled. She didn't doubt they discussed Sîu as they wandered back down the hall.

"You're sure you're safe?"

Kinesee swung her legs over the edge of the bed and strolled to the chair in which the ghost had sat. It was empty, and she put her palm to the seat. "It's warm."

Meliu stepped inside. "What do you mean?"

"When I awoke, a ghost sat in this chair. She spoke to me. Would a ghost leave a chair warm?"

Meliu sucked a breath and shrugged. "Hells if I know. There are no treatises on ghosts that I'm aware of."

Sîu said, "What ghost?" The short silk robe she wore covered her privates, but not by much.

"She sat in this chair and spoke to me. She said something like, '*nesemê râ putolum enoi*'. She was asking me something."

Meliu's lips pouted limp, her eyes darting. She swallowed before speaking. "I... It's canonic Silone. Or real close. Your pronunciation is a little different than we spoke it in Istinjoln."

"How is that possible? What did she say?"

"Who are you, sleeping in my bed?"

Kinesee's skin crawled from toe to scalp, and her knees weakened. "You're saying that in my dream, I understood her?"

"Either that or you've concocted an elaborate joke."

"No joke." She sat in the chair without thinking, and her eyes flew wide. "Gods, I hope I didn't just sit on her."

"Was she threatening? Hostile at all?"

"No. I was dreaming, I was deep beneath this place and came upon a mural with two maned lions fight—"

"One red and one white."

"Yes, how did you know?"

"Sol and Rin, the brothers battled at the creation of the universe."

Kinesee could tell she was hiding something from her, but she didn't push. "The white lion in the painting turned its gaze on me. That's when the ghost spoke, and I awakened."

Meliu paced as Sîu kneeled beside her, staring. The islander gave her the creeps; it was bad enough to be told she was a pregnant Spirit-Ear; she didn't want to know what came next. "The white in your aura flickers."

"What does that mean?"

"I don't know."

"Good! I don't want to know." Kinesee laughed as she rubbed the bump of her belly.

Meliu stopped her pacing and turned with hands on her hips. "Do you think you could find this place beneath us?"

Kinesee snorted and grinned. "No. The place wasn't real. It was deep underground but opened to a universe of stars. It was a dream, one to be forgotten."

Sîu said, "Not all dreams should be dismissed. They can be messages."

Meliu nodded and strode to the door. "A dream in which you understand canonic Silone is one of those. Bontore, or someone, was trying to tell you something. Do you think you could follow the route you took in your dream?"

Kinesee cocked her head, closed her eyes. She recalled that the dream began with her walking from this room alone, but a flicker before she'd not remembered the detail. "I might."

She led them into the hall, and Harlik and Budôê trotted from down the passage to catch up with them. They passed Meliu's room and turned right. She knocked on the door and Alu appeared a flicker later. "What the hells are you doing?"

Kinesee smiled, beginning to enjoy this like some game from her childhood. "Do you want to take a dream walk?"

"I was already dream walking before you woke me."

"Come on. It's not like you have a husband in your bed right now." Tudwan and Adinvan hopped on crude barges and floated south with their army six days ago.

"Fine. A walk. To where?"

"To the creation of the universe. Maybe." She giggled as she walked away, and Alu slipped into their midst while wearing a nightgown and carrying grandfather's sword.

Kinesee led them to the end of the hall and opened a door on the left. Several rooms on this level of the tower still bore furnishings: beds, tables, lamps, chairs, rugs, everything one would expect in a palace, but this one was barren, just walls of empty bookcases. The walls, ceiling, and floor were paneled in burl oak. She gazed around the room while struggling to remember where her dream took her next. There was no way out except the way they came, at least not that she could see. "I'm sure it was this room."

"Well, sis, that was one short walk."

Kinesee closed her eyes, and the image of climbing through a trapdoor appeared in her head, but its location remained vague. "There's a door in the floor somewhere."

Meliu's Light grew bright, the better to see any cracks. They wandered, sometimes hunched and sometimes stomping until they'd covered the room several times. When Kinesee's eye landed on a knot of wood in the wall, a memory returned in a flash. She stuck her finger inside, pointing down, and turned counterclockwise to catch a tiny lever. Two steps to her left a door opened in the floor.

Kinesee gazed into the black shaft. "I see a rung set in the wall."

Meliu arrived a flicker later and directed Light down the hole. She couldn't tell how far down it went but wagered that the rungs led all the way beneath the ground floor.

"Dreams are supposed to be dreams."

Meliu said, "You weren't dreaming. Not exactly at least. Somebody or something was trying to tell you something."

"The gods, ghosts, Rin?"

"I don't know, but I'll go down first."

Harlik said, "We should go down first."

"No offense to you men, but boys with pants on go last."

Harlik grinned. "We won't look up."

Meliu strode for the hole. "Ain't happening. I'm goin' down."

Kinesee stared down the shaft of pure Light, watching until the priestess reached bottom. Meliu looked around and yelled, "Come on, there's nothing here to eat us."

Kinesee climbed with a death grip on the cold steel rungs, but after thirty or so feet, she relaxed. The rungs were sturdy, and though not textured to the point of being rough, they weren't slick either. She reached bottom to find the tunnel splitting in two directions. "I think we go this way."

They waited for everyone else to arrive and headed… was it east? Kinesee was already turned around. "We should've brought a Kingdomer so we don't get lost."

Meliu said, "I'm pretty good in tunnels, but you have a point." The woman bowed her head, and a point of intense Light about the size of her fist appeared on the ceiling above them. "Keep me alive, and you shouldn't get lost."

Kinesee grinned. "Anyone got chalk just in case?"

Sîu said, "We don't even have a lantern if she dies."

Kinesee grimaced. "This is by far the worst planned expedition ever. So, let's make certain she doesn't die." She turned and led them down the hall, cornered left, then right, and left again before descending a flight of stairs. Two more right turns and two more left turns, and they reached the spiral stair of her dream. It was far more ominous in reality.

"This should lead to... well, the stars."

"Skywatch is a building, but inside there are stars. It's more possible than you think."

Kinesee had heard of Skywatch while on Herald's Watch, but figured people were feeding her tales. "I'd rather it be impossible."

They headed into the spiraling deep able to see only a few feet in front of them, and unlike in the dream, they reached bottom after maybe a hundred steps, and the landing was small—broad enough for ten people maybe—and a door blocked their path. Kinesee breathed deep, gripped the door's handle, and pulled. It opened without a sound, and when Meliu's Light lit an ordinary room, relief and disappointment battled within her.

The room was squared with walls a hundred paces long and appointed with tables and chairs, and bookcases lined the walls. A dozen oil-lamp chandeliers hung from the ceiling, all silver except for the most massive hanging over a table in the middle of the room.

Kinesee wandered toward the center. "This is nothing like my dream."

Sîu said, "And yet your dream led us here. There must be a reason."

Kinesee gasped; the central table was oblong and four fingers thick, a single piece probably cut from one of the massive trees in the forest, but it was the carving which stole her breath. A master craftsman had carved the likeness of the city into the wood with meticulous detail. "How in the world did they get this down here?"

Meliu said, "In pieces, I suspect, unless there's another route."

Alu said, "It's beautiful. But what is this place?"

"I don't know. So deep beneath the surface, beneath the fortress. Defensive planning?"

Harlik said, "Might be, but it doesn't show anything outside the city. I'd wanna have space to mark where the enemy is."

Meliu nodded. "If this is from the Age of God Wars, there's no telling what it might've been. But it gives a great view. Ivin was right, if you look over in the section south of the Temirân river, that has to be militia. The ships docked here have rams, and this barren field bears a crossed sword and ax. The rest of the city is organized, but not like the buildings here."

Budôê said, "Aye, it even reminds me a little of how the Tek arranged their camps."

Kinesee was more fascinated with its beauty. "There are tiny gems set in places. A ruby here."

Meliu leaned over to examine the stone Kinesee pointed at. "Red Latcu, I think, but it could be ruby."

"It's a cut stone."

"During the God Wars, Latcu could be cut."

"Oh. Well, they must mean something. This map must mean something. Why else would my dream send us here?"

Alu said, "Maybe for this?" She held up a heavy tome.

Meliu's eyes flew wide, and she would've fallen over with a poke. "Where the hells did you get that?"

"A drawer in the table here."

Kinesee huffed. Leave it to Meliu to be thrilled over a book. It looked an awful lot like the one Meliu toted around, studying all the time. "What is it?"

Alu set the book on the table. "I don't know. It's locked."

Meliu hovered over the tome and pulled a chain with a key from over her neck. "We've explored a lot of city without seeing a book, not even a single parchment." She stuck the key in the lock, and a click echoed through the room.

Sîu said, "How could you have a key that fits?"

"This key is for the *Codex of Sol.*"

Kinesee said, "And it just happens to work on this book?"

The priestess flipped a page, then another, and slumped to her haunches to stare at the ceiling. "Heavens."

"What is it?"

"The book, it's the *Codex of Sol.* The original, unencrypted."

"How is that possible?"

"How did a ghost speak canonic Silone? The ghosts of Endelêun *are* Silone. This city *is* Silone... Lord Priest Ulrikt didn't drive our people from their homes to a foreign land. He drove us from a foreign land to *find* our home." Her legs buckled and folded until she sat with legs crossed.

Alu said, "You aren't making sense."

"I'm not sure how I didn't see it before. Lord Priest Imrok Girn read the *Codex of Sol* and started a war. Why?"

Harlik laughed. "Power. He wanted it."

"Power, yes. He wanted to be king priest. But what would he have done with it? He would've followed the *Codex of Sol* to lead his people home. It's what Ulrikt did."

Kinesee glowered. "Tens of thousands died, were Taken, just so we could reach this bedeviled place?"

"I'm not justifying what he did, I'm explaining it. After five hundred years... longer even, the Silone have come home to Endelêun."

Kinesee fumed, glared at the book, glared at Meliu. Visions of her pa Taken and gramma dead along with the rest of her family terrorized her mind. She wanted to scream, wanted to cry, wanted to throw the cursed book across the room, but instead, she turned and walked for the door. "I'm done with this nightmare. Bring your Forges-be-damned codex and leave this place."

Meliu clapped the book shut and her footsteps trotted to catch her. "The dream wanted you to know we're home. It's not all bad."

"And if it was Rin sending me here? What purpose then?"

Silence followed her steps.

Sixty-Eight

Trial in Fire

The scintillating eye in the pigmented sky
of red and orange and black,
the Fire of the Dame and dancing wings of the Kī.
She knows She says She speaks She lives She breathes She breeds.
Beware the Lesser Children.

—*Tomes of the Touched*

Jinbin rang a small bell sitting on his desk as he overlooked the courtyard dockside of the first gate into the upper city. "Temeru, High Oracle of Skywatch, you may proceed." Eliles didn't recall ever seeing the man so formal when not speaking of beer; she joked to herself that he might be the Face, but figured the Face wouldn't be so obvious.

Temeru stood from her chair, behind which stood thirty-four priests. She sauntered to the middle of their outdoor courtroom. "All of us here, whether adherents of Sol or common folks, are still Sol's faithful, except for one man. It is said that to kill an adherent of Sol without just cause is tantamount to assaulting the gods themselves. This one among us is none other than Reinus Neharl, who confessed to murdering Niktir of Lulmus."

She twined her hands behind her back and turned to face Eliles. "Our esteemed queen shield will argue that the man who confessed his murder was, in fact, not Reinus, but rather, a bogeyman, a changeling, a demon... a legend of Istinjoln's scaredy-white tales, named the Lord Priest's Face."

Eliles stood. "Is the ax going to make the shield's case for her? If not, proceed with your own."

Jinbin dinged his bell. "The arbiter concurs."

Temeru smiled as she turned to face the holies. "Very well. I call my first witness, Priestess Helin of Dojil."

The priestess marched to the front of the court to stand beside Jinbin. Eliles didn't know Helin from a dozen young oracles here; she'd seen many from a distance but spoken to few. Her hometown of Dojil was near Emudar Fost if memory served. She was in her mid-twenties and attractive, albeit in an ordinary way, with long brown hair. But the question that mattered was whether her waves of hair were her own or a creation through prayer.

Eliles panicked. *What if the Face comes as they truly are? There would be no prayer to end.* She breathed deep and regained control over her heart. It was possible, but Eliles doubted the Face's ego could resist the temptation.

"Helin of Dojil, were you present at the murder of Niktir of Lulmus?"

"I was."

"Did you witness the capture of the accused—"

Eliles stood with a grin, aiming to annoy the high oracle. "It should be noted that all uses of 'accused' which relate to the capture should be understood to include the word perceived, as it is our contention that the man captured was not Reinus Neharl."

Jinbin dinged his bell. "So ordered."

"Did you witness the capture of the accused and his admission of guilt?"

"I remained at the gardens, so I didn't see the man running nor his capture, but I was there when they brought him back. He admitted to killing Niktir."

Eliles stood. "Did Reinus speak the words 'I killed Niktir' or anything similar? Recall that there are many witnesses to come."

The priestess' smug smile faded. "No, he did not. But he intimated his guilt, saying he didn't mean to run."

"So, his plea of guilt is your interpretation of what he said." Eliles sat, knowing she'd caught Temeru off-guard; no doubt, the woman expected her to stick to the Face argument.

Temeru cleared her throat before speaking. "You interpreted his words, which is the basis of language. Does the shield also contend that the crossbow is open for interpretation?"

"No." The whole point was to keep Temeru on her toes.

"Helin, did you see the crossbow? And did those who caught Reinus confirm that it was his?"

"Yes, they did."

"I have no further questions. The ax calls Sulumor of Senon."

Temeru called the remainder of her six witnesses, and they all followed the same pattern of questions and answers with nothing new offered. The entire case rested on the perceived confession, the crossbow, and Reinus' motive, but it was more than adequate for a declaration of guilt.

Temeru stood in the middle of the courtyard with arms behind her back, back straight and standing tall. "The ax yields the court to the shield and her scaredy-white tales."

Eliles grabbed a pack hidden beneath the frills of her chair and slung it over her shoulder as she strolled to the middle of the congregation. "Ladies and gentlemen, there were two murders on Herald's Watch in our short time here, and it is my contention that they were committed by the same person. The adherents of Sol have heard the stories of the Lord Priest's Face, at least those from Istinjoln. I am uncertain as to whether other Lord Priests were said to have such a servant. The first murder was Wilu Neharl—"

Temeru stood. "What motivation would such a being have to kill Wilu?"

"I'm glad you asked. A key. The key to the garden, but much more. A skeleton key capable of unlocking doors all around the island, from the temple to Herald's Keep."

"You mentioned this theory, but what proof have you?"

"I have the key." She reached into her pack and pulled out the brass for all to see. "Many of you will recognize the key and confirm it is the key Wilu carried."

"If Wilu's murderer stole the key, then it seems you are the best suspect. But either way, what need would this haunt have for a key?"

Eliles smiled at the gathered priests and oracles, knowing they'd be most interested in her next revelation. "There is a shrine dedicated to Bontore on Herald's Watch." Murmurs shuffled through the oracles. "It was buried by Kotin Choerkin after the death of his wife, Peneluple, and in it kneels a snake-bit skeleton, the only one I know to exist."

Murmurs turned to silent shock until Temeru broke it. "Shrines are never keyed; they are open to the faithful."

"The shrine, yes. I found this key along with Artus Choerkin and Jinbin, our fine arbiter who also discovered the entrance." She knew Jinbin would appreciate the credit and caught his smile. "The key rested in the skeleton's mouth."

"Your belief is that the Lord Priest's Face, a legend, killed Wilu for her key and placed it in the mouth for you to find? I find this irrelevant to your case, but fascinating. Why would this Face do such a thing?"

"What you should be asking yourself is why this one snake-bit skeleton remained while all the others were removed. Why? What would make this one of singular importance? The reason is that the skeleton pointed to a secret treasure, a holy treasure, something so precious that they couldn't risk losing it." She reached into her pack and raised the crown above her head, the gems sparkling in the sun. "Seven points for the heavens above twelve sapphires for the hells."

The islanders stood mute, but an uproar came from the adherents, and Temeru had to wave them back lest they rush Eliles.

Temeru's voice came strong, but Eliles noted that it cracked. "While fascinating, this is irrelevant."

Jinbin intoned, "Denied."

"The ax requests a sojourn to study this development."

"Denied, for now. But this request may be revisited in the future."

Temeru glared at Eliles. "It seems the queen has found a crown."

Eliles smirked. "We found a crown, but what crown? Is this the King Priest's crown?"

"Why would the Face point you to the crown of the King Priests?" The strength of Temeru's gaze suggested she wanted an answer, not that it was a part of the trial. But there was a condescension in the tone different than she'd heard from Temeru before; the woman became her prime suspect.

"If you are the Face, you tell me? Wherever you are among us, answer the ax's question." Of course, no one responded, but at least several of the holy looked around. "The Face's motivations in showing the way to the crown are unknown."

"The Face isn't even real."

"Not only is the Face real, but I doubt they could resist showing up today. Be that as it may... The crown was found before Niktir's death, and I informed Reinus that I didn't believe Niktir committed the murder, and he promised to do nothing foolish."

"And all men's promises are unbreakable stone, please spare us."

"No. Like you, I believed Reinus killed Niktir; it was the only thing that made sense... until I went to the docks, having left the Reinus caught in jail, and saw Reinus and his brother, Barold, fishing. I call Barold as my first witness."

The man refrained from breaking into a jog. "I'm here."

"Barold, when did you and Reinus start fishing that morning?"

"We hit the docks sometime after dawn. Seden saw us that mornin', but no one I know of after that."

Temeru stood. "Barold, would you lie to save your brother's life?"

The man stared before answering. "I would, but I don't need to."

"But you would, that's all we need to know."

Eliles said, "Anyone might lie, but it doesn't mean they are. Barold, you may step away." As the man left, she turned to stare at Temeru and the priests. "As I said, I contend the Face is here." She sent a surge of Elemental energies through Temeru; she expected the woman to turn into the Face.

She didn't.

Eliles' assumption of who the Face was proved in error or her assumption of being able to reveal the Face was. Her heart thudded in her chest, and she turned away. "I call Artus Choerkin."

Artus strode to stand beside Jinbin. "Ask away."

"You locked the Reinus captured at the gardens in the jail, did you not?"

"I did."

"And yet the cell was empty and the door wide open when I returned ten wicks later with the real Reinus. How is that possible?"

"The power of prayer is my only explanation. There ain't no way I slumbered in a natural way. I've no idea how he got out of the cell."

Temeru said, "Pure conjecture which assumes any of this story to be true." She stared at Eliles. "Your defense is simple: Reveal this Lord Priest's Face. You claim he is here. Prove it. Show him to us."

Eliles glanced away, but a flicker later, she returned Temeru's stare. "Would it surprise you that I know the name of the priest sacrificed, the snake-bit skeleton? His name was Elimwoth."

"A name as any other you might source from your imagination."

"He was a man with a lazy eye. In the same way that I know this, I know that the Lord Priest's Face is not a him, but a *her.*"

Temeru twitched, and Eliles thought for sure she had the Face. She drove more energy into the oracle. Life. Spirit. A combination of both. Nothing.

"Are you accusing *me* of being the Face?" She laughed.

Eliles stalked toward Artus and Jinbin convinced, but without a shred of how to reveal this truth. *I changed my eyes as a child without thinking on it. Dareun said I reminded him of his sister. His sister, how would I know that?* She couldn't know it; only the person seeing her could know it.

She leaned on Jinbin's desk, willing him to see her eyes as red, and willed Artus to see her eyes as yellow. "Both of you, what color are my eyes?"

Artus said, "Blue."

Jinbin said, "Red... you figured it out?"

"Artus, look... what color?"

"Gods! They're yellow."

Eliles stood and spun to face Temeru. She understood now. The face didn't change who they looked like; they controlled how others saw them with precision guided by expectations. There was no need to mimic their voice. People would hear them as they expected to hear them. It was perfect. It was flawless. It was a power imaginable, albeit astounding. And if true, would surging Spirit into everyone around her reveal the Face?

"I need a wick to gather my thoughts."

"A wick? Take a day to gather your foolishness."

She funneled Spirit into herself, but Temeru remained unchanged. Not just Spirit, Spirit with the will to control a mind. Would it even work on herself? She funneled the power and willed it to reveal the truth. Temeru blurred, and it was enough to convince her.

"High Oracle Temeru, I accuse you of being the Face." She sent a surge of Spirit into every soul standing around her, including herself.

Nothing happened, andEliles stood dazed. No one bore a look of surprise. Temeru laughed, but her laugh faded as people around gasped. They all stared past her.

She spun and saw Jinbin, but beside him stood a woman in plain black priestess robes, not Artus. She was short, maybe forty years of age, with hair draping down to her knees. A flicker later Eliles' shock turned to fury, and she stormed toward her. It made sense, the first time she'd asked, he'd called her eyes blue. He'd been unaffected by her magic. "Where is Artus? What have you done with him?"

The woman smiled with yellowed teeth turning black as she chewed. "He is well." The priestess collapsed before either could say another word.

"No!" Eliles dropped to her knees. She flooded Life into the dying woman, but she died in Eliles' grip. For a flicker, the temptation to summon the full power of the Sliver rose within her, but the words of the Twelfth Star Prophecy held her back. *What use to win, only to raise the next king... queen priest.*

She stood and turned to look at Temeru and her blank expression. "We need to find Artus. Where is he?"

Temeru stared in silence until Sulumor spoke up. "I might know where he is. Follow me."

Eliles and every person on the island followed the priest. He was a healer steeped in Life, not an oracle, so Eliles hoped he didn't lead them to some sort of trap. They entered Skywatch, but, instead of climbing for the stars as she expected, they opened the library and climbed down. Sulumor turned south, and there in the floor sat another hole.

"There was a second level this whole time."

"Sort of, it leads to a room beneath the bathhouse across the street." Eliles followed him until reaching a room lit by a lantern coming close to guttering dark after running dry of kerosene. Artus sat tied with his back to the wall, snoring. "We kept him here while we held him prisoner the last time."

She strolled over, kicked his foot, and he snorted awake. "Hey! Ho! Well, about godsdamned time someone found me."

"How long have you been here?"

"The last thing I remember was unlocking Reinus' cell, but even that was a blur. The Face?"

"Dead. She killed herself when I revealed it wasn't you at the trial."

"Trial? Eh, whatever, just get me the hells out of here."

Jinbin kneeled with a knife and cut his ties. It was then that Eliles realized they had a large audience. The only person she knew to be missing was Temeru.

"Things should be much more peaceful around here, but the Face's death leaves many questions we'll never get answered."

Artus stood and rubbed his wrists. "It seems we have an eternity to answer them."

Eliles laughed. "So it does." She turned to the group. "We need to tend to the Face's body, but after that, how about we *all* sit down and eat at the Salty Frog?"

The food was delicious, and the beer and whiskey flowed, but by then, they didn't need to tend the body. It was already gone. She chose to believe that Temeru moved the corpse; any other explanation would've left her tongue and palate dry.

Sixty-Nine

Answers in the Dark

Free men fighting a war for a cause they favor will defeat an army of slaves nine times of ten. Queen Boduholu never learned this lesson, because her slaves were always the one of ten.

—*Oxeum Codex*

Glimdrem didn't know what his trial would look like. He hoped for some flashy show of Edan arrogance. He wished to make a spectacle of himself in front of the masses. All he'd done was share his theory that Trelelunin were once Edan before the Forgettings robbed them of their glow. Was that so much?

Oh, they'd tacked on stealing the *Oxeum Codex* and copying it, but it wasn't as if he had kept the original. And there was the little matter of insulting Inslok and Edan in general while on their little mission. In Glimdrem's heart, he believed himself guilty of trifles, not sedition, but he also believed the Volvrolan would have him killed. Therefore, he wanted to go out like a thunderstick rather than a firefly underfoot.

When Glimdrem arrived, there was no pomp and circumstance. Just Inslok, Limereu, Fesele, and the Minister of Justice, Respedelu Belus. Respedelu was a noted Edan scholar of law during the God Wars, her position as Minister of Justice little known, as this was the first trial since the last Forgetting.

Inslok didn't so much as blink, despite the days and weeks the two had spent together. "The Volvrolan has judged you; today, Minister Respedelu will decide which of two sentences will be carried out, while the Edan here will assist in this decision. We will consider your words."

So much for facing the Volvrolan himself. Glimdrem snorted and twined his hands behind his back. "Do I stand before you as a Trelelunin to be hanged or beheaded? No one has bothered to explain what fate awaits the riddle's answer, so I will neither rant and threaten as the lunatic you believe me to be nor will I play the supplicant you demand of my people and me."

Glimdrem strolled to stand within strides of Inslok, indeed, within reach of the Edan's saber. "Inslok, the one Edan I would dare call a friend... You and I spent time on the island of Kaludor. Do you recall the wild boars? If nothing else, their fine taste?"

A single blink. "I remember them well. Aggressive beasts."

He turned his back on the Edan. "For the remainder of you who've never seen Kaludor, these wild boars are relatives of the peccaries who wander the Eleris and the Elers to the south. But they are monsters with tusks longer than your hand, they weigh half as much as a horse and charge their hunters as fast. But on the island of Berul, where the Silone live unharried by the Shadows and Taken, they raise pigs near as big. They do not have any tusks, and instead of crushing you beneath their hooves, they accept your hand to pat their head like might a dog. They take food from your grip with intelligent eyes, and they are indeed bright animals."

"You are comparing the Trelelunin to pigs?"

Glimdrem laughed. "No. But when these pigs on Berul escape into the wild, they grow tusks in a matter of months! Their hair thickens to stave off the bitter winter. Their tame, complacent personalities return to a feral state. They become wild boars, violent at a hint of threat. Neither Edan nor Trelelunin is like a pig; this is not my point. Or maybe it is my point... Why do the Edan no longer leave the Mother Wood? Because a Forgetting could keep them from the Eleris, and when not in the Eleris, they *change.* Does a soul here argue this?"

"Those who were lost entered the Father Wood upon their return."

Glimdrem paced. "Did they? How do we know? Yes, yes, because it is written. But instead, what if I and all Trelelunin are those *lost.* The lost who instead of fleeing to the Father, stayed in the Mother! Edan who, like the pigs of Berul, changed while lost in the wild. Is there insanity in this proposition?"

"There is no evidence."

"All I ask is that you consider the possibility."

"The possibility has been considered and deemed specious. What you ask for in truth is that we accept your proposition without a scintilla of evidence and grant you all the privileges of Edan status despite the fact you are incapable of that which the Edan do."

In his heart, Glimdrem fumed, and his clenched jaw clicked from restraining the urge to scream. "Do? The Edan do?" Glimdrem marched to stand nose to nose with Inslok, his breath puffing like an angered bull. "By the Eleris, what do the Edan do except live in serenity while sending Trelelunin to die? All in the name of greater knowledge! What? What is it you do?" If the Edan had drawn his sword and struck his head from his shoulders, Glimdrem wouldn't have been surprised, but there was no emotion, just the same placid stare as always.

But the answer burrowed into the marrow of his bones. "If you were Edan, you would know."

All the air and anger fled Glimdrem's body and soul, and he tossed his hands in the air as he spun with an exasperated laugh. "I'm done! Finished. Talking with an Edan is like holding a conversation with a book; the story never changes."

"I am one book, and you are another."

"No, no! I have changed, I have seen the truth of the rulers of the Eleris. An Edan never changes... Almost." He pointed to Limereu. "This woman came to us from the Father Wood with a sparkle in her eye and a wit on her tongue. She laughed and smiled when she met joy, and she mocked foolishness with a self-satisfied smirk. She held a glorious glow that your auras will never match because she *knew* joy and experienced it for what it is. Living. Now I look upon her, and I wish to weep! No smiles, no tears, just the stare of a frozen pond like all of you share."

He turned back to Inslok. "Pig. Oaf. Whoreson! Or better, Almost. Somewhere in that head of yours, amidst the intellect, you must know you should be angry and want to punch me, but instead, you blink. Insults mean nothing. But somehow, my wanting the Edan to respect me as an equal is a crime."

"You are aware that you misstate facts."

"In the Eleris, the facts are whatever the Edan say they are." He raised his hand to stop the retort. "Don't bother. I said I was done and meant it, even if I forgot for a moment. You have passed judgment, now pass sentence. I accept your words without exception. Speak them."

In unison, the Minister of Justice stepped forward as Inslok stepped back. Her voice rang clear with precise enunciation. "Glimdrem of the Trelelunin, you are remanded to the wide world and shall never return to the Eleris, unless there comes a time you can prove the impossible to prove. The Volvrolan will give you a ship, and you shall travel from the Eleris with all those who choose to follow—"

"I would like two weeks to talk to as many Trelelunin as possible. It'll take more than one ship." The flippant comment would've been more satisfying if they weren't Edan. He wasn't certain how many would follow him, but he hoped half or more of the warriors who had traveled to Kaludor with him, would.

"The Edan do not seek to keep any so foolish as to believe your falsehood. You are given one week. You will be given ships as required, and you shall travel from the Eleris with all those who choose to follow, and they too shall never return on pain of death, unless such time as your sentence is overturned by evidentiary writ. You have ten days to gather before setting sail."

The council turned their backs on him and strode away like a flock of geese turning south for the winter. Glimdrem waved. "Thank you. I appreciate it. Very generous." He chuckled, but Ilsferu cocked her head and glared.

"Comparing the Edan to pigs? Were you trying to get yourself killed?"

"My sentence was set in Edan stone." Like most Trelelunin who followed him, despite stating otherwise, deep down, she didn't understand just how different and dead to the world the Edan were. "Whether I called him a hero or a worm, it mattered not to Inslok. Only the Touched... Only the Touched is capable of ruffling his feathers without invading his body as Marukane does." Inslok was unflappable as steel until faced with the skeleton or the demon.

Why didn't you see this before? Came the voice of the vine.

That doesn't matter... the question is, was it the man who riled him, or the place?

Or being outside the Eleris.

He loathed that the vine had a point, but Ilsferu stared at him as if he was losing his mind. She'd said something. He muttered, "What?"

"I asked where we will go?"

The sad eyes and wrinkled brow told him that she didn't believe he had a plan. But he did. "The Luck of the Twenty-Fifth has passed us by, my love. We will fill our ships with every supply the Edan will spare, and we sail for Sutan by way of Anduras and Kutu."

"Sutan? What in the world for?"

"The Twenty-Fifth lied. Uvin told me Ôxêum sank beneath the sea, but it did not; it rose to the clouds, and we will find it. But not straight away. We have time."

"Time for what?"

"To find allies and a home."

But the vine answered, *To kill our enemies.*

Glimdrem stepped from his cabin and onto the rolling deck of the *Flaming Wing* clueless as to why he stared at the island of Mevelensa. They sat anchored on the edge of what the Edan considered their territorial waters without a hint as to why the eleven ships had stopped. He yawned and strolled to the helm.

"What word, Captain?"

The man coughed. "We've company, and we aren't out of Edan waters quite yet."

Glimdrem squinted, searching for a ship ahead, but saw nothing. "I'm at a loss..."

"Behind us, my lord."

Glimdrem turned with a snort, and at first, still saw nothing but a shimmer on the sea's surface, a sparkle of lights. The trouble was, the scintillating play of light moved straight toward them. He swallowed. "Is that what I think it is?"

"*Besbelu*, yes. Four hundred years ago, I saw an Edan ride the surf, leaving for Mevelensa and the *Sarlean*. Or so the elders spoke."

"It isn't heading for the island. How did you even see it?"

"Pardons, my lord, but I was warned to keep my eye behind me for just this."

Glimdrem stifled a twitch of fury. "You were warned and didn't inform me?"

"Inslok warned me not to say a thing. My apologies."

"Of course, Inslok." Glimdrem huffed and stared. His first notion was that the Volvrolan and the Eternal Court had changed Glimdrem's sentence from banishment to death, reasonable enough. The second flicker of reasoning was that the court condemned him to enter the Sarlean, which he doubted. Condemned to paradise felt optimistic.

He descended the helm's stair as the sparkling wave drew closer at the speed of a bird with the wind driving its wings, and within wicks, he discerned Inslok's face amid the spray of light.

Shimmering waters lifted Inslok to the edge of the ship; his body didn't rock or waver, as if the Edan stood on a boulder instead of an Elemental wave.

Glimdrem cast him a hard stare, figuring his death was nigh. "I thought I was rid of you."

The Edan's hands twined behind his back, an expression that may have been born by an uncaring, ceramic doll. "I had words with the Volvrolan after my return to the Eleris. I convinced him of one final offer."

Glimdrem rocked back on his heels with a deep and cynical breath. "Offers from the Edan end ill for me."

"I offer an answer to your question. Come." He gestured to the wave and stepped back to make space.

"To borrow a phrase from your human friends, what the hells are you talking about? I don't trust you any more than I can kill you. If you're here to kill me, do it."

"If I were here to kill you, you'd be dead. Come."

Glimdrem chuckled despite knowing the man had no sense of humor. "An answer?"

"If you choose to know."

Glimdrem glanced behind him; twenty Trelelunin stared at him. "So be it." He reached out a tentative foot and brought it back soaked. If this Edan had developed humor, he was about to get a lot wetter, and he imagined falling into the sea to drown.

But his foot found the wave firm and stable; with Inslok holding a shoulder, he didn't fall, and flickers later he stood secure without assistance. The wave descended with Glimdrem drenched to the knees and a rainbow spray licking his face, then it glided toward Mevelensa smooth as riding ice. He stretched his arms like wings and smiled with the wind in his face. "It is sad you fail to enjoy this." No response, as expected, so he did what he took pleasure in what the Edan could not.

Wicks later, the wave settled them on the shore of the island at a speed that required frantic steps to retain his balance. Inslok strode straight past without stopping, leading him up a trail that had no marks. It had been years since last he made this journey, but he understood where the Edan led him.

"You're taking me to *Sarlean*? Why not just give me the answer?"

"The Volvrolan informed you that not a soul in the Eleris knows the answer to your question. He did not lie."

"You weren't in the Eleris at the time. A convenience if you happen to know."

"I do not."

"A pity."

They arrived at the clearing and the dark maw leading to the Elerean. On his prior visit, Sarlean held an unexplainable presence, this time, it spoke to him: *Come home to the Father.* He shook his head, blinking.

Inslok gestured. "The answer to your question reveals itself to you; all you must be is willing to walk far enough to ask the question."

Glimdrem's heart pounded the rock he swallowed. "You're saying..."

"Instead of banished, you may choose to live forever in the Elerean. Now, with the welcome of the Volvrolan. The Father will not turn you away."

"I need to know if I was once Edan."

"And the only way to know for certain is to take these steps. The Father will know."

Glimdrem stared at the dark crevice in the world and licked his lips. "What do you believe? Honest words, no mimicry."

"What we believe only matters until we know what *is*. Only one on this side of the Father knows the answer you seek, and I doubt he'd share the answer."

The Touched. Glimdrem turned to Inslok, more relaxed than the situation warranted. "I want your simple answer."

"No."

"No? No, what?"

"I don't believe you were once Edan. The Trelelunin were not born from the Mother and the Father, but you were welcomed once into their folds and are welcomed again to discover if I am wrong." He gestured to Sarlean.

But Glimdrem's eyes pinned Inslok's. "And if I do this, my people?"

"They are welcome to return to the Eleris or sail onward as planned. No grievance will be held."

Only the Edan could make an emotionless promise like that. Other Trelelunin might not be so kind to those who forsook the Eleris once. He turned to the cave and sauntered toward its entrance. Did it matter? To step into the Father Wood would be a singular moment of pride.

Pride is a pitiable trait, don't you agree? Glimdrem clenched his eyes shut, willing Uvîn's voice from his head.

A warm breeze wafted from the cavern's entrance, its currents awash with the scent of roses and lilac... flowers his olfactory had never consumed before. And so too came overlapping whispers:

Come home to the Father.

Truth is a paid-for whore.

You aren't who you think you are...

Spread your wings without fear.

You are more.

All your questions are answered in the beyond.

And facts may crush the soul.

A step into darkness...

The Blind Monkey has tasted your blood.

And you will fly into the woods, my child.

Glimdrem's lead foot struck the shadows inside the cave's entrance before he realized he was walking, and at the same time came Ilsferu's voice, freezing his stride.

Love. Me.

Shivers racked his spine, pimpled his skin, and he stared into the dark, seeing nothing ahead.

It is they who should be leaving the world.

All baby birds fear to fly, but in the end, they all do.

Love is never a pitiable trait.

He lurched from the cave, stumbling, his hands splayed to catch himself against Inslok's shoulder and chest. Shallow rapid breaths, his mind fogged: "Return me to the Flaming Wing."

The Edan grabbed his shoulders and stood him straight, genuine curiosity in his perfect eyes. "What did you see?"

His voice rasped. "See? I saw nothing."

"The Father, he welcomed you?"

"He did. He offered me answers."

Inslok's brow twitched, enough to convey his surprise. "And you declined."

Glimdrem steadied himself. "What good are answers you can never share?"

Inslok stepped back, and Glimdrem prided himself on finding an answer the Edan would accept. "I will return you to your people."

A candle later, Glimdrem and his Trelelunin sailed into the wide world, and for the first time, he did so as a free man.

SEVENTY

Prophetic Defiance

In victory does every Warlord find his calling; in defeat does every Warlord find their education, or their head taken.

—*Codex of Sol*

Ivin rode across Far-Horizon Bridge as a victorious conqueror, not just a successful defender, and he sat taller in the saddle for it. Until now, so many stories folks uttered about him resonated with pride in survival rather than victory, and that tidbit irked him. The Razing of Fôlgumhiêr would be a tale his ears wouldn't shy from. A tale of being on the offensive, and with any luck, it would send a message to the Histê that would make it the last tale of battle for years to come.

The battle of Fôlgumhiêr was a rout, the complete annihilation of the enemy with only two hundred and seventy-two dead and another three hundred with serious injuries they'd survive. One army destroyed and the other victorious; on one side the masters fleeing their burning homes, and on the other slaves freed to go home at last. Brutal, bloody, and bold, but also showing mercy for the defeated.

Kingdomers and Silone alike awaited them at the end of the bridge, and he was shocked to see how many women and children were here already. But then it occurred to him that they'd been gone for over a month and that the road leading from the north might be cleared by now, even if not finished.

Folks cheered, waved, and chanted, and Morik leaned in his saddle so Ivin could hear him. "I see ghosts didn't keep your people away."

"What're ghosts compared to demons?" Ivin smiled as he absorbed the adulation of the throng, even if it wasn't all for him. "It's a victory that won't last long, I fear."

"Let us pray otherwise. What's the matter with that one? Got a saddle horn up his ass?"

Leto rode to his left, and he glowered as his body swayed in the saddle. Ivin raised a hand to catch a garland of red flowers tossed his way by a pack of children that screamed his title and name. He raised the wreath high and smiled at the young ones. "Ravinrin! Enjoy the victory. You earned it."

"Seems to me they're cheering you and Morik."

The Kingdomer wore a shit-eating grin. "That's 'cause we're that much better looking than you."

Leto snorted but grinned. "My ribs ache more than my saddle-sore ass, and that's saying something."

Ivin chuckled, but something was amiss, though he didn't doubt the man's word after his horse rolled on him. He plopped the flowers on his head and craned his neck to look at Solineus. He sat his saddle as if not recognizing people cheered their return. "Twelve Hells, you too?"

It took a flicker for the man to even realize Ivin spoke to him. "What?"

"Ah, hells, nothing." Ivin plucked the flowers from his head and tossed them to a young girl.

With his joyous wings clipped, Ivin's smile faded. He waved and nodded to folks, but by the time they reached the gate, the thrill had ebbed from torrent to trickle. They clopped down the empty streets, a reminder that the crowd greeting them was an illusion that didn't match the size and grandeur of the city. When they reached the fortress, his clipped wings broke; Kinesee stood in the courtyard to greet him, but Meliu was by her side. It was good to see the two getting along, but bosom buddies was getting awkward.

He leaped from the saddle and hugged Kinesee, but before he said a word, Meliu sawed his wings off.

"We need to talk."

He slumped, curses muttered in his head. "So talk. Forget that we've been in the saddle every day for forty days."

"The fewer ears, the better."

That narrowed the problem down to the Face of Ulrikt, some prophecy, or a combination of both. "Fine. In whichever bedroom Kinesee picked, because I'm going to fall asleep as soon as you close the door behind you." They took three steps, and Solineus was on their heels. "The high priestess said the fewer ears, the better."

"And eight ears is the best she's gonna do."

Ivin chuckled and slapped the man's shoulder. "If there's a man here I'm not going to argue with, it's you."

When they stepped into the bedroom, Ivin had to blink twice. An ebony bed with a silk canopy, carved with griffons, dominated the room, but there was also a dresser with a mirror, a wardrobe, two tables, chairs, and brass lanterns affixed every six feet or so along the walls. "Where the hells did all this furniture come from?"

Kinesee smiled. "It was all here. The rooms in the castle, the palace, are all furnished."

"The rest of the city was empty."

She shrugged. "It's Endelêun, the city of ghosts. I'm sure there's an explanation, but I don't know it."

He sat at a table he figured was intended for eating and offered Solineus a seat. "Did this room come with ale?"

Meliu ignored him. "Kinesee dreamed of a secret passage down the hall and a white lion—"

Solineus said, "I've been warned of a White Lion."

Meliu eyeballed him before continuing. "We're assuming the White Lion is Rin. But it turned out the passage was real. We followed it deep beneath the city and found a room that contained a copy of the *Codex of Sol*. An original. Maybe *the* original, as it wasn't in code."

"How the shittin' Forges is that possible?"

"We really could've used some ale... maybe whiskey. This won't be easy to swallow without it. I think the Silone have come home to Endelêun." She sighed and held up a hand to stop his retort. "Also, Kinesee saw and heard a ghost in this room. It spoke in canonic Silone."

Ivin stared at Kinesee. "The ghost was a priest?"

"We don't think so."

Meliu said, "I think these ghosts are from the Age of God Wars. I don't think the language is canonic at all. That's just what we called it after the Great Forgetting. I suspect it might be what you'd call High Silone, the language of priests and nobility, while there was a Low Silone. But it doesn't matter. What matters is that Endelêun is a Silone city. It's our *home*. Not Kaludor."

"Someone go steal a keg of the Broldun's whiskey, so this starts making sense."

"What we call the *Codex of Sol* is probably one book of many. All the prophecies relate to one thing, the Silone returning to Endelêun. Warlords, Kings, Queens, King Priests, who lives, who dies, it was gravy on the steak of reaching this city. I should've seen it before. A migration south is the one constant."

Solineus said, "What you're prancing around is that while we were fighting to survive, we did what Ulrikt wanted."

"Yes."

Ivin said, "It's over then. We're here. He's won. The gods won."

Solineus snorted. "We can't go looking at it that way. We fought too hard and too long, we've planted our feet on a new land, we've new friends and allies, and our people will flourish. That's winning. If Ulrikt won it was a long time ago, the flicker we sailed from Kaludor. From that point on, our goals just happened to be the same. Safety. Survival."

Meliu exhaled a heavy breath. "There's one thing left in the game. The Warlord Choerkin needs to die. In almost every prophecy, this is so."

"Well, that's another game now, I reckon."

Ivin drummed the table with his fingers. "I've been thinking of this every flicker of the ride back. What happens in the prophecies that I don't die?"

"You are crowned king."

"Leto hounds me about talk of giving me a crown. He and I wager a lot of clan-blood fear this end. What do you want to bet the Face is behind the movement to make me king?"

"It wouldn't surprise me, but the prophecies around a Silone kingdom are more cryptic than the rest. I still haven't read them all, let alone understand them. Just because they aren't encrypted doesn't mean they're clear."

How handy would it be if some oracle spoke concise words? "I wager he's waiting to see which prophetic direction is taking hold. Should I die or become king? Two unappealing options that lead us to number three: Killing the Face."

Solineus squinted with a sinister grin. "That's the plan I like, whatever the hells it is."

Kinesee said, "Why not take the crown? There's too much to live for to risk dying now. We need you."

Ivin glanced at her; she was leaving something out, but he couldn't grasp the unspoken. "The Silone haven't had a king since the Age of God Wars, and then it was a king priest; we don't need a king. I don't want to be king."

Solineus leaned back on two legs of his chair. "So we kill this Face and keep you breathing. How?"

"We give him what he wants. We want a small group of people so the Face can't hide amid a crowd—one representative from each of the Clans. We spread rumors of the clans offering me the crown, give it a week or two to turn into a fever among the people. We hold the meeting, find the Face, and kill him."

Meliu took a deep breath. "Hold the meeting atop Tomarok; it's isolated and where the King Priests were once crowned. But there's no guarantee he shows up, and if he does, there's no way to tell which one he is."

"I will visit everyone before the meeting and mark them, that's one chance. If you have Elemental ink that'd be perfect, people won't know they're marked until you shine Light on them."

Meliu grimaced. "I don't have much ink."

"Just a dab on the hand. It's all we need. Soon as you leave, come back with ink, and I'll mark the back of your neck. And don't wash that spot in one of your soaks. Next, we'll introduce everyone to Sîu so she can see their auras. She might spot something unusual. We study these folks until the meeting atop Tomarok. Speech patterns, mannerisms... something is going to give him away."

"And if none of these work?"

"We figure it out or we walk away."

"Or he kills you."

Solineus said, "I reckon it's a risky plan, and that's before we get to killing him."

Ivin grunted and looked him in the eye. "Downright fearful if we get so far. When you attacked Sedut in the wagon, what did she do?"

"Fire, the Twins cut through it."

Meliu said, "Odds on, Sedut would pray for Lightning if startled; it was her path of priesthood before wielding the artifact."

"Which means I met the Face while Ivin was with the real Sedut?"

"Probable. Ulrikt was a Fire Priest."

Ivin said, "Which means we need you and your Twins with us."

Kinesee said, "None of you take any chances, if you figure it out, kill him."

"Aye, this is no time for a fair fight, that's one we might lose."

Solineus said, "I was sent to kill Ulrikt once, so I don't see a problem killing his Face."

Ivin cast his glance at all their determined faces. "If he falls into our lap in the meantime, great; if not, let's keep the king's crown whispers going. Start saying I might be amenable to the idea."

Solineus leaned on the table. "Just one question: What if *you* are the Face?"

Ivin stifled a laugh, but his tone and hard stare made him consider. "It'll be easy to tell if it's me, he'll want the crown. So cut my head off."

Seventy-One

Reckoning Forces

The gift of the greatest warlord is not to force men to their will, it is to inspire men to execute the warlord's aims at whatever cost.

—*Codex of Sol*

Peace pervaded over Endelêun for the next month, so long as you didn't count squabbles over homes and businesses. Trains of wagons and people rolled and strolled into the city at least once per week, laying claim to homes and buildings on a first-come basis. This led to fisticuffs on more than a few occasions, and one death, so Ivin and Leto claimed a building of their own and declared it the Council of Ownership and put two members of every clan in leadership. At the same time, a host of Kingdomers assisted in mapping for clarity in ownership. If not for the size of the city, it would've been chaos, but even if every Silone on Kaludor had survived the trip, Endelêun would've been populated with a quarter of its potential. Maybe less.

The world settled into calm around her, but Meliu's mind was a blur every waking moment. She read the Codex and spent as much time as she could getting to know the delegates invited to Tomarok.

She awoke the day before the gathering on Tomarok to find the morning already hot and humid. She stepped from bed, and a breeze through the window cooled her skin, then she looked at her robes with a snarl. The Church needed to rethink its style choices this far south. She glanced to where Sîu's gift lay draped over a chair. When Meliu complained of the heat one day, the girl had brought her an outfit more to her islander tastes, which meant it covered almost nothing. It was a long loincloth belted by gold-plated chains and a strip of silk to wrap over her breasts, which in Sîu's opinion was a bit of foolish modesty. No doubt it would be cooler, but she wasn't going to recommend it as the new uniform of the faithful.

Still... She wandered to the chair and clasped the loincloth's link around her waist and strapped the top tight. The breeze through the window swayed the cloth covering her butt and she giggled. "Oh, goodness." She stepped to a mirror that was tall as she was and appraised herself. Bottom line? If Ivin saw her in this, there might be another last, last time.

Knuckles rapped her door, and Deelee's voice whispered, "High Priestess Sedut wishes to speak with you."

Meliu threw her high priest's robes over the islander outfit in a hurry and stepped into the hall. "What for?" The girl planted her foot and stared, hands hidden in her postulant's robes. "All right, take me to her."

Deelee led her from the palace and turned southeast to cross the bridge over the Temirân River on the way to the military compound. The direction surprised her until she realized that they headed for the Southeastern Gate. "Where is she?"

"A building at the foot of Tomarok's mountain. She and several other priests have been living there."

It didn't surprise Meliu a lick, Sedut always shied away from people when given a choice, even as most of the adherents coming south lived, prayed, and worked on the ruins surrounding Tomarok. "So, that's where she's been holing up."

A stone trail led them into the woods at the foothills of the mountain, and it was half a candle before stone structures came into view. They resembled the buildings of the temple above, chiseled stone blocks with open portals for doors. Still, they were a step above tents in permanence, if nothing else.

She strolled inside and no one was there. Worse, no furnishings at all. "So, where is she?" When she turned, it was her own face smiling at her. Meliu froze before the thought of a prayer entered her mind.

The voice was Ulrikt's. "It's good to see you again."

Meliu found her mouth able to move, but nothing else. "Why are you doing this to me? What do you want?"

"What do I want? I want the Warlord Choerkin to be king."

"It's a popular opinion these days."

"Your opinion might be valuable to the Choerkin. Will you push him to take the crown?"

"If that is the Church's desire."

"It is the desire of the gods."

"Their will be done."

He strolled to stand behind her, but she wasn't able to follow his path. "All the right words from a child of a dirty cook. This inflates my concern. No fight. No lip from a mouthy girl. Do not take my words wrong, it is a trait I admire in you."

"Would to the hells with you make you more comfortable?"

He returned to stand in front of her as Lord Priest Ulrikt and smiled. "Too late." He pulled a vial from his robes and popped its tiny cork. "Drink." The vial touched her lips, warm, but whatever he poured into her mouth burned like the juice of hot peppers poured across her tongue. Her throat did as he commanded, and she swallowed. She wasn't sure which was worse, swallowing poison, or the fact she couldn't make her body defy his command.

"Remove your robes and boots. Give them to me. Wearing you should be perfect, such a beauty." She pulled her robes over her head and handed them to him without a twitch or whisper of defiance. A flicker later, she stared into false Meliu eyes wearing her robes, and her vision blurred. Pain struck her gut, so sharp she would've buckled if allowed, screamed if allowed, vomited if allowed, but she wasn't.

"Goodbye, Meliu."

She collapsed to her knees and flopped to her side, body convulsing and slicked in sweat. She tried to curse him, but her throat constricted. Flickers later, the shakes stopped, and the fever subsided, but not a muscle obeyed her commands. The pain faded and every stretch of skin numbed; she assumed she would be dead soon. The only thing giving her hope was the faint aftertaste of lemon. Dreamwater. Why stifle her prayers if she was about to die? Her eyes sagged shut.

Kinesee awoke before Ivin on the morning of the gathering atop Tomarok. Instead of climbing out of bed to pace in the dark as her feet desired, she nestled her head into his shoulder, stared at the wall, and promised herself that today was the day she would tell him she was pregnant. The oaf led armies and outwitted enemies, but he hadn't noticed her belly. She blamed him for it despite her attempts to conceal it.

He awoke, kissed her, and rolled out of bed. He dressed, strapped Eredin's Glass and his shield to his back, and said goodbye. She didn't say a word about being pregnant. She didn't get out of bed and get dressed until he left.

She ate breakfast and sulked. And then she sulked with nausea until a knock on her door. Meliu's head poked in when Kinesee failed to answer. "How are you this morning?"

"Ill and hating myself, thank you."

"Come on, we've time for a bath, a little girl time."

"The baths are getting a little crowded for my tastes."

Meliu stepped inside with a playful smile. "Not all of them. I found a small bathhouse just east of here. They aren't allowing people to claim houses there yet, so I don't think no one but Kingdomers have probably found it, and they don't bathe so often."

"You're sure?"

"If it's busy, we turn around and leave."

Kinesee wasn't thrilled, but it sounded better to soak than sulk, so she followed Meliu out of the palace and through the gate into city streets. She didn't notice until then that her guards weren't with them. "Where are Harlik and Bodêû?"

Meliu glanced around. "How funny. We must've slipped by them or something."

On the one hand, their absence concerned her, but her mind was fogged by too many other worries to force deeper questions. Her feet followed as if by their own will, even when they passed into a building with a long hall filled with doors, even when she realized she no longer followed Meliu. She followed a broad-shouldered man with greasy black hair. Something wasn't right, but her thoughts refused to focus.

"Have you ever heard the story of the Starving Man and the Five Bunnies?" She didn't recognize the voice, and she couldn't answer. "It was a harsh year on Kaludor, and Delun was a farmer whose crop failed. Come the brutal winter, he and his family survived on what meager supplies the garden had provided: carrots, potatoes, radishes, onions, and wheat flour ran short fast. But Delun was a hunter as well, a talented archer, but after fighting off a bear one time and wolves another while trapped in a tree, his count of arrows ran low as their food. Worse, a great lone wolf hunted the region, snatching up deer and coney for its own meals.

"Delun and his family starved for meat and grew weak, but one day, hunting after a fresh snow, he came across rabbit prints. A whole mess of them, and the brambles in which they hid their hole. He slipped behind a log just downhill, laying flat, yet so that he could draw and loose the last arrow in his quiver. He waited and waited until his toes ached and went numb, but his reward came when one fat rabbit hopped from its hole. But in a flicker, more came, and they lined up one by one with whiskers twitching. He drew the string taut and aimed, and just then, the lone wolf appeared, silent and bearing down on the unaware rabbits. He loosed his arrow, skewering five bunnies and putting the arrow down the fool wolf's throat! Delun's family feasted on rabbit and wolf, and they survived until spring.

"There are many morals a person can take from this tale, the most famous being that if you have only one arrow, make it count. But of course, we aren't talking about literal arrows. Another is don't be a dumb bunny and make the hunter's job easy. From the lone wolf's perspective, one might say: When you see an easy meal be sure you are the only one on the hunt. It could also be a tale of patience for the hunter, as Delun could have taken the first bunny and spooked the others and the wolf away. Maybe the wolf would even have eaten him."

He stopped and looked at her with brilliant blue eyes and a gentle smile. "You ask yourself, what is this fool's point? Am I right? Like the morals, I have more than one point. However, I do want you to know that you aren't one of the dumb bunnies nor a wolf. I wish you no harm. No. You, my girl, are the bow in this story. The weapon that launches the projectile. I wanted you to know, so you don't worry after yourself and the little Choerkin inside of you."

The Face removed the pearl necklace from her neck, and she panicked, but he placed the pearl in her hands before binding her wrists, then he gagged her with a knot of silk. "I will light a candle. When it burns halfway, rub the pearl." He grabbed the rope and her wrists and tugged, guiding her down the hall to a doorway. Inside stood five priests, their faces hidden in cowls. The room contained a steaming bath and stools, mirrors and tables, bowls and jugs for hot water, accoutrements to help a lady make herself pretty. Funny that the Face had told a certain amount of truth.

"You're late."

Her guide said, "You have a terrible sense of time. Gentlemen, I present you with your prize, Kinesee Choerkin. The Warlord Choerkin will come looking for her soon." He pulled a candle from his pouch, lit it with a torch set in the wall, and placed it in a silver candle holder. "If this candle burns out before he comes, kill her. Otherwise, when the Warlord arrives, kill him but leave her alive. Rin demands it. If any harm comes to her, at all, before then, I will flay each of you."

A priest snagged her wrists and forced her to sit on a stool. "Understood."

"Praise Rin."

"Praise Rin."

Kinesee's mind cleared, her muscles became her own again, and she relaxed with the pearl clutched tight. She didn't know the Face's game, but she knew it wasn't Ivin that would be coming for her. The question then became whether these priests were the five bunnies, or if they were only the first lined up in his greater hunt.

Solineus sat along the edge of the fountain depicting a mounted warrior and griffons in the middle of the central square, a space large enough to hold a crowd of thousands, nibbling at banana bread. He did his best to pretend it was an ordinary day, but on that account, Sîu notched a finer performance. If not a rock, she was a graceful tree swaying in a gentle breeze, and she caught the eye of every passerby with her choice of clothing. But at least she wore clothes.

The candles passed like a sailing ship on a windless day, but high sun was only a candle away.

Sîu broke off a piece of bread and stuffed it into her mouth. "Are you nervous?"

"More impatient." Solineus wanted to head straight to Tomarok, but everyone agreed to avoid the place so they didn't build on any suspicions the Face might have.

"It isn't long now."

Solineus broke a chunk of bread and tossed crumbs to pigeons and starlings gathered nearby, but giant feet tromped close and scared them away. "Fancy meetin' the likes of you here, mmm?"

Solineus raised his eyes to find Polus standing above him with his beard trimmed, and his hair combed back and wet. "Don't tell me you bathed after all this time?"

"Ha! The wife figured if we were going to crown a king today that I should clean up."

"So, Clan Broldun is behind offering Ivin the crown?" No one knew of the plan who didn't need to know, so Polus and the others remained in the dark.

"I'm torn, but my sister is willing so long as there are proper limitations, allowing for some autonomy for the clans. Them were her words, not mine. Kings make me nervous, but I'm of a mind Ivin will turn it down anyhow."

Solineus stood with a chuckle. "The offer would have to be unanimous, I reckon. And I think you're right, Ivin doesn't want to be king."

"If he becomes king, you prolly don't wanna know who folks are talking about as the new warlord." The smirk said it all.

"That settled that, I reckon there's no way I vote for a crown if I have to be the next warlord."

Polus laughed. "You two are somethin'. Folks give themselves to you and you try to turn them away." He glanced at Sîu. "And some of them are beautiful."

Solineus ducked to hide from Sîu's grin. "So, you'd wear the crown, would you?"

"Oh! Ho. Mmm. I'd be better suited to making war than laws. I'd grow fat and lazy and even more drunk sitting on some godsdamned throne. But if people were fool enough to offer me a crown, I don't know if I'd say no neither. And if I had that boy Choerkin's wits? Aye, I'd accept the weight on my brow."

"You aren't the fool you paint yourself as, Broldun."

Sîu stood and stretched like a lean feline. "He does have good taste in ladies."

"And somehow, I married the only bad choices I ever made." His laugh sputtered at Sîu's pursed lips.

"You love that woman more than you let on, making people think you're an oaf. I bet the heated things you say in her bed are the opposite of everything you say outside of it." She reached up and plucked a stray whisker from his chin, a long one he'd missed with his trim. "Your aura doesn't lie."

"Ouch! Damn it, girl, that hurt."

Solineus said, "The whisker or the truth?"

"Both. Don't let it get around. We best be heading for Tomarok lest we miss the fun."

"I reckon fun is no one's goal."

It was a long walk, but they'd leave their horses behind in the trek to Tomarok anyhow, so they chose their feet. They were passing through the northeast gate when Solineus felt the twinge. Flickers later, the pearl clutched his heart, and he froze in his tracks. *The Face brought me to the Heretics of Rin.*

I'm coming, sweet girl. "The Heretics have Kinesee. You two go on without me. I'll catch up." He spun to the southwest; he faced her dead on, but it was a big city, and one he didn't know his way around.

"What the hells are you talking about?"

"Kinesee is in trouble."

Sîu grabbed his arm as he walked, but he dragged her with him. "Ivin needs you."

"No. Ivin needs you to find the Face."

"You are the voice of Emudar and his friend."

"Kinesee is my daughter." He stopped and stared into the distance. "She's there, and she's in danger."

Polus bellowed, "What're you doing?"

"Go! Tell Ivin I'll be there when I can. Don't tell him about Kinesee, I'll handle it."

The Broldun nodded and disappeared within the gate's shadows.

Sîu said, "She's across the river if you're right. You'll need to take the bridge."

"Go to Tomarok." He pulled loose of her grip and tromped away. When he glanced back, she stood in the middle of the road, but flickers later, she reached his side.

"I'm going with you, I might be able to help."

He broke into a trot with Sîu by his side. He knew where he was going, but had no idea how to get there.

Ivin was the first to arrive atop Tomarok, but it might've taken him a candle longer if he didn't have a guide. The long steps up the pyramid led to an entrance well below the peak, and although it wasn't a maze inside, the entry to the stair leading up was cut into a narrow cleft easy to pass without seeing it. The treads were narrow and the climb steep, but stepping outside atop Tomarok made the labored breaths and claustrophobia worth it.

"This must've been what it was like for Solineus in the Dragonspans." Forests and plains and rivers stretched to distant horizons, beautiful and tranquil. He gazed south, imagining he might see all the way to the Monsoon Strait, set eyes on Tudwan and Adinvan, maybe the sails of longships.

"Seven Heavens, that is a view."

Ivin turned to see Leto. With Tudwan in the south and Danwek still missing, the young Ravinrin was Tedeu's representative to the gathering.

"The world is beautiful and peaceful from here." He turned to look out over Endelêun. Horses were specks from this distance, and the view reminded him of the carved table sitting beneath the palace. Kinesee had shown him the room, and he'd puzzled over it since without finding an adequate answer for why the table had been shaped.

"I thought you didn't want to be king."

Ivin faced him, wanting to tell him the whole truth, but there was no way to know whether the man was the Face or the real Leto. "I don't. I hope this meeting will end the calls for a crown so we can get back to rebuilding our people."

Relief swept across Leto's face, but the man was still on edge. "Lady Tedeu backs offering you the crown. I will have to go against both of our wills to serve her."

"I understand."

"Rumor is the northern clans will concur, with limitations. How the Twelve Hells that happened I'll never know. They can't seem to agree on who's the drunker, so I'm not sure how they came to accept a king."

"If it's true. If."

"That leaves Broldun and Emudar, seeing as the only vote the Choerkin have is to accept or not."

"Adinvan said no, and Polus—

"Nobody here cares what Adinvan thinks, and Polus doesn't head the Broldun. If Solineus cracks—"

"He won't."

"I hope you're right."

Budern Mulharth, Selik Tuvrikt, and Norvil Bulubar arrived next, hailing him and Leto, but keeping their distance. Right behind them strode Meliu in her high priestess robes.

"Dancing Bastards, these robes are hot."

Ivin pointed to the southeast and clouds. "And within a candle, they'll be wet with rain."

She looked around. "We're only missing Solineus and Polus?"

"Aye, I'd expect them soon. A word in private?"

Meliu stepped to the side with him and uncovered her neck. With a quick prayer for Light, the ink beneath her ear glowed. "Any idea who the Face is?"

"I've been talking to Leto and can't say there's anything unusual."

Meliu bowed her head and a flicker later Light ignited around them. A fingerprint-sized glow emanated from the backs of every man's right hand. "Now that I have your attention, I just wanted everyone to know that the Church will abide by whatever decision the Seven Clans reach today. Thank you."

The Light faded and she turned with a shrug. "They're all marked."

"That leaves Solineus, Sîu, and Polus."

"*If you've got three targets, the softest is your first choice...* so reads the Book of Leds."

"Sîu?"

"I was thinking of the Broldun since he was drunk last night. But Sîu might pose the biggest risk. Ridding himself of her might be wise."

"Or no marks matter because the Face is on to us."

"I don't see how, but he's been underestimated more often than not."

"Solineus?"

Meliu giggled. "My gut says that ain't gonna happen. If for no other reason than the swords."

"I suppose you're right. Killin' that one has been tried before."

"Choerkin!" Polus strode from the dark of the pyramid with arms high and a smile on his face. As he approached, Meliu flashed Light on his hand, and it glowed. "What the Forges was that? My hand lit up."

Ivin grinned, his nerves bunching. "Nothing. Have you seen Solineus and Sîu?"

The Broldun hesitated. "I did."

"Where?"

"We were at the northeast gate... they turned back. I can't say why."

It didn't take a flicker for his feet to move toward the pyramid's entry. "Kinesee—"

"You guessed it, so I can't be in trouble." Polus' hand clutched his shoulder. "Whoa, Choerkin. He told me he'd take care of her. Whatever the trouble is, he'll kill it before you've even reached the city gate."

Meliu said, "He's right. Let Solineus handle it."

"Shits! Don't you get it? The Face knows... he's keeping them from us, and he's here. If not one of us, then hiding in the pyramid. Waiting." Ivin glared at Meliu.

Polus stared at both of them with an open mouth. "What the hells are you two going on about?"

Ivin grunted, deciding to trust his instincts and ink that this was the real Polus. The Face wouldn't have cleaned himself up, it would've been too obvious. "One of these people probably isn't who they look like. Someone who can change their face is here, and this whole thing was a trap to catch him."

Polus' stare didn't flinch. "I'm thinkin' you just lost me more than I already was."

"I'll explain it all later, just know that one of those four men is an enemy."

Meliu's tongue still burned the first time she awakened. It was either dark, or she was blind, and she couldn't feel her arms and legs; for all she knew they might be amputated or being gnawed on by varmints. Her heart beat, and her chest rose with weak breaths, so at least she hadn't been condemned to the Forges just yet. She tried to roll over but failed, and her stomach boiled and threatened to vomit.

She relaxed, content to die, but then a determination set in. She strained and rolled back and forth the best she could until her stomach could take no more. Bile belched from her mouth, splattering on the floor straight in front of her nose; her tongue burned anew, her nostrils flared with the acidic reek, and she did her best to squirm from the mess before passing out.

The sun was rising over the trees the next time she awoke, and she could feel every aching part of her body, even her tingling hands and feet, but they were weak and all but useless. She squirmed toward the entry using her elbows and knees more than hands and feet, and she felt like some pathetic snake or wounded lizard.

She managed her way to the door. No help. No enemy. No enemy except exhaustion. She flopped flat, tried to pray, but dreamwater blocked the energy of the gods. Not dreamwater, something worse.

Wicks later, she struggled her way outside and raised her head. A puddle of rainwater twenty paces from her face taunted her and she wriggled and flopped in its direction. It might have taken her a candle or just a handful of wicks, but she made it to the muddy puddle and stared. Curses sputtered from her mouth as parched rasps. She tried to ease her face to the water, but her neck failed her and she splashed, bubbling until she rolled sideways enough to get air while still able to suck the water into her mouth.

In three sips, the pain eased and her throat opened. In six, she breathed easier. In nine, she'd perfected the art of drinking from a puddle and took sucking gulps until her belly swelled.

She rolled onto her back and meditated.

Kinesee watched the candle burn while the men stared at the door, fidgeting, pacing, fingering the hilts of weapons, and muttering short prayers. She stared and wondered if she should wait or rub the pearl now. There was a reason the Face wanted her to wait to rub the pearl, but she wondered if that reason benefitted only the Face, or her as well? The whole situation was crazy, difficult to believe. A little girl, a fisherman's daughter orphaned, being adopted by clan-blood and marrying the Warlord Choerkin, only to find herself caught in a web of deceit whose threads dated to hundreds of years in the past.

To the Forges with the candle. Kinesee rubbed her palms together and did her best to shield its glow. She didn't know for how long Solineus would hear her, if he would hear her at all. *The Face brought me to the Heretics of Rin.*

Solineus' voice came clear between her ears. *I'm coming, sweet girl.*

Tears welled in her eyes, and she smiled despite the silk stuffed in her mouth. She looked at the men and mumbled through her gag. "You will all be dead soon. You should leave now."

The men stared, and the one she presumed the leader said, "Shut your mouth, child."

Kinesee shrugged. If they took off her gag, she might try to explain what was about to happen, that they'd been betrayed by an enemy wearing a friend's face. On the other hand, maybe she wouldn't. Just maybe, they needed to die.

Solineus crossed the bridge leading to the palace and turned east with folks staring as he ran past, but he didn't even bother to ask for help. Besides, half the men stared at Sîu instead of him. His mind was focused, and their faces were blurs anyhow; they weren't the ones holding Kinesee. He slowed when the main road forked into three. Straight or southeast? The pearl drew him, but it didn't draw a map.

"Damn it." He stopped, closed his eyes, and breathed deep. *Lady, if you're there—* A force grabbed his chest; it didn't move him but tugged him southeast. He ran and Sîu followed. He turned north then east again before stopping to stare at a building several hundred strides long and three stories high. Pillars lined its front, and windows and doors were everywhere. He reckoned it some sort of bazaar for traders. "She's in there. Somewhere."

"That's a big somewhere."

He trotted until reaching a door and peeked inside. It was a rectangle without an exit. "We need the main door."

He backed out, and Sîu pointed. "There."

He ran through the door and stopped to stare down a long hall with doors on the interior side; Kinesee was close, but up a level. He ran down the hall looking for a stairwell, and the fifth door led up. He slowed, walking on the edges of his feet. He wore mail underneath a silk waistcoat, less obvious than his Kingdomer breastplate, but otherwise felt naked.

He drew the Twins, welcoming their whispers, and poked his head through the door. Another long hall, but with doors on both sides, and it ran in either direction. The pearl told him she was to his right, about seven doors down. He turned to Sîu and held up seven fingers and pointed across the hall. She pulled a short blowgun from the back of her skirt's waist and loaded a poison dart.

They crept down the hall until he could hear breathing, smell the scent of man, and the oil preserving their steel. He took a step, but the Brother hissed, and he stopped in his tracks. *They know we're here.* The Sister hissed. *Heretics of Rin, priests. Prayers.* The Twins hissed in unison. Fighting priests wasn't something he knew much about. He recalled Kinesee's first rescue and how a Twin struck the Face's Fire, but he'd been singed. He held the blades in front of his face, crossed them in an X, and they hissed. No, not a hiss, they made the sound of a blade crossing a blade... *The hiss of blades crossing.*

He nodded to Sîu and crept forward, took a deep breath, burst into the room. He crossed the blades and Latcu sang as the Twins slid against one another; lightning flared, pushing him backward but forking around him to strikes the walls. A concussion rocked the room. He saw nothing but a flare in his eyes and shadows, and his ears buzzed, but he followed the trail of light and struck. He felt steel, flesh, and bone severed and heard the splashing-flop of a body, but the Sister already moved for the next shadow, tip piercing mid-face. The Brother screamed, and Solineus spun as his vision faded back to reality; the blade clipped a man's shadowy forearm from his body, and he bellowed in agony before the sister took his head. The Twins hushed, and after a dozen blinks, he saw Kinesee sitting, tied and gagged, staring at the blood spatters all over her dress. Two other priests lay dead as well, but darts poked from their faces.

"Sorry about your dress."

Sîu stood over the girl and unbound the gag. The flicker her mouth was free Kinesee said, "We need to get to Ivin."

"I reckon so. Take a breath, then we'll find horses."

Meliu took a deep breath, curled her knees to stare at her feet, lowered them, and lifted again. She clenched her fists and rolled to her belly for another drink, this time propped on her hands and knees. The water tasted dirty, she hadn't noticed that before, but she still didn't care. She managed to raise herself straight on her knees, and her head swam, but she remained upright despite her wobble. That was a fine first step. She brought a foot around and wobbled on one knee before lurching to her feet. She stumbled and fell forward, catching a tree to stay upright. Her lungs and heart labored in her chest, and she thought she might vomit the precious water, but didn't. She looked at her shaking knees and prayed for Life, felt a gentle stream of energy, the most she'd managed so far. Her legs and heart steadied, and her mind cleared enough to think straight.

The sun was a candle, maybe two, from reaching its zenith.

"I need to get to Tomarok." She stared up the mountain. It was right there, yet so godsdamned far away. If she were a bird, she'd make the trip in wicks. She coughed, dropped back to her knees, cupped her hands, drank more water, ignored the wriggling thing on her tongue, and swallowed.

She glanced back the way the Face had brought her. She was half a candle from the gate and crossing the city would take twice as long or more because of the river she'd need to cross. She could skirt the outer wall... She looked up. It wasn't the easiest route, and it wasn't a route that guaranteed getting her where she needed to be, but it was the only one that gave her a chance.

She took a deep breath and prayed. *Elinwe, bring Light and Life and with it the energy to climb.* Power flooded into her soul; it was less than she'd hoped but enough to begin a journey. Within wicks, she stood at the foot of a trail leading into rocky crags, and it grew steep within strides.

"Dancing Bastards." She looked down at her bare feet. "I don't suppose the gods could send me some boots?" She sighed and leaned, hands to the rocks, and fought the desire to cry. She prayed again with dry eyes and more energy streamed. She took every step with caution and clutched at any nook or root or branch to pull herself higher.

She broke free from the steep crevice, granted a reprieve to follow a ridge, but she couldn't unharness the Life and Light, as they both kept her moving and healed the cuts and punctures from rocks and twigs and thorns. When looking back, she saw a bloody footprint here and there on bare rock, but she was healing fast enough that the blood loss wouldn't stop her.

The next crevice leading up that she found was wider, steeper, and longer. She would save lots of time, but it could also kill her. She leaned palm to stones and prayed, a flood of energy came, but exhaustion on top of everything else kept her from holding onto all the power. She screamed and slammed her fists to the wall, releasing the energy along with tears as she dropped to hands and knees. She stared at the drips from her face wetting the rock in front of her, her mind whirling in the chaos of frustration, and all she could do was breathe and cry.

A cold puff struck her shoulders and neck; tears dried, and she stopped breathing; instinct told her that something breathed on her. She turned her head in tiny, terrified jerks until she saw red eyes, whiskers, and a black nose. Cold air puffed down her back a second time, chill but refreshing, before the White Lion strode to her side and passed her by, climbing the crag with massive paws and claws that dug into the stone like a cat would a tree.

She stood and stumbled forward, grabbing his tail above the tuft of fur at its tip. *Erginle, give me Life.* The prayer came with a surge, not enough to carry her on its own, but with the lion powering her climb, all she needed to do was keep her footing and grip.

Ivin delayed the discussion for as long as he could, but with afternoon rains heading in, and the fact that this was an informal meeting without the heads of the clans present, it didn't last long. In the first wicks of chatter, he was shocked by the amount of agreement among the clans.

Polus grunted at the Mulharth demand for clan controlled taxes on interclan trade of whiskey, beers, and wines. "Now why the hells would you want to torment yer own people by making Broldun whiskey expensive? Ain't you bastards done enough folks blind with your cheap swill already?"

"There ain't no accountin' for your piss-water taste, but I'm just sayin' the Mulharth want control over taxation of imports."

Ivin took the whole thing with a dollop of sugar, in particular, because he never intended for any of this bickering to lead to anything. So, he figured he might as well enjoy it. "If the clans joined under a king's banner, trade between clans couldn't be considered import and export, but simply trade. That said, a standard collection rate for funds is fair. By this I mean, if the Mulharth tax the production of whiskey within clan borders, then it stands to reason to tax incoming product of the same nature at the same rate. But it would be unfair to slap punitive dues on a competitor."

"The Broldun will cheat."

"And so will your distilleries, unless you have a man staring at their every move. Who the hells doesn't cheat when it comes to taxes?"

Half the table laughed, but Leto remained stiff-lipped. "I agree with Ivin. Common trade and taxation. Now that the clans are settling down, there's a problem that needs settled, king or no king: The minting of songs for trade. We've had nothing but trouble since reaching the Dragonspans with every clan's coins. It's been polite enough, but the copper, tin, silver, and gold content of coins is up and down the mountain and scattered to the ten winds. We need a standard for fair trade."

It was good to hear something useful. "Aye, as the Choerkin here, I concur on this matter. It'll be tricky, but it needs doing, if for no other reason than to cut down on forgery."

The Bulubar bellowed, "Aye! This is all grand, but we're talking up a wind when we need to strike at the heart of the matter: Will the clans accept a king at all? Considering the Emudar haven't no one here, I suggest we start in the north with the Tuvrikt and see what folks have to say."

"Clan Tuvrikt is open to a king with acceptable provisos."

"Clan Bulubar is as well."

"Clan Mulharth concurs."

Polus stared hard at the three men before sighing. "My personal opinion is no, and that's no slap at the Warlord Choerkin, but Clan Broldun leans toward a king."

Leto looked as if he was about to choke. "I concur with Polus on a personal level. The Silone Clans haven't had a king within memory, and I don't think we need one now. But, Clan Ravinrin could accept a crown, by word of Lady Tedeu, not mine own. This gives us five clans who would, or could, see Ivin Choerkin as king, but the Clan Emudar isn't here. Maybe most important, what is the opinion of Clan Choerkin?"

Ivin looked at each of them in turn. If the Face was among them, his transformation remained perfect throughout. "The mind of the Clan Choerkin is undecided; mine is undecided." Grumbles from around the table. He raised his hands for silence. A desire to bare the bones of this meeting grew within him. "It would be an honor of a magnitude I never imagined to be your king, a king chosen, but

I want what is best for the clans. All of the clans. First, Solineus of Clan Emudar was delayed on a matter of great importance, and I am uncertain of Adinvan Mikjehemlut's disposition, but I suspect it was negative."

Mulharth said, "And what opinion of his should matter when most Emudar are a thousand horizons away?"

"The opinions of every clan matter. But there is a second and more troubling issue at hand. I believe one of you isn't who you say you are." Everyone but Polus and Meliu gave him a confused stare. "One of you is a Lord Priest's Face."

Bulubar snorted. "We're talkin' clans and kings, not cockamamie scaredy-white tales."

"The Face is real. He might even be Lord Priest Ulrikt himself."

Mulharth stood. "This is ludicrous. The warlord is making a fool of himself."

Tuvrikt said, "I don't know what the Forges you're even talking about. A Face?"

Ivin remained in his seat and kept his voice steady. "I might be making a fool of myself, aye, but when Solineus and Sîu arrive, we'll find out for certain."

Bulubar stood beside the Mulharth. "To hells with this childish game. We came to speak of you maybe becoming king, not horse-shit. To be judged by some southern Emudar and his foreign, islander whore."

Ivin's fingers tingled with a clenched fury as he held his temper at bay. "If you aren't the Face, you've nothing to worry about. Now, sit."

"I have you to worry about. You ain't the king, and this isn't a war. You don't command me nor a single godsdamned soul here."

Mulharth stared at Tuvrikt. "I agree. Does the north walk from the meeting united?"

Tuvrikt shrugged as he stood. "I'm confused as the Twelve Hells, but I'll walk with my brothers."

Hope faded fast and Ivin held nothing to fall back upon. "Please—"

"No." Leto stood. "The northerners are right. This meeting should never have been held."

Polus said, "Whoa! I'm right there with Tuvrikt with not knowin' what the shits he's talkin' about, but if I've learned anythin' over the past few years, it's to trust the warlord's gut."

"The warlord's gut didn't win us the Battle of Tarmujon."

Ivin's fists clenched, but Polus came to his defense before he said a word. "The warlord's gut gave everyone else time to cross the Gediswon. You were there by his side, *little* Leto."

Mulharth and Bulubar turned their backs and walked away. Tuvrikt said, "I don't know, lads. We'll have to revisit this another day. I am sorry."

Ivin did his best to keep calm. "Wait, please. Sîu will be able to see through the Face's disguise. Just wait." But the northerners didn't slow. They strode toward the pyramid's dark entry.

Leto turned to him with a smirk. "This isn't settled. Not yet."

A flash of blinding light. An explosion threw him backward, toppling his chair; Ivin's head struck stone, and he crawled to his knees while fumbling for his shield. Bulubar's blackened, smoking body landed in front of him. *Lightning.*

Meliu lay crumpled several feet away, dazed but alive, and when he turned, he saw the clan-blood struggling to their feet and screaming priests running their way with weapons in hand. His mind struggled to take it in as his head pounded. *The Face wasn't here. I was wrong. I failed.*

He brought his shield to bear and swept his arming sword from its sheath, wishing that Eredin's Glass wasn't so awkward one-handed. Flames roared, and he hid his face behind the shield and charged. His trousers smoked and licked with flames, but when the Fire ceased, he peeked over the brim of the shield. The priest wasn't a warrior and wasn't prepared. The man's blade hewed, but Ivin attacked his arm with the shield, striking the elbow so hard the blade flew from his fingers. He wrenched and twisted the edge of the shield straight into the man's throat while driving the blade of his sword through the solar plexus and out his back.

Ivin pulled his sword free, and a flash of lightning lit the area, less powerful than the first, but the Broldun flew backward. Arms flailing. Shield smoldering. But keeping his feet until he tumbled over the step of the pyramid. "No!" Ivin bull-rushed the lightning priest, and the bastard with arms raised in prayer never saw him coming. He rammed his sword through the man's ribcage from the side, puncturing both lungs and driving him strides sideways.

The man collapsed, his fall stripping the sword from Ivin's grip, and from the corner of his eye saw brilliant flames. He raised his shield and took a knee for better cover.

Meliu scrambled behind the White Lion. The soles of her feet sliced on edges of shale and she screamed, but Life flowed as sure as the lion's steady steps. Her feet healed to cut again a dozen steps later, and this time she dropped to her knees.

"Wait. Wait."

The White Lion stopped and turned as she let go of his tail, dropping her hands to the rocks, exhausted. His red eyes showed no pity, no emotion at all. "Whose child are you?"

"I am Meliu, daughter of Kibole. Daughter of Erginle."

"Whose child are you?"

She laughed, but her voice was hoarse. "I am the daughter of a violent piece of shit cook and a drunken serving wench."

"Whose child are you?"

"A bird shit me a fence post, and the sun hatched me." She cackled and dropped flat to the ground. "Just go ahead and eat me."

"Whose child are you?"

"I am not the daughter of Erginle, as you said. But a young girl who heals the lick of the Maimer's Lash, she is the true daughter of Erginle."

"The priests would have both of you believe you're daughters of Erginle, this is why I called you such. You and she are sisters, daughters of the Forgotten Stars."

Meliu huffed with her cheek pressed to stone. "Shits. I don't even know what that means. Just eat me and put me out of my misery."

She grinned, but when she felt his cold breath on her bare back she cringed, and when icy teeth clenched ribs from both sides, she was horrified that the beast was taking her offer. She squirmed, flailed, and squealed in the grip of the massive jaws as the great cat's body tensed, then sprung into a lope up the mountainside.

After twenty strides, she sagged limp, her back and sides going numb with cold. Hauled around like some dead mouse wasn't something even her worst and craziest dreams had conjured. And she was damned-near naked at that. *Gods, this could only get worse if my father was here to laugh at me.*

She half expected for him to appear and for this all to be a nightmare brought on by the Face's poison, but instead, the White Lion carried her to the ledge of the mountain and dropped her to the ground.

She rolled over, numb from waist to shoulders, and when she crawled to hands and knees, her eyes spotted Tomarok across a wide mountain valley. A flash of lightning lit the pyramid's peak. A ridge led toward the city below, but a deep crevice made the journey impossible.

"What's happening?"

"Stand and see."

She stood, bracing herself with a hand to the lion's chest. "I can't—" Her vision doubled and her head spun. She closed her eyes, but could still see Tomarok. And she saw it from the vision of a soaring bird. "They're fighting. Priests. Fire. Shit, Polus! Ivin killed one, and—" She saw herself standing and watching not far from Ivin's side. "Godsdamn it."

She stumbled forward confused by the double vision, as if somehow she would run or fly to Ivin's side, to tell him of the false Meliu. She stopped short steps before walking off a cliff to die as the bird's vision faded. She stared even though she could no longer see what was happening.

"If you're Rin, take me there."

But when she turned, there wasn't a White Lion. She was alone. Tiny in a gigantic world and tinier yet in an even greater universe, and still somehow, she mattered. She needed to matter. She needed to send a message.

She steadied her feet and prayed to Erginle for Life and Light, then prayed to Kibole for Dark, and the gods answered in a furious torrent of energies that rocked her body and rippled reality in her eyes.

Somehow, she kept her footing; somehow, she held onto the energies; somehow, she would make herself matter.

They took two horses when they reached the palace stables—though Sîu had learned to ride, she wasn't eager to sit a running horse—and rode bareback through the city. The islander girl was petite, but her death grip around his waist in a dead run squeezed hard enough to hurt. Folks going about their day leaped from their path as he and Kinesee yelled, and they stared, no doubt wondering what madness had taken the trio.

Shod hooves clopped down the streets and carried them outside to pound the dirt, and by the time they reached the trail to Tomarok, their mounts blew foam. He reined in hard and threw his reins to one of two priests who watched the trail and slipped from his saddle. Nehek stood close, bright yellow eyes focused on them.

He flashed a smile. "We're running late."

A priest answered. "Yes, Lord Mikjehemlut. You were expected alone."

As well as the man said his name, he must've been from Emudar. He lifted Sîu from the saddle and dropped her to the ground. "There was a change in plans. Does the path go straight to Tomarok?"

The priest turned to Nehek, who nodded, then eyed Kinesee's bloody dress. "Yes. Stay on the main trail and—"

Solineus didn't wait for more, he took off at a jog and the ladies followed. The path was cobble and gravel, cleared and repaired in the steepest places, and it wound switchback up the slopes. It was aggravating as the Twelfth Hell to make so little climb with so many steps in some places, and he was tempted to cut straight up, but if he fell, he'd lose even more time, so he stuck to the main path as suggested. They rounded a corner three quarters up and could see the buildings around the pyramid base, see priests and monks going about their duties when thunder rolled across the valley. He slowed to stare; the storm clouds in the distance were too far away to make such a noise.

Nobody said a word, but they picked up their pace. They jogged around three more bends before the next explosion, and though it was weaker this time, he caught the flash from atop the pyramid the flicker they reached the ridge leading to the first low pyramid. Holies scrambled all around the compound, and when they reached the great pyramid's base, he could see priests congregating at the top of the climb.

He ran harder, leaving the ladies behind, puffing hard by the time he reached the priests. Iron bars blocked the holies from entry. He drew the Twins. "Out of my way! Move your asses!" He elbowed his way through. "Stand back!" But the fools pressed close, making it difficult to swing without hurting someone. He swept the Sister high; Latcu sang and two bars of steel split in twain. This got everyone's attention, and priests started shoving others back to give him space.

A hush fell over the crowd, and he turned to see Kinesee and Sîu reaching the top, but it was a ribbon of Light stretching across the sky from another mountain to the top of the pyramid that everyone stared at.

He pulled Eredin's Glass from behind his back, and when the flames subsided, Ivin charged, leaping over Mulharth's twitching, smoldering body to strike. His shield struck broadside and the priest stumbled; he drove high and swept low. Latcu took the man's leg off at the knee, but another priest in prayer stood strides away. He dropped his shield, took the sword in both hands and lunged forward. Lightning crackled and died as Latcu pierced the priest's sternum with the resistance of a canvas sack.

Meliu stood in front of him in prayer, and an instant later, Light flashed behind him. He spun and cleaved a charging priest in half. His eyes scanned the top of Tomarok. Bodies littered the area, dead or dying. He thought of the Broldun, toppled over the edge, but Leto's rasping breath caught his ear and brought him to his side first. Singed hair and blood, blackened skin, Ivin couldn't tell what wounds were worse, or even what blood was his. "You'll be all right. We'll get help."

Meliu leaned by his side and prayed. "He's dying, my Life is too weak."

The wind shifted and the air cooled, and Dark clouds blocked the sun. Rain wasn't far away. But a flash of Light caught his eye, and he stood, staring straight up. A ribbon of Light fluttered against the darkening sky. Perfect Light. His eye followed its shimmer southwest until he spotted a patch of black on a distant mountain. The darkness grew, swelling, but it was ringed by light. Soon, it covered half the mountain top, and it was the source of the ribbon of Light above. He stared, Meliu stared. "What the hells is that?" It wasn't darkness, it was Dark, and the ring of light was Light. He only knew one priestess capable of such a thing.

He turned to Meliu and she backed up a step. "It's a trick."

"Is it? Tell me something. Why did we end up sleeping together the first time?"

She stared at him and smiled. "Because... It seems the game is over." She laughed, but the voice faded into the bass of Lord Priest Ulrikt. "Of all the questions I learned the answers to, that wasn't one." Meliu's face shifted and she grew taller until the lord priest himself stood before him. Or at least, it appeared that way.

"Heal Leto."

"I saved your life, that isn't enough?"

Ivin stepped closer with Eredin's Glass raised. "Saved me? You brought those men."

"No! You brought them. These are the Heretics of Rin. They don't want a Silone king, but I *do*. Come, look." Ulrikt led him to a dead priest, lifted the man's leg, and pulled his boot off. "Four scars on the sole of his foot, the mark of Rin's claws."

Ivin turned and huffed back to Leto, and he heard the Face's steps coming close. "Heal him like you healed Meliu."

"I won't. Five clan-bloods ambushed and murdered by the Heretics of Rin, there is no better way to guarantee you the crown."

Ivin relaxed every muscle in his body even as his mind settled on the answer: The only way to guarantee Ivin was crowned king was for the Face to become Ivin. "On my honor, I will take the crown if you don't let Leto die."

"A noble offer indeed, and I accept. I will be king."

Ivin leaped and spun, Eredin's Glass flashed, and a streak of red opened from Ulrikt's left shoulder to his right hip. Ulrikt gasped, and

Meliu's dagger clattered to the ground from his limp fingers, its edges covered in a black, oily slick. Ivin put his foot to the blade and slid it behind him, making sure Ulrikt wouldn't reach it. But the dying man was no longer Ulrikt. He was blond with gray eyes. A round, unwrinkled face gawked at him, blood trickling from the corners of his mouth. He was in his thirties or forties and wasn't familiar at all. "Who the hells are you?"

"The Face of Ulrikt." A sputtering laugh and bloody cough.

"Who were you?"

"A hooded falcon who forgot his name a long, long time ago."

"You've lost, whoever the hells you are. You lost. I win."

He coughed blood and smiled. "No, my job is done. You *will* be king or die."

The holy's bloody smile brought a surge of anger. He raised Eredin's Glass to swing. As the blade fell and the man's head left his body, he felt a slice to his calf and an unnatural burn.

He spun, and Meliu's dagger fell from Leto's fingers. He glanced at the poisoned blade and felt blood seeping into his boot. "What the hells have you done?"

Leto's breaths rasped, and his head slumped. "I've killed you."

Ivin's mind whirled even as a burn crept into his foot and spread up his leg. He raised his sword in a heart-sunken fury. "Why!"

"You heard him! That *thing* wanted you as king! The Silone need no king!"

"It didn't matter to him whether I lived, only that I took the crown or died!" Ivin's arms trembled, and Leto stared up at him. Ivin saw a broken man before him, tortured by pain.

"Go ahead, end my suffering."

Ivin screamed, intending to take the Ravinrin's life. It was only right, a life for a life, but with a shuddering breath he lowered his sword. He huffed, struggling to breathe. "If I'm to die, my last act in this world will not be to kill a friend." He turned and sat beside Leto. He tore cloth from his shirt and stuffed it in the hole beneath the man's ribs to slow the bleeding. "But know this, you did what he wanted." The burn of poison spread into his chest and he cringed, breaths sharp with pain.

"You were to be king. He—"he coughed and sputtered"— was willing to die to give you the crown."

"In most of the prophecies the Warlord Choerkin dies, in one by the hand of a friend. He didn't care *which* prophecy came true."

"They lied to me." Leto sat silent, his breathing weak. "I die a fool, then."

The world around Ivin faded to gray in his eyes, and shivers shook his body. "We both do. But if you live, swear to me to look after Kinesee."

Leto crumpled by Ivin's side and didn't answer.

Ivin's breaths grew shallow and he wondered on all the things he would miss. He closed his eyes and couldn't open them again, even when he heard Kinesee's screams and felt her hands, her cheek next to his. "You can't die. You must live to meet your son and daughter. They need their father. They must have their father."

Ivin said, "I love you," or at least he hoped he did.

The sounds around him faded and a field of stars opened before his eyes. They were brilliant and bright, stealing the pain from his mortal end. "I've a daughter and son..." He swallowed and exhaled, but there was neither, just a memory of a mortal shell that did such things. The stars swayed before his eyes, and a shape emerged, a cluster stretching like a bridge, and he took two steps forward before he stopped. Something held his soul from its destined journey.

Kinesee burst through the dark tunnel right behind Solineus, and all she could see was death. Blood and bodies. She spotted Leto first, and as he slumped she saw Ivin sitting, dying. She screamed and bloodied her knees as she slid to his side, clutching his shoulders. She hugged him close, his cheek cold against hers. "You can't die. You must live to meet your son and daughter. They need their father. They must have their father."

He faded in her arms without a word, his head lolling limp. Solineus' hand rested on her shoulder as he kneeled with tears in his eyes. A priestess knelt beside them, praying.

"Save him. Save him. He can't die."

The woman closed her eyes and spoke, "It's poison. I've healed the wound, but... It's strong—" The woman sucked a breath, and her back straightened. Her throat gurgled. She fell backward and writhed in convulsions.

Kinesee screamed again and clutched Ivin tight, tears flowing, and muttering "no" over and over as she rocked him.

Priests drug the felled healer away, and Sîu said, "Let me have him. Kinesee. Let go for a flicker."

She couldn't let go. Her arms squeezed and trembled. They wouldn't let go. Until Solineus said, "Sweet girl." She loosened her grip, and Ivin slumped, but Siû eased his head into her lap. She removed the necklace from around her throat and placed it around Ivin's neck, resting the stone on his chest. "This is a soul catcher. Ivin's body needs to heal, this will keep his soul here with his body, with us."

Kinesee nodded even if she didn't understand, then folded to lay her head on Ivin's silent chest.

Meliu released Light and Dark but held on to Life. Instead of going down the mountain the way she came, she shimmied halfway down a cliff before jumping. She landed and rolled, jarring the breath from her body, but by the time she scrambled to her feet, she walked on soil instead of rock. Life healed and invigorated her, and she managed to trot the length of the ridge before reaching a chasm.

It was a twenty-foot drop and at least ten across, and it might've been her prayer for Life giving her confidence, but she stepped back several strides and eyeballed her path. Visualized the jump. Stared. "What the hells am I thinking?" If she had Kinesee's long legs, she figured it'd be an easy jump.

"One, two... Dancing bastards!" She landed on the other side and didn't bother to stop. She ran up and down the low pyramid and sprinted across the courtyard, wound her way to the foot of the pyramid and climbed the long stair. Iron bars dropped from the ceiling, but someone had sliced through them.

She dashed through, passing priests and climbing the stairs to the top of the pyramid. Thunder rumbled from the sky, but the bodies stole her breath. Life flowed from her, her heart skipped a beat, and when she saw Kinesee rocking on her knees, she knew.

She backed against the wall and sat, clutching her knees, afraid to go any farther because of what she might see. Three priests hauled a convulsing healer past her, and she closed her eyes when priests carried men wrapped in bloodied linens into the pyramid, but still Kinesee kneeled with Ivin. Solineus and Sîu stood not so far away, and as she stared, Alu ran out to sit with her sister.

Her mind struggled to accept whatever happened as reality; it was a nightmare she should awaken from. Lightning crackled the sky and winds howled, whipping the pyramid's flat top. She stared at her toes, praying to waken and find herself in another time and place, so when they hauled Ivin by on a litter, it startled her. *He's not in linen.*

She clutched Solineus' leg as he walked past. "He's not dead?"

"No, but he ain't alive neither. Poison."

"The Face?"

"Dead, we think."

He pulled his leg away, followed Ivin, and she bowed her head with a sigh. Hope stirred in her breast, but priests would've purged a normal poison before carrying him away. Soon, she sat alone. Lost. Forgotten.

Wind blew, lightning crackled, and drops of rain as big as her eye fell from the sky, splattering splotches on the stone until it turned dark and wet. She stared at the rain, her breaths so slow she questioned whether they were her imagination.

A hand flashed above the edge of the pyramid's step.

She squinted, figuring it an illusion of lightning or a bird, until it appeared again. She stood and ran into the storm; her hair was slick and dripping by the time she reached the edge, and when she leaned, she spotted Polus Broldun staring up at her.

"Hells, girl! Who stole your clothes?"

Her hair hung limp and dripped rain like a waterfall. "Leave it to you to notice. What happened to you?"

"Pull me up, and I'll tell you what little I remember. Either that or I've got a long crawl down this godsdamned pyramid."

She ran and grabbed one of the chairs and stuck it over the edge. He yanked it from her hands, plopped on the stone, and clambered up. He stared across the empty plateau. "Where the hells is everybody? Priests attacked us."

She nodded and ran for the entrance to escape the rain, and he ducked inside flickers after her. "What happened up here?"

A dumbfounded stare. "Mmm, what the hell do you mean? You were there."

"No, I wasn't. That was the Face. He left me poisoned outside the northeast gate and took my robes and boots."

Polus blanched and stared. "So, you didn't change clothes just for me."

"What happened?"

"Priests rushed from the tunnel here and attacked. It's a blur. Lightning struck my shield, I stumbled... Next thing I know, I'm drenched wet on the pyramid's step. Did they kill the Face?"

"Solineus thinks so." She hid her face, wiping rain and tears with an arm too wet to dry them away. "Polus, everybody's dead. Ivin, he... he's poisoned."

He stared, his face blank. "So, they didn't just ferget about me." He swept his drenched hair back. Swiped water from his chin. "But he'll live?"

"I don't know."

"Well, best we aren't sittin' round here feelin' sorry. Let's find him. He's the Warlord Choerkin. He won't die that easy."

"You've never been more right, Broldun." She didn't bother to mention how many Warlord Choerkins had died before him.

Seventy-Two

Queen of the Mountain

Sorrow is the breaker and the builder. Sorrow sets fires and blows smoke. Sorrow freezes blood and frosts the soul. Sorrow sometimes turns the bereaved to nothing. Remember, the broken may come back stronger.

—*Codex of Sol*

Kinesee stood alone in the dark, staring at the stars from the heights of the tallest of the twenty-one towers of the Palace of Ghosts. She'd blown out the lanterns candles ago, unwilling to see the sorrow of this room. Her hand worked her pearl as her mind wandered to simpler times. In all ways, she seemed an eternity from the young fisherman's daughter who had a child's crush on the man who'd enchanted the pearl and promised he would return in her need. Her heart raced with memories of how he saved two sisters hiding in a chicken coop, how badly he had been needed and how he appeared as if sent by the heavens. She called for him with the pearl, and he heeded her beckoning.

The pearl grew warm in her grip, but she didn't expect him to come for her. She cast her eyes to the shadows and sighed. She waited alone beside her dying husband with nothing to be done for him. Ivin's shallow breaths from the darkness told her he still lived, but no one knew for how long. The poison pulsing in his blood knew no cure, not even from the medicinals of Lelishen. Healers took away his every scratch, and Sîu's stone held his soul to the mortal realm, but time was an ever-encroaching enemy. Lelishen claimed even the wonders of the Edan would struggle to save him now, but whatever hope the Eleris held was months away, and by then, if he were not dead already, the poison would be incurable.

Her hands palmed the pearl and rubbed before she caught herself; she stopped with a tear-choked chortle. There was nothing her father could do for her. In moments the pearl glowed as it ever did, but its soft light shone brighter in abject darkness, allowing her to see things from which she tried to hide. Ivin lay motionless on the bed, his breaths moving the wool blanket spread across his chest with minuscule rises and falls. The tinted light of the pearl made him appear less alive than even the yellow flicker of lanterns or torches. She regretted rubbing the pearl more than she could say, and tears would have washed her cheeks if the hairs on the back of her neck didn't prickle and stand. She wasn't alone.

She spun on her heel and faced a figure who sat in Ivin's favorite chair.

"Hello, Kinesee."

She gazed into Solineus' eyes. "I didn't expect you to come. Have you found hope?" She wiped tears with her dress and struggled to laugh through a sorrow clenched throat. "No one offers me hope anymore."

He stood and hugged her. "I'm not sure if the hope I have is one you'll like."

She clung tight, then pushed him back to gaze into his eyes. "You should've gone to save him, not me."

"No, I will always save you first. For so long as I can. Would he have had me sacrifice you and his children?"

"That isn't fair." She sniffled and shoved him away. "What hope do you bring me?" Kinesee fell into a chair so hard its feet grated on stone, and she cast him a glare she once reserved for Ivin after one of his fool comments. She softened when remembering her husband but couldn't quite let it go. "Will you take him to the Edan?"

He eased back into the chair, hand rubbing his chin. "No. I don't trust them, nor do I know they could."

She threw her face into her palms, stifling a scream. "Then how do you offer hope?"

"By offering to return him to his past." He squirmed in his seat.

"You aren't making sense. If even the Edan couldn't save him, what do you possibly offer to bring my husband back to me?"

"Ivin is lost. To you, to his coming children, the clan, to all the Silonê people, and to me. Time and poison will see to that."

"His destiny then lies in the hands of the gods, not yours."

"Do you expect the gods to be kind after he worked so hard to defy them?"

Great men were said to have favor with the gods, but a great man who had read the Sundering Scroll and fought against Lord Priest Ulrikt and his Face? "I get the feeling you aren't here to help me at all. You're here to help him."

"They aren't the same?" In the dim light of the pearl she struggled to read his expression, but she hoped he could see her glare.

"What is this hope?"

"I take him home."

It was an absurd notion, the island of Kaludor swarmed with Shadows of Man. The only place free from this pestilence was Herald's Watch. Her stomach turned; it made sense. "To the Lady in the Fire?" Returning Ivin to Eliles, his first love—he called this hope? She stared at him in silence until the pearl's glow faded to dark, until he stepped out, and returned with a lantern pilfered from the hall.

Thoughts skittered willy-nilly through her mind, struggling to form any coherence. Her first love offered to return her husband to his first love, if the notion weren't so repulsive, she would've found it funny. "He never did get over her." She knew even if the man never admitted it.

"The Sliver of Star could heal him with little more than a thought."

"And everyone said. Everyone—"her voice reached a few octaves higher than intended, and she swallowed it back"—said that it's impossible to enter or leave her Fire. Ever."

He shifted in his seat. "I believe I can."

"And be trapped forever too?"

"No, I will return to you. Always, so long as we live."

"What makes you believe this could work?"

"The woman from my dreams."

Kinesee laughed, and even if insincere, it was the first belly-laugh in days. "Other women seem my undoing even when they can't be had. What makes you believe her? That you can cross boiling waters and just stroll through a wall of flame and back again."

He shrugged, staring in the lantern's glow. "I've a plan for getting in and out. We both know I'm different, somehow. The energies, I don't expect them to affect me as they would you."

"Raise the chimney, touch that fire, and tell me again how you plan on passing through her Fire alive, let alone with my husband… what, cast over your shoulder?"

He grinned. "We both know that'd hurt like the Twelve Hells."

"Being married to that man was never easy, and to be fair, I wasn't always kind. But we fought through everything. So much blood, so many tears, and now I'm fat with his twins who I never told him about."

"Sweet girl, I'm not offering any happy options here—"

"Tell me, when my time comes, will you whisk me away, save me from my angry gods?"

The grin turned into the crooked smile that had captured her girlish dreams. "There's no need to save you from the gods, the hells, the Slave Fields. They are all far from your destiny."

"The woman in your dreams again?"

"Yes. She spoke to your father once in his sleep, the night before I left your family. I never told you that. She told him I would come back to save you, and I swore I would, and the look in his eyes… It was a relief to know his daughters would outlive him. She also told me you would be important one day, and you are."

She shook her head in a fit, lending a quaking insanity to her laugh. Solineus had more faith in her than she did. She was important, mother of Choerkin heirs, but she could be no more, and they would be children unprepared for such responsibility without a father. It seemed he expected more of her than she did herself. "I can't hold the clans together, not with Ivin gone— Roplin is the leader of Clan Choerkin."

"Some will follow Roplin, but he and the people will need you. You hold an impenetrable city-fortress in a land more fertile than our people have ever known, and you alone hold the key to alliances that will keep the Histê from overrunning every Silone."

"You overestimate my sway with the Kingdomers and Helelindin."

"It is you who underestimates herself. Morik and the Ironwing are smitten with you, and whatever the Dark Waters wants with Tomarok, the Kingdomers will make certain you don't fall."

She poured a glass of wine and took a long drink, and as the wine brought warmth to her chest, her anger faded. There were so few choices. "So, maybe you are here to help me after all."

"I'm here to help everyone I care about. Sol will torture Ivin as no soul has been tortured before, he'll never make the Twelve Hells or the Slave Fields. I don't offer guarantees, just an option. I offer one small hope."

She couldn't see the wine in her goblet, but she stared into it anyhow. "You've my permission. Take him. Be gone, but don't forget you're needed back here."

"I'll need you to make some arrangements."

She nodded and raised her glass in salute before draining the last drops. "Everything you need, of course. Make a list, but give us time to say our goodbyes."

He rose and kissed her on the forehead. "It's the right choice."

He walked from the chamber, leaving her to sit with Ivin and his shallow breaths. She dropped the pearl and its chain into her empty goblet and swirled, the oblong treasure skidding and bouncing before gaining a rhythm to ride the walls. She wished she had only her children to protect, that the Choerkin name could be carried on by someone other than her and her own, that death wasn't taking the true bearer of the name.

She stood and sauntered to Ivin's side, wiped his clammy brow before laying a kiss. His eyes fluttered and his lips twitched into what she imagined a smile, but only for a flicker, before lapsing into his dead sleep. She wiped away a tear. "You doomed me, my love. But it's a doom I bear willingly, if not happily."

Endelêun had been in a state of mourning, or rather, a state of near mourning for the past two weeks. Rinold had heard every rumor, ranging from Ivin murdered by a ghost or Taken by a demon, to some viper god having poisoned him. Some rumors spoke of him already dead, others that he hid, waiting to return and kill his attacker.

The truth was, in many ways, stranger than the rumors. Poisoned and all but dead, but his soul trapped within by some gem.

He stood on the balcony of his home, holding his baby girl, and wondering by what luck he'd managed to survive while Ivin suffered this fate. His scar twitched, and instead of brooding on the topic further looked at little Moldanu and smiled. "Your father is lucky to have ever seen you."

Puxele slipped to his side. "We're both lucky to have you back."

He kissed his wife. "We're all lucky." Lucky but unhappy, despite the blessing held in his arms. "I want to leave this place. Move to the mountains. It's too godsdamned hot here."

"Moldanu and I would be happier where we can see snow."

"I love you both." A horn blew in the distance and a rumble grew in his throat. "Hells, what now?" His first fear was an enemy, but then the horn called two more times, short and long. He handed over their daughter. "Southwest gate. Let's hope it's good news."

He strolled from his home but ran straight to the stable as soon as he was out of sight. He threw on a saddle and rode hard, and by the time he reached the gate, it was wide open. Tudwan rode at the head of the army. It was a thrill to see the man alive, but then it struck him: Leto walked the Starry Road, and they didn't find Daksin at Fôlgumhîêr. In practical terms, Tudwan was the last of three brothers, and his brother-in-law lay comatose from poison.

Rinold squeezed his knees and his horse trotted to the head of the army. He swung in beside the Ravinrin. "How did it go in the south?"

"We sent the Histê running back west and got Adinvan shoved off.

If the weather held, he should be close to Pôn by now."

"Aye, that's good."

"Fôlgumhîêr?"

"We knocked down every wall of every home; found almost a hundred of our people and Kingdomers, but luck be damned, no Daksin. But I've got worse news."

Tudwan rode in silence. "Worse?"

How does a man tell another that his kin has passed on? Rinold didn't know if there was a way. "The worst sort of words. Leto, he died in an attack atop Tomarok. Along with other clan-blood and Ivin's been poisoned. He might be dead soon as well."

Tudwan slumped in the saddle and went silent. Rinold's throat closed, and he fought back his own tears, figuring that somehow, he should have said it better.

The clatter of prancing hooves echoed down the road as warriors marched past, and Polus' voice bellowed. "Ravinrin, good to see you alive."

Rinold turned, and he choked before he could say a word, seeing Eredin's Glass riding above the big man's shoulder. Hearing of a thing was never the blow of witnessing its reality.

Tudwan said, "Seems I missed much, little of it good."

Polus' face fell. "No lies, there. But we persist."

Rinold forced a smile. "All godsdamned that just to have a Broldun as Warlord."

"I tried to say no."

Tudwan said, "You always said that knockin' heads was all you were good at; warlord suits you."

"What suits me is whiskey and snowy mountains."

Rinold said, "I ain't got no snow, but I wager a Warlord Broldun has plenty of whiskey. Let us drink to mourn those lost until our tears bring memories of their laughter."

It'd been four weeks since the attack, and every day Meliu visited the top of Tomarok with both copies of the *Codex of Sol*. She sat and read, puzzled over how maybe she'd missed something. Some answer to what the poison was, and how they could cleanse it from Ivin's blood, but all she learned was to be angrier. Angrier at Ulrikt, his Face, and the gods. She wore thin linen or silk robes now, eschewing traditional wool as a small act of defiance, but in the end, she was still a high priestess.

The worst part was... No. There were a lot of worst parts. But one of them was that they didn't know if the Face was dead. A body had worn her robes, covered in blood, and nobody knew the face of the dead man's head, so everybody declared it the Face. Meliu wasn't so sure. She'd seen too many things to believe something that no witness could speak to. And when it came to the Face, it was too often true that you couldn't believe witnesses or even your own eyes.

Neither codex gave the answers she sought, but as she flipped through the historical passages the other day, she noted a peculiar reference to the Crown of the King Priest. When a king or queen priest died, the Council of Lord Priests met to elect a successor. In truth, election wasn't always the most accurate word, as several histories spoke of meetings where only a few lord priests walked out alive to crown the next king priest, but this wasn't the point that caught her attention.

Priests hid the crown atop Tomarok until the Council of Lords selected a successor. The codices also spoke of the crown being rediscovered, and if this was true, then the crown was most apt to be here.

She stood atop the great pyramid humored by her musings because the top of Tomarok was a flat plateau of stones. Any one of them could lift from the surface to reveal their secret, but none of them did. She'd spent parts of four different days jumping up and down on stones, then kicking at each one, then taking her dagger to see if any of them were loose. If the crown was here, it wasn't so easy to find.

But reading books and searching became her distraction from anger and sorrow, so she found herself atop Tomarok again. She paced with the uncoded codex in hand, reading and tromping on stones here and there, just in case, when she read the passage:

Crowns fall upon the heads of good and evil alike, and it takes good and evil to find the value in a crown. The light in the eyes of the wicked king priest, and the dark in the eyes of wholesome queen priest. Light is best seen in the dark, and without light, darkness is all we would know.

"Good and evil, light and dark, to find the value in the crown. Leave out value, and... Could it be so easy?" She prayed for Light and Dark and held the energies. Faint, flickering swirls appeared in the stones of the plateau. "Erginle, give me your Light for vision, and Kibole the Dark, so that the Light becomes easier to see."

The energies flooded her soul, and she could feel her eyes turn black with Kibole's power. The top of the pyramid surged with radiant symbols connecting every stone of its floor into a flowing pattern similar to many she'd seen in tomes dedicated to Bontore. In a way, it was like walking the Road of Living Stars, a path to find the Seven Heavens, or in this case, a crown.

The swirls of Light rose and fell, but they all coalesced on a single stone. She strode to it with the calm of prayer tranquilizing her soul, and she kneeled. Instead of digging at its edges, she placed her hand in its center. The stone wavered as if turning to water, or quicksilver, and a flicker later her hand submerged beneath its surface. It was cool and her palm tingled, but her fingers met warmth. She clutched the heat and lifted a gold crown from a pool of ink with thick silver swirls on its surface. Seven points with seven gems for the Seven Heavens and twelve rubies for the Twelve Hells spaced along its band. An etching of two wingless dragons curled with their meeting at a ruby at what she assumed was the front of the crown.

She released Light and Dark and held it in both hands. She'd never seen anything so beautiful; not even Kinesee's latcu necklace compared. She lifted it high, the gems catching the sun, and with a pulse of her heart eased it onto her head. It was heavy and awkward.

"So, we have a new queen priest?"

Meliu ripped the crown from her head as Sedut's voice broke the silence. "No! No. Not me."

Sedut strolled close. "It looked right handsome on your head."

"It's a lousy fit."

"In that case, you might want to put it back until its rightful owner needs it."

"I will." Meliu grinned, then frowned. "What're you doing up here?"

"I was looking for you. There's news about Ivin."

Meliu's heart thundered. "He's healed? Dead? Don't tease me. What is it?"

"Solineus took him from Endelêun."

Meliu stared dumbfounded. "What the hells do you mean, took him? Where to?"

"They aren't saying, but there is a rumor—"

"Herald's Watch. To Eliles." It was the only answer that made sense. She didn't want to say the next words, but they slipped from her lips before she could stop them. "The Sliver of Star."

Meliu prayed for Light and Dark and slipped the crown back into its resting place. She prayed she didn't know who would wear it next.

She stood with a deep breath. "I think it's time to forget about crowns and kings and worry about our people."

Sedut walked by her side. "If not queen priestess, you might have to consider lord priestess."

Meliu puffed in dismissal and exasperation. Added a snort.

"The Council will select new lord priests one day. Consider it."

Lord Priestess Meliu. She admitted to herself that it had a tempting ring to its tones. "I'll consider it."

Seventy-Three

Braving Fire

Where have you gone, my dreams?
Where have I gone, my dreams?
Nowhere but sad, it seems.

—*Tomes of the Touched*

The Wiirê built a fine litter to carry Ivin, and they gave Solineus escort through the wilderness tribe by tribe along the southern face of the Dragonspans until they reached Ilu territory. Although the Kingdomers offered, the mountains would slow his travel. The Ilu escorted him on to Mulshahar, where he found Captain Edmordô already wheeling and dealing on behalf of Adinvan. He paid exorbitant fees to the Smiling Men to ensure the enterprise's security, then fought tooth and nail with Sîu in the attempt to force her to sail to Pôn with Edmordô. He hired a wagon to take them to Ôfelun and suffered Sîu's prideful smile the entire way, but in the end, he was glad for the company.

Even in a trade city the size of Ôfelun, it took three weeks to find a vessel suitable and willing to sail north to Purdonis Bay and what had become known as the Boiling Island. The ship at hand was Luxun and destined for Edan ports by way of Tek harbors. It took cajoling, a pile of coins, and the promise of Edan bows to convince the captain to bypass trading with the Tek Nations, but gaining passage on a vessel flying the colors of the Luxuns, who reigned supreme on the seas, was worth calling in an Edan favor.

Montênyô Meledên captained the Onyoño Fî. The man bore more pride in his blue skin and feather-hair than seemed reasonable, but despite the flaw of an inflated Luxun ego, the captain proved an affable fellow. After negotiating the wage for passage, Montênyô admitted he'd heard of the Silone and known the Choerkin name from tales passed along by the Luxun crew who helped the Choerkins cross the Parapet Straits when fleeing the demons. This did not, however, alter their agreed-upon fees.

They stayed out of sight of land and avoided any sails they saw on the horizon as they sailed north. A Tek ship spotted the Onyoño Fî and altered course to follow, but the Lûxuns took note, and within half a day they lost sight of the Teks over the horizon, or as the Captain later said: "The Onyoñyo left them in her winds." Despite the chill of ever more arctic air, these were the most pleasant days of the journey to date. Ivin remained stable, and Solineus relaxed below deck with no immediate worries.

Change came the moment they tacked east into the Parapet Straits. The Luxuns doubled the watch, fearful of icebergs and ships from Thon, but they navigated clear without a threat Solineus ever saw. Luxun eyes in the crow's nest spotted the glow of the pillar of flame that marked Herald's Watch the fourth night after turning east, and by morning they'd arrived.

The roiling waters of Purdonis Bay shuffled and tossed Solineus' dinghy, his oars struggling to find water with steady strokes, and it brought a twinge of nausea to his otherwise iron stomach. Ivin rested in the bow of the boat, and Solineus focused his eyes on the man's nose to fight seasickness. Sweat streamed down his face, and he took a moment to wipe his brow and drink from his canteen. The steam-fog had transitioned from light wisps hovering over turbulent waters to a thick barrier that obscured the world, hiding everything except the looming vortex of fire that struck high into the clouds. There was nothing in the world he'd seen to compare it to. Two mountains on top of each other? Maybe three?

Another drink of water grown warm washed down his throat before he set oars to water again. Could she see them through this haze? Did she know they were coming? He grunted as an oar left the water in mid-stroke, throwing him off balance. It wasn't a matter of could. Does she bother to look and see? What did he expect if she knew? A welcome party? A clear route through the pillar of fire?

He grunted with the effort to row, determined to focus on Ivin's nose instead of a young woman he hadn't seen for years. *I wonder if she aged? Damn it. Stroke. Stroke. Stroke.*

Focusing his mind away from useless meanderings was more difficult under the stress of rowing and the oppressive heat. He switched to counting strokes and took a drink every fifty, and when he drained the last drop of his fifth canteen, they were so close to the rush of flames striking the bay's waters that they deafened him and made it hard to think at all.

He dropped two anchors hoping they'd keep the boat in place and dipped a finger into the rumbling waters. He cursed as he shook the beads from his finger: It was damned hot, but he hoped it would only prove deadly with prolonged exposure.

His plan was insanity, but the Luxuns admitted its possibility of success despite misgivings. Ivin was of little worry, the man was in stasis so deep he didn't need to breathe. Solineus would have to rely on a Luxun contraption called a Bullfrog's-belly: an oiled skin filled with air so a person might breathe under the waves. At least for a time. In practice, he spent over five wicks beneath the surface, and he didn't have more than a thousand feet to swim. The scalding waters concerned him more. He lay back on Ivin and strapped the man to his back.

Healthy, Ivin's weight would've been a burden, but now Solineus came to his knees with more effort to balance on the waves than from the man's diminished weight. He tied the third and heaviest anchor to his waist and eased it overboard until the short length of rope strained, and the boat tipped. He took a breath and relaxed as he clutched the

Bullfrog to his chest and brought another heavy oil-skin to cover them entirely before plunging headfirst into the bay.

Heat surged around him, but the anchor pulled hard, dragging him deep so fast it took only a few flickers for the waters to cool around him. He released the anchor's rope and fought the oil-skin, resorting to slicing it with a dagger and swimming through the gap. He bit the breathing tube and inhaled, taking a moment to get his bearings. Flames lit the waters of the bay, a beckoning beacon impossible to miss.

The Bullfrog's-belly worked well, and the Luxun's estimated the ballast with precision. Aside from the deafening roar of flame greeting water, his swim was slow but uneventful. He passed the stone pillars of the docks and crawled up the rocky shore to flop onto the cobbled bricks of the road. He untied Ivin and shrugged him off his back before making him as comfortable as possible. It made no sense, considering Ivin's state, but it felt right to try.

The temperature was pleasant inside the tower, and looking around, the condition of the roads and buildings impressed him. He expected something to have changed, but all he noted was changes to the Salty Frog, as if a fire had struck and repairs made. At the end of a distant dock, he saw a figure sitting with a hat draped over his face and a fishing pole sticking from his chair. If that was the closest thing this island needed for a guard, Ivin was safe.

He strolled the dock until ten feet from the snoring man. He recognized him as if he'd seen him yesterday. "Artus Choerkin."

Artus glanced from beneath his hat, then tumbled out his chair, catching a post to keep from falling into the bay. His voice was a hoarse groan. "Son-of-a-bitch. Solineus?" He patted his hip for a weapon that wasn't there. "Or are you another Face?"

"I'm not a lord priest's Face." Solineus' brows bunched. "You had a Face on Herald's Watch?"

"Aye, we did, we caught her and she killed herself."

"We had our own Face issues down south. Fishing any good?"

Artus relaxed. "Not hardly." He pulled his broad-rimmed hat off and slapped it on his leg. "What the— How the Hells d'you get here? You don't look as if you aged a bit."

Solineus chuckled, shaking water in the man's face to demonstrate his path to the island. "You're as old and ugly as ever."

"Mmm! True that, aye. What are you doing here? By the gods, it's good to see you."

"I've brought Ivin to see her."

"You've what? Young Ivin? Why I, I—"

"He's dead, or might as well be, an enchanted stone keeps his soul with his body and away from the Living Stars."

Artus sucked his teeth, the thoughts that must've been swirling in his head made his face contort. "Shits. Seems I missed a few things."

"Plenty of time to explain later, I need to find Eliles."

Artus scratched his chin with a smirk. "Like as not you'll find her up in the stars. If not there? It's a small island; good luck."

Solineus left Artus with Ivin and headed for Skywatch. Memories of murder and lies couldn't stain the amazing domed structure and its mesmerizing night sky as he entered. He stared in wonder, his eye drawn to a spot in the dark where a false star once traveled, a harbinger of death instead of the glory foretold.

"I would say I was dreaming, if I were able to sleep." The lady's voice echoed from the infinite ceiling, impacting with power and grace found only within this hall. She appeared as if from nowhere in the dark. "Come, join me in the stars."

He followed her up invisible stairs with cautious steps. Stepping into the stars was like rising from the water to find himself in a world he had never known, and his feet played a song. His imagination had suspected the view up here to be more of the same, but it was much more. There was no visible floor beneath him, the stars were everywhere: if he were the world, this would be his view of the universe. And in the middle of it all, full of youth and beauty, stood Eliles, a bemused grin crinkling her face.

"If ever we were to have a mortal visitor, I should've known it would be you. How?"

"It was wet and warm; I assure you." He took chiming steps and hugged her, but she didn't hug back. "It's been a long time, sweet girl."

She sighed when his arms released her. "I am still a girl aren't I? Nothing changes here, not even— Well, never mind that. Why are you here?"

"I brought Ivin—" The look on her face choked the words in his throat.

"Ivin? Where? Where is he?"

"Not yet." His hands grabbed her shoulders, stopping her in mid-stride. "There was a fight, and they poisoned Ivin; his soul would long have passed if not for the gem on his chest. The stone preserves his body, and it keeps his spirit with him, but it took nine months to get here. I need you to realize that his soul may have walked the Living Stars long ago."

"Where is he?"

"The dock." The world shifted and Solineus' head swooned, buckling his knees. By the time he regained his balance, Eliles kneeled at Ivin's side. "Warn me the next time you do that."

"You both should warn me," scoffed Artus, wide-eyed at their sudden appearance. "When the hells did you learn how to do that?"

She ignored them. "His body is weak, frail, but it is healthy. His soul, I believe it is still here." She looked at Solineus. "If I can bring him back, the Fires will trap him here. Will you be able to leave?"

Solineus shook his head. Shrugged.

"You still don't know who you are, do you?"

The memorized words nearly escaped his lips. *I am Solineus Mikjehemlut, warrior…* but he stopped the words with a smile.

Eliles passed her hands over Ivin's chest, and he took his first visible breath since Ôfelun. "I've always been better with Fire than Life, you remember."

"That a'way, cousin. Breathe," said Artus.

Solineus said, "My confidence wasn't misplaced."

Eliles said, "Breathing is a small thing, but it's a start. We should take him to the Salty Frog, where we can sit and talk." She stood and took Solineus' hands in hers. "After all this time, you still don't know who you were."

Solineus' heart missed a beat as he watched her walk away. What did she know?

"I don't suppose she means to just… magic him inside. No, leave the men-folk to haul his ass." Artus gestured for help, and the two of them brought Ivin to his feet with arms locked over their shoulders. It seemed a long walk to the inn, with hope in every step; Solineus expected Ivin to snap from his malaise and take a stride, but instead his toes drug on the dock and cobbles the entire way.

The Salty Frog stood as Solineus remembered, except for a few char marks. They drank grain alcohol Artus distilled, an improved concoction from what Solineus remembered, but it still burned a trail down his throat and promised a painful morning after. They dined on fish and vegetable stew that Seden brought them, a heartier meal than he'd expected. Solineus shared the plight of the Silonê people in as brief but satisfying a manner as his storytelling skills could muster, and in the end, they came to Ivin's victory and his poisoning. The first question wasn't exactly what he expected.

"And why bring him here?" Her stare was brutal, difficult to look away from. "With a wife to mourn his passing, why?"

"So he might live, so that his wife felt she did everything possible."

"A convenient lie, I grant you. Maybe you even believe it."

Artus whistled into his cup before draining it in a single shot. "More liquid hangover?" He poured for himself and Solineus without a proper answer.

Solineus grunted. "It was his time and my time to head north."

"Closer. Why?"

"She needed to move on, Kinesee did. The clans needed her to move on. She needed to move on and to lead her people forward."

"It was an elaborate ploy, you could have buried him anywhere in between."

"I made a promise, and I saw it through. The moment he left you standing on this island, his destiny was never a journey of east or west, north was always his destination. I fulfilled that."

"So you did. And what of your own destiny?"

He shrugged, but the look on her face lacked satisfaction. "A short trip to the island, from there… I don't know."

"Kaludor? Whatever for?"

"Sometimes life is full of circles, and for whatever reason, this is one I must complete."

She laughed, a wholly unexpected reaction. "There's still a woman's voice in your head. Does she yet have a name?"

There was no need to answer, so he slipped past her words. "You asked if I knew who I am. Do you have some answer I don't?"

"No, but I met a woman I believe to be a dragon—"

"Gers'voresh-kûmjotukî?"

"Is that her name? She left, claiming a friend called her. Was it you?"

A chill ran his spine. "I reckon so."

"She mentioned that she spoke to you once, but that you wouldn't remember what she said. Both her and the Touched have visited me. They know each other, and I think they know who you are. And who the woman in your dreams is."

"Nothing else?"

"The Touched mentioned that Almost will return the Gate, when the Touched said he wouldn't. Somehow that changed because someone overheard him. The how and why matter, but he didn't explain a thing."

Solineus pondered this one. "He said something of the sort, but I'm as confused as you."

"There was one final tidbit. The woman, she said she spoke to you before you became you, whatever that means, and you forgot it."

I became who I am the moment the Lady in the blue spoke to me... The first words he could recall came to him: *Open your eyes to blue.* "She said nothing else?"

They stared at each other with Artus getting drunker every passing moment. He cleared his throat. "M'pa always told me when two people are at an impasse, they should either drink or part ways. He could never leave my ma 'cause she'd hunt him down, so he drank every night." He grinned, but nobody shared in his humor, so he tossed back his glass and refilled.

Solineus stood. "There is wisdom in those words, and I've a ship waiting on me."

Ivin stirred, and Eliles stood by his side in a flicker. He laid on the table, his arm flopped, and Solineus helped him sit. His voice was hoarse. "Solineus? Eliles? Am I dead?"

The girl stared, unable to speak, so Solineus answered. "The Face of Ulrikt poisoned you on Tomarok, I've brought you back to Herald's Watch." Solineus caught her glance. "Aye, there was more than one Face."

Eliles held water to Ivin's lips, and he sipped, then she held her hands to his head. His sallow cheeks filled, and his color returned. "I remember being attacked, fighting... I killed the Face—"

There was more, but whatever it was, he didn't care to share. "Don't worry about it, it's over." He took a deep breath. "There is something you need to know. Kinesee is pregnant... she will have had twins by now."

Ivin stared. "I'm a father? I need to go."

Eliles' hand held him from standing. "You can't leave. Once inside the tower, you're trapped. Unless you are—"she glanced at Solineus"—different."

Solineus stood. "Aye, but the longer I stay here, the more difficult it may be to leave. Besides, I have Sîu and a Luxun ship waiting for me." He grabbed Ivin by the neck and put their foreheads together. "I know this isn't perfect, but you're alive. I'll watch over Kinesee and your children."

The man choked on sorrow. "Tell her I love her—the kids. I won't ever know their names. Tell them."

"I swear to it. If ever I can come back, I will." He turned to Artus. "Don't let him drink too much of that whiskey, I'm not sure what that swill will do to a man." He saluted and drained his glass as Artus guffawed. When leaving, he turned to look back on the Salty Frog, considering it might be the last time he saw any of them. The notion seemed perverse and wrong, so he muttered aloud, "Another day."

Aboard the *Onyoño Fî*, Captain Meledên was ecstatic at the return of his valuable passenger, right until he learned Solineus' next destination. Sîu was none too thrilled herself.

"You've gone mad."

Her hands to hip stare was a familiar part of his life by now, but her beautiful and worried stare broke him; he leaned and kissed her on the forehead. "I'll come back; I always do."

Meledên was far more practical. "You want to row to the island? To the island of demons? If you don't want to pay me, pray, just say so rather than commit suicide." His feathers ruffled, but the Captain acquiesced despite a string of expletives that Solineus couldn't understand. They sailed as close to shore as they could to drop anchor, and with only a brief nap, Solineus was back rowing a dinghy. Meledên offered crew to row this time, but he turned the offer down. As he rowed away, his eyes lingered on Sîu, and he wondered if he wasn't falling for her. He blanked that notion from his head quick as he could.

A half-candle later, he reached shore at a very familiar place, the beach in front of the Koest family home, and curiosity forced him to visit. The wooden roof and the chicken coop where he found the sisters hiding lay collapsed except for a couple larger beams, but the stone walls were solid, albeit showing neglect where mortar gave way. It was a remembrance of mixed emotions, finding so many friends dead and yet being able to rescue the two girls he had come for. He sighed. The home was empty of anything of value except memories, and those brought pain.

He stood beside the fire pit outside and glanced inside where he'd burned bodies. Those fortunate enough to die, anyhow. How many were dead and how many Taken he didn't know. Walking back to the beach, he recalled the spot where he'd found the girls fighting for their lives, struggling to shove their boat into the surf. His hands moved to the hilts of the Twins at the memory, and their whispers came hushed and mellow. He passed a scrutinizing gaze over the area. To allow the past to dim his wits could prove fatal, but he didn't see any Shadows of Man.

He backtracked the oldest trail he could remember walking, seeking the place where he washed ashore long ago. The vision in his dream told him to find that place, but the gray sandy beaches and their sparse bushes looked so much the same he concluded it was a fool's errand. Only trouble being that every fool's errand his dreams had put him upon would have been more foolish to ignore.

In the dream, there had been a boulder in the shape of a cross that mirrored his waking pose on the beach, yet his memory of awaking on the icy shore held no such rock. He moseyed with a careful eye glancing from the ground to all around, unwilling to miss the location or sign of a stalking Shadow. He stopped a candle later and turned circles, feeling he had arrived. But what proof? Inland there was no cross, just rocky beach. He stood where the boulder should have been and dropped to his knees.

He was where the Lady meant him to be, but why? He brushed sand and gravel away, thinking the boulder hid beneath the ground. His dagger plunged into the ground and met loose stone, so he dug. Dig or give up, his only two options, and the latter was a character flaw he didn't possess. His trench reached three feet deep when the dagger rang from striking metal. He dug with his fingers, and the sun revealed something black, polished black, and wrapped in strands of silver. Clearing gravel and sand, he realized he'd found the hilt of a sword.

His fingers dug like claws to get a grip, and he pulled with all his strength, but it stayed confined within the soil until he pulled as if drawing it from a sheath. The massive weapon slid clean from the dirt, revealing a magnificent flamberge blade decorated in whorls of blue and gray. The blade was four feet long, but the balance made it light in his hands. Never had he seen such a weapon, not even in his dreams, and when the whorls moved the length of the blade, he nearly dropped the weapon.

God Wars forged, like the Twins. Not even in the Age of Warlords could smiths forge such a weapon. What did it mean that it was here, at the place his history began?

His gaze turned to an inland rise as hair stood on the back of his neck, and his eyes locked with those of a Shadow wearing a human skin. The abomination cried out, soon joined by two Shadows and a Taken wearing a woman. If once he might have known these people, their disfiguring wounds made them impossible to recognize. For this, he was glad.

"Four on one, eh? Fair enough." Stand and fight or run to the water? He hefted the two-hander and waited for the inevitable rush, only it didn't happen. The Taken knelt to their haunches while the faceless Shadows hovered, showing no signs of aggression. "Come on, then. What're you waiting for? Reinforcements?" He'd never seen the demons wait long on an attack, particularly with numbers. Was it the flamberge? That made no sense. Not once had these things shown a fear of death, unless Colok were around.

Leery, he glanced behind him to make sure he wasn't being flanked, then backed to the waters of the Strait. His oiled, sealskin boots saved his feet from an icy chill as he stepped into the water's safety. He grunted. "What the hells are you demons doing?"

Whatever their plan, their dead stares unnerved him, so he waded down the beach toward his boat. The creatures mirrored his travel, always staying in sight, but they only took steps closer to pass barriers and stay within view.

He half expected to find his boat smashed or at least unseaworthy, but it remained untouched. Matching their stares, he cocked his head in thought. Their behavior was peculiar, similar to when they faced Colok, but here he was, a man alone. What kept them from attacking? He grinned when an obvious answer came to him: curiosity, the very reason he stood here now staring back.

But curious of what, of why a man returned to this cursed island? That made sense to his human mind, but he would never have accused these creatures of deeper thoughts before. Maybe it was best not to grasp for what a demon might think, and be thankful they didn't attack.

He stepped from the waters with cautious strides, and they didn't move. Bold strides carried him to his little boat, and he lay the flamberge inside before dragging it back to the surf. He waved to his followers, gave the boat a shove, and jumped in, setting oars to water. Sîu and the Lûxuns waited for him, and there was a long journey ahead. He would lay his head down every night to sleep, and dream, and await the next fool's errand the Lady set for him.

A fragmented Mind, a twisted Soul, a daring Bone in the Eye of jagged Memory,
Stop.
I see you not for what you are but for what you will be, snakes and Snakes and slither.
You, rigid serpent, tracking a straight and boring line in the sand,
whilst you follow the twisting winding path, the brush strokes of serpentine genius,
beautiful and ominous across the face of Desert dunes.
Dooms, doom, doom-speaker? No, Doom-hisses here.
As with following the twisted trail, so is following the twisted soul,
beware the den of the fork-ed tongue,
Twisted Trails lead to Twisted Ends.

—*Tomes of the Touched*

Epilogue

The Face of Edeenu of Sudeez

Slim, slim, slimmer and slime,
brush away the obvious and embrace the sublime,
buried in lime,
and buried in time,
reaching for the sky,
but falling through the pupil of your eye.

—*Tomes of the Touched*

Thirty Days to the Eve of Snows

Edeenu imagined the clatter beneath her shifting weight was no more than a pile of kindling, but it was impossible to forget that she kneeled on the bones of children. A fragment splintered and cracked as her knees touched; a piece of a long-dead child shifted beneath her toe to throw her into a lean, and her hand met the bony grip of fingers half the length of hers to recover her balance. She swallowed and sucked a deep breath before righting herself. She could've lit the Pit of the Vanquished with a simple prayer but preferred not to witness the barbarity of times past. Knowing she rested atop the remains of hundreds of children was torture enough without seeing.

She clasped her hands, bowed her head in the cavern-black chamber, and murmured the start of the prayer she'd intoned every year since Lord Priest Ulrikt saved her bones from mingling with those beneath her. "Praise Sol for his generosity and kindness. Praise Lord Priest Ulrikt for his wisdom in seeing the truth of my devotion."

The hairs on the back of her neck spiked and tingled; she raised her eyes despite staring into blind oblivion. She lowered the cowl of her robes and listened, but heard nothing other than her own breath and heartbeat. No one would come to such a place without a cause such as hers. Twelve years ago, a nameless priestess led her into this chamber and locked the door, leaving her to die alone. Terror, sadness, and confusion overwhelmed a child who ran and played with friends just days before, who slept in a bed beside a fire sparked by her father and with a stomach contented with her mother's cooking. A chicken stew if memory served.

She should be alone.

She should've been alone that day, but she hadn't been.

"Would you starve if I locked the door?" Lord Priest Ulrikt's voice came as an echo of words uttered over a decade before, when he told a terrified child that she needn't fear hunger if her faith was strong.

"No, Lord Priest. I would feast on the prayers of Father Sol and Mother Elinwe." Light ignited the room, the bones brilliant, bleached white, and every fracture, knob, and socket lay clear before her eyes. She looked up at Lord Priest Ulrikt, or rather, a Face mimicking Ulrikt. The Ulrikt who couldn't change his face didn't know where these bones rested. She knew, too, that this person was a True Face.

He smiled upon her, and she felt its warmth on her skin. "I always wondered why you visit this place."

He didn't frame it as a question, but his pause suggested she should answer. "To remind myself of the righteousness of our path."

He nodded, and his teeth glowed in the Light. "Righteousness will reveal the true path through the forests and mountains of possibility."

His words were true; she entrusted her life to this wisdom. "What brings you to speak with me?" A True Face didn't interrupt prayers for small talk.

He puffed his chest with hands twined behind his back. "How fares your transition to Japin of Andweth?"

Edeenu grimaced. She'd spent her early years shifting her face to look like people who resembled her. The process took five years and burned like the Forges, torturing flesh and bone in ways she hadn't imagined. She'd mastered a dozen faces before work began on altering her height and body shape. The latter hadn't been as bad as she'd expected, and this grew her confidence, but taking on the bug-eater's form was pain beyond her imagining. Japin was tall and skinny with a bulging head, his face locked in a snarl of madness, and his muscles twitched even as he slept. The real Japin of Andweth had smoked his way to the Road of Living Stars before she'd arrived at Istinjoln Monastery, but this didn't stop the priest maddened by prayers of Dark from creeping through the underground halls. A man seen but easy to forget, a man whom folks spoke their mind in front of without a second thought, a man who wasn't the mindless priest everyone thought him to be.

"His is a painful trial, my Lord Priest."

Ulrikt nodded, lips pursed in solemn understanding. "You will master his form and rise to master others. Many others."

"It is torture."

"It is a blessing. You can't feel it; you can't see it; you can't conceive it, but soon your bones will mold like clay beneath the fingers of your will, and so your flesh will follow. Someday soon, you will sleep in the shape you wear when laying down your head. Your bones will forget who you once were and only remember who you desire them to be."

The notion exhilarated and frightened her, then raised questions. "Forget? Will I forget, too, who I am?" Rumors abounded among the lessers of how True Faces lost their born identity.

"You will never forget who you were, but... You will learn these truths."

It wasn't an answer she appreciated. "As you say, my Lord Priest."

"But I did not seek you out to bolster your ego and soothe your worries."

Her heart beat faster. "You've a task for me?"

He rubbed the corner of his eye and rolled his shoulders. "The Eve of Snows is a month away."

"The time of the Twelfth Star." Her blurted words brought a hard stare. "My apologies, Lord Priest Ulrikt."

"I am sending you to Herald's Watch. Priest Kôlil of Mastis will serve as your Visioner."

Kôlil was twenty-four years old and lauded as the finest lesser Face of his generation. "As my Visioner? I am not yet ordained a True Face. I may never be."

His smile returned. "I ordained you myself this morning with a dozen witnesses. Kôlil is eager to serve you."

"I haven't passed the Trials—"

"There is no time. I have faith in you because Sol has faith in you, my child."

She swallowed hard, nodding to hide her nerves. "My task?"

"Practice. Achieve the skills of the True Face. Blend in and observe. When Ivin Choerkin leaves for the continent, be with them. Get close. Use your best judgment for whose face to take as your own. Do not hurry the decision. Perfect the vision."

Shadowing Ivin Choerkin? Her mission was greater than she'd imagined. "You want me with him every step?"

"No. Whichever face you choose, don't step out of bounds to be with him. I will see to his survival, and if you've chosen well, he will return to you."

"Understood." Not a lie, but not the full truth. Her mind spun; failing in this cause could be catastrophic in ways she couldn't fathom. She imagined taking the face of a warrior, a lover, a confidant, or even kin. But she knew nothing of this Choerkin, and her thoughts flailed.

He observed her rapid breaths, but instead of speaking, he reached beneath his robes and produced a tome. Leather bound and bearing a brass lock, it reminded her of the *Codex of Sol*. "This is a gift for you, but do not fall to the temptation of reading it until you reach Tomarok. This you can understand?"

"Understood. A copy of the *Codex of Sol*?"

He proffered the tome, and she opened her palms as a resting place for its sacred pages. "It is the *Codex of Crowns*."

Her eyes narrowed, and her mouth dried. "I've never heard of it."

"Nor has another living soul. Nor will they."

If his words were true, it confirmed that she wasn't speaking to any True Face, but the Master. It felt an appropriate time to be repetitive. "Understood."

He dropped a steel key onto the book with a thud. "Risk nothing until Ivin Choerkin is dead in Tomarok, and then, risk little until portents reveal the time has come."

"I will see you in Tomarok? For further instruction?"

"You will, but you will only know when the time is upon us."

She slipped the key into her robes and hugged the book to her bosom as he strolled toward the door. "It is a great honor bestowed upon me."

"With great honor comes a world's weight of responsibility." He took a deep breath before stepping up from the bones. "You *will* be the greatest Face who ever lived. You *will* achieve what every one of us has dreamed. You *will* not fail. You are incapable of failure."

She didn't turn, keeping her blushing smile hidden, but revelation hammered her. "When Ivin is dead, who do I follow?"

Moments passed, and Ulrikt's footfalls echoed down the hall, but then came his voice, strong and sure. "The Daughter of the White Lion. Ivin Choerkin's bride."

So ends Sundering the Gods;
So begins Sundering the Crowns

Sundering the Gods

Eve of Snows

Trail of Pyres

Whispers of Ghosts

Sundering the Crowns

Shadows of Man

Silhouettes in Doom

(coming 2025)

Monsoon Straits Trilogy

The Contessa of Mostul Ûbar

Best Painted in Blood

(coming 2025/26)

Additional Maps and information on the World of the Sister Continents may be found at:

www.LJamesRice.Com

and

www.STGWiki.com

www.ingramcontent.com/pod-product-compliance
Lightning Source LLC
Chambersburg PA
CBHW020615310726
48979CB00008B/1498/J

9781951068073